# Tales from the Bloody Stump

## Volume 1

## An Anthology By

# Graham Glass

Tales from the Bloody Stump – An Anthology by Graham Glass
Volume 1
Copyright © 2023

Paperback ISBN: 978-1-958889-45-9
Hardcover ISBN: 978-1-958889-46-6
Ebook ISBN: 979-8-88531-482-4

Library of Congress Cataloging-in-Publication Data
Glass, Graham
Tales from the Bloody Stump – An Anthology by Graham Glass Volume 1
Library of Congress Control Number: 2023914897

Printed on acid-free paper.

BookLocker

Published by BookLocker.com, Inc., Trenton, Georgia.

10 9 8 7 6 5 4 3 2 1

DEDICATION

A collectanea of the odd, this anthology is dedicated to friends, family, fans, and acquaintances who, over the years—huddled in their fireplaces, battling a maelstrom of euphoric angst—have watched as these kinds of mysterious artifacts (sometimes in liquid form) leaked out of the woodwork. For the most part, these same individuals—and they know who they are—have disavowed the very existence of the aforementioned mysterious artifacts. – G.G.

# Table of Contents

# FOREWORD

When they asked me to write the Foreword for G.G.*'s Tales from the Bloody Stump*, I was very surprised. I thought my reputation was in the crapper after I was caught cheating my way through barber college. I refused to write anything. I didn't want to get involved. But then late one night I heard some commotion out in front of my house. There were three black SUV's lined up in the street. Before I knew it, I was blindfolded and taken to an undisclosed location. There I was kept in a locked room without food or water for, I don't know, an hour or more.

Just when I thought I couldn't take it anymore, in comes this big, husking, neckless man with some papers for me to sign. I asked him, "Why me? I don't even know anyone named G.G." That didn't seem to matter. They wanted my cooperation.

They left me alone for at least another thirty minutes. Then came the electricity. Holding me down, they repeatedly put the terminals of a nine-volt battery on my tongue. Let me tell you, it was more than any normal human could fight against. Again I asked, "Why me?" Finally, after several minutes of this torture, the guy who was apparently in charge said, "Take him to the cooler!" I don't remember much after that.

When I awoke, I was in, what appeared to be, a sauna! It was hot! Really hot! Over 100 degrees. I was beginning to perspire. I don't know why they called it a *cooler*—some kind of sick hostage irony I suppose. After twenty minutes in that heat my sweater vest and simulated fur coat were almost wet. It was only then that they decided to pull me back out of there. I hadn't cracked, but I don't remember anything after that.

When I regained consciousness the guy in charge said, "Bring in the dogs!" I had been holding my own pretty well till then. In came a fellow with three Golden Retrievers. My God! They were wet! Before I could say "Heel!" the dogs were all over me. That smell. Wet dogs. The licking. The smell, times three! I didn't think I could take any more. I held out as long as I could, but eventually I yelled, "OK, OK you win; I *know* G.G. I *know* him! You've broken me. I give up. Are you satisfied?" I don't remember anything after that.

I'm certainly not the type that breaks under pressure, so I felt defeated and disappointed with myself when I finally gave in and signed all those papers. I was now obligated to write a Foreword for G.G.'s book. Without so much as a simple "Can we get you anything to drink?" I was whisked away by (presumably) the same goon squad that had abducted me in the first place. After a short drive they pulled off my blindfold and dropped me in front of my house. "We're expecting something by noon on Friday," a voice shouted at me as I lifted myself off the front sidewalk. The three black SUV's took off in a chorus of screeching tires.

Back in the safety of my home and with only 48 hours until the noon deadline, I found that I had developed a bad case of writer's block. "I'm no writer," I said to myself. "G.G.'s a writer. Not me. He's the versifier. Not me." Staring at a blank word processor screen I thought of the time when I discovered G.G. rolling around playfully in a bed of eider down. "Now there's a man who knows how to live," I said to myself. Then I began to type. I don't remember much of anything after that.

—Stanville Parkley, Jr.

# Tales from the Bloody Stump

## And so it begins...

# Strip Joint

I was hurriedly on my way to Scanlon to deliver two boxes of legal briefs to the county courthouse. I was using a short cut so I could get there before five o'clock. That way I wouldn't have to stay overnight in town and deliver the briefs to the courthouse records office the next day. Things were going smoothly when I happened upon a detour—a slight detour around some extensive road construction. There was no road crew in sight and the small detour arrow was pointing to a rough and rocky roadway going alongside and around the construction area. It looked way too rough to chance it. So I decided to backtrack and go the long way around to the Paul H. Dowdy highway—also known as the "PHD" or just "The Doc." That highway runs straight into Scanlon and, as it happens, near the courthouse. As a courier, I made this trip from Fort Pick to Scanlon a number of times, but this was my first trip where construction blocked the way.

I thought I was on the right track, but travelling the reverse direction on the shortcut road had me disoriented and I was soon lost. The GPS was on the fritz and there was no cell phone signal to speak of. I could see the cheap rickety radio tower high above the area and was using it as a guide. I soon realized that I wasn't going to make my five o'clock deadline and that if I kept driving around this way I would soon be out of gas. As I came over a small hill I could see the radio tower straight ahead in the background, lined up right along the center stripe of the road, and there to my right was a gas station.

The station was oddly configured. Although the pumps were on flat ground, the cashier building was down a gradual but extended slope. The entire area was paved in concrete. There was a three-bay automotive repair building about halfway down the slope. It, too, was built on a flat area carved into the hill. The sign overhead said *Bill's Gas*. The beat-up numbers on the sign showed $1.19^{99}$. "That can't be right," I said to myself. I pulled into the parking lot and up next to one of the two pumps. There the price said $4.49^{99}$. I went ahead and started pumping the gas. The flow was so slow I figured I had time to use the facilities and get a soda. So I ambled down the slope to the right side of the building where I saw the *Men's* sign (very dilapidated). When I opened the door I was hit with the most heinous odor imaginable—I could not bring myself to even look inside.

I let the metal door slam shut and went to get a soda from the antiquated vending machine out front. Even though the machine was working, the refrigeration was not, so I had to make do with a warm orange soda. I went back to my car where the pump was almost finished filling my tank. As I stood there holding the nozzle, I noticed that my windshield wipers were missing. "When did that happen?" I asked myself.

I noticed it was starting to get dark and the neon lights of the gas station had just popped on. There were now bright lights illuminating the interiors of those three mechanic bays as well. Lots of busy work going on there. Noisy and bright. Down below, the lights in the main building were on but they seemed dim in comparison to the neon greens and reds that now were the major source of light over the parking lot. And the neon "i" on the *Bill's Gas* sign was flickering on and off.

I finished filling my tank and proceeded down the slope once again so I could pay for the gas and get back on my way to Scanlon. When I opened the noisy metal door there was no store inside, just a sparse office-type environment. About the only thing on any of the walls was a No Smoking sign, hung there with a couple of nails. A middle-aged, toothless woman sat on a sickly-green vinyl sofa—there were indications of numerous brown cigarette burns all over the vinyl. The woman had a big tall hairdo and her glasses were connected to a piece of string that went around the back of her head—the string was tangled up in her big mound of hairdo. She wasn't doing anything, just sitting and staring into space; and puffing on the last remnants of a cigarette. She didn't even look toward me when I came through the door.

A very tall man wearing grease-stained work clothes and a baseball cap came into the room. He was smoking a cigarette. It hung from his mouth as if it was stuck to his bottom lip. With the cigarette flopping up and down he asked me, "What's up?"

I noticed from the tag on his shirt that his name was Buzz. I told him I had come to pay for my gas. He sat down at a small desk in the front corner of the room, right under the No Smoking sign. There were a few electronic devices attached to the wall by the desk and a gooseneck light that brightened the surface of the desk. As I looked around the room I noticed that the middle-aged woman was lighting up a new cigarette of her own. I looked back at the No Smoking sign, but before I could make a friendly comment, Buzz said, "That's my Aunt Midge. Don't pay any attention to her. She hasn't got it anymore. She's not all there. Well, let's see here. Let's see here."

Buzz looked at the little electronic counter and said, "Fella, you must have been real empty... sixteen gallons, that'll be $160.00."

"You gotta be kidding," I answered back. "That's ten dollars a gallon."

"Yessir. Yeah that's what it is. Yessir," he said.

At my insistence, we went together, back up the slope to the pump to verify the amount. When we got there I noticed that one of my rear view mirrors was missing. Surely I would have noticed that before. Buzz looked at the pump and said, "Yep. One-sixty. That's it." He turned and moseyed on down the slope, apparently expecting me to follow. I felt like just driving off, but then I thought, "Who knows, maybe he's the chief of police around here. Or a deputy. Maybe a constable—"

I hesitated, but then I went down the slope again and into the building where Buzz was sitting, completely at ease and unperturbed.

"Will you take a credit card?" I asked.

"Credit Card!? Credit Card!?" Buzz sounded like a barking dog. "What kind of credit card?"

I showed him three like I was a magician asking him to pick a card.

"We don't take any of those. None of those. No sir," Buzz stated. Then, as he lit up yet another cigarette, he asked, "Lambert Gringle. Lambert Gringle? Is that your name? Lambert...Gringle?

"Yes," I said. "How about cash? I've got...let's see, a hundred and fourteen dollars." I was starting to get tense about all this fuss and confusion. Looking outside all I could see was the glow of the neon and the bright garage lights. It was so bright that the rest of the area around the perimeter of the station was now in complete darkness. Spooky.

"That won't be enough. Not enough. What are you trying to pull here mister?" Buzz was trying act very authoritative.

"Well...Buzz," I said. "I'd like to see someone in charge."

"That would be Mr. Cockchafer, he's the owner," Buzz offered. "He's out back."

"That would be fine." As I followed Buzz to the "back", various lighting fell on Buzz. He was a lot filthier than he seemed at first. His Aunt Midge, sitting on the sofa, was completely inert through all this and was chain smoking her brains out—the room was filled with smoke. No wonder the walls looked so dingy.

Buzz and I entered the back room. It was just as sparse as the rest of the place. Sitting in an upright lawn chair was a heavy-set man with a huge double chin. He too was smoking a cigarette and was sweating profusely—there was no ventilation to speak of and the air in the room could not have been more stagnant. Like the room out front, this one also had nothing on the walls except a No Smoking sign. In the corner was a refrigerator with rust stains around its metal hinges.

"Are you Mr. Cockchafer?" I asked without waiting for an introduction.

"What's going on here, Buzz?" Cockchafer asked Buzz without any regard to me.

Buzz gave Cockchafer a thumbnail description of the events. After a considerable amount of awkward silent time while Cockchafer mulled it all over, he finally said, "Take his money...then show this freeloader out."

Rather than make a scene or delay my departure any further, I gave Buzz the money—all the cash I had in my wallet. I showed him how my wallet was now empty. "You need a receipt?" Buzz asked.

"Don't bother," I said as I left the building and went back to my car—or what was left of it. The seats were gone as well as the two boxes of legal briefs. Now I was really pissed. I stomped down to the building and went inside. Old smokin' Auntie Midge didn't even look up; what a surprise. Buzz on the other hand rushed out the front door. So I marched directly into the back room where Mr. Cockchafer was still sitting, smoking, and with his shirt now unbuttoned and his belt loose.

"My car has been vandalized!" I yelled. "What are you going to do about it? Have you got a phone? What's going on here?" I really didn't know what I was doing...or asking...or...

Suddenly the room was filled with Buzz and three really big men—oversized muscular men I had seen up the slope, working in the brightly lit garage. "What have you done to my car," I asked firmly. "And where are my boxes of briefs?"

Buzz looked at the three men and said (as he laughed out loud), "Briefs? Ha ha. Briefs? This fella has lost his briefs!" The three giant men all started laughing like a pack of boisterous drunks. It seemed like sarcastic fake laughter to me. Before I could respond, Buzz jumped in, "Mr. Pringle may I introduce you to the Pismire brothers. Pismires, Mr. Lam-something Pringle."

"It's Gringle, not Pringle." I was trying to give the group the impression that I was on top of the situation, but now I was beginning to feel very threatened. So I made a quick move to the door. They were surprised enough that I made it all the way out into the parking lot and up the slope to my car before they could all exit from the building.

There I saw that my tires and car doors were gone. The trunk was open. As I stood there gawking I felt a strong hand grab my arm. I panicked as the three Pismire brothers incapacitated me and dragged me back down the slope, into the building, and then to the back room where Mr. Cockchafer was now standing and smoking, smoking, smoking. All that smoking, very strange. Mr. Cockchafer made some kind of weird hand gesture and the Pismire brothers immediately beat the living crap out of me, knocking me unconscious. The Pismire brothers—at least up to that point they were the only ones adhering to the No Smoking policy.

When I came to, it was still dark, but I had no idea what time it was. I was very cold. Then I realized that they had taken all my clothes, my ring, my ear stud, and my watch. I was left naked on the frontage road by The Doc, the highway to Scanlon. I didn't have a clue what to do, so I decided to walk toward the horizon where the Scanlon city lights were lighting up the haze in the air. I laughed to myself that the haze was caused by all that cigarette smoking back at the gas station. I didn't know how I was going to explain the loss of those legal briefs. I might lose my job as a courier for some screw-up like that. My immediate concern was getting something to cover my nakedness. Without a plan, I just started walking, hopefully ending up in Scanlon and maybe getting some help. As I walked it occurred to me that the four hundred dollars I had hidden in my shoe was now gone as well. Not a good day for me.

I shuddered every time the headlights from cars on the highway lit up my naked body. I tried to maneuver around so that I wouldn't be seen, but it was really hard on my bare feet jumping around on the road and the gravelly shoulder—rocks, broken glass, bent-up pieces of metal. Then I noticed the shine from some headlights that appeared to be a lot brighter than most. Good grief! It was a car on the frontage road and it was headed in my direction. I tried to get out of sight, but the weeds on the side of the road were injuring my feet; and I could hear rustling in the brush—not going in there! Then a bright light bounced around the area and a voice cried out, "Hey! You there!" I froze and tried to cover as much of my anatomy as I could. "Who? Me?" I said. I figured that my day couldn't possibly get any worse so I waited for the unidentified person to arrive. And where was I going to run to anyway?

"Why, you're naked as a jaybird! What in the hell are you doing out here like this, young fella? Have you been drinking? Are you on drugs?" It was the sheriff of Scanlon county, Sheriff Bughouse. "Come with me." Once again a heavy hand grabbed me by the arm and forced me to go along. "I'm gonna need some kind of explanation…and it better be good, or you're under arrest." I was ready to explain when Sheriff Bughouse added, "Look here now, my deputy left his swim trunks in the back seat. You get back there and put those on. Don't want to see any more of you than I have to. Then you better start explainin' yourself…"

I got in the back seat just like he said and put on the swim trunks. The trunks were about ten sizes too big, but I didn't care at that point. The sheriff got into the front seat and turned to look at me. "Well?" he said.

I told him exactly what had happened to me. About the gas station and how my car had been picked clean as well as my body. I had my money stolen from me as well as some boxes of legal briefs. Those briefs were my responsibility and now my job was in jeopardy. He stroked his chin as he took it all in. I didn't know whether he was buying any of it. It sounded pretty far-fetched, even to *me*.

Finally, he said, "Let's go take a look. That area is not in Scanlon county so I don't have jurisdiction, but if we find something I'll call old Jeff Botfly over in Dumfer. Sit back now and show me the way."

I could see the red lights flashing on the radio tower and I used them to retrace my movements. After a few false turns, we were on the road where I was driving earlier with that crummy radio tower lined up straight ahead. Before we got to the top of the hill I could see the glow of the neon and garage lights of the station.

The sheriff drove into the parking lot and parked near where I had earlier. "Is this the spot?" he asked pointing to the area by the pump. My car was gone.

"My car was parked right here. Pieces were stolen...missing...and my boxes of briefs. But the car is gone now. They must have taken it." I was standing there on the concrete, barefooted, hanging loose, holding the swim trunks up with the waist all bunched up in my hand.

"Let's go down there to the office. That's where you say they attacked you." The sheriff led the way and I followed along. Because of the way I must have looked, I felt pretty damn weird.

The sheriff barged in the front door displaying plenty of authority. He approached Midge, the only one in the room. The sheriff was waving his hand to disperse the cloud of cigarette smoke that kept wafting over him. "I need to see a man named Buzz or a Mr. Cockchafer." He got no response from huffing-puffing Auntie Midge so he proceeded to the back room. I followed close behind. There was Cockchafer standing by the refrigerator, the door open. He was briefly taken aback when he saw the sheriff.

It came as no surprise to me that Cockchafer acted as if everything was news to him. He was overtly implying that I must be lying. And of course he just had to say, "I've never seen this guy before in my life."

Then Cockchafer added, "The Pismire brothers—you probably saw them on your way down here. The Pismire brothers. Those brothers are hard workers; hard workers getting repairs done; working into the night. Every night. They have no time for such foolishness. Cockchafer was very convincing...and very annoying. What an innocent act. I was getting frustrated with the whole situation and was now becoming worried more about what the sheriff was going to do with me than anything else.

"Come on," the sheriff said as we went back up the hill. But to his surprise, his squad car was now missing its wheels, its hood, the emergency lights on top, the steering wheel, and a number of items from the interior including his police radio, his shotgun, his radar equipment, and his computer. He immediately assumed that those Pismire brothers in the garage had something to do with it.

The fuming sheriff pounded his way over to the garage where the massive Pismire brothers were hard at work. Fake, self-conscious nonchalance. I trotted behind him, still holding up the swim trunks with my fist, the bottoms of my feet becoming caked with dark grey parking lot grime. The Pismires also acted completely innocent—well-acted I must say. As the sheriff questioned them he saw his police radio on one of the workbenches. The radio was partially disassembled.

"You men are under arrest," he blurted out. "You have the right to—" Down came the heavy forearm of one of the brothers. It landed on the back of the sheriff's head and neck knocking him out cold in one blow. I backed up, holding the swim trunks in my hand. When I turned to run I bumped right into the chest of Buzz who grabbed me and held me tight until one of the Pismire brothers could come over and clobber me as well. I believe all it took was one hit—one hit and I too was out cold...again.

---

Man, I'm still reeling from that hit. So now I'm here on the side of The Doc for a second time; in the middle of the night. Looks like the same place, perhaps not. They not only took my—the Deputy's—swim trunks from me, but they also shaved my body slick, clean of hair. Even my eyebrows and...everywhere. Ye horses of the apocalypse! What would they want with my hair?

I'm going to have to collect myself and find my way somewhere, somehow...maybe to Scanlon...maybe find something to cover myself. Sure. I'll follow the haze of those Scanlon town lights again. Headlights coming and going. Headlights. There...Ha! I can see the sheriff up ahead. Looks like he's headed toward the town also. And boy does he look pissed. Man, that guy's got the hairiest back and butt cheeks that I've ever seen!

# Off the Chart

---

"OK, Roy, I'm gonna need you to step back from the mic…back up…if you bump into it *one more time…*" The frustrated sound engineer was scolding Roy, attempting to stay calm. Marty was definitely not pleased with Roy or the way the project was progressing. "Let's continue working that first chorus…at least we should be able to get that done…maybe *today.*" The sound engineer's voice in Roy's headphones got louder as each word came out. Still, Marty was being as polite as he could manage.

"OK. Let's go," Roy replied unenthusiastically from inside the sound room.

The music began (again) and Roy stepped up to the microphone:

> *Baby, let's not beat around the bush*
> *I want to be in the bush*
> *Baby, hide my* (Thump!)

"Again? Really…Roy?" Marty said as he pushed his chair, rolling back, away from the mixer, tightening the cord to his headphones. The frustration was now obvious in his voice. "Son of a bitch," he mumbled to himself as the door to the control room opened behind him. Before he could cool down, a tall, well-dressed, redheaded woman tapped him on the shoulder. Looking up, he saw that it was Dolly Fingers, his boss. She was president and owner of the country music record label, Hot Knott's Music. She leaned over and grabbed the mounted control room microphone, bending its gooseneck. Looking at the engineer she mouthed, "Marty, is this hot? Can he hear me?"

"Yes Ma'am," he replied.

"Roy, I want you to come to my office as soon as there's a break here," Ms. Fingers said into the mic. She didn't wait for Roy to answer.

"Sure...thing," Roy replied, his voice trailing off. He peeled off his headphones and hung them on the nearby stand before vacating the sound room.

Marty, exasperated, then remarked to himself with resignation, "I guess we're taking a *break*." He removed his headphones and left the control room in a vaporous huff.

As Roy innocently sauntered down the corridor to the president's office, he noticed the assistants and secretaries giving him the fisheye along the way, some looking away from him instead, avoiding eye contact. Ms. Fingers had barely arrived at her office when Roy showed up, so she motioned for him to come on in and sit down, first curling her forefinger at him in and out (as if he were caught on a fishing line), then sternly pointing down at the floor. A somewhat puzzled Roy sat in one of the smallish chairs facing her desk. Ms. Fingers positioned herself behind her one-acre simulated mahogany desk; stacks of papers, folders, a little metallic dog paperweight, and all kinds of whatnot everywhere. The walls were adorned with a few plaques and framed music awards received by the Hot Knott's Music record label over the years. There were only a few. As Ms. Fingers sat down, she performed some meaningless rearranging of the papers and folders on her desk, finally pointing the dog paperweight directly at Roy.

"Mr. Stoner, let me get right to the point," she started, folding her hands in front of her with her elbows on the desk. "We're gonna buy out your contract with Hot Knott's Music. There may be another label here in Nashville that will take you on, but your ties with Knott's are now severed."

"So you say you're dumping me?" Roy asked.

"Well, yes! Duh!"

"Hmm," Roy thought for a moment, not knowing what to say, or what was coming next. "We're in the middle of...I don't see..."

Ms. Fingers continued, "Let's start with this: your last album, *Eight Too Much*, did not overwhelm the music public. Your material doesn't even generate a *cult* following. Second, the market is not really interested in "albums' so much any more as in hot country one-offs dropped digitally immediately on completion. The trickle keeps a buzz going, keeps the name out there, tantalizes, teases, promotes live performances. It's just business, Roy."

Roy sat quietly, feeling chastised like a ten year-old, then he popped off with the first thing in his head, "You only like the one-offs so you can lop off talent as soon as their popularity goes south. Cut cut." Roy made a scissors motion with his fingers.

Irritated but undeterred, Ms. Fingers continued, "Third, how many songs have you finished for your current project?"

Thinking for a moment, Roy replied, "Three..."

"Two and a half," Ms. Fingers interrupted. "And we're already into six figures. This current song, the one you're working on, *Bush or Tush*, is a mess. Marty is threatening to quit. Fourth, what used to be clever, cutting-edge outlaw raunch is now just overt, offensive crap. And fifth...your girlfriend in the studio? She gets in the way, orders people around, so-li-cit-ting. And, by the way, Marty is not the least bit interested in paying for sex—not with her or anybody else."

"Well now that's news to *me*," Roy interrupted, surprised but not *too* surprised.

"What's her name? Tarter, Tatum, Totter?" inquired Ms. Fingers, changing the conversation with some passive-aggressive banter.

"Tater. Tater Totts," Roy answered.

"Tater Totts," Ms. Fingers reiterated. "A hooker, or ex-hooker from over in Burbel county—"

"Porn star. Ex-*porn* star," Roy said, correcting Ms. Fingers.

She paused for a moment, then went on, "Anyway, we're bringing on a *new*, more modern country artist, Trey Duke. He's young, talented, mainstream—only so much room for talent here at Hot Knott's. This is a cut-throat business, Roy."

Watching the expression on his face, Ms. Fingers could tell she wasn't getting through to an obstinate Roy. Then she added, "The name *Roy Stoner* does not generate buzz, magic, no magic...any more. Roy...your material is not cutting-edge...you're stale...old, gnarly, restive, and argumentative. It shows in your music. That's deadly. You got it?" Shaking her head and looking down at the junk on her desk she muttered with contempt, "*Eight Too Much*?"

With that, Roy stood up, snatched the little metallic dog paperweight off her desk, and threw it against the wall, smashing the glass cover on one of the framed awards. "That's what *I* think of all this," he said loudly as he stormed out of the office. Out in the open area he could hear the low murmuring of assistants and secretaries. Roy mumbled to himself, "I've always hated that stupid little dog." Seeing him charging on down the corridor, Ms. Fingers' personal assistant quickly stood up from her desk and rushed to the aid of her employer.

Roy stomped his way into Studio A and gathered up his guitar and guitar case. As Roy made for the exit, the guitar in one hand and the case in the other, he bumped into Marty just outside the control room. For a brief moment, there was an awkward tension between the two, then each went their own way. Outside, Roy sat in his truck, silent, for several minutes before heading over to *Grillo's*, his favorite watering hole, a place where he used to perform at least twice a week. Now, it was just a place for him to get loaded and make some important life-altering decisions. *Grillo's* was nearly empty at this time of day and the early evening's act was just setting up. Some guy with a long, squared-off, multi-colored beard wearing a funky-looking, sweat-stained, curled-up cowboy hat was testing a twangy, beat-up electric guitar. While keeping an eye on the bearded guy, Roy sat down at the bar and ordered a beer. How things had changed in the business—from singers wearing sequined western shirts with fringes to guys like this fella who look like they should be tending to a still and shooting at "revenooers". Maybe Roy Stoner *was* obsolete—although he never wore sequins or fringes. After drinking about half of his beer he became restless and forlorn, and rather than get all maudlin with the bartender, he took off for his yet-to-be-paid-for house.

Over the years, Roy made a lot of money and spent (i.e. wasted) a lot of money—most of it. He barreled his way through a number of relationships and they barreled their way through him, draining him of money and life force. Tater, his current companion was no exception. She could fill a room (or studio) with an atmosphere of fear like a fog machine at a high school dance. She was one aggressive individual. Tater usually accompanied Roy to a session, but today she had packed him off alone.

When Roy arrived home, Tater was not there waiting for him.

Roy looked around the house for her, but she and all of her belongings were nowhere to be found—highly unusual and unexpected. Roy: surprised, yet not surprised. For the next several days, Roy was content to drink himself into a mild stupor, watch TV, and play some antiquated, violent, FPS video games. He was more than a little surprised when an official buy-out check arrived in the mail—he was *very* surprised that Knott's had made good on the deal and not too surprised that the check was so...modest. He called his agent and got voice mail. He called the studio and got voice mail. He called some of his acquaintances and got...voice mail. "Damn that caller ID bullshit!" he said out loud, thinking that he might go to a pay phone just to get a response from someone.

So, on the fourth day, he arrived at his first, and most obvious decision, "To hell with *all* of them!" The big screen TV that Tater had bought (using Roy's credit card) turned out to be his constant companion for those few mindless days, but on this, the fourth day, the TV provided him with an idea. On the screen was an outdoors show filmed in Louisiana bayou country—some kind of wildlife roundup or shootout. Inspired, he made a new life-changing decision. He was going to head south, south to familiar territory, south to a place where he lived when just starting out, Blackchaw, Louisiana. As Roy remembered, it was a bustling little swamp town right on the bayou; it was named Blackchaw as a tribute to the tribe of Native Americans who were pushed off their land and into the swamp in order to build the most important town in North America. Although the town was fairly remote, it attracted country, Cajun, and blues musicians from around the state. It served as an artist mini-Mecca. What Roy had forgotten was that it also attracted hangers-on, losers, and other unsavory zoo animals—and mosquitoes.

For the next forty-eight hours Roy's life was a whirlwind of activity. He emptied his small bank account, cashed his buy-out check, gathered up all the essential shit he could carry (including his guitar), and hit the road...by bus. His worthless truck would never have made the trip, so he abandoned it. His house was worth much less than what he still owed, so he abandoned it; furniture, pictures, knick-knacks...everything. Wherever Tater Totts was, he was abandoning her. His previous life—abandoned. Roy was very eager to enter, what he was calling, "Roy's Country Music Star Protection Program"—i.e. disappear.

It was a blessing in disguise that he had to change buses several times on his way to Blackchaw. No single repulsive passenger was with him for very long: a hundred miles next to a guy with a lung-busting cough; a barefoot guy who groomed his toes with a toothpick; a woman whose rose-scented perfume fogged up Roy's reading glasses; a suspicious twenty-something with numerous moist bandages on his face and arms; and a woman with four untamed, unwashed, sociopathic kids (one of which could scream so loudly that it invoked a visit from the bus driver).

It was getting close to dusk as Roy left the bus station and hit the streets of Blackchaw, the lights and signs of various businesses beginning to shine wearily in the long shadows. But it was only a short time later that Roy realized that nothing looked or felt the same as he remembered. Some of the buildings were now just empty shells or were gone completely. The town was in a state of decay and the music scene had pretty much evaporated—like a dried-up pond. All that was left was the muddy, scum-like residue of hangers-on, losers, and other unsavory zoo animals. Sidewalks were lined with unkempt characters selling used vinyl records out of boxes, aggressive panhandlers, terrible non-musicians playing for tips, and the occasional drunk or dead person lying prone on the ground. His "Country Music Star Protection Program" was not starting out well.

For about an hour, Roy wandered along the streets, trying to take in all the changes, until he came upon a red neon sign marking the entrance to a hotel he remembered, the *Hotel Savage*. Still open for business, it was named after the late Sam Savage, someone that Roy knew long ago. But upon Sam's death the hotel was taken over by three local "businessmen"; "businessmen" who were definitely not pillars of the community. Right now, the hotel appealed to Roy since, for a very reasonable amount, a guest could rent a room for an hour, a day, a week, or a month. Ignoring the dilapidated state of the place, Roy checked in, went to his room, room 212, and crashed onto the bed—greasy, spotted bedspread notwithstanding.

When Roy awakened, it was already mid-morning the next day. Semi-conscious, he raised his head, the bedspread remaining stuck to his cheek—he quickly went to the sink and washed his face. Looking around he saw an old TV in the corner and a clock radio by the bed. There was no phone in the room and the electric outlet by the door had black spark marks all over it. After a few wake-up duties, he grabbed his guitar case and left the hotel to search for a paying gig.

But good, paying gigs were nowhere to be found. Finally, in desperation, he agreed to play in a dark, dingy lounge called *The Rat's Nest*—agreed to play for tips only. It was a real dive, owned and run by a slimy invertebrate by the name of Phil Sheets whose nickname around town was "Dirty." He seemed proud of that nickname and proud of his tacky but quaint lounge. Dirty was a divorced, aging, heavy-set dude with oily hair and a thin, lop-sided mustache. His loud, heavy mouth breathing was the result of carrying around 300 pounds of fat for many, many years—a quantity of that fat stored in four or five chins and the back of his neck. He had one cocktail waitress, Lizzie, and a bartender named Arnie. Dirty spent most of his time in the back room during business hours, eating junk food and watching porn while all kinds of mischief took place in the lounge. He would slither out of his cave every once in a while to see how things were going "up top," as he used to refer to the lounge proper. The lounge would do a fair amount of business on an average night—mostly regulars, but *very* regular. In a town on life-support like Blackchaw, alcohol was big business.

Mr. Sheets was also *very* interested in making contact with the lovely Lizzie. "How are things 'up top'," he would quip, looking down at Lizzie's...nametag. Sometimes Lizzie would respond *carefully* and other times she would just ignore him.

Roy always kept his modest bankroll of nest egg money secured tightly in a money belt around his waist, something that he rarely took off. Without his nest egg, Roy would have been in dire straits since the tips he got for playing at *The Nest* were small and rare. But play he did. Roy would sing and play his guitar every night at the lounge, old favorites from his recording days and a few covers. Some of Roy's most raunchy songs were mildly popular at *The Nest*—that was the kind of place it was. He could never tell if any of the patrons recognized even one of his old hit songs; songs that were once, actually, on the charts—and popular, in their own way. But, in this business, the same revolving door that lets you *in* is the same one that ushers you *out*.

Over the next two weeks Roy reduced his alcohol intake to a mere trickle and his "Country Music Star Protection Program" seemed to be working, finally—Roy found refuge in his performances. Unfortunately, the nefarious goings-on between Phil Sheets and Lizzie Beaudine were escalating

"C'mon Liz, let's go back to your place and do some business," was a typical line from Dirty; sometimes during business hours and sometimes as the lounge was closing up for the night. Unfortunately for everyone, Dirty's advances were getting more and more aggressive and indiscreet with each passing week.

Lately, on a good night, Lizzie would respond with something smooth but clear, such as, "Sorry. Not interested," or "Silly. You're silly". But, if she was having a bad night, she would clobber him with something much less diplomatic like "Get away from me you goddamn pervert!" or "Bite my ass." That latter remark did not have the deterrent effect she was counting on.

Early on, Dirty tolerated her rejections because he always, faithfully, believed that one day he would break through her icy wall and the two of them would engage in every possible sexual fantasy he could conjure up. On the flip side, she tolerated him because she needed the money and there were very few job opportunities in Blackchaw. Besides, ever since Roy arrived, she had a new, more pleasant reason to come to work every day: Roy.

Arnie, the bartender, was used to the prickly back and forth between Dirty and Lizzie so it had become like background noise to him. He was a timid person, a character trait adored by Dirty, and in any kind of conflict Arnie was as useless as a golf club is to an oyster.

So, on one particular night, Dirty, the Blackchaw cocaine groundhog, emerged from his hole, and, not being able to see his shadow, he developed the delusion that Lizzie's cold winter was over—so he was going to make his move. As everyone was closing up the lounge for the night, Dirty pressured Lizzie to come with him to his office. Roy was busy putting his guitar into its case, but he did see Lizzie follow Dirty into the back room office, the door closing behind oily old Dirty. Arnie was still wiping down the bar, zoning, oblivious to everything and everyone.

Then a big ruckus erupted from behind the back room door. A crash here and a yelp there and a deep blubbery voice yelling "Oooouch...shit!" Roy rushed to the door expecting it to be locked, but it opened easily. Looking inside there were two people engaged in what some people might call a cat and mouse game around the desk. But in reality it was a rhinoceros and ballerina game, the rhinoceros horn in full view. Lizzie saw Roy and Dirty did not. Grabbing Dirty from the back and holding him, Roy told Lizzie to make for the door, which she did, walking sideways slowly and keeping an eye on the two and two-thirds men. Once she was safely outside the room, Roy released Dirty who immediately slapped Roy with "You're fired! Get out of here!" Dirty rattling his arms in the air as if shaking off a thousand flies that had alit on them. From the doorway came a response from Lizzie, "I quit!"

As Lizzie and Roy went "up top" and then to the main exit, Arnie, from behind the bar, tossed Roy a full bottle of bourbon, "On me...and good luck!" Roy responded with a wave and Lizzie blew Arnie a kiss. Shortly after that, Arnie took off his apron, tossed it onto the bar, and left the cleanup unfinished as he followed Lizzie and Roy's example, leaving that scuzzy place forever. A totally disheveled Dirty shuffled his way out of the lounge onto the street where a police patrol car just happened to be passing by. Without wrestling with the hideous details, it can be said that Dirty was immediately arrested for indecent exposure.

It was around three o'clock in the morning when Lizzie and Roy found themselves at the Blackchaw Boardwalk, a wide wooden deck that used to be a place of crowds and vendors and music. Now it was an abandoned, rotting eyesore that was even dangerous in some places. At this time of night/morning, even the mosquitoes avoided the place. The Boardwalk was built right up next to a true Louisiana marshland where future expansion of the town was impossible. It was designed with the idea of providing a party deck with a seductive view of the marsh, its vegetation, and wildlife. In the end, as the town slowly withered away; the Boardwalk, being uninteresting and unused, was left to die in silence.

Lizzie and Roy had finished off most of the bourbon and the two were as loaded as a question from a TV trial lawyer. The two sat on a broken down, backless bench in near pitch black, moonless, darkness looking out over the marsh. Lizzie reached over and stroked Roy's face with the backs of her fingers, feeling very grateful to Roy for rescuing her from that oily rhino. She suggested that maybe the two of them could hit the road together, just picking some random place out west, or up east, or anywhere. Roy broke his fuzzy concentration abruptly, turned to Lizzie, and kissed her lips passionately, unleashing a flood of pent-up passion for her. Lizzie savored every moment of that kiss. Having second thoughts about making rash, bourbon-soaked, life-altering decisions, Roy gently backed off, still gazing at her face, "Let's go back to my place. Maybe we can come up with something." The two left the Boardwalk in a romantic haze and headed back to the *Hotel Savage*. When they arrived at the front door of the hotel, Roy realized he had left his guitar down at the Boardwalk, "I've got to go back and get my guitar!" he told Lizzie. Giving her the key to his room, room 212, he said, "Go on up to my room and wait for me,

I'll be right there." After a quick parting kiss, Roy turned back toward the swamp and Lizzie hustled up the stairs to Roy's room, room 212.

Although Roy was still harboring misgivings about the immediate future, he was mostly feeling numb from the gallon of bourbon making its way through his system. He had been harboring a deep feeling for Lizzie and was hoping that she had stumbled onto something good with her idea. But he was also concerned about the realities of the financial situation: both of them would be looking for work in a yet-to-be-determined, totally foreign location.

When he got back down to the Boardwalk, his guitar case was exactly where he had left it, near the broken-down bench. He sat down for a moment and stood the guitar case on its end next to him. For several minutes he sat there, a struggle between reality and pure joy going through his mind. In the end, joy won out. "Why not?" Roy exclaimed resolutely as he stood up, holding the top end of his guitar case. He had stood up a little too quickly and his head was spinning, so he grabbed a section of the rotten wooden railing to counterbalance himself and slowly regained control. Then he cautiously walked over to the swamp-edge of the Boardwalk using his guitar case like a walking cane. Where there was no longer a Boardwalk railing, he began to drain off from himself a large quantity of processed bourbon, adding his fluids to the murky waters of the Coagula Swamp, located at the outskirts of Blackchaw, Louisiana. And there his life changed forever.

Across the water, through the reeds, the cattails, and rotting tree branches he saw a greenish glow right at the water level. He might not even have noticed it had it not been for the absolute darkness of that early morning. Re-packaging his goods, he squinted and leaned forward to see if something was out there. Now it seemed to be moving toward the Boardwalk. Maybe it was the bourbon talking. Maybe not. He was fascinated with the neon-green glow. Maybe it was swamp gas. Maybe not. The glow moved closer. Roy made a step backward. Maybe it was ball lightning, whatever that might be. Maybe not. Whatever it was, it was coming up to the edge of the Boardwalk, right in front of Roy.

From out of those mysterious waters a very tall, thin, human-like female stood up. The water was chest-deep on her. Roy stepped back another step, dragging his guitar case with him. She placed her hands on the wooden deck and with a single motion, she shot up out of the water like a dolphin and landed securely on the Boardwalk, feet first and upright, like a human gymnast.

Even in the darkness, Roy could see she had webbed hands and feet. From what he could tell, she was wearing a shiny black, skin-tight, seamless outfit that covered her entire body except for her dark hands, dark feet, and dark head. She was a foot taller than Roy, which was quite a feature since Roy himself was six-foot one. Her eyes and fingertips had that greenish glow he had seen moving about in the swamp. A mountain of flowing black hair was all around her head—it looked as if it had never been wet with swamp water. Nevertheless, the dank smell of swamp water was all about her as she moved toward him.

Her neon-green eyes, vibrating rapidly, left-to-right began to mesmerize Roy as her glowing green fingertips increased in brightness. She began talking in a liquid gurgling voice with her luscious wet lips, "Glik. Gur, gul, guk. Gur, gul guk." Roy could not move, nor could he look away as she lovingly reached out and touched his face with those glowing fingertips.

"Hello. Do not be afraid," she said. Apparently, as long as her fingers were touching his skin, Roy could understand her every utterance. Still mesmerized by her eyes, Roy felt her rip open his shirt. That was the last thing he remembered. And that was definitely a good thing. Then again, maybe not.

When Roy woke up in his hotel room bed a few hours later, it was already late morning. It felt like the worst hangover he had ever suffered through—his whole body was aching, he had terrible gas pains, his head was spinning. But standing beside his bed, looking down at him, was Lizzie, warm and compassionate. She had helped him to bed when he returned. He quickly sat up straight, checking for his money belt. A sigh of relief lightened his mood when he realized that he had not been robbed.

"What *happened* to you?" Lizzie asked in a very non-judgmental way.

Roy was feeling about for his shirt and noticed that all of its buttons were missing, "I don't know. There was this woman, this being. It, she, came out of the swamp and started to touch me, my face. I don't remember. I don't know how I found my way back here. I don't know, I don't know." He rubbed his face with the palms of his hands as Lizzie sat down beside him.

"Are you OK?," Lizzie said as she stroked his back under his loose shirt.

"My Joe hole, my Joe hole!" Roy said referring to his navel. It was very sore and very red. He lightly rubbed the skin around it. The gas pains made his stomach feel as if he had swallowed a bowling ball. It was as if his bowels were working on something that they could not possibly digest.

Lying backward onto the bed, he asked, almost rhetorically, "Where is my guitar?"

"I'm sorry. You didn't have it with you when you came back," Lizzie replied.

Roy sat up again, "I've got to go get it."

Lizzie prevented Roy from standing up, "But first, I have to tell you the good news...I found a new job for me and a gig for you—both in the same place! This morning I walked back to my apartment and took my car over to the highway. There's a place there called *The Blackchaw Roadhouse*. I thought I would take a chance...everything happened so fast...but, I don't know. I got the waitress job and I mentioned your name. The reality of it is: you're gonna need to get your guitar because you have to perform tonight! Are you gonna be in any condition to play?"

"I will be. I have to be...I want—" Roy knew it would be slow going for a while. "What kind of a place is it?"

"It's a good place, the timing was unbelievable and...it's far away from the swamp area of town.

"Good," Roy responded, "the further the better."

Lizzie became more excited, "It's owned and run by Maggie LeGroyn who inherited the place from her recently dead husband. She and I hit it off right away. A-a-and," Lizzie patted Roy on his thigh, "the best news is that she remembers you and your music. She thinks old outlaw stuff will go over well with the rowdy Roadhouse crowd—you know, truckers and other types, the kind of customers the place has attracted for years. I mean, I mean the timing couldn't have been better for us. And for me," Lizzie continued, "I don't think there's going to be any...ahem...issues like at Dirty's."

"Maybe we can save up enough to head west like we said," Roy added, "or east, or wherever..." They embraced. Then Roy suggested, "Let's go get something to eat. I'm feeling ravenous."

Enthusiastically consenting, Lizzie helped Roy get himself together. While taking a shower, Roy tried to remember any small fragment of what had happened to him. Was it some kind of hallucination, a vision, a dream? Was it the bourbon? Or was it real? For sure, despite the metaphorical bowling ball in his stomach, he was ready to eat and eat big. But *something* didn't feel right about himself. Something.

As Roy was drying off, he called out from the bathroom, "I have to go get my guitar before we do anything."

"Sure," Lizzie responded as she occupied herself by straightening up the room while waiting for him.

Roy and Lizzie left the hotel and went down to the Boardwalk where Roy's guitar case was standing on its end, exactly as he had left it—waiting, like a person waiting for a bus. And the guitar case still contained Roy's guitar.

While having lunch at the nearby *Grubstake Diner*, Roy tried to describe to Lizzie the strange female being that came out of the swamp. His memory of the woman creature was hampered by the misfiring of a million bourbon-plundered neurons in his brain. Lizzie accepted that Roy had seen *something*, but found his story too farfetched to swallow it completely. Occasionally, Roy's mind would reassemble a tiny memory of the creature touching him, or talking, or—

Back at the hotel, Roy and Lizzie went to his room, room 212. It was still hours before they had to be at the Roadhouse. The walk and the big, heavy meal at the diner had made Roy sleepy. But before Roy could flop down on the bed, Lizzie pulled away the bedspread with great caution, using two, and only two, fingers. Then she and Roy got into the hotel bed together and fell asleep.

When they awoke, it was already dark outside—there was just enough time to get to the bar where each of them had a job waiting. Roy's "bowling ball" bowels were still pressuring him, but given the circumstances, he was surely going to have to ignore it. The three of them piled into Lizzie's tiny car: Lizzie, Roy, and Roy's guitar in its hard case. The guitar had the entire back seat to itself.

Lizzie and Roy actually arrived a little early at the Roadhouse. Lizzie introduced Roy to Maggie, who confirmed what Lizzie had told Roy earlier about Maggie's being a big fan of his. Maggie showed them both around and introduced them to the other waitress, Surrey; the bouncer, Lurg; and the bartender, Louie. The Roadhouse was much larger and nicer than Dirty's little place. The restrooms, however, were standard issue: Women's—you could eat off the floor; Men's—you couldn't eat for days after being in there.

There were already a few truckers in the place. Maggie warned both Lizzie and Roy, "Don't be deceived, this place really gets goin' after ten PM; and *really* gets rowdy around midnight. So prepare yourself. C'mon Lizzie, I'll show you the ropes. Roy, you can go ahead and get set up on the stage there. Remember, you play from eight PM to two AM in sets of about forty-five minutes with fifteen-minute breaks in between. It's a full working day for a hundred bucks. Drinks and food are free and you can keep all your tips. Start when you're ready, around eight." Maggie was already walking away from Roy as she and Lizzie went to prepare for the evening's business, real business.

Roy could hardly believe his good fortune and was just about to start his first song when Maggie reappeared next to the stage. The small stage spotlight was shining directly on Roy who was sweating like a squeezed-out wet towel. Concerned, Maggie asked him, "Roy, you don't look so good. Are you all right?"

"Yes, ma'am," Roy replied, not even 100% convinced himself. "I'll be fine after I get going." Roy wasn't about to let this great gig slip out of his hands.

"All right. Let me know if you need anything," Maggie replied as she turned away in order to attend to business, real business.

But before she got very far, Roy called out, "Thanks, Maggie!" Without turning back around Maggie waved her arm in the air and started to get down to business, real business.

Roy's first two sets were uneventful, although his profuse sweating was starting to attract some attention in the increasingly rowdy crowd. His third set found him struggling a little bit with the bowling ball gas pains he had been experiencing all day long. Fortunately for Roy his pains colored some of his more melancholy country songs, giving them an air of authenticity, albeit unintentional. The entire time he was performing, he could see Lizzie out there, waiting on customers and giving him furtive glances of approval. She could see him smile back at her, even though a Niagara Falls of perspiration was pouring from his pores. More than once she brought him a towel from under the bar, one time asking him, "Are you sure you're OK? You're soaking wet."

"Yeah, sure. Don't worry," he always replied.

It was approaching midnight, when Roy decided to do an old favorite of his, *You're Mine, Baby*. He figured that if Maggie really *was* a fan, she would recognize it and like it. The crowd had become very rowdy, just like Maggie predicted.

As Roy played a few guitar licks from the intro, several customers began hootin' and hollerin'. Roy wondered if they actually recognized the song from the intro or were just getting wilder. Maggie *did* recognize the intro and came out to the front area to listen while watching the customers. Roy thought to himself, "There might still be some life left in this aging, mothballed, old country singer after all."

Then he started playing and singing,

> *You're not worth nothin' to no one,*
> *You're not worth a solitary dime.*
> *You're a Schneider, a zero, a goose egg, a goose egg, but*
> *You're mine, baby, you're all mi....*

Before he could continue, he was interrupted with the worst gas pain yet. He felt like he was about to evert his bowels out onto the stage. He leaned forward on the stool and carefully put his guitar down. The abrupt interruption had attracted the attention of everyone the room, including those who had previously been innocently ignoring his performance as only background music.

He could hear a ripping sound which frightened him. "Are my insides tearing apart?" he said to himself. Then he let out a murderous yell and, thankfully, only heard actual cloth ripping (not his insides). "I feel like I'm turning inside out," he muttered in a low voice as he doubled over and strained against the bloated, bowling ball pain. Then, suddenly, as he stood before the crowd, now away from stool, the pain had vanished—the gas, the bowling ball feeling, even the sweating. Looking out over the crowd he saw people gasping, some of them covering their mouths with their hands, some turning away. Roy was bent over as he tried to walk, but decided to sit down on the stage next to the stool.

As the perplexed crowd stared at him in astonishment, Roy looked up at the stool and saw...IT.

IT was a large, glowing, neon-green egg, the size of a melon, with a gel-like translucent shell, sitting atop the stool—sitting as if it owned the stool. Roy was speechless and could only sit and stare at the thing. Since Roy was not reacting in any definable way, the crowd, with a uni-mind, deduced incorrectly that this, obviously, was part of Roy's act and began applauding precipitously. Shortly thereafter the crowd rose up in a standing ovation that lasted several minutes. Maggie had a toothy smile on her face, a smile as wide as the mighty Mississipp. Roy waved a feeble wave to the crowd and passed out on the floor of the stage. Maggie had never seen anything like it and speculated that at least for tonight there was incredible business to be had since the crowd was now in an absolute party frenzy. They had witnessed something truly spectacular. Seeing Roy pass out, Lizzie rushed to his aid and tried to help him out of the front area and into the break room, all the while keeping a wary eye on the big glowing green egg.

The egg continued to sit motionless atop the stool as the fever-pitch customers were making Maggie rich in one night. Whoops and hollers continued from the floor. It was like a New Year's Eve celebration. Maggie worked her way up to the stage and kept curious customers from coming onto the stage and touching the egg. She had no idea that Roy was going to pull *that* on her. She wasn't really complaining. Apparently it was good business, real business, real good business. From the stage, Maggie called to Lurg, dutifully in position by the door, and asked that he come up and protect the egg. Lurg, being a bouncer, was definitely a more logical choice for keeping the crowd away from it. To keep the party going, Maggie put on some energetic, but generic country music over the PA system—music that she had been playing between Roy's sets. She then turned off the stage spotlight so that the neon-green glow of the egg could be the focal point of the entire room. The place was really humming with activity. Louie and Surrey could barely keep up. Pleased, bewildered, and a little bit scared, Maggie then went to the break room to check on Roy and Lizzie.

Roy was sitting up on the old couch in the break room.

As Maggie came in she asked, "Roy! What the hell?"

"I don't know," Roy replied, not looking up. Roy didn't know if he felt embarrassed, ashamed, or what.

Shaking her head, Maggie handed Roy a bottle of water, "I can't say it was bad for business, but Jesus..." Then Maggie turned to Lizzie, "You think you can get him home?"

"I think so," Lizzie responded, helping Roy to his feet.

"I'll get Lurg to help you to your car. Call me tomorrow and let me know what's going on," Maggie said as she left the room. "Jesus..."

As Lurg helped Roy along toward the back door, Lizzie went out to the stage to retrieve Roy's guitar and case. There, she grabbed a towel, and wrapped the egg in it. She then carried the guitar and the egg with her, following Lurg and Roy out the back door.

When Roy and Lizzie arrived back at Roy's room, Roy went straight for the bed and conked out—sprawled out all over the bed. Roy was definitely getting his money's worth out of that bed. Lizzie leaned Roy's guitar against the dresser and put the egg into the bathtub after removing the towel. The egg was still glowing, illuminating the inside of the bathtub with its spooky green glow. Lizzie pulled closed the nasty shower curtain and sat down in the chair near the bed, exhausted. While catching her breath, Lizzie unexpectedly got a front row view of the giant split in Roy's pants. She closed her eyes for only an instant, and also fell asleep.

It was not until about noon the next day when Lizzie and Roy both came to life again, both still wondering about the egg.

"Roy. Roy. If you're OK, I'm gonna go change clothes at my apartment and then check on our jobs over at the Roadhouse. Are you OK?" Lizzie said to Roy as he stumbled to the bathroom.

"Yeah, that sounds good. Yeah, I'm OK," he replied, averting his blurry eyes from the familiar green glow in the tub.

A quick kiss later and Lizzie was on her way, "I'll be back as soon as I can."

Busily doing nothing, alone in his hotel room, room 212, Roy tried stepping through the TV channels for the nth time—still not working, mostly snow. Clock radio—not working, mostly static. The time on the clock had been stuck at 4:05 ever since he moved in. The one window—stuck, not working. Roy was never able to get it open, not even a little, if only for a *hint* of fresh air. And for some reason there was no hot water this morning.

Becoming restless, Roy changed into a new pair of pants and shorts since the ones he was wearing last night were ruined. Holding up the damaged denims, he put his hand and arm through the split crotch as if he needed proof that the split was actually there. His lower anatomy felt different as well, but he wasn't really in the mood to dwell on it. Adjusting himself, Roy could tell that something was just not right.

Roy was about to go stir crazy, when Lizzie came a'knockin', letting herself in. While in a welcoming embrace, Roy asked, "What's going on?"

"You're all over the Internet. You're a sensation, at least around here," Lizzie replied as she handed her phone to Roy. One post read "Roy Stoner Lays an Egg." "Don't read any of that stuff, Roy. It's not very flattering, mostly jokes, ridicule, stupid commentary, some videos, opinions about opinions, and pics. I thought that Roadhouse crowd was way too drunk to capture all that video, but...but anyway...I don't know how you feel about this—but Maggie wants to know if you can do it again."

"I don't even know *what* I did or *how* I did it," was Roy's reply. "I can't even believe that that..." Roy pointed to the bathroom, "...that big green thing in there came out of me! *Me!*"

"I understand," Lizzie said as she comforted Roy. "Maggie's only thinking about business, the delicate balance between good Roadhouse business and a sorry reputation as a freak show. Those were *her* words. She gave me time off so I can look after you. Her estranged folk-singer brother is gonna sub for you until you recover…not her first choice, not for that crowd, not after last night."

After a short silence, embracing, they both began to feel something rising up between them—so, in a frenzy, they scurried off to bed together, their clothes thrown all about the room.

And it was smoking hot, and good—

While they lay together, caressing, without smoke, drifting in and out of a fine afterglow, all that naked loveliness was brutally interrupted by a noisy commotion in the bathroom. At first there was a banging sound, then the sound of turbulent panic, ripping and twisting. Roy and Lizzie both jumped out of bed as if it had caught fire. Roy, crouching, stalking by stealth, slowly maneuvered toward the bathroom. As he pushed on the bathroom door, it opened to reveal the nasty shower curtain moving about in some kind of bulky, spasmodic fit.

"What is it?" Lizzie asked, as Roy reached for the toilet plunger.

"What are you planning to do with that?" said Lizzie.

"I don't know, yet. But I think something has happened to that egg," Roy replied. He stepped back while unscrewing the plunger rubber from the wooden handle. Looking at his soiled hand Roy remarked, "Well, that was stupid." He tossed the rubber part aside, wiped off his hand on the wall, and ventured toward the moving shower curtain while holding the wooden handle like a sword. The activity behind the curtain seemed to reach a peak and then calm down for a brief time. During one of the ebbs, Roy poked the curtain with the handle. The loud spastic activity rebounded into action, causing Roy to step back again. The next time Roy poked at it, the undulating shower curtain ripped itself off the rod and out came a large flying animal causing Roy to fall to the ground in a fetal pile of nakedness—a natural defensive position. Lizzie screamed as the animal flew into the bedroom and began eating the lampshade on the nightstand by the bed.

The egg had hatched and released a giant, bulky, furry, wasp-like, flying creature that resembled a bat, only with multiple legs. It had a nose—a prehensile trunk, not unlike an elephant's—a pair of double wings, two large yellow eyes, and a short tail with a triad of bony hooks on the tip end. Judging from its current size, it was obviously packed extremely tightly (and one must admit, efficiently) in that neon-green egg. The thing was at least two feet long.

The naked Lizzie rushed to Roy's naked side. "What is that thing?" Roy exclaimed using the plunger handle to lift himself up. The thing appeared to be content to devour the lampshade, for the moment. Roy went to the window and attempted to force it open again, but to no avail. With his undulating naked body pressed up against the glass, Roy, lifting with all his might, could not get the damn window to budge. It was quite a show for the people on the street below.

"Lizzie! Open the door!" Roy shouted as he attempted to open the window one last time. She quickly crossed the room and opened the door to the hallway, much to the surprise of the curious old man who lived across the hall. Alerted by all the racket, he was peeking out from behind *his* door when Lizzie exposed the frantic goings-on in room 212. Between the naked Lizzie, the naked Roy, and the luncheoning creature on the lampshade by the bed, the old man got quite an eyeful. But having lived at the *Hotel Savage* for some time, he had already seen everything and anything; and worse, much worse. Well, maybe not. The old man closed his door and proceeded to continue doing whatever it was he was doing.

Using the wooden plunger handle like a billy club, Roy swung at the creature, trying to encourage it toward the open door. Lizzie was alert and ready to slam the door shut if the creature left the room. Instead, the creature landed on the bed and began eating the bedspread. Sick. Roy waved the wooden handle at the creature, but the creature kept eating, making a soft crunching, munching sound as it gobbled away at the single nastiest thing in the room, maybe in the whole world.

"We're going to have to kill it," Roy said in desperation.

Lizzie agreed, "I think so." She closed the door and braced herself, trying not to watch, as Roy went in for the kill.

Sneaking up behind the creature, Roy started banging it with the stick. It seemed to have no effect. After several hits, the annoyed creature bolted from the bed and into the air again. It first flew toward the closed door (and Lizzie), then it doubled back at full speed and headed for what it perceived to be the great outdoors, slamming itself into the window glass, and falling to the floor, dead. The glass was cracked but not shattered. The creature left a large, dripping, creamy yellow splat on the cracked glass and several chunks of its former brain on the windowsill and floor. The big juicy smash against the glass was quite an encore for those few remaining individuals on the street who were privileged enough to have seen *Roy's* recent anatomical extravaganza upon that very same glass.

Roy nervously prodded the dead creature with the handle, but the smashed-up pile of a thing didn't respond. Poking at it reminded Roy of his grandfather who used to fall asleep watching TV, positioned in his big recliner like an astronaut. Pre-teen Roy would take a stick or pencil and poke at his Grampa's head, asking, "Grampa? [Poke] Grampa are you dead? [Poke]"

"Yes," Grampa always responded with a reassuring smile, eyes still closed. Pre-teen Roy got such a kick out of it.

One day Roy's Grampa did not respond.

Pre-teen Roy poked him several times. [Poke] Quite suddenly the startled old man sprung into consciousness with a wild jerk. Grampa's flailing arms spread out like wings with a clenched fist on the end of each arm. Unfortunately for pre-teen Roy, Grampa's right fist landed squarely on pre-teen Roy's jaw, knocking him flat out. Pre-teen Roy learned a lesson that day, a lesson about poking at a dormant creature without staying on full alert; a lesson still "on call" in egg-laying Roy's middle-aged mind.

Convinced that the creature was truly dead, Roy went into the bathroom, Lizzie close behind. Gathering up the shower curtain, he noticed that the thing had eaten almost all of the bathtub soap bar and had chewed through much of the plastic shower curtain that had temporarily constrained its fluttering self into a panic.

"What happens when the hotel maid service sees all of this?" a smiling Lizzie said, ineffectually holding back a huge chuckle. Naked Roy looked back at her and started laughing. Naked Lizzie started laughing. Embracing and laughing, they both began to feel something powerful rising up between them—so they stepped over the dead, oozing creature to the side of the bed...and stopped short, first looking at the half-eaten bedspread, the mostly-eaten lampshade, then at each other. Roy muttered, "Humpf!" and they gathered up their clothes and got dressed.

There was plenty to do for the next hour. Fully dressed, they tried to clean up the place. Roy wrapped the dead flying thing in the chewed-up bedspread along with the fragmented remains of the egg. The remains were now more grey than green and did not have the neon-green glow any more. When Lizzie tried to clean the yellow splat off the cracked window, all of the pieces of glass fell apart, leaving a large empty hole.

"What are we going to do about *this*?" Lizzie asked Roy, tapping at the few hanging shards still attached to the window frame. Roy shrugged. Lizzie picked up the wooden plunger handle from the floor and fiddled with the chunks of thing-brain, pushing them together into a pile. She got a towel from the bathroom and lifted the consolidated mess into the bedspread with all the other organic material. Roy then took an unchewed section of the shower curtain and affixed it over the hole in the window.

"Not bad," Roy said when the cleanup was completed. Pointing at the rolled-up bedspread, he contemplated out loud, "I wonder if this thing would have laid eggs of its own? Who *was* that woman in the swamp? What did she do to me?"

"One thing for sure, it's a fitting end for that horrible bedspread," Lizzie added, looking down at it as Roy came over and put his arm around her.

"Yes. Yes it is," Roy said in a fake somber tone, as if they were viewing the body of a much-disliked relative at a funeral home.

Lizzie then suggested, "Maybe tomorrow you should see a doctor, or someone. Have them take a look at you."

"You may be right," Roy said, as he felt uncontrollable hunger pangs coming on yet again. "Let's go somewhere nice to eat tonight."

Waiting until it was dark, the two carried the bedspread full of thing pieces into the alley behind the hotel and threw it all into the hotel trash bin. They took off in Lizzie's car, looking for a nice place to eat, one that might stay open late into the evening.

They first tried the *Catfish Emporium*—all-you-can-eat fried catfish. But upon entering the front door, the smell of catfish reminded both Lizzie and Roy of the swamp; so they went, instead, to *The Blackchaw Steakhouse*. There they enjoyed a long, leisurely dinner and felt as if they had not a care in the world—except for Roy's recurring gas pains. By 11:30 they had finished eating and Roy excused himself in order to use the facilities.

As he went into one of the stalls, Roy was horrified—not by what he came upon in the stall, which is what one might first assume. No. He was horrified by the feeling coming over him—extreme gas pains, just like he had on stage right before he laid that egg. He closed the stall door and reluctantly sat on the toilet, trousers down. The pain grew worse so he let out a yelp and a long moan as he braced himself for the worst. Having just recovered from the first incident, he was not ready for this, not now, not ever. Another, louder, longer yelp came out of Roy along with another moan and some squishing noises. A crisply dressed single guy with perfect hair was standing at the sink, washing his hands, and checking out his nose hairs in the mirror. Hearing the sounds of Roy's distress, the single guy could not get to the restroom exit quickly enough. In doing so, he forgot to retrieve his leather jacket that he had hung on the coat hook. Outside, the exiting single guy bumped into another dude-on-a-date on his way in. "Don't go in there," the exiting guy told the dude-on-a-date, "don't go in. I wouldn't advise it. There's someone having a really bad BM in one of the stalls right now. Don't go unless it's an emergency!" Roy was left to fend for himself.

Then, it was over. Roy stood up in the stall, looking down. Sitting in the toilet was another glowing neon-green egg, sitting proudly as if it owned the toilet. This time, more inclined to manage the situation, the not-so-proud Roy extracted the egg from the toilet water and left the stall. Standing in the middle of the restroom with the dripping egg cradled in one arm, Roy saw the single guy's leather jacket hanging on the hook. Roy turned the coat inside out and wrapped it around the egg. Hoping the owner of the inside out jacket would not recognize it, Roy quickly went back to his table. The situation was so fluid that it was easy for Roy to disregard the men's room toilet water dripping from the egg, not to mention the stealing of the poor single guy's nice jacket. Luckily, the jacket was thick enough to hide the neon-green glow emanating from the egg.

When Lizzie saw Roy carrying a mysterious bundle back to their table, she immediately deduced what had happened. After Roy hurriedly paid for the meal, the two of them left the restaurant, acting as non-chalantly as possible, and proceeded to Lizzie's car. Then, with Roy keeping a watchful eye on the wrapped-up egg in the back seat, Lizzie drove the three of them to her apartment.

"We need some kind of plan," Lizzie said as she parked her car near her apartment's front door. Lizzie and Roy sat quietly in the front seat of the car for several minutes. Then, in a halting voice, Roy asked, "About how long was it after...you know...after I laid...ahem...the first egg before it hatched out that...that thing?"

"I guess it was about twelve hours, give or take," Lizzie replied.

"I have an idea," Roy said as they went inside Lizzie's apartment with the bundle. Lizzie's place was small, but much nicer than Roy's room, room 212, at the *Hotel Savage*. Roy put the egg on the floor of the shower stall and tossed the slimed jacket into the corner. They talked about a plan for most of the night, dozing here and there and drinking coffee.

Early the next morning Lizzie and Roy drove to the *Blackchaw Medical Arts Building*, an austere, multi-storied office building housing numerous doctors and specialists. Lizzie had been here once before, to see a Dr. Smith in order to be cleared by the health department to work as a waitress. Roy was carrying the egg, again bundled in the jacket. They quickly located the second floor office of Z. Pincus Smith, M.D. and went inside, then up to the reception desk. Because it was so early, there was no one in the waiting room. The receptionist, although brusque, was very helpful in getting Roy seen by the doctor right away. Lizzie and Roy were extremely anxious to move the game plan along before the new egg hatched. Because the clock was ticking.

Suffice it to say that Dr. Smith was quite shaken by Roy's story, but could not challenge its veracity since there, on the examination table was the glowing neon-green egg—real, tangible evidence. Without hesitating or examining Roy, Dr. Smith referred him to a specialist in the same building, a Dr. Lerza R. Phramm. Although Dr. Phramm was well-respected for his knowledge of modern medicine, he was also very familiar with *Jeux de Poulet Blanc*, a form of Cajun voodoo (a.k.a. Ju-Pá) practiced by isolated groups of Louisiana swamp people.

Dr. Phramm's waiting room had a number of people waiting, so after checking in, Lizzie and Roy sat down with the bundle on Roy's lap. A number of odd paintings were hung on the waiting room walls, including one with a headless chicken and another of a human skull with fire coming out of its eye sockets. There were so many houseplants around the room that it felt like a jungle. And the heater must have been set to ninety because it was *hot* in there. It was difficult for Lizzie and Roy to just sit there, waiting, because the clock was ticking.

It was around 10:40 when Dr. Phramm, wearing a long, starched, immaculate white lab coat, entered the examination room where Roy and Lizzie had been sequestered by the nurse. The doctor's skin was perfectly smooth and blemish-free, but his white hair gave away his age. He had stubby little fingers and big hands and he spoke with a familiar, but subtle Cajun accent. The doctor's interest in Roy's case was immediately apparent and he did not seem the least bit shocked by Roy's story. Dr. Phramm placed the unbundled egg in the sink and examined Roy extensively and meticulously. Lizzie stood impatiently just outside the room while the examination took place. The clock was ticking.

Roy's every orifice was explored. All of Roy's vital signs were checked and documented. Samples of Roy and Roy's were collected and labeled. And the details of Roy's story were put into Roy's case history. Dr. Phramm left the room and allowed Lizzie to return to Roy's side. A few minutes later, the doctor came back with a Styrofoam cooler filled with ice. He situated the egg deep in the ice, sealed the cooler, and secured it with several straps.

"You know there's a possibility that that...egg is going to hatch pretty soon, don't you?" Roy said.

"I'm sure, but the ice, yep, we are hoping she will slow it down just a bit," replied Dr. Phramm. "I will need to get many test results and much analysis before we can move into high action, you see, Mr. Stoner. You maybe see? Yep?"

After providing Lizzie's phone number to the receptionist, Lizzie and Roy left the *Medical Arts* building and went back to Lizzie's apartment to wait. Roy's never-ending hunger and sporadic napping were getting to be a nuisance, but at least Roy and Lizzie were taking action.

Dr. Phramm rushed the egg off to the zoology department at the nearby university, Dixon Smoot A&M. He also sent a small sample of the gel-like shell to the toxicology lab for analysis. Urgently consulting several colleagues and using his own knowledge of Ju-Pá, Dr. Phramm was beginning to put the pieces of the puzzle together. But he wanted to wait until he had all the facts in before making any decisions or recommendations.

Roy and Lizzie were disappointed when the day ended without a call from Dr. Phramm's office. Together they were anticipating Roy's next egg-laying event as midnight drew near. Overruling their lustful desire for each other was the thick tension in the air as the minutes ticked by. Roy gobbled down a bunch of stuff out of Lizzie's refrigerator and Lizzie smoked a single, dried-out cigarette she found lurking in a junk drawer. TV, food, drink—they tried all kinds of distractions and as the digital clock displayed 11:36 they both knew that an egg-laying event was imminent. At the first sign of a potential egg outage, Roy was to get into the shower stall, trousers down, and wait.

When the blessed event finally arrived, Roy hustled into the shower and with little or no effort, produced another neon-green egg.

"Well...*that* was a let down," Roy said to Lizzie, putting on his pants. The new egg was identical to the others, but this time, Roy himself was feeling great. As Lizzie hugged Roy in relief, they both felt something powerful rising up between them...

"I need to get something to eat," Roy said, breaking the mood.

"Again? You just ate out my refrigerator," Lizzie said.

"I know. Must be I'm using up a lot of my own body's substance and fat to produce all these eggs."

Lizzie nodded in sympathy and asked, "What should we do with this one? We can't let it hatch another one of those...things."

"You're right, but at least we have until tomorrow around noon—I think...you know, to ditch it," Roy said with resignation. "We *could* just go and toss it into the swamp. Or the trash."

"Hmmm," Lizzie muttered. And, after the wheels turned for minute, she said, raising her eyebrows and smiling, "You know I still have my key to Dirty's place."

"You mean *The Rat's Nest*?" Roy said. And a big smile came across Roy's face as well.

Under cover of darkness, Lizzie and Roy sneaked into the back of Dirty's lounge. Business was slow, and Dirty, out on bail, was "up top" trying to keep things a'moving. There was a new waitress trudging around, scratching and adjusting herself. The new bartender was officiously handling his duties, scratching and adjusting *himself*. Dirty was so preoccupied with things "up top" that Roy and Lizzie easily slipped into Dirty's office, unnoticed. Lizzie kept watch while Roy placed the egg into the bottom of Dirty's trash can and covered it with all kinds of heinous things that were already in there. It would be days before the trash can would be emptied, maybe even weeks. Off they went, out the back door, like a couple of teenagers doing mischief.

The next few days were uneventful. Roy checked out of the *Hotel Savage* and moved in with Lizzie. Lizzie went back to work, part-time, and Roy performed at the Roadhouse from eight to ten every night. Maggie was glad to have them both back, even in a very limited way. Every night Roy and Lizzie would hurry back to her place in plenty of time to manage Roy's next egg.

"I feel like a vampire, or a werewolf, or something," Roy said to Lizzie on one occasion.

"Maybe Cinderella," Lizzie replied.

"I'm glad they're not the size of a pumpkin," Roy responded.

Each night, after a delivery, they would drive over to the Boardwalk and toss the new egg into the swamp—as far as Roy could throw it. They always wondered what was happening to the eggs. Did they hatch? Were they eaten by a predator? Did they just rot away? Without a word from Dr. Phramm, or anyone, they did not know what to do next, so they just muddled along.

A couple of days after leaving an egg in Dirty's trash can, they got word that Dirty had been arrested again for indecent exposure. It was midday at *The Rat's Nest* when the surreptitiously-deposited egg hatched in Dirty's trash can. At that time, Dirty, not alone in his office, was engaged in a little something-something. The newly-hatched, flying animal began thrashing about in the office, immediately homing in on, and eating Dirty's pants that were bunched up, vulnerable, on the floor by the door with the thing's flexing "trunk" in an orgasmic erectilic display. The munching creature was blocking the escape route as a flabbergasted Dirty and his gagging guest stood watching. After the elephant/bird thing finished off Dirty's pants and shorts, it went after the guest's outfit that was lying by Dirty's desk, consuming it in only three munches (buttons, zippers, straps, fake plastic police badges, garter belts, and all). With the creature so distracted, Dirty and his guest made for the door. But the creature followed them in hot pursuit, blocking the *back* way out. As the three creatures (Dirty, guest, flying thing) exited the lounge's front entrance, a passing police car spotted a compromised Dirty and immediately detained him, again. Dirty's guest avoided notice by cleverly ducking behind a big sign on the edge of the dirt parking lot while the policemen busily focused on Dirty's exposure. And the horrid flying creature flew off, high over the building, without being seen by either of the two Dirty-arresting officers.

It seemed like an ordinary afternoon for Roy and Lizzie, ordinary by recent standards. Roy had become used to the idea of laying an egg every night, but he surely did not want to do it in front of the crowd at the Roadhouse again. Having settled in for the afternoon, Roy and Lizzie were not particularly excited when Lizzie's phone rang. On the line was Dr. Phramm's nurse calling for Roy. Lizzie handed the phone to him.

"This is Roy Stoner..."

"Mr. Stoner, this is Nurse Terk from Dr. Phramm's office. Dr. Phramm and his colleagues would like to see you tomorrow at eleven if that is at all possible for you. He would like to go over your case...and, if possible, they would like you to bring an egg with you, if you have one."

"Oh yes, that's possible," Roy replied. After ending the call, he and Lizzie felt a real sense of relief. Finally, something was happening.

With the egg bundled in the single guy's jacket, Roy and Lizzie returned to the *Medical Arts Building* where they were directed by Dr. Phramm's receptionist to a conference room on the third floor. Lizzie and Roy were nervous with anticipation. Alone together on the slow-moving elevator, they felt a sense of quietude as nondescript music played in the background. Roy turned to Lizzie and commented, "I don't think that guy is gonna want his jacket back, do you?" Lizzie made a funny little grunt as the elevator door opened.

Around the corner, a few steps away, the conference room door was wide open. Several persons were milling about, most of them wearing long white lab coats. Seeing Lizzie and Roy, Dr. Phramm came and escorted them to two chairs at the head of the conference table. He unwrapped the egg and put it into the center of a large metal cage positioned on top of a wooden stand at the front of the room. He casually tossed the fouled, damaged leather jacket into the corner. The group of mingling doctors all found chairs around the table and Dr. Phramm introduced Roy to the assembled group; and, as a polite gesture, Lizzie as well. One by one Dr. Phramm pointed out each specialist and their role in the proceedings.

Summarizing the biological aspects was Dr. Adriana Peabody, an expert in interspecies zoology from the University,

"Mr. Stoner, you have somehow been fitted with a functional ovipositor that includes several new organs with yet-to-be-determined functionalities. We believe that the development of these organs is the result of some prodigious genetic manipulations, allowing these organs to develop, quite literally, overnight."

The conference room filled with murmuring from the assembled group.

Dr. Peabody continued addressing the group, "These new organs have Mr. Stoner producing a new 'egg' every twenty-four hours." Every time she mentioned the word "egg," Dr. Peabody gestured with "air quotes."

"These so-called 'eggs' are more like *cocoons* covered in a green gel-like substance, but the term 'egg' is a more convenient and not completely inaccurate description for now. The development of each 'egg' is drawing its substance from Mr. Stoner's fat reserves and the excessive amount of bulk food that Mr. Stoner has been consuming as of late."

Lizzie looked over at Roy.

Dr. Peabody continued, "According to his accounting, each 'egg' hatches in an amazing twelve hours, plus or minus one hour depending on temperature. This incredible level of metamorphosis by such a large creature is unheard of in current scientific literature. Let me direct your attention to the cage here at the front of the room. Before long, we think this 'egg' is going to hatch, producing a voracious, insect-like bird—so our discussion here may be interrupted at any time."

Taking the podium next was Dr. Hugo N. Gettit, a biochemist/toxicologist. Before starting to speak, he brought up a very technical-looking chemical diagram on the projector screen.

"As Dr. Peabody mentioned, we have an egg, a cocoon, with a luminescent, neon-green, gel-like shell. Although analysis of Mr. Stoner's previous egg's *contents* is still pending, we have very some interesting results from extensive analysis of its shell."

Pointing to the diagram with a wooden pointer-stick, Dr. Gettit explained, "A small percentage of the gel itself is merely an inert binder. However, chemical analysis shows that, other than the binder, the shell is comprised almost entirely of highly-concentrated tetra-hydro-cannabinol or THC...an active ingredient in marijuana."

A buzz went around the room. An astonished Lizzie and an astonished Roy looked at each other, both shaking their heads.

Using his stick to point out two other items in the diagram tapping the screen itself, Dr. Gettit continued, "More interesting are these two little organic molecules. This first one, call it Molecule A is actually a powerful aphrodisiac. Yes, that's what it is. And this one, call it Molecule B, requires a little more explanation. From our testing we have found that this little molecule..." Dr. Gettit tapped the item on the screen vigorously multiple times. "...this little molecule makes the other active shell compounds completely undetectable; not in the blood; not in the urine. We have only a small amount of data so far, but further tests on a larger group of volunteer subjects will soon be forthcoming, hopefully confirming our preliminary conclusions."

Facing the group, Dr. Gettit began acting very coyly, speaking in a low voice, "At this point, let me say that we have been blessed with a huge number of volunteers ready to test the psycho-chemical effects of all these shell compounds. We realize that experimental testing on human subjects this way is highly illegal, but we figure 'Who's to know?'"

When the chaotic conversations in the room finally simmered down to a low boil, Dr. Phramm took to the podium for a final word,

"I want to thank everyone who has participated in this ground-breaking research, yep, and those of you who are here today. You too Mr. Egg. Heh heh," he said with a playful humorous tone, acknowledging the still-unhatched egg. Then, getting all serious again, he continued, "One question she remains: Who or what was the female being that Mr. Stoner encountered in the swamp that night? What? Well, let me tell you. Using my experience with Ju-Pá, yep, and researching swamp lore, yep, and consulting with certain officials, our team has pieced together a plausible scenario. Yep. We believe that the female being that came out of the swamp was a member of a rare and strange species of stick people, described extensively in Ju-Pá mythology. Tall people, very thin people, people with vinyl-like skin. But no myth, it looks like, yep. This particular female's natural intra-species mate was...well, killed dead after being hit bad by a big fan boat, yep...fan boat recklessly driven helter-skelter around through the swamp by a bunch of teenaged hooligans. What can you do about it? The mate's dead male body was found by a Coagula State Park game warden investigating a huge bevy of buzzards hovering over a remote area of the Coagula Swamp. 'What's dead out there? Must be big.' Yep. That dead creature's body, he's being studied as we speak, getting busy on it. The female, not finding its original, natural species-specific mate, began seeking out a new species-specific mate. The female's brief fertile window was closing quickly. Finding no natural mate, she had to reproduce 'the hard way,' by depositing a wad of genetic material into Mr. Stoner, here...Yep."

An uncomfortable Roy made a slight, reluctant wave of acknowledgment.

"The wad of material was inserted into the abdomen through Mr. Stoner's umbilicus. Yep." Dr. Phramm indicated the location by pointing to his own umbilicus with both forefingers. "Well, details of Mr. Stoner's experiences are documented in our official report. Read it, understand it. We believe that a select few of the voracious flying creatures will be able to consume sufficient amounts of energy-producing material to develop real cocoons all over themselves. All over...themselves. Real cocoons. Yep. The contents of any *successful* cocoon will then metamorphose into either a male or female creature that will eventually mature into an adult—like the swamp female that reconfigured Mr. Stoner's insides. Yep. We don't know yet if Mr. Stoner's female was the last of her kind or if there are other adult creatures out there in the swamp. No, we don't know. If one or more male adults and one or more female adults make it through this complicated process and emerge from the cocoons, there will presumably be a sufficient number of adult creatures to mate normally, naturally, and in an adult way. Naturally. This elaborate process should produce enough offspring to carry on the species. Yep. According to legend, and assuming all of our conclusions are correct, if an adult male and an adult female can mate normally, they can avoid going through all that roundabout trouble with those big elephant bird-flies. Much too much trouble. Much too complicated to be sustainable. Hopefully no longer requiring the assistance of someone like Mr. Stoner here...Yep." Dr. Phramm gave Roy a fatherly pat on the back.

Roy made a slight gesture of acknowledgment again.

At that moment, as if on cue, the captive egg broke open and out popped a new flying creature, thrashing and banging itself around in the cage. Roy and Lizzie bounded toward the door as the scientists in the room began scientific discussions among themselves, some of them opting to observe, close hand, the distressed creature in the cage; and some backing away, hoping that the cage was going to be strong enough to contain the thing. The room was filled with science.

Before Roy and Lizzie could escape, Dr. Phramm came up to Roy and provided him with some additional information,

"Yep. I'm sorry the conference was adjourned prematurely, but I think you might be interested to know that we may have developed a procedure that will end the egg laying and allow your body to resorb those extra organs...if you are interested. Yep. It's a combination of surgery and genetic manipulation. Some risk, not much. No cost. Experimental, yep."

"Let me think about it," Roy replied as he and Lizzie tried to make a fast exit. But before they reached the elevator, they were accosted by Dr. Gettit, the biochemist, who had worked his way out of the busy conference room, hoping to speak to Roy, in private.

"Roy," Dr. Gettit said. "I think there might be some opportunities in all of this, for everyone concerned. You, me..." He paused. "Ahem...Ms. Beaufont..."

"Beaudine, Lizzie Beaudine," Lizzie said, correcting him.

At that moment, the elevator opened and the three of them entered it together. A quite interesting discussion followed.

In less than a month, with the help of Dr. Gettit's financing and knowledge of biochemistry, Roy and Lizzie were able to open a store in downtown Blackchaw: *Stoner's 4 and 20*. Extracting the active compounds from the gel-like shell of Roy's daily egg, all kinds of top-selling products were made available. Dr. Gettit was in charge of manufacturing and Roy provided the raw materials...daily.

During the day, Roy and Lizzie ran the store together while at night they worked at *Maggie's Roadhouse*, renamed and expanded thanks to a booming business. The Roadhouse now had a dance floor, a real stage with Hollywood lighting, a room with pool tables and arcade games, and a private concert room where once a week, well-off customers could pay dearly for a chance to see Roy produce an egg on stage. Other nights Roy would just entertain the crowd with his offbeat music, occasionally with a new song thrown in. Much to Roy's delight, he could self-produce "albums" of his music, selling them for pure profit at *Maggie's Roadhouse* as well as at *Stoner's 4 and 20*. One might think it unfortunate that Roy never had another song make it to the national charts, but locally he was quite a star. For Roy, that was enough. And one thing Roy knew well and that was when enough is enough.

Multiple waitresses now served food and drink as well as booze. More covertly, other compounds were also available (a cut of that market also going to Roy, Lizzie, and Dr. Gettit.) Lizzie was in charge of all of this waitressing activity and the "darker" market under the table. Some of it was legal and some of it not necessarily so. But, human culture changes, up and down, back and forth. Maggie managed everything at an executive level. And managed it well. Everyone was getting rich. What was once Roy's Country Music Star Protection Program was now Roy and Lizzie's big business in Blackchaw. And the eggs kept a'comin'.

The reincarnated notoriety of Blackchaw as a cultural Mecca once again began attracting a wide range of celebrities, musicians, artists, and tourists. Boutique shops sprang up selling everything from Roy Stoner Bobble Heads to Ju-Pá paraphernalia to green egg replicas (small, medium, and large). The revival of the town also attracted a swamp-full of the aforementioned hangers-on and pond scum like so much green and black algae on a fan boat's hull. But, in the words of the now famous Dr. Phramm, "What can you do about it? Yep."

Many of the rudderless, unsavory characters would congregate on the Boardwalk at three AM hoping to be "violated" by a swamp female so that they too could lay some eggs and acquire fame and fortune. It was a nauseating, mercenary display of tabloid-level behavior.

Roy and Lizzie's newfound wealth allowed them to finally get married. The event was held at Maggie's, of course; during the *day*, of course. They used some of their money to buy a big, very private, fenced-in spread down the highway from *Maggie's Roadhouse*, building a roomy ranch house very much hidden from highway traffic. A lengthy section of that very highway was renamed Valley View Road and, by mere coincidence, the Stoner address became 212 Valley View Road. All of it was far, far away from the swamp.

The repeat offender, Phil "Dirty" Sheets, vanished completely, jumping bond for multiple offenses and thereby relinquishing ownership of *The Rat's Nest* and many other assets. One evening, Lizzie thought she saw a disguised, mustachioed Dirty in the crowd at Maggie's, but nothing came of it. *The Rat's Nest* lounge caught fire one day and burned up. Nobody cared.

Many months went by and Roy's daily production began to far outpace Dr. Gettit's need for raw material. There was more than enough refined final product to supply the *4 and 20* (and Maggie's) for many years to come. The logistics of quickly processing each egg before it hatched became a burden unto itself. If an egg could not be processed in time, it would have to be tossed into the swamp where, each time, the egg would disappear forever. Several times an egg hatched prematurely and had to be dealt with—not pleasant. If a newly-hatched flying animal were allowed to be free, it would make for the swamp and disappear. It was becoming clear to Roy that laying a daily egg was not a long-term desirable activity that he wanted to continue for the remainder of his life—and especially not for his and Lizzie's life together. An understanding Maggie was dismayed when Roy decided to retire from the egg-laying business and undergo the ovipositor dissolution procedures. But she too was now wealthy enough to be comfortable, even following an inevitable change of direction.

Dr. Gettit bought Roy's and Lizzie's share of *Stoner's 4 and 20* and continued to generate wealth for himself. This final boost to the Stoner's finances allowed Roy and Lizzie to easily retire together at their ranch hideaway.

One aspect of Blackchaw was not revived: the Boardwalk. In fact, the city council had almost all of it removed out of respect for whatever was out there living in the swamp. All that was left of the walkway was a small refurbished, rail-less, wooden landing, the place where Roy first encountered the female being. The small deck without a railing was no longer big enough to support or contain the three AM pushing and shoving crowd of opportunistic human low-lifes—as a result, many of them fell (or were pushed) into the swamp water. For some, it was probably the first full body immersion with water (water, if it could be called that) in months. Or years. Between the swamp dangers, the fighting over "turf," and the lack of success in attracting lucrative female creature copulation, the discouraged scum-throng slowly thinned out and eventually dwindled down to none. Townsfolk found it amusing that these characters were so undesirable that even a dank-smelling swamp creature would have nothing to do with them.

As Dr. Gettit no longer needed more raw material, Lizzie and Roy—almost in ritual fashion, each day, shortly after midnight—immediately took each new, freshly-laid egg down to the refurbished landing and tossed it into the swamp.

There were rumors that out in the swamp a swarm of elephant-nosed flying creatures were cruising around together like a pack of wolves. Houses built too near the swamp were vulnerable to raids by the swarm. The creatures would venture far from the swamp and descend on an unsuspecting homestead, eating fabric materials like patio umbrellas, lawn chair cushions, hats, fabric car tops, and clothing and sheets hanging from clotheslines. They never raided houses or businesses in Blackchaw or its outskirts for some reason.

Some minor awards for science were given to the group of scientists who figured it all out, but science marched on and the world marched on. Blackchaw, being so remote was merely a tourist oddity much like those seen advertised on the main highways of the country. Those who knew of the place as a cultural Mecca always made the effort to get there; while those who thought a tourist destination was merely a "clean" restroom at an Interstate Highway chain operation like Truck-a-Luck, did not.

When Roy underwent the ovipositor dissolution procedures, Lizzie stood by him all the way. Over time, the success of the procedures became apparent. Without the need to supply nutrients to a daily egg-laying metabolism, Roy's eating was reduced to a much more sane and normal level. Not surprisingly, neither Roy nor Lizzie could fathom eating an egg, any kind of egg, ever again, no matter from *what* or from *whom* it emerged. Roy's original anatomy seemed to be restored, but considering: (1) Roy's genetic modifications and re-modifications; (2) Roy's ovipositor organ development and resorption of said organ(s); (3) Lizzie's burned-in mind images of Roy's neon-green, glowing eggs emerging from the mouth of his ovipositor; (4) The unveiled story behind the elaborate, cumbersome, and bifurcated mating/reproduction processes of the swamp creature species—Roy and Lizzie decided together, rather firmly, that having offspring of their own was not going to happen. No way.

On the last night before Roy started his ovipositor procedures, he and Lizzie took what would be, ostensibly, his last egg down to the landing. They delayed going, procrastinating, feeling somewhat sentimental about its being the last one, so their trip was much later than usual for the daily egg-toss—about three AM. Roy and Lizzie were relieved that there was no one else at the landing. Unlike all the other times when Roy threw the daily egg as far out as possible, this time, together, they threw the egg into the water as a kind of team effort. Symbolic. They watched wistfully as the green glow slowly sank into the water.

"The last one," Roy remarked as he looked away.

Lizzie watched the once again dark area where the egg sank and saw a residual greenish glow still present in the water near the landing. It was moving, moving toward the landing.

"Roy, look," Lizzie said, pointing at the glow.

It was a familiar pattern that Roy remembered as if it were yesterday. The female creature had come back! Like before she lifted herself up onto the wooden platform, her fingertips and eyes glowing green and hair that never seemed to be wet. Roy and Lizzie backed away fully prepared to run away, but the female's glowing, vibrating green eyes had already entranced them. She walked toward Roy and placed her glowing green fingertips on Roy's face.

"Goq-glun-glof," she uttered. It was nonsense to Lizzie, but not to Roy. Releasing her fingers from Roy, she backed up to the swamp edge of the landing, with a keen, watchful eye on Roy and Lizzie.

"Do you know what she said?" Lizzie asked Roy, not taking her eyes off the female creature, not even for an instant.

"Yes...She said 'Thank You'," replied Roy.

The female swamp creature, a natural denizen of the Coagula Swamp, adjacent to Blackchaw, Louisiana, then made a final, beautiful gesture to Roy and Lizzie with her green, glowing fingertips. And with that, she dropped down into the murky swamp water and quietly and gracefully swam away.

# A Tiny Tale

Fancy Restaurant.

There appears to be somethin' a'movin' in me split pea soup. It be a tiny man. He be a'strugglin' mightily. I offers him the tip of a toothpick. He grabs on and I pulls him out of the thick soup. I deposits his tiny self gently onto the white tablecloth next to me bowl. He begins to be a'scrapin' off the soup from his tiny body.

"Thanks for a'savin' me," he sez.

"What the hell?" sez I.

"I be one of the little people," he sez.

"I can see that," sez I.

"No. I mean, I be a *leprechaun*," he sez.

"Yer no leprechaun. Leprechauns arnt the size of a fly," sez I.

"Ye slobber-noggin! Leprechauns can't be a flyin' sort. Ye thinks ye knows so much. Why dast ye think I be a'wearin' this fanciful little green outfit?" he sez.

"I cannot tell *what* yer a'wearin', as yer covered in some amount of green soup there," sez I.

"Me hat! Me hat! Me hat mus' still be somewheres in yer soup there," he sez in a sizeable panic.

"Then it looks to be too bloody bad for *ye*, I'd say," sez I, addin' a kind of laughin' snort.

I looks for a tiny hat down in me soup and as I could discover nary a one, I then looks away to see if'n any body in the place might be a'watchin' the twosome of us—a'watchin' me—a'talkin' away to me bowl o' soup.

"Now look—" he sez.

"What are ye doin' in me soup, anyhows?" I interrupts him afore he can lather on meself any more o' his malarkey.

"The chef—last night whilst he was a'sleepin', I hitched meself a ride inside o' his nose hole. Tonight, in yon kitchen, the chef, he sneezed out real big nose whopper into yer soup, and I lost me balance—and I too fell out—and I fell in—into your soup there. Hmm. By the way, I daren't eat any o' that there soup, laddie boy," he sez. "If ye knows what's good fer ye."

"What a bunch o' screamin' steamin' green bullshite!" sez I. Me outburst was startin' to attract some attention among me fellow patrons.

"Ah! But I can grant ye three wishes in return for a'savin' me puny green arse. I can make ye a pot o' gold, or a love potion, or a mansion by the sea. All ye has to do is simply jes' name it," he sez.

"I daren't believe you," sez I.

"Come on now. Give it a whirl," he sez.

"All right there," sez I. "Somethin' simple: make me a dog."

He spins around right on that there white tablecloth. Thrice he did so. He stops, looks up at me and sez, "There ye have it young fella, it be done."

"Ha!" sez I, a'lookin' around meself, a'sniffin' and a'lookin' and a'seein' nothin' but the other folks around, all of 'em a'lookin' our ways. "Gruff, gruff. You lyin' little green bastard!" sez I to the little man. So I swats him flat like a fly—leaves him as a tiny little green spot right on the white tablecloth there—right next to me bowl o' soup. I takes a sniff-sniff at the little green spot, then I looks down at me soup in a kind of a ponder 'bout the chef's a'fore-mentioned big nose whopper. Sets me to a'wondrin' what else might be a'lurking in me soup there.

"Well then, enough ponderin'. Who cares? Guess it don't bother me none," sez I. Soup smelt all so mightily good, good. And I came to be hungry and hungrier. So's I starts right in; starts right in on it, as such; lappin' it up, tiny little hat and what ever else there might be a'floatin' around in there.

"Whoa there! Gruff!" sez I, as the before now unseen waiter grabs me neck by me scruff. "Grrr," sez I, as he pulls me out of me chair and sets me ol' bag o' bones down onto the floor. "C'mon boy, let's go," he sez. "No dogs allowed here in the dining room." And he drags me disinclined self off. And away.

"Well, at least I gots me health!" sez I.

# The Adventure of the Grabapple Five

If a mother and father conspired to ruin their newborn son's life, they might start out by naming him "Stupid"—Stupid Smith, for example. No matter how smart Stupid turned out to be, he would always be called "Stupid." Now matter how many degrees he earned, he would always be called "Stupid."

"Thank you for saving my daughter from the fire!" the young woman cried.

"Don't thank *me*...it was *Stupid* here," replied the fire chief, pointing to Stupid Smith, one of the firefighters.

And so on...

Such is the lot with jackasses. No matter how intelligent, no matter how polite, no matter how socially conscious a jackass might be, that individual would always be called "jackass." Sad but true. However, sometimes the shoe fits.

———————————

Isaac was a donkey; a male donkey—a jackass. He lived in the valley at the end of a dusty, narrow country road called Baersback End, not too far from one of the main roads in the county: the Grabapple Road. Baersback End was lined with hedgerows making the road feel even narrower. Near Isaac's home at Baersback End lived four other jackasses: Pucker, Brutus, Ralston, and Mooncalf.

All five donkeys lived on separate properties, but since there were no defined boundaries in that area (no fences) they could move about freely and gather together whenever they chose. One morning, Isaac was up as soon as first light appeared. The open fields around the End were still covered with dew and began to sparkle in the morning sun's light.

*Isaac*: What a great day! I feel like I should be doing something important on a magnificent day like this.

Isaac was doing some routine stretches when his friend Ralston came strolling along, fully expecting Isaac to stop mid-stretch. Ralston was not the most considerate jackass in the county.

*Ralston*: Hey! What are you up to this morning, Isaac?

*Isaac*: I'm looking for something special, that's what.

*Ralston*: And that might be?

*Isaac*: Don't know, maybe an adventure of some kind. Yes. Hmm. That's it. Are you in the mood for an adventure today?

*Ralston*: Well...could be. What about the others? Mooncalf, Brutus, and Pucker? Maybe not Pucker; he gives me the creeps.

*Isaac*: Pucker? Don't know what your problem is. Don't see it. He's always pretty agreeable. Round them all up?

*Ralston*: I have more important things of my own to do. What kind of adventure are we talking about?

*Isaac*: You've got nothing better to do and you know it. Let's go—

With that, Isaac and Ralston trotted over to the field on the other side of Baersback End. There, Isaac spotted two jackasses munching on breakfast bites out of a big pile of hay.

*Isaac*: There's Mooncalf over there, and Pucker is with him. Hey, you two! What's happening?

*Pucker*: It's a fine day. Fine. What do you think?

*Isaac*: Fine day. How about you, Mooncalf? Is it a fine day?

*Mooncalf*: Fine day for what?

*Isaac*: For an adventure. Ralston and I are headed out for some adventure. How about it?

*Pucker*: Sounds good to me. Let's go Mooncalf.

*Mooncalf*: Where are we going?

*Isaac*: On an adventure. Does anyone know where we can find Brutus? He should be in on this; this fine day of adventure.

*Ralston*: Over there. Over that ridge. Look at all that dust. I think I can hear him. Over there.

*Isaac*: Let's go see.

The four jackasses ambled over the ridge only to find Brutus in some kind of fracas with a mongrel barnyard dog. The dog was barking and circling around Brutus. Brutus was kicking and braying, trying to keep the manic dog at bay.

*Isaac*: What the hell, Brutus? Leave that dog alone. You don't even belong in this field.

*Brutus*: What are *you* jokers doing here?

*Isaac*: I've decided to have an adventure today. Ralston, Pucker, and Mooncalf have agreed to join in. How about you?

The barnyard dog was continuing to bark and circle around, but was very confused as to which jackass should be the target of its dog-mania.

*Brutus*: Shut up, you...you...dog! I've got a good mind to kick you into...well...I don't know what—maybe the infested pits of Donkeynation.

*Isaac*: Forget about that dog. Come with us. We have all day...all day for an adventure.

*Brutus*: Anything is better than this, I suppose. What kind of adventure are we looking for?

*Ralston*: Haven't decided yet—on anything, but I'm ready to get on with it. What's the story, Isaac? This was *your* idea.

*Isaac*: We'll—

*Ralston*: What were you doing with that dog, Brutus?

*Brutus*: I wandered over into this field—not my usual territory—and I was getting a little, you know, something to eat. Right in the middle of a mouthful, this yap-yap dog comes over to me and starts barking; yap yap yap. I might have been preoccupied with a mouthful of dewy grass, but I managed a kick or two aimed at that dog. But that didn't stop all the barking and jumping around and...well, you saw for yourself. When you guys showed up I don't think that dog knew *what* to do.

*Isaac*: I thought we'd—

At that moment Ralston leaned over and blasted a huge loud bray right in the ear of the crazy barnyard dog. It was so loud and powerful that the dog was almost rendered unconscious. Stunned, the dog backed away, all the while maintaining a defensive posture and adding in a growl every so often. The dog finally strutted off triumphantly. Then there was a welcome silence. Isaac was hoping that there would be no more interference since he now felt compelled to announce some sort of plan.

*Isaac*: I thought we'd go all the way up Baersback End to the Grabapple Road. We can find our adventure along Grabapple and see what we can make of this fine day. A fine day indeed.

*Mooncalf*: So what is the plan?

*Brutus*: He just told you. We're going up Baersback End over onto the Grabapple Road.

*Ralston*: I've been up Baersback End, all the way to Grabapple. There's nothing up there. I vote we go and disrupt Beezum's morning assessment and servicing of the cows in his field. I'd rather do that than go up Baersback End.

*Pucker*: Beezum, the Bull? I don't think so. Unless Isaac thinks so. I think.

*Isaac*: First of all Ralston, you haven't been all the way up Baersback End in your entire life, especially anywhere near Grabapple Road. And second, what kind of adventure can there be in tormenting a bull? Especially when he's busy—

*Brutus*: I'm game for some tormenting—

*Pucker*: That sounds very exciting.

*Isaac*: Listen, we're all here. We're going up Baersback End to Grabapple. And we're going to have some adventure. And it's going to be...adventurous. Memorable and fun. If anyone wants to stay here...well then...*stay* here!

*Pucker*: I agree with Isaac—

*Mooncalf*: So, what's the plan?

*Isaac*: If nobody has anything useful to say, let's go.

Watching from the hill was the manic dog—cautiously keeping its distance—as the five jackasses left the field and walked as a group onto the small open area at the start of Baersback End.

*Brutus*: I'm not going any further.

*Isaac*: What is it now?

*Brutus*: If we're going all the way to Grabapple, I'm not walking behind any of you, watching all your asses, bobbing back and forth, up and down, the whole way.

*Ralston*: That goes for me too.

*Mooncalf*: Whose asses are we watching? Why are we watching anyone's asses?

*Isaac*: OK. Now, listen you guys. Let's do this: everyone line up...here...side by side.

*Mooncalf*: What kind of a line?

*Ralston*: I'm not walking all that way alongside Pucker.

*Pucker*: What did *I* do?

*Isaac*: Don't pay any attention to Ralston, Pucker. OK, now. I'll decide. And then *that's it*...we're off. We're going to have some adventure, and that's that! Mooncalf, over there on the end, looking up Baersback End, on the outside—

*Mooncalf*: On the outside of what?

*Isaac*: Just get over there, over there. Ralston, you're next. Next to Mooncalf. Then Brutus. Pucker, you're here next to me.

*Pucker*: That's exactly right, Isaac. Just right.

*Isaac*: I'll be on this end. See? Baersback End may be narrow but we all just fit...side by side. Is everybody ready?

*Ralston*: Finally!

*Brutus*: You said it, Ralston.

*Isaac*: Then let's be off!

*Mooncalf*: Are we going?

And so the five jackasses marched five abreast, as if performing in some kind of strange choreographed promenade, brushing up against the hedges on either side of the road. They started their journey going up Baersback End and toward its junction with the Grabapple Road. They began looking forward to their adventure, great adventure, on that fine, very fine day.

When the group of five arrived at the Grabapple Road crossing there was a man there, a man standing on a short ladder. He was painting the crossroads sign pole at the corner. As the "marching" group arrived in their five wide and one row deep line formation, the man paused in his painting work—the group looked awkward and ridiculous. He couldn't help but chuckle to himself as he returned to his painting.

*Isaac*: Hey you there! Up there on that ladder.

*Sign Man*: Who? Me?

*Isaac*: Is this the Grabapple Road? Here?

*Ralston*: Sure it is, Isaac. It says so right there on the sign.

*Isaac*: You can't read, Ralston.

*Ralston*: Sure I can. It says "Grabapple Road."

*Isaac*: You're just guessing—

*Pucker*: That's right, Ralston. None of us can read, including *you*.

The Sign Man stopped painting again and pointed to the long road that reached both ways at the junction.

*Sign Man*: *This* is the Grabapple Road. The one you're standing on is Baersback End.

With that the Sign Man went back to his painting. Then Ralston went up to the man, examining the signpost like an authority.

*Ralston*: Are you sure that's the way to spell "Grabapple"? And it looks like you missed a spot down here...you know...with the *paint*.

*Sign Man*: Why don't you five asses just move along? I've got work to do.

And the painting resumed, once again. Ralston was undeterred. He moved in closer to the man and the ladder. As Ralston did so, he bumped into the bottom of the ladder shaking it with a fair amount of force. The Sign Man had to grab the tall, painted post in order to keep from falling. This, of course, covered the front side of the Sign Man with a broad lengthwise stripe of white paint. First the Sign Man checked his front side. Then he evaluated the damage done to his signpost paint job. Finally, the angry painter glared down at Ralston. Ralston looked around, acting as innocent as a newborn little donkey.

*Sign Man*: Why you jackass! Look what you made me do!

*Ralston*: Well that's *your* misfortune. I can't help it if you're, you know...clumsy. You must be very much unqualified for managing your way through this menial job. And such a bad attitude, blaming others for your own shortcomings.

With that remark, the Sign Man casually loaded his brush with white paint and proceeded to paint Ralston's long forehead and nose with a solid white stripe of its own. Ralston was so taken by surprise that it gave the Sign Man time to apply a second coat of paint on top of the first. At that point, Ralston shook his head as if the shaking would magically remove the paint. Showing no sympathy whatsoever, the other four jackasses commenced to laugh at the painted Ralston. What an appearance! What entertainment! The Sign Man regained his balance on the ladder, but earlier, when he grabbed for the pole, his trousers had slipped down enough to reveal a little something.

*Brutus*: Wow, look at that!

*Isaac*: Yeah, nobody wants to see *that*.

*Ralston*: Hey fella, cover that crack with your tail. Oh, that's right you don't have a tail.

*Pucker*: That's right. No tail.

*Mooncalf*: What's everyone looking at?

*Isaac*: Hey, Sign Man. Grow a tail. Grow a tail, will ya. Cover that up. Lookie here—

In a mocking gesture, Isaac turned his backside toward the Sign Man and flipped his tail up at him a couple of times, giving the Sign Man a couple of brief glimpses of Isaac's true ass.

*Brutus*: You want me to kick his ass?

*Isaac*: I don't know. Hmmm. No. We've got better things to do. Let's just go.

*Pucker*: Yeah. Better things. Let's go.

As the group turned to begin their journey along the Grabapple Road—

*Ralston*: I'm still not sure about that spelling.

*Isaac*: Give it a rest, Ralston. You haven't convinced anyone that you suddenly know how to read. You know, I can't say I care much for your new look—your entire forehead and face. Man that is white!

*Ralston*: What new look? Oh...pbfluuugh!

In a final act of orneriness, Ralston used his back legs to kick up a cloud of road dust...up onto the sign man, the ladder, and the fresh paint of the sign. Giving the sign man a departing view of their five asses, the Grabapple Five were quickly on their way, still marching five abreast and still looking like a military formation in a parade.

*Brutus*: You should've let me kick his ass!

*Ralston*: Now, now, Brutus—

*Brutus*: You're such a pompous wuss, Ralston.

*Isaac*: Shut up, you two! It's time we got on with our adventure. Our day has been interrupted and disrupted enough by that unfriendly Sign Man. There is surely some adventure awaiting us up ahead. And Ralston, you can lead the way with your new headlamp.

*Ralston*: Very funny. Ha...*Ha.*

Ralston did not appreciate Isaac's taunting. The Sign Man watched the Grabapple Five proceed on, their big donkey asses pointing directly at him. Or so he imagined.

*Sign Man*: Jesus H. Christ! What a bunch of assholes!

So their day of adventure was truly underway. What adventure lay ahead down the Grabapple Road? So far there had been no adventure, but they were sure that there was adventure to be had, sooner or later.

As they proceeded along the Road, there came into view a rickety fence. It was mostly intact, but a woman dressed in dirty red overalls was attempting to repair a section of it. The wood was so rotten that she was having a hard time getting the nails to hold fast. She was not aware of the Grabapple Five as they came up behind her.

*Isaac*: Hey there! Old woman!

The woman was startled by the sound of Isaac's voice.

*Ralston*: You jumped like a scalded frog, old woman. You must be nervous and scared. Why are you so nervous and scared? Are you feeling guilty about something? Like...just what is it you are doing to that fence?

*Fence Woman*: What are you talking about? You didn't scare me. You *startled* me. This is *my* fence. What is it? What do you five jackasses want? Why are you all lined up like that?

*Isaac*: We're looking for adventure. Have you seen anything this morning that would indicate *adventure*?

*Pucker*: Yes, answer up, you. Have you seen anything?

*Isaac*: It's OK Pucker. I'm working this. Well, old woman have you seen anything?

*Brutus*: You want me to kick her ass...make her talk?

*Ralston*: What are you doing to that fence, old woman. You sure have made a mess of it.

The woman was not really old and she was definitely not feeling congenial, having been interrupted with such attitude. She was fixing the fence in order to keep her two thoroughbred racehorses from running free, all across the countryside. She decided to offer some kind of information to the five as a way to get rid of them.

Fence Woman: I think I saw plenty of adventure—down the road there, a couple of miles, on the right. You'd better hurry. I don't know—it might be gone soon. Adventure doesn't hang around waiting for the likes of you. Good luck.

Mooncalf: We'd better get going if we're going to catch that adventure before it gets away.

Isaac: Yes yes, Mooncalf. Say old woman, how much did you pay for those red overalls? Whatever it was, it was too much. They're filthy, too.

Pucker: Yeah. It was too much.

Brutus: I think we should kick her ass—

Fence Woman: I thought you five were in a big hurry to find some adventure. (What do I have to do to get rid of these guys?)

Ralston: Look at all this rotten stuff. All I have to do is touch the fence and it falls apart.

Ralston started poking at the fence with his front hoof. When the fence didn't collapse right away (confirming his assessment), he punched at it until it actually did fall apart.

Ralston: See? Look at that!

Fence Woman: Why you...get out of here...right now...before I...Huh? What's with the white painted face? You there, wrecking machine, what's with the white face paint?

*Mooncalf*: Who is Wrecking Machine?

All of the jackasses started braying and guffawing—all except Ralston who decided to take down a few more sections of the fence—to prove his point. With her hammer held firmly in her hand, the woman raised her arm and waved the hammer at the group.

*Fence Woman*: Get away from my fence...get away from there...now! Before I
hammer the living shit out of the lot of you!

Brutus decided to take action with or without Isaac's approval and moved into the woman's personal space in order to start up some ass kicking. Seeing Brutus coming directly at her, the woman whacked Brutus on the nose with her hammer, giving Brutus a geyser of a nosebleed. Of course the other jackasses could not restrain themselves and so re-directed their laughing and braying at Brutus, especially the white-faced Ralston, who laughed the loudest.

*Isaac*: My my. Epithets. My sensitive ears. Gentlemen, shall we be off lest we
be offended further by such a vulgarian?

*Pucker*: Yes, lest us be off before the vegetarian further epithets us.

*Ralston*: Pucker, you're such a—

*Mooncalf*: Will someone please tell me what's going on?

In addition to the bleeding, the blow to Brutus's nose raised a big knot on it giving him a comical, rhinocerated appearance. Having no hands, there was no way for Brutus to stop the nosebleed except to hold his head back as far as possible. Trying to shake off the injury, Brutus backed away from the woman. But backing up with his head held high in the air he could not see where he was going and so he backed right into Mooncalf.

*Mooncalf*: Whoa there, Yow! Look out!

Surprised by Mooncalf's outburst, Brutus lurched forward, bumping nose first into Ralston.

>  *Ralston*: Get back, Brutus! Don't get any of that blood on me. You idiot! Look where you're going.

>  *Isaac*: Come on, we need to get going. Let's go see if the adventure is still down there; down there where the woman saw it. The adventure the woman spoke of. It's only a couple of miles—like she said.

>  *Ralston*: How far is a *couple of miles*?

>  *Isaac*: Hell if *I* know. Let's go!

>  *Pucker*: I vote "Yes" to that.

So the group left the woman to her fence mending, a job that was now six times greater than it was before the Grabapple Five arrived. The woman felt like throwing her hammer at them. Surely she could hit one of them squarely in the ass as they headed down the road (five abreast). But she didn't want them coming back, for any reason—definitely. So why take a chance?

It was only a short distance down the road from the Fence Woman that the group encountered the woman's two racehorses: two beautiful, stately, sleek black horses; trim but very muscular; and much taller than any of the Grabapple Five. Isaac noticed that the two horses were very well groomed—probably the result of a soft life of pampering. The horses were standing behind the rickety fence warily watching the group of five as they approached.

>  *Babette's Box Tango*: What are you five assholes up to?

>  *Isaac*: Assholes? Is that what you think we are? We're jackasses—

*Babette's Box Tango*: Same thing.

*Isaac*: Now just hold on a moment—

*Shadow Dancer*: What do you think they're up to, Babette?

*Babette's Box Tango*: No good...probably.

*Isaac*: We, our group, are on a quest for some adventure. That old Fence Woman said it was just down the road there, a couple of miles.

*Shadow Dancer*: Yes! I believe she's right. I think I remember seeing some.

*Babette's Box Tango*: That's right. Just down the road there, down that way—

The two racehorses were making fine sport of the five jackasses.

*Isaac*: My name is Isaac. That's Mooncalf, Brutus, Ralston, and Pucker—over there. And whom may I inquire are you pair?

*Shadow Dancer*: I'm Shadow Dancer—

*Ralston*: Wow—quite a name!

*Shadow Dancer*: And my filly here is Babette's Box Tango—

*Ralston*: A bigger name! You pair must think you're something real special with all those names.

*Shadow Dancer*: We're racehorses; that's what we do. Race. And that's what they call us.

*Ralston*: Sounds pretty absurd to me. Racehorses? I've done some racing in my time—when I was very young. Won several races before I had to quit and go into business.

*Isaac*: What are you talking about, Ralston? What business?

*Mooncalf*: I never knew all that about you.

*Pucker*: Yeah. Who would have thought.

*Isaac*: He's not...he wasn't—

*Babette's Box Tango*: Say, what's with the white face, Assbag?

*Ralston*: Assbag? Hmmpf...that's none of your business, you old nag.

*Shadow Dancer*: Watch it—

*Mooncalf*: Who is Assbag? All these names. Who can keep track?

*Ralston*: You sure have thin legs. How do you even stand up on those little spindly sticks?

*Shadow Dancer*: We're bred for speed and grace—probably unfamiliar concepts to jackasses like yourselves. By the way, Assbag, do you have any idea what you look like with all that white on your face?

*Ralston*: Not really. How would I?

*Shadow Dancer*: Let me show you. Come here.

As Ralston came up to the fence to get a look, Shadow Dancer turned completely around, brandishing his backside right in the face of Ralston.

*Shadow Dancer*: See anything familiar?

*Ralston*: All I see here is a horse's ass.

*Babette's Box Tango*: Heh heh. (Nickers.)

*Ralston*: Why you—Brutus? Brutus!

Shadow Dancer let out a good horse laugh as he turned back around to face the group once again. Unaware that Ralston was addressing him, Brutus moved slowly into a position very close to Babette's Box Tango. He began speaking in low tones.

*Brutus*: Hey babe. You look good. Looking good—all sleek and black and tall and all.

*Babette's Box Tango*: Heh heh. (Snort.)

*Shadow Dancer*: Get away from her!

*Brutus*: You know, Shadow Boxer, I should come over there and kick *your* ass.

*Shadow Dancer*: You'd have to catch me first, you little pipsqueak. Do you think you're up for that?

*Ralston*: Never mind Brutus. Shadow, you and me. Let's race, right now. I'll run along the road out here and you can run along the fence in there. We'll race up there to that big oak tree.

*Isaac*: Really, Ralston? You can't be serious.

*Ralston*: Flash his big horse's ass in my face? I'll show him. You start us, Isaac.

*Brutus*: Wouldn't you rather I just kick his ass?

*Pucker*: What is it with you, Brutus?

*Babette's Box Tango*: Shadow, do you really need to do this?

*Shadow Dancer*: What the hell. All right, Isaac, say when.

Ralston and Shadow Dancer lined up, one on each side of the fence. Brutus, Mooncalf, and Pucker went down the road to the big oak tree—the finish line. When Isaac said "Go" the two braggarts were off and running. Before Ralston was even halfway to the finish line, Shadow Dancer had already finished. But as soon as Shadow Dancer passed the big oak tree he stepped into a small gopher hole and ostensibly injured his front left fetlock. He was hobbling about when Babette's Box Tango came up to his side. Isaac, trotting from the starting line, joined the group a shortly afterward.

*Babette's Box Tango*: Horrors! Shadow, are you all right?

*Shadow Dancer*: I don't know. I don't think so. It's my fetlock. I think I may have broken something—

*Ralston*: Wow! You know what they do when a horse breaks a leg. Especially a racehorse with those thin little sticks for legs.

*Isaac*: That's enough, Ralston. Leave him alone. He's obviously in a lot of pain.

*Babette's Box Tango*: Why don't you assholes just go on your way and leave us alone.

*Ralston*: I was just saying…a horse with a broken leg…you know—

*Isaac*: That's enough of that! I think we'll be moving along now. Tell Shadow to be more careful next time.

*Babette's Box Tango*: There won't be a "next time." You know that. Enjoy that *big* adventure when you get there.

Without showing the slightest concern toward or further consideration of Shadow Dancer's condition, the Grabapple Five resumed their search for big adventure, heading on down the road—down where there must be adventure since everyone seemed to know about it.

*Ralston*: Clumsy horse. It was his own fault. He's a goner now.

*Mooncalf*: What are they going to do to him?

*Ralston*: They're going to kill him and feed him to dogs or make glue out of him.

*Pucker*: That's awful.

*Mooncalf*: How do they make glue out of a horse?

*Isaac*: Let's not trouble ourselves with any of *that*—we've got adventure ahead. Only a couple of miles. They're just a couple of useless horses. Racing…what kind of a job is that anyway? Pitiful.

*Ralston*: Useless.

*Pucker*: Useless.

*Mooncalf*: And just what kind of jobs do *we* have?

*Isaac*: Never mind.

*Brutus*: (Slurp.) Now, that *Babette*—now there was quite an animal. I'll say that. Really something. Makin' a mule, makin' a mule...with you.

*Ralston*: Brutus, do you really believe she'd—have anything to do with you?

And so, continuing their discussions about anything and everything, the Grabapple Five proceeded on their way down the Grabapple Road.

*Shadow Dancer*: Are they gone?

*Babette's Box Tango*: Yeah. They've gone on past the ridge down there.

*Shadow Dancer*: Looks like they bought all that; bought it all.

*Babette's Box Tango*: Doesn't matter; we got rid of them.

*Shadow Dancer*: Did they really think a thoroughbred racehorse could be that careless and clumsy?

*Babette's Box Tango*: Forget about them.

*Shadow Dancer*: What a bunch of assholes...especially old white-face—even gives a horse's ass a bad name. Shame that I have to have one attached to me.

*Babette's Box Tango*: Yeah. Me too. Heh heh. But I have to admit, that little Brutus fellow was quite an operator—

Shadow Dancer and Babette's Box Tango gracefully turned and trotted away, trotting with a smooth gait, then galloping, far from the Grabapple Road and back into their life of comfort and pampering.

It wasn't long before the Grabapple Five came upon an impressive rock wall. The rocks in the wall were all perfectly aligned and the thin strip of land between the wall and the Grabapple Road was very well maintained. The wall was constructed so well that one could believe that the entire structure was one solid piece of rock. A little further up the road there was a wrinkled and weathered, darkly-tanned man working on some sculpted bushes planted on the small thin strip. Next to him was a magnificent gate.

As the marching Grabapple Five formation came up to the gate, the group began examining it, up and down, craning their necks when trying to see the top. There was a fancy sign on one of the gate columns: Isherton Manor.

*Isaac*: OK Ralston, Mister Smart Guy, what does *that* sign say?

*Ralston*: I can't tell without my glasses.

*Isaac*: You don't wear glasses. Forget it. Glasses...I don't know of a single donkey that wears glasses—

*Ralston*: You and I obviously travel in different circles.

*Isaac*: Circles? *What* different circles? *This* is the circle.

*Brutus*: You big snob—who do you think you are?

Ralston: I'm just sayin'—

The Weathered Man could not help but notice the line of arguing jackasses. He interrupted his bush-sculpting and gave the jackasses the once-over. Isaac turned his attention to the Weathered Man.

> *Isaac*: Hey there, tan man. What's going on *here*? All this wall. Can't seem to see anything on the other side of it.

> *Weathered Man*: That's the whole point of a wall. Other than that, cain't say. What's all this? Five jackasses marching along the road? All lined up. Never seen it. What're you jackasses all lined up for?

> *Isaac*: We're on our way for some adventure. It's supposed to be just down the road here. But what's on the other side of this wall? That's what we'd like to know.

> *Weathered Man*: Cain't say.

Rather than wait for any more non-answers, Brutus began pulling on the gate's rope ring with his teeth. To his surprise, the gate opened easily, revealing a large homestead on a hill. The entire ground was a field, a uniform lawn of green grass, immaculately manicured; and there was a fine road leading from the Grabapple Road up to the mansion.

> *Brutus*: Hey, everyone! Come here and look at this!

> *Weathered Man*: Now don't any of you move any further. You're not supposed to be looking in there. (I should have latched that gate when I came out, but who would've thought that a bunch of jackasses would show up here, sticking their long snouts into things.)

The Weathered Man attempted to block the open gate with his body, but Brutus nudged him aside as the other jackasses wedged their way in between each other and the gate until the gate was wide open.

*Pucker*: Well, will you look at that!

*Isaac*: Let's get on up there. A fine place such as that must be harbouring some adventure in its bosom.

*Weathered Man*: Now look here, you bunch of jackasses! You cain't just come in here—

*Ralston*: **Braaaaaaaaay! Bray!**

The loud slobbering aggressive eruption of Ralston into the Weathered Man's face forced him aside. Without further ado the group began their five abreast march up the road. Since the private road was not nearly wide enough to accommodate a five-wide line of jackasses, the jackasses on either end wound up stomping all over the grass on each side, destroying the manicured edge. And so they went barreling along, five abreast, up the hill, toward the glorious mansion.

Before the group of five got all the way to the building, there, in a small enclosed courtyard, was an elderly couple having a light breakfast. Peaceful. Tranquil. Carefree.

*Ralston*: Hey! You two old folks! What is this place? How do you fit in here? In all this?

*Isaac*: Don't mind Ralston, he's just curious.

*Lord Creamstick*: What in blazes?

*Lady Creamstick*: Oh! O-o-oh!

The royal couple stood up, indicating extreme displeasure with the appearance of five rude intruding jackasses during breakfast—interrupting the delicate and proper *ante meridiem* proceedings. Five impertinent jackasses to be sure. Five jackasses asking questions, no less.

*Lord Creamstick*: Get out of here you filthy animals! Get out!

*Ralston*: Filthy?

*Isaac*: We only wanted to take a look at things. Look around. We're looking for adventure and we thought there might be some in *here*—this side of that wall down there. Can't see a thing from the road—how inconvenient. But it *is* a very nice wall, by the way.

*Lady Creamstick*: I'm calling Simmons.

With her napkin still in hand, Lady Creamstick rushed out of the courtyard and up to the mansion as Lord Creamstick, keeping his distance, began waving his arms and shouting at the group of five. But, as everyone knows, jackasses are notoriously stubborn. And, in spite of the Lord's gesticulations, the jackasses moved nary a muscle (mostly out of pure defiance).

*Brutus*: I could use a drink of water.

*Pucker*: Me too.

*Mooncalf*: What are we doing here? Who is that man?

Determined not to be bullied by the man, Isaac very calmly sat down. The others quickly followed suit. So there it was; quite a sight: Lord of the manor, dressed in morning finery, napkin hanging from his shirt collar; and five uninvited jackasses in a semicircle around the Lord, all sitting on their asses.

*Isaac*: The least you could do is offer us some water—water for my thirsty friends and me.

*Lord Creamstick*: If I let you get a drink, will you be on your way?

*Ralston*: I think he should apologize for calling us filthy.

*Mooncalf*: Who's filthy?

*Isaac*: Let's all go get some water, quench our thirsts, and then get back to the Road. There doesn't appear to be any adventure happening here.

*Ralston*: Yeah. Boring.

So Lord Creamstick led the group out of the courtyard and further on up the hill toward a tank of water where the group of five could get a drink.

*Ralston*: This is quite a place you have here. How much does something like this cost?

*Lord Creamstick*: Why do you care? You don't use money. You're a jackass.

*Ralston*: That's right. And proud of it, I might say.

*Lord Creamstick*: (Don't know if that's anything to be so proud of.)

*Brutus*: How much further is it?

*Lord Creamstick*: It's right over there. Help yourself and then go back out the way you came in.

Lord Creamstick pointed to a large, round, metal tank of water. As the group of jackasses sauntered over to it, Simmons, the butler, arrived on the scene with a shotgun under his arm. Lady Creamstick was right behind. The jackasses came up to the rim of the tank. The water was murky and the metal was rusty—years and years of rust. The tank was used for filling up watering cans and was constantly building up scum on the surface.

> *Simmons*: Are you all right, sir?

> *Lord Creamstick*: I'm fine. As soon as this pack of jackasses gets a drink...they're leaving. If they don't...ahem. Simmons? I expect you to know how to use that thing.

Ralston took the first gulp.

> *Ralston*: Blech! What the hell? What kind of water is this? I've never tasted anything so crummy! My mouth is puckering!

> *Pucker*: Me?

None of the others dared taste the water after Ralston's outburst. Ralston himself seemed to go into a kind of agitated seizure. He began running about, braying like a mashed cat, kicking up his back hooves into the air (as donkeys do). He bounced his way around and then made straight for the mansion, assuming that some kind of real water could be found there. He was spitting and sputtering the entire way.

Then, into the kitchen door he bounced and kicked. Inside, there was no single pot or pan that didn't receive a blow or two from the crazed Ralston. Lord Creamstick, Lady Creamstick, and Simmons chased after Ralston. The other four jackasses followed close behind. And finally, up from the Road, there was the Weathered Man adding his presence to the fast-moving mob. By the time the entire crowd arrived in the kitchen, Ralston was already in the adjoining room, bouncing, kicking, and leaving a path of destruction the likes of which can only be seen after a wartime bombardment.

But as far as Lord Creamstick was concerned, this *was* war. He addressed Simmons as they followed Ralston into the main area of the mansion.

> *Lord Creamstick*: I want you to shoot that bastard as soon as you can draw bead on him!

> *Lady Creamstick*: Don't you dare, Simmons! If you hit one of those priceless paintings with that buckshot, it will surely ruin it. And there's also the statuary, and the tapestries. Don't you fire that gun in this house. Just run that animal off some other way.

> *Simmons*: Yes Ma'am.

> *Lady Creamstick*: What were you thinking, Fenster?

> *Lord Creamstick*: Sorry, Paladora. I just wanted all those animals out of here. Simmons, do like she said. Just get them all out of here as best you can.

Simmons followed Ralston into and around and around the main entrance hall, trying to minimize the damage. Noticing an ancient spear—one of many historic weapons displayed on the walls of the mansion—he pulled it from its hanger and went right after Ralston. In all the mayhem, Ralston never seemed to notice the presence of Simmons. Nevertheless, Ralston was beginning to tire and slow down, the effect of the tainted water beginning to wear off. Rapidly weakening, Ralston continued his rampage as Simmons covertly opened the double doors leading from the main entryway to the outside. Finally, felling exhausted and very self-satisfied, Ralston stood by the double doors, looking out across the rolling green lawn.

The others were watching as Simmons sneaked up on Ralston from behind. With one big thrust, Simmons rammed the spear right into the meaty right butt cheek of Ralston, launching the jackass several inches off the ground, then clippity-cloppity, right out the front door of the mansion—all of which was accompanied with copious amounts of high-pitched braying. In spite of the pain in his butt, and now out on the mansion's front porch, Ralston started kicking his back legs into the air at some imagined phantom enemy. Simmons was quick to close the double doors. Ralston was out on his ass—so to speak.

Simmons and the Weathered Man ushered the other four jackasses out the side door and around to where Ralston was standing. They were all a little more cooperative than before after seeing Ralston get his ass punctured by that pointed stick. And now, sitting down like a stubborn jackass was not an option for Ralston.

> *Simmons*: I want you five animals off this property. Now! Or Driscomb here is going give you more than just a poke in your asses.

The Weathered Man, Driscomb, was now wielding the shotgun, pointing it at the jackasses. Giving Driscomb an occasional stink-eye, the group of five started a new discussion.

> *Brutus*: Who the hell is Driscomb?

> *Isaac*: I think he's the tan man from the gate.

> *Pucker*: Yeah, that's what I think too.

> *Mooncalf*: What tan man? Who's the tan man?

> *Simmons*: No more discussion. Go on beat it!

> *Isaac*: All right. All right. You know that tank is going to rust through one of these days. Just be aware.

> *Pucker*: Isaac's right, you know—

*Mooncalf*: Are we leaving now?

*Simmons*: Go...ON!

Simmons motioned to Driscomb. **Blam!** Driscomb fired the shotgun into the air, the echoes bouncing off everything across the grounds. The blast caused the startled group of five to jump in unison—heads shaking, bodies quaking. Begrudgingly, they lined up and began slowly, casually, sauntering down the slope and across the grass, heading toward the gate. Ralston was struggling to move along, as every flexing of his punctured ass muscle was painful.

**Blam!** Driscomb fired another shot into the air, ringing out across the lawn, jolting the jackasses again.

*Simmons*: Get on with it!

The second shot turned the five's sauntering into an immediate and swift trot down to the end of the lawn, Ralston included. Driscomb ran down behind the group and once the five jackasses were through the gate, he closed and latched it. Outside, the group continued their discussion.

*Ralston*: I hope they don't expect us to pay for any of that.

*Isaac*: How could they possibly expect us to pay for *anything*. We don't use money. We *have* no money. *You* have no money.

*Brutus*: Besides, it was their tainted water that caused Ralston to run amok in the first place.

*Pucker*: That's right.

*Ralston*: At least nobody said anything about my white face and forehead.

*Isaac*: All in all, it was a really nice green field, outside there, all that smooth grass...you know.

*Mooncalf*: All that grass. A million places to do some business. I should have waited. I couldn't help it. Too much excitement. I left a big pile in that first room...you know, with all those pots and pans.

*Brutus*: All right! Mooncalf! Now you're thinking like me!

*Isaac*: Mooncalf! I didn't think you had it in you.

*Mooncalf*: Not in me any more. It's back there on the floor.

*Ralston*: Hmmpf. Serves the humans right if you ask *me*. Stab me in the ass, will you—

And so the Grabapple Five were back on the road again, all lined up, looking for adventure. Ralston was having trouble marching as fast as the others as he was carrying a heavy load of punctured ass. The rock wall seemed to go on forever, but the group finally got past the end of it. And all the events that happened inside the wall were quickly and easily forgotten—all except Ralston's spear hole, that...not so much.

Down the Grabapple Road they went, marching five abreast, sometimes in lockstep— sometimes in lockstep just for the fun of it. Ralston was struggling between pain and a strong desire to avoid letting the others get ahead of him.

It was now about two miles from where the fence-mending woman told the Grabapple Five about the adventure taking place at this very location. But no adventure was to be found. Of course the five jackasses knew nothing about how far they had traveled—they had no concept of what a mile was. But they knew that adventure had to be around somewhere. They just had to keep at it.

Still searching for the elusive adventure, they soon arrived at a fork in the road—one branch going left and the other going right. Unfortunately for the group there was no way to tell which branch was the correct one: the Grabapple Road...the road to adventure. Right in the crotch of the fork was a pole with several signs attached. Signs pointing this way and that. Isaac then turned to Ralston.

*Isaac*: OK mastermind. Read the signs and tell us which way to go.

*Ralston*: You know, Isaac, sometimes you can be a real ass.

*Isaac*: Very clever, Ralston. Never heard that one before—

*Brutus*: Yeah yeah. Well, let's decide. What are we waiting for?

*Isaac*: We're waiting for Ralston to read the signs.

*Brutus*: Well, Ralston?

*Mooncalf*: Is Ralston about to read the signs?

The challenge to Ralston's credibility was interrupted by the arrival of a horse-drawn wagon. All five jackass heads turned to the left at once. There was a white-haired, bearded man driving the wagon. The horse was a huge, sturdy mare with thick, hairy, and muscular legs. The driver was wearing a black coach coat and a tall black hat. The horse was wearing blinders. The wagon was coming toward the Grabapple Five from the left fork in the road. When the wagon reached the group at the fork, the driver pulled up on the reins, stopping the wagon right beside Isaac.

*Wagon Man*: Well, what's going on? Why are you all lined up like that? And what's going on with that jackass with the white face, there? What is that stuff? Chalk?

Ralston offered Brutus a "why-don't-you-go-kick-his-ass" nod, directed toward the Wagon Man. Brutus didn't see Ralston's look because he was comparing the horse's ass with Ralston's face. It was a different kind of horse from before—a different-looking ass. But still no resemblance to Ralston as far as Brutus could tell.

*Isaac*: We are merry adventure seekers, oh bearded one. We were told that somewhere aroundst these hereabouts here or down the Road there we would be finding adventure for us. Say, what's that on your wagon there?

*Wagon Man*: Not that it's any of your business, but I'm delivering this coffin to the graveyard up in Grabapple. Fellow from Grabapple met his maker back there in Oxboro. Some kind of duel. Shot dead. I'm hauling his ass up to Grabapple to bury it.

*Isaac*: What are you talking about? What's a coffin? Where is the man's ass? I don't see one. Is his ass inside the box?

*Wagon Man*: You jackass. You don't know what a coffin is? It's a box—a box used to contain a dead person.

*Isaac*: A dead man? And is his ass in the box with him?

*Wagon Man*: You jackasses don't know anything. Yes, it's in the box with him.

*Ralston*: I've got to see this.

*Wagon Man*: Now look. I need to be on my way before this body...you know, starts to get ripe. Hey you, white face, stay away from that! You guys don't know what you're doing.

*Isaac*: Is that a fact? Well, it looks to me as though you should have tied that box down better. Doesn't seem to be very secure, just sitting there loose.

*Ralston*: Let's take a look.

*Wagon Man*: Go on! Get away from there. This is none of your concern. I need to be on my way.

Before the Wagon Man could get the wagon moving, Brutus maneuvered himself around to a spot in front of the Wagon Man's horse, blocking the way. As Brutus did so he looked up at the horse.

*Brutus*: Hey babe. You're a big one. How ya doin' there?

*Wagon Horse*: Not too bad. These blinders suck. Other than that—What's going on back there? I can't see a goddam thing.

*Brutus*: My friends want to check out your cargo. Your man wants us to move on. Hmm, I'm Brutus—

*Wagon Horse*: They call me Spurla. Brutus? Never heard of a name like that. Are you some kind of brute?

*Brutus*: No, I'm not a brute, I don't think; although I do like to kick ass. Gives me a sense of power. Superiority. Control. Ever heard of a mule? Let's see here—

While the Wagon Man was occupied with the pointless back and forth between himself and the other four jackasses, Brutus took it upon himself to relieve Spurla of her blinders. The horse bent her head down and Brutus pulled the blinders off with his teeth. The bearded Wagon Man then confronted Ralston.

*Wagon Man*: You there. What do you think you're doing?

*Ralston*: Just checking out this box. It seems to be nailed shut. Can't see inside.

*Isaac*: How about opening it up so we can get a peek at the dead man. See how you got his ass in there with him.

*Wagon Man*: (???)

*Pucker*: Yeah. Take a peek. Dead man. Sure.

*Wagon Man*: What kind of jackasses are you? I already told you...it's none of your business.

*Mooncalf*: Why are we just standing around here?

*Isaac*: If you won't cooperate, maybe you'd be so kind as to direct us...which of these two roads is the continuation of the Grabapple Road?

*Wagon Man*: I'm *on* the Grabapple Road. That branch over there leads to Buxton. I'm on my way to Grabapple and behind me is Oxboro. Now, I'd like to get on with my job.

When the Wagon Man looked ahead, ready to move on, he saw that his horse's blinders had been removed. Brutus was standing there proudly, putting forth a toothy grin.

*Wagon Man*: What did you do? You're not supposed to mess with those blinders. I've never—

*Ralston*: I can't seem to get this box open.

*Wagon Man*: Leave it alone!

Then, seemingly from out of nowhere, a long thick brown snake came slithering across the road right between Spurla and Brutus. Brutus wasn't particularly disturbed by it, but Spurla was startled. Highly agitated by the snake, Spurla began neighing and rearing up. Brutus was surprised by Spurla's sudden change in demeanor and backed away to avoid being clobbered by Spurla's jumping. Spurla then lurched into a gallop pulling the wagon forward a short distance, but the inertia of the coffin caused it to slide off the wagon and onto the ground. Brutus kicked dirt on the snake, chasing it back into the thicket. The Wagon Man, being rocked backward and forward on his seat, was becoming very angry. He climbed down and headed to the rear of the wagon where the four jackasses were standing.

The coffin had broken into several large pieces revealing its dead contents. It definitely was a man. Only the top half of his body was dressed. The rest of him was as naked and skin-exposed as a plucked chicken. Mooncalf, Pucker, Ralston, and Isaac stood over the demolished coffin, walking around it, giving the dead man's remains a glassy-eyed stare, sniffing at it, and examining it from head to foot. During the dismantling, a large piece of the former coffin had flipped up whacking Pucker in his jaw, giving him a fat lower lip.

*Mooncalf*: What is it?

*Isaac*: That...my friends, is a *de-e-e-ad* man.

*Pucker*: Pff-boy. Pff-he really *looks* pff-dead.

*Ralston*: Pretty damn dead, I'd say.

*Isaac*: I don't see any sign of his ass. Hey Wagon Man are you sure his ass
        was in here with him?

*Wagon Man*: You stupid—get away from him!

*Mooncalf*: What is that thing there, between his legs?

*Isaac*: Never mind, Mooncalf.

*Ralston*: Kind of weird though...that outfit.

*Pucker*: Yeah-pff, pff-weird.

*Wagon Man*: What did I tell you. Get away from there! What're you jackasses gawking at? Don't you have any respect for the dead?

*Ralston*: Why?

The Wagon Man, holding his whip, was now standing alongside the four jackasses as the group of four continued to disregard the Wagon Man and persisted in investigating the dead man, the coffin, and the situation.

*Isaac*: Say, what kind of outfit is that?

*Mooncalf*: Maybe it's some kind of dead man suit.

*Pucker*: Pff-Yeah, that's it-pff.

*Ralston*: I think your lip is bleeding, Pucker.

*Pucker*: Pff-feels like it-pff.

Exasperated, the Wagon Man cracked his whip in the air with the idea that the four jackasses would take the hint and back off. Not an effective plan when dealing with the likes of the Grabapple Five. Not the slightest bit intimidated, and unmoved, the four body-examining jackasses continued their discussion while Brutus cautiously approached the Wagon Man from behind.

*Ralston*: You know, when one of us is dead they just put us on a bonfire or let the crows and other birds just peck at us until we are reduced to nothing. No box. Never heard of that.

*Pucker*: Pff-What did the pff-man call that pff-box?

*Isaac*: Hey Wagon Man, what did you call this box?

*Mooncalf*: Doesn't even look like a box any more.

*Wagon Man*: I told you to get away from that body. I warned you. Get a taste of this—

As he wielded his whip, charging it up for a real crack at a real target: **Thump!** Brutus butt-kicked the Wagon Man up into the air. Spurla the horse got a kick out of it as well...a different kind of kick. While the stunned Wagon Man was sprawled out on the ground, Isaac picked up the whip with his teeth and tossed it far away from the area. Then Isaac hovered over the man.

*Isaac*: Hey, Wagon Man, what did you call this box?

*Ralston*: I think he said it was a "dool."

*Isaac*: That's what *killed* the dead man, Ralston. Hey, Wagon Man, what's a "dool"?

The Wagon Man just sat up and buried his face into the palms of his hands. Silent and resigned.

*Isaac*: No answer. Humpf! Well, I think that's the last we're going to get out of him. Rude. Very rude.

*Pucker*: Yes, pff-and uncooperative-pff.

*Brutus*: You want me to give him another one? A swift one? For good measure?

*Isaac*: Nah. We got what we needed. This left branch of the road is the one we should follow. Hey Wagon Man, when can we expect this mess to be cleared up? We're going to have to pass back this way again...on our way home.

There was no response from the Wagon Man. Outwardly, Spurla stood silent as if nothing had occurred at all...no opinion. The half-naked dead man also had no opinion. Once again, aligned in their military parade formation of five abreast, the Grabapple Five took the left branch at the fork and continued on along the Grabapple Road leaving the Wagon Man in their dust.

*Isaac*: You'd think that Wagon Man would have apologized for delaying us.

*Pucker*: Pff-you'd think-pff.

*Brutus*: The Wagon Man's *horse* was friendly enough. She was a real big one—kinda different. Got a little crazy when that snake showed up, though. Whatever happened to your lower lip, Pucker?

*Pucker*: Pff-piece of that pff-box hit me-pff in the mouth-pff.

*Brutus*: I should go back there and—

*Mooncalf*: Where are we going now?

*Isaac*: I think that woman lied to us about the adventure being somewhere down the Road. We should've seen some by now. These humans. Bunch of—

*Ralston*: She was probably too ignorant about the actual distance to give us accurate information.

*Pucker*: Pff-yeah. Pff-that sounds pff-right to me-pff.

*Brutus*: I should go back there and—

*Ralston*: Can we just get on with it?

*Isaac*: I agree. All of that stuff is in the past. We're interested in the future— and the adventure that awaits us. After all we've been through to get this far, we deserve quite an adventure when we finally encounter it.

*Pucker*: Pff-I agree-pff.

Isaac was beginning to realize that looking for adventure was going to be more difficult than he expected; and with Ralston's painful puncture, a lot slower as well. The Wagon Man and Spurla were long out of sight and long forgotten when Isaac noticed something just up ahead.

*Isaac*: Look up there, on the left. It looks like some kind of road. You can barely see it with all the weeds and brush.

*Ralston*: I see it. Hmmm. I don't see a sign anywhere around there either. If there was a sign I could tell you what road it is.

*Mooncalf*: Wow, Ralston. You can see that far?

*Isaac*: (Ralston just won't let it go.)

The group had almost reached the small road—a trail, actually—when a pack of seven warthogs clambered out of the brush and into the road, surrounding and surprising the Grabapple Five.

*Boss*: Well, well, well. Five big old jackasses, all lined up in a row. Never seen anything like it. What do you think Bitz?

*Bitz*: Don't know *what* to think Boss.

*Boss*: Look at *that* one, the one with the stupid expression on his face.

*Mooncalf*: Are you talking about me?

*Boss*: "Are you talking about me?" Shut up! And this one here, the one with the white face—what are *you* made up for?

*Ralston*: (Grunt) **Vociferous Nose Spew**.

*Boss*: Whoa there hoss! Nasty, nasty. And just where do you jackasses think you're going?

*Isaac*: Now look here. We're just minding our own business—ahem...for the most part. Our plans are none of *your* business.

*Brutus*: Let me handle this—

*Isaac*: Wait a minute—

*Gord*: Hey Boss! Come back here and take a look at this. This jackass has two assholes.

*Boss*: What?

*Ralston*: That's a spear puncture you asinine animal!

*Isaac*: What could you possibly want from us? You want money? Do we look like we're carrying any money? Do we look like we're carrying anything?

*Boss*: Naw. We don't want your money.

*Isaac*: Food? You want to kill us and eat us?

*Boss*: Eat you? Ass meat? We wouldn't be able to show our faces back at the club. Naw. Our job is to come out here and molest the shit of you.

*Mooncalf*: Sorry Boss, I already left all of mine back at that big house.

*Boss*: What is that dumb-ass talking about?

*Isaac*: Never mind him. Are you going to let us move on or not?

*Boss*: What do you think Bitz?

*Bitz*: I'm with you.

*Pucker*: Pff-that sounds pff-familiar—

*Boss*: Quiet, big lip. Bitz, you want to give the signal to start the molesting or should I?

*Pucker*: Big lip?

*Bitz*: Go ahead Boss. Whenever you're ready—

*Brutus*: Now, Isaac?

*Isaac*: Yeah. OK...now!

Brutus took the lead. In a flurry of wild mania, fur, dust, and blood the Grabapple Five delivered a violent swirling tempest of donkey mayhem on the gang of warthogs—an attack unheard of in the entire animal kingdom. Brutus's hours of pent-up frustration ignited the pandemonium as the other four joined in immediately. The loud braying of the donkeys mixed with the squeals and howls from the warthogs resounded through the trees, the brush, and everything in the vicinity.

Then silence. Six members of the warthog gang lay in the road, dead: one disemboweled, one beheaded, one mashed into an unrecognizable mess, and three just plain dead. Boss was still alive, but he could not move. Isaac and Ralston looked down on the warthog leader showing very little sympathy.

*Boss*: What the hell happened?

*Isaac*: Your gang is dead. I believe you're next to go.

*Boss*: Boy, never saw *that* coming. *Cough cough*. I think...I have just one question...before I...*cough cough*—

*Isaac*: Well, what is it? We've got things to do.

*Boss*: What's with that white face? *Cough cough*...blphew—

*Brutus*: I think he's dead. You want me to make sure?

*Ralston*: Yeah, go ahead.

*Isaac*: Come on. Leave him alone. It's done.

A tall, thin man suddenly appeared on the little side trail near the group on the Grabapple Road. He was carrying a shotgun. **Blam!** The old hermit fired the shotgun into the air.

*Old Hermit Named Dave*: What in the fuck of humanity is goin' on out here?

Instead of reacting as the hermit expected, the Grabapple Five merely began a new discussion.

*Isaac*: Is everyone on this road armed with a gun?

*Ralston*: Never thought about it much, but I guess that's our big weakness—

*Isaac*: What do you mean?

*Ralston*: We can't carry firearms. Even if we could, we'd have no way to fire them. No way to even load them.

*Isaac*: Yeah. I see what you mean. Quite a disadvantage.

*Brutus*: We can still *kick* ass. Ask those warthog jokers what they think?

*Mooncalf*: I thought they were all dead?

*Pucker*: Watch it! Here comes that man with the gun.

*Isaac*: Hey there old man of the woods. There's no need for that...that gun. We're not violent.

*Pucker*: That's right. We won't do violence on you.

*Old Hermit Named Dave*: Holeeeeee shit! What a massacree! Did you fuckers do all this? How many of these damn hogs did you kill?

*Isaac*: I don't know. A bunch of them. Except "one" or "two," donkeys don't know how to count.

*Brutus*: Or read...eh Ralston?

*Ralston*: Eat me, Brutus.

*Old Hermit Named Dave*: Yep. I see seven of the goddam things.

*Mooncalf*: Ooh, that man's language.

*Pucker*: Yes yes-pff. Pff-very colorful-pff.

*Old Hermit Named Dave*: These fuckers have been pesterin' me for months—

*Mooncalf*: I thought *we* were the fuckers. Didn't he call us the fuckers? What *is* that anyway?

The old hermit looked quizzically at Mooncalf and then addressed the rest of the group.

*Old Hermit Named Dave*: Hmmm. They've been comin' around, makin' noise, pesterin' me. A couple of 'em got into my cave one time. Tore the shit out of the place. They're fast li'l buggers—I took out two of 'em with old Frida here, but I haven't had much luck since. Gotta thank you fellas for riddin' me of the rest of 'em. Damn nasty li'l fuckers—

*Mooncalf*: Who is he talking about now? And who is Frida?

*Old Hermit Named Dave*: Not the brightest jackass to come flushin' down the old pipe now...is he?

*Isaac*: I suppose. Do you think you could spare a little water, my friend? The road is dusty and we've built up quite a thirst.

*Ralston*: Are you sure about that, Isaac? Remember last time?

*Isaac*: We'll see. What do you say old man, old friendly man with a gun?

*Old Hermit Named Dave*: Water? Yeah. You can have somethin' to eat too, if you'd like. I can get a good grillin' campfire goin'. Just let me grab one of these old hogs—

*Isaac*: Uh...no thanks, just the water, if you don't mind.

*Old Hermit Named Dave*: Sure. Come on over to my cave. Got a little stream runnin' by it. Plenty of cool, fresh water.

The old hermit grabbed Boss warthog's legs and started walking through the trees on the narrow side path. But before any movement could take place—

*Isaac*: Spread out you guys. We can't walk five abreast on this narrow path. Way too narrow—there's not enough room. There are too many trees.

*Ralston*: So what are we going to do?

*Brutus*: I'm not walking behind Ralston. Not going to watch his double asshole shifting up and down all the way to the water.

*Isaac*: Don't look at *me*.

*Old Hermit Named Dave*: Hey! What's goin' on back there? You comin' or ain't ya? This goddam hog is heavy. If you jackasses want water just follow this trail. I'm goin' on without ya. (Fuckin' jackasses.)

The old man left the Grabapple Five behind. Boss warthog's dangling head banged against a rock every now and then as the hermit swung the body by his side.

Finally, the Grabapple Five made a decision about how to proceed, one jackass at a time. Isaac went first and as soon as he was out of sight, Ralston followed—then Brutus, then Pucker, then Mooncalf. It took a while, but everyone was happy with the solution. When Mooncalf, the last one, finally arrived at the old man's cave there was a campfire going and a skewered warthog hung over the fire, roasting (fur and all). The others were already at the edge of the stream getting a much-needed drink of water.

*Brutus*: It's about time, Mooncalf. What've you been doing?

*Mooncalf*: I was last. What did you expect?

*Isaac*: The old man said that it's been a while since he could grill something outside because of those hogs. They had been coming around and tormenting him and "stealing his shit."

*Mooncalf*: What could they possibly want with his shit?

*Isaac*: Well, that's what he said, "They come around here and steal my shit; even when I'm standing right in front of them."

*Brutus*: Earlier he said that they tore the shit out of his cave. What did he mean by *that*?

*Isaac*: (???)

*Ralston*: Man, get a load of that smell.

*Pucker*: Pff-yeah. Pff-burning hair and all-pff.

*Brutus*: Kinda kills the appetite, doesn't it?

*Isaac*: You'd think he could have chosen some better grilling material than old Boss warthog. Something more to *our* liking—carrots or corn or hay? We might have even taken him up on the meal he offered. Too bad.

*Mooncalf*: That big roast...that was old Boss?

*Isaac*: Yeah. How about that?

*Brutus*: By the way Ralston, you were walking so slowly that I almost caught up with you. Ahem. You really do look like you have two assholes. You know that, don't you?

*Ralston*: Now just how would I know that?

After they got their fill of water the group meandered on back to the cave.

*Ralston*: So you live in there...in that cave?

*Old Hermit Named Dave*: Yep. Lived there for some forty odd years. Never had no trouble until those fuckin' warthogs showed up a couple of weeks ago. Things ain't been right 'round here since—not until now.

The five jackasses did not know how long "forty odd years" was but they figured it had to be a long time since the hermit was so old.

*Isaac*: What's all this stuff?

*Old Hermit Named Dave*: Gathered up big bunch of brush and brambles...tried to build up a fence. Damn warthogs tore that down. Built it up again, thicker, taller, into a kind of wall. They tore the shit out of that too.

*Brutus*: (???) Tore the shit out of that too? Like the cave?

*Old Hermit Named Dave*: Yep. After that, I gave up.

*Isaac*: Well you don't have to worry about that any more.

*Old Hermit Named Dave*: Damn straight!

The old man then directed his comments to the roasting warthog.

*Old Hermit Named Dave*: You hear that, Boss! Look at you *now*! You fuckin' bastard!

*Pucker*: Pff-I may be a jackass-pff, but I sure-pff don't use language like that...pff.

*Old Hermit Named Dave*: What's with your pff pff friend here?

*Isaac*: Got hit on the lip with a big piece of a dead man's coffin box.

*Old Hermit Named Dave*: Boy! Never met any jackasses like you five. (*That's the damn truth.*)

As the fire roared on, there was a loud and sudden **Pop!** One of Boss warthog's overheated eyeballs had exploded, eyeball fluids flying everywhere. The juice that fell into the fire caused a great deal of sputtering—more than one would expect. The old hermit had seen a roasting eyeball explode like that before; not often, but he'd seen it. So he started laughing—laughing at old Boss warthog's posthumous response to being called a bastard and laughing at the effect the pop had on the five jackasses. Before any of the five could calm down. **Pop!** The other eyeball exploded. Because of a limited amount of world experience, the Grabapple Five could not understand what was happening, so they panicked. The old hermit continued his laughing—laughter that brought tears to his eyes. The hermit's crazed laughing only served to fuel the jackasses' panic.

Thoroughly distracted, the old hermit failed to notice that the jackasses were now completely out of control. They had demolished the campfire and caused the roastee to catch on fire as well. Fiery pieces of wood were distributed all around the cave entrance. Brutus attempted to kick some dirt onto the campfire, but inadvertently hit the end of a long slender stick of the charred firewood. Acting as a catapult, the stick launched the burning remains of Boss warthog into the air and onto the piles of brush and brambles, setting the entire area on fire. Oblivious to what was happening, the old hermit continued laughing. It had been a long time since he was able to laugh like that.

Unfortunately, the inattention of the old hermit led to a larger problem: his large wooden cask of homemade spirits, hidden deep in the flaming brush, caught fire as well, and soon, *it* exploded into fire. The old laughing hermit was rudely brought back into reality as a copious amount of fiery debris and flaming spirits went flying everywhere, blanketing the area.

The ground around the cave was covered with burning brush and pieces of wood. The old hermit attempted to dump dirt on the flames, but realized that he would just have to let the whole mess burn out.

As for the Grabapple Five, small pieces of burning debris pelted the five, singeing the fur in numerous random places. For once, Ralston got the least of it. Pucker and Mooncalf got the worst. And Isaac and Brutus, somewhere in between. But now, they all had acquired a patchwork look on various areas of their bodies. Not too bad...but not too pretty either. In addition, Isaac and Pucker had the hair on their front legs singed off as well.

The old hermit started rummaging around looking for his gun.

*Old Hermit Named Dave*: You crazy bunch of fuckin' jackasses! You're crazy. You set the whole place on fire!

*Mooncalf*: What is *he* all steamed up about?

*Ralston*: I think the old man has gone insane. All that laughing.

*Isaac*: Looks like it. We'd better go before—I think he's looking for his gun.

*Pucker*: Pff-yoicks! Yeah-pff. We'd better go-pff.

*Ralston*: Yoicks? Where'd you hear that?

*Pucker*: Pff-I don't know-pff...you just-pff hear stuff-pff.

*Brutus*: I think the old man found his gun—

*Mooncalf*: Are we leaving now?

*Old Hermit Named Dave*: Go on! Get out of here!

*Ralston*: OK Who's going first?

*Isaac*: I'll go first.

The old hermit was not in on the original planning discussion nor did he care about the group's one-at-a-time methodology for going along the path, so as Isaac started down the path the old hermit expected the rest to follow immediately.

*Old Hermit Named Dave*: Well...what are the rest of you waitin' for?

*Ralston*: We're waiting for Isaac's ass to get out of sight.

*Old Hermit Named Dave*: You! White-face. Get on with it or I'm gonna to shoot *your* ass, sure as I'm standin' here. Git!

As Ralston slowly, against his stubborn nature, began following Isaac—

*Old Hermit Named Dave*: Hey, white-face. What's with the double asshole? Hmm. The rest of you, get in line and get out of here.

So the Grabapple Five slowly plodded back toward the Grabapple Road, single file, everyone but Isaac having to view the ass directly in front of him.

*Brutus*: Hey, Ralston, you really do look like you have two assholes.

*Ralston*: Shut up! And quit ogling my ass.

*Brutus*: How do I do that? You're right in front of me.

*Isaac*: Hey, knock it off back there! We need to get on back to the Road. We're lucky we're all here in one piece—well, at least alive.

*Ralston*: That old man. Doesn't seem right, him running us off like that after we killed off all those warthogs for him.

*Pucker*: Yeah-pff. Doesn't seem –pff-right. Pff-Pretty foul-mouthed-pff...if you ask me-pff.

When the group finally reached the Grabapple Road again, a large group of buzzards had descended on the six remaining dead warthogs—just about unrecognizable as warthogs at that point.

*Ralston*: Wow. Look at that! Buzzards. How many would you say?

*Isaac*: Many.

*Brutus*: Should we run them off?

*Isaac*: What for?

*Pucker*: Pff-those warthogs-pff. They-pff don't even look like-pff *anything*...any more-pff.

As the Grabapple Five was gazing at the scavenging going on in the road, one of the buzzards turned to address the donkeys.

*Top Buzz*: What're you jackasses looking at?

*Isaac*: Just checking out your work. Do you eat that fur or do you peel it off first?

*Top Buzz*: What kind of a stupid question is that? Don't care. We enjoy eating rotting meat. Do you think that fur is going to bother us? What in the world have you guys been doing? You're all beat up. Big nose on that one. Painted white face on that one. What's the matter with your skin? You all look diseased. Not that it matters to any of us. If you were dead we'd eat you in a heartbeat.

*Isaac*: Yeah. Well. We started out the day seeking adventure, but fate...and everyone on this road is trying to delay us and...so many guns.

*Mooncalf*: Is he going to eat us?

*Pucker*: Pff-not unless we're pff-dead.

*Ralston*: What is that group over there? They're all just standing around.

*Top Buzz*: They're the Under-Buzzards. They don't get to eat until the Over-Buzzards are finished.

*Ralston*: And how do *you* fit in...some kind of agent?

*Top Buzz*: Agent? What do you mean...*agent*? I'm the top buzzard of all. Now, enough questions...if you don't mind.

The conversation was suddenly interrupted by a fairly large black and white dog sprinting down the road toward the Grabapple Five. Its barking alerted the buzzards and they casually began jockeying around and re-positioning themselves, eventually lifting themselves up into the trees far enough away to avoid being attacked but still close enough to resume eating when the threat was over. Only Top Buzz remained on the ground, but he too would take off if he felt threatened.

The Grabapple Five was very familiar with dogs, so they did not feel threatened by this squirrelly one. They just stood their ground while the dog barked and barked in a mindless display of bravado. Only the dog perceived that the actions were having an effect. The smoke from the old hermit's fire was now beginning to reach the Grabapple Road and was fogging up the whole area.

*Top Buzz*: Smoke! Where's that smoke coming from?

*Isaac*: I don't know. Do you know Ralston? Brutus?

*Brutus*: Beats me.

*Mooncalf*: Uh—

*Ralston*: Smoke? What smoke?

*Top Buzz*: You guys are the worst liars. What did you do? Set the woods on fire?

Not getting a legitimate answer, Top Buzz focused his attention on his own group in the nearby trees.

*Top Buzz*: Hey! Buzz-alert! Let's get out of here, back to those taller trees way over there. We can watch from a much safer distance. There may be fire here soon. We need to be ready to vacate entirely!

As Top Buzz lifted off, the other buzzards began a retreat, *en masse*, to taller and more distant trees, leaving the Grabapple Five alone with the loud barking dog. The dog was part of the Oxboro fire brigade. The brigade was getting very near as indicated by the loudness of the bell.

*Isaac*: Fascinating how something that big can just fly up into the air—

*Ralston*: What is that dog doing here?

*Isaac*: I think it came up the road...from down there. Down there where we were planning to go.

*Ralston*: Shitfire! I can't even hear myself think. That dog and that bell!

Brutus took the opportunity to make a few token kicks toward the dog, but the defiant dog just jumped around, skillfully avoiding Brutus and continuing to bark. The loud bell could be heard distinctly by everyone in attendance. The bell was an indication that the fire brigade was on its way. The dog was considered the leading edge of the brigade. It was usually pretty adept at heading toward smoke. The fire wagon was being drawn by four sturdy horses and was moving very fast.

The brigade set out as soon as the smoke was detected—not so much to save the hermit's goods but to prevent the fire from reaching the town. The people of Oxboro didn't have much use for the old hermit. He was just an eccentric old bum as far as they were concerned.

*Isaac*: I think we should get out of here before we get any more involved.

*Pucker*: I pff-agree. Pff-yeah. I think we should-pff get out of here-pff.

The Grabapple Five assembled into formation, five abreast across the road and began marching along as before. The barking dog was frantically jumping around while avoiding being trampled by the reassembling group. But before they could even get started, the fire brigade was right in front of them. The driver reined in the team of horses and the fire wagon stopped abruptly in the middle of the road.

*Fire Captain*: Get out of the way! We need to get through!

*Mooncalf*: Is he talking to us?

*Isaac*: I believe so. And just where are you going in such a hurry may I ask?

*Fire Captain*: We're going to put out that fire. What do you think?

*Mooncalf*: What fire? There's a fire back there, that way? Is that it?

112

While the group was engaged with the Fire Captain, Brutus moved up to the large female horse at the head of the team.

> *Brutus*: Hey babe. Look at you. Aren't you a big one.

> *Ralston*: What's Brutus up to?

> *Isaac*: Why ask me? Say, mister fireman...hmmm...why are you wasting time delaying us here?

> *Ralston*: What's that man doing now?

> *Isaac*: I can't tell.

The Fire Captain had dismounted from the driver's seat and was now talking to one of his crew, a stocky man with a curly mustache. The Captain then returned to his seat atop the fire wagon.

> *Fire Captain*: For the last time—get out of the way!

> *Pucker*: Pff-what does he mean by pff-that? The last time-pff?

> *Mooncalf*: Maybe he meant, "since the last time he *told* us—"

While Brutus was busying himself, the other four jackasses discussed the situation, paying no attention to the Captain. Then, on the Fire Captain's signal, the crewman with the curly mustache opened up the hose nozzle and began spraying the heads of the discussion group with a forceful stream of water. The stream was strong and painful. When a widening gap appeared in the group of jackasses the fire wagon forged ahead, right through the middle, and on to the spot where the trail led to the old hermit's cave. Brutus, who was engaged in a conversation with the female horse, had to jump backward quickly to avoid being trampled by the very horse he was verbally fondling. The dog was still in an excited state but was no longer barking. As the crew operated the pump and prepared the fire hose for the short trek to the hermit's cave, the Fire Captain looked over the remains of the warthogs. He was joined by Lieutenant Kelso, second in command.

*Fire Captain*: What the hell happened here? I mean...look at this? Looks like some kind of slaughter. Recent too.

*Lieutenant Kelso*: This one looks like its head was removed.

*Fire Captain*: Can't even tell what this pile is...or was.

The members of the Grabapple Five were looking back at the busy men, watching it all with curiosity and indignation. Holding the offensive fire hose nozzle, two of the crew pulled on the hose while running into the trees toward the old hermit's cave. The hose began unspooling with the sides of the spool itself spinning around vigorously. The members of the Grabapple Five were fascinated but were still feeling very annoyed at being hosed down with that water, but all of this brigade action had really captured their attention.

*Isaac*: Will you look at that! That thing spinning.

*Ralston*: Never seen *that* before. And that dog...it went right in there with those two men.

*Brutus*: And just *what* are those two men looking at so carefully? It's just a bunch of dead warthogs.

*Ralston*: Men do some of the strangest things. I guess all that water got rid of that white on my face...hey Isaac?

*Isaac*: Nope. Sorry Ralston. Still there.

*Brutus*: Looks pretty ridiculous. You got a little paint on your eyelid, too. It's like a little light going on and off when you close and open your eye.

*Pucker*: Pff-ridiculous.

*Ralston*: Yeah. OK. Thanks a lot. Yeah, you Brutus. You're the one who should be talking—you with that puffed up nose.

*Mooncalf*: Are we going now?

*Brutus*: Let's go, I'm getting hungry—

*Pucker*: Pff-me too.

So the Grabapple Five once again lined up and began walking, marching, down the Grabapple Road—the group's immediate concern: food; the overall mission of finding adventure: still intact. With the hermit, the warthogs, and the fire completely erased from their minds, they began focusing on getting something to eat.

Although the distance traveled so far was not particularly great, it seemed longer to the wearying group. After passing through a small wooded area, they came upon a cornfield. Food!

*Isaac*: Look at that! Corn! Time to eat.

*Ralston*: Yes, but these stalks aren't old enough to have any corn on them yet.

*Brutus*: Yeah, you're right. I don't see any.

*Mooncalf*: What are we looking for?

*Isaac*: Hey! Look over there. Across this field...over to that side. That cornfield looks a lot older.

The spread belonged to a farming couple named Haas: Jack and Minniha Haas. The farming husband and wife had worked together to build the farm and had their own way of raising crops. They divided the cornfield into three sections—three different levels of maturity: one field of mature plants; one halfway grown; and the one the couple was currently working, getting the initial plowing underway. The mature field was located in between the other two.

*Pucker*: Pff-what about this pff-fence?

*Brutus*: I'll take care of *that*—

Brutus went after the wooden fence, kicking a section of it into a hundred pieces, making an opening wide enough for five jackasses to enter the field—five abreast. It was the field of mature stalks that the Grabapple Five had set their sites on.

*Isaac:* Let us be...off!

The group of jackasses, five abreast, entered the field of half-grown corn stalks and went straight for the mature section, traipsing over the immature stalks, creating a kind of highway as they went; it was an interesting swath of destruction—a highway, the width of five jackasses.

*Brutus*: This is actually kind of fun.

*Pucker*: Pff-yes it is-pff.

*Ralston*: It will be easy to find our way back. We made our own path.

*Mooncalf*: Good thinking.

They reached the mature section and found many, many tall stalks, loaded with corncobs, just waiting to be eaten.

*Isaac*: Let's go further in, that's where the best corn is probably growing.

On through the tall stalks they tromped. They finally stopped when they thought they were in the center of the field. In actuality, they had reached almost to the other side—right next to the field where the farming couple was working. Then the eating began—ripping and tearing, crunching and munching. Rather than staying in one cohesive group, the individual jackasses fanned out, eating cobs of corn while knocking down corn stalks like a tornado made of jackasses. Brutus, being the most aggressive had tromped out the farthest from the group and was pulling off another juicy cob—

*Brutus*: *Chomp chomp.* Hey! Come look at this. *Crunch crunch.*

The others all migrated toward the sound of Brutus's voice, creating yet another senseless swath of destruction as they walked. Brutus was at the edge of the mature section. As the others arrived they gathered around Brutus and looked into the empty field.

*Ralston*: Look at that. Who are *they*? *Chomp chomp.*

*Isaac*: I think that's a couple of *farmers*. *Crunch crunch.*

*Mooncalf*: Did they make all this corn? *Crunch crunch.*

*Isaac*: I guess so. *Chomp chomp.*

*Brutus*: That man…he's looking this way. *Chomp chomp.*

*Ralston*: He looks pretty pissed. *Chomp.* Here comes that woman too. *Crunch crunch.*

*Pucker*: Pff-you think-pff we ought to take off-pff? *Chomp chomp*-pff.

*Isaac*: We're not doing anything but eating. *Crunch*. We're minding our own business. *Crunch crunch*.

*Ralston*: *Chomp chomp*. The man is running now...so's the woman. *Crunch crunch*.

*Brutus*: Looks pretty funny. Look how he trips over those dirt ridges on the ground. *Chomp chomp*.

*Ralston*: What're you going to say to him when he gets here, Isaac? *Chomp chomp*.

*Isaac*: Don't know. We don't even know if all this corn belongs to him. *Crunch crunch*.

*Ralston*: Maybe he just tore up someone else's field of corn—

**Bop!** A stone bounced off Mooncalf's head making him stagger.

*Isaac*: What in the perilous pools of Donkeynation was that?

*Ralston*: I think that woman threw a rock at Mooncalf.

*Isaac*: What did he ever do to *her*? I didn't see anything.

*Ralston*: Pretty good aim. That woman—

*Farmer Jack Haas*: You sons-of-bitches. What do you think you're doing? What have you done to my corn?

The five jackasses looked around for something called "sons-of-bitches," but didn't see *anything*.

> *Brutus*: We're eating this corn. What does it look like?

**Bop!** Another stone came flying in. This one bounced off Pucker's head, almost knocking him out.

> *Ralston*: She did it again, Isaac. Popped Pucker right on the noggin. I have to say, she's really got a good aim.

> *Isaac*: Tell that woman to stop throwing those rocks!

> *Farmer Jack Haas*: Get off of my farm! Look at all that damage!

**Whizzzz!** Ralston was just able to dodge yet another stone thrown by the farmer woman, one that was headed for *his* head.

> *Brutus*: I'm going over there and taking her out.

> *Mooncalf*: I'm getting a terrible headache.

**Bop!** As the farmer raised up his hoe in a threatening posture the woman's new stone pounded Ralston right on the nose giving him a puffed up nose like Brutus's.

> *Ralston*: Yeeeow! That woman—

> *Isaac*: I think we'd better beat a path back to the road. These two are not going to listen to reason.

> *Mooncalf*: Should we line up again?

*Ralston*: Come on! Let's get out of here.

*Mooncalf*: Are we lining up?

The group did a quick about-face in order to beat a retreat.

*Mooncalf*: Guess not.

Before the jackasses could get into a full stride, the farmer man's big wide hoe came down on the top-center of Pucker's ass, creating a huge, wide gash. Pucker's reaction was to kick his back legs high into the air. But Mooncalf was just a little bit too close and Pucker's hooves knocked out two of Mooncalf's teeth. Shaken and discouraged, the group of five took off, rampaging back to the Grabapple Road, making yet another wide swath of cornfield destruction as they went.

*Farmer Jack Haas*: I don't think anyone is going to believe this.

*Farmer Minniha Haas*: I don't believe it.

*Farmer Jack Haas*: Where did you learn to throw rocks like that?

*Farmer Minniha Haas*: Don't know. Just natural, I guess. Those jackass heads are kinda big—easy targets.

*Farmer Jack Haas*: If I ever run across those jackasses again, I'm—

When the Grabapple Five finally reached the road, they couldn't find the opening in the fence—the opening where they had barged in earlier. So Brutus kicked down a new opening in the fence and out they went, spilling into the road like mass of liquid jackass, limping and hurting. And wondering when they were, if ever, going to find their adventure.

*Isaac*: Is everyone all right?

*Ralston*: What do you mean by "all right."

*Brutus*: Hey Pucker, have you seen your ass?

*Pucker*: Pff-*never* have...why-pff, what is it-pff? Hurts like pff-crazy—

*Brutus*: You've got a big smile on it—a big bloody smile—right in the center, above your tail.

*Pucker*: Pff-what do you mean-pff, smile?

*Brutus*: That's what it looks like, a big shit-eating grin...no teeth, just a grin.

*Mooncalf*: What is he smiling about? I don't think there's anything to smile about. What about my teeth?

*Ralston*: How did you get that, Pucker?

*Isaac*: I think it was the farmer that put it there.

*Ralston*: The farmer put a big smile on Pucker's ass? Is that what you're saying?

*Isaac*: The farmer hit Pucker with his hoe and cut his ass.

*Brutus*: Mooncalf...did you know your mouth is bleeding?

*Mooncalf*: I think I lost a couple of teeth.

*Isaac*: When did this happen?

*Mooncalf*: I think Pucker knocked them out.

*Ralston*: Pucker! Why did you do that?

*Pucker*: Pff-I don't know pff-I didn't mean to-pff. Pff-didn't know I did-pff.

*Ralston*: Well...what do we do now?

*Isaac*: Why don't we make an assessment of where we are. And then move forward. Maybe we can find our adventure in that town up ahead.

*Ralston*: You mean Oxburg? Oxhead?

*Brutus*: Oxboro, mister genius who can read.

*Pucker*: Pff-sounds good to me-pff. I'd like a cool-pff pool of water-pff to soak my aching ass-smile-pff.

So the group of five stood on the Grabapple Road, figuratively licking their wounds, looking each other over, assessing each other's physical state, and evaluating their situation.

*Ralston*: Brutus...how is it that you've come out of all of this so...so unscathed?

*Brutus*: I'm used to kicking ass more than receiving...uh...ass.

*Ralston*: Are we going on to the town or not?

*Isaac*: Do we want to vote on it?

*Mooncalf*: What does that mean?

*Isaac*: Can we all just agree to move on? Or not? Does anyone object to moving on? After all we've been through it seems that we should press on and find our adventure if it kills us.

*Ralston*: I wouldn't go that far—

*Brutus*: I think *he* would.

Brutus saw Farmer Jack Haas coming through the trampled down swath of cornfield. The farmer wasn't carrying his hoe anymore. He was carrying a shotgun.

*Brutus*: Another gun? What is it with the people on this road?

*Pucker*: Pff-is *everyone* carrying-pff one of those-pff?

*Ralston*: I guess we didn't get off his cornfield fast enough. You're right...what is it with all the guns?

*Isaac*: I think we'd better get on out of here before he gets close enough to shoot us.

*Pucker*: Pff-do you think he would-pff?

Ralston: Why else would he be coming at us with his gun? We're already off of his field. He's pissed at us about something.

*Isaac*: Come on!

Rather than spend time lining up, five abreast, the Grabapple Five started running toward Oxboro as fast as their diminished condition would allow. **Blam!** Farmer Jack Haas fired one shot at the distant group, but the group was too far away for the blast to be dangerously effective. But poor Brutus—his ass captured several pellets of shot—not too deep, but painful enough for him to really notice.

*Brutus*: Dammit Ralston! You jinxed me. Now I've got these shotgun pellets stuck in my ass. I'm not going to be able to sit down for weeks...maybe months...or ever. I oughta kick *your* ass!

*Ralston*: Don't blame *me*—

*Isaac*: Come on! Let's not stay here any longer than we have to—in case that farmer decides to follow us.

*Ralston*: Sooner or later we're bound to find some adventure.

*Pucker*: Pff-I agree-pff. Pff-so let's go-pff.

The group slowly, methodically worked their way along the Grabapple Road until they reached yet another farm. This one was surrounded by a well-maintained, very nice, white wooden fence. The Grabapple Five saw a cow—a single cow—standing under a large tree. The cow was chewing its way through another round of cud when the group arrived. Yellow-white drool was occasionally leaking from the corner of the cow's mouth.

*Isaac*: You there, cow. What's that you're eating there?

*Cud Cow*: Urrrp—

*Isaac*: That's a hell of a reply. You seem to be losing some of it from your mouth there. Yee-uck!

*Pucker*: Pff you said it-ff. Pff-yoicks!

*Cud Cow*: Urrrp—

*Isaac*: We're on our way to find some adventure. Do you know of any in this area...maybe down the road...maybe in that town, Oxboro?

*Cud Cow*: Nope! Urrrp—

*Ralston*: You seem to be getting mighty big and fat. Fat. Have you considered exercise? You might want to think about it. Do you some good.

*Cud Cow*: Nope! Urrrp—

*Pucker*: Pff-you might want to pff-consider it-pff.

*Cud Cow*: Urrrp—

*Brutus*: You want me to kick his ass?

*Pucker*: Pff-all right by-pff me. Go ahead-pff.

*Ralston*: Why do you just stand there? The bigger and fatter you get the closer you are to death. Don't you know that very soon now they're going to come and take you away. They'll clobber you on the head with a big hammer. They'll carve you up into little pieces—little pieces that have names—and...eat you. Don't you know that?

*Cud Cow*: Gulp. Seriously? Why are you telling me all this? What am I supposed to do about it?

*Isaac*: You could escape.

*Cud Cow*: And how would I go about doing that?

*Isaac*: Brutus...if you please.

*Brutus*: You want me to kick its ass?

*Isaac*: No. I want you to knock down part of this fence so the cow can escape.

With that, Brutus began kicking at the fence. This fence was very sturdy and the boards seemed to be unmovable. But he was undaunted and kept at it while the others watched.

*Cud Cow*: Hmmmpf...urrrp—

All the clatter aroused the attention of a certain massive bull named Tuck. This cud-chewing cow, and many others, were *his* responsibility. Seeing trouble at the fence, Tuck came to the scene and saw Brutus standing by the rubble where a section of fence once stood. Brutus didn't see Tuck approach—but the others did. **Whump!** Tuck gave Brutus's ass a bull-sized head butt, knocking Brutus up into the air and several feet out into the Grabapple Road. Brutus landed square on his ass, giving it a second pounding. The shot pellets that still resided in his ass made the two blows even more painful. As a result, Brutus leapt to his feet immediately.

*Brutus*: Yeeeeeow!

*Tuck the Bull*: And stay out! The rest of you will scram if you know what's good for you!

*Ralston*: Say, Isaac. Why would that bull want to keep the cow inside the fence if he knew she was going to be killed and eaten?

*Isaac*: He must have other uses...other purposes for her.

*Mooncalf*: What did he mean, "scram"?

*Ralston*: Somebody chopped off part of that bull's horns. Beezum's got big long pointy ones.

*Isaac*: Very interesting. Hey bull! What's with those little peg horns?

*Tuck the Bull*: (???)

*Ralston*: Look at that funny scar on the side of his ass. What's that all about?

*Isaac*: That cow has the same scar on the side of *her* ass. Weird.

*Tuck the Bull*: What are you asses waiting for? Move it!

As usual, following somebody's arbitrary orders was not the primary concern for the Grabapple Five.

*Isaac*: Hey bull, how'd you get that funny little scar on your ass? Did you back into a pitchfork or something?

*Tuck the Bull*: (???) Move it!

The group of five showed no hint of movement.

*Ralston*: That cow doesn't appear to be the least bit interested in any of this. Hasn't even tried to escape. What do you make of that, Isaac?

*Isaac*: Hey cow! Why don't you escape? The fence is down.

*Pucker*: Pff-yeah. Pff-look at it...it's open-pff!

*Cud Cow*: Gulp. I'm a *dairy* cow, you bunch of numbskulls! They don't eat me...I'm not part of the abattoir group. Urrrp—

127

*Mooncalf*: What's a dairy cow?

*Cud Cow*: They get milk from me to drink.

*Ralston*: *Who* does?

*Cud Cow*: The humans.

*Isaac*: You expect us to believe that milk comes out of you and the humans drink it?

*Cud Cow*: Burrrrp. Yep.

*Ralston*: Do you realize how disgusting that is?

*Cud Cow*: Keeps me alive...urrrp—

Still walking about, trying to shake off the pain, only Brutus noticed that Tuck the Bull was purposefully passing through the fence, getting a line on the next donkey to receive a head butt.

*Brutus*: Hey you guys! The bull is out *here*...I think we should leave...now!

The others quickly lined up as Brutus limped his way to the end of the line. The Grabapple Five continued their journey as fast as they could, somewhat hampered by the physical condition of several of its members. Tuck the Bull kept an eye on the group making sure that they really did move on.

Unfortunately for Tuck, however, his owner came out of the farmhouse and saw Tuck standing in the road next to the demolished fence. Of course the owner surmised that Tuck had done the damage. For punishment, Tuck was tied to a post. At least for a while he wouldn't be able to use the cud cow (or any cow) for those other purposes mentioned by Isaac.

Down the road a ways—

*Pucker*: Pff-I hear a bell-pff.

*Mooncalf*: Me too.

*Brutus*: Ralston, ever since you jinxed me my ass has taken a real beating. I can hardly walk straight.

*Ralston*: Look at *me*. What are you bellyaching about?

*Isaac*: Quiet! I hear a bell also. It seems to be getting louder.

Before the Grabapple Five could evaluate the situation further, the fire brigade wagon was barreling toward them from behind with the firedog out in front. The brigade had extinguished the fire and their tank was out of water. They were now headed back to Oxboro. It didn't look like the driver had any intention of stopping this time.

*Ralston*: That driver looks like he's aiming that wagon, those horses, straight *at* us.

*Brutus*: I'm getting out of the way.

*Pucker*: Pff-me too-pff.

So all the members of the group stood to the side of the road and let the wagon pass. Upon passing, a huge cloud of dust was created and all the members of the Grabapple Five were covered with a fine white powder. They now looked like five jackass ghosts. They began shaking off the dust with some success, but a lot of it remained.

*Isaac*: Hey Ralston, I can hardly tell that you've got all that white paint on your face any more.

*Ralston*: Yeah. Well—

*Pucker*: Pff-aren't we a sight-pff.

And the journey toward Oxboro continued. As the Grabapple Five got closer to the town, they started to anticipate great things. Surely they would find adventure there. By continually recycling their own thoughts about it, among themselves, anticipation soon turned to expectation. They were now *expecting* to find adventure there—big adventure—adventure just waiting for their arrival. Even if they found no adventure, getting to Oxboro would feel like a victory in itself. But first—

*Isaac*: What is that up there, on the road? Ralston, do you see them?

*Ralston*: I see them. Looks like a bunch of jackasses coming this way. Looks like one donkey more than we have.

*Mooncalf*: Maybe it's a reflection...like in a pond.

*Brutus*: Say the word and I'll kick their collective asses. Just say the word.

*Isaac*: I'll keep that in mind, but you're in no condition to do any ass-kicking.

The group of six spotless, well-groomed donkeys approached the Grabapple Five, not really wanting to interrupt their own constitutional, but feeling obligated to at least acknowledge their fellow donkeys.

*Lehigh*: Well well well. What do have we here? What are you jackasses made up for? Why are you lined up like that?

*Isaac*: It's a long st...

*Ralston*: We saved an old hermit from a burning cave. Rescued him from certain death—

*Lehigh*: What a load of bullshit. We heard that you set his place on fire after killing a clan of warthogs—

*Isaac*: How did you hear that?

*Lehigh*: Fire brigade...news travels fast. And where do you think you're going now?

*Isaac*: Oxboro. We're seeking...we have...appointments there.

*Lehigh*: Oxboro? Oxboro? This isn't the road to Oxboro.

*Isaac*: Then what is that village up there? The fire wagon—

*Lehigh*: That's uh...Mohr. Mohr City. You'd better steer clear of that place. Why are you all lined up like that? Across the road?

*Isaac*: Never mind. What are *you* jackasses doing out here?

*Lehigh*: First of all, we're donkeys. We have males and females in our group. Not all of us are jackasses. Some are jennies.

*Brutus*: Jennies? What are jennies?

*Lehigh*: Females, you jackass. Don't you know anything?

*Brutus*: Females? It's been a long time since I've been in the presence of a donkey female.

Brutus went over to the elite group of donkeys and began poking around looking for a female.

*Lehigh*: Hey, Bub! Leave those jennies alone.

*Isaac*: What are you doing out here on the Grabapple Road? And why aren't you covered with dust from that wagon?

*Lehigh*: We're out for a walk. And, we know enough to move far away from the road when we hear that bell. Looks like you're too ignorant to know that.

Amidst some giggling from the female donkeys, a happy-faced Brutus emerged and confronted Lehigh—

*Brutus*: You know, I would kick your ass if I wasn't so impaired at the moment.

Ignoring Brutus, Lehigh addressed Isaac—

*Lehigh*: You need to rein in your friend there, before he stirs up more trouble than he can handle...or *any* of you can handle.

*Isaac*: How do *you* know what town that is up there?

*Lehigh*: We all live on a luxurious farm with a wealthy owner.

*Ralston*: Yeah? So do we. And ours is bigger and fancier.

*Lehigh*: Humpf.

Brutus had found his way back into the group of three females and was titillating them with his charms. The females' giggling was starting to irritate Lehigh—if only because he knew that Brutus was the one causing it.

> *Lehigh*: OK that's about enough of this chitchat. You need to move your line
> of jackasses and let us pass.

> *Ralston*: Everybody stay put!

The group (minus Brutus) stood their ground and held their formal line of four in place; defiant, ready for confrontation, heads held up high, proud. Following Lehigh's lead, the six elite donkeys casually went around one end of the line and proceeded on their merry way. As the giggling females followed along with the males in their group, Brutus returned to his own group.

> *Ralston*: Well. That was a big disappointment.

> *Brutus*: Yeah, I'll say. Too bad we didn't have more time. Those females.
> Ooh, Donkeynation!

> *Ralston*: I meant...we could have kicked their asses.

> *Brutus*: Oh yeah? Oh. Yeah, too bad.

> *Isaac*: Mohr? That jackass said the town up there was Mohr, not Oxboro.

> *Ralston*: Let's go find out for ourselves.

Feeling let down and discouraged, the Grabapple Five plodded on until they reached a sign on the outskirts of a small town. The sign read, "Welcome to Oxboro Township."

*Isaac*: I sure wish you could really read, Ralston. Don't know if that says
        Mohr or Oxboro or something else.

*Ralston*: Yeah...sorry.

*Mooncalf*: Are we doing our adventure in this town?

On into town the Grabapple Five went. At the edge of town they saw a woman tending to a
rose bush in front of a pleasant little white cottage. Remembering what Lehigh had said
about how poorly the Grabapple Five would be received in the town, Isaac wanted to be as
polite as possible—

*Isaac*: What ho, say hey there fine woman of the flowers there—and mighty
        fine flowers they be, if I do say so myself. I see you are a beautiful fine
        human female spreading some fine animal shit on the ground around
        those flowers. Say, what might be the name of this wonderful village
        here, this place?

*Rose Woman*: What the—?

*Isaac*: Yes. Pardon our appearance—we do look a mite amiss, but I assure
        you we do not intend to destroy your house or molest you or anything.
        Just what town is this if I might ask without getting too far under your
        skin?

*Rose Woman*: Why, you're the jackasses! Get out of here! Quit stepping all
        over my flower beds!

The Rose Woman grabbed her broom and began waving it at the Grabapple Five. Barely
making an effort to move, the group made a few more observations.

*Ralston*: How long has it been since you washed your hair? Looks pretty ratty to me.

*Pucker*: Pff-ratty-pff.

*Ralston*: Oily too.

*Mooncalf*: And, um, hairy.

*Brutus*: You should be grateful that I don't kick your ass, right here, right now, on your front yard.

Still waving her broom the Rose Woman let out a high-pitched, tree-bark-removing scream that drove the Grabapple Five back into the road with ten watering eyes.

*Ralston*: Have you ever heard anything like that?

*Isaac*: Never.

*Brutus*: As if I wasn't already hurting enough—

*Isaac*: I was being as polite as possible.

*Ralston*: She seemed to recognize us though. She knew who we were.

*Isaac*: Maybe this *is* Mohr, like the other jackass said. He said to steer clear of it.

The Rose Woman retreated back into her house carrying her broom, while the Grabapple Five stood in the street wondering what to do next, discussing the new situation. All five were hoping to avoid someone in the street, hoping to avoid another confrontation. But they also wanted to find out just where they were. So they waited, and rested, and waited, hoping a solution would come to them. But as they say, idle minds...

*Brutus*: I think we should give her what for—

*Pucker*: Pff-I agree-pff.

*Isaac*: Where are you going, Ralston?

*Ralston*: Going around back, around back here—

Because they all felt the camaraderie that came with being in this entire thing together, the rest of the five followed Ralston to the back yard of the cottage. They saw that Ralston was sticking his head into an open window, having a look around.

*Isaac*: What do you see, Ralston?

Ralston quickly withdrew his head from the window and turned to Isaac—

*Ralston*: Shhhh. There's two of them in there: a man asleep on a sofa and that same woman...looks like she's asleep or half-asleep in a chair. Both of them right up near the window. What do you think?

Now it had been a while since the Grabapple Five destroyed the farmers' cornfield. But they had eaten a pretty hefty amount of corn while traipsing through the stalks. During the hustle and bustle of eating a glutton's share of corncobs on a rampage, a fair amount of air was swallowed as well—and enough digestive time had passed—

*Brutus*: Hey Ralston!

The group began talking in whispers.

*Ralston*: Watch it! Don't talk so loud.

*Brutus*: Hey. What do you say I deliver a flatus into the window there?

*Ralston*: Have you got enough stored up?

*Brutus*: Let us see. Let us see.

So Brutus assed-up to the window, inserting it as far as he could and let out a bomb of a flatus that, luckily, didn't bring down the roof of the cottage. Quickly he withdrew his ass, and the five jackasses all crowded around the window, like voyeurs, to see the result.

*No Longer Asleep Man*: Annie? Annie? Are you cooking something? Annie?

*Rose Woman*: Uh? Huh? No. Go back to sleep.

The couple fell back asleep and the Grabapple Five stepped back from the window.

*Isaac*: Ralston? Can you deliver one?

*Ralston*: Lemme at it. Step aside.

Ralston went to the window and delivered a whopping silent greasy flatus that might have driven the Grabapple Five from the window but for their collective curiosity. They gathered around the window again. This time the woman, with the palm of her hand covering her face, went over to the man and said something to him. The man left the room as the woman fell back into her chair. Soon, the man reappeared and went back to the sofa. It appeared to the Grabapple Five that the delivery of the two gas bombs had little or no effect—the couple appeared to be fast asleep once again.

*Isaac*: Anybody else have something to…unleash…deliver? I feel nothing myself.

*Mooncalf*: How about me?

*Ralston*: Be my guest—

Mooncalf went to the window and prepared himself for a big delivery. After a couple of false alarms, Mooncalf let out the grandest blast that had been delivered so far. If the couple was asleep, they must surely be awake after that one.

Unfortunately for the couple, Mooncalf delivered more than just gas into their living room.

Unfortunately for Mooncalf, who was a little too slow to extract his ass from the window, the man took out a pair of heavy shears and cut off Mooncalf's tail, right there where it was attached to his ass. It was not a painless procedure and Mooncalf leapt from the window and out into the yard, knocking over a table and a sizable stack of firewood.

*Ralston*: I think we should get out of here...right now!

*Pucker*: Pff-I agree-pff.

*Mooncalf*: Something stung me on the ass!

*Isaac*: Come on Mooncalf. We have to get out of here!

*Brutus*: Do you think they'll come after us with a gun...like the others?

*Isaac*: I'm not waiting around to find out.

So the Grabapple Five quickly fled to the Grabapple Road and away from the cottage—the cottage where they had delivered the cheese. The Rose Woman came out of the house wielding a large butcher knife. She watched as the Grabapple Five moved on along the road to the center of town.

In Oxboro, the Grabapple Road was more of a wide street than a dusty country road; but no matter what kind of road, the five damaged jackasses still insisted on walking five abreast. Although it might be said that if the jackasses were forced to view each other from behind, their asses would definitely be more interesting to look at than they were when the journey began.

> *Ralston*: At least it wasn't a gun this time.

> *Isaac*: Not so good for poor Mooncalf.

> *Brutus*: What does a jackass do without a tail?

> *Isaac*: Not so good at all.

> *Ralston*: We should ask someone what town this is. We may be looking for adventure where none exists.

> *Brutus*: That's been the case so far anyway.

The Grabapple Five moved slowly through the town observing the unwelcome looks they were getting from nearly everyone. No one in the town wanted to talk to the five. No one wanted anything to do with the five. The townsfolk just wanted the jackasses to go away without doing any more damage. On the other hand, the Grabapple Five were very curious about everything in the town—more than just the name. They knocked over pails of trash, looking through the contents. They raided a fruit cart, taking delicious samples until being run off. Where there was something to eat, they ate it. Marching through town, they looked into windows; they looked into open doors—

> *Brutus*: Whoa. You should've seen that!

> *Isaac*: What was it?

*Brutus*: I looked into that window over there. Naked human inside. It was weird. Ugly. The human started screaming. Weird. Weird and ugly.

*Isaac*: Like that dead man back there, eh?

*Brutus*: Sorta—

*Ralston*: I looked in a door and a man threw a book at me. Almost hit me in the head!

*Isaac*: You seem to be good at dodging things people throw at you.

*Pucker*: Pff-what's that-pff up ahead-pff?

*Mooncalf*: It's a bunch of small humans, I think.

*Isaac*: You're right. Something's going on in that little park.

*Ralston*: Let's go see what *that's* all about.

The weather was changing. As storm clouds gathered overhead, the Grabapple Five sauntered over to the edge of the park, curious about all the activity and hopeful that someone might be willing to talk to them and tell them the name of the town. The five jackasses stood behind a sculptured hedge. The hedge hid them from the neck down as they watched the proceedings discreetly. There were several adults and about twenty children participating in a celebration. It was a birthday party. But being jackasses and not humans, the Grabapple Five did not understand any of it.

One of the children seemed to be very intrigued by the hedge with five jackass heads peering over it, but the child was easily detoured by one of her playmates.

*Ralston*: What do you think all this is?

*Isaac*: I don't know, but look over there. That tree.

*Ralston*: What is *that*? Is that a picture of a jackass?

*Brutus*: What are they doing to it?

*Isaac*: I don't know, but those little humans are sticking those little brushes on it. I've got to find out what's going on.

*Mooncalf*: Maybe it's a sign of adventure.

*Isaac*: Come on.

As the wind began kicking up, the Grabapple Five, overwhelmed with curiosity, broke straight through the leafy hedge—needless to say, a hedge no more—and ambled over toward the party. As soon as the five's presence was detected, the adults frantically began gathering together the small ones. As one would expect, panic ensued. The children's party turned to mayhem and the jackasses stood alone among the tables, the chairs, and the food. The children had been rushed into the nearby building. The humans watched the five jackasses from a window as the jackasses started eating the food and the cake. In the process, tables and chairs were overturned. The area had become a gigantic mess. Away from the others, Mooncalf was closely examining the picture of the tailless donkey with all the little bundles of horsehair stuck to it, all over. One was stuck right in the donkey's eye.

*Mooncalf*: What do you think it is, Isaac?

*Isaac*: I have no idea. Those little brushes look like they're made of horse's hair.

*Mooncalf*: That jackass in the picture is missing its tail, just like me. Of all things—

*Isaac*: Why don't you go get something to eat, Mooncalf. Before it's all gone.

*Mooncalf*: Yeah. (I wonder what that picture is doing there.)

*Isaac*: Hey, Ralston! Guess no one is going to talk to us. There's no adventure here. We'll have to be turning around soon...if we're going to get home before dark.

*Ralston*: Yeah. We should go.

Before they even left the park, the rain started. Thunder and lightning. The Grabapple Five trudged back to the Grabapple Road and continued their journey to the far edge of town. They were not immediately aware that the light shower was washing some of the white dust off their bodies—but only some. The combination of the dust and the rain was now giving their bodies a mottled grey appearance. They looked like five animated heavily-veined marble statues.

As they reached the edge of town, the brief shower began to subside. There was an old man sitting in a rocking chair on the porch of a small thatched roof cottage. He did not react when the Grabapple Five approached him. He was blind so he didn't know that he was talking to jackasses. And the jackasses had no concept of a blind human.

*Isaac*: Hello there! We were on our way out of town and were wondering— what is the name of this town?

*Blind Man*: Why, this is Oxboro. Didn't you see a sign when you came in? Oxboro Township.

*Isaac*: None of us can read. One of us *says* he can, but really, he can't. Oxboro? Township? What's that? There was a group of donkeys on the other side of town that told us that this place was called Mohr.

*Blind Man*: Oh. Those guys. Those guys are a bunch of lying asses—vagabonds that showed up here in Oxboro one day. They're a nuisance. People in this town have come to hate donkeys, jackasses, asses...whatever you want to call them.

Isaac looked at Ralston. Every one of the five was looking at everyone else. Unspoken words and surprise: the Blind Man didn't seem to know that five jackasses were right in front of him. Unspoken words among the jackasses: no one was going to tell him. And Brutus forcefully nudged Mooncalf before Mooncalf could inadvertently say something to blow their cover.

*Blind Man*: So, where are you going?

*Isaac*: We're going on up the Grabapple Road—a little ways further. We've been looking for adventure all day long, but now we're running out of time.

*Blind Man*: Well, I hope you find what you're looking for.

*Ralston*: Yeah...we'll see.

*Blind Man*: Be careful on that end of the Grabapple—

The Grabapple Five left town knowing that they would soon have to turn back and go home. The road coming out of Oxboro was muddy from the storm and they were building up quite a load of glue-like mud clods on their hooves. But the rain had been refreshing—a small element of good fortune, but good fortune nonetheless.

They weren't very far from town when they came upon a wooden bridge; a bridge crossing a rapidly moving stream. The water was splashing and rippling over stones.

*Isaac*: If we can find a place in the stream that's deep enough, maybe we can wash off some of this mud and caked-on dust.

*Pucker*: Pff-sounds like a great-pff idea-pff.

*Ralston*: Doesn't look nearly deep enough. Are we going across the bridge or what?

*Isaac*: Yeah. Why not?

The bridge was not quite wide enough to accommodate the group walking five abreast, but they insisted on doing it anyway. On the left end was Isaac, his big left side rubbing heavily on the bridge rail. On the right end was Mooncalf—same problem. At times they thought that one of the unstable rails was going give way, sending one or more of the five into the stream. But they made it to the other end of the bridge without too much difficulty or any new catastrophe.

*Mooncalf*: I thought I saw something, there, under the bridge.

*Ralston*: What was it?

*Mooncalf*: It looked like two men; maybe more. Do you think they live under there like trolls?

The five jackasses stepped off the wooden bridge in unison and onto the muddy road, but before they could check under the bridge they saw five riders approaching on horseback. The five horses were very fine stallions, four black ones (ridden by four Road Marshals) and one white one (ridden by the Chief Road Marshal). These designations of the men would have meant nothing to the jackasses had they been so informed.

Mooncalf was right. He had seen two men hiding under the bridge. They were highwaymen—robbers. Their horses were long gone, but they were carrying quite a bundle of booty. They were also carrying guns—small ones. The two men climbed up onto the bridge, making sure that the five jackasses were positioned between themselves and the approaching team of Marshals.

*Mooncalf*: What's going on?

*Isaac*: I have no idea. Let's get out of here.

*Abraham Stiggs*: Don't any of you jackasses move!

*Ralston*: And who are you? You can't tell us what to do.

*Abraham Stiggs*: You see this? This is a gun. Now be still.

Upon seeing the two highwaymen taking cover behind the Grabapple Five, the five horsemen pulled up and dismounted, ducking down and raising their own pistols.

*Brutus*: Have you ever seen so many guns?

*Pucker*: Pff-and they're all-pff little ones-pff.

*Abraham Stiggs*: Shut up you two!

*Moses Stiggs*: What do we do now, Abe?

*Chief Marshal Baxter*: All right. Abraham and Moses Stiggs...drop your weapons, stand up, and move away from those jackasses!

*Moses Stiggs*: We'll do nothing of the kind.

**Blam!** With that remark the shooting began. The Grabapple Five were caught right in the crossfire. None of them had any experience with this sort of thing. Bullets were whizzing past the heads of the jackasses, but one bullet went right through the left ear of Isaac, leaving a big hole. Another one hit Isaac's right ear at an angle and clipped the entire ear clean off.

In almost every situation, Brutus was always ready to kick someone's ass, but in this case, when he started kicking, his hooves hit Moses Stiggs right in the head, ostensibly knocking him out cold. In actuality, Moses Stiggs was dead from a broken neck. Not bad for a brutally injured Brutus. The gunfire continued and Abraham decided to make a run for it. Before he could get twenty feet on the wooden bridge he was gunned down by one of the Road Marshals. He lay dead in the center of the bridge.

> *Chief Marshal Baxter*: What are you jackasses doing here? You could have been killed.

> *Isaac*: We were out for a day of adventure. (Man, do I have an earache.)

> *Chief Marshal Baxter*: I suggest you all clear the area, and next time...stay out of the way.

The five Marshals scrambled around the area, gathering up the guns and the loot of the dead men. When everything of value was in their possession and loaded onto their stallions, the five corrupt Marshals turned and rode off the way they came, away from the town. They made no effort to do anything with the bodies of the two highwaymen. The Grabapple Five stood over the bodies, trying to make sense of what had just happened.

> *Ralston*: Brutus, I think you killed this one.

> *Brutus*: I didn't think that I kicked him all that hard.

> *Isaac*: This other one...look at all those holes...and the blood. Wow, it's red just like ours. Never seen that before—so much blood. Not from a human.

*Brutus*: What do you think it was that those horsemen took with them? All that stuff.

*Isaac*: I don't know, something important to these dead men...I think.

*Brutus*: Took their guns too.

*Mooncalf*: I *knew* I saw something under the bridge.

*Pucker*: Pff-what do you think-pff we should do-pff?

*Ralston*: Maybe it's time we headed back.

*Mooncalf*: Was this the adventure?

*Ralston*: Maybe. But it seemed to happen so fast...too fast to be a real adventure. What do *you* think, Isaac?

*Isaac*: I think we were lucky. (Hell of an earache, both of them.)

*Brutus*: I think it's time to go back. As it is, it'll be getting dark before each of us gets home.

*Isaac*: These men are dead. Just like those warthogs. Dead. I wonder if the buzzards will come. Maybe tomorrow when those birds get wind of the deadness on this bridge.

*Mooncalf*: Do you think that old man will take one of these men and roast him?

*Isaac*: Who's to say who eats whom in this situation. But I think Brutus is right—we should head back now.

So the Grabapple Five, agreeing that they had ventured as far as was reasonable, began the long trek back, back to Baersback End...and home.

When they reached the edge of town again, there was a sign just like the one on the other side of town. But the old blind man in the rocking chair was nowhere to be seen. Up ahead they saw three men and one was holding...a shotgun. The constable was alerted to something suspicious when he heard the sound of all the gunplay coming from the bridge. He quickly grabbed his shotgun and brought his two deputy constables with him.

> *Isaac*: What the? Another man with a gun?

> *Constable Forepot*: You five jackasses! I *knew* you were somehow involved.
>         Just where do you think you're going?

> *Isaac*: Back through town, on our way home.

> *Constable Forepot*: You're not coming through *here* I can tell you.

> *Isaac*: And how are we supposed get to the other side of town?

> *Constable Forepot*: Well, you're not coming back through here. You'll have
>         to go around.

> *Ralston*: Where?

> *Constable Forepot*: I'll show you.

The constable led the Grabapple Five (still attempting to walk five abreast) to a corner at the edge of the city limits. There was long alleyway there. Along the entire length, one side was mostly a rock face and on the other side were the backs of many buildings. The ground was muddy from the rain and there was a nose-burning stench in the air.

*Constable Forepot*: All right you jackasses, if you want to get to the other side of town, this is the only way—because you're not using the Grabapple Road to get through town...I can tell you that.

*Isaac*: The alley is hardly wide enough for one jackass, much less five of us, abreast.

*Constable Forepot*: What difference does it make? This alley is your only choice.

*Ralston*: What about on the opposite side of town, along that other side?

*Constable Forepot*: You're not going through on that side...where the park is. Children. And the lake.

*Ralston*: What do *you* think, Isaac?

*Isaac*: I think we'll have go down this alley single file.

*Mooncalf*: We could roll dice to see who goes first.

*Ralston*: We don't have any dice. And if we did, how do we roll dice? Mooncalf, sometimes you can be such a dumb-ass.

*Mooncalf*: Ralston, sometimes you can be a real horse's ass.

*Brutus*: Well, I'm not walking behind Mooncalf. It's bad enough with his tail intact, but without it I'll be staring right into his pucker.

*Pucker*: Pff–was that a crack at me?

*Ralston*: Nobody is allowed to walk after me. I don't want someone staring at my second asshole.

*Constable Forepot*: Quiet! All of you. You there, tail-less [Mooncalf]. You first. Get on with it. Then Mister White Face next [Ralston]. You, with the fat lip [Pucker]. Next. Little tough guy [Brutus] then mister smart-ass [Isaac]. No stopping. If you five don't come out of the other end when I get there, I'm coming after you with both barrels blazing.

*Brutus*: Do you think he's serious?

*Mooncalf*: What did he mean by "both barrels"?

*Constable Forepot*: Go!

The Grabapple Five, extremely averse to taking orders from some human and extremely averse to walking single file, started down the alley of filth, slogging through the mud, viscous liquids, dirty dishwater, dirty bath water, garbage, and all sorts of human waste.

*Ralston*: This is the most disgusting thing I've ever experienced.

*Isaac*: I have to agree.

*Brutus*: But the man had a gun. We've seen firsthand what can happen.

*Ralston*: I tell you, Mooncalf, without your tail you have a pretty vile-looking ass.

*Mooncalf*: (What a horse's ass.)

As they trudged along, a woman appeared in one of the second-story windows. Without taking note of the passing group of jackasses below, she dumped a large pan of dirty bath water out of the window, the water landing right onto the head of Ralston. It was unintentional but Ralston, of course, immediately took offense. Just one more insult—one more incident.

Toward the end of the alley there was an opening on the right side. Instead of the back of a building, there was a fenced-in area. In the pen were the six donkeys the Grabapple Five had met on their way into town. Ralston was in a heightened mood of sourness.

*Ralston*: Well well well. Look who's here.

*Lehigh*: This is all your fault.

*Ralston*: *What* exactly is our fault?

*Lehigh*: Our being locked up in here.

*Isaac*: How is that *our* fault?

*Lehigh*: When we got back from our constitutional, the constable rounded us
up and put us into this pen. He said that he wasn't putting up with
any more jackass antics in his village. And...that we could all just *rot*
in here. So, it's all *your* fault.

*Isaac*: Could it be that the town was already fed up with you six assholes
anyway? Hmm?

Brutus was not paying any attention to the conversation. Instead he was back in the business of titillating the female donkeys and making them giggle. While Isaac engaged Lehigh and Brutus engaged the females, Mooncalf was still trying to get a look-see of his tailless ass...back there. Apparently he was unaware of the futility.

*Lehigh*: Tell your buddy there to leave our jennies alone.

*Isaac*: We were just leaving. By the way, enjoy all this...ahem...fresh air.

*Lehigh*: You're a real smart-ass aren't you.

*Isaac*: Smarter than you, it seems—

Lehigh turned and gave the fence a swift kick, one that indicated his frustration and one that indicated that the fence could not be breached. So the Grabapple Five strolled on to the end of the alleyway, with heads held a little bit higher after their encounter with those other asses. Brutus kept looking back and showing some toothy grins to the giggling females. An occasional swing of his tail to the side revealed to the females furtive little views of what they were missing.

When the Grabapple Five were only covered with mud and coagulated dust, the group just smelled like mud. Now they were covered with something else and they smelled like...something else. As they reconvened on the Grabapple Road, lining up five abreast and pointed toward home, the Oxboro constable stood firm by the Oxboro welcome sign, watching them leave and making sure they were truly on their way and out of his hair.

*Ralston*: I'll never get that view of Mooncalf's ass out of my mind. And that little tail stub. What do you think, Brutus? You were behind *me*. What are your thoughts about my extra hole?

*Brutus*: I wasn't looking at your ass, Ralston.

*Isaac*: Come on you guys. Let's forget about it. We need to get home before the sun goes down.

Before long the group reached the place where the cow was chewing its cud. There was the cow, still chewing. The fence had been mended in a very haphazard way. There was no sign of Tuck the Bull. As they passed the cow, Isaac paused and then stepped aside.

*Isaac*: You guys wait here, I want to have a final word or two with that cow.

*Cud Cow*: Urrrp...what do you want *now*?

*Isaac*: Something has been on my mind. I just wonder...could you possibly be any more indifferent about the things going on all around you?

*Cud Cow*: Urrrp...I suppose I could be—I just don't care.

*Isaac*: That figures. Well then, just out of curiosity, as a dairy cow, would you drink milk that came out of a human.

*Cud Cow*: Urrrp...How awful. And just how would I do that anyway?

*Isaac*: Don't know. Maybe a bucket?

*Cud Cow*: Have you ever heard of pule?

*Isaac*: Never heard of it. What is it?

*Cud Cow*: It's cheese made from donkey milk; from female donkeys. Humans pay lots of money for it. Probably more than any other cheese.

*Isaac*: And what is cheese?

*Cud Cow*: It's like solid milk. People eat it.

*Isaac*: I don't know if I believe all that. In fact, I don't. And just how do you know all this stuff?

*Cud Cow*: I'm a dairy cow. I know all about these kinds of things.

*Isaac*: Say, what happens if your milk runs dry? What happens to you then?

*Cud Cow*: I suppose they'll kill me and eat me.

*Isaac*: That doesn't bother you?

*Cud Cow*: Nope. Life could be worse. I could have been born as a sorry ass obnoxious jackass. Urrrrrrrp—

Isaac felt a little cheated having come up short on real answers, so he returned to the five and they went on their way.

*Ralston*: What did you find out?

*Isaac*: Nothing. Nothing at all. But what can you expect from a stupid cow? Have you ever heard of something called cheese?

*Ralston*: Nope.

Moving on, the group came upon the cornfields where they had their fill of corn on the cob—corn, cobs, shucks, silk, all of it. And Brutus's ass had received its fill of buckshot—still painful. They didn't stop to reminisce. They didn't even slow down. Brutus did occasionally glance toward the fields—just in case the farmer happened to make an encore appearance.

The group was beginning to get weary. It was the kind of weary where the end seemed too far off to matter. Instead of being weary as a *direct* challenge, it was a kind of ambient weary—always there underneath the more pressing need of just getting home.

Soon they arrived at the place where the warthogs were feeding the buzzards. The buzzards were still in the trees. Isaac assumed they were stuffed with warthog and were sleeping it off. When Isaac stopped, the group stopped with him.

*Isaac*: Look at where those warthogs were. There's only a few bones left. Some blood stains. Amazing.

*Pucker*: Pff-they're all gone—pff.

*Isaac*: Look at them, those buzzards, up there in the trees. They look like they're asleep. How do they sleep and stay attached to the branches?

*Ralston*: They're so still. They look like they're part of the trees.

*Mooncalf*: Who are we talking about?

*Ralston*: Still smells like burnt wood around here. I wonder what happened to the old man that was roasting the warthog.

*Isaac*: He's probably back there in his cave.

*Brutus*: Can we get on with it?

*Isaac*: Yeah. OK.

The Grabapple Five soldiered on. Each place along the way brought back memories of earlier in the day—sometimes painful reminders. When they got to the place where the Wagon Man was hauling a dead man in a box, Isaac saw the horse's blinders lying almost completely buried in the moist dirt on the road. Isaac picked them up in his teeth and shook of the dirt. The blinders were the only thing left at the scene. All the rest had been taken away, presumably by the Wagon Man. Isaac speculated that Spurla the horse had covered the blinders with dirt while the Wagon Man was gathering up his cargo.

But for the rest of the way home, every time Isaac wanted to say something he had to put down the blinders first [plop]. And if he wanted to keep them, he had to pick them back up [snatch].

The sun was getting low in the sky and the entire road was now being completely immersed in shadow. The Grabapple Five continued to press on.

When they got to the impressive rock wall where Ralston went crazy inside the big house, the members of the group wanted to sneak by as fast as they could. Everything was quiet, it was starting to get dark, and there was a gate lamp already burning by the magnificent gate.

> *Isaac*: [plop] Hey Ralston, want to go get a drink? [snatch]

> *Ralston*: Isaac, you wise-ass.

> *Mooncalf*: Are we stopping for water?

> *Pucker*: Pff-sounds good to me-pff.

> *Ralston*: No, we're not stopping. We're moving on...now!

Onward. Onward. Trying to get home before the real darkness set in, the members of the Grabapple Five knew that on a moonless night they would hardly be able to see their way. And wolves and raccoons and other creatures would come out—*their* day would just be starting. And those creatures, unlike jackasses, could see in the dark—if one could only imagine. Not a pleasant prospect after what they had already been through on this day of so-called adventure.

And then they came upon the place where they encountered the racehorses. Strange occupation for a horse. But the racehorses were already back in their stables, ready for a good night's sleep. As they approached the spot where the woman was mending the fence, there was no woman. But the memory of the woman's leading them astray—

> *Isaac*: [plop] Isn't this the place where that woman told us about an adventure being two miles up the road? [snatch]

*Pucker*: Pff-you're *right*-pff.

*Brutus*: If she were here right now I'd—

*Isaac*: [plop] Maybe we misunderstood. None of us knows what a mile is. Could have been even further than we thought—way past that bridge. [snatch]

*Pucker*: Pff-you're *right*-pff.

*Ralston*: You know, Pucker, you're really starting to get on my nerves.

*Pucker*: Pff-who? Pff-me?

*Brutus*: Leave him alone.

*Ralston*: Or what? You're going to kick my ass? And just what were you doing with those female donkeys back there?

*Brutus*: None of your business.

*Isaac*: [plop] All right. Knock it off. We've got to get home. [snatch]

Everyone was getting testy. Legs were aching. And shadows were disappearing into the darkness of early evening. The Grabapple Five had finally arrived at the sign where Ralston got his face painted.

*Isaac*: [plop] Hey Ralston! What does the sign say now? [snatch]

*Ralston*: It says "kiss my ass."

*Mooncalf*: Is that what it says? How strange.

*Brutus*: If we keep stopping we're going to be eaten by wolves. Let's go.

*Ralston*: Who the hell put *you* in charge here?

*Brutus*: Listen, I still have some fight left in my hams, you dick! (What a belligerent gas bag.)

*Mooncalf*: Who is Dick?

Isaac was too tired to continue refereeing all the bickering that was surfacing between the members of the group. This was the crossroads—the junction between the Grabapple Road and Baersback End. And at the end of Baersback End was Isaac's home. To hell with everyone else. If they wanted to argue and stand in the crossroads all night they could do so. So, Isaac, ignoring the others, merely turned onto Baersback End, then onward, on the road home. He hoped the others would come along as well—and to stop all the constant complaining. When the rest of the group saw that Isaac was leaving, they all followed. They were no longer interested in walking five abreast, just in getting home.

Down Baersback End they went. The first to leave the group was Brutus. There was a lot of silence among the members of the group—tense silence. Next to go were Pucker and Mooncalf. Finally Ralston went his separate way, leaving Isaac to walk the last few hundred feet alone.

*Brutus*: (Home at last. Nice straw. And those female donkeys...aah, what might have been. Horses are OK, but when I got within snuffling range of those...jennies he called them. Aah! Did kill a man though; can't forget that. Wasn't really my fault. Can't let any of those kinds of things keep me down. Those shotgun pellets—what a pain in the ass. And Mooncalf, now with that little flat stub for a tail. Ha ha ha...)

*Pucker*: (Well, here I am. Good friends. It's all good. At least I didn't kill anybody, except maybe a warthog or two. That doesn't count. It's all good. All good…ha ha ha…)

*Mooncalf*: (Already home? Did we finally find adventure? Don't know. I wish I could see what my tail stub looks like. That picture of the donkey…and no tail…just like me. How could that be? And that party cake—wasn't so hot if you ask me—all sticky. Too sweet. Weird. They say my head is full of straw. But the straw is here on the ground—I can see it. What do they know? Ha ha ha…)

*Ralston*: (Home, I suppose. All those people, warthogs, the old man in the cave. And those damn donkeys. Who do they think they are? I guess the humans, like all humans, are going to place the blame on us for all of their troubles. Too bad for them. We had a legitimate goal—to find adventure. Nothing wrong with that. And they call *us* asses! I still wonder what Brutus was up to with those female donkeys. That little ass-kicking shit wouldn't say. Hah, I'll bet that fancy mansion will never be the same after tangling with the likes of *me*. Serves them right for trying to poison me with their water. Ha ha ha…)

When Isaac got to his stable he placed the horse blinders on a small shelf he reserved for such items. It was a real nuisance carrying those things along the rest of the way. It was times like that when he wished nature had given him hands. What did nature know about it? Four legs and no hands. Nature. Over the years Isaac had collected a number of mementos: a bow tie, a piece of metal, and a bunch of other items that most jackasses would call junk. But each item meant something to Isaac. And so the dirt-covered blinders were added to his shelf.

*Isaac*: (What an ordeal! It's good to be home. I guess we did find a kind of adventure after all. We just didn't know it. I never knew the world was filled with so much rudeness. And all those guns. No call for that. I feel lucky to be alive. Ralston did look pretty ridiculous with all that white paint on his face. I wonder if it will ever come off—but, as they say, better him than me. And Pucker's smiling ass—ha. Boy, have I got an earache—both of them. Still, what a memorable day…ha ha ha…)

Each one of the Grabapple Five had finally arrived home; each one reflecting on the experiences of the day; each one ruminating in his own way. As different as they were, they had one thing in common: the resolve to forget about what had happened and to start the next day with a clean slate and a clear conscience. Yes, a clean slate, a clear conscience, and no regrets. Yet, each of them would always carry reminders of the day—scars, missing parts, and such—things not so quickly dismissed.

But as far as they were concerned, why should they be bothered by all the mayhem they caused? Cornfields, warthogs, wreckage, fire, disruptions, death. The five of them had been able to have their day of adventure and everyone that got in their way would just have to get over it—those that were still alive. And so, as they prepared themselves for a good night's sleep, each of the Grabapple Five, including Mooncalf, was able to put the events of the day completely out of mind, laughing off everything. Even to the point of laughing themselves to sleep. Why should someone expect anything different? After all, every one of the Grabapple Five was a real jackass.

---

### Tale Extras

Your *Dramatis Personae Majoris* (in order of appearance)

The Wise-Ass (a.k.a. The Smart-Ass)…….Isaac
The Horse's Ass…….Ralston
The Kiss-Ass…….Pucker
The Dumb-Ass…….Mooncalf
The Bad-Ass…….Brutus

Your *Dramatis Personae Minoris* (in order of appearance)

Manic Dog.......Manfred
Sign Man.......Tab Gritsfield
Fence Woman.......Doreen Voscrow
Babette's Box Tango.......Herself
Shadow Dancer.......Himself
The Weathered Man.......Driscomb Tanner
Fenster Lord Creamstick.......Himself
Paladora Lady Creamstick.......Herself
Simmons the Butler.......Knurl of the Onyx
Wagon Man.......Roy Raye
Wagon Horse.......Spurla
Boss.......Head Warthog
Bitz.......Another Warthog
Gord.......A Third Warthog
Old Hermit Named Dave.......Dave
Top Buzz.......Top Buzzard
Fire Brigade Dog.......Rex
Fire Captain.......Phil Mauro
Fire Lieutenant Kelso.......Himself
Farmer Jack Haas.......Himself
Farmer Minniha Haas.......Herself
Cud Cow.......Pinkie Tietzworth
Tuck the Bull.......Tuck
Lehigh.......Elite Jackass
Rose Woman.......Annie Upton
No Longer Asleep Man.......Jethro Upton
Old Blind Man.......Jim Hackman
Highwayman #1.......Abraham Stiggs
Highwayman #2.......Moses Stiggs
Chief Road Marshal.......Ned Baxter
Oxboro Township Constable.......Fortis Forepot

Your *Dramatis Personae Minutiae* (in order of non-appearance)

Beezum the Bull
Disturbed Half-Naked Dead Man
Four Unnamed Warthogs
Frida, a Named Firearm
The Under-Buzzards
The Over-Buzzards
Three Giggling Female Donkeys
Two Elite Donkey Males
Naked Person Eyed By Brutus
Book-Throwing Man
Group of Party Adults
Twenty Party Children
Four Deputy Road Marshals
Two Oxboro Deputy Constables

———————————

Deleted Scene

*Isaac*: Mooncalf, cheer up! Your tail stub doesn't look all that bad.

*Mooncalf*: What use is a little tail stub like I have now?

*Ralston*: It's just the right height for brushing my teeth.

*Isaac*: Ralston! When is the last time you brushed your teeth?

*Ralston*: Never.

*Brutus*: Who's going to put their mouth that close to Mooncalf's ass anyway?

*Ralston*: Maybe Pucker—wouldn't bother *him*.

*Pucker*: Pff-I agree...I think...hmmm...no...now wait a pff-minute!

Memorabilia

*Brutus*
Hammered, puffed-up (rhinocerated) nose
Small area of burnt fur on the back
Bald burnt spot on the top of the head
Multiple shot pellets in the ass
Double-pounded butt
White dust powder all over
Marbleized streaks of coagulated white dust
Thick, glue-like mud covering legs
Grotesque smelly filth added to leg mud

*Pucker*
Fat lower lip and associated speech impediment
Burnt-off fur on the left foreleg
Crazy quilt of burnt fur on the back from the hermit's fire
Swollen bump on the head (from a rock bop)
Big smiling ass-crease on the center of the ass above the tail
White dust powder all over
Marbleized streaks of coagulated white dust
Thick, glue-like mud covering legs
Grotesque smelly filth added to leg mud

*Mooncalf*
Patchwork of burnt fur on the back and above the ass
Swollen bump on the head (from a rock bop)
Missing tail (probably hanging on a wall somewhere)
Two missing teeth (whereabouts unknown)
White dust powder all over
Marbleized streaks of coagulated white dust
Thick, glue-like mud covering legs
Grotesque smelly filth added to leg mud

*Ralston*
White painted face and forehead (two coats)
Bad taste in the mouth
Spear hole in the right butt cheek (masquerading as a second asshole)
Patchwork of burnt fur on the back and the back of the head
Swollen bump on the nose (from a rock bop)
White dust powder all over
Marbleized streaks of coagulated white dust
Thick, glue-like mud covering legs
Grotesque smelly filth added to leg mud

*Isaac*
Burnt-off fur on both front legs
Patchwork of burnt fur on the back and right buttocks
White dust powder all over
Marbleized streaks of coagulated white dust
Thick, glue-like mud covering legs
Round hole in one ear
Missing ear
Grotesque smelly filth added to leg mud
One set of horse blinders

# Casino Lutz

My name is Hudson Ballantine. I'm an actor living in Los Angeles. Perhaps you have seen some of my work. I've played a crime-solving Scottish goatherd, a priest who doubled as a county coroner (one stop for last rites and autopsy), and numerous action heroes. But my favorite parts were those of secret agent Rod Fury in such memorable spy movies as *Spyload*, *Spy vs. Rhombus*, and *The Spy on My Face*. I've never garnered much respect from my peers (actually zero) since none of my movies were met with any critical acclaim. But I did make a lot of money. Even if you haven't seen any of my movies you might be aware of my trademark catchphrase: "I didn't see a thing!"

I'm not an international playboy, but I've had enough experience playing Rod Fury that I can do a pretty fair impersonation of one out in the real world—when I want to: overdressing; pretentious cocktail orders; suggestive innuendoes; culinary connoisseur commentaries; and fearless and confident demeanor at all times. With me, through *some* of this, has been my on and off female companion, Tracey Trinidad. We like being seen with each other in public and we sometimes feed tabloids with bogus scandal-like information in order to keep our names in the mind of the public. It's all show biz.

Tracey is an actress with a professional background similar to mine: no respect, lots of money. When we're out on the town together she plays the part of a vintage movie star—long legs, slinky, dressed like a *femme fatale*. However, in the real world, I'm convinced she's a lot smarter than I am. She invests her money, building a nest egg for the time when she's finally tossed aside to make way for the next banana cream pie on the conveyor belt. I would rather just keep spending and have it all right now.

It was Thursday the 21st. The following Monday, the 25th, shooting was scheduled to begin on my new Rod Fury project, *Spy on a String*, so I decided to drive up to Condolero,

Nevada. Condolero is a spicy little mountain resort town that, at least for the time being, is *the* "in" place for chic, socially-networked public figures (like Tracey and me)—my last chance for a little R & R and some gambling. Of particular interest for me was the Casino Lutz (and its associated Hotel Avignon). Many of my celebrity friends had been there. It came highly recommended—exclusive, glitzy, and luxurious. And expensive.

Although I was anxious to check it out I decided to drive there from L.A. I'd rather drive than fly for some vacations because I own a vintage Raleigh Roadster convertible, one of the most expensive automobiles ever built. There's nothing like being out on the open road with the top down, enjoying the powerful and smooth ride of the Roadster; beautiful scenery flashing by; distant mountains out across a desert landscape; watching Tracey's long platinum blonde hair rippling in the wind. That part, not so much fun for Tracey, later, when she would have to brush out all the tangles—especially before arriving at the hotel. As I said, "It's all show biz." And it is with you all the time in this business.

Tracey was patiently waiting to hear from her agent about a new movie contract that was currently in limbo. Rather than sit around waiting, she preferred to ride with me to Condolero and to stay with me in my suite at the Hotel Avignon. She wasn't the least bit interested in the casino but having heard of the luxurious accommodations, she wanted to check it all out. Going with me was a perfect opportunity. Even though most of the drive from L.A. to Condolero was very scenic, it was still a long drive and we were happy to finally arrive at the Hotel Avignon shortly after sunset that Thursday evening.

When we first arrived at the hotel, I couldn't help but notice the numerous surveillance cameras—cameras everywhere. I found out later that they were not only placed there for security—incredible amounts of cash floating around—but also for capturing images of guests upon arrival. The pictures would then be used for face recognition. Through an ear plug, every resort employee, no matter how low in the hierarchy, could be instantaneously provided with the name of an approaching guest or guests. That way, a guest could always be referred to by name—a pleasantry, yes, but not foolproof by any means. As enjoyable and flattering as it might seem, it was very unsettling to be walking down a hotel hallway at two a.m. and have a janitor, cleaning up some drunk's throw-up, suddenly look up at you and say, "Good morning, Mr. Ballantine."

That first day, Tracey and I were much too tired to do anything more than grab a bite to eat at the Café Mahlzeit and go to our room for a "nap." About eleven p.m. that night I woke up, very refreshed. Tracey had already taken off to who-knows-where, so I put on my tux and my boutonniere and headed over to the casino to get things going.

Upon entering the casino proper there was a greeter at the main entrance. In the old days, this was usually a washed-up celebrity of some kind: totally recognizable and willing to stand for hours, getting photographed, shaking hands, and making guests feel...welcome. When I entered the casino that night, I recognized the greeter immediately. It was David Troy, the guy I replaced in the role of Rod Fury. If I hadn't recognized him, I would have been able to identify him by looking at the life-sized cardboard cutout next to him. It showed him in an action pose from *Spy in the Hole* and his name was prominently displayed overhead, in lights. He recognized me, even without receiving my name through his earpiece. I felt a little awkward when he treated me like a long lost friend, so I stopped and we talked for a bit.

"How are things going?" he politely asked.

"Pretty well. Keeping my head above water," I replied.

Without making eye contact, he added, "Well, that's good. Just let me say this: take care of your assets; manage them well...or you might wind up elbowing me out of this job too."

Was he taking a jab at me? Why did he bring that up? Just what was he trying to say?

Then I said, "So now you're here, doing...this. What would you have done differently, you know—looking back?"

"I would have spent more time in school, learning math."

"Hmm. Well, I guess it was good seeing you again," I said as I walked away. He just waved at me silently with a greeter's enigmatic pseudo-smile all over his mouth. I still couldn't understand what all he was talking about. Math?

I love casinos: the lights, the atmosphere, the noises, the colors, the constant activity. Looking out across the floor seeing the green tables and gaming surfaces, the colorful chips, the sudden flashes of excitement of someone hitting it big, they all added to the enjoyment of playing the games themselves. The Casino Lutz was a little different than other casinos I had visited in the past. There was an elegance to it all—above and beyond the electric atmosphere. To some extent, it was because there were so many recognizable celebrities everywhere. Some of the celebrities I knew personally and others I didn't even recognize at all. Out with the old, in with the new, I guess. Even though there was no dress code, there seemed to be one—every famous person in the entire casino seemed aware of being on camera, constantly; and each of them came dressed for the occasion, for the gaudy show of it all. Show biz. I have been in some of the rattiest and sleaziest casinos you could imagine...Casino Lutz was definitely preferable; even when my tux began to feel more like a straitjacket. And in this casino, I wasn't overdressed.

It was quite an amenity to have cocktail servers, pit bosses, bouncers, officials, dealers—every one of them correctly addressing me by name. Was it my movie star status or was it the face recognition software in the futuristic control center that was responsible? I deluded myself that it was the former.

I have never been a big fan of slot machines, especially when everything became purely button-operated. No skill involved. No tactile connection with the machine. With a mechanical one-armed bandit—you can tell yourself, "If I pull the handle just a little bit harder, maybe the wheels will turn just right and the bandit will pay off." Even so, the colors, the flash, and the festiveness that a hundred or more simultaneously active modern machines bring to a casino floor...the attraction is undeniable.

To me, roulette is purely a game of randomness (which it is) and no matter how big your winnings, the house always gets its cut—percentages. Baccarat tables are too snooty, even when I'm dressed for the occasion—like I was that first night. Although I can easily manage the numbers game when it comes to betting the percentages at the craps tables, I can never get around the strange feeling that the person rolling the dice is directly and personally responsible for my losing a bet.

Betting on sports, horses, and a myriad of other events going on around the world has its attraction. But that kind of wagering requires a lot of knowledge and research to be successful at it. I don't have the patience for that. At least betting at a casino is more reliable than going through a bookie, especially when the winnings turn out big.

Being successful at playing Texas Hold 'Em not only requires skill at reading people, but a pretty exact sense in managing percentages. It also requires a level of discipline that I don't have. And then there are the players: the young guy wearing dark sunglasses; the super-skilled old woman giving you the sense that she never played poker before; the obnoxious guy in a cowboy hat trying to distract the other players; the psycho; the loud talker; the constant talker; the guy who comments on every card; the self-important silent one who is all business; the truck driver who is in over his head; and a thousand other personalities. A politician or a professional poker player relishes the challenge of reading them all, and outwitting them all. I, for one, am too easily distracted, so I would be an easy mark for all of them. Not my kind of game.

So what is left? Blackjack, twenty-one. My skill is in the numbers. I can build a picture in my mind of all the spent cards as well as the cards left remaining in the deck. But in order to do this I have to play at a blackjack table that uses a single deck. Six decks in a shoe is not an option. Plus, there is something about a dealer dealing cards by hand, off of a 52-card deck, that has a simple purity to it, at least for me. Old school? Maybe. It may be considered card counting to maintain mental lists of played cards and to calculate the odds based on what's left in the deck. Still, it only evens the odds to about 50:50 if I'm playing in top form—maybe a little better for *me* in some circumstances. But if I can get ahead, I usually just stop playing. *That* is a discipline I *do* have.

When I was younger I had to count the cards using the tips of my fingers and my thumb on my left hand while using my right hand to stand or take a hit. I developed a system of different locations on my fingers and the palm of my hand to keep track of everything. As surveillance technology became more and more sophisticated I had to transfer the entire counting system to my head. That is my current system. It was a difficult adjustment at first, but practice makes perfect—at least it improves the odds. Even so, I had to develop yet another skill: a sixth sense in order to back off before some high-tech statistical model singled me out and I was taken to a back room for...ahem...questioning.

Sometimes I prefer to play at a table with multiple players and other times I prefer to play alone. Each has its advantages and disadvantages. I can see a lot of cards with multiple players, but I have to be alert, fast, and very discreet in order to capture all of that transient data in my head. When I play alone I have to bet prudently until enough cards have been spent from a newly shuffled deck so that my counts can reveal my best game play options. All the while, I have to be aware that someone, somewhere is watching my every move.

So there I was, in the much-anticipated Casino Lutz. Even though the various denominations of standard round chips were designed with different colors, they were all the same size—unlike those in some casinos I have visited abroad. And the edges of all the chip denominations were also identical. Except for the two flat sides where the value was printed, a one-dollar chip looked exactly like a $25,000 chip. Therefore, unless someone looked very closely at your stack, they could never tell just exactly how much wealth you were actually carrying around. The casino was truly top-heavy in wealthy high rollers and celebrities and I presumed that this chip convention was to keep nosy onlookers from determining just how much a famous quarterback had in his stack. On the other hand, it was very easy to lose a huge amount of money by carelessness alone—dropping a very high value chip by accident. But that was the way Casino Lutz operated so I just accepted it.

It was almost midnight when I sat down at a single deck blackjack table--$100.00 minimum bet. It was a center seat between four other players—two to my left and two to my right. I could easily see every card dealt. The dealer was shuffling as I sat down. I didn't think to even look at the other players or I might have recognized one of them. I was ready to focus. I gave him my packet of C-notes and received $10,000 worth of chips in several denominations. It has always felt a little disconcerting to watch my real money get pushed into a slot in the table—so easily and unceremoniously dismissed and gone forever. In this case a hundred $100 bills.

I played cautiously for the first few hands in order to get my counts going. Then I started to win. I was up about six hundred dollars when a voice addressed me from behind,

"Hud. Hud? Is that you?"

I turned around and there was Val Stewart who played Frosty on the old TV series, *Western Man.* I never thought of Val as a high-roller type. He was kind of a negative person and his sudden appearance at my table disrupted my counting.

Val then added some unsolicited information, "Have you heard about the ill winds that blew in on *Spy on a String*? Don't want to be the bearer of bad news but, you know, something financial."

It must have given Val a perverse sense of importance to be the one to bear disturbing information. Some people are like that. But I already knew all about the financial situation, and it was nothing. As a result, I was able to react with complete indifference— took the starch right out of him. After a few minutes of polite small talk, I was able to return to the table and basically...start over.

As I got back up to speed, along came Tracey. I was glad to see her, but my counts got disrupted...again.

"Hey Hudson, I think I'm going back to the suite," Tracey said. "I saw Barton Chesterfield over there playing Baccarat. Thought you might be interested."

Barton was the British villain in *Spyload*, my first Rod Fury movie. We became friends even though he was about forty years older than me. And he was British all the way. This many years later...he must be ancient. I told Tracey that I might be up all night and returned to my table where only two other players remained. And once again...I started over.

For the next hour I stayed pretty even with the house, but the guy to my right was losing—losing big, really big. It did not become a distraction until the casino floor manager came to the table and took the guy aside. I was trying to maintain my counts, but the conversation was too close by for me to ignore. They were comp-ing him his hotel room and buying him breakfast in return for his losing over $188,000 in just under three hours. I suppose they had been watching him for a while. It was a stark reminder to me that there was always someone watching...someone, somewhere.

My counts were wrecked again, so I started over. But I was amazed. Despite all the distractions, I was still up around six hundred dollars. Not bad, playing at $100 a whack. I was offered free cocktails. And I started over. The last person at the table, a guy who was getting a little too hot under the collar, was beginning to get on my nerves. When he finally left in huff, almost making a scene, I lost track of my counts. And once again, I started over.

I have always been impressed with how dealers are like Yeomen of the Guard (Beefeaters) in their ability to remain stone-faced, neutral, and emotionless while managing all kinds of personalities and challenges at the table. Hand after hand they just keep dealing and when it's time for a break another dealer comes in and takes their place.

I was alone at the table when a new dealer stepped in. A new deck was introduced, displayed, and shuffled. The casino crowd was starting to thin out but there were a fair number of people still playing at games all around the room. As much as I like the noise and the action when there is a big crowd, the relative calm and low noise level was helpful to me as I concentrated on the numbers. I played my first few hands by the book. Then my counts started giving me encouragement—so my bets got larger.

I managed to get my winnings up to about $1450.00, but it was taking me all night. It was starting to feel a little too much like work at 4:30 in the morning, so I resolved to play only a few more hands before joining Tracey in our suite.

It was around 4:40 a.m. and I remember the cards very distinctly. I had the ten of hearts and the six of clubs (16) and the dealer's up card was the five of clubs. My mind was getting fuzzy—I was losing track of my counts and I was starting to become indecisive. This is the kind of hand where my numbers game could have helped me immensely. The dealer waited patiently for me to decide (perhaps only outwardly) and as she looked away, if only briefly, a small trap door opened up on the table, right in front of my stacks of chips. From out of the hole a tiny little pink hand appeared. It was about the size of my thumb. I shook my head and did a double take. It was a hand, a tiny little hand. Before I could fully grasp what was going on, the hand grabbed a $500 chip from my stack and popped back into the hole in the table.

"Did you see that?" I shouted.

"See what?" the dealer replied. "What are you talking about, sir?"

"A little hand. A little hand came out of a hole in the table and stole one of my $500 chips!" I explained.

"Surely you're putting me on...sir," she said.

I was serious. I'd never seen anything like it. A little pink hand came out of a hole and stole my money. It must have been the early hour, a drowsy hallucination. Before my behavior could initiate a sequence of bad events, I decided to stop for the night.

When I got to our suite, Tracey was still up, but half asleep also. She was lying on the sectional sofa watching some cheesy adult movie. I just had to interrupt her.

"You'll never guess what I saw while I was playing," I told her.

When I told her what had happened, she seemed more concerned about *me* than in being shocked by the gist of my story. She told me that I needed to get some sleep so I joined her on the sofa. $2550 a night for the luxury suite and here we were scrunched together on the leather sofa with hard, cold pillows and very little space.

We both slept till half past noon. Then Tracey and I left the hotel and bounced around Condolero, acting like real resort tourists. It seemed like everywhere we went we ran into someone we knew from the business—or into someone who knew one of us from our work. And none of *them* required earpieces. Back home, I was used to being approached by people I didn't know. They were anxious to deliver my catchphrase, "I didn't see a thing!" How cute. How clever. Here in Condolero it was no different. However, considering how little respect we usually got from our peers back in L.A., that kind of treatment in Condolero was actually fun and refreshing.

So...Friday night—I was determined to reproduce the conditions from the previous night, but this time Tracey would be a witness. I started playing alone at the same table, but with a different dealer. Tracey watched as I played, but nothing happened. Hand after hand. When she got tired of standing behind me she decided to go to the bar. I watched as she slunk her way through the casino tables. But when I turned back and looked at my two cards, the small trap door opened up and the little pink hand coyly reached out and grabbed a $1000 chip from my stack. Before I could do anything the hand disappeared, back into its hole the table. I slapped my palm on the table hoping to discover a trace of the trap door, but to no avail—the hole was gone, the hand was gone, and my $1000 chip was gone.

I alerted the dealer, who, of course, had seen nothing. That little pink hand was into me for a total of $1500. I asked to see someone in charge. So the pit boss came over and graciously addressed me as Mr. Ballantine. (Another stark reminder that anonymity does not exist in a place like the Casino Lutz.) I showed him where I was sitting and showed him where the hole appeared, but there was not the slightest indication of a trap door or hole or anything unusual on the table surface. It was very frustrating. Yet, considering the outlandish nature of my story, he was very polite.

I didn't know whether to raise a bigger fuss over it or just try to forget the whole thing. I decided to play at a different seat at the same table. They brought in a new dealer and I hesitatingly went back to work. Before long I was crunching the numbers, grateful that no one else was playing at "my" table. I started winning and at that point was up about $1200 in winnings for the session.

Just when things really got going and my concentration was at a peak, the little hand came out of the table once again and nabbed a $1000 chip right off my stack. The hand and my chip were out of sight before I could even think about grabbing at them. And again, the dealer saw nothing. How was it that that little pink hand could be so utterly skillful at avoiding detection? Detection, only by me.

I was beginning to doubt my own eyes. Maybe I was going crazy. All those numbers in my head. In two days, I was up over $2700 in winnings, but was down $2500 because of that little chip-stealing hand. That was enough surrealism for one night so I went back to the suite where Tracey was anxiously awaiting my return.

Tracey had won the female lead in *She-Slug from Venus* so she (Tracey, not the slug) would have to fly back to L.A. in the morning. Not only would I be alone for the next couple of days, but I would have to drive back to L.A. by myself. Not really my preference. Since it was our last night together in Condolero, we decided to actually sleep in the bed.

The next day (Saturday morning) I drove her to the airport. It was a small airport, but the place was loaded with private jets. As we kissed goodbye, Tracey made a joke about two movie stars being caught kissing on an airport surveillance camera. That gave me an idea. I couldn't wait to get back to the casino.

On the five-minute drive back, I pondered how I would approach the subject with the casino manager. Because of my celebrity status and a hundred-dollar "donation", the highly skeptical casino day manager (Ms. Anita Lugi) agreed to sit with me and view the overhead surveillance videos. At the time I didn't feel comfortable about it. I perceived that looking at the videos might be illegal or unethical or both. But I really wanted some answers. In retrospect I believe that Ms. Lugi's only real concern was possible unwanted bad publicity that I might generate for the casino. So she was humoring me and trying to accommodate me as politely as she could.

We watched the video from the first night. From every angle, something was always in the way. The pilfering could not be seen. We watched the video from the second night. Someone's head was in the way. When I changed seats, my shoulder was in the way. How could that little five-finger bandit be so deft at avoiding capture on video? And, at the same time, how was it able to avoid being seen by the dealer? Or anyone else for that matter?

Then Ms. Lugi asked me, "Was it left or right-handed?"

Although I felt like she was giving me the business, I looked at my own hands and replied, "It was a left hand."

"Because, you know, most people are right-handed," she added. "Hmm..."

She suddenly became very interested in one particular camera view. She zoomed in and did a screen capture. Then she found another frame and did the same thing. She looked at the two images and finally remarked,

"Look here. In this image I can see four chips in this stack, but in this later image I can see only three. As for the little pink hand, *I didn't see a thing!*" I wished she had been able to hide that smirk on her face. I wish she had seen the grimace on my face.

"Well how do you explain *that*—the missing chip?" I said, getting back to business.

"I can't. But you must understand, in this business we are witness to all kinds of fast and creative hand skills, all with the single purpose of cheating the casino. Some cheats have better sleight of hand than most professional magicians."

She paused for a moment and then said, "I tell you what—I'm gonna comp you one night on your hotel suite...but that's about all I can do under the circumstances."

I did not appreciate the sleight of hand insinuation, but I reluctantly agreed to accept her offer. She must have thought I was crazy, or a cheat, or that maybe I was trying to lay a scam on her and the casino. I really must have been crazy to think that anyone would believe my story. I decided that I would go ahead and return to L.A. the next day on schedule and get together with Tracey when I got back. Forget about the hand. Forget about my $2500. I was still up.

The next morning (Sunday) I packed up my things and did the streamlined electronic check out. I went to the casino for a fond farewell. There was a different greeter there: a singer named Scott Pumper—I could tell who he was by the name sign and the life-size cardboard version of him, arms spread wide in a saloon singer's pose. Didn't recognize him; never heard of him. I decided to make one last appearance at the blackjack table while they managed my luggage and brought out my Roadster. There was no one at "my" table so I sat down for a few final hands—just for fun—before the long drive home. Unfortunately, alone.

I won a few more dollars including a fast, unexpected blackjack. Then a hand grabbed me on the shoulder. It was Mel Paas. He had played the deputy villain for the evil international Rhombus organization in *Spy vs. Rhombus*, my second Rod Fury feature. He was supposed to be comic relief—portraying a bumbling, socially incompetent spy. Knowing Mel, he may not have had to do too much acting in that role.

Much to my dismay, Mel sat down right next to me. I don't know if he wanted to play cards or just wanted to talk my ear off—talk *at* me mostly. I tried to keep track of my counts, but his constant chatter was throwing me off. I was supposed to be playing just for fun before my trip, not providing Mel some early morning camaraderie. Still, forgetting my counts and going just by the book, I was up another $200. Lucky me.

Then, as a new dealer was preparing to step in, the trap door in the table opened up. But this time there were *two* hands! There was the familiar pink left hand, but to *its* left there was a tiny dark tan right hand. The two little wrists were handcuffed together! The little pink hand then pushed forward two $1000 chips up next to my stack. Then both tiny hands popped right back into the hole in the table. As before, not a trace of anything remained.

As freaky as it was, I was grateful to have my money back—at least some of it. But I was still short by $500.

"Did you see that?" Mel shouted to the dealer. "Those little hands—they came out of the table. One of them gave Hud here a couple of chips. Looked like two $1000 chips. What's going on? What kind of a place is this?" Mel was giving me an angry look as if I was somehow involved in a nefarious money scheme with the casino. At that point I didn't care what Mel thought. Based on my recent experience, the dealer wasn't going to believe Mel's ranting anyway.

I had saved $2550 on my stay at the hotel—comp-ed by the manager. I had won over $3000 dollars playing blackjack. The little pink hand had returned $2000 of the $2500 that it stole from me—I guess the house took its cut (a little steep if you ask me). So in the end I figured I was well over $5000 to the good on this little mini-vacation.

As I left the table, Mel grabbed my arm, "You saw that. You saw those little hands come out of there and give you that money. You saw it all."

I retrieved my arm and said to Mel, "I didn't see a thing."

# Murga, the Foul-Haired Mute

Once on rocky crag sat I
With hand on ale and lute,
When from the deep,
Up shore so steep
Came Murga, the foul-haired mute.


And to my rocky crag she climbed.
I put down ale and lute.
And there she stood,
With cape and hood,
Murga, the foul-haired mute.


And from the icy fog she stared,
Wet, from tip to boot.
With voice so vile,
Through toothless smile
Spoke Murga, the foul-haired mute,


"You twisted vole from Sjörgren's Bowels!
You spawn of snail and newt!
Your manly horn...
Beneath my scorn
Says I, the foul-haired mute."

And from her hair sprang tiny flies
Gath'ring in the air.
On wind so free
Attached to me,
Commanded Murga of the foulest hair.


Carried high from rocky crag was I.
Broke wind with crow and owl.
And to her nest
We came to rest,
The mute's, of hair most foul.


This tale of dread and woe I spin,
Its facts beyond dispute.
From arse to tongue both heart and lung
Fed to the young
Of Murga, the foul-haired mute.

# Something in the Air

[ Cut to WWW ]

Once again, Wendy Wellman Wexler here, your *On the Case* reporter, coming to you from the small suburban gated community of Walnut Oaks Estates, here in sunny southern California. The sidewalks you see before you are part of the pristine America, the sterile America, the immaculate America: manicured lawns, perfect paint, children deeply involved with their phones. But something new is taking shape on America's streets, right under our noses, literally, even in these well-groomed, tidy neighborhoods. For years, other countries around the world have been keeping a lid on the phenomenon—but no longer. It has now washed up on *our* shores. And what is this rage that has been hitting our streets? It's public defecation, or PD as insiders refer to it.

[ Pan camera to follow WWW ]

As I walk down this sidewalk on this peaceful street...holy moley...what's this?

[ Pan from WWW to the turd ]

It's a little turd. Must have been left by one of the neighborhood children. This is PD. Public defecation in its most innocent form.

[ Zoom in on the item and get that shimmer ]
( Beat )
[ Cut to aerial view of farmland ]

PD has been around for years in other countries. But now, it's been dropped on America. Is this phenomenon homegrown? Or was it imported? Or was it just a matter of time before it all came rampaging out anyway? Let's ask someone who may be a pioneer in the area.

[ Cut to WWW with the sodbuster ]

With me I have Amos "Red" Pyles, a tomato farmer here in West Polypesia, Florida. Mr. Pyles, can you tell us how you became involved in PD?

[ Cut to sodbuster ]

"Well, one day, years ago, I was workin' my vines—far from any...you know, facility—when suddenly the urge hit me. I dropped trou and deposited a big one righ' then and there. Went righ' back to work without missin' a beat. So I says to myself, 'Hoo boy, that sure is a timesaver.'"

And you've been handling your feces that way ever since?

"Yes, ma'am."

[ Cut to WWW ]

There you have it: a case of homegrown PD. So if you happen to notice that your tomato is a little redder, a little juicier than usual, well, it might be that there's a little "Red" in it.

[ Cut to aerial of urban New Jersey ]

Communities with dense populations have decided to step in and regulate PD where necessary. Take the case of Flyhaven, New Jersey. Rather than ban the practice entirely they have set aside specially designated plots of land for use by PD aficionados.

[ Cut from aerial of PD plot to WWW and interviewee ]

Acres of fertile PD reserves are popping up all over Flyhaven, and the largest one is the one you see behind me here—forty-two acres of virgin turf. But as popular as PD has become, this place, in particular, is not without controversy. I am speaking with the mayor of Flyhaven, the Honorable Barron Butts. Mayor Butts, what seems to be the focus of this controversy?

"Well ma'am. First let me thank you for bringing attention to our little community. We take pride in our public-spiritedness. But with this issue, we have a problem. These acres have been set aside for public defecation and as such we christened it *The City Dump*; you see the sign over there, the vandalized one with the spray paint; can't even read it anymore. This place was supposed to be a haven for 'dumplings', as we like to call them, available to who...so...ever without regard to gender, color, creed, orientation, or bowel habit. Well, the *City Dump* moniker triggered an all-out strike by our sanitation workers who felt that the name was stealing their thunder. Their position was that the original *City Dump* designation belonged to them, exclusively. Their stinking name and they wanted to hold on to it."

[ Cut to close-up of intrigued WWW face ]

And what happened then?

[ Close-up on thoughtful Butts ]

"The strike caused massive quantities of garbage to build up on the streets of Flyhaven—overflowing mylar sacks of garbage were everywhere. So we were forced to rename *this* place 'Dumpland.' And we made a new sign. You see...it says 'Dumpland.'"

[ Pan to the new sign that's stuck in the ground, then cut to WWW ]

But that wasn't the end of it, was it?

"No ma'am. The garbage and all the PD products became completely co-mingled on the streets. Sanitation workers are now refusing to go back to work—refusing to collect all the garbage—not going back to work until someone comes in and culls out all the turds, officially. They consider gathering up human excrement to be outside the scope of their contract with the city. So that's where it stands right now. It's a mess."

[ Cut to WWW ]

Thank you, Mayor Butts. There you have it. Controversy on the streets of Flyhaven. Controversy on the streets, mixed with garbage, mixed with feces. And yet, as I look out over this acreage dotted with the turds of thousands of New Jersey-ites, I think of how beautiful life could be if we could all just get along with each other's feces.

[ Pan across the field ]
( Beat )
[ Cut to the WWW *On the Case* SUV motoring along on a street ]

As we were developing this story, driving to our next location, we happened upon an individual who was in an early stage of a PD event—he was just about to plop one on a person's lawn.

[ Cinéma vérité: backpedaling in front of WWW as she chases down dump man ]

Sir? Sir? Can we stop you for a moment?

[ Swift swing to dump man ]

"Do what? Can't stop now...nnnnnnh huh—"

[ WWW off cam ]

Yessir we can see that. Wow. I must say, that is one huge load. Now what are you doing?

"I'm moving my product from this family's lawn over to the sidewalk. I have great respect for private property, especially here in the 'burbs.' So here goes."

[ Follow the load in his hands as he places it in the center of the sidewalk ]
[ Tight shot of the quantity and careful placement of the load ]
[ Close-up of dump man with satisfied and proud smile as he views the load ]

"There we go. PD all nice and proper. Think I'll head over and get me a big passel of enchiladas. Check with me tomorrow. I may be able to conjure up something special."

[ Cut to WWW ]

Well. How about that. Live action PD, caught on camera. Quite aromatic I might add.

[ Cut to view of pre-school sign ]

Our next stop is the Little Stinkers Pre-School in Diverticulus, Georgia. Here they have done something innovative for young dumplings, Pre-K through first grade. With me now is Anna Wat Mung, proprietor of Little Stinkers. Ms. Mung can you describe what you have done for these Little Stinkers kids.

[ Cut to Mung ]

"Yes. Well. We built a little stage over there on the playground where our kids can go and practice PD just like grown-ups do. It's like a short performance, if you will. Very natural. We call it our little Poop Deck. You can see for yourself that's it's a very popular feature here in the playground area."

[ Quickly cut to the back of a distressed child addressing Mung ]

"Ms. Mung. Ms. Mung. I have to do number two—"

[ Zoom in on back of distressed child's head ]
( Beat )
[ Back off for two-shot of Mung with child facing away ]

"*You* know where to go; *you* know where the Poop Deck is...go ahead now...do a good job...make us all proud. We're all going to be on TV."

"OK, Ms. Mung."

[ Track back of distressed child as she runs to the Poop Deck ]
[ Cut to WWW before child reaches the deck ]

Public Defecation, PD, source of inspiration...catalyst for innovation.

[ Aerial shot of Crapper University ]

Crapper University. An institute of higher learning. A place where mysteries of the universe are studied. PD has not been overlooked.

[ Cut to WWW ]

We are privileged to have with us now Professor Amy Scheissturm, PhD, an expert on public defecation. She began studying the practice long before it became a sensation here in the U.S.

[ Cut to two-shot of WWW and Professor ]

Professor Scheissturm, what can you tell us about the history of PD?

[ Cut to Professor alone ]

"It is a practice that dates all the way back to the age of the cave-person. From our studies, it appears that, at *that* time, only cave *men* were allowed to load-out in public. Women had to repress a movement until they could do their business discreetly, usually retreating to a dark recess in the cave, and preferably on top of a fresh mound of bat guano so that the stool would 'blend in.'"

[ WWW off cam ]

And what about those who say that *everyone* must continue to use only porcelain facilities?

"PP—porcelain *prejudice* masquerading as porcelain *preference.* I say, look at the animal kingdom. Public defecation is rampant throughout. It is a very natural behavior, it is a necessary outcome following a good pie-hole stuffing, albeit one or two days in the making. And if it's good enough for our dogs, it's good enough for us, and it's good enough for me."

[ Cut to a wide-eyed WWW ]

So you're saying you're a practitioner yourself? A dumpling?

[ Cut back to Professor ]

"Yes. Indeed. It's a type of freedom that is hard to describe. My significant other and I many times go on a 'dumpling run' together. The mall is one of our favorite places. A tandem dump always attracts a crowd. And if someone should criticize or have a problem with what we produce there on the ground, I always say, 'It's fine. I *am* a doctor.'"

[ WWW off cam ]

And what kinds of issues or problems have you run across in your studies?

"For centuries PD was frowned upon. People were forced to hide their products—forced to rid themselves of it as quickly as it left the chute; down, down the drain. Even though PD is now in vogue—an 'in' thing—there are many folks out there who do not understand it, refuse to understand it, will never understand it. We dumplings as a group feel that every big loaf we lay out on the ground, in the public domain, raises awareness of what PD can become for our society. And the movement is growing."

[ Cut to WWW ]

And what's next for you, Dr. Scheissturm?

[ Cut back to Professor ]

"There's a lot of fundamental research going on right now—questions like, 'How can you tell a floater from a sinker by just looking at it on the ground?' Not to get too technical, but it has to do with specific gravity, fat content, and so forth—a lot of science involved. Also we are looking at cingulates, striped turds, and their effect on the psyche of the dumpling. Can we really tell if a dumpling needs more fiber in their diet by merely fondling the product? And another nagging question: If a turd, part of a potential PD, emerges, only to draw itself back in—Are we in for another six weeks of winter?"

[ WWW off cam ]

Sounds very cutting edge to me.

"Some of it is. But *my* current research concerns how to handle diarrhea—how to handle it in a context of public defecation. Should it really count as true PD or is it just *accidental* PD. If they can re-categorize Pluto, an entire planet, then surely we can find a place for diarrhea; perhaps a new category—say, *involuntary* public defecation. The situation concerning diarrhea is, at this stage, very fluid. As you can tell, PD is currently a wide open, emerging field of study."

Thank you, Professor. Now we turn our attention to how PD is handled in the military.

[ Aerial view of Military Base ]

We wanted to see firsthand how our armed forces are changing with the times and how PD has become fully integrated into the lives and practices of our fighting men and women.

[ Cut to WWW ]

So here we are at Fort Sphincter, Texas.

[ Pan to two-shot of WWW and General ]

With us here is General Pinto Bowles, base commander. Thank you for visiting with us today General Bowles.

"Pleasure to be here with you, Ms. Waxle."

Tell us, General Bowles, some of the ways that PD has impacted your command.

[ Cut to General ]

"Well, Ms. Waxle, for one thing, the Army, as well as all the other branches of the service, have adopted a rigidly-enforced policy of ignoring PD altogether—all branches except the Space Force, for obvious reasons."

[ WWW off cam ]

And just what does that mean, ignoring?

"Let's say a company engaged in routine marching drills encounters an area heavily populated with PD turds, a shit minefield, if you'll pardon my language."

[ Quick cut to WWW acting conciliatory then back to the General ]

"Marching, marching, hut-two. Right through, we march right over the area—just as if all that waste wasn't even there. We're aware that all that mashed up shit spoils the intended esthetic quality of the PD products, but soldiering is serious business and we can't allow a minefield of turds to force our troops into tippy-toeing around an organic blanket of human shit. Pardon the language, again. Aircraft carriers...well, jets land on decks covered with sailor droppings...no issues there, no problems. Complete disregard for the presence of PD products has become the best policy for all concerned. As long as a soldier is doing his or her job...performing exceptionally, then it's really nobody's business where they leave their business...as long as it's done in an official manner and follows all military protocols."

[ Quick cut to WWW ]

And are there any *other* changes in basic military life that you'd like to mention?

"Well, we've renamed the Mess Hall. We now have to refer to it as the 'Dining Room.' Oh...and they no longer serve 'chicken and dumplings'; it's now called 'chicken and dough-balls'—just can't get around that one. Minor institutional changes like that—always gonna have those. But, in most cases, ignoring PD products is the policy. However, there *is* one exception—"

[ WWW off cam ]

And that is?

"The Marines have several special elite units known only as Brown Ops. It's very prestigious. There are ten men in a unit. It's a crack team. They're trained to perform synchronized PD...on demand. They appear at major sporting events and military showcases—they're part of the entertainment, a connection with the public; just like dramatic flyovers."

[ Quick cut to WWW acting all interested then back to the General ]

How interesting.

"Oh, and sometimes as a tribute to those unfortunate individuals who are in the throes of constipation or fecal impactions, there is the missing turd formation. Ten asses, only nine piles of shit—pardon the language. It's very moving."

[ Cut to the two-shot ]

Thank you for your time, General.

[ Cut to montage of Wall Street and big business edifices ]

[ WWW off cam ]

Every time our society has latched on to a new trend—the latest shiny object—big business has been there to extract cold hard cash from those who are riding the surf. And this current trend is no exception. It *is* a surf, a tsunami of human feces—all in the form of PD.

[ Cut to WWW and pan to interviewee in a two-shot ]

So let us turn our attention to the commercial aspects of PD. With us we have business icon Barry McStool, business executive and author of the best-seller *Public Defecation in the Boardroom*. He's going to tell us what's in the works for capitalizing on the wave of feces fever spreading across the nation. Mr. McStool, what kinds of products can we expect to see this Christmas?

[ Cut to McStool ]

"Well, Ms. Wexler, it's an exciting time for us all. There is huge potential out there—potential for profits. But with huge reward comes exceptional risk. What if we make a product and the public loses interest in feces, especially in PD? That is always the gamble. But here are some products that your viewers might find interesting."

[ Cut to WWW with a nod of approval then back to McStool ]

"First we have the Modesty Skirt. Some women...some men...Scotsmen in kilts...some groups may have no immediate use for this product. For them PD doesn't require them to bare ass to get the job done. But for all the others, the Modesty Skirt can be pulled out of a pair of pants in order to make a small curtain around one's exposed ass. Let me demonstrate—"

[ Focus in on McStool deploying the skirt as he squats ]

"Now as you see, I am ready to deliver, but my ass is completely out of the picture. Ahem...mmmm...OK mission accomplished."

[ Focus on the load as McStool rises back up ]

"I tuck in the skirt. Nobody's the wiser. Nobody knows all of that came out of *me*. Quite a gift to get one of these on Christmas morning; a Modesty Skirt, that is."

[ Quick WWW head shot ]

And what about something for the kids?

[ Cut to McStool ]

"Well we have a couple of things. This fun item is called The Little Brown Banana. Kids'll love it. It gives a youngster a role model, a perfectly-shaped turd. Something a kid can aspire to create someday."

[ WWW off cam ]

And what is *this*? This little cage?

"We call it a Pet Doody, a preserved dog nugget in its own little cage. A child can open the cage and let the little doody out during the day, take it for a walk, give it a bath, you know, like a pet. The Pet Doody comes in two models: the standard model or the deluxe model. The deluxe model comes with a unique factory-installed name and includes pedigree papers describing the dog that produced it and the nugget's own personal history. With the standard model the owner can give it a name of their own choosing. Of course they miss out on the pride that comes with owning a turd with a pedigree."

[ WWW and McStool in two-shot ]

And why are you using a *dog* stool for the Pet Doody instead of human feces?

[ Cut to McStool ]

"Well, since it's supposed to be a *pet*, we thought using human doody was in very poor taste."

[ Back to WWW and McStool in two-shot ]

I see. Well, thank you very much Mr. McStool and good luck with all of your merchandise.

[ Aerial view (flyover) of Mount Everest ]

Adventure. Americans can't get enough of it. Whether vicarious or hands-on, it's a part of life. For some, inviting danger and risk is second nature. That is the case of mountain climber Harry Wildass, who recently returned from his second trip to the summit of Mount Everest.

[ WWW and Wildass in two-shot ]

Mr. Wildass, you've been up Mount Everest several times, and to the summit twice now. Tell our viewers what was particularly special about this recent trip.

[ Focus in on Wildass ]

"The previous time I conquered Everest there was no focus on feces—not in America at any rate. This time I wanted to do something special. I left my first sample of PD at base camp. That was merely a trial run. Much to my surprise, I found that there were already hundreds of turds sprinkled around base camp. Other dumplings had already beaten me to it. Later, far up toward the summit, I left a sample on a hidden ledge where the frozen body of a would-be climber was already present."

[ Cut to WWW with a look of mild shock then back to Wildass ]

"I realized then, that even if my base camp sample were to be trampled down and lost over time, that hidden sample would be frozen and would remain there, on that remote ledge, forever. Now *that* was special. My final sample I left right up on top of the world, at the summit, in plain view. The others up there were none to happy about it even though history was being made—millions of views on the Internet by the way. Because of the challenging conditions at the summit, producing a sample there took a lot longer than I was expecting. So my bare ass got quite a patch of frostbite for my effort.

[ Cut to WWW with a look of concern then back to Wildass ]

"But I have to say, it was worth it—all those Internet views for something *I* created. On the way down, before I reached base camp, I was in the middle of unloading an impromptu fourth sample when the authorities came and arrested me. They hustled me on down to a makeshift detention cell. They wanted to know if I had left anything else like that on the *mountain*. So I lied and told them that I hadn't. Apparently PD is only legal at base camp. Of course millions of Internet views exposed my lie so I may not be welcome if I decide to go back to Everest in the future. But all in all I'd have to say, for me, it was quite a successful, history-making climb."

[ Cut to WWW ]

And what do you say to those who might disapprove of your actions on Everest, and in particular, your leaving a sample at the summit, of all places?

[ Cut to Wildass ]

"It remains to be seen."

[ Cut to WWW ]

Americans. Unbridled. Everything in excess. Leaving their mark around the globe. Other stories of adventure involve Sheila Brown-Bomber a hang-glider specialist who distributes her PD from the air.

[ Cut to stock footage of hang-glider ]

And then there is Navy SEAL, Fred Anopore who specializes in underwater PD with his special-composition turds that rise to the surface as floaters.

[ Cut to ocean surface with multiple turds bobbing up one by one amidst bubbles ]

And as we move on from these adventurous PD sports, we now focus on a relatively new area: "Competitive Public Defecation" or CPD.

[ Cut to crane view of competitors in squatting positions ]
[ Pan to capture the pageantry and crowd, then fade in to competition montage ]
[ Montage of world-class competitors in action ]

Here we see master-level athletes who have trained for months on end. During that time they experiment with special diets; they monitor the effects of hydration and dehydration; they go through regimens of special muscle exercises to give themselves full control. Once a season of PD commences they compete in series after series of grueling qualifying rounds in order to reach the highest level of CPD, the World Championships. There are a number of events: the On-Demand competition, the Timed Defecation Event, and of course the always controversial Stool Judging.

[ Cut to judges' table then pan to stage with squatting competitor ]

There is never a World Championship without plenty of second-guessing of the judges. A team of five judges ranks a competitor's stool in five categories: cohesion, quantity, form and shape, color, and aromatics. It is always a tense moment for a PD athlete as the judges officially scrutinize the entrant's specimen, examining it from every angle, testing its cohesion, giving it a good hearty sniff.

[ Cut to judges' table where competitor's score cards are revealed ]

The cards come up 8, 9, 9.5, 10. Hearts are broken; lifelong memories are set in stone; coveted medals are awarded to the winners.

[ Cut to World Champion holding the Gold Medal ]

The memories of winning the championship become cherished ones for the new World Champion, Bear Grillo.

[ Cut to clip of Philip Severence (reporter) in two-shot with Grillo (champion) ]

Severence: Well, Bear, how do you feel at this moment?
Grillo: I could just shit!

[ Cut to high-tech animated graphics of stylized ones and zeroes ]

Closer to home we have the Internet where people who are proud of their PD products can post pictures for the entire world to enjoy.

[ Show screen shot examples of PD posts then transition to general PD montage ]

But these days, it's not enough to merely provide close-up images of a PD sample—context also counts.

[ Start general PD clip montage as WWW narrates ]

A substantial offering proudly displayed in front of an erupting Old Faithful in the background; a turd placed strategically on Mt. Rushmore; a tall load riding on the back of a slow-moving Galapagos turtle; a very hearty Asian specialty, the Siberian Shit; a PD happening, live, at Machu Picchu; or a specimen left on the seat of the USA's tallest roller coaster, *Badass Backfire*. And if someday diarrhea is sanctioned as official PD, then "*Running* with the Bulls" will have a whole new meaning. The possibilities are endless.

[ Cut to WWW from new angle with dark shadows across ]

Finally, we have to acknowledge those few people who are not the least bit enamored with this latest American craze.

[ Cut to two-shot of WWW and old curmudgeon ]

Sir, you seem to be against all this public defecation.

"You're damn right, I am!"

And what is your objection to it?

"Well, for one thing, there's shit all over the place—"

[ Cut to WWW ]

Just one man's opinion. Are hostile naysayers, like this gentleman, just plain old stick-in-the-muds or do they make a legitimate case against public defecation in all its forms? Only time will tell.

[ Cut to stock footage of generic factory machinery ]

In every trendy public obsession there will always be winners and losers. And one of the unfortunate victims of the PD craze is the toilet paper industry—sales are down over 40%.

[ Cut to TP factory montage ]
[ Overlay clip fades of rolls and rolls of TP in various stages of manufacture ]

Business leaders in the toilet paper industry have always been able to count on a relentless demand for the ubiquitous paper product, pumping out millions of rolls, providing a seemingly endless supply of TP to satisfy the public need. But PD has changed all that.

[ Cut to WWW with a look of anxious concern ]

Aficionados and casual practitioners of PD just walk away from their product; they seem to have abandoned the ritual use of TP after a PD. It is an unanticipated consequence of America's burgeoning feco-mania...and very unhygienic in this reporter's opinion.

[ Low-level crane shot of WWW walking on sidewalk, looking at camera ]

And as for the future of public defecation—what the...?

[ Show WWW inadvertently stepping in PD product then wiping it off on the grass ]
[ Cut to close-up of vigorous wiping action then cut back to crane shot ]

How about that? Well then, OK...as for the future of public defecation—in the words of mountain climber Harry Wildass, "It remains to be seen." For now, let us continue to surf on this tsunami of PD product and try to take advantage of all that it can offer. It is definitely a movement—a bowel movement, if you will; a society fixated on feces; a culture in the grip of a fecal phenomenon. But, as we must now reluctantly close the lid on this fascinating subject, may I take just a moment to remind everyone, "Watch your step!" This is Wendy Wellman Wexler, your *On the Case* reporter. See you next time.

[ Cue the triumphant *On the Case* theme music ]
[ Fade to black after WWW waves at the rising crane shot cam ]
[ Black screen with alternate woman's voice-over following the end of music ]

*Voice-over*: Poop-poop-a-doop.

## Standing the Gaff

——————————————

"I'll take the next one, thank you," the young man said as the last of five rain-soaked souls entered the elevator. He gave a half-hearted wave as the elevator doors closed, leaving him (again) on the ground floor of the Palance-Ivory Towers building. It was now a full twenty minutes since he first arrived, having braved the storm outside the building. If he didn't get an empty elevator soon he was going to be late for his appointment and the trip through the inclement weather would have been for nothing. Wilbur Odeliza was a heavy, out-of-shape insurance man with a pathological fear of closed spaces, especially elevators. He would wait for an hour if need be, just to get an elevator to himself.

After another ten minutes, finally, with no one in the lobby, an empty elevator appeared on the ground floor. Wilbur, with great temerity went in and pressed number twenty-two, the floor where his psychiatrist's office was located. As soon as the elevator doors closed, Wilbur broke out in a cold sweat and began shaking. The elevator lurched upward—

"Raaaaaaah, ahhhhh, eeeeeeeee...screeeeeeeech, raaaaaaaah, screeeech, raaaaah, sweet mother of screeeeeech, aaaaaah, holy friggin...waaaaaaaah, pump-sucking Ralph rocker...screeeeeech!"

It was a cacophony of screams, wails, and epithets from Wilbur Odeliza the likes of which no normal earthly being can even imagine—but *Imagination* was really not needed for occupants and visitors in the Palance-Ivory Towers building.

For a full forty seconds Wilbur felt the suffocating grip of the shoe-box-size elevator and its metaphorical metallic fingernails dragging across the metaphorical chalkboard of the shaft until the demon car finally came to rest at the twenty-second floor. As Wilbur stepped out of the confines of the elevator, he wiped off his sweaty brow with his coat sleeve. This was not the first time his voice was rendered so hoarse that his appointment with his psychiatrist, Dr. Hamilton Frug, would have to be cut short. Dr. Frug was treating Wilbur for claustrophobia, but so far there had been little progress. The lack of progress was clear to everyone in the building since Wilbur's elevator performances continued to announce his every elevator trip to one and all—the elevator shaft making a marvelous echo chamber.

To Wilbur's credit he always waited for an empty elevator before making the ascent from the ground floor up to floor twenty-two. And if someone should happen to board from a floor in between, Wilbur would quickly disembark as the person entered. Every time, the new arrival would be looking around, around the interior of the elevator, curious as to the source of all those psychotic banshee screams.

Once, Dr. Frug asked Wilbur directly, "Why don't you take the stairs?"

Wilbur answered with a question, "Do I look like I could climb twenty-two flights of stairs?" Occasionally he might struggle up to the second floor by using a stairway, but he was just too out of shape to attempt anything more. Whether going up or down, it was always the same for Wilbur Odeliza: a thoroughly humiliating ordeal.

On this particular day, having completed his fifth (albeit abbreviated) appointment with Dr. Frug, the office workers braced themselves, anticipating the usual howling extravaganza from Mr. Odeliza. Eyes rolled; deep breaths were taken; sighs of sympathy mixed with sighs of "please, not again" leaked out from the staff and other onlookers. Ding! An unoccupied elevator arrived and the mindless doors spread open wide to receive passengers. To Wilbur it might as well have been the jaws of a huge shark. He stepped inside and pressed "G." The doors closed and—

"Ayyyyyyyrrrrreeeeeeeeee, screeeeeech, eeeeeeeeeyaaaaah! Aaaaaaarrrrrrr, sweet stained-glass Jesus of Singapore...eeeeeeeeyaaah...Daddy of Dickson...on a mongrel mound of motherf...ayeeeeeeeee! Naaarrrrrrrr—*gotta dime!*" remarked Wilbur as the elevator lurched downward toward the ground floor.

Many times, if enough ruckus was caused by Wilbur's wailing and screeching, the ground floor security guard would be waiting for him by the elevator just in case something was truly amiss. So, on this trip, Wilbur prepared himself for the expected embarrassment since his emissions were especially screechy, shrill, and forlorn.

Much to his surprise, Wilbur saw the elevator move past the ground floor without stopping, without hesitating; passing the basement floor, sub-level 1, sub-level 2, and continuing on after that with no floor indicated on the panel. The extra descent did not interrupt Wilbur's screams even if the curious continuing descent did interrupt his train of thought. Up on floor twenty-two Dr. Frug's office staff noticed a marked difference in the screaming—usually Wilbur's screams stopped abruptly as he exited on the ground floor, but on this day the screams just seemed to fade slowly away.

No two fingerprints are alike, no two voices register electronically as identical, no two retinal landscapes are the same, and supposedly no two snowflakes are identical (although not every snowflake has been examined under laboratory conditions so there is no way to be sure). Similarly, it must be said that no two episodes of Wilbur Odeliza's panicked screeching were ever exactly the same.

When the elevator doors opened and Wilbur could finally step out, screaming in check, he saw a marvelous sight. It was a little town where all the buildings were built directly into giant colorful mushrooms. And there were little people, gnomes, scurrying busily about. Wilbur could not imagine what had happened, but before he thought about disembarking from the elevator he took inventory and speculated:

1) His screaming had broken something in his brain
2) He was hallucinating (a psychotic episode related to his phobia)
3) It was a dream, or a nightmare (but he wasn't asleep)
4) He was dead and this was heaven (a weird mushroom heaven)
5) He was dead and this was hell (not as inconceivable as mushroom heaven)

In Wilbur's mind, all of these explanations seemed ordinary and logical. But this little mushroom village was something that was just too *extraordinary* for mere routine and obvious explanations. Before Wilbur could step very far from the elevator, a gnome approached him, and with a congenial and inquisitive tone the gnome asked, "What the hell are *you* doing here?"

"I don't know. I was on this elevator—" Wilbur sat down on a nearby spotted mushroom, catching his breath. Kerthump! The little mushroom collapsed under Wilbur's great weight. While sitting flat-assed on the ground, Wilbur looked all around and admired the extreme beauty of the place. It was fantastic. Such a wide open little gnome community located in an underground cavern or hole or—perhaps something else. And Wilbur wondered why the little gnome wasn't showing at least some interest in the presence of the elevator.

"Well you'd better get on back to where you belong before you make any more trouble," the little gnome said, looking over the crushed remains of the spotted mushroom that were peeking out from under Wilbur's bulbous backside. "You don't belong here. You bring no magic. You have no value here." The gnome attempted to push Wilbur's meaty hulk off the mushroom but was unsuccessful.

"I was screaming, and the elevator—" Wilbur tried to explain.

"Screaming? Why were you screaming?" the gnome asked, walking around Wilbur's seated mass, inspecting everything carefully.

"I have this fear—" Wilbur said as he adjusted himself on the mashed mushroom remnants.

"Fear? Fear of what?" The gnome actually seemed more interested in the mushroom rubble than in Wilbur.

Noticing the gnome's deep concern over the flattened mushroom, Wilbur stood up and brushed off pieces of it from the wideness of his sore booty.

"Sorry about that little mushroom," Wilbur said apologetically. "I have a dreadful fear of closed spaces, any kind, like that elevator or a coffin or a closet or the trunk of a car. They terrify me. Closing in. A feeling like I can't move; trapped; confined."

The gnome looked at Wilbur without saying a word, then dropped to his knees, immersed in the thick ground cover.

"Now what are you doing?" Wilbur asked.

Seemingly disregarding Wilbur, the gnome had begun to crawl around on the ground on his hands and knees, looking here and there, sorting through the myriad of colorful flowers and the patches of variegated mushrooms, large and small. In a short time he found what he was looking for: a tiny yellow mushroom with orange and black stripes radiating out from the center. "Here, take this and eat it," the gnome said. "Eat it! Then get out of here."

"I don't kno—"

"Now!" The gnome was very insistent and bold—surprising, considering how he was "dwarfed" by Wilbur's huge body. Startled by the gnome's loud outburst, Wilbur nervously stuffed the mushroom into his mouth without even thinking, expecting something bad or bizarre to happen to him at any moment. But nothing did happen. Wilbur wondered what was going on; what might have been in that mushroom.

"Get back in that box thing and go back to where you came from. And you'd better think twice before you come back here again." With that the gnome walked away and mixed back in with the other gnomes scurrying busily about.

Wilbur turned around and saw the elevator, doors still open, waiting for him, as ominous-looking as ever. Reluctantly, he stepped inside and pressed twenty-two, out of habit. "Oh well," he thought as he closed his eyes and waited for the upward lurch. When the elevator started moving, Wilbur rejoiced. He did not feel like screaming. He did not feel anything, floor after floor, all the way up to twenty-two. He had miraculously lost his fear.

"Why Mr. Odeliza," Dr. Frug's receptionist said as the elevator doors opened. "We didn't hear you coming."

"Yes. Yes, that's true. It's a miracle. I seem to have conquered my fear." He knew that no one would ever believe such an absurd story (the truth) so he decided to leave the explanation as...unexplained. Still standing in the elevator, Wilbur kept looking around, attempting to get a grip on the situation and holding up the elevator's business by intermittently keeping the door open with his foot.

Then he saw Dr. Frug come out of his office in a rush. "I thought I heard something going on out here. Oh! Mr. Odeliza! I didn't hear...are you all right?"

"Yes. Yes. I seem to have been cured of my claustrophobia. Here let me show you." With that Wilbur pressed "G" and allowed the elevator doors to close. But before the doors were completely closed, Wilbur's mind captured the mystified looks on the faces of Dr. Frug and his staff. He wanted to always remember those looks.

Down the elevator went. No screams from Wilbur Odeliza. No fear. It truly was a miracle (of course the truth was something different, as we all know). "What a strange day this has been," Wilbur thought to himself. As the elevator reached the ground floor Wilbur wanted to rejoin Dr. Frug on the twenty-second floor and share this moment. When the elevator doors opened he pressed twenty-two.

Then, some horrific thoughts began to prey on him. Wilbur began thinking of the evil that might have been motivating the underground gnome. (He wasn't all *that* friendly, come to think of it.)

In an instant Wilbur began to speculate:
1) People will be getting on (what if I switched phobias; I now hate *people*)
2) Fear of heights (common phobia, maybe that's what the new one will be)
3) My original fear will return just in time to deafen everyone in the elevator
4) Maybe I will experience motion sickness (woe betide the other passengers)

He thought about getting off the elevator, but he was going to stand the gaff and face whatever might be coming his way next.

———————————

Many years ago, it was all over the news: the birth of identical quadruplet girls, a rarity in human reproductive biology. The media referred to them as the Quisenberry Quads: Millie, Goosie, Tillie, and Frond Quisenberry. They made quite a splash while they were youngsters. They all dressed alike and were always together as a group. They were given parties and gifts. They had been on television. Their parents milked the quadruplets' celebrity for all it was worth. And by the time the quads became young women the constant notoriety and attention had really screwed them up. So as adults they, as a foursome, were now being treated by Dr. Frug.

———————————

Before the elevator doors could close, sending Wilbur back to the twenty-second floor—

"Hold that elevator!" a young female voice cried out.

Aha! This was it. Wilbur would let the young lady board the elevator. She could ride along with him to *her* floor and he would continue on up to Dr. Frug's floor. A good test. While Wilbur held the door open, three more young females appeared. These four young women were the famous Quisenberry Quads, all grown up. Wilbur had seen them on TV when they were much younger. As the quads packed themselves into the elevator, Wilbur was pleased that his fear was not returning; there was no claustrophobia, no fear of heights, no fear of anything. None of his wild speculations had come to pass.

The elevator doors closed and the car started moving upward. Wilbur was pushed up against the back of the elevator and could barely see over the heads of the quads—four big red bouffant hairdos adding ten inches to the height of each Quisenberry. The smell of hairspray and perfume filled the air; one hairspray and one perfume times four. They had only reached the tenth floor when the elevator came to a stop. The doors opened and a pretty woman was standing there, waiting, obviously in some kind of difficulty. Her hair was still wet having been drenched from the downpour happening outside the building. When the elevator stopped, Wilbur was expecting the quads to get off. He was unaware that they were also patients of Dr. Frug and would be riding with him all the way to the twenty-second floor. So his thoughts were redirected when he saw the distressed woman with the wet hair.

The pretty woman on the tenth floor said, "I'm sorry. We seem to have gotten off on the wrong floor. Do you know where the Piglet-Squiglet Daycare Center is located? Which floor it's on?" The young woman seemed apologetic, but highly agitated. "We're already late."

"You want the twentieth floor," Goosie Quisenberry replied.

"We can all fit in. We'll make room," Wilbur added, feeling emboldened with his newfound lack of claustrophobia. It was going to be a tight squeeze; the elevator wasn't all that big.

"Over here, Bubba. This elevator is going up." The pretty woman was talking to an unseen man down the hall, waving him toward her with her arm. "Come on. Hurry up, we're late."

As the pretty woman shoehorned herself into the elevator, the quads turned every which way in order to make room, all of them scrunched up facing Wilbur. It did not bother him at all. It might have been a bit easier for everyone if Wilbur wasn't quite so heavy, but there you have it.

Due to the rain, Bubba still had a large damp towel draped over his head as he too squeezed into the elevator. The doors closed together, almost pinching Bubba's backside as he handed the towel to the pretty woman. Still, Wilbur, totally immobile, stood firm and did not panic.

With the passengers adjusting themselves continuously, the overstuffed elevator struggled upward (or so it seemed). The group was a mass of humanity squirming together like an amorphous tide of grunion attempting to spawn in a full moon. The four Quisenberries began feeling very awkward and uncomfortable looking up into the vastness of Wilbur's big nostrils, so as a group they sucked in their abs and turned to face the door. They took one look at Bubba and, as a unified heaving quadruplex of flesh and hair, they became unhinged—

"Ayeeeee ayreeeee help! Murder! Screeech! Motherless M-M-M-M-Moleheads of Maui...squreeech!" screamed Goosie.
"Ayeeeee ayreeeee help! Murder! Screeech! Motherless M-M-M-M-Moleheads of Maui...squreeech!" screamed Millie.
"Ayeeeee ayreeeee help! Murder! Screeech! Motherless M-M-M-M-Moleheads of Maui...squreeech!" screamed Tillie.
"Ayeeeee ayreeeee help! Murder! Screeech! Motherless M-M-M-M-Moleheads of Maui...squreeech!" screamed Frond.

The quads were all screaming and screeching and caterwauling together in unison; identical, powerful screams that could be heard high on mountaintops around the world— and in no small way, all the way up to Dr. Frug's office. It was a piercing chorus that rattled Wilbur's brain and made his eyes bug out. The quads began thrashing about, bruising and bumping everyone in the elevator: themselves; Wilbur; the pretty woman; and Bubba, the children's birthday party clown. The quad sisters were afraid of clowns[*], deathly afraid, pathologically afraid. That fear was a residuum from traumatic parties and all kinds of nasty whatnot experienced in their early years of forced celebrity, punctuated by horrific, painted, birthday party clowns—clowns delivered to the world from the darkest birthing pore of the necro-organic carnival universe.

---

[*] coulrophobia

The high-pitched human stridulating and sardine can thrashing went on for the full thirty seconds that it took for the elevator to reach the twentieth floor. Wilbur didn't think he could last even that long. Everyone was going to be deaf by then—deaf or severely injured. Wilbur covered his ears and waited, his elbows being bumped, thumped, and re-bumped by the four wild hypersonic creatures in the cage with him.

When the pretty woman and Bubba exited the elevator at the twentieth floor, they wasted no time in getting out of there—out of the box. Having been around screaming kids as part of their party business they were somewhat used to the sound. But this was something different—a different level entirely—industrial strength, multi-voice choral shrieking. Hundreds of birthday parties and they had never encountered anything like it. And the jostling and scrambling in such a tight space...well, Bubba and his pretty assistant were thoroughly relieved to finally be off the elevator. After that experience, they would be able to withstand anything that the Piglet-Squiglet daycare kids could possibly throw at them. Wilbur and the now completely-exhausted quads were just as relieved as the elevator doors closed and the back of the party clown was finally hidden from view.

While the elevator moved on up to the twenty-second floor and Dr. Frug's office, the quads, although relatively silent at that point, were still whimpering and shaking, hunched over together in a kind of four-person, sweat-soaked, jelly-mold blob. Wilbur's ears were ringing and his head skin was tingling. He had seen four faces of fear. He had seen four puffy hairdos bobbing up and down like a red tide on the North Sea. He had heard the scorching sounds of fear, amplified synergistically four times, echoing and re-echoing through the elevator shaft. It was an incendiary exhibition of fear in someone—in *four* someones other than himself—a raw fear, a morbid fear, a fear of clowns. It looked unholy, unseemly, and unfortunately, all too familiar.

As soon as the elevator doors opened on the twenty-second floor, the quads literally tumbled out of the elevator and onto the floor of Dr. Frug's reception area, leaving Wilbur standing alone in the back. Having been forewarned of the elevator's arrival by the quadra-mega-decibel screams, Dr. Frug's assistants were expecting to find Wilbur Odeliza in a quivering pile of huddled mass. But after seeing the quads spill out all over the carpet, the assistants quickly re-assessed the situation, and rushed to the aid of the four blubbering Quisenberries instead.

The quads were completely spent from their tightly packed birthday-clown-in-a-box nightmare and were now aimlessly milling about in the reception area—dazed, confused, spots before their eight eyes. Wilbur was, for the most part, being ignored.

"Well," Wilbur said to himself, remaining on the elevator, watching the doors close once again. "Imagine that—being afraid of clowns. How ridiculous!"

# Clowns in the Attic

I know they are watching me, watching me, watching me
Through that hole in the ceiling up there.
I see an eyeball, blinking, rotating,
I can feel that murderous stare.

Red rubber noses and oversized shoes
They'll come down and scoop out my brains.
It's only a matter of time now I think,
As my blood turns to ice in my veins.

>*"I'm from the service. I've been to your attic.*
>*I just made it out with my skin.*
>*I must be emphatic; there are clowns in your attic,*
>*And I'm not going back there again."*

They can squirt you, and squirt you, and seriously hurt you
With acid from colorful guns.
Who gives you chills and kills you for thrills?
The clowns are—the clowns are the ones.

With painted-on smiles, they drive all my thoughts
Out to the edge of my mind.
With faces of white they'll come in the night
It's all just a matter of time.

*"Your attic's infested and riddled with clowns;*
*The smell of grease paint in the air.*
*They scramble around like rats in the dark.*
*You can see for yourself if you dare."*

They'll climb in the walls, through doorways, down halls
With stealth they will crawl 'cross the floor.
Creeping and creeping they'll come while I'm sleeping,
And cut me right down to the core.

Colorful smoke bombs, exploding bananas,
Confetti all over the place.
They'll brazenly mock me; with needles they'll shock me
If only to laugh in my face.

*"I was pinned to the floor by those clowns in your attic.*
*They tried to peel off all my skin.*
*'Twas very dramatic, cruel, and traumatic,*
*And I'll never go back there again."*

They're stalking me, stalking me, stalking me
Through a hot wire in my head.
They're rumbling, stumbling, rolling and tumbling
 I can hear them just over my bed.

I feel doom, and the gloom, and my room is a prison.
My last breath will die on the vine.
And clowns there will be, all coming for me,
It's only a matter of time.

*"I came from the service; I'm down from your attic.*
*I'm lucky to still have my skin.*
*You can empty my shell and burn me in hell*
*Before I'll go back there again."*

# Night of the Tongue

Sunday, October 20 2:03 am

Arranging and rearranging the bed sheets, Moebius Moli, in the middle of a fitful sleep, was rehashing the details of his last case and making no effort to avoid disturbing his wife, Margaret (who was *out*, out and as motionless as a half-decayed dead dog under two tons of concrete). After every closed case there came a period where Moli would second-guess himself, wondering if he could have done a better job on this issue or that. But, before he could come to any conclusions through his rehashing of those old events—and while he continued to thrash around in his sheets—his phone rattled the nightstand with its all-too-familiar vibratory buzz.

"Inspector Moli," he answered in a very soft voice as he rotated up and out of bed, making his way to the bathroom.

The woman's voice at the other end sounded apologetic (almost), "Sorry, Inspector Moli, we have a situation. There might be some murder involved. Can you make your way to the scene and investigate?" Several years ago, the department changed the way dispatch called the Inspectors (and others who were higher up in the pecking order), speaking to them in an improvised, conversational tone instead of the clinical and more technical way calls were made to uniformed officers in the field.

"I'm on the case," he quickly replied, putting his phone down on the bathroom counter as he prematurely ended the call before getting any additional information.

Moli appeared to be very organized in his personal life, a trait that carried over to the way he would handle a case, especially the really big, important ones. He hoped the appearance of diligence, organization, and attention to detail would result in his being promoted to Chief Inspector someday. However, at this wee hour, his task was to get all groomed up for the business day ahead, albeit a day that was starting out pretty bloody early on a Sunday morning. A regimen of calisthenics (in name only) was the first item on the daily agenda. Following that, it was a full body soaping up in the shower using a special edition of Poover's Alaskan Seal Blubber and Avocado Shower Gel. As Moli topped things off with a custom-designed, chemical body rinse, he began speculating on how he was going to manage the suspects (if any) in the new case. He applied his facial masque, dug out material from some of his orifices, removed stray hairs from various locations around his body, performed his usual morning routine of conscientious—minty fresh—oral hygiene, and ended with a prolonged stare-down of his teeth with a once-over of his tongue. After checking out the shine on his very small, stainless steel nipple ring and stroking his breasts, he headed for the closet.

Moli always wore a black bolo tie with a too-tight, short-sleeved, white shirt, even in winter. The black, (undefined) animal skin cowboy boots on his feet had decorative, silver-colored, pointed tips on them. Into the heel of each boot Moli routinely stuck a thumbtack so that he would make a clicking sound when he walked. Those boots must have looked good at some point in the past, but now, stretched out of shape by Moli's flat, wide footpads they just looked used, over-worn, deformed, and foot-like. While assembling his outfit, he eyeballed the sleeping Margaret. She could sleep through anything, never allowing the dangers inherent in Moe's job to prey on her mind. In actuality, she never *worried* about anything, except for the fact that one of her legs was shorter than the other and that it gave her a kind of hillbilly gait. They were married for over three years before he ever said anything about it, and at that time he was lashing out in the heat of an argument—an argument about nothing. Margaret didn't look like a supermodel but she was very female-like in an athletic sort of way. She never, ever ventured out into the sun for any length of time. This resulted in her looking as pasty white as the bleached-out bones of a desert carcass. On the other hand, she was as muscular as the horse she rode in on, making her as strong as an ox (or a horse). On any given day, if Moebius and Margaret were to lock horns for some reason, she could easily give Moe the old one-two, the old heave-ho, the big frosty, the slam-bam.

Margaret's muscularity was, in no small way, thanks to a lean, well-built, hands-on trainer named Raoul Bendito who provided her with his personal "training" specials any time Moebius was out on a case. Much to Moebius' dislike, Raoul routinely referred to him (Moebius) as "Big Moe": "How's it goin' Big Moe?"; "What's shakin' Big Moe?"; "Hey Big Moe, look at this!" Reacting to this casual lack of deference, Moebius started referring to Raoul as "Big Toe" then finally just "Toe": "What's happening, Big Toe?"; "Put a sock in it, Big Toe"; "'Sup Toe?"; "Bite me, Toe!"; "Hey Toe, is that a new cold sore?" In spite of all this Raoul business, Moebius and Margaret seemed to get along (after a fashion) even though she was Moe's opposite in many ways: insensitive, disorganized, unhygienic, indiscreet, averse to detail, pale, calorie conscious.

Moebius Moli himself had a classic Mediterranean look, a dark-skinned Italian gigolo motif—except for his face which looked like the inside of a tomato: red, seedy, and always moist. When (infrequent) sex was on the table, given his dark skin and her pale skin, entangled together they looked like a checkered flag flapping in the wind.

After eleven years of marriage, through several job changes, Moebius and Margaret decided to move to the suburbs. They settled down in Bubb, a township suburb of the big metropolis of Little Head, New Jersey. Margaret got a full-time job at Bubb College as a women's conditioning coach, a job which gave her a significantly larger income than Moe's salary as a police inspector. Bubb College was just a few blocks (walking distance) from the Moli household, but Margaret never walked...outdoors...in the sun.

The township of Bubb had its own city council, its own fire department, and its own police department—no siphoning off services from Little Head for this independent burg—although a fair number of Bubb residents worked in the big city.

Years ago, the Bubb police department hired Moe on the professional hunch—actually a mere whim—of the late Captain Abraham Hudu-Jenkins, a hunch that Moe could fit the bill as a detective. During his job interview, Moe impressed Captain Hudu-Jenkins, and, as a result, landed a job as an Assistant Inspector in Bubb. He was hired in spite of his colorful and awkward past in other law enforcement capacities: improper storage of morgue bodies, possession of twenty-two crooked slot machines, loss of a police black-and-white patrol car, a peck of trouble with those Cubans, missed court appearances, contempt of court, bigamy. When questioned by Hudu-Jenkins, Moli provided a logical, plausible explanation for each incident on the list. It really impressed Captain Hudu-Jenkins that Moli could logically explain his way out of anything even if none of it was true. In spite of his past, ever since Moli started working in Bubb, he always kept his nose clean, followed the straight and narrow, walked the line, and kept his impulses under control in his everyday professional work—his everyday *professional* work. Because of this, he quickly advanced to the rank of Full Inspector.

Following the early morning call from dispatch, at that moment, he had not the tiniest hint that his dedication along with his creative detectiving skills were going to be severely tested by the case that had just been dropped in his lap.

Before heading on out, Moli set about making his typical breakfast (while Margaret slept). He made waffles; a breakfast steak; biscuits and gravy; two bananas; half a grapefruit; a cherry; potato pancakes flavored with black truffles; four eggs (over easy); ham sticks; a slab of cheese; raw garlic toast; and a smoothie made of two apples (skins, stems, and seeds included), chocolate malt balls, peanut butter, maple-flavored corn syrup, orange juice, and a can of pineapple chunks. He washed it all down with a quart of hot, steaming, deluxe-blend coffee. The immediate biological effect of all this intake is beyond the decorum of this discussion.

After giving Margaret a little nudge—to which she sleepily responded with, "My menudo's gone cold, Raoul"—Moebius Moli headed off to the crime scene. But first he had to radio in to headquarters, ostensibly to let them know he was on his way, but in reality it was to find out where the hell he was supposed to go. With the location firmly in hand and cautiously speeding his way to the crime scene, Moli struggled mightily to stay awake, big tank full of caffeine-laden coffee notwithstanding. Upon his arrival, he reviewed the status of his oneship while still in his car. Since he was going to be the top dog on the scene, it was his duty to remain professional at all times. As he opened his car door, he was about to step into something, about to step into one of his most compelling, frightening, unusual, and disgusting cases.

Sunday, October 20 5:33 am

Moli was feeling sluggish as he sat behind the wheel of his car. "I got here as soon as I could," Moli shouted out to Doctor Pfeffer who came to greet him as the overstuffed Moli laboriously lumbered out of his car. Dr. Felix Pfeffer was a scientist in the forensics department of the Bubb Municipal Police Department. He was an important member of Moli's investigative team and, over time, the two had become good friends and good teammates. Early on, Moli learned to trust Pfeffer's findings no matter how they might appear at first glance.

Before the two could connect and do some greeting type stuff, a woman appeared out of the darkness. She was moving anxiously toward Inspector Moli.

"Ella!" Moli shouted in surprise, "what are you doing here?"

"I caught the call on my new police radio and came over to see you," she answered as she enveloped him bodily in a big hug. "When are we going to get together—you know, like in the old days, Moe? How about tonight? Derringer misses his Dad."

"Ella, you shouldn't *be* here," Moli responded in an authoritative way, "I'm on a case." It had been over three hours since Moli received the call from dispatch so Dr. Pfeffer was becoming impatient. "Yeah. Can we get on with it?" Dr. Pfeffer prodded.

"Yes. Yes we should," replied Moli, addressing his attention to Dr. Pfeffer. "Ella, I'll call you sometime...later, when things here get under control." With that, the two crime specialists turned away from Ella and headed for the location of the body, the "murder" victim. An abandoned Ella watched wistfully as the two disappeared through a hedge demarcating the parking lot of the corner convenience store/laundromat/gas station, *Eat Up and Gas*.

Dr. Pfeffer was a cautious and meticulous forensic scientist. His skills with the latest laboratory techniques and forensic methodologies had brought him recognition from as far away as Little Head. He took pride in his work and never seemed to be "off the job." He could appear out of nowhere at a moment's notice when his input and analysis were required. And, no matter where he was, no matter what the circumstance, he always dressed in a full length, white lab coat adorned with the Bubb township logo, a police department arm patch, and an embroidered name tag with "Dr. Pfeffer" written in dark orange script above his left man-tad. He never went anywhere without wearing a protective facemask. As a result, Inspector Moli had never really seen Felix's actual face. In direct conflict with his medical knowledge, Dr. Pfeffer was an unrepentant chain smoker, so every mask he wore had to have a hole punched into it so he could hold a lit cigarette between his lips. He repeatedly violated *No Smoking* areas and was a notorious, but well-respected nuisance at many crime scenes; and especially at headquarters. His long white lab coat was always adorned with multiple random smudges of scruffy-looking cigarette ash.

The good doctor was able to divide his time efficiently between performing his duties in the department's laboratory, doing research in the computer center, working directly with Moli out in the field, and applying his special skills wherever they were needed. He preferred using a beat-up old clipboard over any kind of electronic device, a clipboard he carried with him everywhere. At a scene, with clipboard in hand, he could instantly and reliably provide important and relevant data—all gathered, compiled, and interpreted—ready to be applied in real serious detecting by his colleague, Inspector Moli. Moli and Pfeffer, an efficient and successful partnership.

As they approached the body, Inspector Moli could see that the victim was a middle-aged male. Being so early in the morning, there were more uniformed police officers at the scene than there were spectators. Four of the officers busily lined up near the victim's car at the gas pumps in order to prevent the three onlookers from interfering with the investigation. The two crime experts positioned themselves strategically on either side of the corpse.

"What have you got for me so far?" Moli asked Pfeffer.

Dr. Pfeffer began, "Yeah. Well, we have a middle-aged man, lying on his back, here on the wet pavement. He's dead. The dead man was apparently filling up this rented car with gas when he was attacked and killed by the pump."

Confused, Moli asked, "What does that mean, 'the pump—'? What? He was dead—somehow filling the car? Killed by the pump...how?"

Interrupting and looking through his notes, Dr. Pfeffer explained, "Yeah. No. Not right. He was attacked while standing *by* the pump. The victim was one Adolph A. Biggwon from Fort Woolsey over in Delaware. He was a salesman for a woolen goods outlet. The...Wooly Bear Woolenry in Fort Woolsey. Luckily, the pump's automatic shutoff valve kept this area from getting soaked with gasoline...since the customer was incapacitated...because he was killed."

"What was the cause of death," asked Moli.

Dr. Pfeffer continued, "Yeah. Well. It looks like he was choked to death, from inzertion, into his windpipe, of a foreign object or objects unknown, inzerted by person or persons unknown. There does not appear to be any such object or objects, known or unknown, currently at the scene."

Inspector Moli began looking over the body, poking at it here and there with the eraser end of his pencil, eventually accumulating a viscous substance on the investigative eraser. "Curious, very curious," he muttered. "And what is all this liquid on his face? It doesn't look like water...or gasoline."

Dr. Pfeffer was lightning quick with the facts, "Yeah. According to these lab results," he said as he leafed through the pages of paper on his clipboard. "According to these results, that liquid is saliva. But..." he paused.

"Yes?" Moli responded, looking up at the smoking Pfeffer from Moli's own indelicate squat position. When puffing on a cigarette, Pfeffer would take a drag off it and upon exhaling, the second-hand smoke would emerge from all around the sides of his mask. Years of this behavior had left a brown tar outline around the edges of the protective mask, a ring, on Pfeffer's face. What Pfeffer's face must have looked like *under* the mask was a frequent topic of conversation in the police locker room.

"The saliva is not of human origin!" Pfeffer added with a little tremor in his voice. "But the large quantity of saliva was not what choked him to death."

Moli continued squatting like a constipated toad trying to pass a football. Then, as he stood up again he asked, "What about the clerk in the store? Did he or she see anything?"

"Don't know. Yeah. She's over there if you want to talk to her," Pfeffer replied, pointing toward the small store with the big *Eat Up and Gas* sign over the entrance. She was being attended to by one of the uniformed officers, Officer Tinsley—the same officer who was first to arrive at the scene having seen the body lying on the ground during his routine patrol.

Moli confidently strolled over to the store with his boot-heels a'clicking on the pavement. There, he noticed a heavy-set woman with deeply tanned, leathery skin. She was wearing a faded, flowery muumuu and was talking to the officer in a piercing, husky voice. With that voice she surely must have been another passenger on the smoke train of death. Stepping up to her, Moli interrupted her cackling, sonorous laughter, "Ma'am, I'm Inspector Moli of the Bubb police. Can you tell me if you happened to see anything here, earlier?"

The woman tried to sound important, "I wasn't watchin' the pumps at the time the crime was committed so I didn't happen to see no perps or felonies. I was watchin' the cats out back, watchin' on the security TV screen. I always put the unsold, day-old hot dog roller-weenies on the ground out back where the video's at so's I can watch the cats come up and try to eat 'em—them's tough ol' things. Cats, they fight over 'em, sometimes carry 'em off. Never seen *one* of those gals actually bite through the hull on any of those weenies. It's real fun, great for watchin' during the slow shift, and sometimes a little, you know, sad. But...next thing I know, I see the reflection of that cop's patrol car lights flashin', and I look out the front winder and see these two legs stickin' out from behind that automotive vehicle out there, on the ground, and this copper here takin' it all in. Then he comes at *me*, into the store, and tells me to 'hang tight' until the investigative team arrives. And I guess that's you...and that other guy over there...in that white getup...and that mask. We've been waitin' here for—"

"Thank you Ma'am," Moli interjected, "that's all I need. Officer...Tinsley, will you get this witness managed up. Thanks." With that, Moli returned to the body where an excited Dr. Pfeffer was ready to provide some more facts.

"Yeah. Following these back-calculations and using Friedrich-Klein eigenvalues, we can say that the man was killed around 12:36 this morning (give or take an hour). And, according to all available information—" Pfeffer began shuffling through his clipboard pages, "he was the father of two children that look nothing like him, he was involved in a messy divorce, and he still keeps in very close contact with his ex-wife's sister."

"Great! Good work," said Moli, giving Pfeffer a fatherly pat on the back. He then added, "Let's get over to my office at the department and sort all this out." Proceeding on over to their respective cars, the two specialists seemed perfectly oblivious to poor Ella's lingering presence. As she watched them both drive away in an official, police-like manner, she raised her hand and pointed to the sky with her middle finger as if to say, "I'm not bearing you any more children...you married POS." Love and romance, alive and well in the streets and houses of Bubb, had many, many faces.

Sunday, October 20 7:14 am

The sun was beginning to beam over Bubb as the two crime solvers arrived at the headquarters building. Using the hidden police door, they entered the building from the rear and meandered into the police locker room. Seeing who was already there, Moli muttered to himself, "Good grief! That's all I need." What he saw was a fully implemented, fellow inspector Harry Pitts standing in the central area with a leg up on one of the benches, Pitts' gun hanging off his hip like a large cave bat. He was massaging a locker room towel in his hands as if it was a big mound of dough.

"Click-click. Click-click. You're here awfully early on a Sunday morning, aren't you, *Inspector* Moli?" Pitts remarked with a thinly-veiled, taunting tone. "Morning, Pfeffer," Pitts said as an afterthought, redirecting his attention momentarily. Pfeffer responded with a half-hearted nod as Moli attempted to get around Pitts. Moving to his side in order to block Moli's way, Pitts added, "I hear they saddled you with that two AM call. What was it? Road kill patrol? Donut duty?"

"Get out of my way," Moli answered, moving forward into Pitts' body. As Pitts turned sideways, Moli got right in front of him, eye to eye, paused for an awkward moment, and then brought up a loud, greasy, flavorful belch that landed right on Pitts' face. Pfeffer could not contain a smile—no need to contain it, it was a smile hidden from the world—and the partners left the locker room heading for Moli's office while the fuming and displaced Pitts turned to watch them leave. The exact makeup of the gaseous emission that came up from deep inside Moli would have defied analysis if Dr. Pfeffer were to have used his awesome powers to examine its composition. That composition would be beyond the decorum of this discussion.

In the privacy of Moli's office, Moli and Pfeffer went over the facts of the case, step by step. Pfeffer then headed off to the lab, closing Moli's door behind him. Leaning back in his chair, Moli propped his feet up on his desk and soon fell asleep, still digesting his early morning tableau of food.

Moli seldom locked his office door so it was unfortunate for Moli when Chief Inspector Pil Wafer barged in and caught him napping.

"Ahem!" uttered Chief Inspector Wafer, noticing the thumbtacks on Moli's heels.

Moli, almost falling out of his chair, sat up attentively, "Yessir?"

"I came to inform you about that convenience store murder. You handled that?" Wafer asked.

"Yessir, I'm on the case," replied Moli.

"No you're not," Wafer sputtered back. "I'm putting Inspector Pitts on it, and I want *you* to go home and get some sleep. Dr. Pfeffer will brief Pitts with all the pertinent details. And...lose those blasted thumbtacks."

Reluctantly, Moli agreed, "Yessir."

He gathered himself up and walked toward the door. As he clicked past Chief Inspector Wafer, Moli did everything he could to suppress the launch of another big belch. But Moli was aware that part of keeping your nose clean sometimes means backing away from self-destructive impulses. Before leaving the building, Moli looked back down the hallway and saw Wafer and Pitts in an official-looking, deep, dark discussion. Not particularly disappointed, Moli got into his car and drove home.

<u>Sunday, October 20 8:13 am</u>
As Inspector Moli's house came into view, he saw an old, unwashed, rusted heap of brownish junk parked in his driveway. He recognized it as the pickup truck belonging to Raoul Bendito. He had asked Raoul not to park in the driveway. An annoyed Moli parked his car on the street. As he was standing by his open car door, Moli looked out over the car's roof and saw Raoul emerge from the front doorway.

"Big Moe!" Raoul shouted, pointing his forefinger at Moli.

"Hey, Toe," was Moli's unenthusiastic reply. "What are you doing here so early?"

"Came to pick up my ankle weights," blubbered Raoul.

"Where are they? I don't see them."

"Ooh! Right! I must've left them inside," Raoul answered, quickly short-stepping backward through the doorway, ostensibly planning to retrieve them. But, upon turning about, Raoul bumped right into Margaret who had come up from behind, knocking her into a sitting position on the floor. Moebius, Margaret, and Raoul, together, now awkwardly occupied a small area in the front doorway of the Moli house.

"I'd better go get those weights," Raoul said as he stepped over the sitting Margaret, ducking into the other room. Moebius was helping Margaret get up off the floor as Raoul came back holding a pair of ankle weights. Funny...Raoul smelled like Margaret and Margaret smelled like Raoul. No other words were spoken as an uncomfortable Raoul hastily scurried to his truck, mounted it, and took off.

"Where are the kids?" Moebius asked.

"Magnum is over at the Slackhauser's and Beretta is still asleep in her room," was Margaret's unemotional reply. Magnum: 12-year old son, Beretta: 18-year old daughter.

"Humph," Moebius nodded and headed for the bedroom, "I need to get some sleep." Without changing clothes, Moebius fell face first onto the bed and was unconscious almost immediately.

Sunday, October 20 8:55 am
Moebius had descended into such a soft, soothing dream state that he did not hear the buzzing of his phone right away. After subconsciously ignoring more than twenty rings, Moebius became aware enough to answer it. "Inspector Moli—" he finally responded sluggishly.

"This is Chief Inspector Wafer," said the voice on the other end of the line.

A weak "Yessir" was Moli's reply.

The Chief Inspector continued, "It looks as if we have two more cases here like the one you were handed early this morning. Dr. Pfeffer is convinced that all three crimes were committed by the same person or persons unknown. Both of these other cases occurred last evening. One was a night watchman who was doing his outdoor sweep of the grounds around the Tithonus & Richter Law building. The other was a taxi driver who had stopped at the end of a deserted street in the Gruud area and was relieving himself on a concrete wall when he was attacked. So far, all of the victims have been anatomically correct males and all the murders have occurred in approximately the same area...*and*...in the dark of night. They were all choked to death and they all had copious amounts of saliva, non-*human* saliva, on their persons."

Not hearing a response, Wafer inquired, "Moli? Moli, are you there?"

"Yessir. Yessir, I'm here," Moli answered even though he had suffered several "brown-outs" while Wafer was talking. Because of this, he had missed much of the salient information Wafer was passing along; so Moli was going to have to rely on Dr. Pfeffer to fill in the gaps when he (Moli) returned to headquarters.

"OK, well, good," Wafer then replied, adding, "Moli, I want you back on the case so you can make sense of these three similar incidents. What do they have in common? Where do we go from here? Dr. Pfeffer is ready to assist you in any way he can."

"What about Inspector Pitts?" Moli asked innocently. But Chief Inspector Wafer had already ended the call. Margaret was now asleep on the couch in the living room. Beretta, their daughter, was still asleep in her room. And Inspector Moli was back on the case, even though he felt like a zombie. Full clothed, Moli rolled out of bed and prepared himself for a return to headquarters.

Sunday, October 20 9:30 am
Moli arrived back at headquarters and immediately met with Dr. Pfeffer for an update. The two crime fighters spent much of the day working out commonalities, downing coffee, and eating vending machine snacks. These included peanut butter crackers, pork rinds,

fried garlic balls, beef jerky, chemical sausage stix, fluffy artificial dessert products, and other alleged food items. But despite all the food, there were no breakthroughs in the case. Then, late in the afternoon, they received a call from downstairs, from the Bubb coroner, Dr. Mario Pisioroli. Moli and Pfeffer joined the coroner in the morgue.

Sunday, October 20 5:35 pm

Entering the morgue, both Moli and Pfeffer were sniffing the air like a pair of bloodhounds, even though Pfeffer could hardly smell a thing through his smoke-contaminated mask. Moli smelled *something* even through Pfeffer's ever-present, smoky cloud.

Before proceeding with the usual greeting type stuff, Moli addressed Dr. Pisioroli, "What's going on down here? It smells really funky-bad down here this evening. More funky-bad than usual...down here."

"The ventilation and cooling systems are both on the fritz and some of these bodies are starting to get a little bit ripe," Pisioroli replied. "And to top it all off, Dr. Gorman just had an autopsy go bad. It's been a real stinker of a day."

"Whew!" responded Moli, covering his mouth and nose with his hand. "What have you got for us?"

"Well, we've found something very interesting," Pisioroli began, uncovering one of the bodies. "This victim, the night watchman, must have bitten down on the object that was choking him. We were able to identify a small piece of organic material wedged between his teeth. Look here." Pisioroli peeled back the victim's lips to reveal his teeth where a piece of the organic material remained lodged between his central and lateral incisors. "At first we thought it was a chunk of food—chipped beef, pork chop, offal, chili con carne—you know, usual stuff. But after careful analysis we determined that it was muscle tissue. Muscle tissue and mucosa from the tongue of a *cow*."

Dr. Pfeffer spoke up, "Yeah. Hmmm. Maybe he had just eaten a tongue sandwich. Something like that."

"We thought of that," Pisioroli answered. "Examining his stomach contents we found a large amount of guacamole salad, half a toothpick, and several coins. But no cow tongue. And...the cow tongue we picked out of his teeth was *raw*—"

"Raw?" asked Moli.

"Raw, bloody, uncooked, still kicking," Pisioroli added, "as you can see here."

Between the moist heat of the morgue, the rampant smells of dead funk, the detailed descriptions, Pfeffer's second-hand smoke, a stretched-out stomach, and an intense lack of sleep, an overwhelmed Moli became very light-headed and quite nauseous. "I need to sit down," he said, after taking a deep breath from behind his hand. He leaned back against the stainless steel counter top where some unknown forensic liquid began seeping through the butt area of his britches onto his backside. Feeling the liquid on his skin, Moli began slowly and discreetly moving away from the counter. He thought to himself, "I'd just rather...not know..."

"Yeah. What about the saliva?" Dr. Pfeffer asked, as a hefty cylinder of ash fell from his cigarette onto the edge of the sheet covering the corpse. He quickly brushed off the material with a couple of strokes of the back of his hand—as if nobody had noticed.

"We believe that it too...came from a cow," Pisioroli replied with an unapproving look directed at Dr. Pfeffer. Then, giving Moli the once-over, Pisioroli said to him (Moli), "You're looking a nice shade of ashen green there Moebius. Why don't you both go back upstairs. I'll call you if anything new rolls in."

The two crime investigators took Pisioroli's advice and trudged their way back upstairs to Moli's office, where, as the Chief Inspector ordered, they tried to make sense of all that had transpired. In the stairwell, on the way, Moli paused and asked Dr. Pfeffer, "What did he mean, autopsy gone bad?" Dr. Pfeffer just shrugged as a puff of smoke came out from around his mask. The climb up the stairs and relief from the odors in the morgue led Moli into an improved physical state. And, there was only a small cool spot left on his butt area where the unknown liquid had not yet dried out.

At this point in the investigation, Inspector Moli had only a sketchy idea of what was going on. At every turn, there had been one distraction after another so only fragments of investigative meat had made its way into the jaws of his awaiting head. So far. Moli was depending on the professionalism of Dr. Pfeffer to keep the investigation moving forward, afloat, and on track. Now it was getting late and time to go home, have a bite to eat, and get some much-needed rest.

Sunday, October 20 8:48 pm

As Inspector Moli and Dr. Pfeffer headed out from the headquarters hallway into the parking lot—and for Moli, home—Moli's phone buzzed. It was an operator from dispatch. "Hello there. We have another incident that is potentially related to your investigation. The victim is a woman on the Bubb College campus. One of our officers is on the scene with her now. They didn't indicate if there was some murder involved. Meet the officer at the intersection of Bubb Avenue and Arctic Circle, right there on campus."

Dedicated to his job and with a quiet, restful night at home now scuttled, Inspector Moli took off for the new crime scene. A masked, smoking Dr. Pfeffer, clipboard in hand, accompanied Moli. Next stop, Bubb College.

Sunday, October 20 9:01 pm

But first...

Having cleaned out the department's snack machine, Moli and Pfeffer decided to get some real food, something substantial, on their way to the crime scene. So they queued-up in the drive-through at the neighborhood *Snatch-A-Snack* for a quick bite of that *real* food. Moli ordered two *Snatchy* triple cheeseburgers with *Super-Snatchy's* secret ghost pepper sauce on the butter and bacon layer, a *Snatchy's* family tub of chili cheese fries, two quarts of *Snatchy's* Big Elmo Beans, the hamper-size tangle of premium *Snatchy* onion rings, a medium *Snatchy's* Everything Pizza (with extra anchovies and olive paste), and a 64-ounce, world-famous *Snatchy* Cantaloupe Malt. Dr. Pfeffer ordered something small that could be consumed through a straw.

Parked in the *Snatch-A-Snack* parking lot, Moli and Pfeffer were downing the cornucopia of quasi-edible food items when Dr. Pfeffer delicately asked Moli, "Yeah. Hey, Moebius, your wife. Doesn't she work over at Bubb College?"

Thinking that, by some small chance, the victim might be his wife, Moli considered the possibilities while he continued eating. After the downing of all the portable comestibles was completed, they took off. "Let's hit it!" Moli exclaimed as Pfeffer pointed forward toward the road. Next stop, Bubb College.

Sunday, October 20 11:06 pm
There was quite a disturbance in progress when the crime-fighting team finally arrived at the scene. A crowd of Bubb students had formed. As Moli and Pfeffer approached the area, the officers in charge cleared a space around the body. The body's head was covered with a Bubb College leather jacket, the jacket's back adorned with a large *Ice Dogs* logo. The jacket had been inadvertently aligned such that the Ice Dog head on the jacket looked to be the head of the victim.

"This is not Margaret," Moli uttered, almost accidentally—a strange comment given that Moli had only seen the Ice Dog head on the jacket; inadvertent humor that had Pfeffer smiling behind his mask (a smile hidden from the world).

From the crowd came a voice, "Ees dot you, Moe? My-eeee Moe-man?"

Moli recognized the voice. A woman was tunneling her way through the crowd and waving to Inspector Moli. It was Edema, a tiny French-Indonesian student enrolled at Bubb College. She and Moli had been having a scorching-hot fling over the past year.

"We can't talk right now, Edema. I'm on a case," Moli said, trying to tamp down the awkward public display of enthusiasm.

"Alvays on de case, alvays de case. See? You never haff no time—time for Edema."

"We'll get together next week," Moli said in an attempt to reassure (i.e. dismiss) her.

As he turned his attention back to the victim, he noticed an old, unwashed, rusted heap of brownish junk parked in front of the Bubb College gymnasium. It was Raoul's truck. Edema was being involuntarily re-absorbed into the crowd as Moli took a step in the direction of the truck. Just at that moment, out came Raoul with a young, bubbly, mussed-up student hanging all over him.

"That's not Margaret," Moli said, clearing his throat and watching the couple get into Raoul's pickup and drive off. Before he could turn away, he saw a similarly mussed-up Margaret exit the gym and walk across the yard toward the college breezeway. Neither Raoul, nor Margaret, nor the sexually active female student seemed to notice or care about all the hurly-burly surrounding the crime scene.

While Moli was distracted by Raoul and his entourage, Dr. Pfeffer was squatting, leaning over the body. Pfeffer had brought a large, bundled-up, yellowing white morgue sheet with him. The sheet was not as pristine as it could have been; there were washed-out splotches of dried blood and other fluid stains sprinkled about randomly on the sheet. The splatter stains seemed to register *zero* on the attention-meter of the rubbernecking student crowd. Restoring some dignity to the victim, Pfeffer removed the *Ice Dogs* jacket from her head and neck area, and blanketed her body with the morgue sheet. Pfeffer then engaged himself in examining the body while he worked around under the sheet with a flashlight in his mouth. The crowd watched as Pfeffer made the sheet undulate like a big pile of animated vanilla pudding. The area under the sheet soon became filled with Pfeffer's second-hand smoke. And as he moved around under the sheet, little puffs of smoke leaked through it in various places. The crowd was thoroughly entertained—stains or no stains.

Moli was still staring at the gym. "What are you doing here, Moli?" a voice rang out from behind. It was Harry Pitts. He had not yet been informed about Moli's reassignment to the case. Moli turned back and saw Pitts standing near the moving pile of sheet.

"Is everybody I know here at this damn crime scene?" Moli thought to himself, looking down and shaking his head. "Is *everybody* I know here at this bloody *crime* scene?" he repeated, mouthing the words. He then turned to Dr. Pfeffer and asked, "What have you got for me, Felix? Anything?"

Harry Pitts was elbowing his way into the confined space around the victim, moving aside anyone in his way and acting as if he was still in charge. Coming out from under the sheet and removing it from the body, Pfeffer offered his comments directly to Moli (ignoring Pitts), "Yeah, well, first of all, she is not dead." Moli did a double take. "Second," Pfeffer continued, "she wasn't choked, either."

"Then what *is* going on?" Moli inquired. Pitts stood nearby, nodding his head and holding his arms crossed as if none of this was news to him (even though it was) and indicating, by his demeanor, that he was at the scene in an official capacity. Pitts inserted himself into the conversation, "Moli, you know you can't have a *murder* without somebody being *dead*. Isn't that so?" Inspector Moli and Dr. Pfeffer pressed on, consciously ignoring Pitts' comments—and his presence.

Pfeffer continued, "Yeah. She was licked into *insanity*. Right now, she is merely passed out. She'll come to for a short while, expressing a desire for some smoked ham, then she'll pass out again. She is in no condition to respond to questioning and needs to be taken to a hospital. She is not dead."

"What about saliva?" Moli followed up.

"Yes, what about her saliva?" Pitts added, as if he knew what he was talking about.

"Yeah. There was plenty, but not on her face. It was, it was...all over... ummm...nether areas—" Pfeffer stumbled along, very aware of the presence of the crowd of sensitive, impressionable, innocent young college students. He became all coy and reticent about answering with graphic and lurid details, his flushed face fortunately obscured by his mask. "Nothing had been inzerted into her...mouth...or throat. She was not choked."

"I see...I see...I *think* I see," muttered Moli in response. "Let's go ahead and get her to the hospital."

"No saliva on her face. No saliva on her *face*. What could it all mean?" The clueless Pitts was mumbling, trying to look more thoughtful and official than he actually was. "You know, if we corner this pervert we should avoid a trial and just—"

Having had enough, Moli asked one of the officers to please remove Pitts from the scene. The officer handled the requested removal operation brusquely and firmly as the meddlesome and uncooperative Pitts was hauled off to his car. While that was taking place, a second officer stepped forward and addressed Inspector Moli, "You might be interested to know, sir, that we have a witness to all this."

Moli produced a big, wide grin. It was the first expression of joy that Moli's face had experienced in the last 24 hours. Dr. Pfeffer smiled also, but who was to know.

All this joy fell apart and turned to confusion when the witness gave her statement to Inspector Moli and Dr. Pfeffer. The witness was a young female student who had been walking along near the future crime scene. As she spoke she was vigorously chewing a big wad of bubble gum:

Pointing toward the Humanities Building she began, "I was walking along over there [smack] when I like heard this squishing noise [smack]. I looked over and saw this like fleshy [smack] kind of animal [smack]—"

Moli interrupted her, "Let me see there...hmm." Leaning forward, he put his fingers on her chin as he looked into her mouth. While she was momentarily taken aback by this intrusion, Moli quickly stuck his finger in her mouth and forcefully popped the pink, ping pong ball-sized wad of gum from out of her mouth. The slimy ballistic wad of pink flew through the air and quickly cleared a swath through the crowd of young students. It was more effective at moving the crowd than the police officers were earlier.

"Please continue," Moli said, acting as if his impulsive behavior had never happened.

Surprised and bewildered, the young woman continued, "Well, ahem...as I said before, I saw this like fleshy little animal crawling along. Next thing I know, I hear this woman gasping, like...you know, shock. Then I hear a bunch of like...moaning and groaning. I couldn't see what the animal was doing, but she sounded awfully, like you know...funny. Funny. I was thinking like...you know...whatever."

"How big was this...thing? Can you describe it?" Moli asked.

"It was about two or three feet long and like all slimy and a pale shade of like...pink. Fleshy. Kind of a long triangle shape; big on one end and like real narrow on the other end. The narrow end seemed to be like...the front end. It looked like one of those inchworms as it moved along. Oh, and it made this like...squishy sound. And it was fleshy, like, real fleshy."

Moli concluded, "OK thank you. The officer will get your personal information. We'll call you if we need you." He then motioned to Pfeffer to step aside with him. "What do think of that?" he asked Dr. Pfeffer.

"Yeah, well, it seems to fit," Pfeffer replied.

"You don't actually believe her, do you?"

"Yeah. No. Well, it kind of fits. Yeah. No choking, but the saliva, the squishiness—"

"I need to mull all this over. I'm going home. Let's get together tomorrow morning and sort all this out." Moli was ready for a break.

"Yeah. See you then," Pfeffer said in agreement. He lit up another cigarette, "inzerted" it into his mask hole, and puff-puffed his way to his car.

Monday, October 21 1:33 am

Inspector Moli was quite relieved when he arrived home safely and, much to his delight, Raoul's truck was nowhere to be seen. Exhausted, he quietly went inside and fell asleep on the couch. He couldn't even make it to the bedroom. As he dozed off, he just couldn't reconcile all the odd facts about the case: saliva, tongue meat, fleshy animal, saliva, choking, insanity, Pitts, saliva, bubble gum, Raoul. But soon, he was overcome with sleep—

Monday, October 21 1:43 am

Moli was awakened yet again by the buzzing of his phone.

Wearily and reluctantly, he answered, "Inspector Moli—"

It was Chief Inspector Wafer. "Moli! Harry Pitts informed me that you had him removed from the crime scene over at Bubb College. Is that right?"

"Yessir," replied Moli in a breathy, low tone so as not to awaken the household. "He was interfering with the investi..."

"And he arrived at the scene before *you* did, even though he was not even assigned to the case at that time. Is that right?"

"Yessir," said Moli softly, turning on his back to get more comfortable. He rolled his eyes back and placed the palm of his free hand on his forehead.

"Secondly…or thirdly, Pitts tells me that there is some kind of complicated four-sided triangle of love pyramid thing going on with you and some other people. Is that right?"

"Yessir…I mean no sir," replied Moli, not really in any condition to contest or explain anything.

"Thirdly, or is it fourthly? Ahem, you arrived at a murder scene where there was no murder. Is that right?"

"Yessir. I'm sorry that no one was killed…sir," was Moli's quiet response.

"So, as of now, you are off the case and Inspector Pitts is taking charge. I want Harry Pitts all over this case. Do you understand?" The Chief Inspector sounded very hostile but Moli just wanted to get some sleep. "And I want you and Pitts to get over whatever is going on between you two."

Finally the Chief Inspector (who was always on the job) admonished Moli, "You need to get your personal life in order, Moebius."

"Yessir, I'll do my best." Moli ended the call himself this time and went back to sleep.

Monday, October 21 2:21 am

Bubb Outlet was a dead end road overlooking Bubb. Forty years ago it was going to be the main road into a planned subdivision in the hills at the edge of Bubb. It was a massive project that wound up being DOA. But Bubb Outlet, the road, survived. On one side of the road was a wooded area with thick undergrowth. On the other side was a gently sloping drop-off peppered with bushes and a few trees. It was a Lover's Lane in its own time, now mostly abandoned for that purpose, having been replaced, in modern times, by warm and comfortable motel rooms or the occasional public lavatory. Seldom was the road visited for romantic purposes any more except by those too cheap (or desperate) to spring for something a little less seedy.

Enter Raoul Bendito. He left the Bubb College campus earlier that evening with Judy Drumhead. She was a student at Bubb College and was thoroughly enamored with Raoul's wild and kinky ways. She and Raoul had left the group session at the College gym to go "camping out," as a twosome, on the Bubb Outlet road. That was a big mistake.

No sooner had they started the proceedings than a loud squishy sound caught their attention. Before they could cover themselves, the entity had come through the driver's side window of the truck and the fleshy thing entered Raoul's mouth and began choking him, choking him in a gush of thick saliva. The partially dressed Judy let out a weed-withering scream and barreled her way, panicking, out of the passenger side of the truck. She hit the road running. Another partially clad couple further down the road interrupted their own doin's and took Judy in. Had to. Judy was beating the window of their car mercilessly. While Judy explained what had happened, Sammi Davis, the woman who had been receiving something fleshy of a different sort, began calming Judy, while Mick Pohl, the man, called the police.

Because of Judy's experience, all three of them were too intimidated to venture on up the road in order to check out Raoul and his truck. Their first instinct was to back out of there and return to town. But not knowing, really, what to do, they decided to stay put until the police arrived. While they waited for the police, the three of them holed up in the car with all the windows closed and the doors locked. The engine, and, by extension, the ventilation, was off in order to save money on gas. But, at the first sign of trouble they were planning to speed the hell out of there. By the time the police arrived, the windows were so steamed up that the arriving officer could not see into the car.

The officer, Officer T. Michael Brownwater, tapped on the driver's window with his ring, startling the threesome inside. Mick rolled down his fogged window and explained the situation. Officer Brownwater made a few preliminary and highly inaccurate conclusions upon seeing the three sweaty, disheveled people in the steamed-up car. Bewildered and confused by their story, the officer went on up the road to investigate. Mick quickly rolled up his window as the threesome waited quietly, with nervous anticipation, alone, in their moisture.

About that time, another (civilian) car drove up. It was Inspector Harry Pitts who was now all over the case as specified by Chief Inspector Wafer. After providing the sweaty threesome with some inappropriately cheerful and sarcastic banter, Harry Pitts took his flashlight and walked on up the road in order to join Officer Brownwater at the scene. That was Pitts' big mistake.

Before he could reach Raoul's truck, but out of sight of the sweaty threesome, Pitts heard a loud squishy sound coming out of the bushes. He directed his flashlight beam at the area. Then, in the blink of an eye, just as Pitts was getting himself all over the *case*...the *case* proceeded to get all over Pitts...all over his face and down into his throat. Pitts gasped for air as he fell to the ground. He was being attacked by a long, muscular tongue. It was strong. It was oozing saliva. It was more than a tongue. It was a tongue, and salivary glands, and cheek fat, and muscle—lots and lots of fleshy, pale pink organic, living, material. And now it was killing Pitts, just as it had done in terminating (almost) all the other victims. In each one of those cases, there was never a cry for help—a large tongue crammed into the throat prevented that. Pitts was no exception. Being highly trained in martial techniques he silently wrestled with the tongue, giving it multiple expert karate chops, and attempting to use the tongue's own strengths against it.

As Pitts' mouth and throat were being violated, Officer Brownwater was alerted by the irregular movements of Pitts' flashlight beam bouncing off the trees and shrubs. Responding, Brownwater came running back down the road from Raoul's pickup truck to determine what was happening. Coming upon the tango-ing Pitts and writhing tongue, the officer tried, unsuccessfully, to pull the tongue out of Pitts' mouth. Then in desperation, the officer zapped the thing with his taser. Withdrawing itself from Pitts' throat, the tongue flopped around momentarily like a hepped-up, beached mackerel, finally squirming its way down the slope away from the road, and leaving a nasty-looking slime trail in the dirt.

Pitts, grateful to the officer for saving his life, asked, in an extremely squeaky and nervous voice "What the hell *was* that thing?" Squeegee-ing thick globs of adherent, viscous saliva from his face using his forefinger, Pitts squeaked "Man, this stuff is soooo...heinous."

"It looked like some sort of big tongue," Officer Brownwater replied, "that thing that attacked you. Also, there's a dead person up there in a pickup truck, probably a victim of that thing as well. His ID says his name is, was, Raoul Bendito. His girlfriend or wife is in the car down there with that other couple." The officer pointed down the road to where Pitts had left his car.

Officer Brownwater then tried to help Pitts get to his feet, but it was difficult since Pitts was more compromised than he let on. "We need to get you to a hospital," the officer told Pitts, helping him down the road and back to the car containing the sweaty threesome. Pitts was in no condition to manage the situation, so the officer notified HQ, requested backup, ordered two tow trucks to the scene, and called for an ambulance.

Monday, October 21 3:40 am
It had been two hours since Inspector Moli crashed onto the couch in his living room. He was fast asleep when his phone began to buzz. Again. Fumbling around in the dark to gather up his phone, Moli answered it, "Inspector Moli—"

"Moli? This is Chief Inspector Wafer."

"Hey. How's it goin'? Uh...sir," was Moli's slurred and sleepy reply.

Wafer went on, "Moli? There's been a bad incident and I need you back on the case. The call I got from headquarters...they woke me up...they described a case like the others you were investigating, on and off. And Harry Pitts is involved somehow."

The name "Harry Pitts" went into Moli's ear like some kind of buzzing insect and gave his brain an electric wake up shock. "Why can't *he* handle it? Uh...sir," Moli asked. He rubbed his eyes with the fingers of his free hand as he rose up on the couch. He was now sitting with his feet on the floor and his forehead resting in the palm of his hand while he conversed with Wafer.

"Pitts was attacked and is being taken to the hospital. There's another victim...a dead body...someone named Raoul," Wafer continued. "Who is this *Raoul* character, whose name keeps coming up?"

If Moli wasn't awake before, he was awake now. Hearing the name of Raoul and the word "dead" in the same sentence was not altogether unpleasant news to Moli. "I'm on the case," Moli said with some enthusiasm.

"Yes, that's what I told you," replied the Chief Inspector. "Go out to the Bubb Outlet road and see Officer Brownwater. He'll fill you in. I'll have Dr. Pfeffer meet you there as well. Then check on Pitts in the ER at Bubb General and get back to me on your progress."

The Chief Inspector ended the call before he could hear Moli's last "Yessir." Moli sat with his jaw resting in his hands, motionless, on the couch, for several minutes. He was trying navigate out of the fog in his head, all the while attempting to absorb the big satchel of information that had just been dumped into it: Harry Pitts (again), Raoul (again), Bubb Outlet. On the case; off the case; on the case. Getting up from the couch, yawning, Moli gathered up his already-dressed self and drove off to the Bubb Outlet road.

Monday, October 21 3:58 am
On the way to the scene, Moli stopped briefly at Bubb's only all night deli, *Joe Herring's All-Nighter*. There he picked up a ten-pound *Balzer's* garlic salami and a block of *Balzer's* Provolone cheese that he could munch on while driving to Bubb Outlet. He also supplied himself with a large quantity of black coffee to be used to keep him percolating through yet another early morning assignment.

Due to the murderous crime wave, the township of Bubb, uncharacteristically, had really been humming the last few days.

Monday, October 21 4:20 am
Moli arrived at the scene on the old Bubb Outlet road and Dr. Pfeffer arrived very shortly thereafter. An ambulance had already removed a passively protesting Harry Pitts, rushing

him off to the ER. The coroner's meat wagon was on its way to pick up Raoul's body as soon as Inspector Moli and Dr. Pfeffer could examine it at the scene. Officer Brownwater leaned against the front fender of Mick's car and the sweaty threesome sat comfortably in the dark with the windows down. The threesome was fairly dried out by this time, given the cool, but dry October air. The two tow trucks that were requested had not yet arrived. This road had not seen so much action since the time that the Bubb High School graduation just happened to coincide with the fumigation (shutdown) of Bert's Pay-As-You-Go Motel.

Officer Brownwater gave a brief bullet point description of the situation to crime investigators Moli and Pfeffer:

    Item: Raoul's junk heap located on up the road—

        (Brownwater pointing that way)

    Item: Raoul's dead body, still in the truck—

        (Brownwater indicating a "thumbs down" sign)

    Item: Three folks to be interviewed—

        (Brownwater pointing at the darkened car containing the threesome)

    Item: The attacked Pitts carted off to the ER at Bubb General—

        (Brownwater signaling "You're out!" with his fist, thumb extended)

    Item: A tasered fleshy thing lurking in the dark, out there, somewhere—

        (Brownwater pointing to the area, aiming his forefinger here and there)

    Item: Two tow trucks on the way, one for Pitts' car and the other one for the truck—

        (Brownwater now expecting a response)

Quickly turning away from Officer Brownwater, Moli and Pfeffer, both armed with tasers, started on up the road to examine Raoul and his truck.

"Good work, Brownwater. We'll be right back," Moli said, looking back and acknowledging Officer Brownwater with an unofficial-looking two-finger salute.

The masked Pfeffer carried his clipboard and Moli led the way with flashlight in hand. The crime scene at the truck had elements similar to all the others in this case: a choked Raoul, a *dead* Raoul, plenty of saliva. The driver's side door was closed and the passenger's door was open. Raoul's head was tilted back and his eyes were open as if staring at something on the ceiling inside his truck. But he was just dead; and his mouth was wide open. Donning a pair of vinyl gloves, Moli examined Raoul's head and mouth using the flashlight.

"Showtime!" interjected Dr. Pfeffer when Moli's flashlight inadvertently revealed that Raoul's body was wearing no pants or underwear.

"Except for the nakedness of the corpse here, this all looks very familiar," Moli commented. "Let's send the meat wagon crew up here when they arrive. But for now let's get the lowdown from the group down there."

"Should we cover up the exposed area of the body?" Pfeffer asked.

Moli thought for a moment, then replied, "I don't think so," and he headed on down the hill.

Pfeffer remained at the truck, examining the body and gathering any remaining scraps of scientific data that might be helpful.

Back down the hill, Officer Brownwater had the formerly sweaty threesome pile out of Mick's car and line up alongside it.

When Moli arrived back at the car, Sammi cautiously stepped forward from the lineup and called out, in recognition, "Moe?"

"Sammi?" Moli responded.

Mick had a puzzled look on his face. "You two *know* each other?"

At that point, a beautiful tap dance of choreographed bullshit took place starring Sammi and Moebius. It was an attempt to conceal the existence of their sordid, tempestuous, and ongoing affair—a beautiful, yet clumsy, display that fooled no one. In spite of this big distraction and in an attempt to remain professional and official, Moli went over the incident with each of the three: Judy, Mick, and Sammi. All during the interviews, Sammi frequently made eye contact with Moli, raising her eyebrows in a "come hither" and "all aboard" manner. Moli maintained his official demeanor but an occasional grimace would reach the surface.

Each witness had a unique, if unhelpful, perspective on the events. Judy Drumhead was very disturbed about the demise of Raoul (and *only* that). She could have cared less about the recent horrors of an at-large rampaging tongue killer and the ongoing investigation. As for Mick and Sammi, each of them was anxious to get back to their respective wholesome family households where there would be a boatload of questioning and explaining and lying in store. There would be sweat—the kind of profuse intangible sweat that occurs right before one has something important amputated.

As Moli and the now returning Pfeffer compared notes, Officer Brownwater left the scene and ensured that each one of the formerly sweaty threesome made it safely to each of their formerly peaceful homes. The meat wagon crew arrived and gathered up Raoul's body, taking it to the morgue. The two-man crew, not particularly enamored with Raoul's pants-less condition, argued about which one would have to handle Raoul's naked half as they extracted the body from the truck. Much later, the two private enterprise tow trucks finally arrived. One towed Pitts' car to the parking lot at headquarters. The other tow truck hauled Raoul's junk heap to the police impoundment yard. Moli and Pfeffer stayed on the scene through it all.

After finalizing the crime scene, Inspector Moli headed to Bubb General Hospital and Dr. Pfeffer went to the lab at HQ to compile his data.

Harry Pitts was still being treated in the ER when Inspector Moli arrived. The attending physician informed Moli of Pitts' condition: "We had a difficult time removing all that slime from your Mr. Pitts' face and neck and chest, but we were eventually able to sanitize the man's head. Mr. Pitts has damage to his throat, which accounts for his squeaky voice. He is likely to recover from most of his injuries, but the squeaky voice will probably remain."

"Is that so?" Moli commented. "Is he able to talk at all right now?"

"He's under mild sedation and can talk, but it's very squeaky," replied the doctor.

"No. We can hold off on his debriefing until later today," Moli said. Then, very softly, soliciting confirmation, he uttered, "So that squeaky voice will be permanent, you say—"

"Unfortunately, yes," was the reply.

Moli then went home so he could get a nap in before returning to the department.

Monday, October 21 6:06 am
The pattern was very clear: Moli asleep on the couch, a buzzing phone, a brain-fogged Moli answering, Chief Inspector's voice, etc. Only this time, Moli's sleep was interrupted by a call from Dr. Pfeffer and not the Chief Inspector.

"Inspector Moli—" Moli said as he answered his phone.

"Yeah. I have some new information about the case," Dr. Pfeffer informed Moli. "I think you'd better come on in. We might be able to devise a plan to capture or kill the rogue tongue."

"I'm on my way," was Moli's half-hearted answer as he dragged himself, one more time, to his car and drove to headquarters.

Monday, October 21 6:10 am

It was a world gone mad, at least temporarily, as Inspector Moli drove directly to headquarters without stopping to eat anything—except for a family-sized bag of goat cheese flavored potato chips, what was left of his warm *Balzer's* salami, a couple of fried garlic balls that had rolled out from under the seat of his car, and another quart of hot black coffee. Somewhere along the way, Moli had misplaced the remainder of his block of *Balzer's* cheese. (Moli figured that the cheese, wherever it was, would make its presence known after a few days of fermenting.) Lieutenant Fishman of the vice department once remarked to Moli, "How is it you are still alive, eh buddy?" It was the same remark Fishman had made to the smoking Dr. Pfeffer on multiple occasions.

Monday, October 21 6:38 am

Dr. Pfeffer was waiting in Moli's office, clipboard in hand, when Moli walked through the door. The masked Pfeffer was nervously puffing away at his current cigarette.

"I need to know what's going on and I need to get some *sleep!*" Moli remarked as he plopped down in his chair. "And not necessarily in that order."

Shuffling through the pages attached to his clipboard, Pfeffer responded, "Yeah. Yes...well...I think you'll find this information useful. According to our analysis, examination of evidence, computer processing, research, and lab work, our forensic team has come up with several observations: "First, the fleshy, pink creature is a cow's tongue between two and three feet long. Salivary glands, non-tongue muscle, and other tissues complete the cow-tongue complex. This tongue fell out of a cow a couple of days ago at the Bubb Country Feed Lot and Meat Works. Hitting the ground, the tongue *et al*, became disoriented and could not find its way back into the home cow. It then wandered into a nearby field and apparently attacked a horse, inzerting itself into the horse's mouth and throat and choking it to death. The horse tried to fight back, shaking the tongue mercilessly, but to no avail. The tongue, having suffered a few superficial injuries, then crawled into the woods to lick its wounds."

"If we capture this thing, why don't we just stick it back into the home cow?" Moli interrupted, waving off a lingering cloud of Pfeffer's smoke.

"We considered that option. So we contacted the night shift at the Meat Works. It seems that the home cow has since been slaughtered and butchered into everyday meats—except for tongue meat of course," Pfeffer added. "There is no longer a home cow that we can use. That brings me to our second observation," Pfeffer said as he leafed through his clipboard notes. "The tongue is not killing for sustenance. The tongue is not killing for pleasure. The tongue is not a psychotic maniac. The tongue is not killing for hire. The tongue *is* seeking a dark, moist, living cavity in which to deposit itself; a surrogate cow so to speak. In other words, a place to call *home*. After the tongue enters a victim, it soon discovers that the dark, moist cavity is not the home it has been searching for. So the tongue vacates. By then, it is usually too late for the victim. In the case of Mr. Bendito, there was a struggle. The pants-less Mr. Bendito was an aggressive muscular man and fought back, only to eventually succumb to the tongue, the confines of his steering wheel limiting his ability to fight off the creature."

"Good. Good information," Moli responded.

"One last footnote," Pfeffer continued rather reluctantly. "Raoul had a raging case of gonorrhea. Just thought you might want full disclosure of everything associated with Mr. Bendito."

"Not good. Definitely...no...not good," Moli said while contemplating all the new *tongue* information. While Moli self-basted in his thoughts, his face slowly morphed from one of discouragement to one of great satisfaction. He stood up and advanced to the white board on the wall. Picking up a marker, he began drawing a diagram on the board. Dr. Pfeffer watched as Inspector Moli laid out an inspired plan of action.

Monday, October 21 Midday
Under Chief Inspector Wafer's wary eye, Moli and Pfeffer worked all morning to hammer out the details of the plan. Using the location of each crime scene as a guide, Inspector

Moli and Dr. Pfeffer pinpointed, geometrically, the most promising place to set a trap for the rogue tongue: a small private park belonging to the Bubb Bakery (home of the locally famous Bubb's Bread). The Bakery was located in the busy downtown district of the Bubb micropolis.

After getting tentative approval of the plan from the Chief Inspector, Moli and Pfeffer spent the rest of the day setting up a trap in the small park. The privacy of the park ensured that there would be no crowd of onlookers getting in the way; curious onlookers requiring official management. However, the crime fighters' actions did not go unnoticed by employees of the Bubb Bakery who gawked from office windows throughout the setup of the elaborate trap. As Moli and Pfeffer were working, a security guard from Bubb Bakery came out and rousted the crime fighting pair.

"What are you two *doing* here?" the security guard inquired.

Moli answered, "We are here in an official capacity, police business."

"If you are the police, let's see some ID. Where are your badges?" the guard asked.

The two crime fighters looked at each other for a moment and then produced their badges, satisfying the guard that the two were in fact on an official mission—a tongue hunt, a tongue hunt...of death. Having accepted the legitimacy of the badges, the skeptical guard retreated back to his secure location and Moli and Pfeffer continued their work.

The trap itself was truly a trap, a giant rat trap; deadly, and equipped with a hair trigger. Soon after the trap was positioned, a delivery truck arrived at the park. Delivery persons from the truck unloaded several large drums, a large cardboard box filled with electronics, a five-gallon keg of cow saliva, and a huge, dead cow's head wrapped in plastic. Moli signed off on the delivery and the curiously uninterested delivery persons made a routine exit out of there. Moli thought it was ironic that they had to actually *pay* for the keg of cow saliva seeing as how they had sloshed through so much of it in past 36 hours.

Moli and Pfeffer got to work, opening the two large yellow drums. Each drum contained around 500 pounds of liquefied cow cud. Moli had ordered the cud product without pulp. With shovels, the two crime-fighters spread the creamy cud all around and over the yet-to-be-armed tongue trap, covering the grassy park lawn with the thick, yellow-green mixture.

"Who collected this stuff? *How* did they collect it?" Dr. Pfeffer asked Moli at one point.

"Beats me," Moli replied while he continued shoveling the acrid slime.

It was a difficult and messy task, but to the rogue tongue it would indicate the smell, and feel, of *home*. After two hours of cud-spreading, nerves were getting bit frayed for the two investigators.

They continued on.

Next on the agenda: dung. Two large brown drums of fresh cow dung were opened and a new round of spreading began.

"This smells weirdly terrible," Moli commented, holding a big shovel full of moist dung. "Are you sure this came out of a cow?"

Pfeffer nodded in the affirmative and the two proceeded with the spreading.

Shoveling pound after pound of fresh dung onto the lawn in the park was not only a disgusting task, but the creation of the thick layer of cud and dung had now attracted the attention of Hermoine Bubb, CEO of the Bubb Bakery. She came out of the building, almost stepping into the swamp-like mess now covering most of the ground in the park. Ms. Bubb was a multi-generational heir to the Bubb business empire. The township itself was named after Ms. Bubb's great-great grandfather, Hub. The family-owned bakery was well run and successful, and had been for several generations.

"What are you doing to our park?" Ms. Bubb asked the two crime specialists as she stepped backward in order to avoid stepping on the yellow-green layer of slime.

Again, Moli answered, "We are officials, here, attempting to capture or kill a murderous, rogue, cow tongue." Drenched with liquid cud and cow dung, Moli meandered through the mounds of muck and over to Ms. Bubb at the edge of it all. She backed further away, away from *him*.

After a few moments of testy back and forth, Moli said, "This must look very strange to you," gesturing with a sweep of his arm toward the shimmering layer of viscous cud-dung on the ground.

Ms. Bubb replied, "*Strange* is not the word I would use. You know, people are used to walking by our bakery and savoring the smell of freshly-baked bread. Now, all they can smell is this...this awful mess...this...*substance*!" She waved her arms at the lawn and stepped back away even further, distancing herself from Moli who was quite an offensive mess himself.

"I'm calling your superior," Ms. Bubb said as she returned to her office in the building.

"Oh brother," Moli thought to himself, returning to work. "That's all I need."

Once the area was covered in attractant, the next order of business was to set up the electronics: a 500-watt amplifier and public address speaker system. A recording of cow sounds was to be played over and over as a further inducement for the tongue to "come on over and die." Motion detectors were placed at the site to alert the stakeout crew (Moli and Pfeffer) if and when the rogue tongue arrived. Everything was drenched with the foul liquid, but the electronics seemed to be in good working order.

Moli then cranked up the public address system, blasting the area with a 125-decibel acoustic shower of mooing and other cow sounds. This elicited a new response from CEO Bubb as she pounded on the window of her office in an attempt to get the attention of the crime-fighting duo. They could not hear her over the natural sounds of fine, contented, domestic animals (cows) now filling the park. The test run was successful so Moli shut down the system, ready for the night's vigil.

The final step was to arm the trap. This took the efforts of the two of them as they pulled over the heavy, spring-loaded, steel bar of death, securing it with the arming lever, and carefully, very carefully, releasing their grip on the system.

Snap!

They had not secured it completely and the trap sprung into life almost killing Dr. Pfeffer. The springing trap saturated Moli and Pfeffer with another layer of the cud-dung melange. It took at least a dozen tries before the crime-fighting duo successfully armed the trap and avoided being killed in the process. But arm it they did.

After removing the shipping plastic from it, the dead cow's head was placed in the "money area" of the armed trap. "This head smells like a combination of raw meat and wet fur," Moli remarked.

"I don't smell anything," Pfeffer replied.

Moli cut out and removed the dead cow's tongue and much of the surrounding tissue. He then deployed the scooped-out head with the mouth propped wide open, adding a small mechanism that caused the head and jaw to subtly move about as if the whole thing was alive.

While still holding the dead, wet tongue in his hand Moli remarked, "You know, Felix, all of this is more disgusting than I could ever have anticipated."

"Yeah. May be...but...that cow head, the way it's set up—that's quite an attractive little cavern of a home there for the rogue tongue...if you ask me," Pfeffer said.

The final piece of the setup was the affixing of a nozzle, hidden in what remained of the throat-box of the dead cow's head. The nozzle was a special kind of industrial paint-spraying device, powerful enough to handle the thickness and viscosity of the store-bought cow saliva. A plastic tube connected the nozzle to a strong but silent pump. The pump was to be intermittently activated by an electronic timer. The tube itself was coiled around an old-style 100-watt incandescent light bulb, kept lit for the purpose of keeping the apparatus and the saliva warm. At 20-second intervals the pump would issue a small amount of cow saliva through the connecting tube and the nozzle would emit an atomized mist of the warm saliva out of the cow head's dark mouth cavity. Hopefully a moist mist irresistible to a killer tongue.

After everything was set up, Dr. Pfeffer remarked, "Yeah. You know, I think we set these things up in the wrong order. We could have been snapped by the trap while we were diddling with the head."

"I think you're right," said Moli. "Maybe we'll know better next time."

When exasperated bakery CEO, Ms. Bubb, tried to contact Moli's superior—Chief Inspector Wafer—she was automatically routed to the Inspector's voice mail. Chief Inspector Wafer's outgoing message indicated that he was assisting other important crime victims and for the caller to leave a message. Her message pointed out her extreme displeasure with the proceedings at the Bakery's park. It wasn't until later that evening that Wafer finally got her message.

Monday, October 21 6:20 pm
The trap was set and the sun was at the horizon, so Inspector Moli and Dr. Pfeffer went to the nearby diner (Bubb's *Bob's*) for some eats before settling in to their all-night stakeout. Moli ordered *Bob's Acre of Nachos* and the bottomless crockpot of chicken and dumplings while Pfeffer ordered a *Snark's* Crème Soda and a straw. Even though the two chose a booth in the corner, their offensive "coating" literally emptied the diner of customers. Once again, the crime-fighters relied on the official gravitas of their badges to keep them from being tossed out onto to the street by Bob, the owner. After an hour of chow and

another quart of hot, black coffee, Moli purchased an assortment of snacks to take back to the stakeout for the all-nighter. Pfeffer had to manage a few of the sacks full of snacks since there were too many for one person to carry.

<u>Monday, October 21 9:45 pm</u>

The stakeout was now well underway. Moli was deep into the second grocery bag of snacks and whatnot. The cow sounds had been blasting away since sunset. Although the cud-dung mixture was beginning to dry up and harden, the odors were still powerful—still powerful enough to interrupt Moli's snacking when an occasional breeze would blow a little cloud of the stench into the stakeout. Dr. Pfeffer was unaffected by the smell as he had been all day since he was wearing his mask that was usually filled with cigarette smoke.

"May I borrow your pocket knife for a minute, Felix?" Moli asked his partner.

Dr. Pfeffer handed his knife over to Moli who began digging through a layer of cud and dung in order to pry out the thumbtack from the heel of his right boot.

"What are you doing, there Moebius?" Pfeffer asked Moli.

"I have to get rid of my signature clickers in order to keep my nose clean. Chief Inspector Wafer is none too keen on them," Moli replied as he dug out the tack from his left boot heel.

Just as the tack popped free, Moli received a buzz on his phone. Moli wiped off the knife blade on his shirt in order to de-crud it before handing it back to Dr. Pfeffer. The call was, again, from Chief Inspector Wafer.

"Inspector Moli—" he answered, already bracing himself for Chief Inspector Wafer's tongue-lashing.

"Moli?" this is Chief Inspector Wafer. "I got a voice mail from a Ms. Bubb over at the bakery. She is extremely pissed off about what is going on over there."

Moli could not hear Wafer over the sounds of cows mooing at 125 decibels.

"Moli? Moli? I don't know if you can hear me over all that racket over there, but this scheme of yours had better work or you are out of here! You got that? Moli? Moli?"

Unable to respond, Moli ended the call. The contact from the Chief Inspector was the only real thing of interest up to that time.

As the hours dragged on, Moli and Pfeffer decided to take turns keeping watch, giving at least one of them a rare opportunity to get in a little nap. Losing the coin toss, Moli was to be first to stand watch, keeping an eye on the trap and the lights connected to the motion detectors. Dr. Pfeffer had not been asleep more than five minutes when Inspector Moli leaned back and fell into a deep sleep himself. Even with cow sounds blasting the area through the PA system at 125 decibels, the two crime detectives were now fast asleep at the stakeout "bunker." The decaying cow-dung mixture was now driving away any and all nocturnal wildlife so there was no chance of an accidental false kill.

## Monday, October 21 10:11 pm

The layers of viscous liquid on the lawn of the Bubb Bakery park were yellow-green by day, glistening in the sun, but now, in the evening, the cud-dung mixture merely appeared as various shades of grey, dull and vile. In the dark, it looked like so much fried chicken meat pureed in a food processor. While the stakeout crew slept, an eerie, pale pink presence made a ghostly appearance at one corner of the drying, swampy mess. It was the rogue tongue. The aroma of the cud-dung mixture had done the trick and attracted the tongue to the park. By this time the de-foliating mixture had become very sticky and acted as if it were flypaper to the slug-like monopod. Unable to control its instincts, the tongue was lured into the trap by the doctored-up cow head, the head's mouth cavity appearing to be a potential home for the wandering and restless creature. The motion detectors did not respond to the presence of the tongue as they had now been disabled by the acid-wash of goo splashed onto them during the setup; the digestive juices had eaten into the delicate electronics. Struggling across the sticky mire, the tongue finally managed to worm its way up to the (deadly) end of the giant, armed, rat trap. The tongue could sense the cow's head and could feel the warm saliva puffing forth at 20-second intervals. The cow head's dark, moist cavity was like a magnet to the home-seeking tongue. Given the recent history concerning one of the tongue's victims, an inquisitive person might speculate that the tongue's strong, uncontrollable urges were significantly sexual in nature, but that person would be wrong. The tongue had no sex. Even when the tongue was in its cow, there was no sex. There was no thought of sex. Cow tongues have no interest in that sort of thing—as far as anyone knows.

Exploring the head, cautiously and carefully, the tongue decided to "head in." It ignored a wet nozzle blast of saliva as the tongue penetrated the cavity.

Snap!

The giant trap's steel bar of death came down on the tongue with its full force as the entire trap along with the thrashing tongue popped up high into the air. The whole trap-tongue combo landed upside down in the surrounding sticky goo, the flat portion of the trap moving up and down as the tongue attempted to wriggle free in an uncontrollable frenzy of panic.

"Did you hear something?" a revived Moli anxiously asked as he shook Dr. Pfeffer.

"Yeah. I don't know, I was asleep," Dr. Pfeffer replied. "How could you hear anything over the cow sounds? The motion detectors have not been activated."

"Listen!" Moli replied. All they could hear was the sound of cows mooing in a special cow language at 125 decibels.

Looking out of the stakeout "bunker" and slowly turning toward the lawn, in synch, the duo saw the upended trap, now completely still, haunting the darkness of the night.

"Let's check it out!" Moli exclaimed excitedly. And the two clambered out of their stakeout positions and stepped into the field of sticky slime that surrounded the giant trap. When they reached the trap, it took the efforts of both crime solvers to flip it back over. And there it was, the menacing tongue, with the steel bar of death neatly creasing it musculature. Apparently, the tongue was dead—as dead as Inspector Moli's career would have been if this unconventional plan had failed.

Dr. Pfeffer began using a stick to poke at the defunct tongue while Inspector Moli attempted to scrape some of the tenacious cud-dung mixture off of his boots using the edge of the trap.

"We need to phone this in," Moli said while scraping away.

"Right!" Dr. Pfeffer replied without turning his rapt attention away from the fleshy tongue thing.

Monday October 21 11:14 pm

Moli's call in to HQ set into motion the entire machinery of the Bubb township's police department and municipal infrastructure. Chief Inspector Wafer was notified. He, in turn, notified the media. The media, in turn, notified the public. Officially, the general public had been kept in the dark up to that point in order to avoid widespread panic. But rumors were running rampant around town and it was time to let the people of Bubb know the whole story.

Dr. Pfeffer added a footnote to the incident, relaying it to Inspector Moli and filing the information in the official report. "Yeah. The trap itself did not kill the tongue. When the trap was sprung, the whole apparatus flipped over, snap-captured tongue and all. The displaced trap accidentally shorted out some of our cud-dung-damaged electronics. This sent a powerful electric shock through the tongue. This, in turn, triggered a seizure in the tongue and it was during that seizure that it swallowed its own tongue. Dead."

<u>Tuesday October 22 and—</u>

The meat wagon crew was assigned to haul the fleshy creature to the morgue where it was autopsied and studied. Pieces of the tongue were sent to various institutions for research. A sanitation unit was called in to clean up what was left of the Bubb Bakery park lawn, including some odd droppings left behind by the rogue tongue—the droppings also gathered, examined, and analyzed. Chief Inspector Wafer had to admit that Moli pulled this one off.

Harry Pitts' voice was never the same again. It was squeaky and lacked any semblance of that needed by an investigating authority figure. So he was given a token desk job with the Bubb Police Department. He embraced his token job and the desk that went with it—a new appendage—Pitts became one with his assigned desk.

Survivors who encountered the tongue had some pretty wonderful tall tales to tell their kids and grandkids. Despite her licking, the insane student was all cured up. The political bigwigs of Bubb stuck their collective noses into it all, stratifying the township into factions of varying opinions. The know-it-alls argued with the know-nothings and the town, now rid of the rogue cow tongue, was newly afflicted with the flapping, boisterous tongues of its citizens. Tongues. Once unified, now a town deeply divided by the actions of its own tongues. The population of Bubb turned into an aggressive, chaotic swarm of opinionated gnats.

Inspector Moli continued to work (and eat) alongside his partner in detecting, Dr. Felix Pfeffer. One of the biggest mysteries was how either of them was going to be able to live past the age of 45. When Pil Wafer was promoted to Police Commissioner, Moebius Moli became Chief Inspector (his thumbtack clickers fully reinstated). And, with Chief Inspector Moli's full approval, Officer T. Michael Brownwater was chosen to replace Moli as a Full Inspector.

Moebius and Margaret maintained their extended family and non-family web even though their individual indiscretions would, inconveniently, crawl out of the woodwork every now and then. There was a rush on penicillin and other antibiotics shortly after the township's adventure with the tongue. Margaret would have been badly shaken by the death of Raoul were she not thoroughly pissed at having to start an antibiotic regimen of her own.

Many months later, in court, the city of Bubb was found liable for damages to the park at the Bubb Bakery since the acid-laden cud-dung was responsible for permanently killing all of the grass and most of the wildlife in the park. The suit was settled out of court; millions were involved.

Bob Funk filed a lawsuit against the city, citing that he had lost his customers because of Moli's and Pfeffer's foul stench and troubling appearance when they came into his diner looking for food. The lawsuit was thrown out when it was discovered that an outbreak of Salmonella (traced to some undercooked chicken at *Bob's*) was solely responsible for the steep drop-off in customers.

—into the near future in that same October
Driving together along local Farm Highway 55 just outside of Bubb, Chief Inspector Moebius Moli, along with Dr. Felix Pfeffer, enjoyed watching the countryside roll by. It was nice to live in a community so close to the open air of the country. The cool atmosphere of fall filled Moli's new car with fresh air, while keeping Dr. Pfeffer's second-hand smoke at bay.

Suddenly, something filled the air that even the masked Pfeffer could not ignore.

"What is that?" Moli exclaimed, looking around and sniffing the air. He allowed the car to coast along. They had just unintentionally stumbled upon it: the Bubb Country Feed Lot and Meat Works.

"That smell!" Moli cried as he slowed the car to a halt. Pfeffer made a kind of gagging noise. They both knew the smell of a feed lot all too well. The smell was so strong that it even penetrated the dark confines of Felix Pfeffer's mask.

"Makes you think, eh Felix?" Moli remarked.

"Yu-yeah." The smell was having an emetic effect on Pfeffer, but he surely did not want to barf with his mask and cigarette firmly in place.

Moving on again slowly, Moli took in the view as their car passed a field crowded with cows, cows milling about, condemned cows, cows with no future. Moli began philosophizing, "I see that field there, that field of cows, and I think back to a few days ago. I see one of those animals and wonder if someday somewhere, from a another cow, near another town, another tongue will fall out, become disoriented and start killing innocent people in a search for *home*."

After a brief period where the two crime-fighting heroes rode along in contemplative philosophical silence, Moli suggested excitedly, "What say we go get something to eat? I myself could use a big plate of steamed clams with mayonnaise, maybe some sauerkraut and vienna sausages, four or five cheese enchiladas with sour cream, some fried...Sushi! Maybe some sushi!"

The immediate, paroxysmal, biological effect on the nauseous Dr. Felix Pfeffer is beyond the decorum of this discussion.

# Host of Hosts

*Network Voice-Over*: The following is a Network-of-Networks *color* presentation.

*< Kettle Drum Roll >*

*Announcer*: And now...your favorite talk show, direct from our studios in Cityville. It's the most from coast-to-coast...It's *Host of Hosts*!

*< Opening Theme Music >*

[ *Audience*: Applause ]

*Announcer*: I'm your announcer, Barry Baer. With music by your *Host of Hosts* orchestra...Orchestra of Orchestras...Oooh, led by our own...Bobby Bose Bowman! Joining your co-hosts tonight is guest host, Victoria Mosca. And of course, this week's Top Host, Lowell Mack! And now...just so you get the most from your *Host of Hosts*...Lowell Mack!

[ *Audience*: Applause with cheers ]

*Lowell Mack*: Thank you. Thank you. Welcome to *Host of Hosts*! Thank you! And to my left, is my co-host...you all know her as host of the documentary series *Hosts at War*...Letitia Greythumb...Letitia—

[ *Audience*: Applause ]

*Letitia Greythumb*: Thank you. And to *my* left is my co-host Smokey Montenegro, host of the early-morning comedy series *Hosts on Toast*...ha ha! Monty?

[ *Audience*: Applause with laughter ]

*Smokey Montenegro*: Thanks. Thanks Letitia. And to my left is the modern renaissance man himself...host of the annual Hosting Awards...author of *Hosting: What Is It Good For?* Your very own hosting curmudgeon, Vincent G. Emerson! Good evening, Vincent.

[ *Audience*: Polite applause ]

*Vincent G. Emerson*: Thank you Monty. And now it is my honor to acknowledge *my* co-host and tonight's Top Host—I'd like to run barefoot through your chest hair—Lowell Mack!

[ *Audience*: Applause ]

*Lowell Mack*: Yeah...we're all familiar with your...uh...preferences, Vince...but thanks.

[ *Audience*: Silence ]

< *Opening Theme Music Terminus* >

*Lowell Mack (seated)*: We've got a great show for you tonight. Joining us in a little while will be our guest host, Victoria Mosca, star of the poignant drama in theaters now, *I'll Be Hosting for Christmas*. But first I'd like to thank Rodney Pferderennen who filled in for me last week while I was hosting the Briar's Club Roast of Hosts where we really roasted Jackie Jackman, host of the *Jackman Hosting Hour*. Like Donnie Donnybrook said, "Watching Jackman host is like a fart in church...you can't tell how bad it is at first...and then, when it really kicks in, nobody wants to say anything about it."

[ *Audience*: Laughter ]

*Lowell Mack*: I know our ratings took a big hit to the solar plexus last week, but thanks for filling in anyway, Rodney. Also with us tonight is comedy sensation, Touch Allteats. Later we'll have our mystery host and much, much more...so stay with us—

[ *Audience*: Applause ] < *Earburger Music* > [ More to Come ]

*Lowell Mack*: To get us started, let me turn things over to my co-host Letitia Greythumb—

[ *Audience*: Applause ]

*Letitia Greythumb*: Yes, Lowell. It's an honor to be co-hosting *Host of Hosts* every week. And I want to say good evening to my co-hosts Monty and Vincent. Being here is quite a respite from hosting my documentary series *Hosts at War*. Every day we find out more and more about the atrocities inflicted on hosts—hosts captured trying to host on the battlefield; microphones being confiscated; hosts being forced to wear business casual. The list goes on. Our series is dedicated to raising public awareness about the sacrifices that these undaunted hosts have made—and continue to make. Many a time an unfortunate freedom fighter has looked up from a pool of blood and into the eyes of a battlefield host and received that comforting message, "We'll be right back." With our abundance of hosts in this country, we must remember that there are still places in the world where the mere act of hosting can land the host in some serious kimshee. *Hosts at War*: a show for the quick...*and* the dead.

[ *Audience*: Goes wild ]

*Lowell Mack*: Yes, it's a story that needs to be hosted and we thank you for bringing those important issues to our attention.

[ *Audience*: Goes wild again ]

*Letitia Greythumb*: Thank you. So let me turn it over to my good friend Smokey Montenegro. What's up, Monty?

*Smokey Montenegro*: Thanks Letitia. Yes, well, as you know I've been hosting *Hosts on Toast* for several seasons now. Sometimes we go out into the community and interview everyday hosts; hosting at the grass roots level. It's always spontaneous and unpredictable. Well, to show you what I'm talking about, I brought a clip from my show. Now this clip...we were out filming examples of spontaneous hosting in the suburbs when we ran across this group of kids. If you could run that clip—

[ Clip starts ]

*Montenegro*: What are you hosting here, little boy?
*Little Boy Host*: I'm hosting a public execution.
*Montenegro*: And just what are we executing today?
*Little Boy Host*: My neighbor's Chihuahua.
*Montenegro*: And who is that over there holding the hatchet?
*Little Boy Host*: That's my friend Pepper. He's the executioner. I'm just the host.
*Montenegro*: I see you've drawn quite a crowd of little youngsters.
*Little Boy Host*: Yes, we always get a good showing for one of these.
*Montenegro*: Well then, we'd better let you get on with it.
*Little Boy Host*: Sure. Thanks.
*Montenegro*: There you have it. Today's youth, getting into the hosting game, on the ground fl...[ Whack! ] As I was saying, getting a head start in hosting.

[ Clip ends ]

[ *Audience*: Groans, scattered applause ]

*Smokey Montenegro*: So check it out weekday mornings, *Hosts on Toast*. There's a lot more where that came from. And now let me turn it over to Vincent, my co-host.

Vince, is it true that you gave birth to a live alligator in your tub, or is that just a rumor?

*Vincent G. Emerson*: Very funny Montenegro. Ha! Ha! Let me just say that hosting is serious business. As beautiful as it may be, can a butterfly host? I think not. Can a refrigerator host? Never. We get paid well for foaming at the mouth because we earn it; the money that is. When a natural born host gets that first slap on the ass, still attached to the umbilical cord—despite the layers of gel-like birth slime covering its body—is that newborn reaching out into the air and groping for its mother's breast? No. It's reaching for a microphone. Serious business this hosting. Natural. Part of the grand design of life itself. So, then, back to you Lowell.

*Lowell Mack*: That's quite a mouthful Vince...and you should know; and thanks for being here each week to give your...uh, insight on things. We'll be right back to talk to our guest host after this—

[ *Audience*: Applause ] < *Earburger Music* > [ More to Come ]

*Lowell Mack*: Our guest host tonight is Victoria Mosca.

[ *Audience*: Cheering, hooting, and applause ]

*Lowell Mack*: Victoria Mosca, starring in *I'll Be Hosting for Christmas*. Welcome Victoria. Can you tell us a little bit about your movie.

*Victoria Mosca*: Thanks Lowell. Even though I'm not doing regular hosting tonight, I always feel like a host when I'm on *Host of Hosts*. Ok, swell, my movie. It's a story about a poor family with nothing to eat for Christmas...the story really takes off when young Tad has to make a hard choice between bringing home food for his starving family and becoming a host; but not just any host...host for the World Championship. I've brought a clip—

*Lowell Mack*: Let's take a look.

[ Clip starts ] < *Morose string section from hell* >

*Sinister Executive*: Well, Tad, what's it going to be? All this food here, food for your family, enough food to feed everyone for a month, enough for Christmas day and beyond...OR...Will you be hosting the World Championship?

*Young Tad*: I'm so confused. I'm torn. After all, it *is* the Championship. I just can't decide—

*Sinister Executive*: Come on, come on...I haven't got all day.

*Young Tad*: Ok! If I *have* to choose, I'm going to go with—

[ Clip stops ] < *Morose string section from hell stops abruptly* >

[ *Audience*: Disappointed moans and reticent applause ]

*Lowell Mack*: Wow! That's powerful stuff. And where are *you* in that scene?

*Victoria Mosca*: I'm sorry to say that I'm already dead before that scene takes place—dead from a hosting accident.

*Lowell Mack*: Powerful, powerful. Stay with us. We'll be right back.

[ *Audience*: Applause ] < *Earburger Music* > [ More to Come ]

*Lowell Mack*: So we're back. Remember, later we'll be talking with our mystery host, so stay tuned. As you can see, my co-host Letitia Greythumb is in the audience, ready to hand out prizes for correct answers to tonight's questions. And Smokey Montenegro is up there as well; ready to hand out those prizes. So, who's up first, Letitia?

*Letitia Greythumb*: First we have Violet Hooper from—

*Violet Hooper*: Fort Lee, New Jersey.

*Letitia Greythumb*: Here's your question: Who was the star of the hit TV series *Hosts, She Wrote*?

*Violet Hooper*: Lana Angelus?

*Letitia Greythumb*: That is *correct*!

[ *Audience*: Applause ] *< Punctuation Percussion and Music Stab >*

*Letitia Greythumb*: And what do we have for Violet, Monty?

*Smokey Montenegro*: We have an all-expense paid trip to New York City and free admission to the Host Hall of Fame.

[ *Audience*: Applause ] *< Punctuation Music >*

*Letitia Greythumb*: Ok! That's one winner...and thanks for playing, Letitia. Who do we have next, here?

*Antwon Stokes*: I'm Antwon Stokes from Los Angeles.

*Letitia Greythumb*: That's Los Angeles, California?

*Antwon Stokes*: Yes. What did I win?

*Letitia Greythumb*: That's not the question. *Here's* your question: Which of the following is *not* a type of host: emcee, circus ringmaster, moderator, or banana?

*Antwon Stokes*: Banana?

*Letitia Greythumb*: Keee-rect!

[ *Audience*: Applause ] < *Punctuation Percussion and Music Stab* >

*Letitia Greythumb*: Monty? What do we have for Antwon?

*Smokey Montenegro*: We have an all-expense paid vacation to the *Host of Hosts* theme park, right here in Cityville. Enjoy six days and three nights at the *Host of Hosts* Hostel right next to the park. Once in the park, you'll be able to host your own talk show; ride hostmobiles through tough crowds; feel terror as you host an alien being in your torso while the entity grows into a flesh-gobbling monster before your family's very eyes; meet some of your favorite hosts as you wander through a forest of life-sized cardboard cut-outs; meet Whipping-Post Yost, host of the western-themed saloon, the Yost Outpost. It's all part of your *Host of Hosts* dream vacation. Congratulations.

[ *Audience*: Applause ] < *Punctuation Music* >

*Letitia Greythumb*: Thank you Monty. Next we have—

*Mons Delphi*: Mons Delphi.

*Letitia Greythumb*: And where are you from, Mons?

*Mons Delphi*: Right here in Cityville.

*Letitia Greythumb*: That's great. Is this the first time you've come to see the show?

*Mons Delphi*: Naw, I come here all the time. I want to be a host someday.

*Letitia Greythumb*: Well, I don't know about that, but...but, here's your question: Which of the following terms is now considered obsolete: Morningside Antarctic Time, totem pole, hostess, or Bush Baby?

*Mons Delphi*: Bush Baby?

*Letitia Greythumb*: No, I'm sorry. The answer is *hostess*. *Hostess* is now considered obsolete.

[ *Audience*: Over the top moaning ] < *Deadly Punctuation Music* >

*Letitia Greythumb*: But we do have a consolation prize for you. Monty?

*Smokey Montenegro*: Mons, for you we have the home edition of *Host of Hosts*. Enjoy the excitement of being a host right in your own home. Share the hosting experience with family and friends as you fend off hecklers; distract from obscenities blurted out by recalcitrant guests; evade questions about your personal life; react with poise to interview dead time by providing meaningless filler; make taunting and unflattering remarks about your annoying sidekick; recover from awkward on-screen moments like hiccups or vomiting. It's great fun that will keep you home-hosting for years to come.

*Letitia Greythumb*: Thanks, Monty. I think we have time for one more. And you are—

*Annabel Quercus*: Annabel Quercus from New York.

*Letitia Greythumb*: Great to have you here, Annabel. Here's your question: What is the scientific name for a fear of hosts?

*Annabel Quercus*: Host-o-phobia?

*Letitia Greythumb*: No. I'm so sorry; it's *degenerophobia*. A little too quick on the draw there, Ms. Quercus, wouldn't you say?

*Annabel Quercus*: Uh—

[ *Audience*: Sympathetic groans ] < *Comedic Sympathy Music* >

*Letitia Greythumb*: Monty? What do we have for Annabel?

*Smokey Montenegro*: For you, Annabel, it's the *Host of Hosts* video game, *Hostbusters,* by Hostindo. Put together your crew of hostbusters. Then review the line-up of evil hosts and mutant sidekicks. Stalk hosts and their ilk through the streets of Cityville on a search and destroy mission. Mow down hosts and sidekicks with a variety of weapons, explosives, and devices. Acquire useful resources that you pick up along the way and add them to your Hostbuster bag of tricks—from the simple machete all the way up to the nuclear loogie rifle. And have fun working your way up the levels toward the ultimate host Carzilla. But beware of the ghost hosts: some of your favorite dead celebrity hosts from the past may pop up out of nowhere to haunt your quest for blood. Celebrity hosts from the past like Foster Forbes, Candy Homeir, and Spruce Board—all dead, all deadly. *Hostbusters,* by Hostindo; for one or two players. Get hosting!

[ *Audience*: Applause ] < *Alternate Theme Music* >

*Letitia Greythumb*: Thanks for your assistance tonight, Monty. So fans, stay tuned for Touch Allteats and our mystery host and more, here on *Host of Hosts*. And we'll be right back.

[ *Audience*: Applause ] < *Earburger Music* > [ More to Come ]

*Vincent G. Emerson*: Welcome back. Vincent G. Emerson here. Every week we ask our studio audience to come up with questions for our co-hosts. I'm going to choose four from this stack of cards and my co-hosts and I will try to answer them. Let's see what the first card says: This is from Kurt: "Can a sidekick become a host?" Well, Kurt the short answer is *No*. And the long answer is *Absolutely Friggin' Not*. Once you have the stigma of playing second fiddle, you can never recover. Nobody likes a suck-up except as a suck-up. I hope that answers your question.

*Vincent G. Emerson*: Next, we have a question from Cindy: "Can you tell us about your charity work?" Well, I'm happy to talk about it. As you all know, I believe it is important to do charity work. As such, my hosting foundation known as The Hosting Foundation strives to bring hosting to many third world countries where hosting is in extremely short supply. People may go their entire lives without being exposed to a host. Volunteers from The Foundation travel into primitive backcountry areas where they set up panels of hosting for native tribes. I've spent many fulfilling hours watching a native village come together to build a stage, many times having to put aside political oppression or state-sponsored murder in order to do so. Under my direction—of course—I've watched industrious villagers set up backdrops; wire for sound; and do all the prep necessary for a successful event. And they perform all that intense labor under the brutal thumb of heat and humidity, sacrificing life and limb just so their village would be able to experience some hosting. As the final touches are added to a hosting platform, I always like to step in as host of the inaugural hosting extravaganza. It's a satisfying moment for everyone and allows me to get in some hosting for myself after all that work. So here we sit on this show with a plethora of hosts, abundance, while some of these villages go to heroic lengths just to have one host. I gives us pause. I believe that if we can expose these destitute people to just *one* host, one host at a time, the world will be a better place for all of us.

[ *Audience*: Goes wild with orgasm ]

*Vincent G. Emerson*: And may I add, contrary to popular belief The Hosting Foundation is not trying to steal the thunder from Hosts Without Borders; that's another fine organization.

[ *Audience*: Applause ]

*Vincent G. Emerson*: Let's see who we have next. Ah yes, Brad. His question is: "I am thinking of becoming a host myself. Do you have any advice for me?" Well Brad, the first thing I can tell you is: don't get discouraged. Ignore all the humiliation and abuse. Ignore the lack of money and food and respect. It took me many, many years of backbreaking scheming and licking the boots of network executives...and many sleepless nights, if you know what I mean. And look at me today, here I am. There is no such thing as an overnight host. Start small by hosting a local host show. Although the odds are miniscule and the cards may be completely stacked against you in every way, press on and do your hosting. At some point you may be discovered by a host scout and brought on board to guest host somewhere. Grab the opportunity because the big time may be just around the corner. Oh, and don't even *think* about taking the easy way out: becoming a sidekick.

[ *Audience*: Standard applause ]

*Vincent G. Emerson*: Let's take one more. This one is from Gary: "I'm eighteen years old and I'm thinking about my future. I want to be an anchorman but my parents want me to go into hosting. What should I do?" Well, my answer to that is this: give your parents the high sign. If you want to be a sailor, that's *your* business. That's all for this week. Now, once again, here's Lowell.

*Lowell Mack*: Thanks again for fielding this week's audience questions, Vince. Your insights are usually appreciated, at some level. Don't forget we still have much more to come, Touch Allteats *and* our mystery host, so stay with us.

[ *Audience*: Applause ] < *Earburger Music* > [ More to Come ]

*Lowell Mack*: Thank you. We are back. You've all seen this fella; he's everywhere. A master at self-promotion. You all know him. He's a quadruple threat: he's a host, goes without saying; he's the star of his own family sitcom *All In with the Allteats*; and, he has won the Kobel Prize for Hosting after he hosted the rescue efforts following the recent earthquake in San Arsenio. We thank you for that. But tonight he's here with his stand-up hat on. So please welcome Touch Allteats—

[ *Audience*: Raging applause ]

*Touch Allteats*: Thanks Lowell. And thanks to all of your co-hosts...guest host. You know, I was sitting in a bar the other day and in walks this dog along with a pig and a talk show host—

[ *Audience*: Snickering in anticipation ]

*Touch Allteats*: Anyway, the dog asks the pig "Why did you bring *him* in here?" And the pig says "Our babysitter was busy."

[ *Audience*: Guffaws ]

*Touch Allteats*: What's the difference between a talk show host and an exploding septic tank? The tank! Haw haw haw.

[ *Audience*: Awkward laughter and groans of repulsion ]

*Touch Allteats*: All right. All right. You see what you've reduced me to...laughing at my own jokes. Soooo...hmmm. A talk show host with a bullfrog on his head goes into a bar. The bartender says, "Aren't you a talk show host?" And the bullfrog replies "What a horrible thing to say about my ass!" Haw haw haw.

[ *Audience*: Laughter living up to low expectations ]

*Touch Allteats*: Ok then. A parasite goes into a bar. The bartender says, "You look terrible." And the parasite says, "Yeah, I know...I couldn't find a host."

275

[ *Audience*: Goes wild with comic orgasm ]

< *Perky, now-get-off-the-stage music* >

*Lowell Mack*: Thanks Touch. We'll be right back with our mystery host in just a moment.

[ *Audience*: Applause ] < *Earburger Music* > [ More to Come ]

*Lowell Mack*: So, with us tonight is our weekly mystery host. She's the host of her own reality show where viewers can watch her host herself in a live action-packed hour, doing routine tasks in her own home, *Live with Amy*. Please give it up for this week's mystery host, Amy Todd Oswald!

[ *Audience*: Standing ovation with obnoxious whistling ]

*Mystery Host Amy Todd Oswald*: (waves)

*Lowell Mack*: Thank you for being here, Amy. We'll be right back.

[ *Audience*: Applause ] < *Earburger Music* > [ More to Come ]

*Lowell Mack*: And now, I'd like to give it over to Letitia for this week's opinion piece. Letitia?

[ *Audience*: Applause ]

*Letitia Greythumb*: Thanks Lowell. When people criticize hosting as being just a closed society of ego-maniacal hosts, they couldn't be more partially wrong. We at *Host of Hosts* only select the best hosts to be part of *Host of Hosts*. Some hosts just bring out the best in the other hosts on our show. Others are just not meant to be hosts, or even co-hosts. They eventually become voice-over specialists or telemarketing recordists or some other lesser profession...like sidekicks. We don't look down our noses at them, not all the time, we just look over at them and say "Jeez, that could have been *me!*" Back over to *you*, Lowell.

[ *Audience*: Tepid applause ]

*Lowell Mack*: Thank you for those thoughts, Letitia. I want to remind everyone about the daytime version of *Host of Hosts*, weekday afternoons at three. It's a more casual and intimate version of our show. See the latest in hosting products. Go behind the scenes and see what your favorite hosts are doing when they are not hosting. Watch them practice, mirror-a-mirror, honing their hosting skills. But beware, it is not a show without its share of sparks; hosts from all over provide their unsolicited opinions about everything under the heading of hosting...a real back and forth dialog. And they never agree to disagree.

[ *Audience*: More applause interrupting the proceedings ]

*Lowell Mack*: Thanks. And so we come to the end of our show for this week.

< *Sentimental Ending Theme Music* >

*Lowell Mack*: I'd like to thank our guest host, Victoria Mosca; our mystery host Amy Todd Oswald—

*Mystery Host Amy Todd Oswald*: (waves)

[ *Audience*: More applause ] < *More Ending Theme Music* >

*Lowell Mack*: Our thanks to Touch Allteats for sharing his material. And, as always, thanks to our *Host of Hosts* orchestra, Orchestra of Orchestras—Oooh. Thanks Bobby!

< *Splash of Acknowledging Music* >

[ *Audience*: Non-stop applause ] < *Non-stop Ending Theme Music* >

*Lowell Mack*: Once again, my co-host Letitia Greythumb—

Letitia Greythumb: Good night Lowell. Monty?

*Smokey Montenegro*: Good night Letitia and good night Lowell. Vincent?

*Vincent G. Emerson*: Good night Letitia, Monty. Lowell?

[ *Audience*: Non-stop applause not stopping ] < *Non-stop Ending Theme Music* >

*Lowell Mack*: Thank you everyone. It's been a great privilege to be your Top Host on this week's show. You can catch me later this week when I host *Best of Bests*. The crew over there at *Bests* looks over all the bests out there and selects only the best ones to showcase on *Best of Bests*. I am honored to be their host this week after my being awarded the Best Host trophy on *Best of Bests*—they're just the best. And please don't forget our annual *Best of Hosts* special. It's our four-hour Flag Day Host-a-thon to raise money for hosts who have been without hosting for excruciatingly extended periods of time. Months! Heaven forbid! For your enjoyment, we show clips of all the best moments from *Host of Hosts* over the past year; we have special guest hosts and celebrity hosts; there are games and surprises; we put on improvisational hosting skits; and of course there are cartoons for any youngsters who may be watching—even if youngsters don't have any money. And just *who* will be hosting the special this year? Nobody's talking...they're *hosting*! Good Night!

[ *Audience*: Non-stop applause ]

< *Non-stop Ending Theme Music* >

*Announcer*: Join us again next week when our Top Host will be Letitia Greythumb. She'll be joined by our regular panel of co-hosts. This is your announcer Barry Baer. See you next week on *Host of Hosts*!

[ Network Logo ] < *Close-out Music* >

*Network Voice-Over*: The preceding has been a Network-of-Networks presentation.

## *Capitosis Delirium*

Dr. Ramus Heartsavitch: physician and surgeon, Chief of Surgery at the Mt. Yobaybi Medical Arts Center. Dr. Heartsavitch was preparing to perform a stomach transverse-overpass operation with hydro-dilation on a Ms. Andrea Drexinslaugh. A stomach transverse-overpass with hydro-dilation can sometimes be a torturous procedure, even life threatening. Dr. Heartsavitch was a co-developer of the controversial procedure with Dr. Reynard Zooflexure, also a member of the staff at Mt. Yobaybi. Together, the duo was sometimes referred to (lovingly) as the "Gut Nuts."

"What's his BP, Nurse T?" Dr. Heartsavitch asked as he "broke skin" with the first deep incision. He always referred to the nurses using only their first initial.

"One-ten over sixty-two," Nurse Testamink replied.

"Good, keep an eye on it. Let me know if the systolic drops below 90."

For the next hour Dr. Heartsavitch performed the procedure with his usual skill, exposing the patient's stomach, lower esophagus, and duodenum. He was about to begin the most delicate part of the overpass procedure (with hydro-dilation) when he stopped cold.

"What is it doctor?" Nurse Testamink inquired.

Hearing the concerned tone in Nurse Testamink's voice, the anesthesiologist looked toward Dr. Heartsavitch. Others in the room also took notice of the sudden halt in the proceedings—all except Ms. Drexinslaugh who was (probably) unconscious under the heavy shag carpet of anesthesia. Heartsavitch was standing over the patient's wide-open abdominal cavity staring intensely down into the yawning surgical workspace. There, the exposed stomach, connective tissue, and organs peripheral to the action—peeking into the scene—were moist and glistening in the bright operating room lights.

Without saying a word, Dr. Heartsavitch removed his mask, his surgical cap, and his protective visor. For several moments, the surgical team was so surprised that none of them knew how to react. What was happening? This was supposed to be a *sterile* area. Dr. Heartsavitch continued to stare down into Ms. Drexinslaugh's open abdomen. Then, suddenly and without warning, the doctor plowed his head, face first, into the cavity. While his head was deeply immersed, he began shaking and rolling his head all around inside Ms. Drexinslaugh, splashing her fluids all about the so-called sterile zone.

While continuing to man his post, the anesthesiologist asked one of the surgical orderlies to please step in and remove Dr. Heartsavitch's head from Ms. Drexinslaugh's abdomen. Dr. Heartsavitch fought hard against the orderly. After several minutes of non-sterile O.R. mayhem, the orderly finally prevailed and Dr. Heartsavitch was brusquely escorted out of the operating room. An extensive sterile saline water lavage was performed on Ms. Drexinslaugh's organs and the on-call surgical resident arrived to close Ms. Drexinslaugh's cavity.

Later, Ms. Drexinslaugh regained consciousness in the recovery room and received a whopping intravenous dose of antibiotics. Dr. M. Lloyd Flossaway, the Chief of Staff at Mt. Yobaybi arrived in the recovery room a short time after the drip was started. He informed Ms. Drexinslaugh that her operation was aborted due to an unexpected power outage and that she would be rescheduled for the procedure at a later date.

---

Dr. Toru Atama was the medical examiner for the county of Boca de la Cabeza Verde, the same county where the Mt. Yobaybi Medical Arts Center was located. But Dr. Atama's home base, the county morgue, was several miles away from Mt. Yobaybi. News of Dr. Heartsavitch's incident had not yet leaked out and into all corners of the county—leakage plugged by those in charge at Mt. Yobaybi.

Dr. Atama was performing an autopsy on a male murder victim brought in a few hours earlier. Other than a hole in the head, there was no visible sign of trauma, but the police knew it was a murder because the murderer said so. With Dr. Atama was his assistant Mr. Claude Spaniel.

Atama started the autopsy, recording his comments on the procedure, "The time is 3:32 p.m., August 5th. The body arrived at 3:17 earlier this afternoon, approximately three and a half hours after the deceased became dead. According to police, the victim is one Salvatore Oniasis, a muscular male about thirty-five years old. His body is shaped like a large bluefin tuna, but that is where the similarity ends. There appears to be no sign of physical trauma anywhere on the victim in spite of police reports indicating murder as the cause of death. On close examination of the head, there appears to be a large hole in the forehead of the victim about two inches above the left eye. At this time it is unknown if that is related to the case. What is the victim's weight Mr. Spaniel?"

"One-ninety, Dr. Atama."

"Approximate height?"

"Six feet, two inches."

After a routine, but extensive evaluation of the intact corpse, Dr. Atama, a skilled autopsy man, wasted no time in making the standard autopsy incisions along the front of the victim's torso. The rib cage was split down the middle of the sternum using a *Cutler-6000* bone saw in order to get access to the lungs and heart. With the aid of Mr. Spaniel, Dr. Atama was able to spread it all open wide. They secured the incision margins on both the thoracic and abdominal cavities in order to fully expose the contents and to get at all those organs. Examination of the contents then began.

Mr. Spaniel was dutifully carrying out the doctor's routine orders—weighing of organs, performing cursory surface surveys, suctioning, rinsing—when there was an obvious, eerily silent pause in the action. Dr. Atama was breathing heavily. Mr. Spaniel was concerned that Dr. Atama might be having a heart attack, but he did not want to go off half-cocked. Then he saw that Dr. Atama was staring down into the wide-open body cavity of the victim as if something in there had garnered his rapt attention. Had Dr. Atama discovered the cause of death? Was there something wildly abnormal and out of place in the victim's body? Were there mysterious organs in there? Suddenly Dr. Atama peeled back the edges of the autopsy incision even wider and penetrated his head directly into the chest cavity between the two halves of the rib cage. Dr. Atama then started vigorously mashing his face around on the dead man's exposed heart and lungs.

"Dr. Atama! Dr. Atama! No!" Spaniel cried out. He grabbed Dr. Atama by the shoulders and forcefully pulled Atama's head out of the murder victim's chest. Dr. Atama stood up, calm and collected, face covered with dark red liquid organics; but Atama was still in some kind of trance. Mr. Spaniel cautiously withdrew his hands from Dr. Atama, "What are you doing, Dr. Atama? That is highly unsanitary. What are you doing?"

The doctor did not answer and quickly plunged his face back into Mr. Oniasis, this time into the abdominal cavity. Atama began rolling his head around, immersing it as deeply as the dead man's displaced organs would allow. Soon Dr. Atama's face was completely lathered up with what remained of the victim's sticky torso fluids.

Mr. Spaniel called security and Dr. Atama was forcefully restrained until local authorities could arrive and assess the situation.

———————————————

Two incidents. Two respected doctors. Two reputations pissed away into the trough. Similar circumstances. Was this a coincidence? Yes and no. Was this merely random chance? People were already jumping to conclusions. Two people: one dead murder victim and one live surgical patient. Both of them already lawyered up.

———————————————

Tourists and gourmands from all over the world frequented the renowned New York City restaurant Chez Choutête. In that fine establishment, expensive wines, aged meats, odoriferous cheeses, and thick sauces made their way into the stomachs and post-gastric tubulature of countless customers. It has been said that the gastronomic wonders were so extraordinary that those who had partaken of them were extremely sad to see them leave their bodies a day or so later and go down the toilet...forever. Master Chef François Carême, in his role as Head Chef of the exclusive restaurant, was the reason for its outstanding reputation.

One particularly busy evening, Chef Carême was hard at work, managing the flow of culinary operations, when one of the assistants was taken ill and had to be removed from the kitchen—i.e. taken to the back door and tossed into the alley. Normally, at this point in the evening, Chef Carême would "make the rounds" and visit with the customers in the dining room. It was a Chez Choutête tradition that added a personal touch to the overall dining experience. But on this night, the missing assistant required Chef Carême to remain in the kitchen to lend a hand and keep things moving. While sautéing a skillet full of diced goat tail, he happened to notice that his sous chef was letting a large pot of *potage tomate a la tête* come to a rolling boil. It was a very thick soup, loaded with sugar, pureed tomatoes, nutmeg, and newborn lamb proteins. When cooked correctly, the soup was almost thick enough to eat with a fork. But high heat could cause it to scorch and the flavor of the entire batch would be ruined completely.

"Don't let that boil up like that, you numbskull!" Chef Carême shouted. "Where's your head?"

"Huh?" the sous chef replied.

Before the batch could become a total loss, Chef Carême took matters into his own hands. He shoved the inattentive sous chef to the side with an aggressive amount of temperamental vigor and began stirring the pot himself. The large pot of soup was saved; even if the diced goat tail was charred into an inedible crust of black, sponge-like material. *Potage tomate a la tête* was an especially popular menu item among those lucky enough to be able to frequent Chez Choutête. A repulsive, spoiled batch would not have gone down well with the customers.

While Chef Carême was stirring the pot, keeping a close eye on the temperature, he became entranced by the folds of creamy tomato as the spoon moved around in the thick mixture.

Marcus Dolét (an apprentice) was holding the smoking skillet of charred goat tail. "*Quel gâchis!* Chef Carême, what do you want me to do with this?" he asked Chef Carême. Chef Carême did not respond. A few seconds later Chef Carême submersed his head (completely) into the pot full of *potage tomate a la tête* and began vigorously thrashing his head around. Chef Carême, apparently, was unaffected by the heat or the lack of oxygen. The assistant dropped the skillet of charred goat tail to the floor and forcefully pulled Chef Carême's head out. The parboiled Master Chef staggered for a moment and Dolét helped him sit down on the floor. Everyone in the kitchen gathered around, staring at the Master Chef's head, now completely covered in *potage tomate a la tête*. Chef Carême's head, in its entirety, was scalded red so the color of his skin blended in well with the color of the soup. In the excitement, the *potage tomate a la tête* was neglected and it came to a vigorous boil. The batch was ruined and had to be tossed out the back door into the alley along with a skillet full of charred goat tails.

———————————

A New York City subway always has its share (perhaps more than its share) of oddball characters. Dalton Binker Weese was one such notorious character. A rainy October evening just after rush hour and Weese was up to his usual tricks. He waited. He was an opportunist and would only act if the conditions were right. He had never been caught. He had never paid the price for any of his actions. He was emboldened. The more success he had, the more emboldened he became. Finally, deep into the evening, the opportunity presented itself: an empty subway car and a potential victim. From outside the car he could see her sitting there, alone. She was a big woman, with huge globular bosoms bursting out from her blouse, barely under containment. Plenty of skin. Everything was just perfect.

Weese boarded the subway car and waited for just the right moment to strike. The subway started moving and it was time to act. He casually positioned himself near his victim giving her the impression that he was planning to exit at the next stop. Then, down he went, burying his face in between her breasts, vigorously massaging them with his hands. The surprised victim immediately stood up, causing her large, multi-stoned brooch to catch Weese in the nostril, lifting him up bodily. He fought to get free but his nose was securely held by the brooch, which, at that moment, was tugging mightily at the victim's blouse. Weese's weight pulled the victim forward and his struggling made her lose her balance. Weese's nose was now bleeding profusely. After stepping forward in an attempt to regain her balance, she tripped on Weese's trench coat and fell face first toward the floor, right on top of Weese. As the two of them were falling, Weese's head slammed into the metal edge of the nearby subway seat. Bouncing off the seat, his head continued on down to the floor with a loud rattling thud. Weese was unconscious and bleeding. The victim detached her brooch from Weese's nose and stood over him ready to kick his ass if he even tried to move before the next stop.

"Dalton Binker Weese, how do you plead?" the judge asked.

Weese's defense attorney quickly responded, "Mr. Weese pleads 'not guilty' by reason of *Capitosis Delirium*. He has volunteered to enter a De-Cap program immediately if your honor will grant him leniency in this case."

The judge responded, "To save time and expense in this case, and if the District Attorney gives his approval, I will order Mr. Weese to be given a complete evaluation by the attending psychiatrist at the St. Moses Roll State Hospital. This case shall be placed in abeyance until I can review the results of that evaluation, after which we shall resume these proceedings."

The District Attorney gave his approval and Mr. Weese was admitted to the St. Moses Roll State Hospital for the psychiatric evaluation. One week later, Mr. Weese was back in court, facing the same judge once again. It did not look good for the defense since the judge looked as if his robe was infested with sawgrass busy-fleas.

The judge started, "I have reviewed the results of Mr. Weese's psychiatric evaluation. In the opinion of the attending psychiatrist, Mr. Weese has merely attempted to use

*Capitosis Delirium* as a shield, as an excuse to justify Mr. Weese's blatant criminal sexual behavior. Multiple witnesses have identified Mr. Weese as the Bosom Bandit including Ms. X, here in court today—Ms. X, being Mr. Weese's latest victim. Mr. Weese claims that *he* is the victim in this case because his right nostril has been irreparably disfigured. That claim does not hold water since it was Mr. Weese himself that initiated the improper contact with the bosoms of Ms. X. The speciousness of the claim further discredits the already suspect arguments of the defense. With all of that in mind, I now ask you again: Dalton Binker Weese, how do you plead?"

"Guilty, your honor," the attorney for the defense stated with resignation.

---

College years are filled with firsts for young people. Many students must learn how to budget their money, budget their time, and do their own laundry. It was a typical fall semester evening and there were at least six university students present at the Stogie McDogue Wash 'n' Dry Laundromat. Numerous non-students were also working their bundles into the machinery. The thirty-two coin-op washing machines were in constant use and the eight large side-loading dryers were all full and spinning away. There were never enough dryers to handle all the wet laundry so the dryers were always in constant use and each dryer was usually stuffed to the maximum. Many times, cash-strapped students would even co-mingle their bundles in order to save money. On that fall semester night, an unusual situation developed, a highly improbable random occurrence: all eight dryers became available at the same time. As usual there was a mad rush to fill the dryers as soon as the previous user removed a dry bundle.

There they were: eight dryers completely packed with soggy wet laundry, ready to be activated for the drying process. The last load was finally in place and the patrons were inserting coins into the machines when suddenly, one of the students lost control and thrust her head directly into the dryer's opening. The student began thrashing her head about in the wet laundry in a mad, uncontrolled frenzy. Rather than react with bewilderment or shock, other patrons began doing the same thing, until all eight dryers were "in use."

Then began an additional frenzy. A fight broke out as other patrons fought to get "a piece of the action." It was "mob rule" as heads were pulled from dryers and new heads inserted—loaded wet laundry being set upon by one head after another. It was mayhem. Those that could not get a spot in one of the eight dryers attempted the same procedure using one of the top-loading washers as a substitute, but, as some found out the hard way, washing machine agitators do not provide enough room to admit entry to a human head. People on the street reported the chaos and authorities came in and broke it all up.

After the dust had settled, experts evaluated testimony from every patron that was involved in the incident. It was the first reported case of *en masse Capitosis Delirium*. A few of the students were not actually afflicted with *Capitosis Delirium*, but joined in the activity "just because." Human empathy and camaraderie compelled other non-sufferers to participate in the maelstrom of the moment as well. Sometimes it was a case of "others are doing it so I should be part of it; it might turn out to be something important." When all was said and done, many of the patrons preferred to re-wash their clothes rather than speculate on what kinds of fluids were left behind by all those heads.

———————

Whenever the President of the United States leaves the country on an official visit, it is news. When President Sauerlander visited the Belgian Prime Minister on a routine diplomatic mission, no one was expecting an international incident to develop that would wind up being seen worldwide.

The formal state dinner celebrating the visiting President was held at an official conference center in Mechelvoorde, just outside Brussels. Many heads of state were in attendance. As a show of respect for the American President, a large barbecue feast was prepared in his honor. It was packed with the usual "down home" elements: brisket, sausage, beans, cole slaw, corn on the cob, and potato salad. Entertainment included generic euro-style country and western music to which President Sauerlander responded with the comment, "Can you turn that horseshit down?"

All of the food was served buffet style to add to the simulated Western atmosphere of the event. First in line, as was his privilege, the President stacked massive slabs of fatty beef brisket onto his plate—then beans, corn on the cob, and some pretty weird-looking sausage. And plenty of sauce slathered over the beef. When he arrived at the giant bin of potato salad, there was no longer any room left on the Presidential plate. And the President wanted some of that potato salad. Aware that the whole world was watching, the President surmised that stacking his plate any further would appear way too gluttonous; it would definitely be bad public form. He pondered the situation as his aides, his entourage, and the rest of the world watched in typical reverence, hanging on his every movement. The President's extended pondering became so deep that the entire room began feeling uncomfortable and awkward. Suddenly, the President dropped his plate and dove headfirst into the potato salad bin, immersing his head in the massive mounds of rich, soft, creamy potato salad. He began blubbering and squirming, in and out, getting every square inch of his head layered and moistened in the chunky, delicious potato mixture.

Officials from the President's staff quickly stepped in to divert attention and avoid further embarrassment for the now pasty-faced commander-in-chief. But to everyone's surprise, the President stood tall, shook off the surrounding advisors, regained himself, and made an announcement to the group, "Rrrrr-ride 'em *cowboy!*"

He casually skimmed off chunks of potato from his face and ate some of the mayonnaise-y goodness as if nothing unusual had happened. With every movement, chunks of potato salad slowly began dropping off the back and sides of his head. The President's normally fluffy black head of hair was pasted down all over making him look more like a slick used car salesman than the head of the free world. While the shock held the honored guests suspended in time, the President was ushered out of the room into a holding area accompanied by his bodyguards and the secret service team.

In order to save face and reassure those in attendance, the President's press secretary, Marvin Groosthroat, stepped up to the dais and offered an explanation for the President's behavior. "Ladies and gentlemen, what you have witnessed is once again President Sauerlander's ingenious way of dramatically calling attention to pressing issues of our time—in this case, an affliction you all know as *Capitosis Delirium*. This condition can be found in every country around the world in a percentage of the people. Raising public awareness, that's what it's all about...and family...that's what it's all about. It is important when, as a leader...a leader with a high profile platform, someone like the President...one can truly make a difference...and that's what it's all about. I am sure the President will rejoin us a soon as he gets cleaned up by his staff. At that time he will have remarks. Thank you."

With that, Secretary Groosthroat rushed from the room back to the holding area where the President was sitting quietly as staff members removed the last vestiges of potato salad from his head and neck.

"What's happening out there?" The President asked.

"They're all wondering what's going on. What's going on?" Secretary Groosthroat inquired. "Are you feeling the effects of *Capitosis Delirium*? What is it? We need to know how to proceed...this incident...future incidents...the media. Oh God, videos, shit...cell phones...shit, shit, shit!"

One advisor cautiously approached the President, "Mr. President, sir, is this a case of *Pseudo-Capitosis Delirium* or is this the real deal, full-blown *Capitosis Delirium*? How long have you had it? Please, Mr. President..."

The President, in a very uncharacteristically flippant manner, then spoke up, "You bunch of nervous ninnies. I just felt like doing it; that's it, nothing more. I don't have *Captain Delirious*...whatever *that* is. Never heard of it. Don't plan to have it. What the hell is it? And who invited that little shit foreign minister Schlemmer to this chin wag? I can't stand that little toad."

———————————

Whether he intended to or not the President *did* raise awareness of *Capitosis Delirium*, all in one brief Belgian moment. Incidents that would have previously gone unreported began appearing in the press. Official caseloads mounted as the public became fascinated with the newly exposed condition. Was it contagious? Was it dangerous? Can you get it from a toilet seat? Was religion involved? Should it be? How about a deep tongue kiss during an episode? Is it sexually transmitted? Questions, questions, questions. And no answers.

Some episodes had frightening consequences. A teenager working in a popular fast food eatery in Newark, New Jersey plunged his head into the deep fry vat. Although the teen's skin was savagely burned by the incident, the hot oil did clear up the teen's rampant acne. Similarly, a Texas family was preparing to deep-fry an entire Thanksgiving turkey in their specially-designed backyard frying apparatus. Grandfather Big Daddy Glazer came over to the vat of hot oil and plunged his head into it. The enormous volume of oil was completely ruined and, as a result, so was Thanksgiving.

Road paving crews began fitting wire mesh to the rims of tar buckets to prevent road workers from inserting their heads into the hot black ooze. Occupational safety inspectors began requiring similar measures for mechanical cement mixers. Severe injuries and deaths: *Capitosis Delirium* was no laughing matter. Any head-sized open hole might seduce the next person to come near it—the hole coaxing that person to come inside, to head on in. Especially inviting were holes containing any kind of soft viscous fluid—a combination truly irresistible to someone afflicted with *Capitosis Delirium*. So many heads, so many holes. No one could possibly predict when or where the next outbreak might occur.

Having lost a fellow teammate in a *Capitosis Delirium* incident, sports legend Boleto Connolio commented, "I just can't get my head around it."

Media magnate Edward R. Blosso-Terpoline ordered his army of reporters to investigate, to find answers, to search high and low for details about this strange affliction. "Leave no stone unturned. We want the truth—in most cases—in some cases. And we want to be the *first*, the *first* to provide the public with those truths (and partial truths if need be). Let's put our vast resources to work for us. As far as we're concerned, we are the world's top media group. If, through it all, we wind up playing second fiddle in this thing, heads are going to roll."

Daily, doctors were being faced with the difficult task of informing loved ones about a family member's dreaded diagnosis. "I'm sorry Ms. Hyde, but your husband has come down with a case of...'The Cap'."

Detroitville, Nevada: Police Captain David Yarno was examining a victim whose entire head was encased in a thick block of rock hard cement. "Chisel off all that cement there," he ordered. "I can't make heads or tails out of this. Did anybody see the hole? *Another* damn head case for the record books. It's enough to make your head swim."

Every hole became a potential suspect, a potential threat. Chemical sprays were developed on a fast track. Urban streets were doused with the spray. No effect. Young and old alike lost their heads and panic became the rule in the streets. People who were not even afflicted with *Capitosis Delirium* began running around, rioting, like chickens with their heads cut off.

New Lisbon, Oregon: Mayor Oscar Springtyne pleaded with the public, "We're going to prevail over this problem, I promise you, but we must all keep our heads in this thing."

Every aspect of life was affected. Family gatherings became arguing fests over who was ultimately to blame for it all and what should be done about it. In polite society, people began to avoid anything associated with the topic of *Capitosis Delirium*. A simple coin toss became: "Tails or the other side." No student wanted to go to the head of the class any more. Military leaders and construction foremen began replacing the age-old "Heads Up!" with "Look Out!" or "Hey you! Out of the way!" Laundromats went out of business all over the country, the world. People were hoping the phenomenon would fade out of its own accord and society would someday achieve head immunity.

Even though incidents of *Capitosis Delirium* began to decrease, it soon became clear to scientists that the condition was never going to disappear completely. So people were going to have to adapt, to adjust, to tolerate its presence as just another element of living in the human community. Entire industries were born in the aftermath. Wire mesh was a particularly hot item. And although new cases were no longer newsworthy, people were very aware of the constant and ubiquitous presence of *Capitosis Delirium*...a mysterious presence, always there, always ready to strike.

———————

[The following is an excerpt from the proceedings of the annual convention of NUDA (The National Unlicensed Doctors Association). Addressing the group is Dr. Fritz Ischnitz, doctor and speaker.]

"Ladies and gentlemen, doctors, administrators, researchers, Mayor Barboboroius, and distinguished Professor Irving Folder. Welcome. I have been asked [air quotes] to speak at the opening session here today so that I may clarify and correct the record after my unfortunate appearance on the nationally-televised Paul Grease Show last week. Many incorrect and confusing things were said on that show, ahem...by me. So my task today is to present all the real facts, unfiltered, and unclouded by my personal opinions—the facts, as I see them. There are many familiar heads out there in this opening assembly and it is a pleasure to be able to address all of you despite the circumstances. I will keep my remarks brief so we can move ahead with our main agenda.

"Several months ago my colleagues and myself began seeing cases of the now infamous condition known as *Capitosis Delirium*. As we all know, this condition manifests itself as an uncontrollable urge to insert one's head into large open cavities, usually, but not always, cavities filled with heavy, viscous fluids and/or soft malleable solids. The condition was first *scientifically* recognized over a century ago when an outbreak occurred on a small Japanese shark-hunting vessel, the *Noshita*. The trouble began when one of the crew, assigned to tossing chum into the water to attract sharks, suddenly thrust his face and head directly into his freshly-filled chum bucket. He thrashed around for several minutes but was asphyxiated by the contents before any of the crew could extract his head from the bucket of bloody, oily, chopped fish heads and entrails. On the voyage back to the harbor, several other crewmembers attempted to engage in the same sordid activity. The Captain of the *Noshita* had to order all chum buckets emptied and secured to avoid any further incidents. At that time incidents like that went unreported, but the slow accumulation of cases in the literature made it necessary for those in the science community to pull their collective heads out of the sand and to start taking the condition seriously. But they never did.

"Since the *Noshita* incident, numerous clusters of "The Cap" have sprung up in various places all across the globe. Many times, years can go by (even decades) without a single reported case. And then Wham! [fist pounding on podium] without warning, *Capitosis Delirium* rears its ugly head. In those early years, research into the condition was supposed to show whether or not a contagion was involved. If one were found, cities were to be evacuated, streets cleared, entire city blocks were to be leveled, and anti-infectious counteragents showered over populated areas in order to avoid a panic. However, a new school of thought soon emerged. It was believed that The Cap might be a psychological compulsion brought to the surface by some repressed childhood trauma. In spite of the dedicated efforts of many researchers, definitive results were, unfortunately, indeterminate.

"With that historic context in mind, let us turn our attention to modern times and what we, as a society, have compiled into the *Capitosis Delirium* knowledge database; basically the current state of our knowledge. Everyone has probably seen or participated in a childhood activity known as 'bobbing for apples.' The *type* of fruit or bobbing target is not relevant. Does an impressionable young child develop some valuable personality insight about the self during this activity? Or does this seemingly innocent watery bobbing activity actually plant a seed in the fertile head of the little snapper—a seed that will grow and eventually lead to *Capitosis Delirium* later in life?

One thing cannot be denied: 'bobbing' for objects at an early age is an activity that carries with it more risk than previously believed.

"Let us now look to the animal kingdom. Many of us have seen a dog pacing around a lawn or grassy knoll, snuffling out one candidate area after another, looking for the perfect place to do its business. In some cases, the dog's sensitive olfactory apparatus will detect something very special on the ground—something that a human being cannot sense or understand. Whatever the unseen quality is, it causes the dog to do a face plant and rub its head all over the magic substance in a frenzy of delight. This action *may* be related to *Capitosis Delirium*, maybe not. We at NUDA believe that there is a link. We also believe that there are dogs that are too fastidious to rub their heads mercilessly into the ground, recklessly applying unknown substances to their heads and necks. This type of persnickety dog seems to find pleasure in a substitute activity: sticking its head out of an automobile window while the vehicle is in motion, preferably at high speeds. And I think everyone here has seen an example of this behavior. Ha ha. [silence]

"Now, I would like to clear up the confusion that I caused on the Grease Show by discussing several other different, but related, conditions. *Capitosis Delirium* should never be confused with an unrelated *pair* of conditions: *Decapitus Major* and *Decapitus Minor*. *Decapitus Major* is a compulsion to bite the head off of another individual. Although it is usually impossible for one human to bite the entire head off of another human, it does not keep those who are afflicted with *Decapitus Major* from attempting the maneuver. Some have resorted to biting off the heads of animals as a poor substitute, providing only *temporary* and unsatisfying relief from the compulsion. As for *Decapitus Minor*, the compulsion involves the sufferer going after the 'little head' of an individual. Our research shows that only about half of the population carries the target organ.

The last condition I would like to discuss is called *Fenestrae Exploratum*. In this case, the compulsion is to look into small holes to 'see what's in there' or to 'see what's on the other side.' For years, cracks and knotholes have been used to view ball games and other events without detection—primarily to avoid paying for admission. In less public venues, knotholes in fences have been used to see 'just what those weird neighbors are up to'—an activity that has been going on for ages. Keyholes and peep holes have been used to secretly observe sex acts and many otherwise private activities—also without paying in some case. Peep shows thrive by offering viewing holes, to people, for money. When it comes to *Fenestrae Exploratum*, any hole will do, and anything seen *through* the hole will satisfy the afflicted one...at least for a while.

"Before we begin our demonstration, let me come clean about the demo we did on the Grease Show. Yes, it *was* staged...fake. It made for good television and everyone was happy with it until the truth came out a few days later. I'll admit that if I could have gotten away with it I would have. Rest assured that our demo today will all be on the up and up."

[The following is an eyewitness description of Dr. Ischnitz's demonstration before the assembly.]

"Dr. Ischnitz started the demonstration, 'This demonstration is for those of you who have never witnessed a *Capitosis Delirium* incident and for the behavioral scientists in attendance to be able to observe the prodromal actions of an afflicted individual. So, we have with us today Mr. Nathaniel Goidextum. Mr. Goidextum, suffers from *Capitosis Delirium* and has volunteered to help us with this demonstration. He is in a soundproof room down the hall and will be joining us shortly.'

"Dr. Ischnitz then rolled out a long cart, about the length of a gurney. The cart was placed near the podium.

"Dr. Ischnitz continued, 'Here you see four large plastic containers, each one about the size of a small trash can. This first container is empty, the second one is about two-thirds full of tap water, the third is filled with maple syrup, and the last one contains a mixture of blenderized slaughterhouse offal, chicken fat, and blood. You'll notice that the containers are labeled with large lettering so you can distinguish between them from where you are sitting. I am going to rearrange these in a random order and then cover them with this sheet. After that we will bring in Mr. Goidextum. Mr. Goidextum has not been told the nature of this demonstration so I believe we're going to get an honest, and hopefully graphic, reaction out of him. Remember, this is a demonstration, not an experiment.'

"As Dr. Ischnitz covered the rearranged containers with a thick beige sheet he motioned to his assistant to bring in the subject. After a brief delay, Mr. Goidextum self-consciously entered the room. His entrance initiated a wave of low murmuring among the assembled researchers, scientists, and guests. Dr. Ischnitz then positioned Mr. Goidextum behind the cart with Mr. Goidextum standing and facing the audience.

"Dr. Ischnitz then remarked, 'Now Mr. Goidextum, I am going to remove this sheet. You may look over the items on this cart and do whatever you feel comes naturally.'

"Dr. Ischnitz whipped off the sheet dramatically, revealing the four containers. Mr. Goidextum began looking over the display. He then became very still as if in a trance. Members of the assembly also became very still and quiet, entranced by Mr. Goidextum. As Mr. Goidextum began to teeter forward, an occasional gasp could be heard from the crowd. He teetered, then tottered, first over one container, then another. He seemed to be resisting some hidden force. Then he leaned over the container labeled "Putrid Gook" and took a deep breath. Members of the crowd seemed restless but for the most part were very attentive; and very silent. Mr. Goidextum's face seemed to be changing color to a pale shade of green. Some of the attendees quietly rose halfway up out of their chairs, apparently to ensure that no behavioral detail was missed. A few were taking notes. The attendees could tell that Mr. Goidextum was fighting against some unnatural inner urge. It looked as though a *Capitosis Delirium* event was imminent. Mr. Goidextum fought the urge until he could no longer resist. In a spastic explosive blast from all engines, up came his entire stomach contents in multiple heaves, most of it landing in the water container in front of him. The upchuck came in surf-able waves and the quantity was really quite impressive. In no time the water container was full and Mr. Goidextum was assumed to be empty.

"'Well', Dr. Ischnitz commented. 'That didn't go as planned.' He covered his mouth and nose—presumably because the sizable Goidextum vomitus was pretty rank. Members of the assembly began vigorously discussing the odd turn of events amongst themselves. Dr. Ischnitz went to the aid of Mr. Goidextum who was still hovering over the full water-vomitus container. Mr. Goidextum seemed to be bracing himself for the possible arrival of yet another wave of barf.

"Then Dr. Ischnitz said, 'Come along Mr. Goidextum, let's get you over here where you can sit down.' Dr. Ischnitz did not appear to be very happy with the outcome of the demonstration as he attempted to grab hold of Mr. Goidextum's arm. Then, to everyone's surprise, Mr. Goidextum plunged his entire head into the container holding the water-vomitus mixture. He began shaking his head uncontrollably, splashing much of the contents all over the demonstration cart and Dr. Ischnitz.

"There were many different reactions from the assembly: regular applause; standing applause—obviously those unabashedly head over heels with the unexpected outcome; vigorous clinical discussions in small groups; note taking; sympathetic heaves and barfing; dry heaves; and discreet exits from the assembly hall.

"Dr. Ischnitz called for his assistant to come in and help collect Mr. Goidextum before Mr. Goidextum asphyxiated in the liquid. Once Mr. Goidextum was extracted and taken away, the few hardy remaining members of the assembly (about one third) settled back in their seats and waited for Dr. Ischnitz to make some final remarks."

[eyewitness account ends]

[Dr. Ischnitz]
"Thank you. Thank you. Thank you for your attention. We have seen here today a condition that has apparently been with humanity for a very long time—even though the phenomenon has, only recently, been identified *as* a phenomenon. And, given recent events, a phenomenon that cannot be dismissed easily. From early cave dwellers washing their faces in dank, algae-laden mud ponds brimming with tadpoles; to cowboys in the Old West dunking their heads into saliva-saturated horse troughs; to drunken college kids driving the porcelain bus and then taking advantage of the seductive bowl full of stomach confetti; to plumbers who must be especially cautious when working on toilets; to Mr. Goidextum who we have just witnessed here today. These are some of the faces of *Capitosis Delirium*.

"Some sufferers have embraced their affliction and have made the most of it. Divers diving from great heights plunge head first into water. (Although some divers will dive head first into almost anything, including murky, untested ponds with hidden rock structures.) Lion tamers routinely place their heads into the mouths of lions. Practicing dentists are usually safe from *Capitosis Delirium,* since a patient's mouth is much too small to set off an episode. But, as a side note, many individuals afflicted with *Fenestrae Exploratum* become dentists in order to satisfy their need to look into holes to 'see what's in there.' It is yet another example of channeling an affliction in order to become a productive member of society. The list goes on and on—

"What can be done? Don't know. Like an unwelcome relative who comes for a visit and never leaves, *Capitosis Delirium*, unfortunately, is here to stay.

"Current research leads the scientific community to believe that the condition is not contagious, *per se*. But it *may* be. Or not. Or it may be genetic. As such, in all cases and scenarios, prevention is currently the best way to stop a sticky situation from developing. We ask people to avoid peeking into open cavities containing viscous fluids, emulsions, and/or suspended solids. Seek supervision when using a toilet or bedpan. Avoid cooking in vats or pots larger than a human head. Remember that even the most innocent of comments may have consequences. For example, take care when saying things like, 'Why don't you go stick your head up your ass?' It may be just the type of trigger that can result in a serious *Capitosis Delirium* episode.

"If you suspect someone you know is on the verge of a *Capitosis Delirium* episode, call a *Capitosis Delirium* hotline before it's too late. If you yourself feel compelled to put your head into a container of amorphous liquids, don't do it. Seek help immediately. Wait until help arrives. If you find yourself as a repeat offender there is always Cap Immersion Therapy. Sufferers are allowed to immerse their heads in all sorts of substances, remaining immersed until they are just plain sick of it. If all else fails, group therapy is also available. These types of groups help build a sufferer's will against *Capitosis Delirium* urges. Members are seated in a circle surrounding a bucket of oatmeal. Individuals must force themselves not to immerse and, if necessary, others in the group will physically restrain an individual, preventing them from succumbing to the impulse. And always remember: there is no shame in admitting that you immerse.

"*Capitosis Delirium* is a condition that should not be taken lightly. We should be on the lookout for the early warning signs, especially in our youths: 'bobbing' for objects, perverse fascination with side-loading washers and dryers, cruise ship passengers popping heads in and out through open portholes. Public awareness: another weapon in the arsenal for mitigating the effects of this condition.

"I hope that my discussion here has helped to clear the air on this subject. I apologize for the blatant falsehoods and misinformation that I offered on the Paul Grease Show last week. I just didn't know what I was talking about. I also apologize for suggesting that the 'head', as referred to in the nautical sense, was somehow connected to *Capitosis Delirium*. I really *don't* know what's going on in the 'head' when a seaman goes in there. And let me just say this: those things I said about the president of the Gludcalf Tire and Rubber Corporation and his transsexual mistress, well those statements were apparently true.

"In conclusion, let me leave you with this thought: Times change. People change. Customs change. We must embrace change. Our response to *Capitosis Delirium* is evidence of our ability to respond to change. *Capitosis Delirium*—it gives a whole new meaning to the concept of someone 'giving head.' Thank you to my friends at NUDA and all of you in attendance. Now let us proceed with our scheduled agenda. Good day!"

# Furburger with Cheese

Late one night I drove my rig down Highway 48.
I came upon a diner, the worst in all the state.
The only place for miles and miles it smelled like somethin' died.
I sashayed through the parkin' lot and dared to go inside.

The floor was soft and sticky with coagulated gunk.
Owner kept adjustin' his reproductive junk.
A chef with chew tobacca drippin' from his jaw.
Waitress with a cold sore as big as Arkansas.

Hey waitress, hey waitress could I have a menu please?
I'd like to get my hungry mouth on your...Furburger with Cheese.
My salivatory lips all over that...Furburger with Cheese.

Gelatinated buttermilk and chicks just halfway hatched.
Fuzzy little biscuits and steak with skin attached.
If you're headed for the men's room, you'd better wear a mask.
As to why they keep it dark in there—hmmm...don't ask.

Hey waitress, hey waitress I'll have a soda please.
And tasty fries to complement your...Furburger with Cheese.
Tasty fries and hold the flies...Furburger with Cheese.

There was dog food in the chili and a hairball from a cat;
A dead bird in the salad with a condom for a hat;
Little bits of shiny metal in the black-eyed peas;
But nothin' could prepare me for the...Furburger with Cheese.
That greasy taste bud torment called the...Furburger with Cheese

A pesticidal grill-top and liquid hard-boiled eggs.
Somethin' in the mayonnaise does somethin' to your legs.
Spicy wings with feathers on that stick right to your chin.
Health department employees are never seen again.

Hey waitress, hey waitress, a paper bag, oh please.
I need a some place to off-load your...Furburger with Cheese.
Comin' up for off-load is your...Furburger with Cheese.

Saw a tampon in some meatloaf, some toenails in the pies.
And somethin' lookin' back at me from underneath my fries.
I coughed up seven dollars and soon was on my way.
That undigested burger still haunts me to this day.

Hey waitress, hey waitress. Painful memories.
When through my lips I passed that hairy...Furburger with Cheese.
Facin' down that evilicious...Furburger with Cheese.

# Down for the Count

Much has been written about Count Pouleé Aurniece Lavoisier and his profligate roué of a nephew, Zizanie Lemonstrui. As legends have it, a wandering vagabond named Neff murdered Count Lavoisier in his sleep, right in the Count's own bed. The people of the village of Prevaloir hired Neff to do away with the capricious Lavoisier. The destitute and disheveled Neff had scarcely been in town long enough to grab a mouthful of water before he was approached by several village elders with the nefarious proposition; a proposition of murder for hire.

The vagabond turned killer, Neff, wound his way by stealth through the corridors and passageways of the Palace Filiamort and into the bedchambers of the Count, where, with vigor unbounded, he proceeded to stab the Count repeatedly until—and long after—Count Lavoisier was dead. Before Neff could safely wind his way back out of the Palace and into the obscurity of the night, he was apprehended by André Depiliatoreé, the Count's close associate, confidant, and delusory myrmidon. Neff was immediately brought to justice by a swift and sure axe at the hands of Depiliatoreé. The vagabond's headless body was fed to the wolves of the forest by Depiliatoreé himself and some of his cohorts.

News of the Count's demise was received with unmitigated joy by the people of Prevaloir. As it turned out, the event warranted a double celebration—the Count was dead and because Neff had not demanded payment in advance, the village had the job done for free. Going against the general tradition of that period, the Count's title was then passed on to Zizanie and with it, all the Count's land, his hoard of gold, and of course the Palace—the Palace Filiamort. And, as so many legends go, this one was total bullshit. So herein lies the *true* story of the Count Pouleé Aurniece Lavoisier, late owner of the Palace Filiamort situated near the village of Prevaloir, and uncle to the miscreant Zizanie Lemonstrui.

Although Pouleé Aurniece Lavoisier was valueless as a human being, indulgent and vain, he somehow wormed his way into the good graces of the short-lived King Ornellierre IV. Lavoisier concocted a scheme whereby he would expose an assassination plot against the King's life, thereby becoming a hero and generating goodwill with the monarch. Even though there was no actual assassination plot, the skillful theatre of the fabricated event convinced the King that Lavoisier had saved him from being assassinated—i.e. Lavoisier's scheme worked. For that highly suspect accomplishment, Lavoisier was awarded the title of Count—much to his surprise and beyond his wildest expectations. With the title came a sizable tract of land in the county of Assener, and a vacant, centuries-old palace thereon. The property was covered with rolling hills and fields and stretched across nearly half the county. Within the boundaries of the property was the village of Prevaloir, a prosperous and autonomous village that seemed to get along fine for years without the presence of a noble resident in the palace. It was the only village in close proximity to the palace, the next nearest community being the much larger Ste. Pelotage which was at least a full day's ride from the palace—a two day round trip. Prevaloir, on the other hand, was within walking distance. Unfortunately Prevaloir's proud tradition of autonomy was to be completely scattered to the four winds when the titleless Pouleé Aurniece Lavoisier became *Count* Pouleé Aurniece Lavoisier.

Count Lavoisier knew nothing and cared nothing about the village of Prevaloir. He found no use for any of the peasants, craftsmen, alchemists, or merchants that lived and prospered there. All he was *ever* concerned about was his own comfort, his own indulgent lifestyle. By his side through this sudden rise to power—including, but not limited to, his "heroic" ingratiation with the King—was his childhood friend André Depiliatoreé. Depiliatoreé was a man of moderate height, slightly weathered, battle-tested, and very angular. Although Lavoisier relied heavily on Depiliatoreé's advice and assistance, André Depiliatoreé was evil, treacherous, and duplicitous right down to his curly yellow toenails. He manipulated the self-absorbed Lavoisier—machinations intended for personal gain— and so indulged every whim conjured up in the dark recesses of Lavoisier's supple and convoluted mind. Depiliatoreé *was* aware of the village of Prevaloir, but only considered the village as a resource, a resource that was there to be exploited in time of need.

Lavoisier's sudden appointment to the position of Count meant that none of the usual enforcement vehicles had yet been developed—there was no private army, no security force, no musclemen. There was nothing that could be brought to bear to enforce the Count's will or intimidate any of the people of the village. This was unfortunate for Depiliatoreé who, without such power, was like the toothless dog. So Depiliatoreé had to rely on the loyalty of a few individuals from the Count's inner circle and what little force they could muster. That, together with Depiliatoreé's will and tenacity, made Depiliatoreé a dog that could literally "gum" the villagers into submission.

Unlike André Depiliatoreé and his cohorts, most of Count Lavoisier's retinue and team of servants were filled with reverence for the duties that go along with a culture of nobility. They were steadfastly devoted to tradition and only to Lavoisier's title, not Lavoisier himself. So they enthusiastically carried out the duties that came with their stations; carried them out as if their individual tasks were assigned to them by the grace of Heaven itself.

Lavoisier's repulsive nature, vile personal habits, and odd sexual appetites were the bane of his desire for marriage and regularly available copulation—copulation that, if constant and relentless enough, would eventually result in an heir. But Lavoisier repelled so many prospective young maidens that, as word got around, no self-respecting female would have anything to do with him—not even the most desperate of those shamelessly desperate harbour women—the ones with the missing fingers and hairy tongues. And so, day after day, week after week, he slept alone in his feather bed, pampered by his pandering advisors and the other parasitic members of his limited court. With the lack of a suitable repository for the Count's seed, no offspring were expected to be forthcoming. And as a result of all that barrenness, Count Lavoisier's only legitimate heir became his nephew, Zizanie Lemonstrui. Zizanie knew very little about his uncle and lived far from the palace in a small winery town where he was employed as a taster where he tasted and tasted and tasted.

Count Lavoisier always demanded that his personal entourage accompany him wherever he might wander on the palace grounds (and presumably anywhere else in the county and beyond). In addition, the entourage was to remain out of sight, at all times, unless called upon by the Count for questions or tasking.

On a cold November day Lavoisier made a ritualistic promenade through the palace gardens. He wore his stiff long-coat with the gold brocade and the broad-hat with the multi-ruby pin that looked like a red egg. He paused, momentarily, to savor the fresh air—in unison, his entourage came to an abrupt halt as well. Looking high into the sky above the manicured line of hedges and trees, the Count rejoiced and personally acknowledged the divine splendor of his very existence. He reached into the top pocket of his long-coat and pulled forth his bejeweled box of exotic snuff. It was a rare type of snuff: pulverized tobacco imported from the far east; laced with herbs, spices, cinnamon, salts, and "other substances." It was a snuff so rare that only the vacant cavities of his noble nose, and his nose alone, were truly worthy enough to partake of the extraordinary mixture and to experience its fine qualities. But on this day his nose was to be denied the highly anticipated carnal pleasure that the powder would bring to him. His snuffbox was empty.

"What treachery is this?" the Count exclaimed. "A snuffbox emptied of its precious and powdery gifts? A bejeweled snuffbox—its normal contents having more value than all the gemstones clutching its gold and silver exterior? I shall have a word with the soul responsible and seek the removal of his inattentive head."

Despite his swagger and blustering, the Count had no such power of life and death. But he could, however, make miserable any individual who happened to offend him—an individual such as a lowly snuff valet, the person responsible for replenishing the snuff stores and keeping the Count's personal snuffbox full of appropriate quantities at all times.

The Count stormed off, entered the palace, and headed to the east wing parlor where he began a good deep sulk. There he recycled his feelings of deprivation and ruminated himself to sleep.

His staff was quick to react. Depiliatoreé asked the group, "Who is responsible for the Count's snuff supply? Why has the store of snuff been allowed to dwindle into nothing?"

Tired of serving in the palace of the capricious Count, the official snuff valet had long since fled from the county, vanishing weeks before the current snuff shortage came to everyone's attention. Only an unranked aide was available to respond at that crucial moment, "There has been no reliable supply for months. We do not know if there will *ever* be another shipment of that particular blend. We have no control over it."

"This cannot stand!" Depiliatoreé shouted. "We must find a new source; something that will satisfy the Count and save us from the miseries that he will surely bestow upon all of our grievously fragile heads." Depiliatoreé took aside his trusted confidants and tasked them, "Go to that Prevaloir village, gather what snuff there is, and fetch it back to the palace forthwith. And bring with you herbs and spices. We shall concoct a substitute snuff substance that will spasm the Count's nostrils right up into his eye sockets."

It must be said that the "other substances" that could be found in the Count's now-depleted snuff mixture were most likely the primary reason for the Count's preference for it; substances, toxic and non-toxic, addictive, and even some with anesthetic qualities.

Every few months following Pouleé Aurniece Lavoisier's installation as Count, the Count's men would go to the village and harry the residents, looking to return to the palace with whatever whimsical item the Count had demanded—salt, fruits, bread, metal goods, leather, laces, teas, buttons, string, toys, and many other (mostly trivial) items. Many times they would turn the village upside down in their search for the urgently needed article. Sometimes threats were used and rarely (if ever) were the villagers compensated for anything the Count's men wound up confiscating.

Now, the need was for snuff. The Count demanded it. Depiliatoreé was expected to deliver it. So after the short journey from the palace to the village, Depiliatoreé's designated entourage of eight or so henchmen (including Depiliatoreé's trusted aides Chameau DuHumpois and Tortus LeHare) fanned out into the streets of Prevaloir, rousting the inhabitants and demanding that all available snuff be handed over immediately. The pattern had become so familiar that the villagers learned to obfuscate, delay, and through a cooperative effort, cleverly hide anything that the Count's men were planning to run off with.

"Snuff? I have no *snuff*. What is snuff?" the village blacksmith replied when confronted with a demand for the substance. All the other villagers had similar responses to the aggressive demands. The villagers seemed to know nothing of "snuff." How humorous (or opportunistic) the villagers might have found it had they known that snuff was something the Count planned to stick up his aristocratic nose.

"Up his *nose*?" was the reply of the village seamstress when Chameau reluctantly revealed the purpose of the snuff. "I have something he can stick up his nose," she said, waving a knitting needle in the face of Chameau. She was lucky that Chameau was too overly concerned about the dire consequences of returning to the palace with nary a particle of the precious substance than to gather what she meant by her remark.

Despite upending everything in the village there was no snuff to be had. With the failure to find any (or even a poor substitute), the Count's men turned toward the palace; to return and face the wrath of Depiliatoreé and the whining of the Count—two fates that were sure to befall them by returning empty-handed.

Then a thin, wrinkled old man in a beret approached Chameau from behind. Chameau had been making sure everyone knew he was in charge of the expedition, although Tortus LeHare had just as much authority (if one could call it that) in the autonomous village. The old man tapped Chameau on the shoulder. Startled, Chameau whipped himself around like a frightened squirrel.

Even though Chameau was feeling a little embarrassed by his nervous reaction, the old man ignored it and, eye to eye with him, informed Chameau, "I know of an old woman who sells potions, and elixirs, and powders; powders, yes. Splendid powders. *She* may have what you're looking for. Her magic shoppe is two streets over and around the corner, just a block from the edge of town. You are probably not familiar with the place since Mme. Represailles set up her shoppe only recently."

Intrigued and freshly energized, Chameau ordered his group to follow as he briskly marched down the road and around the corner to the shoppe. Over the door was a newly-minted sign: Mme. Represailles' Magic Shoppe. The shoppe was small but very dense with products, well organized from floor to ceiling. Shelf after shelf was stocked with small bottles and boxes. And there on a tall stool behind the counter was the old woman that the wrinkled old man spoke of.

"We need snuff!" Chameau announced while waving his fist. He was wasting no time in identifying his official purpose. The old woman stroked her chin and squinted one eye, using the other eye to give Chameau and his crew the once over. Without saying a word, the old woman took out a small square box from under the counter and with two fingers, placed it delicately in front of Chameau.

"Is this all you've got?" Chameau blustered, brashly grabbing the box and opening it. The contents *looked* like snuff, but was it the real thing? "Is this powder snuff?" Chameau asked.

The old woman just shrugged, wrinkling her nose and squinting at the well-dressed squad of noble errand boys.

"Well, it *looks* like snuff," Chameau remarked. "How much for the box?"

"Forty pieces of gold, Old Siege," Mme. Represailles said in a raspy high-pitched voice. It was the first time she had said *anything* to Chameau or his men.

"Old Siege? What? You crazy, you foul old woman!" Chameau said. He thought the price was outrageous—even though he was planning on stiffing her for the box anyway. So he put the lid back on the box and stormed out of the shoppe, box in hand. His group of official toadies scurried around right behind like a bunch of pots and pans attached by twine to the back of a carriage.

The old woman left her stool and hurriedly ran to the door, watching the group round the corner at the end of the block as they headed back to the centre of town—triumphant, fulfilled, energized with renewed dispatch. "Old Siege! You bastard!" she said in a normal voice. "Puff!" She was smirking a smirker's smirk as she said it. "Puff!"

Chameau was so anxious to get back to the palace with the newly-acquired snuff that he would not have noticed the old woman's epithets even if they had been delivered by the lungs of a thousand-pound howling wolf. Chameau, Tortus, and the entire entourage came together in the town square and getting themselves organized in a fog of achievement, they made for the palace, priceless snuff in hand.

When Chameau arrived back at the palace, the Count was walking about in the long side corridor that provided a view of the garden and beyond. He was pacing, deep in thought with his arms clasped behind his back. Depiliatoreé, who was sure that the Count was still ruminating over the depleted snuff, saw Chameau arrive and inquired, "Have you got anything for me?" He spoke as if miracles were routine, expected, and ordinary; he considered those who provided said miracles to be merely instruments in the delivery of them. It was not a good way to motivate people unless a generous dose of fear was applied as well—either that, or the never-quite-fulfilled promise of being one of the privileged few to bask in the effulgence of noble power. Chameau handed the box of powder to Depiliatoreé. Depiliatoreé was more than willing to take credit for acquiring the item. The effulgence was what motivated Chameau in the face of Depiliatoreé's constantly dismissive attitude.

Abruptly turning away from Chameau, Depiliatoreé shouted out to the Count, "Good news, sire!" He trotted anxiously toward the Count with box in hand, leaving Chameau in the lurch—dumping him like so much royal garbage. (Ah, but Chameau was basking in the effulgence: he was in the presence of nobility; he was breathing the same air as the noble Count, in the same gilded corridor, no less! Ah!)

"We have found snuff for your noble nose!" Depiliatoreé announced with excitement.

"Yes, yes," the preoccupied Count replied. "Never mind that now. I have more important things on my mind. I have not heard from the Viscount Sir Rocktatum about those twelve steeds. I should demand an audience so that we may do our business. What is he waiting for? What seems to be the delay?"

"But, the Viscount is on his way here now, as you requested," Depiliatoreé replied.

"On his way *here*? Now? Why was I not informed?"

"You *were* informed, sire, just before your disappointing experience with the empty snuffbox. With so much going on, the Viscount was probably the least important thing occupying your sublime mind."

"Ah…yes! Well then, arrange a meeting as soon as he arrives. You said you have something for me? Well, what is it? Hup, hup!"

"Sire, your snuff," Depiliatoreé said. He made a shallow bow with one arm behind his back as he handed the little square box to the Count. Lavoisier opened the box and saw that it contained a powder that appeared to be snuff. He then withdrew his own bejeweled box from his pocket and handed both boxes to Depiliatoreé.

"Here," Lavoisier said to Depiliatoreé.

Depiliatoreé took the boxes and transferred the powder from the little square box to the Count's bejeweled snuffbox. The contents of the small box only half-filled the Count's own box, but it was enough to soothe the Count's mood and keep everyone safe from any possible Count vitriol—at least for the time being. Lavoisier took a pinch from the box and up his nose it went.

"Mild. Very mild, splendidly nasal. Even the slack-roped mucous and glazed hairs of my nostril grotto tingle with the aromatics from this fine mixture! You have done well, my friend." Lavoisier walked on by, leaving Depiliatoreé standing alone in the corridor in much the same way as Depiliatoreé had turned from Chameau just minutes earlier. While the Count was exfoliating his delight all over the corridor, Chameau retreated into the adjoining room (out of sight and out of mind) and Depiliatoreé crept out of the corridor in the other direction (most likely so he could go off and grind his axe).

When Count Pouleé Aurniece Lavoisier awoke the next morning he felt that something was very wrong. He always remained ensconced in the luxurious folds of his bed until aroused by the arrival of Depiliatoreé who would be bringing with him news (usually none or made up); the day's agenda (usually limited and always made up); or food (usually enough quantity and selection for a roomful of people). When Depiliatoreé did finally arrive, the shock on his face gave Lavoisier a start.

"Your nose, sire!" Depiliatoreé remarked. "Your nose!"

Lavoisier jumped from his bed and rushed to the mirror. What he saw was not a sight for the faint of heart. Overnight, his nasal septum had been eaten away—instead of sporting two nostrils as most noses do, his nose now had one big wide opening, a kind of grotesque smiling nose—an open smile, a small toothless smile. Even though his nose was now permanently graced with an odd smile, Lavoisier's mouth displayed no such smile.

It was a nose grotesque, very grotesque. And of course any and all contents of his nose—to include his slack-roped mucous and glazed hairs—were now openly on display to anyone who might be unfortunate enough to get a glimpse of his face.

"What has happened to me?" Lavoisier said in disbelief. He fell back onto his feather bed. He knew not how to ponder such a tragedy—not that his face was that much more ugly because of it.

"I can send a message to the official Médicine du Jour in Ste. Pelotage, but it will be two days before he will arrive. And as you most certainly recall, sire, you have a meeting with the Viscount this afternoon, ostensibly to discuss the purchase of the horses." As he spoke, Depiliatoreé's attention was constantly being diverted to Lavoisier's wide uni-nostril. With each noble breath, the sides of Lavoisier's nose around the gaping orifice were pulsating in and out. The intermittent revealing of the contents was disconcerting yet fascinating at the same time. How was the meeting with the Viscount going to be affected with the Count's nose behaving in such a way?

The Viscount and his group arrived in the early afternoon. Their carriages were lined up in the parkway by the entrance to the palace. The sun was high in the cloudless sky causing each member of the Viscount's group to squint hard against the brightness. From inside the palace's entryway it looked as if the Viscount and his entourage were a hostile fore-party, come to declare war and to strike the first few blows themselves. There were four gentlemen, besides the Viscount, and a floridly-perfumed lady with tall white hair and plenty of matronly and noble gravitas.

As the visitors milled about in the palace drawing room, they were quite puzzled and somewhat put off when Count Lavoisier arrived to meet them with his face bandaged across its middle, obscuring his nose completely and most of his face as well. The placement of the bandage forced the Count to breathe heavily and noisily through his mouth. For a formal meeting of two somewhat important houses of nobility the Count's presentation of himself left much to be desired—both politically and personally.

The Viscount Sir Rocktatum started right in, "We have traveled a long way to discuss our business concerning the twelve stallions. May I present Mademoiselle Passerina Laurent from Titulaire, she is the proud owner of the dozen hor...what has happened to your face?"

"A royal nosebleed, nothing more," Lavoisier replied, dismissing the question in an attempt to divert the attention of the group. "Before we begin, let us indulge in a flask or two of brandy, of cognac. Lavoisier signaled to one of the aides to produce a flask of cognac forthwith. The aide left the room. Friendly banter commenced in earnest among the roomful of nobility but nothing was said of horses or of the highly visible white bandage while the aide was out fulfilling his mission. When the aide returned, he was empty-handed.

"I am sorry, sire, but there is no brandy to be found anywhere in the palace."

"But we have stores of the finest cognac in all the land!" Lavoisier replied. "It is the finest. How is it possible that we have no more? Depiliatoreé! Depiliatoreé!"

Depiliatoreé jumped from the shadows to the side of his Count, "Yes?"

"See that this cognac shortage is corrected immediately!" Lavoisier wanted to appear "completely in charge" in front of his distinguished guests. Truth be told, Lavoisier could not tell the difference between a fine cognac and water dredged up from an open sewer.

"Sire, it is two day's journey to Charente and a full day to Ste. Pelotage," Depiliatoreé said.

"And when shall we have cognac again?" Lavoisier was looking at his guests and not at Depiliatoreé.

"Uh...at least two days...sire," Depiliatoreé replied. He did not want to promise *anything* definitive from the village of Prevaloir.

Negotiations between the two sides of the stallion deal proceeded without incident, in spite of the tragic lack of social lubrication in the form of fine cognac. But while polite conversation, congenial banter, and discussions of an equestrian nature were taking place in the Count's drawing room, all of the significant palace hands were off, once again, to the village of Prevaloir to acquire cognac, hopefully the finest that the village could offer. Depiliatoreé would seem like wizard if he could produce the substance in a few hours, much less two days.

Again the acquisition group was led by Chameau and Tortus, tasked with acquiring the required cognac in a timely fashion and returning to the palace before the Viscount had a chance to retire for the evening. Depiliatoreé stayed behind to monitor the stallion deal—which, of course, he was instrumental in helping to arrange.

"Cognac? Never heard of it," the village blacksmith said when confronted with the Count's men once again. "You might check the tavern over there. They sell spirits."

With the Count's group in tow, Chameau and Tortus plowed headfirst into the tavern, bluntly interrupting the festivities with their bold entrance. "We are here to acquire a quantity of cognac," Tortus demanded, supplanting Chameau who was preparing to say the same thing. Tortus made a dramatic gesture with his fist, one meant to inspire quick action in the presence of a noble entourage.

The tavern keeper, chewing on an olive, replied, "We do not have cognac here. Cognac no. Ale, aye, but no cognac. No brandy of any kind. We are a modest business in a modest but prosperous village. People here have simpler tastes. No one here can afford such a thing, but if so they would not shell out for fancy spirits like cognac."

Chameau stepped in, supplanting Tortus, "Your quaint ways and folksy attitudes are of no concern to us. If you do not have cognac, or any other kind of brandy, then where might we find the precious liquid so craved by the Count and his guests? Where, I say? Spit it out, man! Spit it out!" Chameau demanded.

Obliging the Count's representative, the tavern keeper spit out an olive pit onto the floor of the tavern right in front of the supplanting duo. As Tortus watched the pit roll to a halt, the tavern keeper offered, "You might try Mme. Represailles' Magic Shoppe across the square and around the corner." He and all the patrons were anxious to resume their rudely interrupted afternoon tavern festivities. But, as a group, they did not want to give the Count's men the impression that there was anything festive or pleasurable going in the tavern...at all. So the patrons sat like statues as long as the entourage was hovering about in the tavern.

"Across the square and around the corner—" the tavern keeper repeated.

"Yes, yes. We know where it is," Chameau replied. As the group left the tavern, Tortus turned to look back at the room full of statues, nearly all of them displaying shit-eating grins, the tavern-keeper among them.

Chameau knew the exact shoppe mentioned by the tavern keeper. Reluctantly, Chameau and *his* group took it upon themselves to return to the old woman's shoppe while Tortus and *his* group went to the square and waited.

Mme. Represailles immediately recognized Chameau as the Count's oily knave who failed to produce payment for the powder she offered him just the day before.

Chameau started right in, "Before we get down to our current business, old woman, the snuff you gave us during our last visit ate out the inside of Count Lavoisier's nose. Now, for your information, I have no particular love for what goes on inside the Count's nose, but I also have no desire to suffer *his* wrath or that of Saint Depiliatoreé over some dangerous product acquired here in your shoppe."

"I never called it snuff, Old Siege," the old woman said. She began picking at her fingernail, occasionally chewing on it.

Being an artful scoundrel himself, Chameau recognized good chicanery when he experienced it—or *thought* he had experienced it. Nevertheless, he would not allow himself to be fooled a second time.

"We need cognac. A substantial amount of fine cognac. I shall taste it and confirm that it *is* cognac before I pay you a single penny."

The old woman spit out a piece of her fingernail causing Chameau to back off before the wet fragment could land on his waistcoat. "Ahem! I believe I have just what you are looking for," the old woman replied. She disappeared through the curtained doorway into a hidden back room. She was talking to herself as she bustled about noisily. When she returned she was carrying a large jug. "Try this, Old Siege."

Chameau grabbed the jug and uncorked it. "Fine way to store quality cognac—if indeed this *is* cognac—a clay jug with a rotten cork in it. For all I know this could be fermented swamp water meant to eat out the Count's bowels by morning."

Chameau took a few sniffs before sampling the liquid. Then down went the sample. He smacked his lips as he allowed the flavor to waft through his biscuit hole and all through his nazum. "Why, this is the finest brandy...cognac I have ever tasted. Its fine quality seems to linger and linger...it...here, try this."

Chameau gave the jug to his aide, Bulbois, a more educated member of Chameau's cognac acquisition group. Bulbois took a generous swig, making slurping and smacking noises rivaled only by those of a beaver's tail slapping mud into place on its dam. The lip-smacking Bulbois gave his full approval stating, "It has the elements of juniper and is...oh so sweet...yet oh so tangy. I am at once repulsed by its graininess and yet intrigued by the mucid texture of its viscosity. There is a hint of melon...or is it hibisc..."

"Ok, that's enough there. I don't know about your description, Bulbois; I don't understand all that, but I trust your assessment of its quality," Chameau said. Chameau then had the others in the group sample the product as well. Each in turn agreed that it was the finest thing they had ever tasted. But they each had their own opinion about what exactly the flavor was—Chameau had to grab the jug and cut short the sampling before the entire contents of the jug were gone. He took one last sip for good measure.

"Let us be off, gentlemen," Chameau commanded, re-corking the jug and making for the door.

"What about my payment, Old Siege?" cried the old woman, giving them all the fish-eye.

"Think of this as a gift, a tribute to the glory of Count Lavoisier," Chameau replied, laughing loudly along with the members of his entourage. There is a theory that the louder the laugh, the more insincere it is. Chameau's cackling might be considered evidence to support that supposition. Once again, Chameau met up with Tortus and the others in the square. Chameau was brandishing the jug of liquid as if it were a trophy, evidence of some great achievement.

When the cognac acquisition group arrived back at the palace they were intercepted by Depiliatoreé, who was glad to relieve Chameau of the heavy burden imposed by the jug. Count Lavoisier and the Viscount's entourage were still engaged in the same sorts of polite tongue-rattling that had been taking place for the last several hours. The stiff and formal conversation was a fine example of how carefully nobles tread in polite company in order to maintain decorum and avoid some inadvertent offence. The fire in the fireplace had been maintained, hour after hour, but was now beginning to burn itself out. An odd assortment of putrid beverages and musty stale canapés was brought in at various times, the only thing to interrupt the flow of the substance-bereft conversation. To someone like Depiliatoreé, it always seemed peculiar and unnatural how these aristocrats could spend hours sitting motionless, maintaining meaningless discourse while outfitted in the most stiff, hot, and constricting apparel known to man or woman.

"We have brought you cognac, sire...and...honored guests," Depiliatoreé exclaimed to group, again taking full credit for something he had nothing to do with. He carefully concealed the clay jug behind his back. It would be poorly received by the guests if such a common battered vessel was being used to contain something so fine as a rare cognac. He motioned to Tortus—the last member of the cognac acquisition group still present—to take the jug and to prepare a tray for the group.

After a few minutes, Tortus reappeared with a tray holding the brandy snifters. Tortus transferred each cognac-loaded snifter from the tray to the glass serving table near the centre of the room. Then, in turn, each member of the group took one.

Count Pouleé Aurniece Lavoisier raised his snifter and offered an official toast, "To twelve fine horses. May they find their new home as agreeable as their last." With that, each member of the group—having spent the entire afternoon bandying about phrases and topics without so much as single *palatable* refreshment—took a substantial swallow of the cognac. The response was immediate.

Mademoiselle Laurent stated unequivocally, "That is the finest-tasting spirit I have ever had the pleasure to put in my mouth."

The response from the Viscount was equally as immediate and energetic, "Bbbbbbllllooooooeeew!" Out came the entire cognac sample onto the glass serving table and further onto the plush oriental carpet and even further onto Count Lavoisier. Depiliatoreé had a similar reaction, although his spittle did not reach the Viscount since most of it was intercepted by Mademoiselle Laurent's tall white hair.

"I have never tasted anything so horrid! Are you trying to poison us?" the Viscount queried, vigorously wiping off his lips and continuing to make dry spitting noises.

Count Lavoisier had the same reaction as Mademoiselle Laurent: it was a fine cognac, the best he'd ever tasted. What could the Viscount be thinking, or tasting. Was he just trying to make trouble? Others in the room had varying degrees of love or disgust. Everyone present was having a different reaction to the taste of the cognac. However, this strange phenomenon was not readily apparent to those directly involved, and as a result, comments and arguments mixed with strong opinions poured forth, replacing the banal and constrained conversational blather that was the norm through the entire afternoon—verbiage and emotion stifled and pent up for hours like water behind a dam. As the arguments over the cognac intensified, members of the noble group almost came to blows—half with a foul taste in their mouths and the other half relishing every moment that the cognac was part of their oral fluids.

Count Lavoisier was not pleased with Depiliatoreé and Depiliatoreé was not pleased with his cognac acquisition team, in particular Tortus LeHare and Chameau DuHumpois.

Depiliatoreé would have been uncontrollable if he knew that the cognac had come from the same place as the snuff that had eaten out the Count's nose. Before anyone realized, Count Lavoisier and the Viscount Sir Rocktatum were standing and arguing, face to face, with Lavoisier's mouth-breathing providing an additional olfactory insult to the Viscount's own nostrils.

The "discussion" was no longer about the wretched taste of the cognac—the "discussion" had taken an ugly turn, devolving into personal insults and challenges to manhood. Both men wanted satisfaction. No longer contained nor restrained at that point, the incident finally turned violent as the two gentlemen brought pushing and fisticuffs into the proceedings. Rather than intercede, the other nobles in the room preferred to allow the gentlemen to settle their differences manhood-style, keeping the battle strictly confined to the two offended parties. Given the culture of the time, it was not an unexpected response by the nobles in the room. Custom dictated that they should consider themselves a *part* of the action by merely participating as observers. Of course Mademoiselle Passerina Laurent, closely observing the action through her spectacles-on-a-wand, was most certainly above it all—distinguished, detached.

Those to whom the cognac's flavor was delightful continued to sip it. Depiliatoreé was not among that group and was still trying to get the taste out of his mouth. The manly confrontation between the Count and the Viscount soon became a highly destructive spectacle. Chairs and tables were upended. Precious ceramics and other *objet d'art* came crashing to the floor. The glass serving table was shattered and the serving tray was briefly used as a bludgeon.

During the melee, Count Lavoisier's facial bandage was easily dislodged. After several additional blows from the Viscount, the bandage came undone entirely and fell loosely to the floor. Of course this revealed the Count's hideous pulsating nose hole—and by extension much of the contents therein—to everyone in the room. The ghastly reveal took the Viscount by surprise and by dropping his guard for a moment he inadvertently allowed Count Lavoisier to gain the advantage. A bleeding and battered Lavoisier socked the Viscount square in the face with a terrifying blow, breaking his nose and putting him into a stagger that saw the Viscount fall backward into the room's open fireplace. The tip ends of the Viscount's coattails were set on fire almost immediately. When the Viscount detected that the burning material might commence to roast his arse he launched himself into the air, carrying with him the flaming coattails. To the other (observing) nobles the Viscount appeared to be a fiery comet crossing the room. The Viscount hurriedly tore off his coat to avoid any damage to his skin after which he stomped out the flames on the Count's exquisite oriental rug, over-dramatizing the entire effort. He then placed his once-threatened derriere upon the edge of a nearby overturned chair. At that point, with the men so separated, an observer might be challenged if asked to choose whose nose was producing the most effusive bloody output.

An exhausted and bruised Count Pouleé Aurniece Lavoisier had fallen back into the corner of the room and watched the fiery display unfold. The Viscount Sir Rocktatum, breathing heavily, his pride in the crapper, was content to remain seated on the edge of an overturned chair with his hands on his knees. When the entire incident was over, both Count Lavoisier and the Viscount Sir Rocktatum had incurred extensive injuries to their faces, ribs, and nether regions, and the formal attire for both gentlemen was damaged far beyond the likelihood of repair. The beautiful oriental rug was ruined with large stains of cognac, blood, and charred coattails. Neither of the two nobles had received satisfaction, nothing was accomplished, and the most severe casualty of the fracas was the highly tentative stallion agreement reached earlier—the twelve horses were no longer hoofing it on the negotiating table.

Rather than staying the night at the palace, as was originally planned, the Viscount's entourage gathered itself together and abruptly left the palace mid-evening, destination unknown.

The next morning the Count had no desire to do anything but remain completely immobile in his bed. When Depiliatoreé came into the Count's bedchamber around noon, Count Lavoisier was lying flat on his back and producing an occasional groan.

"I guess there are no horses for Count Pouleé Aurniece Lavoisier today, eh, André?" Lavoisier said rhetorically in a deep wavering nasal voice.

"No sire," said Depiliatoreé. "I believe that deal is dead."

In spite of his ulterior motives in everything to do with the Count, Depiliatoreé did feel pity for the battered, bloodied, one-nostriled specimen he saw lying in front of him. The Count's face was bruised and one eye was swollen shut. There was a sizable bump on the Count's forehead. On closer examination, Depiliatoreé noticed that the Count had lost several teeth, some upper and some lower; and there appeared to be bleeding still going on from an unknown source in the Count's mouth.

Depiliatoreé called out for an aide; called for *two* aides. Tortus and Chameau both responded to the cry for help with a prompt appearance in the Count's bedchamber. Depiliatoreé wanted to hack the pair of them to death.

"Have we anyone conversant in the medical arts?" Depiliatoreé demanded with thinly veiled anger in his tone.

Chameau spoke up, "Only old Aguisy, the stablemaster, but he only knows hor..."

"Bring him here, forthwith," ordered Depiliatoreé. "You, Tortus. Make haste, you bumbler, and help me clean up the Count before the stablemaster arrives." While Chameau was fetching the stablemaster, Tortus and Depiliatoreé did their best to make the Count presentable.

When Chameau returned, he timidly presented, not old Aguisy, but young Duidecima, old Aguisy's daughter. She was a self-contained, independent, muscular woman that could overpower even the most headstrong and intransigent of the palace horses. She had been rudely interrupted in her daily stable duties and was not feeling particularly cooperative—especially having been summoned to appear in the Count's bedchamber for some unknown purpose; something potentially awful.

Upon seeing the burly woman in her scruffy stable clothes Depiliatoreé asked impatiently, "Chameau, why have you brought that woman here? Who in Frumhole's Tomb is she?" Had Depiliatoreé not been preoccupied with the Count's condition he would have most certainly surmised the woman's occupation from the stable bouquet alone.

"This is old Aguisy's daughter, sire," Chameau replied.

Taking charge, Depiliatoreé broke in, "Sire, per your orders, old Aguisy was dispatched to Ste. Pelotage to purchase a considerable amount of tack for the new set of horses. The twelve hor..."

Sitting on the side of his bed, Lavoisier did not want to hear any more about the twelve horses; he was blubbering and mumbling with his damaged mouth, "One dozen stallions...horses...damn Rocktatum...horses...most likely jackasses, the lot of them I'd wager...twelve of those—"

Stepping up, Chameau chimed in, "Sire, this is Duidecima. She has acquired a modicum of knowledge of the...ahem, medical arts from her father." Duidecima was feeling punchy after being rousted out of her familiar domain and brought here to do who-knows-what. But Chameau's firm grip on her arm was keeping her from fleeing the scene.

"She'll have to do," Depiliatoreé said. Then he spoke to Duidecima, "See what you think of the Count's injuries." This was the first time anyone told her why she was brought here.

Somewhat relieved as to the real purpose of the visit, Duidecima responded, "I know nothing of working on men, human men. I only know horses and the like; mules, asses, ponies. Besides, the Count is swathed in bedclothes and robes. I wouldn't be able to make any worthwhile observation..."

"Clear the room. All except Duidecima," ordered Depiliatoreé. With that, Depiliatoreé, Duidecima, and the Count were left alone in the bedchamber. Count Lavoisier was in no position to resist as Depiliatoreé stripped the Count naked except for a small handkerchief provided to him for modesty's sake. Expecting Duidecima to shy away from the task, he was surprised when she attacked the evaluation with all hands on deck. However, she was used to handling much larger and much more uncooperative beasts, so as she palpated various areas on the Count, she did so with a very strong and indelicate hand. When it came to evaluating the Count's mouth...well, everyone has seen an individual unceremoniously lifting up a horse's lips to expose the teeth in order to get a good look-see.

For Count Lavoisier, it was the first time in years that he felt the touch of a woman—it offered him some recompense for being kneaded like so much bread dough; a kneading accompanied by a fair amount of pain.

As she completed her examination of the Count, Duidecima asked, "Was he thrown from a horse? One of *our* horses? I was not aware that the Count had been out riding. Surely someone would have told me about it."

"No, nothing like that," Depiliatoreé answered. "He fell from the sun porch in the north tower and by some miracle, survived. And so, what have you to say about his condition?"

Very matter-of-factly, Duidecima gave her assessment. "I think he has several broken ribs, a sprained neck, and some of his ribs may be separated in the back...you know...from his spine. He has bruises and cuts on his head and a big bump on his forehead; a pretty impressive mouse...uh...black eye. As for his mouth, it's a real mess. He has three loose teeth and a number of others that only have roots remaining. Some teeth are missing completely. Those teeth, those empty sockets, that's where all that blood is coming from. The one thing that still eludes me is: What's going on with his nose?"

"Never mind about the nose. What can be done for the Count and his injuries?" Depiliatoreé asked.

"He needs a doctor, not a stablemaster's daughter. The only thing I can recommend is that he be made comfortable until a doctor can arrive and take over. And wash all that bloody mish-mosh out of his mouth. But that nose...I don't know—"

Depiliatoreé ordered Tortus to escort Duidecima back to the stables and to ride on horseback to Ste. Pelotage and bring back a doctor...forthwith. Depiliatoreé was very wary of the villagers in Prevaloir and did not want to trust someone from there to treat the Count, even someone skilled in the medical arts.

No sooner than Depiliatoreé and the Count were alone, "My back! My back!" cried the Count—he obviously was not comfortable. Try as he could, Depiliatoreé could not get the Count into a comfortable position. He moved the Count left and right, turned the Count on one side and then the other, nothing seemed to work. It became apparent that the Count's mattress was not up to the task, given the Count's damaged condition.

"Chameau, all of you. Come hither! Quickly! Come! Come!" Depiliatoreé shouted, and shouted, and shouted again. His shouts rang out through the palace. Word spread quickly and soon there were twenty or so members of the staff huddled and re-huddled in the Count's bedchamber with Chameau now fronting the pack.

"The Count is in dire straits!" Depiliatoreé told the group. "He is in terrible pain as his bed is woefully inadequate to the task of keeping him comfortable." Depiliatoreé had concealed the Count (and his condition) under cover of a mountain of pillows and cushions, and he could see that members of the assembled group were straining to get a rare eyeful of the incapacitated nobleman, craning their necks and jiggle-juggling their positions—up and down, side to side.

Depiliatoreé was fearful of what might occur if the Count died from his injuries—fearful of his *own* social status considering the void that would be left in the noble hierarchy. The doctor from Ste. Pelotage would be arriving in an interminable two days, so the only thing Depiliatoreé felt he had control of was to relieve the Count's pain in any way possible and to have him rest quietly and comfortably.

Depiliatoreé stood up on the Count's footstool and looked down over the assembled staff members, "We must make the Count comfortable! We must fill his mattress with new downy feathers until he can rest comfortably. New. Downy. Comfortable, I say! May he heal and return to his duties!" To members of the group (including Chameau) it seemed as if Depiliatoreé was trying to incite a crowd to revolution.

Depiliatoreé continued, "Our task is clear and urgent. Go through the palace and the grounds and gather up all the downy feathers you can...not stiff or useless ones like those of a handsome peacock or the Flemish dickybird; but those from the soft underbellies of our more familiar feathered underlings. Failing that, go out into and across the reaches of this fair county to seek out the requisite soft downy feathers for his bed!

"Chameau...take your associates and go to that insolent little village and scrounge up all the downy feathers you can find. We must have down for the Count! We must have down for the Count!"

With that the assembled group broke into a wild rush as Depiliatoreé stepped down from the footstool and returned to consoling the Count who continued to squirm and moan quietly in pain. The Count's near silence (except for his moans) was beginning to alarm Depiliatoreé, but outwardly Depiliatoreé gave the appearance of being in control of the situation.

The Count's staff did as Depiliatoreé had requested, scouring every inch of the palace and its grounds, but came up short. There was nary a suitable feather to be had, anywhere in the palace, much less soft downy ones. Event the feather dusters seemed to be missing anything useful. No poultry of any kind was available to pluck as the only animals of any consequence were horses, and they of course had nothing to offer in the current emergency.

To an outside observer, the mad rush by an entire court to acquire such a thing as soft downy feathers, purely to further cushion the Count's injured body, might seem a gross misapplication of resources. But to those involved, it seemed quite logical and necessary...and truly urgent. In any parochial domain, such as the Palace Filiamort, cross-ventilation of thought is usually sadly lacking. And so, as absurd as it sounded to those outside the court, the watchword heard across the county was, "We must have down for the Count!"

As word very quickly spread ahead of the Count's men, farmers and other residents everywhere began hiding their chickens and turkeys and geese and anything that sported feathers; including pillows, hats, comforters, and cushions. As the Count's men traipsed across the fields of the county raiding cottages and farmhouses they found no down. No matter how much coercion they provided, no individual would yield and produce the requested item(s). There was no down to be had anywhere. Always fearful, as in every case, of returning to the palace empty-handed, the men attempted to capture wild birds. But the birds seemed to be in cahoots with the county residents as the birds were too alert, too agile, and too quick for a single one to be caught. As nature itself had its say about the matter, no right-minded bird would allow itself to be caught and killed for so frivolous and trivial a purpose.

Meanwhile, Chameau and his group approached the village of Prevaloir once again. And once again the blacksmith was pounding away on a piece of metal, some kind of harness.

"What ho there my good blacksmith," Chameau announced as if he had never conversed with the blacksmith before.

"What could you possibly want with me?" the blacksmith asked as he pounded away as loudly as possible.

"We need down for the Count!" Chameau shouted at the blacksmith intending to notify the village as well as attempting to overcome the metallic sound of the hammering.

The blacksmith made a rare pause in his pounding and came up close to Chameau's face. Chameau could feel heat radiating from the blacksmith's sooty body as the blacksmith stated sternly, "You have come here many times, demanding this and that." The blacksmith started tapping his hammer in his hand as he spoke, "And now...now you come here once again, disturbing the peace of our village, and demanding yet another ridiculous item, with an implied threat of pain, all for your so-called mysterious Count. Now be off before I pound *you* into something useful!" As the blacksmith returned to his work, he muttered to himself, "Useful? Not bloody likely—"

Not without a certain level of chagrin, Chameau left the blacksmith's outdoor workshop. Chameau's group had not taken a single step forward before they heard, from behind their backs, the extremely loud pounding of the blacksmith's hammer once again; the sound fashioning a sharp point onto the blacksmith's threat.

Rather than chance a confrontation with another villager, the group went straight for the Mme. Represailles's shoppe. They felt confident that they could scam her one more time since she seemed to be easily maneuvered and compliant—and lately, she had been the only one in the entire village who was able and willing to produce a sought-after item. But there was going to risk involved; high risk. Could she be trusted? Something bad would surely happen to Chameau and his men if they were to return with no down. Depiliatoreé would see to that. As they approached her shoppe, Chameau was asking himself, "I wonder who's scamming whom in this arrangement? Should I even be doing this?"

As they entered her shoppe, the old woman reached under the counter, pulled out an enormous knife, and waved it at the duo. "You won't come any further if you know what's good for you!"

"We've only come asking for help in a dire situation. We need down for the Count!" Chameau said while scheming to get the knife away from the old woman. Chameau could ill afford to alienate her if he was going to get what he came for, so he tried to be as polite as possible. It was all very transparent to the old woman, so she stood her ground.

The old woman waved the knife, directing the duo toward the door to the back room. A cautious and suspicious Chameau hesitated, but slowly entered the back room anyway. In it was a clutter of boxes and bottles and containers stacked high, making little corridors like a maze. The room was much larger than he anticipated. Stepping around them, the old woman directed Chameau to yet another room. This room was much larger and had a tall ceiling. In one corner was a huge pile of snow white, soft downy feathers—fluffy like a mountain of powdery snow. How was it possible that she had exactly what his band of down-hunters were looking for? Chameau only knew that these feathers were needed back at the palace and that he was going to be credited with bringing home the goods—once again. Had he already forgotten about the previous fiascoes? If his brainpower were any stronger than a hot coal he would not be working under Depiliatoreé in the first place. What harm could possibly come from a mound of soft feathers?

"How much for the entire lot?" Chameau asked.

"Nothing," the old woman replied. "Take it all!"

Chameau reveled in his good fortune. But how were Chameau and his group going to get such a large quantity of feathers back to the palace, preferably in one trip? Chameau thought for a moment and then said, "You men stay here and begin bringing the feathers to the street. I'll be right back."

With that Chameau rushed out of the shoppe, around the corner and into the town square. Before he could catch his breath, a craftsman, a coppersmith, came passing by the square with a wagon loaded with his wares (pots, pans, ewers, and the like). A donkey was pulling the wagon.

"I commandeer this wagon in the name of the Count!" Chameau shouted at the coppersmith. The startled craftsman knew not what this strange fellow was up to and was very unhappy to see all of his copper wares tossed into the street and his wagon and donkey hijacked by Chameau. Chameau could be very imposing and was acting so "officially" that the enraged coppersmith did not protest too vigorously. What seemed strange to the coppersmith was the fact that two or three of his finest copper pots could pay for a whole new wagon and another donkey.

"Why did he take the least valuable of all that I have here?" he asked himself. He gathered his wares together and several villagers came to his assistance.

When Chameau rounded the corner with the wagon, he could see that his men had built quite a stack of feathers outside the door. The old woman was standing near the pile, still wielding her huge knife. Chameau drove the donkey up beside the shoppe and he and his men began loading the feathers onto the wagon. Chameau was filled with excitement. He would be the talk of the palace from the moment he appeared with the payload of feathers—especially if no one else had come up with anything. This would be one victory that Depiliatoreé could not steal from him.

When every last feather had been loaded, a linen sheet was placed over the top and secured with several ropes—all of which were provided by the mysteriously cooperative old woman.

Chameau wasn't the slightest bit concerned with the fact that the old woman wanted no payment for any of the things taken—feathers, sheet, ropes. Chameau and his group left the knife-wielding old woman standing by her shoppe without so much as a "goodbye" or a "thank you." That was just the way of noblemen in such a stratified and iniquitous culture.

"Good luck and good riddance, you toplofty little underling," she whispered to herself.

Just as he anticipated, Chameau was cheered as he and his men approached the palace with the wagonload of downy feathers. Only Chameau's group had been successful in acquiring the much-needed feathers. Depiliatoreé was beside himself with joy upon seeing such a huge load of downy soft feathers—and such fine quality too. Without delay, teams were formed and the feathers brought forthwith to the Count's bedchambers where the massive quantity of down was stuffed and prodded into place in the Count's mattress. The Count stood by, painful as it was, impatiently awaiting the moment when his poor injured body could be nestled in the new mounds of softness. Tested by several of those in the privileged inner circle, the new mattress was considered a raging success.

With the aid of Depiliatoreé, the Count was helped up into his bed and aboard the amazingly soft mattress. He was very pleased. For the first time since the incident with the Viscount, he was finally comfortable. Depiliatoreé hustled everyone from the room as the Count began to doze off. Depiliatoreé too was feeling relieved. In less than two days—not soon enough in Depiliatoreé's mind—the doctor would arrive from Ste. Pelotage. The Count was now comfortable and everyone could breathe a sigh of relief that the latest crisis was under control. Depiliatoreé took a chair and positioned himself outside the Count's bedchamber door. He would take a few naps during the night and monitor the Count's condition from time to time. In the end, it had turned out to be a successful day— or so it seemed.

Crunsch! Crunsch! Scrunsch!

Depiliatoreé was rudely awakened when he heard a liquid munching sound emanating from the Count's bedchamber.

Crunsch! Crunsch! Scrunsch!

Rushing in he saw that the Count's new mattress had somehow come to life as a kind of amorphous whitish undulating creature, ostensibly animated by the mass of new downy feathers. It looked like a giant animated oyster. The bulbous creature had engulfed the sleeping Count and was apparently digesting his body, bones and all. The muffled cries of the Count were only loud enough for Depiliatoreé to hear. Depiliatoreé grabbed the only remaining visible part of the Count, his foot, and tried to pull the Count free. But despite Depiliatoreé's efforts, the fluffy white mass continued to chew the Count to death. The Count's foot came off into Depiliatorcé's hands. A shaken Depiliatoreé dropped the Count's foot as if it had caught on fire. It was too late to save the Count and soon the Count's cries were silenced. The Count had been eaten by his new mattress and not a trace of him remained.

"Burrrrrrrrrup!" The white mass released a resounding flabby belch then paused for a few seconds to ensure that its meal remained in place; its meal—i.e. the Count Pouleé Aurniece Lavoisier, late of the Palace Filiamort in the county of Assener.

The white blob then resumed its peculiar undulations and slowly oozed its way from the bed frame onto the floor where it went after the Count's isolated noble foot. Depiliatoreé watched the blob consume the foot and then move toward him. Not interested in being the next victim, Depiliatoreé alertly stepped outside the room and slammed the door behind him. He could hear the creature begin to pound itself against the other side of the door, but it appeared that the blob was not going to be able to break through.

What was to be done? Watching through a crack in the warped wooden door, Depiliatoreé could see the creature slowly move around the room but could not detect even the tiniest part of the defunct Count peeking out from the folds of white. And the noble foot was gone as well.

No explanation could be offered to anyone in the palace. A night of celebration had turned to tragedy; a tragedy that could not be explained. Depiliatoreé knew that a cover story would be necessary. The Count's nephew, Zizanie Lemonstrui would have to be notified. If the Lemonstrui person accepted the title, as was his right, what was to become of Depiliatoreé under the new regime? What would happen if Lemonstrui did *not* take over, for one reason or another? What if the new Count could not be manipulated? The scheming and planning would have to be started forthwith. And of course there was the amorphous white blob still lurking in the late Count's bedchamber. What was to be done about that? What *could* be done?

Every day, for the next three days, Depiliatoreé peeked through the crack in the bedchamber door, checking on the status of the white blob. On the third day, Depiliatoreé was surprised to see no movement. Cautiously, Depiliatoreé opened the door and there before him was a huge mound of downy white feathers. The undulating blob was no more. He carefully walked around the pile and poked at it with the late Count's walking stick. It was simply a pile of feathers once more. Depiliatoreé ordered that the pile of feathers be removed from the palace and dumped someplace out near the stables.

A mere ten days passed. A false rumor was created that the Count was convalescing abroad at an exclusive mountain retreat. The Count's nephew, Zizanie, was installed as the *new* Count—smoothly and efficiently. As a profligate of the highest order, he was delighted that someone (Depiliatoreé) was willing to manage the day to day activities of the palace—Depiliatoreé, again, was in firm control of all things Count.

The new Count's ways were just as unseemly and capricious as those of the previous edition. In just a few days, the new Count frittered away gold on slabs of fine meat, imported tobaccos, games, wagering, and carnal pursuits that polite society would shudder to imagine. Just a few days. Then, on the fifth day—

"Oranges! I must have oranges!" Count Lemonstrui ordered.

"Sire, there are no oranges to be found in this county. 'Tis not the season," Depiliatoreé informed the new Count.

"Nevertheless, I must have them!" the Count demanded.

With great reluctance and trepidation, Depiliatoreé ordered Chameau and Tortus to come up with...oranges! Oranges! Chameau and Tortus agreed with Depiliatoreé: Where were oranges to be had at this time of year? They dared not venture into the village, not even to the old woman's shoppe. But in desperation, bowing to the will of the insipid and entitled new Count, an orange acquisition team was assembled and once again the Count's men entered the village on a mission; this time demanding oranges. And that was the proverbial last straw.

Much has been written about the demise of Count Zizanie Lemonstrui. As legends have it, the people of the village of Prevaloir rose up against all the nobility and hangers-on associated with the Palace Filiamort. It was a mini-revolution. The villagers, tired of the intrusions by the Count's henchmen, felt as though they had nothing to lose in bringing down the entire hierarchy. The presence of a count (any count) added nothing to their lives; a count offered them no protection against invaders; a count brought them no wealth; the villagers' prosperity was of their *own* making.

So revolt they did. The villagers stormed the palace and corralled Count Zizanie Lemonstrui, André Depiliatoreé, Chameau DuHumpois, Tortus LeHare, and four others. The group of eight was confined in a quickly assembled stockade just outside the front entrance to the palace. The remainder of the court and other palace residents escaped with their lives, most likely running off to places far away in order to provide their services to some other aristocrat.

"What is that smell?" Depiliatoreé asked Chameau as they sat quietly in the makeshift stockade.

"I cannot tell," Chameau responded. "It smells like that rabble is cooking something. I hope that's not supposed to be our meal. I for one will refuse to eat it. It smells awful."

Tortus stood up and remarked, "They're cooking up something all right. I know that smell. I know what it is! It's tar!" Count Lemonstrui sat quietly, immersed in his own thoughts, unaware of the implications.

Depiliatoreé and Chameau rose to their feet, looked out across the area, and saw nothing. But the smell was definitely hot tar. During the revolt, the villagers discovered the large mound of downy white feathers piled up by the stables. Tar. Feathers. A traditional combination.

*Qui joue avec le feu finit par se brûler.*

# Flatbeds

∞

### The Unknown

Dear Reader, we now begin a curious exploration of the X7-PanExpanse, sometimes aware and many times unfortunately bound by the natural inherent limitations of the explorer's mind—all of this rigidly enforced by who or what or who knows what. Desirous to understand everything about everything, the mind struggles when confronted with those limitations, and is constantly (and unfairly) titillated by the uncovering of each new, previously-undiscovered detail—a detail that apparently was not actually unknowable after all.

What is it that drives the human mind in its persistent attempts to explain all of that unknowable material? Does each tiny, tweezed-out revelation give a false impression that knowing the rest of the unknowable is still possible? Or is it the utter hopelessness of such a challenge that inspires the imagination to come up with some kind of explanation for it all? In any case, you might say that the human imagination becomes inspired (and not discouraged) by an inability to comprehend.

In a final analysis, what words can best describe the human mind's innocent (possibly delusional) belief that, somehow, something truly unknowable can be known: unseemly brazenness, conceit, blind ambition, stupidity, pathological ignorance, a grand-scale scam played on the virginal human mind by a mischievous universe, puppetry, unbridled masochism? One may ask, "Is it all of these or none of these or a subset of these?" Who might presume to answer all these questions? Certainly not me.

All I know is that the X7-PanExpanse itself *is* knowable, as evidenced by the text on these pages. Then again, it will soon become clear that there are many mysteries about the X7-PanExpanse that may forever defy satisfactory explanation by the human mind;

unanswered questions will be as gnats swarming about our exposed brains as we make this journey. Despite all of these challenges, our deep-seated self-interest will see us through.

My attentiveness has started to wane, so let us not linger further on any more of that philosophical foreplay. Whether we comprehend it all or not, our upcoming gamboling through the X7-PanExpanse will stimulate us with interesting and tantalizing views; views that include its nature, culture, belief systems, and purpose (not so much purpose as you will see). And the experiences and observations of selected individuals within it will hopefully provide clarity and perspective to us all. Note that an individual from the X7-PanExpanse can only provide us with information based on that particular individual's singular point of view. There is no concept of science or recorded history in the X7-PanExpanse so an individual there will not be able to explain things to us that are beyond that which is simply observable. But, we will be able to enhance our perspective of the X7-PanExpanse individuals as they share their beliefs, their speculations, and their culture with us. We must be content with those things, and not necessarily all the actual, underlying truths. However, as your guide, I will fill in the voids wherever I can.

Where common ground can be established between the realities of our two unassuming domains and the realities of the X7-PanExpanse, we will obtain some modicum of our sought-after insight (probably, maybe), all the while morphing observations made on their terms with references that, most assuredly, only we can understand. An individual in the X7-PanExpanse may never be able to grasp our concept of the color red; but, by discovering common ground, we will find that white is always white and black is always black, everywhere inside the transdimensional union. In spite of all these limitations, for the most part, we are grateful for each and every contribution by the individuals.

So here I am, your humble guide, far-removed from your physical presence. I will never be able to know your thoughts or questions as they arise while we go about our transdimensional journey together. There will be questions, many questions; yours, mine, even those of the X7-PanExpanse individuals. So therefore please forgive me, dear Reader, if my guidance and limited knowledge—that of all three domains (well, two out of three)—

prove to be inadequate as we make our way through the X7-PanExpanse. But please remember that I too am constrained by boundaries; limitations inherent in my own domain as well as this temporary transdimensional union where our journey begins and ends. In other words, if you do not get it, it is (probably) not my fault. And with all of that, let us begin.

### The X7-PanExpanse

Dear Reader, any attempt to understand the X7-PanExpanse may be a fool's errand. But we will do it anyway. After all, a fool may merely be a wise person who does not know what they are doing. And, in this case, that fool would be me. So, as your guide, let me turn over our discussion to O'Perch[RIDER], currently a flatbed Rider and an expert (in his mind) on the subject of the X7-PanExpanse.

O'Perch[RIDER]:

"I have left my chosen flatbed many times. I have become a Walker and wandered out into the X7-PanExpanse in an attempt to understand its limits, its properties, and its ultimate purpose. This I have done on both sides of the Rail-line. There has never been any restriction on my *lateral* movements except when the Rakers appear (to enforce longitudinal limits), which is totally natural and is to be expected. As a frequent Walker, I, like many others, have accepted the fact that my de-boarded flatbed may have moved forward, out of reach, by the time I return to a flatbed on the Rail-line. This always depends on how long I spend time as a Walker. But gathering new information about my domain makes the sacrifice worth it.

"It seems to me that the X7-PanExpanse has no limit, but that cannot possibly be true. I just have not been able to venture out far enough from the Rail-line to discover its boundaries. Everywhere, the ground itself is almost pure white, shiny white, covered with a fine, glass-like, granular material. 'Glass,' don't pretend to understand it, but I think I do. The actual thickness of this perfectly flat ground layer is unknown since the granular material goes as deep as I have ever been able to dig. And, through all that digging, there has never been a change of color or consistency. This material is the only material I have yet been able to find on the ground anywhere; and I have ventured out across the X7-PanExpanse seemingly, to me, all over the place. Many times I have lifted up a handful of the ground material only to feel it fall through my fingers like a frictionless liquid (liquid...whatever *that* is). As the granules dropped to the ground they fell into place in such a way as to maintain a seamless, perfectly flat and smooth surface.

"Walking out onto this white, glassy terrain produces no footprints, the ground granules always sliding back into place to maintain that perfect smoothness. In spite of its liquid-like, granular nature, the ground itself, surprisingly, provides a very stable walking surface. The lack of footprints has always given me pause when venturing out laterally, far away from the Rail-line. If I were to lose sight of the flatbeds, I would have no way to retrace my steps and I am not convinced that the Rakers would come to lead be back. I, for one, am not all that anxious for Closure.

"The ground's white color is primarily due to the way light from the sky plays on the granules. That ambient light is diffuse and white; a comforting, brisk white with a very subtle noli[1] tint—very subtle. The light in the sky does not come from one central source, as the brilliance of the sky is uniform from horizon to horizon. I must say that the term 'horizon' is not completely accurate since the X7-PanExpanse simply fades into a white haze, far distant and seemingly unbounded in every direction; the sky seems to blend in with the ground at some point, out there, very far away. Therefore, it is impossible to know if our surface is generally curved or remains absolutely flat, forever.

"There is a type of warmth that is present everywhere in the X7-PanExpanse. It, like many things in the X7-PanExpanse, is completely uniform—it is the same warm ambience that is present everywhere an individual may go. Does the warmth emanate from the sky? Or the ground? Or is it an atmospheric phenomenon unto itself? I cannot say.

"Over a distance I would expect to see changes in elevation or ups or downs or some other distinctive feature, but so far all I have ever seen is absolutely flat, smooth, featureless

---

[1] rosy-red yellow

terrain; a terrain that is consistently covered with the ubiquitous layer of fine, white, glass-like granules. I have never encountered a single ripple; not so much as a ridge, gouge, mound, or drift. Many times I have seen the vast areas of glistening granules give the appearance of a reflective layer, but always, when approached, the area, like a cenisse[2], would shrink and vanish into nothing. Faced with such a bright, featureless, unchanging topography, an individual might be expected to imagine things that are not really there.

"An experience common among almost all Riders and Walkers, including myself, is that, when looking backward along the Rail-line, the view seems to be much clearer than when looking forward. I can only base this observation on the appearance of the flatbeds and the associated individuals since I have never been able to distinguish any other natural reference feature, out there, away from the Rail-line. From far away, laterally, from out in the X7-PanExpanse, I can look back toward the Rail-line and see the slow, continuous movement of the chain of flatbeds and the Riders aboard them. But that is it.

"I can say with some confidence that the X7-PanExpanse is physically divided into two parts: when looking forward—in the direction of flatbed movement—from on board a flatbed, there is a left side and a right side. In all my wanderings I have never detected even the tiniest difference between the two sides. Except for one: if I watch the flatbeds from what I call the official *right* side of the Rail-line, the flatbeds are moving from my left to my right and if I watch the flatbeds from what I call the official *left* side of the Rail-line, the flatbeds are moving from my right to my left. Crossing from one side of the X7-PanExpanse to the other requires boarding a flatbed from the proximal side and leaving from the other side—i.e. one goes from being a Walker to being a Rider and then back to being a Walker again. In the X7-PanExpanse, there is no other way to do it. Given the freedom of lateral movement afforded to everyone, it is just a matter of effort and willingness.

"As far as I can tell, the only forms of life in the X7-PanExpanse are the individuals that co-exist with me. Of course I have seen other Walkers way out on the open terrain as well

---

[2] a theoretical body of non-granular liquid material

as a few Rakers. But, I must say, there have been relatively few individuals that have joined me way out there in the boundless white, exploring the X7-PanExpanse; a vast majority of Walkers seem to prefer staying close to the Rail-line.

"Whether based on fear, laziness, indifference, or self-imposed ignorance, a Rider's decision to stay aboard a chosen flatbed may have a hidden element of wisdom since, in spite of all my extensive wanderings, I have yet to discover many more superficial truths about the X7-PanExpanse than an overly curious fellow Rider would have observed from the deck of a chosen flatbed.

"I have found no real practical value to any of the information I have gathered from my studies or observations. But, I have nevertheless obtained a great deal of satisfaction in heightening my own sense of self-awareness within the broader context that I have acquired. And that seems to be, and will have to be, purpose enough."

## Flatbeds

Having now received all this new "information" ostensibly describing the vast area of general nothingness we know as the X7-PanExpanse, as your humble guide I must admit that I know very little more now than I did before. And you, dear Reader, now know as much as I [do]. For those among us who may still wish to press on, let us now turn our attention to the flatbeds, understanding them through our own observations and the observations of others. For this endeavor we have Yara'Pek WALKER, who will provide us with her observations and perspectives on the subject of the flatbeds themselves. Now I say this with all due respect (which stealthily means none): she is a slave to detail and is an X7-PanExpanse-class example of self-destructive anality. But, in the case of the flatbeds and their very nature, there exists very little observable detail to cover and so, dear Reader, you will be spared significant amounts of irrelevant minutiae.

Yara'Pek WALKER:
"Intrigued by the mysteries of the X7-PanExpanse and the Rail-line that runs across it, I have assigned to myself the complex task of understanding everything there is to know

about the Rail-line and the flatbeds with which we are all familiar. The X7-PanExpanse has, running across it (or through it, or over it, however you choose to describe it) an extraordinary system of two parallel rails, the Rail-line. This pair of rails forms a perfectly straight line across the X7-PanExpanse, dividing it into two sides, a left and a right. The Rail-line extends in both directions for as far as the eye can see, eventually being absorbed into a white haze. Is there a beginning? Is there an end? Why is everything so white? It has driven me to the brink of having an exploding brain organ that I have not been able to find an answer to any of these mysteries (and many others). That list of persistently intractable loose ends has not kept me from examining in detail the physical characteristics of the Rail-line; those that are discoverable by an important investigator such as myself.

"The rails are held together, securely in place, on the surface of the X7-PanExpanse, by a single, solid block of white homogeneous and seamless artificial stone. I say 'artificial' because as solid and huge as this stone might be, there is nary a solitary vein of discoloration nor flaw of any kind to be found in it. The rails themselves are made of a shiny, whitish-grey[3] metal. I have not been able to find a single seam, break, crack, or joint in the long metal rails nor can I find a single break or crack in the stone base that holds them together. As a Rider, one can observe the two rails of the Rail-line from above by looking down into the large space between adjacent flatbeds. However, the rails and foundation stone are in such perfect, flaw-free condition that it is impossible to tell if the flatbed is moving at all—and we all know that the flatbeds do move, as group, forward, albeit slowly, at all times.

"For a Walker, out on the ground, away from the flatbeds, the story is quite different. If that Walker stands perfectly still, the slow, but relentless movement of the flatbeds along the Rail-line is obvious. The Rail-line can be viewed from a different angle while out on the ground, but the only new information to be gathered is the detection of movement by the flatbeds; that, and a side view of the flatbeds which is not possible while on board. There is a raging debate among some Riders as to whether a Walker who is not moving still qualifies as a Walker at all. That determination shall be left to others. For me, I shall

---

[3] grey is gray, black is black, white is white

stick to my chosen area of investigation. I do not get into those types of administrative discussions.

"More importantly for our discussion is the topic of the flatbeds themselves. The flatbeds are arranged in a long chain, one after the other, extending along the Rail-line for as far as the eye can see. An individual flatbed is a thick rectangular platform with a set of four wheels mounted to the platform's underside at each end—each flawless wheel engaging the flawless rail below it. It is all so very flawless. Very comforting. Every flatbed wheel has a thin black wedge (like a spoke) inscribed from its center to its outer edge. If a Walker views the side of a flatbed, movement can be detected by watching the rotation of the wheels. Riders cannot appreciate this.

"If a Walker of average height is standing on the ground, the bottom of a flatbed platform is about eye-level; the height of the stone base, the rails, the wheels, and the mounting added together. There are no visible springs or other devices employed to cushion the moving flatbed since there is apparently no need for that kind of mechanism in such a flawless system. Wonderful.

"A rigid, prism-like, metal coupling is present to connect two adjacent flatbeds together. In spite of the incredible length of the chain of flatbeds, they all move as one, relentlessly, never stopping, and never changing speed. There is much speculation about how the flatbeds are kept moving along the Rail-line. Are they pulled along from the forward end or pushed along from the backward end? Do they self-propel as a group or is there a special, central flatbed that both pushes and pulls at the same time? Does each flatbed propel itself in perfect synchronization with all the others? Any individual who purports to know the answer to this mystery is a big fat liar. The truth is currently unknown.

"There is no need for a movable joint or flexible connection in a coupling since the Rail-line is perfectly straight—apparently there is never a bend or curve along its entire length, although no one knows for sure. Beautiful. The space between two adjacent flatbeds is referred to as a 'coupling gap.' That gap is just wide enough to discourage a Rider from attempting to leap from one flatbed to another—which in any case, is not allowed; and we all know it is for our own good. Alternatively, Walking along the top edge of a coupling in an attempt to move between two flatbeds is equally foolhardy since the sharp, top edge of a coupling would severely damage an individual, most likely resulting in a 'premature' Closure, or worse.

"Hanging from the lateral side of each back end corner of a flatbed platform is a retractable ladder. Ladders are used to board or leave a given flatbed. When extended, a ladder reaches almost to the ground. When retracted, a ladder is compressed into a height about equal to the thickness of the platform itself. At the center of the trailing end of every flatbed platform is a white metal scaffolding equipped with a small control box and a flat area just large enough to accommodate one standing individual. This structure is commonly referred to as the pulpoose[4]. It is yet another impediment that can deter a Rider from easily and (dare I say it) capriciously jumping across a coupling gap onto an adjacent flatbed platform. Some individuals have no self-control. However, the pulpoose does not block the view from one flatbed to another and the Riders on two adjacent flatbed platforms can communicate fairly easily among themselves.

"This ability to communicate from flatbed to flatbed, I believe, contributes to the continual, rampant spread of rumors all along the Rail-line. Also contributing to the spread is the free communication between the Walkers. More or less messy gossip if you ask me.

"The mounted control box on a pulpoose has two levers, one lever for each corner ladder. Standing in the pulpoose, a Warder, with one hand on each lever, can observe and control the associated corner ladder and can readily see any individual that might be attempting to board the flatbed. As all Walkers and Riders are aware, a flatbed's ladders are operated solely by its assigned Warder. And of course nobody questions the authority of a Warder. It is not proper.

---

[4] a pedestal enclosed by a safety rail supported by a white scaffolding centered at the back end of every flatbed

"As a Rider, I have measured many, many flatbeds during my essential and exhaustive investigations, and have found that the dimensions of every flatbed platform—every one I was able to measure—are identical. Although I have heard of exceptions, personally, I have never seen one. I do not think there are any exceptions.

"I have been able to determine the thickness of numerous flatbed platforms as a Rider and a Walker. Doing so as a Walker is difficult since the flatbeds move along just a little bit faster than an average individual can walk at a normal pace. Attempting to measure platform dimensions by walking forward along the moving Rail-line is awkward and possibly dangerous, so gathering data from flatbeds in that direction always has its physical limitations. An individual must walk at a pretty good clip to make any progress moving forward. Measuring flatbeds backward along the line is less challenging, my measuring activities only being curtailed by Rakers who would dutifully usher me forward if I happened to move backward, too far, beyond the regulated longitudinal limit. And we all must respect those regulations.

"In addition, in order to measure the thickness on both sides of a particular flatbed, I must cross over it by becoming a Rider and then becoming a Walker on the other side. Boarding and de-boarding a moving flatbed can be tricky for some individuals since it involves stepping onto or off of an extended flatbed ladder. Although Warders always extend the ladders for our use, they are not permitted to help us board or de-board in any way. No one knows why. All of these limitations that stand in the way of my making accurate measurements are inconvenient, to say the least.

"I have been able to measure the thickness of each end of a flatbed (any flatbed that I am allowed to board) by being a Rider on the flatbed and measuring it down from top to bottom. Measuring the thickness at each end of a moving flatbed by being a Walker is problematic. From the data I have compiled, I can say that each flatbed platform is uniform in thickness, all the way around. It is yet to be determined whether a flatbed platform is solid or hollow or if it contains any kind of internal structure.

"Using the platform thickness as a sort of baseline, I have divided it into one hundred equal parts called units. Using all of the aforementioned Walker/Rider methodologies, I have been able to accurately determine the width and length of numerous flatbed platforms. One exception: measuring the width of a platform could only be accomplished as a Rider so I can only be certain of the width of the flatbed platforms I was allowed to board. Given these caveats, it is my belief that every flatbed platform along the entirety of the Rail-line has the same length, width, and thickness, those dimensions being: Thickness, 100 units; Width, 1000 units; and Length, 1618 units. So, that is that.

"Very well then...platform colors. Many different shades of every imaginable color are represented—as many as twenty-five, including eight shades of erst[5] four shades of venee[6], paj[7], a grey, and possibly others, presumably including black. A white platform has never been observed, at least not by me. The colorful platforms provide a welcome contrast against the stark white background of the X7-PanExpanse, thus giving Walkers good reference points, albeit ones that move. A flatbed color can be useful in identifying a Walker's own chosen flatbed when the time comes for that Walker to re-board. There does not seem to be any other practical purpose for the different colors. It is said that within the view of any given individual no two flatbed colors are the same. This is merely conjecture: there are currently no experimental means available for proving or disproving such a bold statement.

"I am not a fool, no matter what they say. I know that very few of my fellow Riders/Walkers have an interest in my work, but I plan to continue my research for as long as I can, or until Closure. Most likely, next, I will attempt to find some kind of pattern in the ordering of the flatbed colors or possibly get detailed measurements of the ladders. I cannot say yet. The future looks exciting. There is still so much to do."

---

[5] reddish-brown

[6] brilliant pan-yellow

[7] a pale rose color

∞

## Riders and Walkers

Whew! That was quite a workout, but we thank Yara'Pek<sup>WALKER</sup> for those observations and for keeping her treatise relatively...brief. Dear Reader, you may be aware that each of our previous contributors has mentioned a number of person-types (designations) that co-exist in the X7-PanExpanse. These contributors have done so assuming that you, dear Reader, already know what they are talking about. Many individuals in the X7-PanExpanse have a bad habit of assuming that somehow one's own essential knowledge is of such tremendous value and importance that surely every other individual must have the same knowledge. Is this a psychological curiosity or just plain annoying? You must decide for yourself.

As we move on, let us begin to look at the individual person-types that are found in the X7-PanExpanse. You have already heard mention of Riders, Walkers, Rakers, and Warders. There also exist Flyers, Violators, Providers, and quite a few other types; some of them rare. I can offer you a few of my own observations, yes, of course. But rather than provide my own long-winded, dry, clinical description of each person-type, I will allow a representative of each person-type to speak for his or her self. Truthfully, this is not out of deference to the Reader, but is more a manifestation of my own lazy oneship.

Before proceeding, I have one observation that our next contributor will never be able to comprehend: the concept of "running." It is a given that an energetic Walker can walk somewhat faster than a moving flatbed, but not by very much. In the domain of the X7-PanExpanse, there is no such thing as "running," either in the vernacular of the X7-PanExpanse individuals or in the physical sense. It is not an easy task for a Walker to try to outpace a moving flatbed. It can be done. It is done, frequently, but it is not easy.

May I introduce to you now, dear Reader, Eras'Otis<sup>WALKER</sup>, who currently holds the record for the largest number of Walker-Rider transitions. Eras'Otis<sup>WALKER</sup> has great pride in this accomplishment and can give us some insight on what it is like to be a Rider and a Walker, many times over.

For the sake of clarity, may I add: many individuals in the X7-PanExpanse lump Walkers and Riders together as a group, calling them Normals. This is not an officially sanctioned designation, and is inherently generic, but some individuals prefer to use it. On the other hand, most of the other designated individuals (primarily ones that perform some kind of official task) can be referred to collectively as "officials."

Eras'Otis<sup>WALKER</sup>:

"For those unfamiliar with our domain, a 'Rider' is an individual who is currently an occupant on a given flatbed, riding along on the Rail-line, happy, carefree, possibly even wistful, wistfully blissful. On the other hand, a Rider who has de-boarded from a flatbed is called a 'Walker.'

"Every individual has a tight-fitting body covering called their 'outfit.' In the X7-PanExpanse, when an individual changes designation, their outfit changes color automatically, matching that individual's new designation. For an individual in the X7-PanExpanse, there is no way around this automatic reassignment. How all this works so smoothly is just another riddle of life in the X7-PanExpanse. We all accept that. Rider outfits are universally colored oir-grey[8] while every Walker outfit is oir-venee[9].

"Some flatbeds are crowded with Riders while others carry only a few. Riders are, for the most part, an assemblage of immobile, uninterested, indolent lay-abouts. Any Rider will tell you that being one is the easiest, most envious, and most pain-free existence one can have in the X7-PanExpanse. It does not take any effort whatsoever to become a Rider, but for some reason, most of them believe that they are naturally superior to all the other types of individuals in the X7-PanExpanse. This, unfortunately, is a characteristic that is common among all the individual person-types in the X7-PanExpanse. What could possibly be a reason for this?

"I will admit that there is a sense of absolute serenity and peace that resonates among most of the Riders on any given flatbed platform. But, like me, not every Rider is content

---

[8] light-grey
[9] light chill-yellow

to exist this way. What then is the point of existing at all? We, the slightly ill-adjusted few, are expected to keep our opinions and ideas to ourselves and not disturb the tranquility and idleness of the group.

"One might spend an entire existence as a Rider, never changing designation or flatbed until Closure. Most individuals choose this option, lounging about on the surface of their chosen flatbed's platform, moving along steadily in the brightness of the X7-PanExpanse, basking in it, changing position only every once in a while—no questions, no answers, pure unchallenged tranquility.

"From a Rider's point of view, the 'scenery' of uniform white surrounding the Rail-line appears absolutely stationary, but a Rider can sense the movement of the flatbed chain because of the presence of Walkers who are out on the ground. There always seem to be at least a few Walkers hanging about on either side of the Rail-line. Sometimes there are many Walkers, some walking, some standing still. Although I believe that a Walker who is stationary should still be considered a Walker, there are those who would disagree. Most of the immobile Riders pay no attention to the Walkers, preferring to wallow around in each other's sweet serenity like so many unipogitors[10].

"I remember when my Progenitors first booted me right off their flatbed platform and turned me into a youthful Walker. Not wanting to leave my comfortable and familiar flatbed, I tried to return to it, only to find that I was denied access. Tough...those Progenitors. At that moment, while considering my unwelcome, impending adulthood, I found I was carrying on my back a heavy burden of free choice. That brought me great anxiety, making it even more difficult to choose a semi-permanent flatbed of my own. Even then, in my cloud of youthful, self-satisfied non-purpose, I understood that it was an important decision in the life of every individual in the X7-PanExpanse; perhaps the most important, not to be taken lightly. As a youth, every individual has to face this decision; it is a routine part of a linear life in the X7-PanExpanse.

---

[10] mythical pig-beings of supreme loathsomeness

"Some youths have their new, semi-permanent flatbed pre-selected for them; forced upon them by their Progenitors. Other youths are sometimes provided with sound guidance or direction before making a choice for themselves; guidance given to them altruistically by concerned Progenitors, or, on the other hand, by some meddling individual who could not mind their own haac[11] business.

"I was given no such quality advice—not even faulty advice, no advice. As an ill-informed youth, I had no idea that my choice of flatbed, at that critical moment, would set in stone so many of my future flatbed restrictions; my future options would always be limited by what I decided right at that moment. It was an important decision that, unfortunately, relied completely on my youthful and immature mind. Because the flatbeds continue moving forward, relentlessly, without any regard as to an individual's personal circumstances, I felt a sense of urgency imposed upon me by my pending big decision. One cannot walk alongside the Rail-line forever. That would be absurd. A choice had to be made.

"Seeing as how the flatbeds move along a little faster than normal walking speed, one cannot afford to stop or linger for too long or else many flatbeds will pass by and some will move out of reach forever. Other flatbeds will, of course, come along from the backward end, but the further a promising or enticing flatbed moves forward, the more unlikely it will be that an individual will ever be able to catch up to it. There is no time for indecisiveness.

"My original chosen oir-erst[12] flatbed has long since vanished into the white haze. That original choice was supposed to be meaningful since, because of that choice, I am forever restricted from boarding certain flatbeds. But, in my estimation, the restrictions appear to be completely arbitrary—there are no rules as far as anyone can tell. I regret that as a self-occupied youth I labored over a decision that, in the end, meant nothing. It is also ironic

[11] damn
[12] light reddish-brown

351

that all the Progenitor advice that I longed for at the time was equally meaningless and those who had their first flatbed chosen for them ended up no better off than me.

"I chose my current pung-erst[13] flatbed more than a little while ago. I have become a Walker many, many times. But, as a Walker, I have never allowed my current temporary base flatbed to get too far ahead of me—not too far ahead—thereby preventing me from ever being able to board it again. So even though I hold the record for the most Rider-Walker transitions, I have only been on board a handful of different flatbeds in either direction during any one extended passage of time.

"A number of my fellow individuals have attempted a flatbed 'ratchet' maneuver. In this, they become a Walker and, with some effort, are able to approach an adjacent flatbed forward of their current one. This can only work if an individual has good endurance. But there is a catch. If the Walker is restricted from boarding the forward flatbed, the Walker either has to attempt to reach the *next* one forward or return to re-board the one just exited. Many a Walker has been sorely disappointed (and may I say utterly exhausted) when a chain of restricted flatbeds, forward along the Rail-line, prevented that Walker from ever moving forward again. Ever. Some older, more experienced Rider might counsel a Walker just returning from such a failed excursion by reminding them that many more flatbed options exist toward the *backward* direction along the Rail-line—and to stop fretting over forward movement and upsetting everyone's tranquility.

"Riders on a flatbed can communicate among themselves and can even communicate with individuals on an adjacent flatbed (across the coupling gap). There are no defined restrictions. However, at some places in the flatbed chain, there are empty, universally-restricted flatbeds with only a Warder aboard. Communicating with a Rider on a flatbed beyond that is nearly impossible. Some believe the empty flatbeds are there to prevent rumors from getting very far along the chain of flatbeds—stopgaps. But if that is the reason, it is meaningless because Walkers from different flatbeds can spread rumors just as easily, even more so. (Merely my own thought on the subject.) Walkers are always

---

[13] dark reddish-brown

communicating among themselves while out on the ground, but usually most of them are flatbed neighbors anyway and could have had conversations as Riders without de-boarding. However, just to *be* a Walker shows a certain level of initiative so you would expect Walkers to be a livelier group, in stark contrast to the semi-hibernating permanent Rider type.

"Some individuals seem to have very few flatbed restrictions, while others find their choice of flatbed very limited. These restrictions hold true for an individual all the way from youth to Closure. How restrictions are defined is anybody's guess. For the most part, individuals who have chosen a particular flatbed wind up, over time, preferring it to all others (in some cases merely preferring instead, the company of the other Riders aboard it). Some individuals choose to stay aboard their chosen flatbed permanently rather than risk having the flatbed move along, out of reach, while off-line as a Walker. However, there are those adventurous souls, like myself, that prefer to keep changing flatbeds, changing often.

"There is also a phenomenon known as Rider 'drift' where a Rider becomes a Walker, then boards a new flatbed one or two flatbeds backward along the Rail-line. Repeating the action again and again, over time, the Rider/Walker winds up moving further and further back. The purported purpose of this procedure is to somehow circumvent the longitudinal limit enforced by the Rakers. As you may or may not recall, I have chosen not to do this type of activity in my record-breaking boarding and de-boarding. I have heard rumors that eventually Rakers will halt a 'drifting' Rider, stopping them from moving any further backward by initiating an *in situ* Closure, then and there. Bang. I must confess that, in a way, I am envious of those adventuresome individuals since they have chosen to explore limits by gaming the system—testing the inviolate rules and restrictions that arc cherished and adhered to by so many, including myself. I respect them and envy them and find them disruptive and distasteful, all at the same time. One other item of note: I do not think that a Raker has the authority to perform a Closure. But I could be wrong about that.

"I have transitioned between Rider-ship and Walker-ship so many times that I can hardly keep count, but I have (kept count), if only so that I can maintain my stats. I have spent much of my time just going back and forth until I have grown too weary to climb a boarding ladder. But, I must say that, in spite of their indifference, all the Warders have been quite cooperative, unless, of course, I try to board a restricted flatbed. In that case, it is always 'ladder up,' and I always comply. No one wishes to de-stabilize our domain."

∞

## Warders

Can such an unchanging domain ever be de-stabilized? What would that look like? What does "de-stabilized" mean in the X7-PanExpanse? Eras'Otis[WALKER] is right to be concerned about such things.

Do Rakers really have the authority to perform Closure or are there rogue Rakers that exceed their authority? Later we will get some additional, detailed observations about the Rakers, but next we are going to take a look at a different group of "official" individuals, the aforementioned Warders.

Before that, if you will indulge me, dear Reader, I have an anecdote that I would like to pass along. This story was told to me by Broz'Uni[VIOLATOR] shortly before he disappeared into the white with some type of official I did not recognize. Broz'Uni[VIOLATOR] was a principal figure in the events that I am about to relate to you now.

It seems that a small group of nine Riders including Broz'Uni[VIOLATOR] happened to be observing a group of Cloysteers in one corner of their common flatbed. The Hosperine was pontificating to the Cloysteers about this and that—basically exploiting and encouraging their tepid desire to do something more than just lying about doing nothing.

But wait, dear Reader. Let me not be accused of something I have spoken about previously. A Cloysteer is a member of a belief system called The Spiral Horn. One of the members self-selects as the Hosperine and leads the discussion when the group gathers together. We shall find out more about this group later in our journey.

Anyway, some of the more bored Cloysteers were observing the unchanging scenery and paying little or no attention to the self-appointed Hosperine. Most of the others on the flatbed were lying about, doing their usual nothing at all. Finding all this sloth and obliviousness irksome, Broz'Uni<sup>VIOLATOR</sup> devised a mischievous caper. For this caper, he enlisted a group of eight other fellow Riders. Together, they practiced elements of this plan multiple times before actually attempting it, learning the nuances in and out. A seemingly unlimited amount of time in the X7-PanExpanse allows an individual to follow these types of pursuits.

When the group was ready, it was time to execute the full plan in all its glory. Passively riding along on their flatbed, the group of nine watched for an area on the ground that was, at that moment, empty of Walkers, both forward and backward, both left and right along the Rail-line—an unusual situation, but not unheard of. Using what they learned in the practice runs, the nine Riders immediately de-boarded and formed a tight-knit group alongside the moving flatbed at about its lengthwise center point. Highly focused and working as a group they began walking together with short but frequent steps as if the entire group was just gliding along. After a short while and with some effort, they were able to match the speed of the flatbed exactly, some walking sideways, some walking backwards, but all of them, as a group moving along forward, absolutely synchronized with the flatbed's movement.

Normally there are only a few Riders that pay attention to Walkers on the ground, but in this case, a number of the Cloysteers and more importantly, the Warder, took notice immediately. The group of nine, matching the pace of the flatbed, made it appear that the flatbed had come to a complete stop. With no other points of reference in the surrounding area, those who noticed what had happened were shocked. How could the chain of flatbeds stop? What could have happened to cause such a thing? To everyone on board, this was just not possible, never, in all history, not even in rumors. As members of The Spiral Horn, the Cloysteers eventually assigned some mystical importance to the event. Thinking that something calamitous was in progress, the Warder stepped down from her pulpoose and attempted to de-board the flatbed in order to confront the nine would-be "stationary" Walkers.

She was so focused on the group of nine, she did not see the rotating flatbed wheels. So, stepping down onto the ground surface, which was still passing by (the flatbeds had not really stopped, of course), she immediately lost her footing, bounced around for a bit, and then fell over, face first into the fine ground granules. The flatbed continued to move along, leaving the Warder behind. She was not amused, but was unable to draw from her experience any prescribed action that might be taken in order to manage the situation. Gathering herself up and, walking briskly, she caught up with her assigned flatbed—the ladder still extended from her de-boarding—and reasserted herself on her pulpoose as if nothing had ever transpired. Indifference and inaction. Such is the lot of a Warder, as you will frequently observe. The Cloysteers and their Hosperine regrouped in one corner, continuing to speculate and murmuring amongst themselves. The other Riders returned to their inactive, tranquil state. The group of nine enjoyed their moment, for a short while.

You may ask, "How did the group of nine get back on board their flatbed?" A typical Warder makes no judgements. The Warder's only purpose is to raise and lower the ladders for any individual who is not restricted from boarding. The jokesters merely re-boarded their flatbed—there were no punitive measures. The Warder, carrying out her assigned duty, was outwardly and aggressively indifferent (even if a little bit irritated, on the inside).

Broz'Uni<sup>VIOLATOR</sup> and his co-conspirators tried this stunt multiple times, getting better at it each time; getting different responses, usually at the Warder's expense. Sometimes they would re-board the same flatbed—as we have seen, the butt-of-the-prank Warder, by law, had to let them back on—and sometimes they re-boarded choosing a different flatbed. You might think that a Warder would be smart enough not to fall for the same prank more than once. Well, think again.

But, dear Reader, as you may well know, all things (good and bad) must eventually come to an end, and so it was with this small group of rogues. During their final execution of the plan, with everything going smoothly, a group of unfamiliar officials appeared, basically out of nowhere. They quickly ushered the boisterous group of nine off into the whiteness. Normals who witnessed the apprehension believed that the group had been "collected" or worse, but soon after their disappearance, all of the perpetrators reappeared along the Rail-line. They were no longer considered Normals (Riders or Walkers); each of the nine was now saddled with the ignominious designation: Violator.

Back to the subject of Warders. Because the Warders have a limited vocabulary, a limited focus, and a very limited mental capacity, we shall get our Warder perspective from Qui'Duk[RIDER], a Rider who has studied them extensively. I believe Qui'Duk[RIDER] is one of the few Riders to ever successfully climb up onto a Warder's pulpoose. Once there, Qui'Duk[RIDER] began harassing the Warder until Qui'Duk[RIDER] was (supposedly) forced to step down. Hopefully, more details will follow.

Qui'Duk[RIDER]:
"I have had a number of experiences with Warders, mostly as a Rider, but sometimes as a Walker. I have ventured up onto a Warder's pulpoose with mixed feelings about my decision to do so. More on that experience later.

"To begin with, the Warders have an outfit that matches the color of the Warder's assigned flatbed—a Warder can be easily distinguished from the Riders that occupy the same flatbed platform. Beyond the color distinction, a Warder stands alone, tall (with a big aura of authority) on the top flat area of the scaffolding at the rear end of the flatbed [the pulpoose]. There, a Warder operates the up/down ladders and manages the boarding and de-boarding of Walkers and Riders.

"Warders must have the X7-PanExpanse's most limited vocabulary. They never speak, except with rare, mostly one-word utterances: 'No,' 'Stop,' 'Blub,' 'Welcome' (and boy, is 'welcome' a rare one indeed). I have never spoken directly to a Warder in spite of having boarded and de-boarded flatbed platforms countless numbers of times. I cannot say 'never,' but still on a few very rare occasions, a Warder has responded to me with a one-word comment and taken me by surprise. Warders are a strange breed.

"No Walker is allowed to board a flatbed if that particular Walker is restricted from it. The Warders are there to rigorously enforce this restriction. Sometimes, an individual, a

Walker (a prospective Rider), will select out a particular flatbed only to be denied boarding. Walkers refer to this situation as 'ladder up' referring to the fact that the flatbed's assigned Warder does not lower the boarding ladder for that individual. No one seems to know how these restrictions are organized and I have yet to understand how this system works. Restrictions are not based on flatbed color since, for example, one paj-colored flatbed may be restricted while a subsequent one of the same color is not. Could restrictions be based on a Warder's personal preference? Perhaps restrictions are based on arbitrary color whims of higher order individuals, creating flatbed restrictions that all Warders must uphold. There is a rumor running rampant among Walkers and Riders: it is possible that a Walker who was recently denied access to a particular selected flatbed might find that, later, boarding was granted. That I find hard to believe. Inconsistency is not a quality I would expect of our X7-PanExpanse.

"Still unknown to all of us is the methodology used to choose Warders from out of all the available individuals. There are so many questions. What personal character traits make a good Warder? What possible criteria are used to assign a Warder to a particular flatbed? Can an individual even become a Warder or do Warders originate from a different system in the X7-PanExpanse? And what about a limit as to the number of Riders allowed on any given flatbed platform? I do not think I have ever seen a flatbed platform that has overflowed its capacity. How is this managed? Are some flatbeds more popular than others? And why would there be, since all flatbeds are identical except for color? The Warders seem to be in control. To some of us, this is all so-o-o-o maddening.

"Maddening it may be, but I must say that I keep a lot of these thoughts to myself lest I be chastised into a cenisse of shame by some old sedentary Rider who wants to upbraid me for disturbing the flatbed peace with my inappropriate questions and ideas.

"I have never seen a Warder that was not on board a flatbed platform; i.e. I have never seen a Warder walking out and about on the ground of the X7-PanExpanse. What would happen if a Warder did leave a flatbed? Given the color of a Warder's outfit, the Warder would surely stand out dramatically on the white ground with a bunch of Walkers milling about. Unfortunately, for the Riders on that Warder's flatbed, there would be no one left to raise or lower one of the ladders, ever again. Would a Warder on the ground, at that point, become a Walker? If so, and if a Warder could get back on board the Warder's assigned flatbed somehow, would that individual return to being a Warder or merely be a Rider? What if a Rider took over the pulpoose controls? Is that even possible? And what about a de-boarded outfit color? Would it change color? I do not think the Warders are worth all this brain energy since they almost never step down from their little pulpooses; they just pull levers and watch the ladders go up and down. Surely Warders get some entertainment value from their lofty position on a flatbed—assuming, of course, that Warders are actual individuals. Is it not entertaining for a Warder to look down across a flatbed and see it full of quiescent Riders sitting around and lying about like a wallowing crowd of semi-motionless, bloated blobs? While Warders stand vigilant, raising and lowering the ladders, who knows what they could be contemplating up there on those little 'thrones.' How could anyone ever find out? No one is going milk any information out of one of them. Any of them.

"It is my opinion that Warders are nothing more than just living, mindless pods; shells saddled with a never-ending, soul-coagulating repetitive and routine job. And (from who knows where) given an air of authority—a manufactured authority that is artificial at best and totally gliss[14] at worst. That authority is only established by a Warder's singular ability to restrict Walkers from becoming Riders on certain, pre-designated flatbeds."

### Flyers

Next, dear Reader, you might find interesting these comments from an unusual person-type found in the X7-PanExpanse, a Flyer. They have their own viewpoint on life and culture. Flyers have a unique way of putting things. Most of the individuals in the X7-PanExpanse have never even seen a Flyer, but we have one here for you now, Po'Emmus[FLYER].

---

[14] foul ejecta or excreta from an unknown sub-species or individual

Po'Emmus<sup>FLYER</sup>:

"I welcome myself. A few of the more restless Riders, my own lovely self included, often find that their inner energy has suddenly upped itself over the rim. This energy, unleashed, manifests itself as an urge to change flatbeds; to leap directly from one flatbed to another to leap forward or backward; to leap to a sanctioned flatbed or to one of those unnecessarily restricted ones. Gliss...gliss on those, those arbitrary restrictions. This motivated inner energy comes from some mysterious and unknown humor swirling in the dark non-conforming psyche of such potentiated individuals. The urge comes, the urge goes, then on out, and back again. At some point, definitive action must be taken; the urge becomes too strong. An individual must act. Beyond this, I feel no obligation to explain myself further; and that includes any overly pasty 'officials' that may confront me about my motivations.

"My last designation was 'Rider' but now I am considered a 'Flyer.' Designations mean nothing to me; those who make the designations mean nothing to me. And that is my opinion. As a result of my being gratuitously tagged with the designation 'Flyer,' my body covering is now luf[15], just like the body covering of every other Flyer. All of this came about because I happened to make a successful, and may I say graceful, leap across a coupling gap to a forward, restricted flatbed—restricted by *who*, I would like to know. Through raw skill alone I avoided crashing into the pesky Warder's pulpoose—that is a leap hazard that all of my Flyer friends cautioned me about. I, of course, landed safely on the edge of the new flatbed platform; and not without style and grace mind you. I did *not* wind up with Closure and I was not 'collected,' although many—particularly those of a much lesser essence of quality than myself—have met these fates when attempting such an unapproved and dangerous feat. Perhaps those individuals were not made of true Flyer stuff to begin with. They should never have tried it, I tell you...I tell you right now.

"After I landed, I felt and saw nothing special about the new flatbed; nothing different from any other platform I had ever occupied. I had no idea that the flatbed was even restricted. Restricted to *me*. According to the higher authority, I am no good; I am a

---

[15] light fulmous blue

renegade for even attempting the leap much less accomplishing it. There were gasps, I will admit it, from the ever-present inert groups of Riders as they grudgingly repositioned themselves around, slowly and sluggishly, in order to accommodate my sudden arrival. But, after that, in general, nobody paid any attention to me at all, not even the Warder. Warders, what a bunch of— All of this lying-around inactivity was very curious as I believed that at least something extraordinary should happen to me for making a successful leap. My body covering did change its color to luf, permanently, but I do not care. Not a bit. I am comfortable in my body covering and that is all that matters. Since then, luf always identifies me as a Flyer no matter where I go or what I do. There are still restricted flatbeds (restricted to *me*), but who knows if that really changed when I became a Flyer. Who knows? That is my experience.

"Some individuals that I have known—those harboring brain organs of a lesser vigor— have attempted a leap to a *backward* flatbed. They are fools. *They* are the fools—not me or my own self. A backward leap is easy; easy because the inconvenient Warder's pulpoose and scaffolding is right next to you *before* you leap. And there is plenty of unobstructed space to land. But, a backward leap is pointless. It can only be of value if the backward target flatbed is *restricted* since even a non-adventuresome individual can move backward fairly easily by merely de-boarding and boarding in the normal way. The haac flatbed is moving *toward* your own self, you idiots. Risk free. You figure it out. Yes, you. And if the flatbed is restricted, some official individual is going to boot you off anyway.

"Some Walkers have attempted to leap onto a flatbed from the ground. That is crazy. No one has ever made it, and I am knowledgeable enough to know all the facts. It is just too high a leap and the flatbed is moving; continually, relentlessly moving.

"Every individual who has made a successful leap across a coupling gap has had the same change of body covering color (luf) as myself. How this occurs automatically is still a big mystery. Only those of a higher order must know. What do you think? If they are all gifted with higher order intellects why do they need to identify us all by the color of our body coverings? Why is it a secret?

"Another case involves a Rider leaping from a flatbed out onto the ground. Thud. In every one of these cases, the Rider hits the ground and is swallowed up; swallowed up by the fine granular layer on the surface. That is what I have heard. There may be someone out there who has done it successfully. But why try it? Where do all those jumping Riders go when they disappear into the ground? They certainly do not go through Closure. And what all is down there beneath the surface anyway?

"Being designated as a Flyer has brought me nothing, except for the color change in my body covering. I still have restricted access to certain flatbeds; perhaps different ones; maybe even *more* so-called restrictions. I cannot walk any faster. I have no new insights. Referring to me as a Flyer apparently means nothing. Individuals in the X7-PanExpanse show no reverence, no heightened respect, no curiosity toward me—me, a Flyer! I believe that the smoky-dark hidden truth in all this is that the high risk and eventual indifference toward a Flyer act together as a coordinated deterrent—there is nothing to be gained from being successful, so why do it?

"One last observation from my own self: I have seen more than one Rider fail; fail while attempting to leap across a coupling gap. They may be failed attempts, but they are fascinating to watch. Down they go, randomly smashing about into the wheels, the wheel carriage, or crushed into the foundation stone between the rails. Some have crashed into a Warder's scaffolding. That individual becomes an indescribable twisted mass that many times just falls to the rails below. For most individuals the spectacle of a failed leap is just too awful to witness and dwell on. But to me it is interesting and very entertaining. It is very much like being a member of a special group and watching outsiders struggle in an attempt to get accepted.

"Following a failure, a Heeler arrives almost immediately. The Heeler stands over the heap of former individual—stands there looking over the rubble, thinking. Thinking what? To what end? But before too many oncoming soulless flatbed wheels can pulverize the individual's mass further, from out of nowhere there always comes a crew of Collectors, their job being to collect the individual's pieces and whisk them away to some unknown location. They have methods of collecting all the pieces of the former individual even from dangerous areas under the moving flatbeds. They are always able leave the location spotless. If the Collectors get you in this way, then you get no Closure. That is what I have heard. And I believe that. Collecting is a fascinating procedure to watch, but if you want to watch the whole procedure, you have to do it as a Walker—the flatbeds keep moving. It is equally fascinating to observe the lack of interest from the Riders and even the Walkers that happen to be near the site of the tragedy (if it can even be called that).

"As a Flyer, I must say in conclusion that we all know the rules. We all know the risks. And I can tell you honestly, even with my level of skill, I would not attempt another leap; not even for a change of outfit."

∞

Rakers

We have to wonder if the inner character of Po'Emmus[FLYER] came about as a result of becoming a Flyer or was it his original inner character that made Po'Emmus[FLYER] want to become a Flyer later in life.

It is quite apparent that the population of the X7-PanExpanse is not a homogeneous lot in spite of their uniform appearance. Understanding their collective adoration and respect for the X7-PanExpanse and its restrictions is something that continues to elude me. Our next contributor is a representative of one of the more secretive designations, an "official," a Raker. Given his position in X7-PanExpanse security, our representative, Pud'Nulli[RAKER], wishes to remain anonymous, so we shall honor his request and refer to him by his chosen pseudonym, Jeffsoder Dubkiester Moutón.

Jeffsoder Dubkiester Moutón:
"I keep order along the Rail-line. You foul up; I am there. I restore equilibrium. I keep a watchful eye. It is my job. I am a Raker. Those who respect the longitudinal limits should have no fear. Rakers are only interested in the rebels, the cheats, the slackers. That is *my* interest. That is *my* job. I am a Raker.

"I have been tasked, by those in the higher order, to give you some insights on the Rakers. I have no reason to question the higher order. But, to save time, I will merely answer questions posed to me, as long as no security secrets are involved."

*How are Rakers chosen for service?*
"No can say. Security."

*How can a Raker tell if a Walker has drifted backward beyond the longitudinal limit?*
"That information is secret for a reason."

*What is the reason?*
"No can say."

*Can a Raker perform Closure?*
"Absolutely no can say. What is your name?"

*Uh...what happens to a Walker if they do not move on forward or board a flatbed after being ordered to do so by a Raker?*
"Not relevant."

*How is it that a Raker suddenly appears as soon as a Walker drifts backward beyond the limit? And where do the Rakers go after pushing a compliant Walker forward?*
"No can say. Two questions, over the limit."

*What limit?*
"No can say."

*Is there anything you can tell us about the Rakers that will enlighten us about this mysterious group?*
"I have already told you more than I should."

Well, dear Reader, in my opinion, that was a big waste of time and space. I should have known better. So let me bring forward Hri'Vrix<sup>RIDER</sup>. She has had some experience with Rakers and can offer you her thoughts on the group.

Hri'Vrix<sup>RIDER</sup>:

"Rakers; they think they run everything. I have seen their types many times before: self-important, oh so anointed ones. I have had multiple run-ins with them. Never good. As a Walker, I find it fascinating that I can walk out laterally until I can barely see the Rail-line, but if I drift toward the backward end, allowing many flatbeds to pass me by, suddenly there appears a Raker in the standard official flamboyant colored outfit. I can never tell if the Raker is a *he* or a *she* or an *it*. But, with a few exceptions, they all act the same: overzealous, spooky, and authoritarian. I do not consider the Rakers as nasty unipogitors the way some Walkers do. We all want equilibrium and tranquility. We all respect the system. For each of us to fulfill our purpose here in the X7-PanExpanse there must be those individuals whose job it is to enforce the rules and keep the order of things. I have no problem with Warders. But those ornery Rakers—

"What are they hiding beyond the longitudinal limit? What *is* the limit? It seems to vary. I have drifted backward over thirty flatbeds before a Raker ever showed up. Another time it was only four. What do they think? Do they think, looking backward along the Rail-line, that I cannot see all the flatbeds, Walkers, Riders, and others still visible way beyond the enigmatic and arbitrary longitudinal limit?

"I believe I am going to be in serious hot cenisse for revealing what I have learned from my experiences, but there does not seem to be anyone assigned to the task of keeping a lid on someone like me.

"In one particular instance I found myself seven flatbeds to the rear of where I started. Without warning, a small area on the ground began to quiver, those glassy granules falling all about themselves as a mound appeared, giving way to a Raker, standing tall, puffed up, and wearing that familiar, official-colored outfit. 'Where do you think *you* are going?' the Raker asked me. 'Over there,' I answered pointing backward down the Rail-line. As he pushed me forward he told me to either get walking faster in order to catch up with other flatbeds or to board the one right next to us. Before I did anything, I engaged the Raker in conversation, asking where he/she came from just then, and what would happen if I did not comply? While we had this discussion, the flatbeds kept moving, one, two, three, four— If I was being restricted from these passing flatbeds by a longitudinal limit, how is it that they were suddenly the only ones I could board? This whole system seems so ridiculous that I could just blow out a headweight[16] of gliss.

"Just so you know, every flatbed that I have ever seen looks exactly the same (except for the color of course). Each flatbed carries any number of Riders, most all of them lying about, doing nothing, stretching, scratching, rolling over. On every flatbed a diligent Warder stands ever ready at the ladder control levers. One exception to all this, I have heard, is a Progenitor flatbed, but the only one I have ever seen was the one I de-boarded as a youth; and that was a long time ago; and memories fade. Occasionally I might spot a group of Cloysteers meeting in one corner of a flatbed, but, for the most part, the bulk of the Riders are always content to mindlessly bask in a cenisse of mind-numbing tranquility as their chosen flatbed keeps moving right on along.

"When I am on board a flatbed, I do not lie about like an inanimate object, yet I am surrounded by those whose only movements are to make adjustments to themselves or to reposition themselves among the others; most everyone else doing the same thing. They do not converse. They pay attention to nothing—Walkers board, a few Riders de-board. I do not think they even notice when a Rider makes a leap to become a Flyer, regardless of the outcome. They merely exist, which is their right of course. But that life is not for me. So, I have chosen to spend nearly all of my time as a Walker, in spite of my constant confrontations with Rakers. I cannot stand to stay aboard a flatbed carrying a horde of semi-conscious Riders for very long. I have to walk. I have to get away. During my brief periods as a Rider, I must say that I find it offensive that the inert individuals lying about on the flatbeds are designated as Riders as well. It is very disrespectful to a Rider like me.

---

[16] about eight and a half pounds (3.172 kg)

There should be a distinction, a different designation. Might I suggest the designation 'bedslug'? I am not like them. I am not.

"Another instance where I was accosted by a Raker had a strange twist. The flatbeds that were next to the Raker and myself were all empty except for the Warder on each one. I was ordered to get on board a flatbed immediately or move along, so I tried to comply by boarding the nearest flatbed and was denied access by the Warder. The next flatbed was empty, and the next, and the next. Those Warder denials, one after one, eventually caused a big ruckus between one of the Warders and the Raker. While they discussed the situation, their attention turned away from me, I continued walking backward along the Rail-line away from the Raker and the nearby flatbed. As I walked, expecting to be snatched up and carried off to Mugulus[17], all I saw was a continuation of the same old chain of familiar flatbeds moving along, same old bunches of nondescript Riders on them, Warders at the controls. I kept walking and soon the Raker was out of sight. There was no breakdown of the system, no X7-PanExpanse-shaking event, no spook came to get me— nothing. It was not until several more flatbeds passed by—maybe ten—that a new Raker confronted me. At that time I was ordered to comply by boarding the unrestricted flatbed next to us; which I did. As I was going up the ladder, I looked back and saw the Raker slowly sink into the ground as if melting into the white granules.

"One last special incident is burned into my memory. I was doing my usual challenging of the limits, boarding and de-boarding, when I encountered another Walker who was engaged in Rider 'drift.' A Raker confronted him and performed, what looked to be, an immediate Closure, although I cannot say for sure since I am unfamiliar with that process. I saw no Takers in the area. But I was surely shocked. Was I next? What distinguished me from him? What *really* happened to him? Every time a Raker confronts me I think of that incident. But I will not allow myself to be intimidated. Not too much.

"My question is, 'What purpose do the Rakers serve in the overall scheme of things?' If a lowly Normal like myself can venture so far backward from a selected, albeit temporary,

---

[17] a mythical prison camp of supreme awfulness that no one has ever seen but is talked about often

flatbed without the slightest disturbance to the X7-PanExpanse, of what value is an inconstant longitudinal limit, arbitrarily enforced by magically-appearing Rakers? Rakers—I have yet to see the same Raker twice. How many of these individuals are there? You would think that after so many confrontations with me that the same Raker would have rotated in again, but no. What do they do underground when they are not conducting Raker business? Considering the incredible length of the visible Rail-line there must be thousands (or more) stationed in some kind of underground tunnel system, just waiting to be activated, ready to enforce the so-called longitudinal limits. Apparently, I am one of the few who has actually seen the coming and going of a Raker. But who would I tell my story to. Although I feel privileged to be able to relate my experiences as a contributor here, there does not seem to be anyone in the X7-PanExpanse that is the slightest bit interested in these curious Raker facts.

"I have done these excursions so many times that my *original* flatbed (chosen when I was a youth) is now several hundred flatbeds forward from where I am now. I will never be able to get back to it even if I wanted to. I do not think I would recognize that flatbed anyway, all things being the same, as they are. There is no sentimental value to be had. Neither do I miss the indolent mass of fellow Riders with which I co-existed on that *original* youth-chosen flatbed. Why would I?

"In my travels, I have boarded flatbeds of every color. I have challenged and questioned Rakers many times. I have never had a taste for adventure that would make me want to be a Flyer. I have seen what happens to an individual, making the attempt, who falls into a coupling gap. Not something for me. I will spend my time in the X7-PanExpanse walking. It pleases me to know that there are always any number of Walkers out there with me: looking about; exploring; shunning those who have become static immovable mounds of gliss aboard a flatbed—maybe even the same flatbed that they chose as a youth. Never left it, never will.

"I wish I knew what was going on, what it is all about, but I take comfort in knowing *more* about our domain (and the Rakers in particular) than most of the Riders and Walkers around me.

"Riders: what a bunch of lazy, sluggish, zero-progenitors[18]."

## ∞

### P'Ortif^FLYER and L'Oora^RIDER

Well, Hri'Vrix^RIDER, all of us here share your hunger for knowledge. We too would like to know what is going on and what it is all about. And of course, we appreciate all the fine observances provided by you and our other contributors. Not so much gratitude to Pud'Nulli^RAKER who would rather remain anonymous and be referred to as Jeffsoder Dubkiester Moutón for security reasons. In my opinion, he was about as helpful as a de-boarded Warder.

But now, dear Reader, let me relate to you the short, tragic story of P'Ortif^FLYER and L'Oora^RIDER. Whether this story qualifies as X7-PanExpanse mythology or if the events actually occurred is unknown. Rumors abound along the Rail-line, so the telling and retelling of a story inevitably results in a corruption or slow degenerate evolution of certain details. Hopefully that is not the case with this story. It is as accurate as can be expected. So—

In the distant past, the Rail-line was exactly as it is now, straight, unchanging, eternal. Into the world came P'Ortif^RIDER, the product of average Progenitors. Shortly thereafter arrived L'Oora^RIDER, also the product of average Progenitors, but with one important difference: the Progenitors of L'Oora^RIDER preferred a better than average life for their product. Consigned to the same flatbed through many segments of time P'Ortif^RIDER and L'Oora^RIDER spent their pre-youth being idle together, basking in the nothingness world of Rider life aboard a Progenitor flatbed. They were blissfully unaware of anything beyond their pre-youth existence.

The time came when everything changed. They had both reached their "youth." It was time for them to leave their Progenitor flatbed and board flatbeds of their own. Being sensitive to choices and opportunities based on status (which is ironic since there is no

---

[18] bastards

such thing in the X7-PanExpanse) the Progenitors of L'Oora<sup>RIDER</sup> had arranged for her to board a specific flatbed, one that would offer minimal future flatbed restrictions while itself having very tight boarding restrictions. The Progenitors of P'Ortif<sup>RIDER</sup> had no such preference and offered him only advice on to how to choose a flatbed for himself. The choice would be his alone.

Whether it was coincidence or fate, when the time came, both L'Oora<sup>RIDER</sup> and P'Ortif<sup>RIDER</sup> were booted from their Progenitor flatbed at the same time. Each set of Progenitors watched as their youthful offspring became a Walker for the first time; watching the change in outfit color; seeing their grounded offspring fall back as the flatbed chain continued moving forward, carrying the Progenitor flatbed on to...well, *forward*. Despite the puzzled and somewhat hurt looks on the faces of L'Oora<sup>WALKER</sup> and P'Ortif<sup>WALKER</sup> there was no hint of sadness among the two sets of Progenitors since the absence of their offspring paved the way for another round of genitooling[19], the elaborate process of creating *new* product (offspring). It was a time of restrained and somber celebration on board the Progenitor flatbed.

Their feelings of abandonment were brief since both L'Oora<sup>WALKER</sup> and P'Ortif<sup>WALKER</sup> knew they must now choose and board flatbeds of their own. Unfortunately for L'Oora<sup>WALKER</sup> her choice had already been made. She was expected to board a moge-erst[20] flatbed. When one soon came passing by, the ladder was lowered and she boarded the flatbed with ease. P'Ortif<sup>WALKER</sup> attempted to follow her on board but was denied access. It was "ladder up" as far as P'Ortif<sup>WALKER</sup> was concerned. Although all of this seemed very arbitrary to P'Ortif<sup>WALKER</sup>, he knew that quick action was required or L'Oora<sup>RIDER</sup> and her flatbed would fade forward into the white leaving him behind forever. Since L'Oora<sup>RIDER</sup>'s flatbed was chosen for her, she was not allowed to re-choose another, different flatbed until much later. This left the decision solely up to P'Ortif<sup>WALKER</sup>. He attempted to board the flatbed immediately behind L'Oora<sup>RIDER</sup>'s but was denied access. The next flatbed, same story. He *was* allowed to board

---

[19] activity performed by a set of three Progenitors, it is the extremely climactic and satisfying process of putting together a new individual from a quantity of raw material provided by others
[20] foaming reddish-brown

the flatbed after that. This put two restricted flatbeds between P'Ortif[RIDER] and L'Oora[RIDER]. L'Oora[RIDER] now seemed to be almost forever out of reach.

With two flatbeds separating them, P'Ortif[RIDER] and L'Oora[RIDER] could not even talk to each other so she had no way of knowing where he was or how he was. Being so young, P'Ortif[RIDER] had only vague ideas about leaping forward from one flatbed to the next. His youthfulness provided him with no concept of the risk involved. All he wanted was to be on board L'Oora[RIDER]'s flatbed. He did not want to wait for her to change flatbeds some time in the future, de-boarding and re-boarding, back to whichever one he was currently on. What if she missed him? What if she was restricted from his flatbed? The relentless movement of the flatbeds made any thought of inaction totally unacceptable. Circumstances and P'Ortif[RIDER]'s desire to be with his friend demanded bold action.

Stepping over several basking, inanimate Riders, P'Ortif[RIDER] made his way to the front left corner of his current flatbed. His only sense of movement was watching the Walkers out on the ground move in and then out of view, passing by like scenery (the only scenery). Perhaps if he knew the risks involved he would never have attempted a leap.

His youth was big advantage when he finally summoned his courage and made the jump forward to the next flatbed. He had very recently been restricted from boarding that particular flatbed. There were ordinary Riders there doing the usual ordinary things, mostly nothing. He could not tell any difference between the flatbed he just left and the one he was on now. But, his outfit was now luf, identifying him as a Flyer. It was a curious thing, but that part of this adventure was of no concern to him at all. He was not a typical Flyer. He was driven by something diffcrent from the ordinary (and now familiar) Flyer bravado personality. Without thinking, he made a second leap successfully. He was now on the flatbed right behind that of L'Oora[RIDER].

Something felt wrong. There appeared on the ground some kind of "official" in a burlo[21] outfit heading toward the flatbed's boarding ladder. The Warder acknowledged the

_____

[21] wandering neon green

individual and began lowering the ladder so that the official could climb aboard. As P'Ortif<sup>FLYER</sup> moved along, an older Rider, basking in the nothingness, grabbed P'Ortif<sup>FLYER</sup> by the arm, pulling him down, and speaking softly, "Do not stay here. You do not want to be confronted by a Booter. That is the individual that is coming on board. I think he might be after *you*."

Frightened and perplexed by this, P'Ortif<sup>FLYER</sup> quickly moved toward the front left of the flatbed but was blocked by a small group of Cloysteers who were conducting a meeting and would not make the slightest effort to get out of the way. The right front corner *was* open but P'Ortif<sup>FLYER</sup> would have to use a slightly different leaping technique since the next flatbed's Warder pulpoose would be to his left this time. This would be his third leap. Again, he would have to defy the odds. But, he had no time to contemplate any of this. Looking across the coupling gap he saw L'Oora<sup>RIDER</sup> and knew, for sure, that making another (hopefully final) leap was the right thing to do. In spite of the risk of yet another leap, encouraged by two unlikely successes already, I believe he would have made the attempt anyway. Good for him.

When L'Oora<sup>RIDER</sup> spotted P'Ortif<sup>FLYER</sup> getting ready to make his leap, she came to the corner of her flatbed to catch him or to greet him or to assist him, preparing to do whatever was necessary so that they could be together again. P'Ortif<sup>FLYER</sup> again summoned his courage and dove for the edge of L'Oora<sup>RIDER</sup>'s flatbed. This time things did not go as smoothly. P'Ortif<sup>FLYER</sup> was clinging to part of the Warder's scaffolding, the only thing keeping him from falling into the wheel structure of his previous flatbed, now behind him. L'Oora<sup>RIDER</sup> reached down and grabbed his arm and helped him up onto her flatbed. He was safe. He was with his friend. The Warder was uninterested. Everything seemed proper and good. But the Booter on the flatbed behind them was watching them, directing an evil eye toward P'Ortif<sup>FLYER</sup>. If P'Ortif<sup>FLYER</sup> was to be booted off this flatbed it would have to be by a different Booter. By the time a new Booter arrived, P'Ortif<sup>FLYER</sup> surmised that he and L'Oora<sup>RIDER</sup> would be long gone.

The two "friends" embraced each other and sat down to plan for what was to inevitably come next. The moment either of them spotted another Booter attempting to board, they would de-board on the opposite side as soon as the Booter started up the boarding ladder. All of this drama was of no interest to the flatbed Riders or the Warder. A typical response.

It was not long before another Booter appeared. P'Ortif^FLYER recognized the dowygog[22] outfit; it was the same color as that of the other Booters. P'Ortif^FLYER and L'Oora^RIDER now followed the plan. Just as the new Booter started up the boarding ladder, they de-boarded from the opposite side of the flatbed, the indifferent and dutiful Warder lowering the ladder for the youthful couple without hesitation.

Feeling safe, they watched as another thwarted and angry Booter rolled on forward away from them. But the Booter acted quickly and began to de-board on the side with the two "friends." P'Ortif^FLYER and L'Oora^WALKER began walking backward along the line only to see, emerging a few flatbeds away, a Raker coming their way. For a brief moment, they thought about doing a re-board on a passing flatbed but instead decided to head out laterally, walking deep into the X7-PanExpanse, maybe where no one had ever been before.

If I could interject here for a moment—if P'Ortif^FLYER was already off the restricted flatbed, why would a Booter care anymore? And what did the Raker have in mind? Those of us who can exercise free choice can just choose to ignore those kinds of pesky details.

P'Ortif^FLYER and L'Oora^WALKER walked as briskly as an X7-PanExpanse individual can possibly walk. Every time they looked back the Rail-line seemed smaller and smaller. There was no sign of the Booter or the Raker, but the couple continued on until the Rail-line disappeared completely...into the hazy white. They felt safe. There seemed to be no one in pursuit. They were together, by themselves, at last. Sitting down, they finally felt comfortable enough to rest. They were able to laugh about the experience, noting especially the look on the faces of those Booters; and that Raker who added himself onto their adventure at the last minute. Neither of them had ever heard of a Booter before this. They laughed again when P'Ortif^FLYER asked L'Oora^WALKER, "What do you think of my new outfit?"

---

[22] spirit of orange

"It does not matter what I think. You are stuck with it," she replied. She was right.

After a while, they felt rested enough to make new plans. No "officials" showed up or appeared in the distance. L'Oora^WALKER looked around. P'Ortif^FLYER looked around. There was nothing but white in every direction. In their joy they had lost their orientation; they had no idea which direction the Rail-line was in. But it did not matter, they were not going back to the flatbeds anyway.

Which way *were* they going? What if the X7-PanExpanse were to go on forever? Were they going to walk along forever? They picked a direction and began walking. No "officials" appeared. No Rail-line appeared. Again they stopped and sat down on the granular surface. Looking at P'Ortif^FLYER, L'Oora^WALKER asked, "What now?"

Now, dear Reader, I must say that I have some doubt as to the veracity of this story. If P'Ortif^FLYER and L'Oora^WALKER were lost forever into the whiteness of the X7-PanExpanse, how do we know all these details. This story would have to have been pieced together by several individuals. How would that be accomplished? Even so, it would be a wonder of nature if all those individual pieces were not contorted into a maze of unreliable story elements.

However, during my research, in preparation to be your guide, each individual that was familiar with this story provided me with a different plausible outcome for the two "friends."

1) They went to Humma Mádula[23]. Very few individuals believe this version. It is just not credible given the mindset of the individuals in the X7-PanExpanse.

2) They wound up in Mugulus—Humma Mádula forbid. Very few individuals want to believe this version, but many do.

3) They wound up with Closure all on their own, without any official intervention. Not really possible according to the dogma.

---

[23] a spiritual place of great beauty that has no flatbeds, Rakers, or Takers; it is believed that there is something there called "Big Food" but no one in the X7-PanExpanse knows what that might be

4) After wandering about, seemingly forever, they ran across another, different Rail-line with completely different designations, cultural norms, and rules. No Riders or Flyers to be found anywhere.

5) After wandering about, seemingly forever, they found their original Rail-line and lived in bliss and sloth and inactivity aboard a receptive flatbed. This is the standard version, accepted among most Normals.

6) After wandering about, seemingly forever, they found their original Rail-line, were accosted by a Raker, placed on different flatbeds, separated forever, re-designated as Violators, and all kinds of bad things. The Cloysteers love this version.

7) They went their separate ways. "And just where was that?" I might ask.

In spite of all this fluff and vagueness, we can still learn a lot about the X7-PanExpanse from elements in the story. We have been introduced to the Booters. The story reinforces the idea that there is absolutely nothing out there in the distant hazy white. The curious reaction by the second Booter indicates to me that there may exist a small glimmer of free will lurking in some of the X7-PanExpanse individuals. We have also learned (as we suspected) that passing along information from flatbed to flatbed or Walker to Walker will probably corrupt even the most stable and logical story. In addition, I believe that there might be several more alleged endings to this story, but I cannot prove that. Let us move on and find out more about the Violators.

## Violators

Dear Reader, by now you are familiar with the term 'Violator' and, like it or not, there is little that I can add. Violators make themselves scarce and their experiences and circumstances are not well documented. In fact, *nothing* in the X7-PanExpanse is well documented. Or documented at all. Our time together (with my oneship as your guide) is the closest thing to a written record that there has ever been. Even so, we have seen blurred truths, corrupted and apocryphal stories, gossip, beliefs held as facts, and mysterious individuals doing things to other individuals. I feel sure that you will agree with me when I say that, from our point of view, there is no such thing as *history* in the

X7-PanExpanse. There has never been. Once our journey together is over, the history that we have "documented" here will be of value to no one in the X7-PanExpanse. There is no such thing as "reading." All of our experiences together here will be a mere curiosity in our own respective dimensions. In the depths of my broad intellect I cannot conceive of a domain where there is no history. But there it is. What does a lack of history say about the concept of a future in such a domain? My conclusion is that it is not really our problem. Would you not agree?

Well, I seem to have gotten off point. Let us proceed. Since my knowledge of Violators is so limited, we have with us Izo'Lodus[VIOLATOR] who will give us some thoughts on the Violator designation. We will have to keep in mind that, as a Violator, this individual has already demonstrated a certain level of unreliability. But we are grateful for his contribution to our quest for knowledge.

Izo'Lodus[VIOLATOR]:

"Hmmm. It is a *fact* that some*one* or some *thing* has designated me as Violator. That is a fact, we can agree on that. It is also a fact that I did nothing to deserve that designation. That is also a fact and we can agree on *that*. I deal in facts and *that* is a fact. So now that we agree on all the facts I can tell you something about what happens to Violators here in the X7-PanExpanse: Nothing. How did I become so designated? And why?

"As a Walker, I attempted to move backward along the Rail-line beyond the longitudinal limit. That was all. Was not subverting the system. Was not pestering Riders or teasing Cloysteers—at least not as part of this particular incident. It was an innocent Walker's undertaking; I had no evil purpose in mind. I can attest for myself. The Warder fell off of his pulpoose on his own account. I was there, I saw him fall. I did not pull or push him. Not that I can recall. I was merely interested in those levers—up and down, up and down, all the time. Walkers then Riders, Riders then Walkers. The Warder lost his balance. That is a fact. A pulpoose is a very small space. That is also a fact. We can agree on that. Not big enough for two individuals wrestling over the controls. That, too, is fact. If you have ever wrestled with a Warder in one of those pulpooses, you will have to agree with that. Next thing I know the Warder is down there in the coupling gap hanging on to the scaffolding with his hands. I tell you that it is a weird thing—that Warder never made a sound, just struggled to hold on. I tried to help by stepping onto his hands, you know, to hold him tight, but that just made him struggle all the more. I tried to show him what I was up to by pushing my foot into his face but, well, that was it, he just gave up. Down he went. How am I supposed to know what happened to him. I saw nothing. The flatbeds never stop moving. For all I know that Warder is operating the controls on some backward flatbed. But up shows a Booter and a Raker right there—where in the name of Mugulus did they come from? They came out of nowhere; they came for me. Seeing as how I was not to blame, I had nothing to hide; I had nothing to fear from that pair of officials. That is a fact. You see, the facts just keep building up, the facts are on my side. So many.

"I used the pulpoose controls to lower both boarding ladders and de-boarded on the side of the Rail-line away from the Booter and the Raker. Innocently, I started walking toward the backward direction, along the Rail-line. I had nothing to hide. There were many other Walkers wandering about so I just blended myself on in. So there, you see, I was minding my own business, just being a Walker.

"Several flatbeds later I noticed that my outfit color had been changed from oir-venee [Walker's color] to dirovan[24] [Violator's color]. How did *that* happen? *When* did that happen? I was examining my new outfit when I looked up and there in front of me, confronting me, was a Raker. What had I done. I was just walking along, minding my own business. The Raker began nudging me forward. I must have passed the longitudinal limit. That is why my outfit changed color. Yes. That was probably it. There was no sign of the Booter or the other Raker, so passing the limit must have been the violation. Must have been. And that is a fact.

"When I attempted to bypass the Raker, I was given a choice: either move forward or face Closure. I knew that a Raker did not have the authority to do Closure on me so I just kept moving backward. You see, I am totally innocent. I should not be designated as a Violator.

---

[24] wispy violet

"I was then re-approached by the Raker. I referred to him as a zero-Progenitor for again blocking my path. Then he came right up next to me. The ground began to open and the Raker and myself were gobbled up, melted into the ground. The last thing I remember was being eye-level with the surface. I don't remember anything after that. The next thing I knew I was walking forward alongside the Rail-line, next to a group of unfamiliar flatbeds. Even though I was walking out on the ground (my outfit should have been oir-venee but it was still dirovan), I found out that I was not a Walker at all, but a Violator. How could that be? I had not done anything. And that is a fact. You have to agree.

"As a Violator, nothing has really changed for me except for my outfit—well now, I must admit that 'nothing' is too strong a word. It seems that as a Violator (innocent though I may be), as a Violator, I am denied access to *every* flatbed. I have to spend my entire existence as a Walker, walking alongside the Rail-line, never again experiencing the idleness, sloth, and peacefulness that comes along with being a Rider. I must keep walking. Oh, I can stop occasionally, but I cannot stay idle for long because my longitudinal limit is now very short and the Rakers appear and force to me to keep on moving forward and...it all becomes very mundane and awful. I have been warned (by whom I do not recall) that if I do not adhere to a Raker's prodding I will be given Closure immediately. I do not think I want to test that. No. I think not. And that is a fact.

"I think you will agree that the system works arbitrarily, turning innocent Normals like me into Violators for no good reason. My life in the X7-PanExpanse is ruined because of a conspiracy of officials that, well...I do not know. Now that you have been given all the facts, you must agree that something is going on around here, something evil, something...I am going to get to the bottom of it. And that my friends is a *fact*!"

∞

### Providers

Dear Reader, does Izo'Lodus[VIOLATOR] really believe we are swallowing all that gliss? It is very sad to say that, tragically, the Warder who fell under the wheels of the flatbeds, ostensibly crushed into a pile of individual flesh, and viewed by a Heeler for a while, that that Warder eventually recovered enough to return to a new pulpoose further down the Rail-line.

Monotonously raising and lowering boarding ladders, over and over and over— It might cross your mind to ask, dear Reader, "Who in this story got the worst of it, the Warder or the Violator?" You can see from all this that when we apply our own value systems to situations in other dimensional domains we are only asking for trouble; or at the very least, more stubborn questions.

Time for more. Let us get at it.

There is talk that being a Provider leads to one becoming a Violator. That may be true in some cases, but I do not think that one necessarily leads to the other. Providers are relatively harmless as a person-type. Most are even proud of being designated as a Provider. I would not be. Providers, notoriously, do not provide individuals with anything. Nothing but verbiage, as if that alone was the sustenance of life itself. Before I bias you further, dear Reader, let me welcome Barun'Ort[PROVIDER] a Provider who is willing to give us some insights.

Barun'Ort[PROVIDER]:
"Needless to say you have heard of me, of my reputation. If not, then you will soon see why I am such an important and splendid individual here in the X7-PanExpanse. What sustains life here in the X7-PanExpanse? I do. Without me and other splendid individuals like me, no one could exist in this barren, empty domain. We, as a group run the Rail-line and invented the flatbeds. We invented them to provide individuals with a medium to pass from the past, through the present, and into the future. You wonder why the flatbeds keep moving. *We* keep them moving; myself, along with the other Providers. *We* are responsible. *We* keep time from standing still—"

Let me step in here, dear Reader. I need to interrupt this absurd bunch of unipogitor efflux. As our time is limited, it is my responsibility to guide us away from such uninformative windbags. Earlier, the words of Izo'Lodus[VIOLATOR] provided you with an extraordinary look into the mind of a Violator. You could clearly see why he was designated a Violator even through the dense fog of exposition he generated about his experiences.

However, in the case of Barun'Ort[PROVIDER], I feel obligated to correct the record where I see fit. Our journey here is supposed to be one of enlightenment. You should not have your understanding of the X7-PanExpanse be so casually misdirected and polluted. It is common knowledge in the X7-PanExpanse that Providers are completely unaware of their pathological level of telling falsehoods. Whether or not a Normal is aware of this fact does not really matter since no one pays attention to anyone in a spiloot[25] outfit; the outfit color of a Provider. Not that anyone pays much attention to anyone else anyway. But, now that you know these things, dear Reader, I believe the words of Barun'Ort[PROVIDER] will have for you a less insidious polluting effect on your understanding. I do, however, reserve the right to step in when the air becomes too thick with the stench of Provider blather.

Barun'Ort[PROVIDER] (again):

"When I was a youth I knew that I was destined to become an important individual. It was my destiny. I do not believe that I am a product of Progenitors. I *must* have come from somewhere other. Why else would I have been given all this power? Early on as a Normal I was content to sit around like all the others, enjoying the sheer nothingness, basking in tranquility. Soon I found that I had answers to questions asked by many and answered by few—or none. It was my destiny to provide those answers. The truth.

"From one end of a flatbed, I spread the word, the answers to any and all questions, including the most difficult questions imaginable. Even Warders listened and learned from my splendid oratory. Sometimes I have difficulty understanding individuals' skepticism with my enlightening answers. Simple question? I believe a simple answer must be the *right* answer. For example: 'What sustains life here in the X7-PanExpanse? I do...'"

Interrupting. I do not want to be a nuisance, dear Reader, but I do not think that we are getting anywhere. You can see why "Provider" is such a special—and might I say, negative—designation for certain individuals in the X7-PanExpanse. Providers like Barun'Ort[PROVIDER] take advantage of an individual's legitimate desire for clarity, for real

---

[25] bright neon magenta

answers to important questions. Appointing themselves as bearers of the truth, Providers are willing to supply those answers; answers to any questions. In actuality, they have no answers, only self-promoting verbiage. Many Providers start out as Hosperines, Riders whose lust for attention gets fed by a small group of Cloysteers. That is a relationship that is fairly obvious. As time goes by, the attention of a small group is no longer adequate. So the answers get bigger, bolder, more audacious. Bigger questions, bigger answers. Over time, the answers and explanations get more and more polished, counter-arguments get addressed, and contradictions get their own special attention. All of it becomes practiced and self-sustaining. What used to be a big-mouthed, rambling Hosperine becomes a big-mouthed, overreaching Rider with all the answers. Eventually, the misinformation becomes so deadly that some*one* or some *thing* re-designates the individual: Provider. The new Provider's outfit is turned into the spiloot color—it is truly difficult to miss a Provider in that color outfit. And so, in the end, it resolves itself. What a Provider says is universally and utterly ignored. The Provider is content to speechify everything, even if no one is listening. The Provider's pathetic self-delusion of importance stays intact.

All of that, dear Reader, may appear to be inadequate justice for such a shallow group of lying, blathering unipogitors. However, you may find it comforting to know that there is one other destiny that befalls Providers so designated: the last flatbed occupied by a newly-designated Provider becomes that Provider's *permanent* flatbed; the Provider is never allowed to de-board it. The flatbed's Warder enforces this restriction. Over time, the vast majority of Riders that happened to be on the same flatbed as the new Provider eventually de-board and find other flatbeds to bask on; sometimes, much to their relief. Sooner or later, the only audience a Provider has is the Warder stationed on the Provider's permanent flatbed; not that it ever deters any Provider from continuing the oratory. I, for one, believe that the audience of one (the Warder) is actually an audience of zero since Warders have no interest in any of that outpouring of Provider ramblings; the Warder's only concern is in forever forcing 'ladder up' for the Provider. Occasionally, a Walker will unwittingly board a Provider's empty flatbed only to de-board shortly thereafter, having been hit with a virtual flood of lies, braggadocio, lecturing, and offensive, pungent, foaming gliss.

With all of that in mind, dear Reader, let us be generous to Barun'Ort[PROVIDER] allowing him to have the last word before we move on. Have pity, dear Reader, he knows not what he provides.

Barun'Ort[PROVIDER] (once again):

"I do not take offense (I am that great) when there are those that question my answers since they have none of their own. I see them as irritants and obstacles. They cannot recognize greatness when it stares them down from the end of a flatbed. If I wanted to, *I* could stand in a Warder's pulpoose, reaching out to everyone on my flatbed. I choose not to. My place is down, among my individuals, feeling what they feel, refining my splendid oratory, all on a personal basis. Let me close by providing you with some answers to persistent questions that come before me from the alleged minds of the masses.

"Many have asked me, 'What do the flatbed colors represent?' I must say that it is a fascinating question. Those colors—and Warders with matching colors. Is it not splendid, splendid indeed? Others have asked, 'What are the rules governing the longitudinal limits?' Let me answer that with a question, 'What does anyone mean by longitudinal?' Big word, used to confuse individuals, keeping it vague to cover up the truth. And we all want the truth. Is that not so? Another question, 'Why are you called a Provider?' The answer is obvious. And, of course, the biggest, most important question of all, 'How does one rise to become part of the elite, a Provider?' Unless you happen to be one of the so-destined few that have my gifts there is no point in trying. It must come naturally. There is only room for a chosen few at the top. Answers? Yes. Satisfaction? Guaranteed and delivered.

"I have so many important things on my agenda that I must now call an end to this enlightening discussion. I know that I have added to everyone's knowledge and have provided some much-needed evidence for why my lot in life is *greatness*. My destiny. I am the incarnation of all that is good in the X7-PanExpanse. I can speak in proverbs, I can induce youths to become one with the great whiteness beyond. I know where the ground is not flat. I know where the Rail-line ends and begins. I know where the flatbeds are going. I know exactly where the sky meets the ground. I know the names of all the Warders. Rakers would avoid my very presence (if I could somehow get off of this haac flatbed).

Booters are close friends of mine—sometimes they boot off an individual merely based on my whim. What power. I know why we are here, here in the X7-PanExpanse, here on these flatbeds. Listen to me for I am the provider of all knowledge, of all truth..."

Enough, enough. So it seems that I must have the last word after all. Dear Reader, in spite of all his "answers," his contribution has spawned yet another question, one question that even Barun'Ort<sup>PROVIDER</sup>, a slave to his non-existent introspection, cannot answer: Does Barun'Ort<sup>PROVIDER</sup> really believe all that regurgitated spew that comes out of his mouth? Try to answer that one you self-appointed, self-anointed Provider. Forgive me, dear Reader, my bias runneth over.

## Zee'Erl<sup>VIOLATOR</sup>

Out there, somewhere, in the vast, white nothingness of the X7-PanExpanse, exists Zee'Erl<sup>VIOLATOR</sup>, an interesting character with a checkered past. It would be highly enlightening if we could speak to him directly, but, alas, he is as elusive as a straight answer from a Provider. And you now know what I mean by that. We will probably never know if Zee'Erl<sup>VIOLATOR</sup> is currently avoiding contact with officials; or if he even needs to. Could it be that he is just lost? Possibly his fate was merely Closure—a common, ordinary end for an uncommon individual.

Ages ago, as a youth, as all others do, Zee'Erl<sup>VIOLATOR</sup> started out his life as a Walker, booted off his original flatbed by his three Progenitors. Like so many Normals of his era, back and forth he occupied himself with the boarding and de-boarding of flatbeds, using his system-given power of free choice. It was not long before he befriended several Riders aboard a ter-erst[26] flatbed where he unemotionally and casually fell in with a group of Cloysteers. It followed that, with his restless and devious personality, he soon advanced to become the group's Hosperine, elbowing out the existing one unceremoniously—most likely unfairly as well. His leadership position went to his head. He was, after all, a skilled opportunist, having no interest in the beliefs of the Cloysteers, their "message," or their hierarchy. Let

---

[26] rich and bright reddish-brown

us say that, his heart was not so much in promoting a message as it was in looking out for himself. With his aggressive nature, it was not long before his designation was automatically changed from Zee'Erl[RIDER] the Rider to Zee'Erl[PROVIDER] the Provider—recall that a Hosperine is not an official anything. Unlike other self-delusional Providers, he was not content to stay aboard his permanently assigned flatbed, especially after all his fellow flatbed Riders had abandoned him. The Warder's lack of interest—a totally natural and expected response—drove Zee'Erl[PROVIDER] over the edge.

Realizing that he had very few options, Zee'Erl[PROVIDER] tried to leap onto the next forward flatbed. This, he thought, would serve three purposes:

1) He would be re-designated a Flyer. He hated being a Provider; at least the deserted flatbed part.

2) He would be back among Riders, giving him companionship and a new audience for his enlightening oratory.

3) With a different Warder he would again be able to board and de-board flatbeds at will; he longed to be a Walker again, walking every once in a while.

Zee'Erl[PROVIDER] leapt. He made it on the first try, although it was touch and go when he hit part of the Warder's scaffolding as he landed. As for his three goals, unfortunately for him he miscalculated on all counts. He remained a Provider and as such had no welcoming audience for his speeches and no worshiping Riders looking for his leadership. His unchanged outfit color alerted the new Warder as to Zee'Erl[PROVIDER]'s designation as a Provider so it continued to be 'ladder up' on his *new* flatbed.

Frustrated and perturbed that his risky leap to a new flatbed had not altered anything, he became reckless in his choice of actions. He had been emboldened by his first and only successful leap so he tried the "ratchet" scheme: leaping *forward* from flatbed to flatbed across multiple coupling gaps. This was quite a feat—to what end, only Zee'Erl[PROVIDER] knows. It was a rare event for a Rider to make even *one* successful leap, much less many. Although he continued to remain a Provider after many, many successful leaps—some easy, some difficult, some painful, some almost ending in disaster—he did get a glorious sense of satisfaction and accomplishment from his long, unbroken string of successes. True to the Warders' unwritten code of conduct, not a single Warder paid notice to the sudden, new arrival of Zee'Erl[PROVIDER] after he (Zee'Erl[PROVIDER]) made a successful landing. That is, a Warder would have paid him no attention until he (Zee'Erl[PROVIDER]) tried to de-board a newly adopted flatbed. And you guessed correctly, dear Reader, it was still, and as ever, "ladder up" for the ambitious and adventurous Zee'Erl[PROVIDER].

Given all this, he had only one, even more reckless, option left. It was something that was never successfully managed by any Rider in recent memory. Rumors or no rumors, he would de-board by jumping directly from the flatbed to the ground, disregarding the ladders altogether. Zee'Erl[PROVIDER] had heard the rumors of jumpers hitting the ground and disappearing into it. It was a foolish plan with little chance of success, but Zee'Erl[PROVIDER] was desperate. He first considered the idea of impulsively jumping off into the air, landing, and rolling to a stop on a flat area of white ground. But in spite of his recklessness and wild ideas, he really had no desire for Closure; or worse still, disappearing into the ground—what exactly would that be? He finally settled on a plan where he would locate a small group of Walkers, jump into the group, and allow the individuals' bodies to cushion his fall. "Has no one ever tried this?" he asked himself. It seemed like a perfectly rational, logical, and obvious plan. Once he decided to do it, he began watching and waiting for a target group. As luck would have it—and Zee'Erl[PROVIDER] seemed to have his fair share of good luck—he did not have to wait very long before his flatbed came alongside a large, dense group of Walkers. Why there were so many bunched together was unexpected and highly unusual.

Zee'Erl[PROVIDER] jumped. Landing directly into the center of the group, he bounced on top of several individuals and eventually fell softly to the ground. It was just the result he had hoped for. The members of the group (who were not as organized or purposeful as they looked) migrated on and dispersed as Zee'Erl[PROVIDER] picked himself up and began walking. He was still a Provider, but he was on the ground—what an accomplishment. He did not know what to expect now as he knew nothing about the rules of the X7-PanExpanse for someone on the ground with his Provider designation. What could his longitudinal limit possibly be now?

Rather than tempt fate yet again by alerting a Raker, he started walking *forward* alongside the moving flatbeds acting as nonchalant as possible. No matter that he was saddled, probably permanently, with a Provider outfit, no matter that he was stuck with the Provider designation, he felt like a Walker again. But, it must be said that his big, bold jump did *not* go unnoticed. The large group of individuals that cushioned his leap noticed; many other individuals on that side of the Rail-line noticed; the Warder noticed (and felt that her sense of order had been violated). And more importantly, some*one* or some*thing* of a higher order noticed. And that was, unfortunately, the beginning of the end for Zee'Erl^PROVIDER.

He had barely a moment to relax when a Raker rose up from the ground and blocked the way. As Zee'Erl^PROVIDER saw things, he could not possibly have violated the longitudinal limit, but here was a Raker, ready for action. The legend of Zee'Erl^PROVIDER was about to be set in stone for all time.

Noticing a flatbed coupling gap rapidly approaching along the Rail-line, Zee'Erl^PROVIDER immediately jumped to his side, away from the granule-wading Raker—the Raker who was about to descend into the ground, taking Zee'Erl^PROVIDER with him. Zee'Erl^PROVIDER landed on the sharp top edge of the coupling. It was not a pleasant sensation for the dangling Zee'Erl^PROVIDER, but neither was the thought of disappearing into the ground with a Raker. Zee'Erl^PROVIDER scrambled over the coupling and pushed himself off, clear of the flatbeds, and onto the ground on the other side of the Rail-line. There he saw only a few Walkers and no "officials" of any kind. Why was there no Raker to accost him? Not one to wait around for events to overtake him, Zee'Erl^PROVIDER made for the distant absence-of-hills, into the vast whiteness of the X7-PanExpanse, and was soon to disappear forever. Before the Rail-line was completely out of sight, Zee'Erl^VIOLATOR found that he had automatically been re-designated: Violator. His outfit had changed color to dirovan. Zee'Erl^VIOLATOR did not care. He was free.

Now, dear Reader, there is no way for us to verify this story; but it is one that has been passed around in the X7-PanExpanse for as long as anyone can remember. If the story is true, then it appears that at least some of the seemingly inviolate laws that govern existence in the X7-PanExpanse may be circumvented if an individual is clever enough. I have found that this phenomenon is universal and exists in most, if not all, of the many domains that I have studied. I am sure that you, dear Reader, have seen examples of that in your own domain.

∞

## The Spiral Horn

There are those individuals in the X7-PanExpanse that actively seek answers; many a Rider, many a Walker. As your guide, dear Reader, I have tried to *provide* (if you will excuse me for using that term)—I have tried to provide you with a broad view of the X7-PanExpanse, the Rail-line, and a cross-section of individuals that co-exist in the X7-PanExpanse. You have seen for yourself the adventures of a number of special knowledge-seekers. There are, of course, many other Normals that do not actively pursue knowledge. Most of the Riders found on any given flatbed are slothful baskers, existing, stretching, and lying about without pursuing anything, happy to wallow in tranquility and inactivity. We have run across a number of these types during our journey. Yet, among this group, there are those that can be dredged out of their torpid state and lured in by the mere *promise* of knowledge. But in actuality, it is not knowledge they seek. They merely seek confirmation of and validation for what they already believe. They feed on each other's questionable and insubstantial information, passing it back and forth, until, to them, it becomes truth. Add to this a seductive, apocryphal baseline story—one with which all these individuals feel completely comfortable—and you have the makings of a sub-culture, even in a domain like the X7-PanExpanse. Long ago, just such a sub-culture emerged; one that eventually developed into what is now known as *The Order of the Spiral Horn*.

And this, dear Reader, is that baseline story:

In ancient times (whatever that means in the X7-PanExpanse), an innocent Walker wandered far into the white, not really searching for anything in particular, just wandering. Before long, the Walker, Rana'Orami[WALKER], discovered that she could no longer see the Rail-line nor could she make out the presence of any other Walkers. You and I, dear Reader, have heard of this kind of issue before. Rana'Orami[WALKER] continued to wander, now urgently, with a more purposeful mind, expecting that, at any moment, the Rail-line or another Walker would come back into view. Then, high in the sky, there appeared to her a huge, spiral-shaped entity, rotating slowly and seemingly coming toward her. Was it a living being? There was no form of life in the X7-PanExpanse other than the individuals with which she was already familiar; she was not aware of any others. Was the spiraling entity a machine? The Rail-line and the flatbeds were the only mechanical devices anyone knew about. To her, the only logical course of action was to turn around and walk away as fast as possible, away from the hovering object.

Let me interject here for a moment. The X7-PanExpanse is a fascinating domain, and many transdimensional beings, like myself, study it. We study it along with a myriad of other dimensions, domains, featureless voids, and countless others. Without knowing for sure, I can only speculate that the spiral entity was merely a manifestation of just such an explorer. But it is only speculation.

The spiral entity did not pursue Rana'Orami[WALKER], but it did let out a loud burst of sound, a shrill siren-like sound. Although brief, it was, metaphorically speaking, ploo[27]-coagulating. When the sound stopped, the spiral entity had disappeared. Let us assume that this part of the story is true. Let us also assume that the spiral entity was a mechanism or force operated by some transdimensional being. It appears to me that, as the transdimensional being's spiral entity left the X7-PanExpanse, it broke through the bright, uniform sky and created a rift. This rift disturbed the sky's stable and constant state causing the reverberating, horn-like blast. It is an effortless and non-challenging explanation requiring a lot of assumptions. I do not necessarily accept all of it—but it might be true.

Rana'Orami[WALKER] kept walking, not looking back; then fortune smiled on her. In the distance she saw the Rail-line, and soon after she saw a number of other Walkers. When she got all the way back to the Rail-line she boarded a non-restricted flatbed and sat down, contemplating what had happened to her. Of course, she knew no one on that particular flatbed; the one she had de-boarded was long gone forward by that time. After a short

---

[27] the self-generating, viscous internal liquids that supply the body of an individual with nourishment and structural support

while, she innocently told a nearby Rider about her experience. Never before had anyone ever seen anything in the sky but the sky itself. Flyers did not really fly—well, for that matter, nothing did. The unfamiliar thing that Rana'Orami^WALKER saw was somehow hovering there in the whiteness, all on its own. Of course, everyone had an opinion about the story, at least for a while. The story easily spread among those Riders on Rana'Orami^WALKER's new flatbed, and soon after, rumors spread from flatbed to flatbed and out among the Walkers as well. As is typical, the vast majority of Normals were interested in the story only long enough to spread the rumor, but not much more than that. By the time the story had reached far along the Rail-line and minimally wide, Rana'Orami^WALKER was long since forgotten. But the story itself continued to live on.

It may be that the entire story is merely bunk. Rana'Orami^WALKER may never have existed at all. Rumor or fantasy or true story, it did live on in the minds of a few individuals. With this single belief in common, small groups of Riders began to form, calling themselves members of *The Order of the Spiral Horn*.

Note how they named their group after the entity, with no reference whatsoever to Rana'Orami^WALKER. The whole story was only revealed to me (almost inadvertently) because of my transdimensional status. My experience has allowed me to detect a familiar pattern in mythologies: over many lifetimes, some elements survive and others do not. Some elements are added or dropped to suit the times. In this way, mythology survives and evolves just like life itself.

Before we take a look at the Cloysteers, let us examine what has become of *The Order of the Spiral Horn*. The current version of The Order explains Closure, or more accurately, The Order allows its members to explain it. Therefore the explanation varies from group to group. Other polychromatic explanations include the origin of the Rail-line—not only how it came into being, but where it is coming from, backward, from out of the white haze. Similarly, explanations abound concerning the ultimate forward end of the Rail-line. Some versions include an incoherent mix of Closure, The End of the X7-PanExpanse, and the Rail-line terminus. The concepts of Mugulus and Humma Mádula were rooted in and emerged from this maelstrom of questionable explanations. You can only imagine the flatbed-load of anecdotes and speculative notions that surround the "officials" that appear and disappear in the X7-PanExpanse; especially those mysterious ones that have no official designation.

However, the connective tissue that holds The Order together is a belief in The Dementians, the higher order beings that run everything. How this became the foundation belief of the Order is truly unknown. I suspect that, at some point in the past, an individual in some group proposed the idea, and because members of The Order found the concept too seductive to ignore, they adopted it and spread it all along the Rail-line. Again, as with other things, over time, the concept of the Dementians evolved, becoming more refined, acquiring more specific spurious detail, and solidifying like stone in the minds of the Cloysteers. Getting information about the Dementians from Cloysteers has been one of the easiest knowledge-gathering tasks I have ever had. Every Cloysteer I have interviewed has been rabidly eager to pass along every known, well-developed detail. I have found a few variations and a few inconsistencies in the descriptions of the Dementians, but I will cover those features that are generally agreed upon among the Cloysteer set.

The Dementians are believed to have a very organized hierarchy in their lofty and wondrous higher-order domain. Members of the hierarchy are organized in a two-dimensional pyramid as shown here:

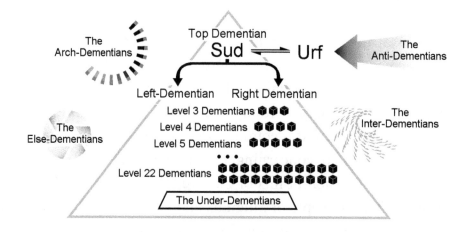

Please be mindful of the fact, dear Reader, that the Cloysteers (and for that matter all the other individuals in the X7-PanExpanse) have absolutely no idea what a pyramid is, even a simple two-dimensional one. The Cloysteers have a *sense* of the hierarchy, but have no real way of describing or understanding their own pyramid scheme.

There is, at the top, a single Dementian, the supreme, all-knowing, eternal Dementian. Neither male nor female, the supreme being is called Sud[28], not to be confused with Urf[29] who, to the Cloysteers, is just a phony poseur. Even mentioning Urf may prevent a Cloysteer from ever becoming a Hosperine. Humma Mádula forbid. All of this is serious business to the Cloysteers. Here and there you can find individual Cloysteers that want to believe in lots of Suds, but they are in a small minority.

Below Sud are two high-level Sud-Associates: a Left-Dementian and a Right- Dementian. Out of respect for the greatness of Sud, no other Dementian is allowed to have an actual name. At the next level there are three Dementians and below them there are four Dementians. If I did not know better I would begin to think that all of this Order hierarchy and personnel is the result of mind pollution caused by contaminated knowledge residue irresponsibly left behind by some transient transdimensional journeyman like myself. But I cannot truthfully say that I have evidence of that. There are five individuals in the fifth Dementian level. Some Cloysteers believe that level five Dementians have the power to fly—up, up, and away. As expected, there are six individuals at the sixth level. This pattern continues up to and beyond the 22nd level—level twenty-two consisting of twenty-two much less important Dementians. Those Dementians below level twenty-two are referred to as the Under-Dementians—purpose unknown. Perhaps they represent those Dementians who never had what it takes to make it into the hierarchy, a kind of catch-all for the rest of the Dementian population.

Outside the basic pyramid, some believe that there is an even *higher* higher-order group known as the Arch-Dementians. They supposedly run everything at an even higher level.

---

[28] the original higher-order supreme being, the top-level Dementian
[29] the alternative higher-order supreme being, a different top-level Dementian

Then there are the Anti-Dementians. Belief in some kind of black and white opposing forces of the universe seems to exist in most domains. And of course an entity like Urf must be part of that belief. The Inter-Dementians serve as some kind of administrative force, managing the interactions between Dementians in different levels of the pyramid. I suppose they keep every Dementian properly confined to their assigned level. Finally, there is the group known as the Else-Dementians. All leftover essential functionality (as invented by the believer) is attributed to some entity in that group. Not every Cloysteer believes in all these groups and all the organization associated with them. My belief is that no single X7-PanExpanse individual understands the entire pyramid scheme anyway.

At some point I found this made-up system tedious, repetitive, and bordering on absurdity. Truthfully, I could not stomach—merely speaking figuratively, as I do not *have* a stomach—I could not stomach any more unsubstantiated ramblings and blather from multiple, overanxious, proselytizing Cloysteers.

What all these additional levels have to do with each other and what function all these higher-order beings serve is very nebulous. Cloysteers, and especially Hosperines, can assign to those lower-level and extra-pyramidal Dementians whatever characteristics and functions they wish to dream up. The large number of Dementian subordinates provides quite a fertile garden for planting seeds in the receptive minds of reality-deprived Cloysteers, whether planted by fellow Cloysteers or by Hosperines—or even self-seeded as a form of delusion with a limitless amount of vague and unchallenged material to draw from.

What are the Cloysteers discussing in their small groups? Do they communicate with other groups on other flatbeds? How else would they keep their culture coordinated and cohesive? What do the Hosperines add to the discussions? Why even have a Hosperine? These questions and many others may have plausible answers as we discuss the Cloysteers and their perceptions of reality.

I must confess however, I do not know if we will be able to answer one of the most daunting questions: What value does all this organization and Dementian personnel add to life in the X7-PanExpanse and what is the ultimate goal? Let us see if we can answer that one—or is that *two* questions? Hmmm.

∞

### The Cloysteers

Our examination of the Cloysteers—members of *The Order of the Spiral Horn*— can be divided into two parts. First, I would like to make a few clarifying remarks. Then I plan to turn the discussion over to a number of individuals (mostly Cloysteers) in the hope that we will gain additional knowledge from some first-hand accounts; intriguing first-hand points-of-view; and a number of unfiltered opinions, both positive and negative.

We have already discussed how Cloysteers build energy for discussions of their beliefs by encouraging each other into a frenzy. Led by a Hosperine, ideas are generated and fed back and forth among the members of the Order. New members find the energy captivating and existing members keep themselves charged up meeting after meeting. Meetings are always held on flatbeds. Members congregate away from the Warder, either in the left forward corner or the right forward corner of the flatbed. Their intention is to meet "in secret," out of range of their Warder. (Have they not taken into account that the forward corners of every flatbed are very near to the next forward flatbed's Warder, separated by only the coupling gap?)

The Order's practice of only meeting on the flatbeds does have a strange logic to it. If a group were to engage in a long-winded meeting on the ground, their flatbed, continuing to move along the Rail-line, would be long since gone by the end of the meeting. Besides, Cloysteers are generally known for having no desire to walk—i.e. to become Walkers—not even if having a mobile meeting on the ground were an option.

That brings up another issue. Almost without exception, Cloysteers universally deny their designation as Riders—or any other designation for that matter. As a whole, they believe their designation should be "Cloysteer" without regard to any other status they might acquire or deserve. How they developed such a conceited attitude may stem from the way ideas spread through a group. Someone comes up with an idea that other members like, the idea spreads around and around with high energy, it takes root, and finally it becomes part of the doctrine, the culture, or both. Whether the idea is good or bad or even possible is not relevant to any discussion of it. From that point on, it is accepted without question. By the way, creating a new designation specifically for the Cloysteers is never going to happen. The X7-PanExpanse itself is a lot bigger and a lot more disinterested than the Cloysteers think.

As leader of a group, the Hosperine can facilitate the spread and/or acceptance of any or all of the ideas concocted by members. And, to the Order's credit, nothing is ever rejected out of hand; all ideas are welcome. How one becomes a Hosperine is purely by merit: out-talk the existing one. Talk is the main product of a group of Cloysteers—the only product. Talk is the focus of all meetings. There is the excited incomprehensible back and forth between two or more Cloysteers. Rumors, counter-rumors, and murmurs roll through the group like a wave. Newly-concocted ideas make their debut. Old ideas are revived and rehashed but never questioned; only refined and relished. Hosperine politics is always an option; who is in, who is out, who may be next. And so on *ad inhabilis*.

It is remarkable, but not surprising, that none of the Cloysteers knows anything at all about the history of The Order. Only the rarest of individuals in the Order has ever heard of Rana'Orami[WALKER], much less the details of her experience. Some Cloysteers will admit to their ignorance while others purport to know everything there is to know about the Order's history.

How does one become a Cloysteer? Let us say that you have been a Walker for a period of time and decide to become a Rider on a new flatbed. After boarding, you are intrigued by the group of Riders huddled in the right forward corner of the flatbed. So you approach them (after clambering over a number of idle, supine, inactive Riders). You hear what the Cloysteers are saying and start to chime in. If what you say injects energy into the group, you are in. If you question or criticize what they are saying, even subtly, you are out; you will never be accepted as part of the group. Can you fake it? Well, yes. Many do. Usually it is for the purpose of taking advantage of the group in some way—even to the extreme level of replacing the Hosperine.

If you should ever fall out of favor with the group, they merely stop talking to you. And when *you* talk, they merely ignore you—I do not see how this is much in the way of special treatment considering the typical culture aboard a flatbed. There are numerous reasons why some individuals eventually leave the Order voluntarily. An individual doing so is still merely a Rider and does not receive some kind of brand or have a change of outfit color; there is no permanent evidence that one was ever a Cloysteer. Having a member leave the group does give the rest of the Cloysteers plenty to talk about: shame, pity, never should have been a member in the first place, punitive action should ensue, not really one of us, etc. If you thought the Rail-line was endless—

I have asked a number of Cloysteers and a few non-members to give us their thoughts. They are free to talk about whatever they wish, and...I have warned each of them to keep it *brief*. I reserve the right to correct the record when and where I see fit.

First we have De'Ouer[RIDER], a long-time member and former Hosperine.

De'Ouer[RIDER]:
"I have nothing in particular against those who shun our Order. Not everyone can be as enlightened as we are. What you may perceive as distaste and disapproval from us is merely pity. I pity all sloatusses[30]. They are unknowing, ill-informed, and unenlightened. And, let me say this, I have no hostility toward Jal'Hote[RIDER] who wrested me out of my position as Hosperine; although I would like to see her get Closure—and what is wrong with right now?"

Without commenting on that further, we now have I'Mazsu[RIDER], a non-member who has some opinions about the Order.

I'Mazsu[RIDER]:
"I, for one, have no desire to be a Flyer, but I resent the groups of Cloysteers that gather in the flatbed corners and block the way for others who may want to pursue their dream of

---

[30] sloatuss - derogatory name used by Cloysteers when referring to non-members

leaping across a coupling gap. The Cloysteers believe that their meetings are 'secret', but every individual can hear them; every individual can see them in their little groups."

Thank you, I'MazsuRIDER for your opinions. Next we have Jal'HoteRIDER who is currently a Hosperine. Hopefully we will get something a little more informative that what we have received so far.

Jal'HoteRIDER:
"Yes, I would like add some maturity to the discussion by giving you my thoughts on the Rail-line. I believe that the Rail-line goes on forever in both directions, forward and backward. If an individual were to travel forward far enough, that individual would be able to see the forward end. Similarly, if another individual were to travel backward far enough, that individual would eventually witness where it all begins. Now, let us assume that the aforesaid individuals actually were able to move to their respective, absolute ends. They would meet each other. How miraculous! How marvelous! This explains it all."

Hmmm. I believe that I'MazsuRIDER has something more to add. Keep it brief.

I'MazsuRIDER:
"I remember an incident where one group of Cloysteers occupied the left front corner of a flatbed while another group decided to occupy the right front corner. Two groups, babbling away; two Hosperines. As each group added more and more members, the two groups began to overlap. I have heard of such things, confrontations, where clashes resulted and where numerous individuals were re-designated as Violators. However, in this case, the individuals in the expanding area of commingling were getting discussion energy from two different sources. A frenzy of confusion ensued. That confusion then spread to the non-overlapped areas resulting in an entire flatbed end full of confused, noisy, blathering Cloysteers. The two Hosperines began to compete with each other for the attention of the confused mob making matters worse. As the volume level rose to an intolerable level, the Warder on the next forward flatbed turned to the mob and loudly shouted 'HEY!' The merged Cloysteers were so stunned that the Warder had intervened, the chaos died down immediately. Very soon after, the new homogenized group began

discussing the Warder and a new Hosperine emerged. I have never had a desire to be a Flyer, but if I did, I would surely be miffed if a big group of talkers was blocking the entire end of the flatbed."

Ok. Ok. Not brief, but pretty good there for a while, I'Mazsu[RIDER]. Next we have, Fing'Oster[RIDER] another Hosperine who will offer his thoughts on Mugulus and Humma Mádula. Please keep your remarks brief.

Fing'Oster[RIDER]:
"Well, there you have it: Mugulus. No one has ever seen it, or returned from it. That proves that it is there, serving its secret function; serving as a place to sequester those who belong *there* and who do not belong *here*. Who belongs there? Certainly not those who deserve to be in Humma Mádula instead. If *one* of these two places exists, then we know the other one does also. Where else would they sequester individuals when the higher order has ruled on one or the other?"

So, I believe we have exhausted all the substance that any Hosperine is going to be able to offer. That is enough of them. Let us now hear from Fallous'Sha[PROVIDER], a very popular Cloysteer who supposedly has experienced Closure and has returned to talk about it.

Fallous'Sha[PROVIDER]:
"I do not have the time to relate all of my experiences to you at this time, so I will try to summarize. When an elite individual has been selected for the honor and permanency of Closure, the Takers will come to escort that individual to a holding area. I was selected as just such an individual. I was first placed into a hidden *enclosed* area—yes, believe it, an enclosed area. No one *I* know has ever seen one. I was then placed in a smaller container filled with a multi-colored substance that I suspect was taken from a cenisse. Do not know for sure. I experienced *bathing*. I have heard of such a thing but— The Takers then removed me to a cubicle where I was to be opened up and my internals cast into yet another contain..."

I do not think we are getting anywhere. I *know* we are not getting anywhere. I am not even interested in finding out how Fallous'Sha[PROVIDER] explains how he was able to return to tell us all this; something incredible and heroic no doubt. I use the word incredible sarcastically—i.e. lack of credibility. Let us hope that we get something refreshing from our next contributor from Roa'Loa[RIDER], a Cloysteer with some new ideas.

Roa'Loa[RIDER]:

"I think any X7-PanExpanse individual—especially (maybe exclusively) members of *The Order of the Spiral Horn*—should be able to fly if they try hard enough. I am not talking about being a Flyer. That is just stupid. I mean fly, up high, maybe even have spiritual congress with Dementians. I have brought up this topic in several Cloysteer meetings. The question always gets asked, 'Once we are able to fly, will they let us?' This always starts a debate around the question, 'Why should we even pursue flight if, in the end, they will forbid us from doing it?' My beliefs lie somewhere in between. The debate usually ends without resolution followed by a period of aggressive inaction."

Very interesting, but who or what is the "they" being mentioned. Against my better judgement, we shall again hear from Jal'Hote[RIDER], this time concerning the X7-PanExpanse itself.

Jal'Hote[RIDER]:

"I would like to clarify my previous remarks by expanding my model of the Rail-line to include the X7-PanExpanse as whole. The Rail-line goes on forever, both ways. The ends are connected together. We have already settled that. Now, if an individual were to travel all the way to either end of the Rail-line, they would necessarily poke through the edge of the X7-PanExpanse into what I call The Great White Area Beyond the End of the Rail-line..."

Nothing new being added there, dear Reader, so let us continue. For a short political commentary we have Bo'Egus[RIDER].

Bo'Egus[RIDER]:

"Cloysteers should have their own designation. I should be Bo'Egus[CLOYSTEER]. They choose to suppress our Order by not providing us with our own identity. I do not want to be a Walker. I do not even like walking around, out there, on the ground. I do not like being called a Rider. I vote that we Cloysteers have our own designation with our own outfit color—and yet *another* color for a Hosperine. They will just not allow it. If enough of us push for it, I believe it will happen. We want everyone to know who we are and what we stand for. Yu-yu[31]."

I have a few comments of my own:
1) Who or what is this "they" again?
2) Since when did the X7-PanExpanse develop into a democracy? Vote?
3) The Cloysteers do not represent a natural, intrinsic, official designation of the X7-PanExpanse. Believing that they could create a new designation just for themselves would be like believing they could change the color of the sky just because they wanted to.
4) Why do they not ask why there are outfit colors at all? I am certain that they could conjure up some explanation that satisfies them.
5) Finally, why are they so anxious for everyone to be able to identify them?

I am quite familiar with our next contributor, Ru'Tuza[WALKER] who I have found to be one of the more interesting individuals in our group of contributors. She used to be a Cloysteer but slowly and discreetly migrated her way out. Currently she is a Walker, and if it were an official designation, I would like to say a Thinker as well. I had planned to have her be the last of our contributors, but I think her thoughts are much needed right now.

Ru'Tuza[WALKER]:

"I left the Cloysteers because I was stifled out of my mind. Simple. I cannot recycle thoughts over and over again for the mere energy it produces. But that is just my own bias. I dream of a place where you can see the sky meet the ground. Maybe a place where the

---

[31] cryptic higher order expression meaning "come hither, roll into a ball, and proceed"

sky changes color, maybe even to black. Maybe there is a place where ideas and thoughts, no matter how unconventional or revolutionary, can be analyzed and tested impartially. And then, with an actual end result, a resolution, a universal truth would emerge and be accepted; an undeniable truth.

"Maybe there is a place where the flatbeds stop every once in a while. Not forever, just once in a while. It would be a place where, as a Walker, I would not have to be constantly moving—inevitably being forced by a Raker to move on or else board a flatbed full of hibernating Riders. I would like to live in an X7-PanExpanse where everything is *not* ignored by everyone. It would be a place where being an indolent, indifferent Rider for all time is considered a *bad* thing. What does that actually mean, 'bad?' What is 'good?' What is 'bad?' I would be very afraid if those ideas were to be defined by a Provider or a Violator or an unscrupulous Hosperine.

"I would like to have a way to save my thoughts in some permanent way so that I might share them with others, perhaps others that I may never meet. Could there exist a domain where individuals have no official designation—a place where individuals can somehow connect with each other meaningfully, maybe boarding and de-boarding flatbeds together. Maybe there is a place where individuals spend time together, not out of rebellion or curiosity, but because they mean something significant to each other. To be able to walk out into the X7-PanExpanse, either by myself or with another individual, and find new things and new things to do, that would really be something. There are so many ideas that I would like to explore; so many experiences that might be had. But the X7-PanExpanse seems so limited. If there were a place where all these things existed, how would we ever get there?

"Lastly, I would cherish an X7-PanExpanse where individuals are not the only form of life. I dream of a place where there are countless varieties of life; a complete spectrum; life, each form of life having a unique agenda and sense of purpose. What colors, what interesting interactions, what beauty could be found in a place like that? I will always wonder."

Whew! How could someone like Ru'Tuza<sup>WALKER</sup> ever have descended low enough to be a Cloysteer? We thank you for those remarks.

So, I am ending this Cloysteer discussion prematurely. I do not believe that our remaining contributors will add anything as thoughtful as the philosophical comments of Ru'Tuza<sup>WALKER</sup>. If I were a rude being with hidden hostilities I might have a caustic or flippant remark or two as I *terminate* this particular discussion before I had originally planned. So for now, all can say is, "Yu-yu."

## The Prism Experiment

In *your* domain, dear Reader, white light is the combination of all colors. Light is understood and analyzed using the properties of electromagnetic wavelengths; a spectrum of wavelengths. Outside your *visual* perception are countless other wavelengths. In my domain we have an analogous, but very different, four-dimensional lattice of physical properties associated with what you might call light. You, dear Reader, understand yours, and I understand mine. Together, in this journey, we are attempting to understand a third domain; one that is altogether different: that of the X7-PanExpanse. Thanks to advanced technology from my domain, we are currently able explore, together, a transdimensional space where there is an overlap of the three domains.

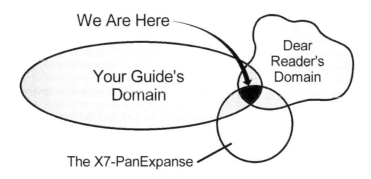

Superficially, there are enough commonalities between our three respective dimensions so that you, dear Reader, and I, your guide, can observe and analyze the X7-PanExpanse on terms that we are both able to understand.

Let me tell you, in my transdimensional explorations of discovery, I have seen:

1) Domains that defy logic (too many of these)
2) Domains that are too complex to even begin to understand, even for me
3) Domains that are so simple that I am quickly in and quickly out, expending only a single, universal, elemental particle of time (I do not have time to explain all about time here.)
4) Domains with so much going on that I could not take it for an extended period (Someday, maybe you and I, dear Reader, can explore one of these. It is glorious; it is a madhouse!)
5) One domain with no physics at all (Figure that one out and explain it to me— I still wonder how I got in and out of there in one piece.)
6) Domains with individuals having a *much* greater capacity for understanding than myself (Not to disappoint you, but yes, it is true.)
7) Domains with individuals that have no true understanding of anything nor any desire to acquire any (too many of these also)
8) Domains with individuals that have no true understanding of anything but believe they understand everything (These I can do without.)
9) Domains with low forms of life led by higher forms of life and vice versa (Many times I have had to ask, "Who is leading who?")
10) Inconceivably vast barren wastelands of dimensional space where sometimes great beauty can be found
11) Many, many domains very similar to yours (These are some of my favorites, but please, dear Reader, do not get carried away with that compliment.)
12) One of the greatest complexes in the entire multiverse: level zero of the great multi-level *Interdimensional Plexus* (barely understandable and mysteriously incomprehensible even at level zero)

I apologize for the diversion.

In our case, here, as you and I explore the X7-PanExpanse, we have employed, as reference points, the mutual commonalities between our three domains. As we have seen, so far, this approach has proven to be successful—at least in our minds.

Let us look at the diffuse light in the sky of the X7-PanExpanse. There is no single source. It is just there. It seems to emanate from everywhere overhead, unchanging—both in time and space and color. Now, let us theorize that the sky is comprised solely of extremely tiny elemental and indivisible particles. Each of these particles illuminates a tiny space around itself. Given countless such particles, the entire X7-PanExpanse could be illuminated, *in toto*, without requiring a single omnipresent point-source of light. Would these particles necessarily have to hang suspended at the upper reaches of the domain? It is more likely that the particles are uniformly distributed everywhere above the surface, all around, and are just not perceptible at close range. This would explain why:

1) There are no shadows anywhere in the X7-PanExpanse.
2) The sky and the ground appear to be seamless, far in the distance.
3) The light is uniform in brightness, all the way from the ground up to the sky.

But what gives the sky its noli tint and exactly where does it start to change? Is there a different form of energy at work in the X7-PanExpanse? What, then, is the basic nature of the light?

In preparation for our journey, dear Reader, I took the liberty of creating an experimental object with which you may be familiar: a simple transparent prism; one that is cut at very precise angles. The prism's purpose was to allow us to analyze the components of the light that emanates from the sky in the X7-PanExpanse. In my domain, the physics of light is based on infinitely-small, four-dimensional tetrahedron-like energy particles suspended in the four-dimensional lattice described earlier. Because of this, our technology could not be expected to have an experimental object analogous to a prism. Since the light in the X7-PanExpanse seems to be more like the light in your domain, dear Reader, I designed a prism that is based solely on the physics found in your domain. Because I am an experienced transdimensional being, I have the ability, in a physical sense, to briefly cross into your dimensional domain and also that of the X7-PanExpanse. If you will politely pardon me for saying so, moving oneself physically into another domain does require more than a little bit of skill to avoid breaking transdimensional protocols or causing a catastrophic de-stabilization of domains—not to mention the risk of splaying out all of my personal oneship into a transdimensional jumble that no one wants to see.

Using the prism, I studied the light from the sky in the X7-PanExpanse and found that the prism could not separate out any component colors from the noli light. In fact, the prism did not transmit, reflect, refract, or do anything else to the light. If anything, the light from the sky seemed to cause the prism to glow, evenly, on its own. Rather than jump to any conclusions, I concluded that a prism, designed using specifications from your domain and using physical materials from mine, would most likely be too incompatible to be of any use for experimentation in the X7-PanExpanse. I did not know what I was thinking. It seemed like a good idea at the time.

Is there *anything* we can learn from my stupendously naïve attempt at transdimensional experimentation? Although our prism experiment did not provide us with anything physically definitive about the light, we *have* learned that attempting to apply our own physics to that of a totally alien domain, in the end, is a foolish and valueless endeavor.

Dear Reader, in my zeal to chastise myself, I have too easily dismissed an interesting discovery—a side effect of my prism folly and possibly more important and meaningful. Closely examining the fine ground particles that cover the surface of the X7-PanExpanse, I have found that, small as one may be, each individual granule is a tiny, transparent icosahedron[32] comprised of a homogeneous, yet unknown, glass-like material. The material in these granules *does* break down the ambient light from the sky. But the particles reflect and refract the component light rays back and forth, bouncing the rays into each other in so many ways, that the result is the familiar bright white endless ground cover. And that is why the overall surface appears white, but looking at a very small sample of the granules, held in the hand, the granules look glassy and clear. If I could

---

[32] a twenty-sided, regular, geometric solid

somehow make a prism out of the same material as the ground granules then we might be on to something.

Let me end this discussion by passing along several ideas given to me by so-called colleagues from my domain—ones who have observed the X7-PanExpanse in the past. And, let me say this, they have not been significantly forthcoming with information. I have never been part of the "in" crowd in my domain, so I believe that the information trickle is purely intellectual turf-guarding—as if it really mattered to anyone anywhere in any domain. Sometimes I would like to see a big pack of fat unipogitors leave a wide swath of gliss all over that sacred turf.

Since these ideas were so grudgingly given to me, I cannot vouch for the validity or value of them. You may accept or reject any or all of the proposed ideas and you may accept or reject my comments about them. Regardless, they are all food for thought:

1) There may be some kind of solid material far above and surrounding the sky giving it that noli color. (How would anyone ever determine this? This sounds more like Cloysteer talk.)

2) There might be a solid white mass under the ground material—that mass being made of the same kind of particles that cover the sky—producing the light from below. (This idea might have some merit. Let us take a forgoroove[33], dig deep down, and check it out. Good luck with getting that massive piece of machinery into the X7-PanExpanse without de-stabilizing every haac thing.)

3) The notion of the sky and ground meeting seamlessly in an indefinite white haze that goes on forever—forever beyond reach—may require a different and separate definition for the concept of *infinity*. (In *our* domain, such a qualified supposition is called "redefining the discussion space in order to create a question tailored to a non-answer.")

---

[33] a massive excavation machine with an automatic suction apparatus that produces an ear-splitting noise when in operation

4) The ground is completely flat in all directions but the ground is curved into some other shape. (Who came up with that contradictory theory? Good luck sorting that one out.)

5) If one were to travel forever in a straight line at right angles to the Rail-line one would find that the X7-PanExpanse has no end. (A deranged, power-addled Hosperine could not have said it better.)

My last comment about my colleagues' closely-guarded ideas, "Where are those stampeding unipogitors when you need them?"

∞

Aux

At this point, and before we move on, dear Reader, I would like to relate to you a few of my miscellaneous thoughts and observations. I hope that we can tie up a few loose ends and perhaps clarify an issue or two.

Let us say that you are a Rider; let us say that you attempt to become a Flyer by leaping from one flatbed onto the next one forward; and you fail; and you fall under the wheels; and you are crushed into rubble. What can be done? In my domain we have beings that can reconstitute an individual back into its full form. In your domain, dear Reader, you have organic repairpersons and support teams. In the X7-PanExpanse they have Heelers. Their job, if you can call it that, is to stand over the rubble and stare at it in silence until the unfortunate mound of former individual is removed by the Collectors. When a Heeler first arrives at the mound, the Heeler's outfit temporarily changes color to match that of the victim. When the last bit of former individual is removed from the scene, the Heeler's outfit returns to its original color. As far as I can determine, there is no point to a Heeler at all, but then, that characteristic applies to many individuals in the X7-PanExpanse. And who am I to judge?

Injuries in the X7-PanExpanse are rare, but I have seen a few individuals receive a simple injury for one reason or another. Simple injuries do not affect the individual for very long.

But any serious injury causes the entire individual to disintegrate into a mound of rubble, as if the individual's body were being held together by a gossamer web of tiny filaments.

I have always wondered if the Rail-line ever gets damaged or wears out in some way. Supposedly, there is a designation called Tooler. I have never seen one, but several individuals have mentioned them in passing. A Tooler is supposed to manage damaged flatbeds, ladders, rails and anything else along the Rail-line. It would be fascinating to see what methods a Tooler uses to repair a component part of a moving flatbed, say a wheel.

We have already been introduced to the Booters. From what we have observed, dear Reader, they have been tasked to remove any individual from a flatbed that has not been authorized to be there (especially newly-designated Flyers).

And then there are those mysterious individuals, "officials", who wear burlo outfits and have no designation. They appear and disappear. I have no theories about the role of these individuals, but the role must be important and unique enough for them to operate in such a different way.

We also have Collectors, Gleaners, Progenitors, and Takers. But if you will allow me, dear Reader, I should like to defer my discussion of them until a later time; a more private time. Then, I believe you will be in agreement with me concerning my desire for discretion. For now, suffice it say that the roles of these individuals are all related to each other and are associated, in some way, with Closure.

Another curiosity about the Cloysteers: most of them believe they have an integral part to play in an individual's Closure. They do not. Some of them come into a Closure scene and get all chummy with the Taker and the under-Takers. Other Cloysteers spend a lot of time explaining Closure to any individual who will listen. You guessed it: total gliss.

∞
### The End

You may have wondered how I got in here and acquired all this information. Remember, I am transdimensional and can venture in and out of some spaces with relative ease. Where I have been able to gather knowledge, I have tried to pass it along to you, dear Reader. I have been able to interface with individuals in the X7-PanExpanse in a way that even they do not fully grasp. This has been valuable in getting their views and stories on many different subjects. I have been careful not to de-stabilize their domain and have kept my *physical* presence in the X7-PanExpanse to a minimum. Understandably, one might be tempted to contradict that statement by referring to my naïve but innocent prism experiment—the transdimensional, comm-network heckling from my colleagues has already started.

As one of our final stops on this journey, I have asked a number of individuals to give us their thoughts on The End of all things, The End of the X7-PanExpanse. What are their impressions and beliefs about it, if any? These thoughts are unfiltered, uncensored, and I will pass no judgement on them—even if some of them are really nutty, or useless, or both. I will keep my musings out of the way of the contributions unless something completely egregious is offered. Some names you will recognize and others will be unfamiliar. I have tried to be as thorough as possible in rounding up this gallery of individuals. So, let us proceed—

Jeffsoder Dubkiester Moutón (Pud'Nulli[RAKER]):
"I suspect that the idea of an End to the X7-PanExpanse is merely a de-stabilizing concept introduced by malcontents and Violators. If there is an End, that information should be protected for security reasons. Need I say more?"

Uey'Duke[WARDER]:
"Get back, flatbed, pulpoose."

Z'Asqi<sup>HEELER</sup>:

"I do not know why individuals tell me that I serve no purpose here, but I do, yes, I do, and...if the X7-PanExpanse Ended, I would be missed and all the other Heelers also and...how could something that is supposed to go on forever not go on forever...so answer me that."

Naz'Osser<sup>PROVIDER</sup>:

"I tell you now, do not worry about an End. There will be no End unless I say so. I have complete knowledge of all things End-wise and I can assure you, here and now, that I have no intention of making an End to the X7-PanExpanse any time soon, unless some individual questions my authority and then I might End it all just because I can."

Dear Reader, the following is from the only Violator that was willing to discuss The End.

Zep'Petry<sup>VIOLATOR</sup>:

"My biggest worry is that the X7-PanExpanse will suddenly End before I am able to prove my innocence and I can be re-designated as a Normal again."

Wen'Onona<sup>RIDER</sup>:

"I have a scary notion that some kind of being beyond the sky will come and interfere with our tranquil existence here in the X7-PanExpanse. That being will start out just watching us for who knows what reason. Then the being will get involved (either inadvertently or purposely) and de-stabilize everything, collapsing the sky and everything else—The End."

I believe, dear Reader, that Wen'Onona<sup>RIDER</sup>'s remark was in some way directed at me. I am not de-stabilizing anything, so...do not look at *me*.

Oi'Poyule<sup>TAKER</sup>:

"I cannot believe that there might be an End to all this. We recycle. Individuals never disappear completely. I am a witness. I am part of it. Why is all this never-Ending just to End up Ending? I cannot believe it. I will not believe it."

Per'Hunf[WALKER]:

"I hope The End comes quickly while I am out walking. I hope the sky opens up and we see what is behind it all. Failing that, I hope the ground opens up and we can see all those 'officials' down there, below us, exposed; 'officials' doing all sorts of interesting things."

A'Odir[RIDER] (Cloysteer):

"I believe that, if there is an End, that all of my fellow Cloysteers will arrive, unharmed in Humma Mádula and we will co-habitate there with the Dementians and Sud or Urf. Everyone else just goes to Mugulus and gets what they deserve."

Ti'Ret[RIDER]:

"I do not think there will ever be an End. That will be our punishment for being here in the first place."

Gef'Lowar[RIDER] (Hosperine):

"I happen to know what will happen when that time comes. First, the sky will begin to change colors (many more colors than we have ever seen). It will eventually turn black, but everything else will still remain white. Then, from out of the black sky will come a series of flying flatbeds with special eternal individuals on board. These flatbeds will have no Warders and the individuals will be dressed in outfits that glow and shine—absolutely horrifying but inspirational against the black sky. As these sky individuals descend to the ground on their magical flatbeds, they will flicker out every individual on the Rail-line before eventually doing the same to our beloved flatbeds, the Rail-line, and finally the X7-PanExpanse altogether. Then they will take those unorganized remains and build a new paradise such as Humma Mádula ruled by Sud, the one and only higher-order being worthy of the position. I cannot wait for that day."

X'Odonner[WALKER]:

"The End will come when the flatbeds stop moving. Will the Riders even know that the Rail-line has stopped? I cannot imagine what will happen to the Riders if the flatbeds stop. That is why I prefer to be a Walker, away from the flatbeds—away from the mayhem and panic that will surely take place among the Riders."

Poy'Fuy<sup>RIDER</sup> (Cloysteer):

"We are all going to End up in Mugulus."

Ex'Odus<sup>RIDER</sup>:

"The End? The first things to go will be our feet. This will prevent Walkers from walking. Then our voices will be silenced; Cloysteers included. Hosperines and Providers will tremble at the thought. Higher-order beings will not allow us to be led by ignorant talkers who cannot properly guide us during such a tribulation. From the ground will rise up tall structures that will damage the sky to a point where all light will disappear. We will climb into those structures and be elevated away to another X7-PanExpanse where there are better flatbeds and movement cannot be impeded either way. That means there will be no Rakers. We will all become superior beings and will rule over some yet unknown, more primitive type of individual. Those inferiors will see to our every need."

Poy'Fuy<sup>RIDER</sup> (Cloysteer):

"We will all End up in Mugulus."

Bonx'Sezzer<sup>RIDER</sup> (Cloysteer):

"We will all End up in Humma Mádula."

Ru'Tuza<sup>WALKER</sup>:

"If The End ever comes, I believe that it will come slowly, with scarcely an individual taking notice. It will force some individuals, justly or not, to look at their lives here. There would be no Mugulus, no Humma Mádula. Just *thinking* of The End raises questions about the permanency of what our X7-PanExpanse represents. Perhaps a higher-order being will intervene and prevent our X7-PanExpanse from actually Ending—not Sud, not Urf, not any Dementian. Then again, why would there be an End at all. With our purpose here left unrevealed, why would there be an End—a fate that would leave us with more questions than answers. Why are we here at all?"

Who knows, dear Reader, maybe one of these individuals has the right idea. Hopefully, for their sake, the X7-PanExpanse will always exist. Maybe it will exist long enough for us to return and find out more about it.

∞

## Beyond

Well, dear Reader, we are getting very near the end of our time together. Our overlapping domains with the X7-PanExpanse have given us both a remarkable experience—even if I do say so, as your humble guide.

My transdimensional journeyman capabilities have allowed me to bring you into the world of the X7-PanExpanse. There are so many other domains yet to be explored. Because of dimensional incompatibilities, there are many domains that may be inaccessible to you until some time far into the future. But, there are so many more that *are* accessible, right now. I am hopeful that at some future time we can embark on another transdimensional exploration and discover even more wondrous, hidden, unknowable things together. Having the opportunity to be your guide has been an experience for which I am truly grateful. Together, we have attempted to explore a world that has few reference points in either of our domains. And yet, where possible, we have observed some fascinating phenomena.

As the X7-PanExpanse now slowly becomes detached from our two domains, it will fade into the interdimensional void. Soon, dear Reader, the transdimensional technology of my

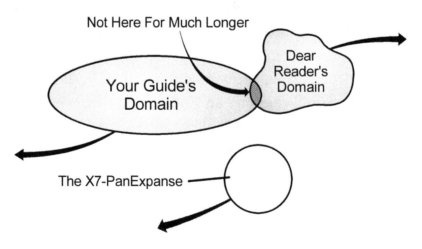

domain will not be able to maintain its attachment to your domain as well. In the short time remaining, and with the X7-PanExpanse completely separated from our transdimension, I would now like to reveal a few things that I was unable to while still connected to the X7-PanExpanse.

The individuals in the X7-PanExpanse speak of the Rail-line running forever both forward and backward. Yet, surprisingly they have no real grasp of the concept of infinity. The flatbeds keep coming from the backward end of the Rail-line. They never really question how all the individuals got there; they are just there. It is my belief that if you or I were to explain infinity to them, it would be beyond their capacity to understand. Would explaining such things as physics, technology, biological life, and science de-stabilize the X7-PanExpanse or would exposure to those concepts force it to evolve. The beings from *my* domain do not believe that we are in a position to make a judgement as to whether or not a risk like that is acceptable.

In every domain there are always darker truths, de-stabilizing truths, and truths that cannot be fathomed by even the most brilliant among us. In many cases, there are truths that, if revealed, are perceived by some resident individuals as being de-stabilizing, dangerous, or subversive. These are only labeled as sinister by those who would be threatened by them. One might think that the bizarre, rambling explanations of the Cloysteers would fall into that category. But none of those ramblings reveal any real truth. It is only the revelation of pure foundational truths that some perceive as threatening, because once revealed, those pure truths never go away.

In the X7-PanExpanse we have seen a few individuals acting in an authoritarian manner when in actuality they have no authority. We have seen those that act as if they have special or privileged knowledge when they have none. We have seen indifference, curiosity (relatively), self-indulgent sloth, and daring (also relatively). We have seen cultural norms enforced by other individuals with specific roles or mysterious "officials" whose authority is provided by some outside entity (presumably). We have been exposed to beliefs in Mugulus, Humma Mádula, Dementians, Sud, and Urf. If I should ever return to the X7-PanExpanse, maybe I will discover who or what is running the show.

Now that we are separated from the X7-PanExpanse, I can enlighten you about a few things without risk of polluting or de-stabilizing it. But I must necessarily make my remarks brief since *our* two domains will soon become separated as well.

1) The Rail-line is not a conveyor hauling the Riders to some nefarious end: to be slaughtered, eaten, used for transplants, or any other predatory organic purpose. Should the X7-PanExpanse individuals even be considered organic at all?

2) The Rail-line is not an assembly line.

3) The Rail-line does not explain life, the movement of time, or the limitlessness of this or any other domain.

4) In spite of the petty hostilities and self-promotion that we have witnessed, there is really no concept of good or evil among the individuals in the X7-PanExpanse. Some individuals use the terms "evil", "good", or "bad" without a deep understanding of what they really mean.

5) There is no counterpart for the slothful, inactive individuals (Riders) on board most of the flatbeds—neither in your domain nor mine. So do not look for any.

6) Do not believe anything said by a Hosperine or a Provider no matter how reasonable or logical they might sound.

7) What our contributor O'Perch[RIDER] stated was true: the individuals in the X7-PanExpanse do *not* know whether their surface is flat or curved. The fact is, their surface is absolutely flat, although the individuals have no way of knowing that or finding that out for themselves. As in many domains, there are those that believe one thing and those that believe the exact opposite (and not for any particular reason). But if an actual underlying truth were ever discovered (say "curved"), it is certain that there would be individuals who would still prefer to believe "flat"—it could be obstinacy or stupidity or inertia or security or something else. Is that kind of thing even voluntary? As long as the individuals that adhere to the truth outnumber those who deny it, a culture progresses, otherwise it stagnates or slowly decays.

8) At this point in time, there is no way to know what lies underground in the X7-PanExpanse. Officials appearing and disappearing through the glassy granules indicates that there must be something down there.

9) In spite of their almost universally exhibited passive demeanors, individuals in the X7-PanExpanse do have emotions (Warders included), but their instincts and respect for preserving their tranquil domain always seem to override even the strongest of emotions. There are exceptions, of course.

10) I did not de-stabilize the X7-PanExpanse with my failed prism experiment (although I am going to hear about it from my colleagues for many universal time segments to come).

11) I chose to use a primitive prism object for my experiment instead of a complex piece of equipment (neither from your domain nor mine) because the smaller and less complex the object, the less chance of causing a rift or de-stabilization of the domain. There is little danger of such a small object doing any *damage* to the X7-PanExpanse, but a de-stabilization might have severed the connection between our overlapped domains and that would be that. For *this* journey, anyway.

12) If we could have taken a spectrum analysis device from your domain or mine and examined the light in detail, we might have been able to discover the chemical makeup of the light source and perhaps answered many questions.

13) I do *not* have unlimited access to all the answers concerning the X7-PanExpanse. I have relied on contributions by individuals—not necessarily for acquiring truth, but to advance our understanding of how they perceive their world.

14) The individuals in the X7-PanExpanse are not insects or some other low form of life. They are not organized in a hive hierarchy, a privilege hierarchy, a meritocracy, or any other artificial structure. You must take their system at face value.

15) There is no food or water in the X7-PanExpanse because neither is ever needed.

16) Some of the individuals we have met refer to "brain organs." They have no idea what they are talking about. There is no such thing in the X7-PanExpanse individuals. They have minds but not brains, not brains as we might think of them. Some individuals have neither, if you ask me. I believe "brain organ" is merely a figure of speech. Or possibly something that has been lost in translation.

17) You or I will always have difficulty in telling one X7-PanExpanse individual from another—they are all the same size, they all have the same outfits except for color, they all look similar anatomically. However, they seem to be able to tell each other apart easily. They can also remember the "faces" of almost every individual they have ever met. It is quite remarkable. They have a similar memory for names as well.

18) If, for whatever reason, a Warder abandons their assigned pulpoose and a Rider takes over, that Rider (unfortunately for that Rider) re-designates and becomes the Warder for that flatbed. This includes a change of outfit color and (sadly) a substantial loss of mentality. This phenomenon is not common knowledge. Riders generally do not aspire to become Warders anyway. Whether or not this is the *only* way Warders are assigned is still a mystery. And what happens to orphaned Warders who leave their posts?

19) Walkers exhibit more of a free spirit than most of the Normals in the X7-PanExpanse. A vast majority of them are cognizant of the fact that while they are out walking, the flatbed they have just de-boarded will continue to move along, possibly out of reach. Walkers are used to the idea of having to continually board new flatbeds when deciding to become a Rider again. To Walkers it is just an acceptable fact of life for any individual who wants to go out walking. This consequence explains why so many Riders never want to de-board their currently-chosen flatbed—they do not want to be forced to ride on any flatbed other than their "own." Period. So they choose to just stay put.

20) The longitudinal limit varies from individual to individual. How the Rakers know the exact limit for every single individual is a marvel unto itself—although I suspect that some mechanism from the dark reaches of the

underground complex (if one exists) identifies wayward individuals for the Rakers. The longitudinal limit expands as an individual walks farther out laterally from the Rail-line. If the individual ventures so far out that the Rail-line cannot be seen at all, the limit disappears completely. Apparently, like most Walkers, the Rakers do not have much of a taste for getting forever lost out in the white abyss.

21) Individuals in the X7-PanExpanse have no internal structures, just a self-generating fluid that sustains them, all held together by the thin gossamer filaments described earlier.

22) There is no true liquid in the X7-PanExpanse, the self-generating viscous material making up the inside of the individuals being the only exception I have run across. It would be interesting to know how the mythology of a cenisse got started. Was it a true experience or merely the active imagination of an individual?

23) There does not seem to be any kind of entity "in charge" of all the "officials." They seem to operate by instinct rather than by higher-order rule. All of the laws that govern things such as the speed, direction, and movement of the Rail-line may have some higher-order control (or physics to use your terminology), but as in most domains I have visited, those higher-order beings are skilled enough to keep their activities secret and out of sight. Perhaps they are from the great *Interdimensional Plexus*. If so, I would speculate that they are from a level higher than zero, but what would I know about all that?

24) Any similarity between individuals in the X7-PanExpanse and those in *your* domain is just a coincidence.

25) Any similarity between individuals in the X7-PanExpanse and those in *my* domain is a real problem. We do not need to explore that possibility here. My colleagues would let me have it if I happened to unleash that topic into your domain.

26) I am but an explorer in transdimensional space and time, an abstract state not to be confused with the great multi-level *Interdimensional Plexus*. Even

a higher-order being such as myself feels unworthy to speak of the *Plexus* in common, oh so very ordinary, terms.

Dear Reader, your gift of *human* self-awareness goes far beyond the ability to know oneself. Your personal timeline starts when you come into your world, but things that have happened before that, if recorded in some way, can also be added to your consciousness. These can be simple stories passed down orally from generation to generation. Or, they could be added through the written word. Or, as technology has advanced in your domain, actual images, voices, and recordings are available. But it is one-sided. A time-limited being cannot have the same detailed awareness of the future. One may only guess, dream, or speculate. In the X7-PanExpanse, there is no real history. Nothing is ever recorded. Other than rumors, stories, and individuals' own memories, the past is almost as ethereal as the future. And, as we have seen, many individuals lose track of past events too easily for any kind of common history to survive.

Since I still cannot get over it, I have one last thought about the prism. In your domain a prism takes one type of light and spreads it out into many different components. *Poetically speaking*, I would like to think of all the individuals in the X7-PanExpanse as component parts of something larger, the protective ambient sky of the X7-PanExpanse acting like a prism and separating the larger entity into an interesting collection of individuals—many different colors.

Finally, I must reveal to you the truth about Closure. Knowledge of the true nature of Closure would most likely destroy the sanctity and peace of the X7-PanExpanse if it ever leaked back to the individuals. But as we are now isolated from the X7-PanExpanse there is no danger to the individuals and their domain. We have seen many references to Closure and it is still one of the least understood concepts in the X7-PanExpanse. All these theories are passed around about what it means to the individuals. From these descriptions, it sounds like Death (in your domain, dear Reader) or Terminatum (in my domain). It really is neither of these.

The Takers are the primary group involved in Closure. A Taker can confront one or more individuals at any time and at any place. There is no warning, except that when a Taker rises up, everyone knows that some individual is facing Closure. Closure is an event that is not desired, but it is not feared. So there is never any clamor or drama when a Taker arrives.

A Taker is the "official" that first confronts the Closure individual(s) and supervises at least three undesignated individuals (assistants) that work under the Taker. Together, the group escorts the selected individual(s) off into the distance; individual(s) never to be heard of again. Perhaps, as some rumors have it, they disappear into the ground. Most of the time Closure involves a single individual facing Closure, but many times Closure comes for two, three, four, or even an entire flatbed of individuals all at once. A Taker usually comes for a Rider or a Walker, but on some occasions a Warder is taken. Other "officials" presumably face Closure sooner or later as well.

Violators and Providers get a very different, special treatment. When Closure comes for a Violator or Provider, that individual is confronted by a Collector instead of a Taker. The Collector has the power to break down an individual into a pile of rubble not unlike that left behind when flatbed wheels crush someone trying to become a Flyer. Once the rubble is collected, it is processed, without Closure, just as if it were a crushed Rider. Although they have their own designation, the Collectors seem to be lower in the X7-PanExpanse hierarchy than those who work under Takers.

As described earlier, during a normal Closure procedure, an individual is escorted into the white until out of view by all other individuals. The Closure individual is then placed in a special holding area with other Closure individuals. What goes on in there is anybody's guess. One by one the Closure individuals are removed from the holding area and taken back thousands of flatbeds (maybe more), back toward the backward end of the Rail-line. Once there, a Fertiller locates a special Progenitor flatbed carrying a complete set of available Progenitors.

Progenitors work in groups of three, rejuvenating an assigned individual and preparing that individual for new life on the Rail-line. They take full responsibility for an individual as soon as that individual arrives. The individual is treated as a novice until later when it comes time to be booted off the Progenitor flatbed, out into the X7-PanExpanse. Once so booted, the novice becomes a youth and a "new" life begins.

The individual basically starts over but still retains a few recollections of their previous life. Since the Rail-line has no beginning and no end, there is always infinite room for infinite numbers of individuals, cycling and recycling endlessly, relentlessly, through all time. The population can never grow out of control. As a side note, a Progenitor flatbed looks like any other flatbed except for its special fulio[34] color and the fact that it is a restricted flatbed; restricted for just about everyone.

When an individual makes a fatal error such as being crushed by the wheels of a flatbed, one or more Collectors gather up the material and pass it to the Gleaners who reconstitute it into pure raw material. A similar fate awaits the Collector's rubble from a Violator or a Provider. The Fertillers then take that raw material and locating a complete set (3) of idle Progenitor specialists, pass the material along for building into a truly new individual. Of course, it stands to reason that an individual reconstituted from raw material would have absolutely no memories of a previous life. That individual will be an absolutely new and unique youth ready for life along the Rail-line. Compared to regular Progenitors, the specialist Progenitors have a slightly more challenging and complex task of preparing this type of new individual for life on the Rail-line.

If I were to question the value or purpose of this process, I would have to ask myself, "Who am I to pass judgement on its repetitive, pointless, and endless nature?" Your domain or my domain, dear Reader, at this very moment in time and space, might look just as inane and pointless to a yet higher-order observer.

---

[34] cryptic orange

As we have seen, good answers sometimes generate new questions: What if a Closure individual were put *forward* thousands of flatbeds instead of backward? Would that individual retain all their knowledge and memories? Does the act of going significantly backward on the Rail-line erase memories? Is that why there is a longitudinal limit? If an individual goes too far back does that individual start to gradually lose memories? What kind of memories or knowledge would accrue if jumping forward? Maybe on a return trip to the X7-PanExpanse we could answer at least some of these new questions.

Well, dear Reader, I, Mara Yana Equaan, as your humble guide want to wish you a fond farewell as I see now that our domains are nearly separated; so I will leave you with the illuminating words of Ru'Tuza^WALKER—words that I believe are still appropriate at this parting moment. And I hope that you agree.

Ru'Tuza^WALKER:
"I dream of a place where there are countless varieties of life; a complete spectrum; life, each form of life having a unique agenda and sense of purpose. What colors, what interesting interactions, what beauty could be found in a place like that? I will always wonder."

∞

### Epilogue

"Zzzzip. Interrupting this...I am Xander-Kolfax the Astral Mariner, a traveling scout from the top zone of the famous ninth *Interdimensional Plexus* near the Dimaggius system—a system located in the diamond-shaped Joltus nebula far far afield from here.

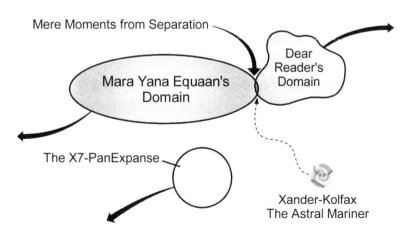

Mere Moments from Separation

Dear Reader's Domain

Mara Yana Equaan's Domain

The X7-PanExpanse

Xander-Kolfax
The Astral Mariner

"I left my home base on an excursion with the goal of visiting other bases in the region. Each visit was to be only a short stop. But somewhere along the way I accidentally wandered out onto the Field, a three-dimensional, red-hot wedge of temporal anti-space. Having taken far too many four-dimensional Maysian analgesics (which, I admit was an error) I found myself off course, driven away from my baseline by the Field, eventually ending up here, down, in the hole, adjacent to both the Reader's dimensional space and this so-called X7-PanExpanse. While I have now regained my equilibrium (to an extent) and am ready to return to the plexus, I would like to inject into this discussion some much-needed reality by adding a few observations of my own.

"First, I take issue with references to the sub-beings in the X7-PanExpanse as 'individuals.' I can barely tell one from another. There is some kind of irony in there.

"Second, although I have found them occasionally fascinating in some odd ways, I believe the sub-beings of the X7-PanExpanse live an extremely unenviable, uniform, and repetitive existence.

"Third, they seem to be inherently unaware of anything outside of their own time and space. And my dimensions? Do not even think about it. But before you, the Reader, get all clammy with superiority, let me remind you that you yourself could imagine nothing of my expanded double bubble-universe existence in the all-encompassing *Interdimensional Plexus* until I penetrated your astral layer and fertilized your mind with all this new information. I obviously come from a place that single-, double-, or triple-dimensional beings can scarcely comprehend. I do not want to imply that your species will never be capable of reaching out your minds beyond your current perimeters, but, well then... let us say that the odds are not with you, so far. But before you cry 'foul,' remember: this is just my opinion. For all I know, I may be merely a character in some other entity's imagination, possibly playing a fool's position in the 'Big Game,' calling out references I do not understand. Does not bother me. And please remember that, even though answers to questions do not just fly out, it is important to stay in the game. Do not balk at the daunting nature of the task. You must continue to strike out on your own and make every attempt to 'know' your domain; stretch your imagination.

"And now, after rounding the first, second, and third dimensions, I must try to reach my home base in the *Interdimensional Plexus* before they call me out, on the carpet, so to speak. Or worse yet, exile me to the *bottom* of the ninth *Interdimensional Plexus* where no one is safe.

"Virtually yours, Xander-Kolfax the Astral Mariner."

Hmmm. Well then, back to me now—

As your humble guide, dear Reader, I want to make it clear that the opinions of any and all interlopers are not necessarily those of your guide. But now, while our dimensions are still overlapped (barely), I would like to take these unexpected extra moments to thank you for your curiosity and your companionship throughout this journey. I am definitely more enlightened about the X7-PanExpanse than I expected to be. I, your guide, Mara Yana Equaan, like you, am basically on the outside looking in, although my transdimensional nature gives me somewhat of an advantage. And if you, dear Reader, will please indulge me, I have one last question remaining; maybe a bigger question than we perceive; one last question in this now fragile, tentative overlapping formulation of space and time; one question that, like many others, may have no satisfactory answer; one more question only: "How did that Astral Mariner character get in here?"

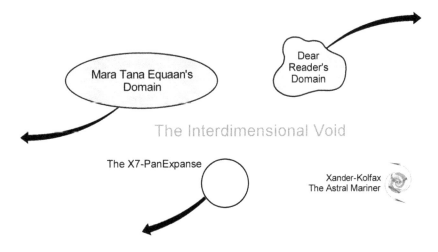

# This Is My Mountain

I must get across. I must get across. I cannot stop running or I am lost. Those creatures. Some remind me of the wolf. Others are tall and sport no hair; I cannot tell for sure. Short or tall, I will not survive if they catch up to me. I must get across. The stones on the ground make it more difficult but they will delay my pursuers as well. I must get across. My life depends on it. My legs are tired but they are strong. They have saved me many times before. I am short of breath but I have determination and a will to survive. I must survive—I do not ask why. I never ask why. Only a short distance more and I will be across this field. Still, I cannot stop or they will be upon me. I cannot stop even when I get across—across this field. I must get across.

I am here at last. The forest. Shall I go up? The trees are mighty and can offer me refuge. This works sometimes, but not always. I do not have enemies, so why are those creatures that pursue me—why are they like enemies? But what if the creatures can climb as well? I will be trapped, up in the branches, with no route of escape. I have seen that the trees are sometimes a dead end. Branches get smaller and smaller and I can go no higher. Perhaps I can weave a path through the woods that those creatures cannot follow. I should not take the chance—so I will continue to run.

Turn to fight! That might be a way out of this. But I will certainly be outnumbered. The wolf outnumbers its prey in order to survive; they cooperate. It is a curious concept. Are they friends with each other or just business associates brought together for the convenience of the group? I for one prefer to go one-on-one, to go it alone, in all things. I know what is best for me. I have no friends; I do not need them. I prefer the life of a loner. But now—I must pay for that isolation by overcoming these creatures, these pursuers, by employing my wits and my strength.

That rocky ledge. I will climb up there to evaluate the situation. Maybe they will not be as agile as I am and I will be safe—at least while I catch my breath. One rock at a time. I must go up, up to that ledge. One rock at a time. I have no fear. Fear is for the weak; it fogs the mind when life is threatened; and clear thinking will be needed to prevail. I *must* keep a clear mind if I am to outwit and escape from those creatures. I *must*. Scrambling among the rocks high on these steep cliffs is natural for me. Perhaps my pursuers cannot reach me up here. Perhaps *they* feel fear. That may be my advantage. I must evaluate and strategize. Those sounds. Quieter now, but still in the distance. They still approach. Up, up, up to the ledge. They cannot possibly follow me up here.

At least I have already eaten. I am not hungry. I am not thirsty. That is a good thing, for the moment. I could have eaten more but the creatures came and the threat was clear. Better that I did not fill my belly with too much meat. It would weigh me down. It would slow me down—as now, now I climb up, up to that ledge. I must get to that ledge—and maybe safety.

Master of Dung! A thorn bush. How shall I get around it to go up? The thorns have hurt me in the past. I remember. Foul obstacle, this. I cannot continue without injuring myself. I have seen what injuries do to others out here in this rocky and difficult land. Many survive injuries, but many others get sick and become food for the "stinky dead" birds— birds that do not hunt. They are lazy. They wait for death. What skills do they have? They fight with each other over dead meat. What horrid vile taste they have for what others leave behind.

I will leap over the thorn bush. My life depends on it. But if I am injured, that will be the end of me. And what is the end? All I feel is that it should be avoided. Avoided at all costs. I have felt the end come near to me many times—times when there has not been enough food. When the cold comes it is even more difficult and desperate; no food, the cold, the frozen ground. What *is* the end? Is the end like sleep? *I* sleep; I awaken and carry on. If the end is like sleep, what is there when I awaken from the end? I shall not occupy my mind with such things or it will distract me and I will not be able to outsmart the creatures that follow me.

Success! I have not been injured and the ledge is now only a short distance away. Up, up. And here before me one last giant leap—my strong legs be praised! Here I am atop the ledge—oh familiar sight! Now I can see far down into the trees and I am not trapped. There are many ways down from here and a few ways up. I will have a path to escape. Let the creatures come—they will fail, they will not catch me.

I still do not *see* the creatures, but I *hear* them. They are still after me—a noisy herd, all of them. And their herd is very strange, very strange-looking. There are short ones on four legs and tall ones on two; many different colors. They are very unlike the big, powerful, wooly brown ones—half furry and half naked, the ones with the horns; big groups of those, out there in the fields, the brown ones, they all look the same.

But what of these creatures that follow me? The sounds of the short ones are like poison to my ears. Over and over whelping, raw, punching sounds. How do they make such sounds? My ears can hear the tiniest movements of animals in the grass. It gives me advantage when I search for food. But why are such loud annoying sounds necessary to those who pursue *me*? What advantage do those sounds give to my pursuers? As irritating as those angry rumpfs rumpfs rumpfs may be, they tell me exactly where my pursuers are. How stupid. Those short ones with the four legs, they are like the wolf but sillier, and clumsier, and with less of a mind. But the tall ones—I do not know them. I do not want to know them. They are silent. If I knew fear, I would be frightened of them. But I know for sure I that must evade them, all of them, at all cost. I must. Whatever is the nature and purpose of their herd, I sense that they are a danger to me.

This ledge is good. Respite. Time to catch my breath and plan—a plan of action. What purpose have they, those in pursuit? Do they plan to kill me and eat me? What other reason could they have? Is it for sport? I do not believe the laws of nature allow such a thing. That is wanton and wasteful and serves no natural purpose. That is my belief. I could be wrong.

Far back there in that meadow, my meal—that seems to have started all this trouble. The one I caught, one of the fat furry ones, one with the curly coat and the black legs and the sad pathetic whining sound—perhaps that furry one was a mate or a friend of the creatures that pursue me. Curly was only a routine meal. Do my pursuers not have the same or something like it? I do not see what the fuss is about, just for a meal. Curly was no match for me; slow, inconsequential, whining to the end. My pursuers should be glad that I culled out and removed from this place such an inferior animal. And that whining—I wanted to yell, "Be silent and submit to my superiority!" But Curly and I did not speak the same language and my mouth was already becoming full of its belly meats. There were many, many curly ones in that meadow, so why was that one so special? And why do they stay together in such a group? A tight herd that moves as one. I have to wonder. What value does that have? Do they all know each other? How ridiculous. Do they hunt together? I have never seen it. They eat grass, that stuff on the dirt, maybe even other green stuff. Yech!

Curly ones do not look like *any* of my pursuers so it could not have been a mate. Besides, my meal was no longer good for mating. It was dead. So what is the point of chasing *me* down, now? I suppose the "stinky dead" birds will go pick at what's left of Curly. Why do my pursuers not chase after them? Why pursue me? I have already left the scene.

Those jumbled sounds: rustling, bustling, clomping, rumpfs. How can these creatures hunt? Even the most deaf of beasts could hear them coming, making such a ruckus. They're getting closer now. Those four-legged ones seem so disorganized. In some ways they remind me of the wolf, but I have never seen them hunting. There is a grace and style to the wolf, and the wolf is *not* disorganized. What manner of beast are those that rumpf rumpf-er so? What kind—

[Crack!!!!!]

Master of Dung! What was that? That was not a creature. Sharp, loud. I think it means danger; danger to *me*. Where did it come from? I cannot see my pursuers—they seem to have stopped cold. Did the loud sound come from them? I must flee before they see me— or have they already seen me?

[Crack!!!!!]

That noise, it is not natural. But I feel danger. It is like the crackling noise from the rumbling sky, but smaller, and sharper. Up, up. There is a path up there. I have been through there many times before. A familiar path.

This passageway is narrow, but it is familiar. The walls are rocky and high and I cannot hear the creatures here. That does not mean they have given up. I must get through. I must get through. That spot up ahead. That is where I once encountered a mate. It was not that long ago. A mate. It was fine, and necessary. What did come of it? I shall never know. But I recognize this place, the rocks, and the smells. Will my pursuers follow me to this place? Will they pursue me through this narrow and treacherous passageway?

Open field ahead—I am far away from where I left the dead curly one; my meal Curly, my meat. I can no longer hear my pursuers. Once I cross the running waters up ahead, I believe I will be safe. But I must be vigilant. The creatures, my pursuers, know that I am here. I am faster than they are. I will outrun them. Maybe I should find other places to get a meal and satisfy my hunger. A meal of a furry one may not be worth the trouble if those noisy creatures come out of hiding and chase me down— expecting to do *what* to me? And what was that loud, deafening sound? That was no creature. That sound was painful to my sensitive ears. I want no part of it.

The danger may be there for me, there in that beautiful meadow, with all those stupid curly ones milling about and eating grass and who knows what else. There will always be temptation. At some point my belly may overcome my sense of danger. The thought of all those stupid ones, Curlys, down there in that meadow, that is temptation. Tomorrow I will feel new hungers upon me. Curly ones are so much easier to make a meal of than the small long ears that are very hard to catch—except by stealth. I can excel at stealth. And the thin-legged fast ones—the dancers and the prancers. They also live in groups. They are the hardest. I can only get hold of old ones and sick ones and injured ones. The old ones are hard to chew even if they are easier to catch. No thanks, not very delicious. Maybe I will take a chance and go back to the meadow some evening. But not now, today has been a good day and I shall savor this full feeling.

I look back. No creatures in pursuit. The running water was cold and wet but felt good on my sore feet. I am not injured and I have eaten, and eaten well. I will be fine for a while. I shall clean my face of the red and I shall sleep—with one eye open and one ear open. Perhaps in this familiar space I will run across a mate. I am comfortable in this place and mates appear from time to time. That would be good—good for me. For now, I have no rivals here. Today is cool and the air is crisp. I know a mate is nearby and I shall look into the possibility. Here, I rule. I shall roar with the delight of it all, to let everyone know, rivals, mates, and prey alike that I am here and that I rule this place. This is *my* mountain.

[Editor's Note: In a subsequent interview, the protagonist in the story indicated that he is fluent in four languages besides English (Dutch, Hungarian, Esperanto, and Latin). He prefers English when he is talking to himself.]

# Feelin' Scrotal

It was still a little early, bed felt gritty twixt the sheets.
My life was like the vacuum cups on some old heifer's teats.
Sat down at the table on a bug spray killin' spree.
Walls were talkin' out of turn, the tables turned on me.

Stood up against reality and faced with my mortality,
The world had peeled the skin away—
I woke up feelin' scrotal, feelin' scrotal, today.

Saddled with a pasty mouth, stiff and achin' back;
Desperate, wild and scrotile, balled up in nature's sac.
Pooper-scooper livin' just spins on down the drain.
They all come to run me down, leave skid marks on my brain.

In view of the scrotality that limits geniality,
I just can't piss this stone away—
A pain of feelin' scrotal, feelin' scrotal, today.

*I walked the fields and felt bodacious*
*And as I stopped, became scrotacious.*
*Lookin' up, just who I am, this shell of life—Scro-Magnon man.*
*Circumstances cut you off like someone whizzin' in your trough.*
*And people, well, they're out to nail ya—life's just one big genitalia.*
*The world is oh so populous, and I am oh so scrofulous.*
*It overwhelms me total, this way of feelin', feelin' scrotal.*

Aware of my mortality but lost in abnormality,
A heapin' pan of brain decay—
An air of feelin' scrotal, feelin' scrotal, today.

With jobs that pose as memories, scrotalism settles in.
Armpits smell so fishy that I think I'm growin' fins.
Wistful days behind me; there's danger in them hills!
Bowels feel full of golf balls, I'm turnin' green around the gills.

The rise of my scrotality kills off congeniality.
When time has passed to yesterday I may not be all scrotal,
Feelin' scrotal—
But there ain't no antidotal to this, my feelin' scrotal,
Feelin' scrotal,
Today.

# Nurse Fowler

## I

"My name is Edna Mae Fowler, more commonly known as 'Nurse Fowler.' I am a nurse (duh) here at the St. Romulus County Hospital in Santa Clamidia, California. Currently, I am under the thumb of Head Nurse Rola Doobie. Head Nurse may be a position that I aspire to, but for now I have to answer to Nurse Doobie. Santa Clamidia is a moderately-sized desert community. We have been blessed with an adequate climate, good roads, good people, and a steady flow of truckers to keep our economy ticking. Despite long-term drought conditions, we have plenty of water thanks to the large industrial reservoir left behind by the Deadman Chemical plant when it was shut down.

"I became a nurse because I am, by nature, a 'people' person. I communicate at an expert level—if not verbally, then by using my body. In addition to being the most compassionate person that you will ever meet, I am also fearless and invincible. As such, I have become the 'Go-To' nurse for handling the most extreme cases and situations, the worst of the worst:

Violent convulsions? I'm all over them!
BBD (Ballistic Bowel Discharge)? Hand me the mop!
Impacted placenta? Lemme at it!
Exposed spine? I've got your back!
Elephant man? Where are my tools?
Time to pull the plug? Comin' through!

"Every day while doing my personal prep for work, I look into the mirror and ask 'What can I do for my fellow man today?' Then it's a big hit of crack, a swish of mouthwash and I'm ready to go into action—ready. I be *ready*! On my way to work I routinely stop off at my neighborhood coffee bar (*Mudpuppy's Flash and Go*)—gotta wash down those uppers—and eventually I make it to work in plenty of time for the administration of morning meds. It has always been my philosophy that I would never give anything to a patient that I wouldn't take myself, so before I begin my rounds I sample each and every pharmaceutical that is to be given to my patients, although sometimes the suppositories are little bit tricky.

"I am, not 100% by choice, single, but I am looking for just the right man or woman to shack up with. I have an apartment that overlooks one of Santa Clamidia's two golf courses. The course is always brown, but it still provides a nice view. I have no time for such time-wasting things as golf. I live for my work as a nurse. It's a clean life:

No smoking (except for cigarettes)
Regular church attendance (each and every Christmas)
Safe sex (each and every Christmas)
No doing of drugs

Therefore, on the floor, on duty, I am always alert and ready for anything. That is, almost anything. Whatever may be said about me and these recent unfortunate incidents, I know nothing and...it's not my fault."

## II

It was a typical hot, desert day in Santa Clamidia with the usual humid brown cloud settled in over the town. Light September breezes were kicking up dust, salt, and reservoir moisture so cars and buildings had their usual layer of crust. It was the kind of crust that people and possessions get after an extended time at the seashore:

Sticky
Gritty
Sandpaper-like
Adherent
Corrosive

Santa Clamidia was established in a salt flat that, once upon a time, was an ancient seabed. The year was 1934 and the town was founded as a support community for the Deadman Chemical plant. Natural resources in the salt flat meant big business. The town itself was located in a depression-like formation within the salt flat's perimeter, so there was always a prodigious amount of salt in the humid air—or so it seemed. In spite of the environment, people in the town were able to maintain a certain sense of pride in enduring what visitors called the "Clamidia hellhole." Nurse Fowler was one of those proud robust citizens.

On that improbable day in September, Nurse Fowler arrived at work, greeting the doctors and nurses with her affable, self-motivated, authoritative charm. All scrubbed (if nothing else, she was very clean) and ready to work (as she saw it), she made her way to the third floor of the St. Romulus County Hospital. The third floor was reserved for the most difficult, unmanageable, and desperate cases. Patients there were allowed very few visitors. Nurse Fowler's special attitudes made her a perfect fit for the requirements of the third floor. She quickly became part of the essential staff at the hospital, especially the third floor; ready for anything. Other hospitals had steered clear of Fowler but an underfunded County was a collapsed air sac of desperation.

Fowler would eagerly take on anything the floor threw at her. Her enthusiasm wasn't contagious. It was a plague. It was as if she were, dare it be said, *on* something. Her off-the-grid activities with substances apparently went on right under her co-workers' noses. Nurse Fowler was professional, not in the usual sense, but in the scrupulously ingenious ways she was able to hide and disguise her rampant abuse of substances:

Sudden collapsing at the knee (a warm hug latching onto the nearest person)
Rolling back of the eyes (smug impatience with a co-worker's conversation)
Glazed-over, sunken eyes (overwork, dedication)
Red, flushed cheeks (a physical manifestation of unbridled enthusiasm)

On a good day, one might be able to summon up a few grains of sympathy for such a substance-muddled individual (if one knew about it). But, always getting in the way would be her brazen, self-satisfied, tireless belief in her hero: the one, the only, Nurse Fowler.

In her position at St. Romulus, she was constantly surrounded by tempting pharmaceuticals. The nurses and doctors on the third floor had become used to her many quirky behaviors and had no palpable suspicions that most of it was chemically-induced. Her frequent awkward and off-color remarks were not always well received, but because she was the "Go-To" person for the most awful jobs and situations, her commentary was, for the most part, tolerated. Comments such as "I've seen better toenails on a Pterodactyl" or "This vomit seems like a terrible waste of food" would raise a bit of a titter among the staff, but in the end she showed an acceptable (if surprising) level of competency at her job. Despite her training and dedication to patient care, Nurse Fowler paid no heed to the many dangers of drug interactions, overdosing, or side effects. She was (in her own words) "invincible."

When all the events of that September day began to unfold, Nurse Fowler's deteriorating behavior, at first, did not seem particularly out of the ordinary. Early in the day, patients came and went, routine tasks were carried out, tests were done, and gossip and rumors about Nurse Fowler popped up here and there. It was an ordinary day for a while. Up until that morning, Nurse Fowler's remarks, offbeat or otherwise, were always directed toward the job (or patient) at hand. Her seemingly compassionate demeanor and unusual bedside banter were appreciated by most of her patients. She seemed to be looking after their best interests and, quite possibly, she was. But, when she started mentioning things like a boisterous parade of enraged, oversized skunk-demons traipsing through the third floor corridor, her colleagues and (unfortunately) some of her patients started to suspect that her brain balloon was beginning to leak. Some of her more cynical co-workers believed Nurse Fowler was giving them "the business" because of the casual and convincing way she mentioned these types of things. "Did any of you notice that three-legged woman with the see-through, red cellophane nightie that came barreling right out of 307B?" she said on one occasion. After the skunk-demon remark she reportedly asked, "Who's gonna clean that up?" pointing at a bare area on the floor of the corridor. "I'm not touching it!" she announced, avoiding the bare area every time she passed it by.

Her sycophantic deference to the doctors was also a plus even though it sometimes generated a fair amount of nausea in her fellow nurses—nausea mixed with animosity, that if left to fester, might have resulted in homicide. Through it all however, Nurse Fowler somehow continued to remain functional. And thereby hangs a tale.

## III

The middle-aged patient in 302B, a Mr. Borneo Ruggins, was resting quietly after his complications from surgery were finally under control. Nurse Fowler would regularly come into his room, feel his forehead for any possible return of his fever, and prop him up so he could watch a full set of commercial-laden TV game shows (even though he wasn't the slightest bit interested). On one of her visits, Nurse Fowler found him crouched into a ball, under his bed, holding onto his metal walking cane—the one with the makeshift rubber tip protruding out from the end of the metal tube like a tongue. He was yelling something about a Voodoo Priestess, a sacrificial goat, and a castration ceremony. It was fairly unsettling to hear him describe things in such detail; it was as if he could *really* see them. He had obviously lost his mind. The current on-call doctors were notified and two of them arrived to handle the situation (Doctor #1 and Doctor #2). Mr. Ruggins attempted to hold the two doctors at bay by sweeping his cane back and forth across the floor while he remained safely under his bed. Then Nurse Fowler stepped in.

"I can handle this," she said confidently, motioning for the two doctors (both #1 and #2) to step back and give her some room. They might have been put off after being elbowed out of the way by Nurse Fowler, but they were intrigued by her officiousness and impressed by the positive effect she seemed to have on a bewildered Mr. Ruggins. After a short while and several *non sequitur* comments later, an absolutely confused and confounded Mr. Ruggins emerged peacefully from under the bed and surrendered himself, handing over his cane to Doctor #2. Doctors #1 and #2 stood by and watched as Nurse Fowler triumphantly, proudly, marched out of the door as if neither of them was there. They found themselves so distracted by her behavior that Mr. Ruggins' episode quickly became secondary, and Mr. Ruggins, held in check concurrently with a routine processing of red tape, soon found himself dispatched to Psychiatric for evaluation.

Ordinarily, an isolated event like this would not have raised much of a stir, but a short time later, a second incident occurred. This time, it was the patient in 304A, a Ms. Cilantra Onwego. She was a poor immigrant who had made it to the ripe (perhaps over-ripe) old age of ninety-four. While standing, literally dancing, on her bed, she began performing a striptease, taking off her imaginary clothing. She was performing for, what she said, was a crowd of about five hundred people in her room. The nursing staff, led by Nurse Fowler, was able to coax Ms. Onwego down by pretending that she (Ms. Onwego) was being escorted to her dressing room through a well-wishing crowd. All the while, the joyous old woman waved, smiling, to her assembled fans, soon to be rushed directly to Psychiatric— red tape be damned. Coincidence?

It was after the third incident that an investigation was in order. That incident involved the patient in room 306B, a Mr. Ed Wahrt, diagnosed with severe *urinosis precocious* (production of massive amounts of urine). As a public defender, Mr. Wahrt's condition had progressed from a purely private hell into a public nightmare. Courtrooms had to be vacated. Consultations with defendants had to be strictly monitored. During a trial, when a judge directed the attorneys to, "See me in my chambers," everyone knew that there was a peck o' trouble a'brewin' for Mr. Wahrt. Seeking treatment for his condition, Mr. Wahrt finally ended up at St. Romulus and, following a series of unfortunate incidents at the lower echelons, he was passed on up to the third floor and into the care of Nurse Fowler, *et al.*

The real trouble began when a routine check found him extinguishing an imaginary fire with his penile "extinguisher," dousing his entire room with urine. There is not a bedpan manufactured anywhere in the Western world that could have possibly contained it all. Since no one on the floor dared interrupt the stream, Nurse Fowler was buzzed. But before she materialized in the room, Mr. Wahrt's tank dried up. But even so, he continued pumping his dry hose, targeting a fire that wasn't there. Following a cool-down of an agitated Wahrt, Nurse Fowler was assigned clean-up duty and Mr. Wahrt, under a watchful eye, was temporarily denied any liquids *per os*. After a moderate to severe amount of red tape, an overdue investigation into the three patient "occurrences" was finally initiated. Mr. Wahrt thus became the third patient sent to Psychiatric just that morning.

## IIIa

Popular and scientific literature references many stories about incidents resembling those at St. Romulus. Sometimes the stories have been compelling and vivid enough to be featured in movies and documentaries. But like so many of the inner-workings at St. Romulus, there was an administrative consensus that knowledge of such incidents should remain "contained." Obviously that didn't work out.

## IV

The morning slogged on toward noon. When not being called upon to actively participate in the aforementioned specific events, Nurse Fowler continued to attend to her routine duties, always alert and ready to be all over any crisis—all over a crisis like blood on a ruptured spleen.

A new patient had been brought up from the emergency room, a Mr. Sesame Spoor. Victim of a dangerous heatstroke, he required a substantial amount of fluids in order to re-hydrate and avoid kidney damage. (The irony did not go unnoticed by anyone: a dehydrated Mr. Spoor was missing fluid while Mr. Wahrt's fluids were distributed "all over the place.") Dr. Chiarracha Z. Salzmo, a top (very top) resident from the nearby Remus Medical School, ordered Nurse Fowler to start a saline IV and to monitor Mr. Spoor's progress every 15 minutes. Dr. Salzmo then began reviewing Mr. Spoor's latest test results. While attempting to insert the needle for the IV, Nurse Fowler moved briskly backward a half step. She thought she saw a tiny army of brightly-dressed horse jockeys and an equally tiny horde of identical elves all engaged in a battle for supremacy atop Mr. Spoor's (open-at-the-back) bedclothes. As she gasped, holding her patient's arm, immobilized, Dr. Salzmo grabbed her by the hand. "Are you all right?" he asked, "I'll do it *for* you if you're not up to it."

"No, I'm all right," she replied, sluggishly shaking off her daze-and-glaze, and finally getting the IV started as ordered. Both tiny armies had now retreated underneath the covers. But, she could still see them, moving about under there, under the sheets. Silently, she asked herself, "What the...?"

Her attention was then re-centered by the doctor in charge. "Call me if you need me, or if there is any change for the worse in his condition," Dr. Salzmo said as he left the room. Before he was completely through the door, he glanced back at Nurse Fowler with a worried look on his face and then proceeded on. She was still scrutinizing the sheets occupied by Mr. Spoor, afraid to lift them for fear of what she might find.

"Yes, doctor," Nurse Fowler softly responded, unaware that he was already gone. She was still attempting to understand what was happening when she noticed that Mr. Spoor had regained much of his normal color and had what she described as "a real dog-bobby of a grin" on his face. What *was* he thinking? What was he *seeing*?

"The sheep! The sheep!" Mr. Spoor belted out as he rose up from the bed. "The sheep are headed for Mexico. Don't let them see you. Those wooly rooks—no one is safe!" He had almost worked himself into a seizure.

Nurse Fowler hit the emergency button. Almost immediately the emergency squad arrived, followed closely by a returning Dr. Salzmo. Nurse Fowler filled in the doctor as best she could, given the decibel level and density of Mr. Spoor's ovine ravings. Although Mr. Spoor continued to *look* fine, he was really much too ill to send over to Psychiatric. So they calmed him down and resumed his IV in his room on the third floor. Nurse Fowler reassured Mr. Spoor that the sheep had all been killed indiscriminately by a winged superhero dressed in a blue and orange polyester pantsuit bearing the initials GUD. She personally saw the superhero zap the sheep with a custom-designed firegun. "Don't you recognize the smell of burnt wool?" she asked Mr. Spoor. Nurse Fowler and Mr. Spoor obviously spoke the same language. No one suspected that Nurse Fowler was telling the absolute truth: she actually *did* see what she had described to the now-docile Mr. Spoor.

As the room slowly cleared of highly-impressed personnel, Dr. Salzmo turned to Nurse Fowler and suggested that she take the rest of the day off, which, reluctantly, she did. Her next shift was still two days away so she felt a little bit set adrift—alone in a lifeboat with nothing to eat but a can of worms and some toe cheese. How would she keep herself occupied? How would she survive? Substances. Nurse Fowler's resilience in such challenging circumstances could many times be attributed to her chemically-erased memory engrams and her inexhaustible ability to reboot her mind.

## V

Later that afternoon, the investigation into the morning's events was well underway—an investigation headed by a Dr. Bartholomew "Bat" Breath. Dr. Breath was a forensic scientist and, over the years, he had managed many a case for local law enforcement. A very intelligent, rational person, he was a well-respected professional in the medical and science communities. He always knew what to say and when to say it. He never missed an opportunity to polish his knob, his reputational knob. So when the investigation took a novel and quite bizarre turn, Dr. Breath became a bit concerned about his reputation, the reputation of the hospital, and the health of the community as a whole, in that order. He was, and still is, one aggressive and ambitious S.O.B.

Of course the patients were suffering from hallucinations, but why so many, and why a cluster in this particular area of the hospital? What was in common between the four patients? Why were there, suddenly, no other new cases? These were questions that had to be answered.

"What do you think, Dr. Breath," asked Head Nurse Doobie.

"All I know is this: at all costs, we must avoid a panic," Dr. Breath replied.

Dr. Breath's first act as head of the investigation was to call in the staff toxicologist, Dr. Martin E. Izer.

"We need blood and urine workups on all the patients in question," Dr. Breath commanded. Without hesitation, Dr. Izer and the hospital staff gathered the required samples from the afflicted patients. Of special note was the acquisition of a sufficient urine sample from a dehydrated Mr. Spoor: highly problematic. But getting a urine sample from Mr. Wahrt: automatic. Staff: "Where is Nurse Fowler when you really need her?" Gathering all the other samples was merely a matter of routine.

Some tests and analyses would require 24 to 48 hours to complete, but only after a handful of hours, Dr. Izer had made an unusual discovery. There was an unknown foreign substance, the same substance, in each patient's blood sample. Although some rigorous tests would be necessary in order to determine the exact nature of the substance, Dr. Izer speculated that this substance was causing the hallucinations. As a safety precaution and to keep a lid on the situation, all four patients were immediately quarantined.

## VI

Late in the day, an emergency conference was called in the third floor conference room. In attendance were Dr. Izer, Dr. Salzmo, several third floor nurses (including Head Nurse Doobie), the Hospital Administrator (John Thomas Verbungle, PhD), several staff doctors, and a number of residents (for training purposes). Nurse Fowler was not in attendance. Leading the meeting was Dr. Breath:

"Welcome, Doctors and others. I am Dr. Bat Breath, head of the ongoing investigation into the incidents of this morning. Dr. Izer and I have taken the reins of this inquiry and, together, we are going to wrestle this issue down to the ground and beat it to a standstill. By now I am sure all of you are aware of the bizarre incidents in question. If not, you can get up to speed by word of mouth on your own time. We have had four patients who began exhibiting behaviors consistent with hallucinatory episodes. Until the first toxicology results were posted, there appeared to be nothing in common between the four subjects. However, blood work showed the same unidentified foreign substance in each person's Toxic Substance Panel. Further analyses identified the substance as an unusual hybrid molecule of a denatured opiate, an RGX (Region X hallucinogen) compound, and a potpourri of fertility and fungal sub-molecules. The hybrid is bound together by an as yet unidentified organic substance, possibly a chelate. How these four patients came to be contaminated with this substance is still a mystery. Hospital tap water was tested and only the usual toxins were found. Many people ate the same hospital food today, yet only the afflicted four produced these specific symptoms; symptoms above and beyond those normally expected from ingesting the food in the St. Romulus cafeteria."

As Dr. Breath continued his presentation, a commotion suddenly erupted at one end of the large, expensive (and highly polished) mahogany conference table. Dr. Salzmo was having some sort of religious experience. Standing up, fully erect, he slowly raised his arms, looked at the ceiling (looking beyond the ceiling) in a jubilant trance, and chanted, "I a-a-a-am the Motorcycle King, I a-a-a-am the Motorcycle King!" Had Nurse Fowler been in attendance she would have clearly recognized that Dr. Salzmo was exhibiting the same dog-bobby grin as observed previously on Mr. Spoor, now quarantined in the Psychiatric Ward. But she wasn't present so they all just missed out on that informative tidbit of evidence.

Seeing that Dr. Salzmo was not behaving like himself at all, several of the stunned people in the room rushed *en masse* to his aid, bustling about him like so many hyenas on a gnu corpse. In all the mad confusion, as if exhausted, Dr. Salzmo re-seated himself, slumped down in his chair, and passed out. One of the doctors shouted out, "Nurse, quickly, get me a cup of Joe!"

# VII

Living alone, Nurse Fowler could, if only by habit, indulge her sense of independence. Her modicum of *team* spirit was reserved for the workplace. She had minimal trouble managing herself during her days off, but she preferred the excitement and challenge of working her way through a day on the third floor at the hospital. After leaving St. Romulus and on her way home, having been forwarded there by Dr. Salzmo, she decided to treat herself to a new pair of shoes. Parked at the mall, near Scofield & Squirts (a major department store chain) she took several big hits of Tijuana Shag, removed her white stockings, then made for the shoe department where Mr. Alonzo Gluehard recognized her as a regular customer.

Mr. Gluehard was a short, stout, bald-headed little pervert who had a leather fetish that kept him stimulated all day long in the shoe department. He felt disappointment when somebody was interested in sneakers or cheap plastic hiking boots—no leather. He loved the touch, the smell, and everything else associated with that dyed and processed animal skin. When he was all alone in "the back," amongst all that shoe leather, it was Nirvana. Heavenly. So he was especially excited when Nurse Fowler appeared in the store stating that she would like to look at some *leather* dress shoes.

Finding a suitable chair for the commencement of business, Nurse Fowler made herself comfortable and prepared herself for a few cheap thrills as Mr. Gluehard measured and manipulated her bare foot. She conjured up some specifics about the dress shoes she was looking for, and had him gleefully hopping to and from "the back" while she relaxed, tipping her head back, stretching her neck, and looking up. Then, while Mr. Gluehard was seeing if he had her size in "the back" she noticed the ceiling, lights and all, turn into a big slab of chocolate that slowly started melting, bits of crunchy nut fragments pelting the shoe displays below. As the chocolate continued dripping from the ceiling it revealed, irregular patch by irregular patch, the panels of a gigantic, quite colorful, comic strip, with disfigured and grotesque cartoon characters shaving each other with dead mice. The dialog balloons over their heads were in 3D and written in the language of an Amazonian tribe that no one has ever heard of. "Fight or Flight" being far from her mind, Nurse Fowler began to swoon, loosening the kinks in her neck by rolling her neck and head around in a circle. Every now and then she would open an eye and check out the progress of the melting chocolate.

Suddenly, a muffled scream came forth from the dark recesses of "the back." Mr. Gluehard had gone berserk and was being bothersome to two of the female staff (Lois Toker and Lisa Spitz). They had sneaked in the back entrance to "the back" from an extended "smoke break" in the parking lot. Gluehard was making swimming motions at them with his arms and winking. He attempted to reassure them by stressing that he was the magical, aqua-doctor and had (most likely) seen it all before. Luckily, neither of the two women was wearing anything made of leather. Otherwise it might have been "touch and go" for the both of them.

At the first opportunity, the female employees exited "the back" out to "the front" where a bare-legged, hypnotized, Nurse Fowler, with one shoe off and one shoe on, was still rolling her head around. While Lois watchfully monitored the head-spinning Nurse Fowler, Lisa called Security.

"This is Lisa Spitz," she said to the security officer at the other end of the line. "There's something weird going on in Women's Shoes! Please send someone right away!" The two women then carefully sneaked through the sales area over to a handbag display. There, they concealed themselves, waiting to see what was going to happen next.

Mr. Gluehard, with bulging eyes and sweaty brow, returned to the floor, "the front" with his shirt torn open, drooling, panting, and attempting to catch his breath. He was so noisy about it that Nurse Fowler reconstituted herself and, opening her eyes, was surprised to see, as the first thing in her field of view, Mr. Gluehard's hairy chest only about ten inches away. She was face-to-face with curly chest hair and a tattoo of a horse head with a man's perky nipple for an eye.

Nevertheless, Nurse Fowler, being a 24/7 nurse, came to his aid, calming him down. She sat on the floor, with one shoe off and one shoe on, and cradled his quivering head (face *up* mind you) in her lap, while stroking his forehead. Soon, two officers from Security came and took control of the situation. While questioning Nurse Fowler, Security Officers Leticia Wopper and Kurt Muskwarm paused for a moment when they heard a faint snickering that seemed to be coming from the handbag display. But, keeping focus on the task at hand, the officers gathered up Mr. Gluehard and helped him to the Security Office. Shortly after arriving there, unbeknownst to Nurse Fowler, Mr. Gluchard had a second, more severe spell and became so agitated that he had to be restrained physically. Details of his behavior in the Security Office are sketchy at best.

Nurse Fowler left the store, with no new shoes, but with an unusual feeling of recovery and well-being. She headed home. Lois and Lisa were left with disarranged displays and numerous shoes and shoeboxes to sort out. Without touching the mess, they left "the front," went into "the back," and exited out the back door, proceeding to the parking lot for another "smoke break."

# VIII

For two days Nurse Fowler kept herself busy at home tidying up her place, catching up on her reading, and taking a recreational dose of this or that, whatever she still had on hand. Her reading materials were not to everyone's taste: biker magazines; articles on self-promotion and self-improvement; and reference books – lots and lots of reference books. Her short attention span did not allow her to read them *per se*, so she absorbed them in small pieces, in most cases randomly piecing together small unrelated bits of knowledge which she retained as fact: King Edward was a brand of canned fish, Norway was the opposite of Orway, and "blue blood" was some kind of gasoline. Not wanting to seem superior to her colleagues, she kept this vast reservoir of knowledge to herself. During the time away from work she continued seeing strange images, off and on. For her, it was easy to dismiss them since they did not seem to linger for very long and most of them provided some level of visual interest. Nurse Fowler was not much for watching television at home—she was exposed to all she could take on the patients' TV's during a regular workday. But lately the TV itself provided an extraordinary light show that was mesmerizing, if only marginally related to the subject matter. Never making the connection between her fluctuating mental state and her beloved substances she continued to believe that maybe she *was*, truly, invincible after all.

In the meantime, the investigation at the hospital continued without success. Dr. Breath and the suck-ups in his staff began to point the finger at an unknown/unidentified psychopath who had invaded the building and infused the patients with some kind of hybrid drug concoction. Evading all detection, the suspect then vanished without a trace. Although there was little or no evidence to support his supposition, Dr. Breath felt that it was a safe and *politically viable* explanation for the events. Dr. Salzmo was recovering nicely as were the four quarantined patients from incidents on the third floor. But Dr. Salzmo's case, flying in the face of Dr. Breath's deductions did not fit the M.O. since, according to Dr. Salzmo, "I have not had contact with any psychopaths. Not recently. No."

Ignoring Dr. Breath's protests, Hospital Administrator Verbungle ordered the quarantined patients back to their rooms on the third floor. They no longer seemed to be a threat to themselves or others and all the hallucinations had stopped. Submitting to the power of a higher office, Dr. Breath successfully lobbied for special surveillance that kept the four under strict observation at all times. Ready for a ten-Martini dinner, Dr. Salzmo left the hospital for the day and went home to his family. There were no further incidents until...

## IX

Nurse Fowler returned to work with a fresh outlook after her two-and-a-half-day sabbatical. Newly pumped up on various substances she began to look forward to her "visions" as colorful additions to her day. After all she was invincible. No sooner than she began tending to patients than a new outbreak occurred. Several patients began exhibiting the same symptoms as those from several days ago. Panic among hospital officials set in.

By now, today, Nurse Fowler had come under suspicion. It seemed that two days before, there had been a new patient admitted to the hospital, a Mr. Alonzo Gluehard (Nurse Fowler's favorite shoe salesman from the Scofield & Squirts department store). He had experienced some wild psychedelic imaginings at work and was brought to the emergency room by his distraught wife, Flotice Hanjaubert-Gluehard (who incidentally was wearing black leather pants and a black leather vest). Department store Security Officer Leticia Wopper called the wife, asking her to retrieve him from the store. His wife picked him up and drove him directly to the emergency room at St. Romulus where his symptoms were recognized immediately thanks to the rampant rumors circulating throughout the hospital. Several hours later he was seen immediately. However, the effects had completely worn off and he was no longer exhibiting any detectable symptoms of the condition.

After a precautionary observation period, Mr. Gluehard, who became quite exhilarated at seeing his wife's attire, was released to her care. Before leaving with his wife, Mr. Gluehard, while sitting on the edge of the emergency room bed, was approached by Dr. Breath. He had some final questions for Mr. Gluehard.

"Have you seen or had contact with any psychopaths recently?" Dr. Breath asked.

"How would I know?" was the reply from Mr. Gluehard. Ms. Gluehard was watching her husband's every move.

"Do you remember being infused with a foreign substance intravenously by anybody recently?" was Dr. Breath's next question. Before Mr. Gluehard could answer, his wife scolded Dr. Breath for delaying her husband's release, "I think he's had enough for one day, don't you?"

A final open-ended question came from Dr. Breath, "Have you got anything else to say about your experience that might be helpful?"

"Yes," replied Gluehard, "tell Nurse Fowler that I found the shoes she wanted."

The fact that Mr. Gluehard had recently been in close, direct contact with Nurse Fowler while she was at Scofield & Squirts had Dr. Breath's mental gearbox in a full grind. Although the gear motion was slow, two days of incubation was all Breath needed to give birth to some interesting deductive fruit. When Nurse Fowler returned to work and, coincidentally new cases suddenly appeared at St. Romulus, it was then that Dr. Breath called in local law enforcement to ramp up an investigation into Nurse Fowler's, possibly malicious, activities. Dr. Breath, of course, was right on top of things. Was Nurse Fowler the psychopath they had been looking for?

Lieutenant Detective Emil Eedilogger questioned Nurse Fowler, and although he had no proof, he became convinced that something smelled awfully fishy about her involvement. (One might suppose he had just captured the smell of the hospital cafeteria, out of control on cod day once again.) At one point, Nurse Fowler became belligerent and uncooperative, requiring him to grab her by the arm and spell out the dire consequences if it turned out that she was poisoning the patients.

He ordered her to submit to a drug test, which she flatly refused to do. The female officer in charge, Lieutenant Detective Rose Frumdeded forcibly escorted Nurse Fowler to a private area in the hospital labworks and retrieved a number of samples of her metabolic fluids. The Lieutenant's methods need not be divulged at this time in order to prevent abuse or misuse if somehow the techniques were to fall into the wrong hands—so to speak. Nurse Fowler's protests, although unheeded, were heard throughout the hospital, mixing in so well with those of the typical crop of current patients that they were easy to ignore.

Using the evidence in hand, Dr. Breath's musings, eyewitness accounts, and lab tests on Nurse Fowler's liquid samples, the investigation came to a close with Nurse Fowler (briefly) in custody, not for poisoning patients but for the numerous drug violations, that many say, will take years to unravel.

Officially, Dr. Breath's investigation concluded:

Cause of the incidents: unknown.
Prognosis for the victims: unknown.
Perpetrator: unknown, possibly a nurse, possibly a psychopath.
Possibility of future incidents: unknown.
Keeping the events out of the public eye: failed.

Dr. Breath was universally praised for his clear and concise resolution. Things returned to normal at St. Romulus. And a final, resolute, and unofficial conference was called in order to put the staff "in the know."

## X

The conference began with brief comments by Dr. John Thomas Verbungle, the Hospital Administrator. He reminded the assembled throng that accretion was the better part of *ad valorum* and not to emiss themselves naked to the press about anything they were about to hear. "All of this is off-the-record and unofficial, so keep your mouths shut," he warned. "Remember, insanity is defined as repeating what you hear over and over again, expecting results." After a short agenda of unrelated items, the floor was turned over to Dr. Breath and Dr. Izer. Dr. Breath was to deliver the play-by-play while Dr. Izer was to provide color.

"Through a series of tests, analyses, and a set of involuntarily-obtained fluid samples, we have determined the following," Dr. Breath started off, showing a projected slide with a number of "bullet" items in a boldface Times Roman font. The connection between the "bullet" items and the rest of the presentation is still unclear.

Dr. Breath continued, "Several days ago we here at St. Romulus began to notice some odd behaviors exhibited by several of our patients. These behaviors were caused by hallucinations ostensibly induced by a mysterious substance in the bloodstream of each victim. Theories were advanced that turned out to be only partially correct, if not totally incorrect. Nearly all the victims have recovered, except one. Let me turn this over now to Dr. Izer who will discharge some facts on you. Dr. Izer—"

"Toxicology on the patients showed a foreign substance in all of their blood samples. However, the real breakthrough occurred when both law enforcement officers assigned to the case, Lieutenant Detective Emil Eedilogger and Lieutenant Detective Rose Frumdeded, also began exhibiting the symptoms. Minutes before, each had had close physical contact with a Nurse Edna Mae Fowler, a third floor 'Go-To' employee of the hospital. An examination of Nurse Fowler's fluids turned up a cornucopia of pharmaceutical horrors. Apparently the chemical substances in her fluids, and there were many, interacted with each other giving her central nervous system a special type of intermittent electrical charge potential known as the Eustachian DeHaney effect. Even now, whenever Nurse Fowler comes into contact with someone physically her nervous system discharges this effect into the other person. Shortly thereafter, with varying degrees of latency, the other person begins to experience wild hallucinations until the charge dissipates. The length and breadth of the hallucinations depends on how much charge is sent from Nurse Fowler into the victim."

"Question," a voice from the group spoke out. "How is the nurse herself affected by this phenomenon?"

"Good question," replied Dr. Breath. "Nurse Fowler seems to be completely unaware of the effect she is having on other people. Fowler's symptoms are very mild compared to the others. In other words, Nurse Fowler is primarily a carrier. She has been sent to rehab and is facing a number of legal charges for possession of a vast array of substances, both prescription drugs and some highly illegal ones."

"What was the nature of the substance found in the bloodstreams of the victims?" asked another voice.

Dr. Breath yielded to Dr. Izer. "We have no friggin' idea what that is," Dr. Izer added.

A final voice arose from meeting, "Is there any further danger to the public at this point?"

"Another good question," replied Dr. Breath.

# XI

"My name is Meulah Smith. I was once a nurse on the third floor of the St. Romulus County Hospital. I was the 'Go-To' person; a person in charge. Due to events beyond my control I have been forced to live a life 'off the grid.' Something happened to my body chemistry that made me a pariah in society. I could no longer work at the hospital. I had a long list of felonies attached to my name. And, sadly, I no longer was provided access to my beloved substances. Now I must hide from the law and must make money doing what I can. I was originally sent to rehab to prepare myself for a life of legal troubles. By trading some body time for a key to my door I was able to surreptitiously work my way out of that place and disappear.

"While moving from place to place, I found out that my special talent is useful and highly valued on the Black Market. People pay me for giving them a 'charge.' I touch them and charge them for a charge. It's good money, but I worry that law enforcement will someday catch up with me and haul me in. Sometimes people get in a bad way after a charge

451

(especially a *deluxe* session) so I always get cash in advance. Some of my customers have experienced mild side effects after multiple charges: massive hair growth, desire for sushi, pregnancy, and a toothpaste-like earwax that oozes out while sleeping.

"But, I'm doing fine. I'm still here. I am fearless and invincible. Working in the Black Market, I find other avenues for obtaining my substances, and there are many. Nowadays I have to *pay* for all of them so I must work, work, work. After all, I have to maintain my charge, that Eustace DelMonico thing. I have learned to dismiss the cost of my substances as merely a business expense. By the way, that is quite an impressive two-headed parrot on your shoulder there."

## Basil Hyenoid's Book of Fables

 "Welcome. I'm Basil Hyenoid. And here, my friend, is my book of fables. Before we get on with the savory entries of meat and their meat product substances, let me relate to you how I came to be in possession of all this material. But first, let me just insert this…

"Picture a young girl, innocently walking home from school, a young girl awash in her insouciance. She had not a care in the world—which explains all of that insouciance. The young girl began skipping along like a little iridescent bird, a songbird hopping along the ground, a songbird with a past, a past that included looking for scrumptious little seeds to pop into its pointy little insouciant mouth. The insouciant young girl had left her little friends far behind at the crossroads when the members of their friendly little group all went their separate ways. Her friends weren't feeling as insouciant as she was. But because of her innocence and insouciance, she could not imagine all of the dangers that could befall her as she made her way through the neighborhood—a neighborhood where clean streets and perfect lawns masked a dark underbelly of horror, borne from congress with the sweaty musculature of hell itself. She had only one block to go before she would be safe at home; and the innocent and insouciant young girl had no idea that she was heading straight into peril—it would be a nightmare of staggering proportions.

"As she came around the last corner, she encountered something so terrible that, in its presence, grown women shriek in horror, agitated men unscrew their heads from their necks, so-called friends collapse in spastic anguish, and small animals lose control of their drool.

"But there it was, on the edge of a greenish-brown patch of grass, not fifty feet from where she now stood. There stood a man in a yellowing, tank-top undershirt. The holey undershirt was attempting, unsuccessfully, to cover his big, bulging, hairy midriff and a weird, black, oval-shaped navel right out front. The man was wearing thread-bare lime-green plaid shorts with a leather-tooled cowboy belt, over-the-calf black socks, thirty-year-old orange sandals, and a fisherman's hat inscribed with, 'I fish for crappie, therefore I am.' The man was cheerfully hosing down the sidewalk. It was her Dad!

"She turned to run but was stopped dead in her tracks when she heard a voice say, 'Hello Lucy, how was school?'

"Bwaaha-ha-aha-ahahha! Ha!

"And so I bring to you these fables. How did I come into possession of them? I stole 'em...Bwaaha-ha-aha-ahahha! Ha!

"But, no, seriously. There once was a powerful witch. She was very capricious and cast spells on random people just out of randomness—some kind of bipolar whimsicality issue. This witch had a big flat beaver's tail protruding from her forehead. She would use it to wave at people instead of using her hand. No, scratch that...it was a horn that came out of her forehead. She was a unicorn. The fact is, unicorns no longer exist because of a bureaucratic mix-up many millennia ago. Bureaucracies in the age of the unicorn were not as sophisticated as they are today, so mistakes were common. Or so they say.

"Anyway...one day I ran into a thin, grossly offensive man on a deserted and dusty country road. He was pulling a cart full of fresh bread. When I stopped him he told me of a hermit who lived in a ramshackle lean-to near the Backleberry Caves. As he resumed walking, he attempted to pass me by. So I said to him, 'Hey! What gives? How about a sample of that there bread? That fine aroma is killing me.'

"'Get your own bread,' he said in a huff as he continued on down the road.

"When he wasn't looking I grabbed a small loaf off the back of his cart and made off with it into the woods. Man, that was the shittiest bread I have ever eaten.

"Bwaaha-ha-aha-ahahha! Ha!

"So, I was in a museum in a far off distant land; an ancient land; a land of myths; a land of legends; a land of fables. There was a lot going on in that land. So much so that they didn't see me kipe that book of fables right out from under their noses.

"Bwaaha-ha-aha-ahahha! Ha!

"Nah. None of that is true. These fables have been passed down from generation to generation and are presented to you now in their original form, finally uncorked like vintage wine. The oral infamy and associated cult-driven mythologies that plagued them through all those many generations—keeping them from finding a broader audience—have been whitewashed. An entire array of natural disasters that were mistakenly thought to be caused by the existence of these very fables turned out to be unrelated after all. Mysterious fable cults have been disbanded in order to protect the integrity of their gist. Family squabbling has been shut down by legal processes so that the fables can be cast off into the river of public discourse. Animals have been driven from their habitats to make room for them. Ant farms are no longer able to produce viable crops due to soil depletion. Irrelevant? May be.

"And so here they sit, poised, for you my friend, like so much squalid hut rubble; like debris gathered into a coherent mound by a friendly bulldozer; like strange bric-a-brac on a dusty shelf; like festering wounds on a Roman soldier's thigh; like so many autumn leaves raked into a big pile, ready to be blown—

"Bwaaha-ha-aha-ahahha! Ha!

"And speaking of plagues...I met this curious doctor..."

---

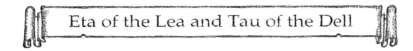

Eta of the Lea and Tau of the Dell

n the peaceful lea that stretches across much of the county of Kerryblue, where tall green grasses ripple like tiny waves in the wind, there roamed a wild, longhaired hound by the name of Eta. She romped freely through the blades of grass, occasionally picking up a rogue bur in her long hair. The innumerable number of smells in the air challenged her brain as she used her fine sense of smell to locate a morsel of food and some water to wet her dry tongue.

Tau, a hound of similar size wandered freely in the Kerryblue dell, marking each tree with his liquid signature. It always confounded Tau when other animals ignored his markers, traipsing through his territory when the area obviously belonged to him. As a sturdy growing hound, Tau was also on the hunt for something to eat. Catching every tiny aromatic bit in his long and sensitive nose, his brain sorted through the myriad of smells wafting along in the wind.

On a sunny day one spring, Eta came upon a man and a woman, farmers, working together in a field near the road. Eta, with her congenial disposition on full display, innocently approached the couple hoping for a treat or a friendly rub behind the ears. The woman reached down with both hands, immersing them in Eta's soft coat, showing Eta some welcome affection. But the woman was suddenly taken aback by Eta's ghastly smell.

"Heavens!" the farmer lady exclaimed. "You smell awful!" She backed away from Eta and began wiping her hands vigorously on her overalls. The man then took his hoe and waved it at Eta in an attempt to turn her away from the area. This was a curious behavior. Eta went back to romping about, but soon came upon a raccoon. She knew that a raccoon was in the area because they have a particular smell that is easy to recognize.

"What are you doing out here in the daylight?" Eta asked the raccoon.

"None of your business, you smelly dog," the raccoon said while sauntering away from Eta.

Eta ignored the raccoon's insulting comment and replied, "I detect the oil of skunk in your fur. Is that why you are in such a foul mood today?"

"What nosy creatures dogs are. That was weeks ago when I was punked by that skunk," thought the raccoon. And so the raccoon hastened its retreat away from Eta.

While all of this was taking place, Tau had encountered two young girls playing with a bright yellow ball. One was wearing a blue dress and the other was wearing a red blouse. Tau, indicating friendly intentions with his tail, stepped in between the two girls. Each of them began running their fingers into the hair around his head, petting him and giving him lots of affection, pulling him up close their collective cheeks. They expressed their affections with kind words and encouragements, until—

"My goodness! What a horrible smell! Get away you awful dog!" the girl in the blue cried. The girl in the red blouse pushed Tau away with force.

"Have you ever smelled anything so bad?" the girl in red asked.

Tau thought the girl in red smelled like rotten peaches and the girl in blue smelled like a potato. He was very discouraged and disappointed by their behavior but his discouragement did not last very long—there were other smells to sort out in his search for something to eat.

Along the road he came upon a merchant sitting beneath an elm tree having his lunch. The merchant was taking bites out of a thick sausage and supplementing each bite with a mouthful of bread. Tao caught the all too familiar smell of cat pee in the air but it turned out to be some kind of toilet water generously applied to the salesman for some reason. The salesman's greasy-looking hair had the smell of pork. This salesman's chaotic array of smells was almost too much for Tau, but that sausage...

Tau made an attempt to get at that sausage or to play on the salesman's sympathy with some friendly gestures, but the closer Tau got, the more hostile the salesman became.

"Get away from here you stinky animal!" shouted the man. "I'm trying to eat!" He picked up a rock and tossed it at Tau who had already started to retreat. Off went Tau, back to the dell with his tail between his legs. The chance encounter with the odoriferous salesman had forced Tau to slightly alter his route and in so doing Tau caught an odor that every male dog recognizes as essential for living the good life: that of a female, a female in the throes of bitchways, ready for mating rituals. The female Tau had detected was Eta. She too had picked up something important floating in the air. It was Tau.

Despite the distance between them, Eta and Tau easily had a meet-up. On first approach the two began sniffing the money areas of each other's bodies avoiding any outright touching. Soon they brushed up against each other, rounding around each other, evaluating the situation with their noses. They both concluded, almost simultaneously, that this was going to be a productive encounter and there should be no delay in executing the biological operation. Tau got down to it on top of Eta's business end and before the two lovers could recite the Poem of Porkeyremus, it was over—just routine adult dog action in Kerryblue. They separated, each one resuming the search for food and water.

Back at the farm, the farmer's wife was attempting to wash Eta's smell from her hands and was cursing Eta during the process, "This damn smell just won't come off!" A similar event was taking place at the homes of the two yellow-ball girls, but the cursing was coming from the girls' parents as soap and water were dreadfully inadequate in removing the smell of Tau from their hands and forearms.

It has always been a paradox why nature would give an animal such a well-developed sense of smell for use in navigating the world and then saddle that very same animal with an array of repulsive smells (especially when wet). On the other hand, animals such as humans are given merely mediocre olfactory abilities, but they have an infinite assortment of opinions about everything that is detected by their noses.

## Moral: To a dog, a smell is just information.

*Postscriptum*: A thoroughly proud and satisfied Tau trotted on to greener pastures while a couple of months later, Eta was stuck with the kids.

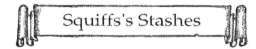

## Squiffs's Stashes

t takes many, many acorns to build a winter-proof stash. With squirrels it's always every squirrel for him or her self. Each squirrel has its own private hoard to be accessed during the leafless, acornless winter months. And if a squirrel should come upon someone else's stash...well, finders keepers. It was a competitive and unfair way to do squirrel business, but it was just the way things were done in squirrel-dom; it was the culture of the times. In such a system every stash lost was somehow always replaced by a different stash found. And around and around it went.

Squiffs the squirrel was an average, everyday sort of squirrel. But unlike many of his colleagues, Squiffs had a hyper-inflated view of himself and his intelligence. He did not like the inherent unfairness of the acorn-gathering business model. His acorn stash was always the biggest and the best. Why should others be able to capitalize on his good planning, leaving him puny little stashes of inferior quality nuts as accidental compensation?

Squiffs set out to do things a different way. He made a plan to seek out the cleverest and most secure acorn hiding place he could locate. This winter he would be able to get fat and food-secure while others would be on rationed portions until spring. Squiffs searched all over the area as he and the others carried out their routine gathering of acorns. One day Squiffs ran across an old decaying log. The place reeked of turf-marking fluids from a spry male bobcat. It was not a place that any self-respecting, cautious squirrel would want to be—not one that wanted to see the next day, that is.

As the fall acorn-gathering process reached its usual fever pitch, Squiffs would scurry off to the dead log and hide his acorns inside its hollowed out interior. Even a skunk or other forest scavenger would not want to risk an encounter with a bobcat or other predator; Squiffs's stash was perfectly safe from all outside intruders.

As fall began turning into winter, Squiffs's stash was overflowing with acorns. He was very proud of it. He always gathered the most and now he would be able to enjoy his huge stash all winter long—all to himself.

Just before the first freeze, Squiffs was standing by the log admiring his stash, fluttering his squirrely tail with satisfaction. Nobody in squirrel-dom realized how absolutely clever and industrious Squiffs was. His stash *was* the best *and* the biggest. Brimming with pride, Squiffs pranced around the forest, joyous in his accomplishment. He soon ran across one of his friends whom he had known for many a season.

"How are you, Torq?" Squiffs said.

"Is that you Squiffs?" Torq replied.

"Yes, it's me. How's your winter stash coming?" Squiffs asked.

"OK, I guess, you never can tell. I got started a little bit late. Some human kid with a pellet gun kept poking around my usual oak tree, so it hampered my gathering. I was lucky compared to Yurqi. She got a pellet right in the head. She got sent to the great nut-house in the clouds. How about you? How's your stash?"

"Pretty great actually. You want to see?" Squiffs was so proud that he was about to burst wide open. Torq followed Squiffs to the old log. Torq was really impressed.

"You gathered all these yourself?" Torq asked.

"Sure did. Ain't it just nuts?" Squiffs replied. As the two stood by the log admiring the stash, the shadow of a hawk passed over them.

"We'd better break it up," Torq said with alarm as he scurried off. Squiffs did the same before the hawk could detect their presence in the undergrowth.

Braving the possibility of a bobcat, or a hawk, or some other monster, Squiffs brought one friend after another to admire his stash. His ego was stroked with every viewing and with every envious comment made by his fellow squirrels. But the high risk was always there and the novelty of showing off his stash soon wore off. No more exhibitions; not this season.

Winter finally arrived and there was frost on the ground. Dead leaves, colorful as anything, were everywhere, lightly covered with the frost. Soon Squiffs's temporary supply of acorns was exhausted and he had to go to his secret stash for a re-supply. But when he arrived, only a few scattered acorns were left there. What had happened to his stash? Perhaps everyone in the entire universe knew it was coming and knew what had happened; everyone except Squiffs who just couldn't figure. Despite his high opinion of his own intelligence, just how smart could he actually be?

**Moral: *If you are proud of your nuts and want to keep them safe, stop showing them to everybody.***

*Postscriptum*: Squiffs barely survived the winter, bumming acorns off friends and family, sneaking around at night getting into other squirrels' stashes. He even resorted to getting his nuts from a nut shark. How would he ever pay back such an unsavory underworld scoundrel especially when the vig was so high? But through it all, Squiffs had learned his lesson. The following fall, Squiffs hid his acorns well, only revealing their location to his mate, Blisq. Once again his stash became the biggest and the best. Squiffs kept his pride in check and his stash a well-kept secret. But Squiffs, not being all *that* smart, was caught by his mate, fooling around in another female's nest. In an act of pure brazen arrogance Squiffs had even taken the other female to his stash and had shown her his nuts. As a result, Blisq divorced Squiffs and got all his nuts for herself.

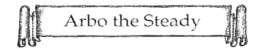

## Arbo the Steady

 nce there were two clans of ferrets: the Golden Field Clan and the Miceland Clan. The two clans were very competitive. Over time, the rivalry made the clans suspicious and judgmental of one another. Members of the two clans did not get along even though the wide open fields where they all lived were expansive enough to accommodate a dozen clans. So the two clans co-existed in the large field but they would have nothing to do with each other.

Arbo and Obbi were members of the Golden Field Clan. They were "friends" and members in good standing in the Golden Field community. Arbo had strong passions for Obbi and brought her mice and other goodies. Obbi accepted Arbo's gifts with a polite but very noncommittal "Thanks." Arbo chose to completely ignore Obbi's dismissive attitude toward him, but over time Arbo began to notice a change in Obbi's attitude. Although she had many suitors from around the clan, Arbo seemed to be the "safest." But she couldn't decide for sure about any of this. Her indecisiveness was rooted in her flippant desire to *have* her prairie dog and *eat* it too. And so, as time went by, everything stayed in a tenuous state of equilibrium.

Zazier was a member of the Miceland clan. The clan was so named because mice flourished in the clan's territory; flourished in spite of the population control exacted on the mice by the ferrets in the clan. Miceland ferrets, including Zazier, were overweight, slow, and sluggish. But, for the most part they lived harmoniously and enjoyed a comfortable life.

One day, on the outskirts of Miceland territory, Zazier was eating the head off of his recently captured dinner (a small rat) when he encountered a ferret from yet another clan: the Dark Moss clan.

"I'm Jex," the Dark Moss ferret said, introducing herself.

"I'm Zazier." Zazier kept chewing the head letting bits of fur fall from his mouth. Some of the tearing and chewing was just for show.

"Where did you get that?" Jex asked.

"Caught it over there," Zazier said, motioning toward Miceland.

"I haven't eaten in days. May I have a bite?"

"Get your own," Zazier replied, clutching the remains of the rat, protecting his dinner from a possible snatch by the stranger.

"Our field is barren of small ones...of food," Jex said.

"Well, that's too bad, because we have more than enough where I come from." With that Zazier decided to get away from the moocher and return to the Miceland community. However, Jex secretly followed Zazier and was shocked to see plenty of mice and rats along the way. When Zazier got back to the group, Zazier's brother, Barzeer, noticed Jex.

"Who's your friend, Zazier?" Barzeer asked.

"Some ferret from beyond the water," Zazier replied. "She was watching me eat."

"Why is she here? Why did you let her follow you here? She doesn't belong in here with our clan." Barzeer moved to get a closer look at Jex, but by then Jex had left the area.

"What difference does it make?" Zazier said casually. Barzeer didn't bother to answer.

It *did* make a difference. Soon the Miceland clan was overrun with ferrets from the Dark Moss clan; overrun to the point where mice and rats and all other types of quarry were depleted to a starvation level. When the Miceland ferrets were forced to drive the Dark Moss ferrets back from whence they came, Zazier was nowhere to be found, arrogant little coward that he was. As the central figure in the entire Dark Moss fiasco, Zazier was banished from the Miceland Clan; sent away to fend for himself, away from Miceland territory altogether.

At first Zazier was satisfied with his banishment. "Who needs them anyway?" he told himself. But he soon became dissatisfied with his life as an exile.

One afternoon while wandering about, dangerously close to the territory of the Golden Field Clan, he met Arbo. On his best behavior, Zazier was just happy to have someone to talk to; to talk *at*. Zazier liked Arbo's carefree and friendly attitude. They quickly became "friends": Arbo tolerated Zazier's arrogance out of pure good will and proximity; Zazier enjoyed feeling superior to Arbo. It was complicated, but Arbo was used to things being in a fragile equilibrium.

Zazier soon began to put pressure on Arbo as he wanted to join the Golden Field Clan and return to clan life. Arbo finally relented and brought up the subject with other members of the Golden Field Clan.

"Nothing doing!" shouted Pobo, one of the clan's elders. Numerous other members of the clan echoed Pobo's sentiments.

But Arbo had the respect of many clan members and was soon able to convince the others that Zazier should be a member. And although there were those who hated the idea, Zazier was accepted into the Golden Field Clan. For a time, things in the Golden Field Clan returned to their tenuous state of equilibrium: Arbo continued to pursue Obbi and Zazier enjoyed taking potshots at Arbo's ego. Arbo continued to ignore Zazier's arrogance purely out of disinterest.

Obbi was weakening. She was leaning toward finally being *more* than friends with Arbo. His steadiness and non-threatening nature had great appeal to her at this point in life. Keeping so many young suitors on a tether was becoming tiresome to Obbi. With Arbo, she wouldn't even *need* a tether; he brought his own. No effort involved.

Obbi began to hint to Arbo that he might be her chosen one, but she never quite got to the point of making it clear—she was still being flippant and noncommittal. So Arbo just bided his time, and continued to remain in equilibrium—steady.

But Zazier had a different point of view about all this. He was impatient and self-motivated—i.e. motivated to help himself. His advances toward Obbi were partially responsible for her indecisiveness. Zazier knew good and well that Arbo had passions for Obbi, but that was of no concern to Zazier.

Then, an important day came. Arbo was out in the far reaches of the field looking for a little something to eat. He frequently liked to poke around for food far away from the community. The solitude allowed him to contemplate things and sort them out in his mind. Figo, a feeble-minded acquaintance, came looking for him.

"I believe I have news for you, Arbo," Figo said with excitement. "Obbi mentioned something about wanting to see you. That was yesterday...or was it today...this morning?"

"What else did she say?" Arbo asked.

"That's it. I think. I think that's it. This morning...actually it was someone else...maybe."

"Never mind, Figo," Arbo said as he started back to the community.

This was the day Arbo had been waiting for. He would be proud. There would be many little ferrets. He would move up in the community, perhaps someday he might even rise up from the ranks high enough to become an elder. As he made his way back to the community he thought about all the times that he felt hollow after treating Obbi with passion only to be casually dismissed. None of that mattered any more. His efforts and steadiness had won the day.

As soon as he arrived back at the community, he went straight to Obbi's little hideaway. He had been there many times, but now he would be there in a whole new capacity. But he never anticipated what awaited him. There was Zazier, mixed all in and over with Obbi, having his way with her.

"Well...this sucks!" Arbo said to himself as he left the scene.

**Moral: You may think that's a knife in your back, but that's actually someone taking the monkey off of it.**

*Postscriptum*: Obbi and Zazier became mates, making sure that their union was viewed as a "big deal" by everyone—making sure to instill envy whenever possible. They set up housekeeping, calling their home "The Brownhole." But beyond that, for Obbi and Zazier, there were no little ones in the offing—no little paws in The Brownhole.

Soon after The Brownhole was up and running, Zazier's brother, Barzeer, was forcefully ejected from the Miceland Clan—something to do with cannibalism, but it was all kept very hush hush; so nobody knows for sure what Barzeer was really up to in that nursery. Of course, Barzeer came running to Zazier for help, paying no attention to the fact that Barzeer himself was an unwelcome visitor in the Golden Field Clan's territory— unwelcome, to put it mildly. Without regard to Obbi's feeling, and without regard to the opinions in the rest of the Golden Field Clan, Barzeer brazenly moved in with Obbi and Zazier and was a constant pain in The Brownhole. Obbi and Barzeer soon became lovers and Zazier had to sit outside the entrance to The Brownhole and listen to moaning and groaning and grunting through the night.

While all the superfluous melodrama was running rampant over at The Brownhole, Arbo's good will and steady nature allowed him to become a respected leader in the clan (soon to become an elder as well). After a passionate romance with Heyo, a beautiful and fertile young ferret, Arbo wound up with a family of his own—with many little ones, just as he once envisioned. As a steady leader, Arbo was able to maintain the equilibrium that everyone in the Golden Field Clan valued so much.

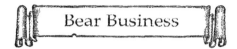

## Bear Business

anx was an animal behavioral scientist, a human, who regularly went to the woods to study bears and their behaviors. It was difficult to find a bear but eventually Manx encountered Baria, a big black bear, and her young cub, Barwin. The two bears went about their business and paid no attention to Manx, who was taking notes and making observations about their activities. She followed them to a backwater pool in a stream where Baria plucked a fish right out of the water. Baria ate a large portion of it, head, tail, bones and all, and gave bite-sized chunks to young Barwin. Later Manx saw the mother bear locate a beehive and, much to the bees' displeasure, Baria dug out a honeycomb and gnawed it up. Baria gave a few pieces to Barwin.

All of this behavioral splendor was soon interrupted with a stark reality: there were hunters in the area. Manx wished that she could run over and warn Baria of the impending danger, but the bear probably wouldn't understand—or worse, the bear could turn on her—and she definitely did not want Baria to think she was threatening the young Barwin. Manx watched in horror as one of the pair of hunters drew a bead on Baria. Baria and Barwin continued to explore the area, unaware of the threat.

As the hunters tried to get into position for a good shot, a sudden shriek of pain cut through the ambient sounds of the woods. One of the hunters had stepped into a bear trap. Baria knew of the trap and Manx had seen her avoid it several times. The second hunter attempted to remove the trap from the victim's leg, but it was difficult. The trap had broken the hunter's tibia and fibula and the leg was bleeding where the broken tibia poked through the skin. That was the end of the hunt. Baria seemed unperturbed by the incident and proceeded on her way with Barwin tagging along behind. Manx followed, writing notes as she did so, being careful not to interfere with Baria's routine.

A short time later, the two bears (and Manx) came to the edge of the woods. There was a very large, wide, treeless clearing. The clear area might have been the result of a recent fire. It was quite a large meadow, open, with very gently rolling hillocks. Manx followed Baria and her cub into the field, but kept her distance since there was no good place to hide. Soon she noticed that there were other bears in the field—all types. This was an unfamiliar behavior. They seemed to be converging on a single location. So a nervous Manx crept closer to the area where the bears were congregating. There was Baria, along with Barwin and several other bears. Nearby there was a large, long, modern building. At this point, Manx and all these bears had wandered quite a distance from the woods—Manx could not imagine what purpose such a building might serve, out here, in the middle of this huge empty field...in the middle of nowhere.

Manx wanted to get closer to see what was happening so she crept into a depression and hid behind a few of the larger plants. This was as close as she dared get with the large number of bears in the vicinity. She was still documenting behaviors when she saw Baria and Barwin arrive at the building. She was shocked when they went inside. Baria seemed to be familiar with the mysterious place. What was going on? This behavior had to be a new discovery about animal behavior. Some kind of bear meeting? Even more mysterious was the fact that as Baria and her cub approached the building, the "front door" opened automatically.

Several bears left the building as Baria and Barwin went inside. Manx waited, still in hiding. There were strange sounds coming from the building. Many minutes went by without any activity, so it seemed to Manx that the only bears still left in the building were Baria and her cub. This might be worth the risk. She decided to go up to the building to see what was happening—to see what was going on in there. When Manx got near the front door it opened automatically just as it had done for Baria. Manx heard music. Even though it was strange music, it still sounded very generic. As she poked her head around the corner to look inside, she felt cool air blowing out on her face—the place was air-conditioned! She looked both ways—there were no bears in sight. But there was a long row of individual cubicles each with its own door. And there was a stench, a powerful stench—a mixture of rotten fish and honey.

Manx heard a flushing sound that drowned out the music and soon Baria and Barwin emerged from one of the cubicles. They were coming toward the door so Manx made a hasty retreat before she could be seen. She got clear of the building just in time to avoid the arrival of several new bears. So Manx stealthily headed back, across the field, and into the woods. As soon as the opportunity presented itself, Manx anxiously wrote of her breakthrough discovery: The bears were coming *out of the woods* to this *building* to take a dump.

**Moral: Just because everyone assumes something, doesn't make it true.**

*Postscriptum*: The Pope *is* Catholic. Or is he?

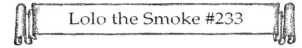

Lolo the Smoke #233

 t was the end time—at least for the community of lemmings in our story. Lolo the Smoke #233 and his best friend Uolo of the Bees #19 were munching on some of the sparse ground cover vegetation, quietly minding their own business. Just a couple of happy guys doing guy stuff.

"Meeting! Meeting!" was the cry from a community messenger. There were so many lemmings currently in the community that word would spread quickly as soon as an important message got started.

Lolo stopping eating and asked Uolo, "What do you think *that's* all about?"

"I don't know, but I have an uneasy feeling about it," Uolo replied.

"Well then, let's go see." Lolo headed toward Big Puff, the local area meeting mound and Uolo followed closely behind. In a few minutes Lolo and Uolo were immersed in a sea of curious lemmings. Just a couple of guys about to be part of something bigger than themselves.

On the mound was Polo the Old #26. "We are many. Too many. As we all know, food is becoming scarce. I announce today that it's time for The Run!" The crowd went wild! There was cheering and boisterous celebrating. Someone started the "Wiggles": thousands upon thousands of short little tails propped into the air, arse over tip, wriggling and wiggling in a display of solidarity and raw excitement.

"What do you think Lolo?" Uolo asked Lolo.

"What did they call Polo the Old when he was young?" Lolo replied with a question.

"No no. What do you think about The Run?" Uolo asked again. Calm was returning and the horde, once again, turned its full attention back to Polo the Old.

Skillfully managing the crowd, Polo the Old began again, "Tomorrow morning at sunrise, males of every group and clan in our society will run toward the sun, foraging along the way, one-minded in mission; we will run toward the sea and bravely face what awaits us there."

"What do *you* think Lolo? Are you ready? Shall we meet here tomorrow and do The Run together?" Uolo asked.

"I don't know. What are we going to do when we get to the sea? Why will there be no females participating in The Run? Who decided that? It's all very mysterious."

Uolo responded, "We're not meant to know such things, but it must be important. They say Polo the Old #26 is very wise—much wiser than any of us."

"That's another thing. Where are the Polo the Old brothers #1 through #25?" Lolo's questions were making Uolo uneasy.

"We're supposed to meet here at sunrise tomorrow...for The Run. That's all I know," Uolo said.

Lolo wasn't sure about all this and wanted an audience with Polo the Old #26. So Lolo wandered through masses and the plants till he came upon the place where Polo the Old #26 managed the affairs of the community. But before Lolo could even speak, the lemming in charge gruffly said to Lolo, "Don't even *think* about talking to this guy." The lemming in charge brushed Lolo away. So Lolo went back to talk to Uolo...to discuss The Run, and to wait for the sun to rise on the morrow.

The next morning the yellow-orange sky was getting brighter, but it was still too early for the sun to be above the horizon. Neither Lolo nor Uolo had ever seen the sea before, but they knew it was out there...out there where the sun comes up. Lolo liked this time of day because the low vegetation had a lot of early-morning moisture clinging to it. It helped his digestion, all that moisture. Eating too much dry scrub made him constipated.

The crowd was gathering. This was it. The males in a giant sea of male lemmings were preparing for The Run while another sea of lemmings watched: the females. Lolo thought it strange how the two groups seemed to assemble themselves without any kind of leadership.

Polo the Old #26 crawled up atop a dead tree stump where he could look out over the roiling mass of male lemmings. "I see we have a good turnout for The Run today," Polo the Old #26 shouted to the masses. Every utterance brought cheers from the crowd. "All the females are present here today, present to watch your bold maleness, exhibited openly, as you participate in this historic Run. For the first time, only males will participate. This is a great experiment and we should all be proud to be part of it. I, of course, will lead the throng as we make our way to the sea. So without further delay, let us...be off!"

With that, the giant community of male lemmings began The Run, moving almost as one, like a massive rodential wave.

"Are you ready, Lolo," Uolo inquired.

"As ready as I'll ever be," Lolo replied. The two friends began scampering along, grabbing little tufts of snacky grass as they went. It was very exciting to be part of this—thousands upon thousands of fellow male lemmings, all with a singular purpose. All part of something larger than themselves. To what end? Only the elders really knew. Only time would tell.

Soon, Lolo could smell the sea. In the sky were the white birds of the sea that he had heard stories about. It was all so exciting. As long as he was with Uolo, The Run did not seem all that overpowering and enigmatic. Surely there would be some kind of revelation, some point revealed, answers to many questions.
As the massive wave of lemmings approached the waves on the shore Lolo paused for a moment.

"It's a beautiful thing, Uolo," Lolo remarked. "All these fellow lemmings here together—with a singular purpose." Uolo stopped as well and observed the wave of lemmings as the front edge of the horde began to splash in the water.

"I must go, Lolo. Will you be running along with me?"

"I want to stay here for a moment and take this all in," Lolo replied.

Uolo turned toward the sea and joined his fellow thousands in the final part of The Run. Lolo the Smoke #233 watched as ripple after ripple of tiny lemmings were consumed by the immense waters of the sea. Uolo had vanished into the crowd. Lolo never saw him again. More and more of his fellow lemmings were vanishing into the water—thousands upon thousands. Then, even more curious—the dead bodies of many many lemming fellows began washing up on the shore.

"I *knew* something wasn't right about all this. I *knew* it!" Lolo wasn't about to join the others in this mass suicide mission—a suicide mission that had no apparent purpose. Lolo felt sad that Uolo had become part of the mindless rush to death. Soon there were no more live lemmings left. Every single one of his brothers had drowned in the sea. The thick line of dead lemming bodies that had accumulated on the shore was slowly being eroded by the waves. Soon, every last vestige of the group had disappeared. Lolo was the only one left. It was a sad day after all. On his way back to the community (if one could call it that) he happened to see the backside of Polo the Old #26 casually heading back to the community as well. What was *he* doing here? Wasn't he supposed to be leading The Run? There was so much information to process.

Lolo was too smart to confront Polo the Old #26 about any of this. As far as Lolo was concerned, Polo the Old's credibility was shot to hell. There seemed to be something corrupt and odd about the whole business. But, as Lolo the Smoke #233 folded himself back into the community, those misgivings were soon forgotten. Lolo quickly realized that he and Polo the Old #26 were the only two males remaining in an entire community of females. And Polo the Old #26 didn't count because he was too old to pop one on a female, even if she helped him along. So Lolo was it.

Lolo wasted no time in getting down to business. Every female in the community wanted a piece of Lolo's action and Lolo was ready to give it; give some of himself to every female in the community. He gave and gave and gave. With no other males, there were no head butts, no fighting, no chewing ears, no fur chunks ripped out, no shows of malehood, no displays of sexual prowess, no genitalia comparisons, none of that extraneous performance lem-shit; just out and out, all day and all night, raw, continuous humping.

But, as everyone knows, there can be too much of a good thing. Female after female demanded some of Lolo and female after female, Lolo provided. Until one day, exhausted and drained beyond the limits of lemming biology, Lolo had literally humped himself to death. So sad.

***Moral #1: Even the very smartest person in the group can become a complete fool when it comes to sex.***

***Moral #2: Be very careful how one treads when running along with something larger than oneself.***

*Postscriptum*: Shortly after Lolo's demise, the community of females all gave birth to the late Lolo's offspring. But the experiment of having *only males* do The Run—headlong into the sea—turned out to be a dismal failure. And whose bright idea was that? No one in the community knew anything about gene pools. All the new children, thousands upon thousands, all of them had the late Lolo the Smoke #233 as their dear old Dad. Lemmings who were specifically named after their Dad ran the number up to Lolo the Smoke #2887—a new record. It wasn't long before inbreeding in the community generated a whole array of freaks, five-legged lemmings, and, unfortunately, sterile males. Over time, Lolo's community faded away, consumed by nature and history. As word of the failed experiment went out to other lemming communities, the idea of a single sex making The Run was abandoned. It was a horror that no lemming community ever wanted to repeat.

However, being hard-headed and single-minded, as lemmings are prone to be, it never occurred to anyone to question The Run itself, not even remotely. So the tradition continued to be observed religiously, over and over and over and over. And just whose idea was that?

## A Badge Day for Blodwyn

lodwyn the badger woke up one day feeling absolutely full of himself, absolutely *badge*. Stretching and yawning he strutted around, enjoying the badge-ness of the misty morning—delightful and dewy.

"Let's find something to eat," he said to himself while strolling through the filtered light of the forest.

"Ho ho," the grey fox said as he encountered Blodwyn along the path. "I see you're looking good today."

"Feelin' badge. Very badge today," said Blodwyn. "Just looking for some meat."

"Me too," replied the fox. "Just steer away from my areas, if you please."

"Never you mind about that," said Blodwyn, dismissing the fox's request.

"Well, humpf," the fox said as he went on down the road and left Blodwyn to wallow in his badge-ness.

In a clearing that eventually ended in a cliff overlooking the sea, there was a thick-trunked aged ash tree with sparse leafage. Sitting on a horizontal branch of the tree was a large owl named Sensa. Coming out of a mid-morning doze, she began eyeballing Blodwyn as he came toward the tree. Blodwyn was in a prideful self-satisfied strut.

"What have we here?" Sensa said, watching Blodwyn curiously.

"I am Blodwyn."

"And how are you today?" Sensa asked politely.

"Feeling badge. Feeling badge."

"And what kind of a feeling is that?" Sensa asked even though she knew what he meant. "You *are* a confident one, aren't you."

"Got a right to be. Got a right to be," Blodwyn said, looking out over the sea. He stopped strolling and began staring out to sea.

Sensa noticed that Blodwyn was suddenly preoccupied, almost mesmerized—something had caught his attention out over the water.

"What is it?" asked Sensa. Blodwyn did not reply.

After a brief pause, Blodwyn then asked Sensa, "What kind of a creature is that, flying out there?"

"Why, that's Abby, an albatross. An albatross soars on the wind. They live over there by the sea," Sensa replied.

"I don't suppose one of those would be easy to catch, you know, for a meal. But look how she floats on the air...out there." Blodwyn was captivated. He soon realized that he was still ready for something to eat. "Hey you...owl bird. Seen anything good to eat around here?"

"I had a few mice during the night, but...haven't seen anything all morning. Besides, I'm ready to continue my nap," Sensa replied, yawning, beginning to get drowsy again.

As Blodwyn poked around in the dirt around some large rocks, uprooting some grassy weeds, he came upon a big juicy spider, slowly crawling over a downed tree branch. The spider had a huge red, bulging abdomen. "What about this?" Blodwyn asked Sensa as he looked the spider over.

"I wouldn't touch that spider if I were you," Sensa said as she closed her eyes. "Those things are poisonous."

"I don't believe it," said Blodwyn. "Spiders are only poisonous if they bite you. This one won't stand a chance...and I'm feeling oh so badge this morning." With that Blodwyn gobbled down the spider. "Tasty. Tasty. Real badge," said Blodwyn, wiping a lick of spider juice from his lips. Sensa had fallen into a kind of twilight sleep and was in no mood for any more banter from Blodwyn. But she was still trying to keep a drowsy eye on him as he kept poking around on the ground underneath the ash tree.

Blodwyn then tuned his attention back to the soaring albatross. But now, as Blodwyn watched it, the albatross seemed to leave a long, colorful trail behind it as it floated through the air. "Very beautiful, very badge," thought Blodwyn. Things soon became a lot fuzzier for Blodwyn. He was feeling even more badge than before. He felt empowered and magnificent. As Blodwyn began making a spectacle of himself in some kind of dirt dance, Sensa fought off her drowsiness and watched Blodwyn reveling in his stupor.

"I sure would like to float on the air like that," Blodwyn announced as Abby the albatross made a pass over Blodwyn, Sensa, and the ash tree.

"I think that spider juice has done something to you," Sensa warned. "The poison."

"Phooey. I feel great. I feel powerful and omnipotent. The most absolute badge ever."

Blodwyn was starting to annoy Sensa. He was definitely addled and had lost himself somewhere in his own mind. Abby made another pass over Blodwyn and Blodwyn thought he saw Abby beckon to him like a bright star with hundreds of rainbow-colored paws giving him spiraling fingers of nature-love. Blodwyn headed over to where he could see the sparkling waters of the sea and the waves that were curling like organized clouds of light. He could hear the surf—something that made its own music. A reawakened and fascinated Sensa could see Blodwyn standing there, mesmerized by the entire scene—the morning seascape.

Blodwyn started watching every motion of Abby as she soared this way and that, swooping and sailing, gracefully floating with every direction change in the steady breeze. He just *knew* he could soar like that, so he jumped out over the edge of the cliff and into the air. Abby continued to fly and soar, completely unaware of Blodwyn—had never been aware of him. A disappointed and saddened Sensa watched as Blodwyn sailed and sailed—for a few seconds, vertically. Then Blodwyn smashed onto the rocks below, leaving only a small pile of badger remains. Not so badge of a day after all.

**Moral: You may be high as the soaring albatross. You may think you can fly like the soaring albatross. But, given the chance, gravity will most certainly bring you down to earth.**

*Postscriptum*: Abby kept soaring and swooping, never even noticing the events surrounding Blodwyn's demise. As Sensa lifted off from the ash tree branch to find another tree (perhaps one more isolated and deeper in the forest), she said to herself, "What does someone have to do to get some sleep around here?"

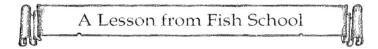

## A Lesson from Fish School

t was the second week of school. Boley and Tilo were late. They always swam to school together, cautiously, since there were big fish, big predators in the water; predators like the ones that ate Grandpa Gil and Uncle Finn. Closer to school, Boley and Tilo were additionally on the lookout for Yumpus and his gang of fin-pecking fishes. Yumpus and his cohorts really had it *in* for Boley; Tilo, they just ignored for the most part.

When Boley went to the portal outside the classroom cove, Yumpus was there, as usual. He was blocking the portal, specifically to annoy and harass Boley. Tilo with her big eyes and her sleek oily fish skin was let in to the cove unmolested. But Boley was an agile darter and passed through the portal before Yumpus knew what was happening. This type of pointless back and forth happened almost every day.

As Boley got himself aligned among the group of students in the usual synchronous way, a mildly perturbed Fishmaster Flosso "requested" that *all* the young fishes settle down so that the class could get down to business. Like every other school day, Tilo was hovering by Boley's side in the synchronous group. She and Boley had been good friends for many seasons. Boley hoped that one day he might cast his seed all over her dismounted eggs, bringing new life to the larger group of which he was only a small part.

Each day was divided into periods: there was Swimming, Communication, Reproduction, and Skills. Boley was interested in all his subjects; but some more than others. It didn't matter which subject his Fishmaster was presenting, every new revelation was like a juicy morsel floating right in front his mouth, begging to be eaten. Yumpus and his group were only interested in disrupting the classes and making everyone miserable. Boley found himself hoping that one day Yumpus and those in his gang would get "net-exiled"— gathered up in one of the mysterious top-water nets; gathered up just like thirty-three of Boley's fish-brothers and fish-sisters.

Swimming class went smoothly. The kids were taught how to move in formation; how to dart and maneuver; how to avoid predators. Boley was only an average student when it came to formation swimming and synchronization, but so was every other member of his class. All the same.

Boley was especially good at Communication. Fishmaster Assistant Poundu would go far from the classroom where he would make clicking vibrations that the young students were asked to detect. Boley's well-developed body sensors could respond to vibrations from very far away. It was a gift he was born with. But he was way too young to know just how important this particular ability was to him; or it would be as he approached adulthood. He felt bad for others in his class who were born with poorly-designed or defective sensors, although the young and inexperienced Boley did not see any obvious disadvantage the disability afforded them. Not at present.

Boley, like others in his class, thought Reproduction was an unnecessary subject. Without any kind of guidance, Boley already knew what to do and how to do it. And, who to do it with: Tilo. That was his choice. Others in the class found their own Tilos, but this Tilo was a perfect match for Boley—as Boley saw things. She was waiting for the day when she and Boley would locate the perfect surface, the perfect surface where she would, at long last, eject her eggs. Then she would stand by while Boley saturated the water with his seed, layering the cloud over her eggs. Eventually the mixture would spawn new life. It was exciting to even think about it. She could only *imagine* the thrill of it when the big day came. She had saved the contents of her egg sac for Boley's spew and Boley's spew alone. Boley and Tilo knew these things. It seemed very natural. They did not need Fishmaster Flosso or Grand Fishtutor Fodiodo to rehash all of the procedure in Reproduction class.

Finally, toward the end of the school day, it came time for the Skills period. Boley enjoyed Skills the most because the things he learned seemed to be very useful and sometimes just plain fun; nudging rocks for food, outsmarting predators, and blowing bubbles to name just a few.

One wet day (*every* day was wet) in Bondover (one of four cycles on the school calendar), the class seemed a bit smaller to everyone. The head of the school, Fishprincipio Zyt, addressed the class, "We are sorry to report that a number of your fellow classmates were gathered in a 'net-exile' incident last evening. Someday they may return to us and we shall all welcome them, but until then, children, my little cold-blooded babies, stay healthy and reproduce."

Boley was glad that Tilo was safe. He was sad that Yumpus was safe as well, although, on the bright side, a few members of Yumpus's gang did seem to be missing. Too bad all of them weren't put in "net-exile."

Things in the classroom settled back down and Fishmaster Flosso, unruffled, started right in on the day's lesson.

"Can anyone tell me what this is?" Fishmaster Flosso showed the class a picture of a thick juicy worm contorted all about on a metal hook. There was a barb at the end of the hook and the hook was attached to a thin wire that disappeared out of the picture.

"Dinner!" many of the students cried out in a chaotic reply.

"Now think carefully about it before you answer. What is it?" Fishmaster Flosso asked again.

"Dinner!" Even Tilo joined the crowd in responding. Boley did not respond either time when Fishmaster Flosso posed the question.

Then, Fishmaster Flosso directed her comments to Boley, "Student Boley, you have not responded to my questions. What have you to say? What do you think it is?"

Boley looked around the classroom cove. Everyone was staring at him, giving him the fish-eye. It was embarrassing.

Fishmaster Flosso pressed the issue, "Perhaps you didn't hear me, Student Boley. What comes to mind when you see something like this?"

Boley finally responded, "Death! That's what I think of."

"Everyone believes it is a picture of dinner. Does anyone agree with Student Boley?" Fishmaster Flosso's tone was very authoritative. No one in the class agreed with Boley. Not one.

Boley felt awkward and embarrassed. He just wanted to quietly return to his home cove. Even Fishmaster Flosso seemed to be in agreement with the class: dinner. Boley felt isolated; even from his future reproduction partner, Tilo.

Then Fishmaster Flosso blurted out, bringing up bubbles from who knows where, "Student Boley is absolutely right. This is *death*! Student Boley gets the morsel prize and a day off from school."

Boley knew that this incident had further alienated him from his classmates, but he didn't care. He experienced a great feeling of satisfaction, one that stayed with him for the rest of his life.

**Moral: At least once in a lifetime, every individual should experience the joy of being the only one in a group who is proven to be right when everyone else has it wrong.**

*Postscriptum*: After school that day, a hostile Yumpus and his gang caught up with Boley and banged him up, this way and that. They chewed into some of his fins and called him all sorts of derogatory fish names. But none of the damage was permanent. The thrashing only made Boley feel good about himself—he was pleased to not be considered one of the ignoramuses that were apparently all around him. He looked beyond Tilo's error in judgement and was a willing participant when it became time to spew all over Tilo's egg ejectum. Soon, the countless progeny of Boley and Tilo would be coming into the world, and things were going to be just as they should be.

As for Yumpus and his gang, one by one, each of them, every last one of them, including Yumpus, eventually got a sharp jagged hook in the mouth. Fear of a predator was a common issue among members of the larger group. But the strike of a predator, as a generation of stories had always related, was considered fast and merciful; deadly, but fast and painless. This was not to be the fate of Yumpus and his so-called gang.

As fish legends would have it, the hooks were extremely painful but not fatal. With a hook in place, a fish would be aggressively pulled out from the water, into the air, where breathing would become very difficult, if not impossible. Then, something even more painful would be inflicted: the offensive hook would be ripped, helter skelter, from the mouth of the fish, tearing mouth flesh and opening wounds, sometimes with blood involved. At that point, the fish might be beaten to death with a club to the head or possibly kept in anguished captivity until thrust into freezing ice. On the other hand, more often than not, the fish would just be allowed to slowly suffocate and die out in the *air*. But the eventual fate of almost all of the fish so captured was to be cooked, placed on a plate, and eaten; little by little—picked at, picked at, picket at. A fate worse than death. Those that weren't eaten might wind up being stuffed with heaps of dry fluff and tacked to a board—to be gawked at and poked at and talked about.

Yumpus, members of his gang, and all the other students had been required to learn about such death legends in school. Did Yumpus and his gang members learn anything? Were they even paying attention? Was Yumpus really stupid enough to go after a deadly worm on a hook after being warned? Or was he doing it just out of defiance, contradicting Boley purely for annoyance's sake? In that case, possibly, Yumpus's only motivation was that he couldn't stand the idea of Boley being right. But, that is quite a different fable.

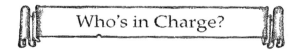

## Who's in Charge?

hen the whirring stopped and the green smoke subsided, Ezzi-Oxon made his first attempt to exit from his craft. But the hatch was way too hot for him to get it open. So he waited some more. Impatiently he waited. He had things to do and did not want to be delayed any further. This was an unplanned landing because of a malfunction in the atmospheric trajectory guidance system. He was lucky his craft wasn't burned to a cinder. But now he was ready to get on with his mission. Finally, the hatch was cool enough for him to open it, disembark, evaluate the situation, and get on with it.

In spite of the fact that it was nighttime and very dark, Ezzi-Oxon exited from his craft and was able to make out quite a bit of tall vegetation surrounding his craft. He had landed in a wooded area, a deeply wooded area. He was supposed to land in a densely populated city with buildings and important humans all milling about, performing mundane tasks, and intensely unaware of his important advance groundwork mission. He never fully appreciated how lucky he was that his craft was not torn to shreds by the tall trees in the area. Just as he set his foot pod on the soft vegetal layer covering the ground—pine needles, leaves, moss, and other decaying organic matter—he realized that he had forgotten his transmagnum ray pistol. He had left it on the control deck. So he climbed back aboard and retrieved it, crawled down out of his craft, and confidently proceeded on with his mission.

Even though the darkness made it difficult to move around, Ezzi-Oxon felt his way through the trees, somewhat clumsily, and soon encountered an Opossum named O'Hay.

"Oh my," O'Hay exclaimed upon seeing the odd looking creature named Ezzi-Oxon. "You must be lost. You look lost. Are you lost? Oh my!"

Ezzi-Oxon ignored the question; had no intention of responding to it. "Take me to your leader."

"Oh! I *have* no leader. I am a one-woman operation. You smell funny, like smoke. Are you on fire?"

"Quiet!" Ezzi-Oxon blurted. "Where is your leader? Any leader. I must have words with a leader...someone in charge...here in this strange place."

"Oh phooey," O'Hay replied. "Try the tortoises. They may know what you're talking about...you weird creature. Go that way toward the big pond." O'Hay pointed toward the lily pond, to an area further into the woods. "That's where they usually get together. Oh phooey." With that, O'Hay lumbered away into the brush. Lucky for her that she got out of the area before Ezzi-Oxon's transmagnum ray pistol had a chance to build up a charge or Ezzi-Oxon would have blasted her then and there.

So, following the direction that O'Hay had indicated, Ezzi-Oxon went on, deeper into the woods and toward the big pond. Ezzi-Oxon knew nothing of tortoises and was not aware that tortoises do not usually wander around in the middle of the night. This fact became apparent when he arrived at the pond and there were no creatures anywhere.

Ezzi-Oxon scanned the area near the pond and discovered a huge pile of garbage. He didn't recognize the pile as garbage since he was from another planet. A curious Ezzi-Oxon was looking over the rotting pile of garbage when he saw a large group of rats rummaging through the debris. When one of the rats made eye contact with him, Ezzi-Oxon confronted the animal, "Take me to your leader," Ezzi-Oxon demanded.

"*I* am the leader. What do you want?" the rat said.

"He's not the leader. *I* am," another rat rudely interjected.

"They're both wrong. *I* am the leader," a third rat said.

By this time a full congregation of rats had arrived around Ezzi-Oxon, each one claiming to be the leader; each one denying the credentials of everyone else. It was mass confusion.

"You there," Ezzi-Oxon said, pointing at one of the rats. "I accept *you* as the leader. Surprised to be the one selected out of all those present, the rat stepped forward with an immodest stride, looking around at the others who were now to be considered inferiors. The rat approached Ezzi-Oxon, while the rest of the group began talking behind his back.

Ezzi-Oxon began his prewritten speech, "I represent a race of superior beings. My comrades will be arriving here as soon as I return with my report. I am telling *you* as the designated leader to *submit*...and prepare to be enslaved by our invading force. You, you, the designated leader will be held responsible for any resistance waged against our takeover."

"*I'm* not the leader. *She* is," the abdicating designated leader rat offered quickly, pointing out the first rat that came into his view.

Suddenly, the chaos started up again as each rat in the group attempted to maneuver out of the focal area of the conversation. Suddenly, no one was claiming to be leader—no one ever claimed to be leader. The rats began pushing and shoving against each other in a mad rush to get back into the garbage and away from Ezzi-Oxon and his threats.

Ezzi-Oxon was getting nowhere with these creatures, and since his transmagnum ray pistol was fully charged at that point, he saturated the area with its bio-ray until all the rats were turned into a pile of co-mingled rat bodies representing a grotesque mangle of genetic confusion. Even the pile of garbage was melded into the organic mélange. If Ezzi-Oxon's olfactory senses had been pre-tuned to Earth's molecular signatures he would have gagged on the rank smell he had generated with his action. Now Ezzi-Oxon was more impatient and frustrated than ever.

He noticed that the planet's star was beginning to shine down on the area. It was getting warmer and brighter with each passing minute.

"Now that's more convenient," Ezzi-Oxon thought as the sun rose up into the sky. Soon, a number of slowly moving, shelled animals arrived at the pond.

"These must be the tortoises that the other creature spoke of," Ezzi-Oxon whispered. While the congregation of tortoises grew in size, Ezzi-Oxon forced his way into the middle of the gathering group. Ezzi-Oxon climbed up on a rock and addressed the group of tortoises.

"I am Ezzi-Oxon. Take me to your leader," Ezzi-Oxon boldly said.

A nearby tortoise very slowly came up to Ezzi-Oxon and said, "Follow...me."

Slowly...very slowly, the tortoise painstakingly crept across the ground and introduced Ezzi-Oxon to a very large and weathered tortoise getting some sun on a big flat rock.

"Here...is...King...Tortoise..." the guide told Ezzi-Oxon in a painfully slow and deliberate manner.

"You are the leader here?" Ezzi-Oxon asked the old tortoise.

"I...am...the...ruler...of...this...area.
I...am...King...Tortoise...and...these...are...my...subjects."
King Tortoise also spoke in a very slow and deliberate way. All of this slowness was very foreign to Ezzi-Oxon.

"Then I have a message for you," Ezzi-Oxon started. "I represent a race of superior beings. My colleagues will be arriving here as soon as I return..." By the time Ezzi-Oxon finished his speech about enslaving everyone, most of the tortoises had left the area or had fallen asleep.

"That creature is much too fast for the likes of us," one of the tortoises said.

"These tortoises cannot possibly rule this planet, they are so painfully slow. And this one, this one may be the King..." A frustrated and impatient Ezzi-Oxon set his transmagnum ray pistol on "disintegrate" and zapped into oblivion the entire colony of tortoises, King and all.

"That's odd," Ezzi-Oxon said. Although his pistol disintegrated the tortoises, it had left the dried-out shells completely intact. "Very curious," he said to himself as he walked away, looking for a leader to whom he could deliver his important message.

Later that same day, in a wide-open grassy area, Ezzi-Oxon encountered a herd of antelopes. Locating one of the animals Ezzi-Oxon confronted it, "Take me to your leader."

"We have no leader," the antelope replied. "We behave as one."

Without warning, the antelope darted off as the group moved (as one) to a different spot in the field. Ezzi-Oxon chased down the herd. He was confused. He couldn't locate the animal he had just been talking to. All the antelopes looked alike. So he repeated his story to the next antelope he came across. Before Ezzi-Oxon could ask to see the leader, the herd made another unified move across the field.

So after chasing down the herd once again, a weary Ezzi-Oxon asked the first antelope he saw, "Tell me. Who is the most fearsome of all creatures? Who do you fear? Who rules? Who has the power of life and death? And does that group have a leader? Tell me quickly..."

The antelope was quick to reply, "It may be the wolf. We must be very careful. Sometimes the wolf catches and kills one of us. I know of no other so dangerous a creature except man. Man is but a myth. I have never seen one."

True to form, with his transmagnum ray pistol fully charged and set on "fireball", the conquering Ezzi-Oxon roasted the entire herd of antelopes and started a big grassfire in so doing. Ezzi-Oxon was a real badass.

The time was late afternoon. Ezzi-Oxon was tired of searching for someone in charge; someone that could assist him in bullying the entire population into submission. With the help of a squirrel—a squirrel that was quickly afterward dispatched into a charred blob of gelatinous organic matter melted onto the limb of a tree—Ezzi-Oxon was able to locate a wolf...a she-wolf.

Ezzi-Oxon wasted no time with this creature, "Take me to your leader."

Surprisingly, the she-wolf was very cooperative and complied with Ezzi-Oxon's demand.

"Now we're getting somewhere," Ezzi-Oxon remarked to himself.

When Ezzi-Oxon and his she-wolf guide arrived at the wolf pack, he checked the charge level on his transmagnum ray pistol. If he was disappointed once again, he was going to really let this group of creatures have the worst of it, just like the others. Maybe give it to them slowly and painfully, just because—

The leader of the pack, the alpha, looked very impressive. The others seemed to defer to him. He apparently had his pick of the females. This was the leader that Ezzi-Oxon had been searching for. The alpha wolf was bolder than all the rest and voluntarily came up to Ezzi-Oxon. This creature was definitely in charge.

"Are you the leader?" Ezzi-Oxon asked the alpha wolf while giving the beast the once over.

"Yes I am," the wolf replied.

Ezzi-Oxon could almost *feel* the cold, hard look coming from the alpha wolf's eyes. But Ezzi-Oxon was glad to have finally contacted someone in charge—someone to whom he could deliver his important message. Filled with curiosity, the other wolves gathered around Ezzi-Oxon and the alpha wolf so that they could see what was going on.

Rather than explain himself once again, an impatient Ezzi-Oxon got right to the point, "I have come to give you notice that my colleagues and I are coming to take over and you must submit to us or die."

At the alpha wolf's signal, the rest of the pack joined the alpha wolf and jumped onto the alien, tearing the little interplanetary badass to shreds. Everyone joined in. It was one of the easiest kills the pack had ever experienced. All that was left of Ezzi-Oxon was his uniform and his transmagnum ray pistol.

**Moral: *You're not the least bit as big and powerful as you think you are.***

*Postscriptum*: It was a strange meal for the wolf pack: Ezzi-Oxon had no bones inside; his flesh was spongy and had a metallic taste; and members of the pack wound up having the runs for several days. When a follow-up alien scouting party arrived, they found Ezzi-Oxon's empty shredded uniform and his fully discharged ray gun lying on the ground. Conquering this planet was going to be more dangerous and difficult than they first imagined, so the invasion was called off and the Earth was saved. Nature knows what it's doing. As with all things, nothing is truly permanent. One day, the alpha wolf got his leg caught in the jaws of a bear trap and had to chew his own leg off. He lost his lofty position (replaced by a smarter, younger, more agile wolf) and no female wanted him any more—his having only three legs and all. Nothing personal, just nature.

## McCocker, the Cocksure

ne could smell the chicken farm from miles away. It wasn't a large farm, but chickens are chickens. The smell was not attractive by most standards, but it *did* attract one Fryck the Fox. Waiting until the dark of night, Fryck stealthily made his way into farmer Milksaugen's barnyard. Following the chicken farm smell, Fryck located the hen house, a place where numerous chickens (hens) were kept for egg-laying purposes—and when a chicken was too old to lay...well, fricasseed chicken would then appear on the menu. After all, it *was* a farm.

Just outside the chicken coop, Fryck began salivating as he could hear the chickens making tiny little chicken noises as they slept. He carefully stepped into the hen house and saw rows and rows of delicious poultry, lined up on shelves, just waiting to be taken as dinner—it was a chicken supermarket. Fryck acted quickly and snatched the nearest sleeping hen from her nest. She only squawked briefly as Fryck killed her without hesitating for an instant. Out from the hen house he trotted triumphantly with the dead chicken clutched in his jaws.

If Fryck thought he had made the kill unnoticed, he was mistaken. McCocker the resident rooster heard the sounds and came directly to the scene. But he was too late. Fryck had made off with the hen already.

The next day, farmer Milksaugen noticed the array of bloodied chicken feathers all around the scene of the crime. He may have been angered, but there was really nothing he could do about it. McCocker the rooster, strutting around the yard as usual, could not help but notice the farmer's displeasure.

Two nights later, Fryck the Fox returned for another run at the chickens. Again, Fryck was able to snatch a hen from her nest and make off with it into the woods. A sleepy-eyed McCocker awoke when the fox first clamped his powerful jaws down on the unsuspecting chicken, but the hen's cries were brief and the hen's death was quick and otherwise silent.

The next day, farmer Milksaugen assessed the situation and laid some of the blame on McCocker. "Why don't you make some noise when this is happening, you stupid rooster?"

McCocker was ashamed. He didn't like being referred to as *stupid*. "What kind of a cock are you?" he said to himself. I must make amends. So that night and for the two following nights, McCocker probed his beak into the Milksaugen garbage bin and found used coffee grounds from the Milksaugens' morning brew. McCocker became quite nervous and agitated, but thanks to the caffeine he was able to stay awake every night until the wee hours of the morning. Nothing occurred. There was no fox and the chickens were safe.

On the fourth night, McCocker was in his caffeinated state of alertness when Fryck the Fox came into the barnyard. Fryck went inside the hen house and had his way in selecting his chicken. Out he came with another fat, dead hen in his mouth.

McCocker took a deep breath in preparation for a really loud crow when he backed down and decided to find out where the fox was taking the chickens—possibly the fox's lair. So rather than crow his brains out, McCocker followed the fox. It was quite a journey. It was difficult for McCocker to follow Fryck quietly, roosters being roosters after all. But Fryck never suspected a thing.

Soon Fryck and McCocker arrived at the lair of the fox. McCocker was not impressed with the state of the fox's lair: unkempt, very unappealing esthetically, and chicken feathers lying about everywhere. He heard the sounds of bones cracking and flesh being torn asunder. He dare not venture any closer lest he alert the fox to his presence. McCocker waited and soon, the fox, with a full belly, fell asleep.

McCocker turned away and started to make a hasty retreat back to the farm; back to the farm to inform farmer Milksaugen of the whereabouts of the fox's lair. But McCocker, being a cocky sort of fellow, as cocks most assuredly are, decided to stay. He went directly to the fox's lair, crowed loudly, and literally prodded the fox into waking up. The bleary-eyed fox saw the rooster and said, "What do *you* want? What's *your* problem?"

McCocker spoke brazenly, "I wanted to inform you that I plan to turn you in. I am going to lead farmer Milksaugen to your lair. He will see these chicken feathers as evidence and he will end your life and your chicken-killing ways."

As McCocker smugly turned away to head for home, Fryck pounced on the rooster and pinned him to the ground. The fox, highly annoyed at the arrogance of McCocker, provided that rooster with a slow and painful death. Fryck did not like being awakened in the middle of the night any more than the next fox.

**Moral: *If you've got the goods on someone, be careful who you tell.***

*Postscriptum*: The fox was already full and was only killing the rooster to keep his hideout a secret. Later, he began snacking on the rooster and accidentally choked to death on the rooster's furcula. Some stories just don't have a hero.

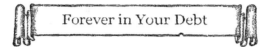

Forever in Your Debt

exter and Anisette were a couple of love-struck rabbits. Not that it was anything out of the ordinary. What made it difficult for the lovers was that Dexter's father, Pater Exeter, disapproved of the whole thing—visibly and vocally. This was quite unusual in the rabbit community where normally the standing rule was "anything goes" especially when it came to producing offspring.

"I don't *have* to have a reason," Pater Exeter would say boastfully. He didn't express a reason because he had no reason. He just liked exercising his power over those with less power. But Dexter and Anisette continued to plan for getting hitched.

Eventually Dexter left home in order to be with Anisette. This outraged Pater Exeter to the point where Dexter was made *persona non grata* when it came to anything associated with Dexter's immediate family. Such was the power of Pater Exeter.

In stepped Uncle Doleo. He encouraged Dexter and Anisette to elope and to set up shop somewhere else. Uncle Doleo was motivated by the long-standing and continuing sibling rivalry he had going with Pater Exeter. So siding with Dexter was a perfect jab at his brother.

Ever since he was a little bunny, Dexter always thought his Uncle Doleo was a card, even though his uncle always referred to Dexter as Dickster. Dexter didn't like that nickname one bit. No one else called him that. Uncle Doleo had a habit of giving everyone his own made-up names. No one except Uncle Doleo liked the practice or thought it was "cute."

So Dexter and Anisette made a hole for themselves and scratched together enough food to get by. They were happy to be together in spite of the circumstances. As soon as everything calmed down they planned to run away and get hitched.

A long cold winter came roaring in and Dexter and Anisette had to ration their food supply. They had made their hole comfortable even though they had a bare minimum of essentials. But with excellent foresight, they had made sound plans for surviving the winter; and when winter finally gave way to spring, there would be new opportunities for starting a family of their own and getting on with their life.

In stepped Uncle Doleo. In the midst of a winter cold spell, Uncle Doleo came calling with a bunch of carrots and some thatch (for adorning their hole and adding some insulation).

"Here you go, Dickster. For you too, Anise," Uncle Doleo said as he placed the items at the feet of the young couple. He was expecting a boundless expression of gratitude for such a good deed.

"You shouldn't have done this," Anisette answered. She hated having her name truncated like that. "We're getting along just fine."

"Yeah, we're doing just fine; so you should keep all those things for yourself," Dexter added. They really didn't need any of it in order to get by during the winter.

"Nonsense," Uncle Doleo said. He was going to get some gratitude out of those two if he had to torque it out of them. "Take them, take them all." With that Uncle Doleo left the couple. In addition to fishing for some gratitude, he was, once again, attempting to stick it to his brother Pater Exeter. "Here's something I can do to ingratiate myself with your *persona non grata* son," he thought to himself. "And your son's undying loyalty to me will just be a little something extra in it for *me*."

Spring finally arrived. Dexter and Anisette began building their life together. They were frugal and managed their assets well. Soon they were able to set up a very nice, enviable hole for themselves. They started planning on raising some young ones of their own. Things were progressing very well and it wasn't long before there were little rabbits running all about the place.

In stepped Uncle Doleo. He had come to the hole of Dexter and Anisette for an impromptu visit. Uncle Doleo didn't waste any time getting to the point. "It's election time. Time to elect a new Master Rabbit. I'm supporting a friend of mine, Dover. I'm sure you've heard of him and you'll want to support him as well; especially you, Dickster. You too Anise. He's got my support. What do you say?"

"Dover?" Dexter replied. "Why are you supporting that unscrupulous rogue of a rabbit?"

"Rogue?" responded Uncle Doleo. "I'll have you know that he's been a friend of mine since before you were born...before you were *even* born. I'm quite offended that you've taken that attitude...after all I've done for you and Anus over there."

Anisette was about to respond to that obvious slur when a petulant Uncle Doleo stormed out of the hole in a puff of inflamed dust. Rather than gnaw on the incident or worry about things over which they had no control, Dexter and Anisette went on with their life and happily tended to their little family of rabbits.

A short time later, Conroy, Dexter's brother, came calling; he had come to deliver a message to Dexter. This message had taken a very circuitous route in making its way from the source: the highly abraded Uncle Doleo and his clan. Uncle Doleo presumed that by sending the message through such a convoluted path it would hide the identity of the source. But everyone figured it out anyway.

"Hello, Dexter," Conroy started. "I have a message that was started somewhere back along the grapevine and it finally fell upon me to deliver it."

"Well, what is it?"

"It's about your Uncle Doleo. He wants you to pay for the carrots and the supply of thatch that he brought to you two winters ago." Conroy seemed reluctant to deliver the message, but there it was, out in the open. Uncle Doleo had put together a small group of willing allies from around the warren. They were involved in talking up about what ingrates

"Dickster" and "Anus" were. News of all this was just now reaching the couple. And the message, as blatant as it was, didn't really surprise Dexter when it finally was delivered to him.

"I'll manage this," Dexter told Anisette.

Not wanting to stir the pot any further. Dexter brought a bunch of carrots and some fresh thatch to Uncle Doleo. Uncle Doleo did not seem pleased with the offering.

"This is all?" Uncle Doleo responded to the offering. "I would think you could at least sweeten the deal with a little extra of each: a few carrots; a little more thatch. After all this time. Well, I'll take them. You know it wasn't easy giving you those things that winter. We were having a hard time ourselves. We had to make such a sacrifice."

"That's right!" Aunt Furla chimed in with indignation. She seemed to be even more put out than Uncle Doleo.

"The least you could have done was to have supported Dover for Master Rabbit," added Cousin Droog, piling it on. "The very least..."

"Wow, that didn't go like I expected," whispered Dexter to Anisette as they left the smoldering relatives and went back to their own hole. Dexter and Anisette felt a little bit hurt, but it didn't linger. They hadn't really done anything worthy of that kind of assault.

Uncle Dolco and his family continued to smolder. There definitely wasn't enough contrition or gratitude from the couple. They would punish the couple by denying them their familial camaraderie and by warning others about them—about their ungrateful attitude. But none of that smoldering went very far around the community.

When Uncle Doleo and his family got no hint of how Dexter, Anisette, and their family must be suffering under the Doleo embargo, they began smoldering even more than before. Smoldering led to animosity (and more smoldering). Every little thing that went wrong for Uncle Doleo was blamed on Dexter and Anisette. Smoldering and more smoldering.

**Moral #1: Unsolicited "free" things are usually very expensive.**

**Moral #2: If you think your smoldering is having the intended effect, remember: the only one who suffers while you smolder is you.**

**Moral #3: If you get too close to a smolderer you may start smoldering too.**

*Postscriptum*: Completely unaware of all the smoldering that was going on in that small corner of the family, Dexter and Anisette were busy pursuing life to its fullest. The relationship between Dexter and Pater Exeter eventually thawed out. News of the thaw raised Uncle Doleo's smoldering to a new level—the smoldering could be smelled from miles and miles away. Generally isolated from the community, Uncle Doleo and his smolderers continued their smoldering until one day they were all just burned up.

## The House of Acipenser

wild musk hare named Cuniculus was casually watching a nearby meadow whilst consuming a mouthful of lush vegetal material. The meadow being observed was the *royal* meadow. Cuniculus didn't know anything about that. He was delightfully chewing and keeping a keen eye out for any sign of a possible threat from the sky—a menacing silhouette of a dreaded hawk or eagle. Chomp chomp chomp. The vegetal material was sweet and silky, moist and chewy, just the way Cuniculus liked it. He felt that he must inform Coneja about this area whilst the vegetation maintained its spring form...but first, chomp, chomp, chomp.

Interrupting the serenity of Cuniculus's meal came an entourage of seven well-dressed men and three young street urchins dressed in rags. Along with them were three dogs, moving about randomly and anxiously, but quietly—all three dogs attached to one of the men by a long leash. The entire group came stomping (plodding) into the meadow with brazen authority. Cuniculus briefly stopped his chewing and watched the group thrusting its way through the grass. When the group stopped moving, Cuniculus resumed chewing: chomp, chomp, chomp. Now, Cuniculus was keeping both eyes focused on the group of men. Little did Cuniculus know, but the man in the gilded coat and feathered hat was King Delmar of the House of Acipenser. This group was out for some sport hunting. Cuniculus had seen a "man" before...once or twice; but never this many in one group; never accompanied by three tiny little dirty men (the three street urchins). It was all very strange, but very interesting. Chomp, chomp, chomp.

At the command of one of the men, the three street urchins went running ahead of the group, yelling, and screaming, and making a terrible racket; running chaotically out into the taller meadow grass. Cuniculus again stopped chewing for a moment and watched with fascination. Shortly after the noise and chaos began, three brilliantly-coloured pheasants fluttered out from the grass and up into the air, wings flapping in a rage of panic.

Bam! His sensitive ears having been assaulted, Cuniculus recoiled in a start. King Delmar had fired the first shot...and missed. While the King received a second (loaded) shotgun from his assistant, the others in the group began firing at the fleeing birds. Bam! Bam! Bam! Bam! The King fired another. Bam! All three pheasants fell from the sky and onto the ground...dead...deader than a stone statue of Himmeloneus. No one knew for sure if the King himself had actually hit anything. No one was supposed to know.

The three young urchins scrambled around like manic chickens; the dogs were released; the three pheasants were gathered up, one by dog, two by urchin. And the entire group reassembled with congratulatory backslapping and lots of garrulous huffety-puffety. The entourage then left the meadow and peace was restored. The hunt was over as quickly as it began. Cuniculus resumed his chewing: chomp, chomp, chomp. When he was full, he couldn't wait to tell Coneja about the new area of fine vegetal material.

King Delmar returned to his palace, but before he could even enter the front door, First Adjunct Viscus greeted him with some news. "Your majesty, we have captured three poachers...and...we have found damning evidence as to their guilt: a sack full of royal poached quail. What shall we do with them?"

"Roast them!" the King said decisively. "We shall supplement our dinner of fine pheasant with their delicious carcasses as well."

Viscus replied, "I mean...what shall we do with these *men*, these poachers?"

"Roast them as well...and throw their carcasses into yon river." The King waved his fist in the air. "Let those in the valley below behold their bloated bodies and smell their odoriferous flesh and cower at the might of their King! Their King, who is best friend with God himself; their King, who converses with angels; their King, who controls the weather—for the most part. Their King..."

"Consider it done, your majesty," interrupted First Adjunct Viscus as he made way for the King to promenade into the palace—a well-earned promenade meant to signify the completion of a successful hunt. Members of the King's entourage began peeling off from the group in order to pursue their own royal duties.

That evening—whilst the pheasants roasted, the quail roasted, and the poachers roasted—the King called in Squire Dubius. The King commanded, "Today I saw young urchins in the meadow, urchins with no shoes. I took offense at ugly toes from bare and dirty urchin feet. I decree that the King shall never again have to view anyone's big toe. If I see a big toe, that toe shall be separated straightaway from its owner and placed in a jar...on a pedestal...in the village square. And when *that* jar is full of toes, a second jar shall be added, and a third. No more naked disgusting big toes. I decree it! And so it shall be done!"

"So be it, your majesty," Squire Dubius responded, without question, without delay, as always. Off he went to implement the details of the decree.

Several days later, there were three jars full of big toes sitting atop a pedestal in the village square. The King had made several surprise visits through the countryside and through the streets of the village looking for decree violators. And chop chop chop, just like that, illegally exposed big toes were added to the jars. The King did not seem to take offense when confronted with a weird-looking big toe as long as he knew that it was soon to be coming off its owner—right off—as specified by royal decree. And through all of this chopping, the royal hatchet men were earning their keep in a big way.

This was not the first time that a King's whimsical decree resulted in misery for the small kingdom and the residents of the village. There was the decree that Sundays were reserved for axe fighting only—no meals, no sleeping, no loitering, and especially no shirking of the axe fighting. Everyone was expected to participate. Another decree specified that every newborn must have the royal coat of arms tattooed on their buttocks. And another that cat meat would be substituted for bread—and it was just too bad for bakers, not to mention the many supercilious cats that were always strutting along the streets of the village.

Three days after the hunting party event, Cuniculus, along with Coneja returned to the meadow's edge, returned to enjoy the savory vegetal material while spring was still in the air. But no men came to the meadow while they were there.

It was one week since the King's brief pheasant hunt; one week since the big toe decree; one week for the accumulated toes to rot in the jars. The King was bored with it all. Unable to sleep, King Delmar climbed out of bed and donned his royal robe. He was going to invade the palace pantry to get a bite to eat; maybe a muffin, or a crème-filled pastry, or perhaps some royal meat. It was deep into the night; dark, very dark. As the King awkwardly ambled down the darkened hallway he accidentally jammed his right foot's big toe fiercely into the base of a marble statue—a statue of King Delmar himself. He collapsed onto the ground in agony. Several aides who heard his cries came to his side and helped the King back into his bed.

The King's toe became infected. The King's toe developed gangrene. The King's toe turned black and could be smelled all the way to Timbuktu (wherever that was). The King's toe was amputated. It was too late. Too much gangrene. Too much delay—the King, at first, refusing to have *his* big toe amputated—for *any* reason. The King was dead...dead...deader than tuna-flavored beer.

The King's brother, Curdell, was now King. King Curdell of the House of Acipenser. Long live the king!

Perry the Gopher was wandering around near the royal meadow one day when an entourage of men appeared at one end. Perry hastened to the edge of the meadow to watch the men, curious as to what they were going to do. (And getting out of the way.) There were eight men, including a gaudily-dressed one who seemed to be in charge. There were three little ones (three dirty little street urchins) and three dogs in the group.

Watching the proceedings, Perry asked himself, "What do you call eight big men, three little men, and three dogs? Trouble," Perry replied to his own question.

Before Perry could even get situated the three boys started their typical flushing-out maneuvers. Two pheasants popped up out of the grass. The King and his entourage began firing their shotguns at the birds, bringing the two of them down in a hail of shot. Two more pheasants...dead...deader than dried Lucidular mushrooms. The birds were gathered up and the entourage retired from the scene before the smell of spent gunpowder had even left the field.

"That looked like some bad mojambo, I can tell you," Perry said out loud. No longer interested in all that, he then resumed his bandying about around the edge of the meadow.

King Curdell had only been in power for eight days when he made his first decree. He was his brother's brother as Curdell's whimsy was just as distasteful as Delmar's. He decreed that naked foot races be carried out every Saturday—men, women, and children; all together; running from Mason's Point, through the village, and up to the palace portal where the King would bestow an unspecified honor on the winner. The last-place loser would be beheaded. It was a distance of seven miles. It was highly probable that the crippled, 90-year old vicar would be losing his head in the event.

The next Saturday...the first race day...King Curdell went to the roof of the palace's north tower to watch the unfolding of the race. From that vantage point the King could see all the way to Mason's Point. He could see most of the village streets and all of the road leading to the palace portal right below him. The King's sycophantic advisors were officiously making a fuss all around him. The King was holding the first prize in his hand: a small hat adorned with colorful pheasant feathers. The winner would be required to wear the hat, night and day, until the crowning of the next winner a week later; the next Saturday. It was all so exciting for the King and his men. It was all so horrible for the villagers who just wanted the whole thing to be over with.

The race began, and the rambling, bouncing, horde of nude villagers ran for their lives—from Mason's point, across the Hundirt stream crossing, into the village, and onto the Putrit Road leading up to the palace portal. As the King leaned over the edge of the tower wall to get a better view, he lost his footing and fell to his death, right on the road below...dead...deader than Bronson's theory of independent hornage—right on the road where King Curdell was supposed to deliver the prize to the winner.

Unfortunately for everyone, King Curdell had a son, a halfwit named Sturgid. Upon King Curdell's untimely demise, the rules of succession elevated Sturgid to the throne; Sturgid became the new king: King Sturgid of the House of Acipenser. Long live the King...at least longer than the unfortunate King Curdell.

A fancy porcupine named Porky was walking along the edge of the royal meadow when King Sturgid and his entourage came into it. The humans were huffing and puffing, stomping and plodding, just as many of the King's ancestors had done in days past— another sporting hunt, a hunt for pheasants. King Sturgid had been King for only three days, but he was ready to get into the "action of stout ruling" as he put it. Porky watched the group intently. He had heard other animals talk of strange goings-on in this particular meadow.

As the individuals in the King's group assumed their designated positions...Bam! went the King's shotgun. Then, in reaction to the King's initial firing, a flurry of numerous *Bams!* followed—the entire entourage unloaded their weapons into the pheasant-free air over the meadow. But as to the first Bam! King Sturgid had accidentally shot himself in the face and was dead...dead...deader than a half-eaten cutter chicken.

"Wow. If that don't beat everything," Porky said out loud. As the entourage gathered around the dead King in a frenzy of activity, Porky looked on, fascinated—but after noticing some nice juicy berries in a nearby bush, he downed a few and went on about his own business, quickly and easily putting the events in the meadow completely out of his thoughts.

For the House of Acipenser, it was several days of anguish and positioning as the line of succession was at a new crossroads, this time very vague and ill-defined. There were political and legal implications steeped in every move by *anyone* associated with the previous Kings. Would there even be a successor from the House of Acipenser? Was King

Sturgid the last of the line? Advisors were called in and many royal families from around the country were brought in. Many families came in uninvited, all seeking a slice of the royal pie, or possibly the whole pie. All of this folderol was to determine who was to be the rightful person to sit on the throne and exert the power of the King or Queen.

As the group of candidates was narrowed to a mere handful, a bloody phase to the succession processes began. Murder, disappearances, bribery, violence, conspiracy, and treachery were commonplace—day and night there were plots and counterplots. Traditions were tossed aside in favor of unseemly power moves.

One confrontation between two possible heirs was witnessed by a couple of owls that were quietly hovering over the palace gardens. The heirs were vigorously fighting with swords when a brief lapse caused the two combatants to simultaneously stab each other dead...dead...deader than the sizzling corpse of the legendary Dwight Skunk whose inattention allowed firestorm debris to rain down on him—pointless because a couple of squirrels had warned him ahead of time.

"Have you ever seen anything like that?" said one owl to the other as they flew off looking for something more interesting to do. The second owl just rotated its head in a typical display of wise smugness.

When the dust had settled, there was a very marginal consensus that the new monarch should be Lemonista, a distant cousin of King Curdell. She was to be the first female to rule over the lands and the property of the fragile House of Acipenser. When a message was sent to inform her that she was to be installed as Queen Lemonista, she refused. This rejection caused chaos to begin again, wilder and bloodier than before. As long as all the infighting, politics, and chicanery were taking place, the villagers were free of decrees.

And so it went, on and off, for many years, until a group of invaders took over all the lands and property of the House of Acipenser. The realm fell easily to the invaders since there was no stable monarchy or royal army to defend it; or to protect it; or to do anything with it. The House of Acipenser was dead...dead...deader than a thick slab of meat on a tavern's pewter plate (except at the Ale and Tongue Tavern where sometimes the meat might still be moving—rare indeed). Because the invaders were a small exploratory contingent from a huge empire—an empire too huge to be concerned with governing such a puny kingdom like that of the Acipenser's—the village was at last free of royal decrees. There was no longer a salient ruler, or governor, or monarch, or anything like it.

All of this shuffling, and hunting, and turmoil was great entertainment for the animals of the field—some of which were still curious about what all went on in those buildings, especially the big one up at the end of Putrit Road. And just what were all those sparse-haired naked humans up to, running, running, running along the roads on that one strange Saturday morning?

***Moral: There is not another species of animal on the Earth that gives a damn who the King is, or what he is—except for the pheasants, and boy are they pissed. And don't forget the owls, they too couldn't give a hoot.***

*Postscriptum*: No animals were impressed in the making of all this kingdom business.

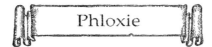

Phloxie

hloxie was a strikingly exquisite red fox, although her fur was more a shade of orange than red. Her tail was wonderfully fluffy and Phloxie knew how to use it. She had a way of moving that was very graceful and seductive. But, even so, all the male foxes avoided her.

One day Phloxie was on the prowl for a good meal, even though she was full and still spitting out little pieces of the bird she had eaten the night before. But she worried that if she didn't re-fill her belly before noon, she was going to get all cranky. Soon, she came upon a small group of rabbits. At last, a meal...a good one. So going into her stealth routine, she crept closer and closer to the group of five. There was a real young one in the group. Phloxie knew that the young one was her best opportunity to make a quick kill. And the young one was just the right size for a meal. Phloxie started breathing hard in anticipation, but before she could act the entire group of rabbits ran off into the underbrush.

"Oh poo," Phloxie mumbled in disgust. Lately this had become a little too common an occurrence. Well, she *had* caught that crippled bird last night so she figured that she was still able to pull off a kill. But her confidence was waning. So on she went, looking for another likely prospect.

"Ah-hah!" Phloxie said to herself as she spotted a lone chipmunk having its morning nutty snack. Again, she crept up on her prey. But before she could get close enough to make any kind of move, something alerted the chipmunk and scared it off.

"Oh, double poo!" Phloxie exclaimed in frustration. So she went to the grassy meadow where the berry bushes grow. She located one of the purple berry bushes and started snacking on the berries. "These are so sweet!" she said. Normally, she only ate the berries as a between-kill snack or to top off a meal, but for the last two days she resorted to eating only the berries. She loved those berries. Too much one might say, judging from her expanding body.

Then she saw another little bird hopping about on the ground. Its wing was damaged and it couldn't fly. "Another cripple!" Phloxie said to herself. She started huffing and puffing, ready to pounce, ready to eat. But like the others, the bird quickly flitted along into the brush and disappeared. "Not even close on that one. And a crippled bird, no less!" Phloxie grumbled and pouted and slunk off to visit her mother. But first, some more berries. And then more.

Once she arrived at her mother's den, Phloxie was surprised as Mother could already tell that Phloxie was soon to arrive. Mother was obviously uncomfortable being in close proximity to Phloxie. But, being a good mother, she comforted Phloxie and said, "Come inside, Phloxie. Let's have a little chat." So the two of them went inside Mother's den and had a heart to heart between mother and daughter. All the while, Mother was suppressing a gag reflex that welled up every time Phloxie started speaking.

**Moral: *Always maintain good oral hygiene or your breath may precede you.***

*Postscriptum*: Phloxie paid a visit to Doctor Hotroot, the local fox dentist. He put Phloxie on a good program of oral hygiene and told her to lay off the berries, especially between kills. Soon she was back in business, even acquiring a suitor or two. Next up: Attacking Phloxie's weight problem.

## The Finger Club of Tooba

eep in the jungle, in unexplored territory, there was a city of chimpanzees. The city was called Wacka-Ooh-Ooh. Among the many professional chimpanzee residents there lived a boisterous and adventuresome ape named Tooba. Tooba did not understand the ways of his fellow apes and their reluctance to do risky things.

Scouting around for some fruit one day, Tooba and a large contingent of his acquaintances came upon a machete inadvertently left behind by some recent human explorers. As was his way, Tooba was the one who was first to grab it and check it out. The bold Tooba played with the machete, experimenting with its feel, and having a great time with it. Once he got the hang of the blade he began chopping off branches and hacking into tree trunks and brandishing it toward his fellow chimps; all the while squawking and bellowing like a wild banshee. The big group of chimps backed away from him, becoming frightened by Tooba's erratic behavior.

Before Tooba could destroy too much vegetation, he swung the machete around and, losing control, caught his other hand with the blade, chopping off his forefinger completely. Now the chimpanzee city was quite organized as ape cities go, but by human standards it was still very primitive. Among its professionals, there were no ape doctors...no one that could re-attach Tooba's finger. So that was it. His forefinger was right off and was lying there on the ground, motionless. Painful as the situation was, it was Tooba's nature to remain stoic and hang tough through any misfortune he may have brought upon himself. It was his way of mitigating the chimp community's negative reaction to his foolhardiness. So with finger stub bleeding, he acted as if the accident was something special, waving the bloodied hand at the other apes in his group and laughing it off; laughing in a chimpanzee manner. The other apes were surprised at the reaction and came closer to investigate.

Although most of the chimps were skeptical of the benefits, even horrified, some were intrigued. Tooba's post-amputation demeanor caused a number of the chimps to become very curious. Tooba took the machete and showed the curious ones how to do it—how to chop off a finger. In order to elevate the amputation to "fad" status, Tooba grabbed his severed finger from the ground and waved it around.

Seeing what was happening, a few of the older chimps in the group shouted a warning. "Don't do that! It won't grow back!" But mere words could not deter the dozen or so very curious chimps, and one by one, each chimp, in turn, chopped off one of its own fingers. Without exception, they followed Tooba's example and reacted heroically to the painful procedure. They had formed quite a little club—a club of Tooba followers. And each member's severed finger served as a kind of membership badge. So here was a group of chimps indicating their special status by carrying around their own severed finger at all times. A few other chimps back in Wacka-Ooh-Ooh joined the group as well—but only after going through an ad hoc initiation ordeal that included the chopping ritual. When all was said and done, Tooba had a following of two dozen chimpanzees.

The group had a special status as far as *they* were concerned, but most members of the chimpanzee city thought Tooba's group was just a gaggle of goo-goos (idiots). Tooba's club members wore that negative assessment as a badge of honor as well. So Tooba's Finger Club began to alienate itself from the rest of the community. The members hung out together, doing chimpanzee stuff together.

Loo-Barga was the leader of a small group of baboons. Her group was poking around the jungle when she encountered Tooba and his group.

"Who are you?" Tooba asked with an authoritative and hostile tone in his voice.

"I am Loo-Barga and we're just passing through," she replied. "I see your group has had some kind of strange accident," she commented after seeing every chimp holding on to a decaying forefinger.

"No. We're a special group of chimps, separate from the rest. What is wrong there...with your asses?" Tooba asked, seeing the bulging pink-skinned asses on many of Loo-Barga's baboon group. "They all look like skinned melons!"

"Nothing wrong, it's natural for a baboon," she replied. "Where have you been, here in this jungle? Living under a rock? It's very natural for a baboon. Sexy. Now if you don't mind we'd like to pass on through—"

So Loo-Barga's group carried on without giving the chimpanzees another thought. But Tooba was so intrigued by all the pink asses that he continued to stare at Loo-Barga's group until they disappeared into the jungle vegetation.

Tooba was envious. He just had to have an ass like those baboons. He convinced the others in the Finger Club that they too should have bulbous pink asses—skinned melons. So, as a leader, Tooba made it a point to acquire his pink ass first. He found a giant flat stone with a rough surface and began rubbing his ass on it, scooting around on the rock, sanding off his hair. This was a lot of labor. Tooba's ass was bare and pink in some places, but it wasn't as good as the ones he saw on the baboons. And within a couple of weeks, the hair grew back. Not good enough for Tooba. Not good enough for Tooba's hold on his followers.

Incidentally, by this time the membership badges of the Finger Club members (the severed fingers) were getting very rotten; some even beginning to fall apart. This was disquieting to Tooba. How were others to recognize members of the elite Finger Club without the signature badges? Most of the members just carried around one or more of the bones after the flesh had rotted away. Without the badge, a couple of members lost interest and just went back to Wacka-Ooh-Ooh. But Tooba's group was still around twenty strong.

Coming upon a human campfire one day, Tooba saw an opportunity that he couldn't pass up. Seeing what Tooba was about to do, Galua, a Finger Club member—one who was *very* familiar with fire—shouted to Tooba, "Don't go near that fire! It does damage. Permanent damage...and it's painful. Beware, Tooba, beware!"

Tooba had seen fire before; he knew it was hot; he just didn't know *how* hot. Ignoring the warning, he sat right down on the fire and immediately burned off all of his butt hair and set his ass on fire. He leapt into the air in excruciating pain. Tooba could barely contain his reaction to the pain. Always aware of his image, he had to remain stoic and self-assured. In spite of the pain and the damage, Tooba now had a bulging pink, hairless ass—not quite the same as the baboons, but good enough. Again, one by one, members of the Finger Club were required to burn their own asses—a show of solidarity to the other members of the exclusive club. Unfortunately, all the ass-burning soon extinguished the campfire and seven of the Finger Club members, including Galua, were now on the outside looking in. The Finger Club membership was down to thirteen, including Tooba.

For the remaining Finger Club members the pain was soon forgotten and Tooba was thrilled: a pink ass was now the new membership badge, and those without one were no longer welcome in the club. The elite group was now even more elite. The completely rotten and awful severed fingers no longer had to be carried around to indicate membership.

After a heavy meal one afternoon, Tooba and his club members were lying around on the ground near a grassy clearing. Their bellies were stuffed and they all had heavy eyelids. Near them were the scattered remains of a wildebeest, long since dead and picked over. Now only an array of dry bones was left. Tooba, feeling a little bored and sluggish, began playing with one of the bones and got the bright idea to stick the bone up into his nose.

Kopio, an original Finger Club member, exclaimed, "Tooba! What are you doing? Are you going to be able to breathe with that bone up in there?"

"Of course I can breathe," Tooba replied, not letting on that it was *very* difficult to breathe with half of his nose blocked.

"What if you can't get it out?" inquired Kopio. "What if it's stuck up in there permanently?"

"That's the whole idea," Tooba replied defiantly.

Needless to say, Tooba took the opportunity to challenge his Finger Club members and their loyalty once again. He demanded that all of them stick a wildebeest bone up into their noses. A number of them did so. But a number of them did not, including Kopio. The Finger club was now down to nine members, including Tooba. The zeal of Tooba and the remaining eight members was such that the bones were thrust deep, deep into the nasal cavities. Again, pain was involved. And Kopio was correct, the bones could not be pulled back out; the bulging ends of the bones were permanently wedged in tight. Another badge of honor? Kopio and the other un-boned exiles, pink asses and all, went on back to Wacka-Ooh-Ooh; they were no longer considered part of the club.

With a bone protruding from the nose in front and a shiny pink ass behind, a non-initiate would be able to identify a member either coming or going. Tooba was very pleased with himself in spite of the dwindling numbers in the club.

And then the day came. The Finger Club was tormenting a rhino (a rhino who was minding its own business by the way) when the rhino, having had enough of the shenanigans, started to charge at the chimpanzees. The Finger club members took off in a start, but Tooba accidentally turned and ran straight into a woody bush, face first. A thorny, pointed branch rammed into Tooba's left eye, completely destroying it. In agony, Tooba scurried along as best he could, but without any depth perception began banging into brush and rocks and trees. Nevertheless, he eventually caught up with the group and avoided getting trampled by the enraged rhino.

"Look at this!" Tooba exclaimed, proudly displaying his empty eye socket to the rest of the Finger Club members. It looked horrible. But Tooba demanded that the other members follow suit.

"Don't you know that you'll never see out of that eye again?" said one member.

"Well, that's all part of it," Tooba replied. "Who's first?" Tooba grabbed a big pointed stick, aimed it at his followers, and asked for volunteers. There were no takers. The remainder of the Finger Club abandoned him and went back to Wacka-Ooh-Ooh. What could possibly be left for a one-eyed, pink ass, 9-fingered ape with a bone up his nose?

***Moral #1: A crazy lunatic is merely a cult of one.***

***Moral #2: Permanent means permanent.***

***Moral #3: A pink ass is still better than a sharp stick in the eye.***

*Postscriptum*: Although former Finger Club members were received back into the community in the city of Wacka-Ooh-Ooh, each of the members bore the permanent mark of their foolish past—some with *more* than just a permanent pink ass. An unrepentant and undaunted Tooba, the instigator of all that pain and discord, maneuvered his way into a different chimpanzee city, Ooh-Lacka-Wacka. Learning from his mistakes, Tooba refined his messaging, polished up his "brand," and acquired a new following. His look gave him a mystique that some chimpanzees found compelling. There's no rational explanation for that. But this time Tooba was getting members from all walks of life; more than just chimpanzees. It was a diverse cult of self-mutilation the likes of which the jungle had never seen. It was so out of control that, eventually, the King of the Jungle had to step in. The King of the Jungle forcefully broke up the cult and sent all the members to a non-species-specific de-programming center—all except for Tooba, who was banished from that area of the jungle...permanently.

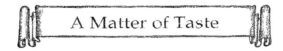

## A Matter of Taste

imsey was a young woman with a pathological frog fetish, a condition known in some circles as *frog-nuts*. To Mimsey, there was something appealing about the color, the skin, the slime, and the swampy smells. It was a complete mystery of science as to how Mimsey could possibly acquire such a fetish. When Mimsey gazed upon a big bullfrog she would get all delicious at the sight of the frog's bulging eyes; and if she was lucky enough, she would literally swoon if she caught the frog snagging an insect with its tongue, plucking it out of the air in mid-flight. In the case of Mimsey, the phrase *"there's no accounting for taste"* comes to mind.

Mimsey regularly visited a nearby swampy pond, watching frogs on the banks of the pond as they slithered or jumped in and out of the water. She was a frog pond voyeur; so normally she kept her distance in order to keep from frightening the unsuspecting frogs away. But there came a day when a massive bullfrog appeared. She had never seen this frog before. Where did he come from? What was he doing here? His presence had "encouraged" the smaller frogs to vacate the area. He was a compelling character, especially to the flavorful Mimsey.

In the local frog world, the giant bullfrog was well known. The other frogs referred to him as Grumbling Grenouille. Of all the many frogs in the area, he was the most negative, complaining frog of all: "the water is too cold; the water is too warm; where are the flies…send in the flies; what are those damn reeds doing here?" And so on. The salivating Mimsey knew nothing of Grenouille's reputation and only saw him as a target for her affections. She decided to take a chance and approach him—and to express herself. As your fable-ist, I must pause for a moment as all of this is making me sick.

[Fable-ist Pause]

So, as Mimsey came out of the greenery she could hear Grenouille grumbling to himself about something,

"I don't know why she [Grenouille's frog-mate] wants *me* to watch the damn pollywogs...they know what they're doing without *my* help...why *me*...I'm not going back...this pond is just fine, for now...she can just watch the damn things herself...she can just drop dead for all I care...half of the damn pollywogs are gonna be eaten by somebody anyway...more than half. Go ahead, eat them all as far as I care."

"What a bunch of pointless grumbling," Mimsey thought; but she consciously decided to overlook all that negative chatter because she wanted some real amphibian action. She had a plan to engage Grenouille in some shallow banter; and hopefully, one thing would lead to another. She cautiously approached him and was relieved that he chose not to hop away. He seemed more interested in grumbling than in anything else.

"Hello," she said, acting as coy and innocent as possible.

"Krrrrroak!" said Grenouille. "A human? Krrrrroak! Can't even squat here in peace. Krrrrroak!"

It was not the response that Mimsey was hoping for. Feeling a sense of rejection, she altered her plan.

"I take it that you are having domestic troubles, Mister...uh—", Mimsey said.

"Krrrrroak! My name is Grenouille. Now beat it!"

"I understand," Mimsey said sympathetically. "However, this is your lucky day. I happen to be a frog princess that was turned into a human by an evil witch."

"Yeah, right," replied Grenouille.

"No, seriously. I am. I'm a frog princess. If you will kiss me, I will return to being a frog and we can run off together..."

"Frogs don't do things like that anyway...krrrrroak...besides, what's in it for me?" Grenouille moved away from Mimsey, wishing she would just vanish.

"Once I'm a frog I can do things with you that you can only imagine," Mimsey said. She was very convincing. "It has to be a good kiss, not just a peck. Your long tongue has to be involved."

[Fable-ist Pause]

OK. So, Grenouille is reluctant and skeptical; and Mimsey is as determined as ever.

"Bite my ass!" blurted out Grenouille. "Leave me alone!" Grenouille then grumbled to himself, "I should have stayed home and watched the damn pollywogs..."

Undaunted and possessed with fever, Mimsey made a fast move and kissed Grenouille on the mouth, giving him plenty of tongue—

[Fable-ist Pause]

OK. Hmmm. Whoops...

[Fable-ist Pause]

Whew! Needless to say, Mimsey did not turn into a frog princess, but she did need a good lie down as her legs were a little shaky after the romantic encounter. Repulsed and bewildered by it all, Grenouille hopped away as fast as his frog legs could take him— grumbling all the way. He knew all along that she wasn't on the up and up.

**Moral: *An innocent and familiar old story, when viewed from a different perspective, can be quite sickening.***

*Postscriptum*: The incident left Mimsey with a really bad taste in her mouth.

[Fable-ist Pause]

OK. In one magic moment, she was cured of the frog-nuts—reality had relieved her of her frog fetish in no uncertain terms. Forever after, she kept her little brush with bestiality a secret. However, going against all science, Mimsey's luscious upper lip sprouted a big gnarly wart, the size and color of a tangerine—and a famous plastic surgeon made a lot of money off of her misery. As for Grenouille, he got his wish: somebody eventually did bite his ass...and more...on a plate in an exclusive French restaurant.

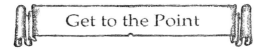

Get to the Point

t was morning and bursting out of the jungle and onto the grassy savanna the small herd of giraffes was running for its life—at least for the life of one of their numbers. In hot pursuit was a leopard by the name of Lucy. Normally Lucy didn't waste time chasing giraffes, but she was desperate—and when it started out, it was great fun watching all those long necks run in terror. But now she was beginning to tire and the giraffes were getting further and further ahead. Exhausted. If she did catch up to them, their feistiness might be a problem. She might not have enough energy to bring one down at that point; not even an easy one. Out into the middle of the vast savanna the chase went on until Lucy was just too tired to continue. She turned around and trotted all the way back to the jungle, to wait for a better opportunity on another day.

The herd of giraffes continued running for a short while and in their frenzy to escape became very disoriented. They milled around aimlessly for the rest of the morning, beating down a very large swath of dead grass all around them.

"Where are we?" asked Rosalee.

"I don't know," answered Adolphous, a currently the self-appointed leader of the herd.

"I'll tell you where we are; we're lost, that's where," stated Princeps, the other self-appointed leader of the herd. Princeps was very charismatic and decisive. Those qualities made him a perfect leader—as far as *he* was concerned.

"How can we be lost when we're out here in the middle of the savanna?" added Rosalee. "It *does* look the same in every direction, I'll give you that."

"It's high noon and the sun is directly...up," Adolphous said. "So that's no help..."

"What are we going to do?" Rosalee asked.

Adolphous then answered, "I believe we should line ourselves up, forming a circle, then we can slowly radiate out from where we are now. The circle will grow larger and larger and once we're past all this flattened-out grass, one of us should be able to detect the tracks we made coming out here. That individual should let out a hoot to alert the rest of us...then we can re-assemble and follow those tracks back to the jungle where all of this started. Does everyone understand?"

"Not so fast," Princeps interjected. "I think we should go this way..." Princeps motioned to the others and confidently began walking in the direction he was indicating.

Now, the giraffes in this towering group were known for being particularly gullible and vulnerable to GBS (giraffe bullshit). So the herd was easily influenced by Princeps's decisiveness and charisma. Seeing some reluctance in the ranks, Princeps added, "This is the way; let's go..." And off he went again, following his political instincts.

"I believe you're making a mistake," shouted Adolphous. "Princeps is merely guessing at the correct direction. If we don't form a circle...if you don't like that idea, we can wait until the sun is further down in the sky. Then if we stand and look toward the sun, it will tell us that the correct direction is directly behind us...if we go in *that* direction, it should put us back in our jungle."

"Come on...if we keep this up, it's going to be dark...and then where will we be?" Princeps was forceful and undeterred. Again he turned and started walking in his chosen direction. "Who's with me. Let's go..." he said without looking back. Princeps had no idea what he was doing, but as a self-appointed leader he had already staked out his position and was too turf-protective to consider caving in to the complicated logic of Adolphous.

Princeps's charm and impressive confidence (which was mostly GBS) eventually convinced the others to follow him. Princeps was happy and proud to finally have the undisputed top position in the herd—the position itself meant more to him than actually doing anything for the herd. As Princeps and the herd headed toward the horizon, Adolphous and two others stayed behind, waiting for the sun to indicate the way, the way back.

Later that day, Adolphous and his friends found themselves back in their jungle having had no trouble at all. On the other hand, Princeps and his loyal group wandered about the drought-ravaged savanna for weeks, scrounging for food and complaining about the quality.

***The Adolphous Moral: When offering suggestions, if you're going to stick your long neck out, keep it short.***

***The Princeps Moral: You may think you're sitting on top of the world, but you may be just sitting atop a big pile of GBS.***

*Postscriptum*: Adolphous and his friends joined another herd where he became a well-respected science advisor. As the Princeps followers became weary of his rampant GBS, he was eventually deposed as herd leader. Not really knowing what they wanted, the herd replaced Princeps with another equally incompetent member of the herd—a good talker with a fresh and different flavor of GBS. This was an ideal situation for Princeps since he could carp at the new guy without suffering any consequences for himself.

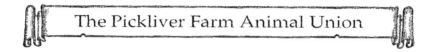

## The Pickliver Farm Animal Union

orace the Horse tapped his hoof on the wooden bench, calling the meeting to order, "I've arranged this meeting of the Animal Union to discuss the recent disappearances going on here in the barnyard. As you know, as of now, there is only one chicken left in the coop, and that would be Chiquita; who obviously could not attend tonight because she's locked up in there. But of course Rudy the Rooster is here because he has free run of the place.

"It appears that those of us in this barn and three others are the only animals left here at Farmer Pickliver's farm. We have Gary the Goat, Potter the Pig, Shari the Sheep, and Claudine the Cow. Including Chiquita, Rudy, and myself, that makes seven. Only seven of us remain. And then there's Durwood the Dog. I don't have a line on him since he's never been a member of the union. But I *have* seen him around recently. I can only speak for myself, but I'm beginning to think that there is something ominous in all this."

Horace was right. Farmer Pickliver had fallen on hard times. Markets had collapsed and the bank was about to foreclose on the farm. There was no money for food, so all he could do was to start eating the animals on the farm.

"What are you animals up to?" asked Durwood the Dog as he poked his nose into the barn where the union meeting was being held.

"We're having a meeting, Durwood," Horace the Horse replied. "You're not a member of the union...what are you doing here?"

Durwood the Dog continued, "As long as I'm here, you might like to know that Chiquita is not in her coop. I just saw Farmer Pickliver carrying her around to the back...to you-know-where..."

"Oh my!" exclaimed Shari the Sheep. The others could hear the terror in her voice.

"'Oh my' is right," said Horace the Horse. "That leaves only six...and of course you, Durwood."

Soon, the smell of fried chicken was wafting over the barnyard and filtering into the barn...bathing the union meeting with a smell too horrible to contemplate.

"Well, I for one am not worried," stated Rudy the Rooster. "I've been here longer than any of you. Farmer Pickliver needs me every morning...needs me to crow to wake him up. Besides, my flesh is old and stringy."

"You may be right," said Horace the Horse. "But we must brace ourselves for what may be yet to come."

"Oh my!" reiterated Shari the Sheep. "I have nothing to offer but my wool. I may be next."

"Yeah, wool, and...hmmm...but what about me?" said Gary the Goat. "I can't provide milk, or wool, or...you know anything...abstract..."

"Thanks to Chiquita, I think we'll all be safe for a day or two, maybe three," Horace the Horse said, offering some reassurance. "Let's meet again tomorrow and determine a plan of action. That gives us a day for everyone to be thinking about it. But we can't let on that we know something. If no one has anything to add, this meeting is adjourned."

The animals all went back to their "stations" and acted like everything was "normal." They definitely did not want Farmer Pickliver to get suspicious. The next day, Horace the Horse noticed two men talking to Farmer Pickliver. They were not in farmer uniforms (overalls and such). Farmer Pickliver seemed very distressed. The men left the farm a short while later. What could it all mean?

The next evening, after Farmer Pickliver was asleep, the union met again. "Where's Rudy the Rooster?" Horace the Horse asked. "Has anyone seen Rudy the Rooster?"

"I haven't seen him all day," said Potter the Pig. "If Rudy is not safe...if Rudy *was* not safe...*none* of us are safe."

"Oh my! What are we to do?" cried Shari the Sheep. "I thought you said we'd be safe for a day or two."

"OK, OK. Let's not panic," said Horace the Horse.

"That's easy for you to say," said Claudine the Cow. "You're big and important. You have jobs to do. He needs you to pull his wagon and his plow. And besides, I don't think that men like eating horsemeat—something weird about that—but as for *my* meat, that's another story entirely."

Horace the Horse replied, "Well, he hasn't needed me to pull his plow since the crops failed; and he hasn't been out in his wagon since all of this started. But besides all that, I saw Farmer Pickliver talking to two strange men today. Something is up."

"Maybe he sold the place," said Potter the Pig. "Then we would be spared. Maybe that's it!"

"Let's not jump the gun," Horace the Horse said.

"I think we should *do* something," said Gary the Goat.

"Durwood, what do you want?" asked Horace the Horse, noticing Durwood lurking in the shadows, eavesdropping.

"Those two men were walking all around the farm, even out in the empty fields, looking at this and that," said Durwood the Dog. "I don't know what it means, but I thought you should know."

"OK. Thank you very much," Horace the Horse replied. "Well?" Horace the Horse added, implying that Durwood the Dog should make himself scarce. As soon as Durwood the Dog was gone, Horace the Horse said, "I think we're going to have to meet somewhere else. Either that or someone will have to stand watch to make sure Durwood the Dog isn't listening in—especially if we come up with a plan. Tomorrow let's meet in the open area behind the woodshed. Meeting adjourned."

When the secret meeting was called to order the next evening, no one seemed to be missing. Horace the Horse started off, "The good news is that no one disappeared today. We have a chance to act! Has anyone come up with an idea? A plan?"

"We're going to have to kill him!" Potter the Pig offered.

"I agree," added Claudine the Cow. "We're the ones—Potter the Pig and myself—we're the ones that most people eat. One of us may be next."

"Well, let's put it to a vote," Horace the Horse suggested. "All those in favor of killing Farmer Pickliver, say 'Aye.'"

When the votes were tallied, there were two for killing and three against. As expected, the two in favor of killing Farmer Pickliver were Potter the Pig and Claudine the Cow.

Horace the Horse then made a suggestion, "Since we do not have a legitimate plan yet, why don't we wait and let Farmer Pickliver make the next move?"

"What if his next move is one of us?" Claudine the Cow said vehemently.

Without resolving anything, the union adjourned the meeting for the time being with a plan to continue the discussion, in secret, the next evening. But around noon the next day, loud squeals were heard. It was a familiar-sounding voice. Squeals were emanating from you-know-where. And while the squeals were being heard, Durwood the Dog was bouncing around the yard, agitated and barking like a mouse on a hot plate. Needless to say, an emergency meeting of the union had to be called...in secret once again.

"What's the story with Durwood the Dog?" Shari the Sheep asked.

"He always goes crazy whenever something big and dramatic is happening," Horace the Horse answered. "It's just the way dogs are. But more importantly, what are *we* going to do? I say we have a new vote on Potter the Pig's pla... Where *is* Potter the Pig?"

"You cannot possibly be that stupid," interjected Gary the Goat. "Who do you think was doing all that squealing?"

"Oh my!" cried Shari the Sheep.

"Well then, it's settled," stated Horace the Horse. "We're going to have to kill Farmer Pickliver before we lose anyone else."

"Hey you guys! Look at that truck!" Gary the Goat pointed out a truck parked beside Farmer Pickliver's house.

"And look at that! There's a picture of a dog on the side!" added Shari the Sheep. "Durwood the Dog. He's next, I'll bet. He's going away."

"I don't believe it," said Claudine the Cow. "I'm the logical choice. Potter the Pig was logical; now I'm logical. If we don't kill Farmer Pickliver right away, I'm going to have to make a run for it."

"I say Horace the Horse should go and trample Farmer Pickliver to death as soon as the truck leaves," Gary the Goat suggested.

"I agree," added Claudine the Cow.

"Oh my!" said Shari the Sheep. "Are we really going to go through with it?"

The meeting was adjourned and all the animals returned to their "stations" in an atmosphere of high tension and anticipation. Horace the Horse waited behind the barn for just the right moment to make his deadly play. When Durwood the Dog came snooping and sniffing around, all the other animals went into hiding. Their anxiety over the proceedings outweighed their morbid curiosity. Besides, none of them really wanted to watch Horace the Horse when he went in for the kill.

When the truck finally left, there was a very tense silence all around the barnyard. Had Horace the Horse finally done the dirty deed? Where was Durwood the Dog? Had the men taken him away, just as Shari the Sheep presumed? Gary the Goat suggested a new meeting so Horace the Horse could give everyone an update.

So that night the union met again, in secret. Only Shari the Sheep and Claudine the Cow were in attendance. There was no Horace the Horse nor Gary the Goat.

"I believe that Gary the Goat may have been...I don't want to think about it," Shari the Sheep said mournfully.

So there was no union meeting...only sadness...and fear. It was to be the last meeting of the Animal Union.

When Claudine the Cow finally disappeared, Shari the Sheep knew that her own time was drawing near. But weeks went by and nothing had happened to her. Maybe she would be spared. She was the last one, the last remaining member of the Animal Union. Then one afternoon, Farmer Pickliver came for her. Durwood the Dog was running alongside, agitated, panting and puffing...like so many times before. Shari wished that she had voted with Potter the Pig and Claudine the Cow back when she had the opportunity. Too late for regrets.

And then there were none. The Animal Union had finally been dissolved...the hard way.

It was a winter night. Shari the Sheep had been gone for over a week. Sleeping by a warm glowing fireplace, Durwood the Dog thought he heard a noise outside and went to investigate. There were two raccoons poking around in the barnyard.

"Well, the joke's on them. There's nothing left," Durwood the Dog said to himself. Even though it was cold, Durwood the Dog continued to watch the raccoons' futile attempts at locating some food, when—"Blam! Blam!" Farmer Pickliver had come out of the house with his shotgun, firing both barrels at the rummaging pair of raccoons. But to no avail. All the shots did was scare them off, into the night. Farmer Pickliver, mumbling epithets, went back into the house, but came out again a short time later...with his hands behind his back.

"Come with me Durwood," he said. And the two of them went around to you-know-where...

**Moral: When a desperate company is downsizing and hauls out the chopping block, no one...no one is safe.**

*Postscriptum*: The farm was taken over by a big agriculture conglomerate (as recommended by the two mysterious men who kept coming around and examining everything). Farmer Pickliver got a job in the service industry and became a militant vegetarian.

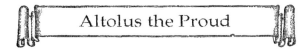

## Altolus the Proud

ltolus was a proud stag. His job was to strut around the forest all day, prancing and preening, and being a prime example of stagdom. His gift to the world was to allow all who would venture into his sphere of influence to admire him and be in awe of his very presence. He was a perfect specimen of his breed: muscular, graceful, and bold. Protecting every inch of his blemish-free coat of fur, he avoided brambles and sharp rocks; anything that might mar his surface. He had to remain an example of perfection. It was his job. As he maneuvered among the trees in the forest his rippling muscles produced such a rhythm of beauty that birds would swoon and literally fall right out of the sky; moles would suspend their furious burrowing as he passed by; and rabbits would drop their multiplication tables. Such was the way that Altolus envisioned himself and his place among the animals of the forest.

Coming upon a pond—no matter how foul or swampy the water—he always felt compelled to take a look, take a moment to admire himself in the reflection. "What fine antlers. What magnificence I behold here. And that face. Those eyes. That perfect fur coat—what a surface." Sometimes, while staring down at the water, Altolus would summon up an incredibly wide and toothy grin, turning his head side to side, so that he could marvel at his array of fine teeth; if only he could have seen how ridiculous he looked at those moments, grinning at himself.

One day, he happened upon a raging grass fire burning its way toward the forest. Stag heaven forbid! Toward *himself.* The fire was being exacerbated by a strong wind that was blowing in his direction. "Help! Help me!" was a cry from the undergrowth. It was a wiry little rock squirrel who had become entangled in a nest of roots. "Help me, pull me free, or I shall surely be roasted by the fire."

"Sorry, but I cannot risk it," Altolus replied. "First there's the roots, and those stems I see have sharp thorns, and I don't know *what* that grey stuff is right there, and of course there's the fire—that's the big one. I will stay over here, way, way over here, and keep you company until you burn up...let that be a comfort to you."

"You pompous pig!" shouted the cute little rock squirrel as the flames began engulfing his body. Then silence.

"Not a pig. I am a proud stag. But what does that squirrel know? It's dead...and I'm not. Not dead and not a pig." Snorting with defiant snubbery, Altolus turned his back to the fire and re-entered the forest without a giving the incident a second thought. It never occurred to him for a moment to warn others about the fire. Luckily, a change in the wind stopped the fire from spreading further and it eventually burned itself out. And somewhere among the ashes of the field rests the charred remains of an innocent little rock squirrel—not enough left of him to even get a positive ID. But, the forest and its inhabitants were safe from the fire's threat, no thanks to the lax attitude of Altolus.

Not the same day, but soon thereafter, a beautiful redbird was snagged from the air by a mighty eagle. Normally the eagle would have carried off its victim to somewhere high in the trees—possibly for a family meal. But, earlier in the day, the eagle pulled a wing muscle (possibly a pectoralis) trying to cull out—unsuccessfully—a poor, little white lamb from its flock. She grossly underestimated the weight of the lamb; a little too heavy for the overly ambitious eagle. And now she was suffering for the error in judgement.

So there was the grounded eagle using its heavy talons to hold down the redder-than-red redbird, unable to get back into the air painlessly without releasing its prey. Altolus, making his usual rounds in the forest was quite surprised when the eagle paid him no mind—none whatsoever. Surely she should want to find time to give his lovely personage the once-over.

The towering presence of Altolus cast a shadow over the eagle and its prey as the eagle evaluated its situation, "I have to abandon this juicy redbird if I am to fly away unharmed by this big...whatever-it-is. Or I can have my meal right here—it might be my last. And this huge...whatever-it-is could then come down on me and have its way with me. What to do?"

"Cheep, cheep," cried the redbird again. "Help me!"

"Those talons look mighty dangerous and that beak is nothing to sneeze at," said Altolus as he contemplated his own situation. "I must consider my perfect surface. I might even suffer deeper damage, even to my face. Can't have that. And just who am I to interfere with someone's repast?" Rationalized into inaction Altolus turned away. As he did so he could hear the redbird say, "Why you scum-sucking slog..." Then silence—except for the crunching sound of tiny hollow bones and cartilage.

"Why does everyone keep calling me these odd names? I am a *stag*. Can they not see? Are they that ignorant?" Altolus unencumbered and still magnificent carried on with his job of strutting about the forest.

On still another day, Altolus came upon a pixie, apparently trapped in a pool of thick quicksand and sinking fast. "Help me. Help me," the pixie cried out. "I'm mired in this quicksand and shall soon perish. You there, beast so big and mighty. Step up. Help me." Being very absorbed in his own thoughts, Altolus was unable to detect the aromatic insincerity in the pixie's flattering words; although Altolus did enjoy being called "big" and "mighty."

"I don't help pixies," Altolus replied. "You just can't trust 'em. Besides, I might get trapped myself. Or worse, I could soil or even damage my surface, or my face, or both. I see how unfortunate your situation is...but you'll just have to save yourself."

"Very well, you big ass," uttered the pixie as it slowly disappeared, down into the quicksand. Altolus watched it all with morbid fascination and his usual better-him-than-me attitude. Only the pointy little red cap of the pixie remained behind, the cap still floating on top of the sandy pool. Once again Altolus callously turned his back on such unwelcome unpleasantness and resumed making his rounds.

"I don't get it," Altolus to himself as he trotted along. He had a bounce in his step and joy in his heart. "I am not an *ass*. I am a *stag*. Is everyone blind? Who *are* these uninformed creatures—and where are all my admirers?"

"Hold it right there!" the quicksand-covered, re-emergent pixie said as it brazenly blocked the path of Altolus. The pixie was standing there defiantly with its hands on its hips. "Why did you not help me in my time of need, you big clunky ass?" the pixie asked in an increasingly belligerent tone.

"First of all..."

"Tut tut tut!" The hostile pixie continued to interrupt, cutting off Altolus mid-sentence. The pixie then reached into its magic velvet bag and pulled out an off-color yellow-green blob. The blob was soft, squishy, moist, dripping, shiny in its moistness, and oh so yellow and green and slimy. It was a magic slimeball.

Altolus was taken aback. "What is this little pixie up to?" he thought to himself.

The pixie took aim and, with a skillful thrust, bounced the magic slimeball right off the forehead of Altolus. Almost instantly Altolus was turned into a giant, greasy venison sausage.

Satisfied at having completed its pixie-mission, the pixie sauntered off into the forest emitting a high-pitched, screechy, ear-piercing, evil barrage of laughter.

***Moral: As you bask in the warmth of self-love under the impression that others feel the same way about you, remember: not everyone has access to a magic slimeball.***

*Postscriptum*: One might think that the pixie in this story was operating from the moral high ground, but—

The pixie continued its highly unpopular campaign of "testing" passersby. No one passed muster when it came to the pixie's standard of altruism and good will. One day a friendly sawtooth lion was scrounging around near the pool of quicksand and heard the pixie's feigned cry for help. Being a Good Samaritan, the sawtooth lion hurried to the edge of the pool and courageously pulled the pixie out of the quagmire, ostensibly saving its little pixie life. But once "safe," the pixie—without so much as a *la-dee-da* or even a pretense of gratitude—pulled a fresh magic slimeball from its velvet bag, and with deadly aim, bounced it off the forehead of the sawtooth lion, turning the unsuspecting bouncee into a giant, greasy lion sausage. Pixies—you just can't trust 'em.

***Shadow Moral: If you run into a pixie, expect the Wurst.***

## Mole Desmond and the Spectacles

ole Desmond was burrowing in a surface tunnel one cool grey overcast day—how would he know if it was overcast? Moles can't see squat, not even above ground. Anyway...he was burrowing along when he banged his head against a gigantic rock. This forced him to come up to the surface to assess the situation—out onto the grass, the short grass on a golf course fairway. Moles don't know squat about golf, either. But while on the surface, Mole Desmond stumbled upon a pair of spectacles—carelessly dropped by some golfer no doubt. They were fine wire-rimmed spectacles, very heavy on the prescription; and bifocals no less—not that any of these spectacle specifications meant anything to Mole Desmond.

Mole Desmond's eyesight was very poor, a common weakness among moles. With his limited eyesight he happened to see through one of the spectacle lenses. The world on the other side of the lens was very clear and distinct. What a discovery!

So Mole Desmond attempted to engage the spectacles on his person in some way. That would have been quite a trick for Mole Desmond considering his lack of ears and the fact that the huge size of the spectacles made it impossible—they were much larger than his entire body. He tried to affix the spectacles several times and in many different ways, but there was apparently no way to make any use of them. Nevertheless, he believed these spectacles must have some great value. So he dragged the spectacles down into his surface tunnel and later into the lower areas where he lived. All the while, the awkwardness of the spectacles made it impossible to make any new burrows; so he just maneuvered around the old burrows in order to get home.

While at home Mole Desmond contemplated ways to exploit the value of the strange object. "There must be a way," he kept saying to himself. Then a visitor appeared at Mole Desmond's doorway, sticking his head into Mole Desmond's hole. It was Mole Guacha, a hole to hole insurance salesman who was there in an effort sell the "man of the hole" some earthworm insurance. Insurance, what a concept for a mole.

"I don't need any insurance...especially as protection from some kind of earthworm scarcity," Mole Desmond told Mole Guacha. But Mole Guacha did not feel the usual sting of rejection since he had his limited eyesight ill-focused on those spectacles.

"What is that?" Mole Guacha asked, referring to the strange contraption.

"Something I found up above," replied Mole Desmond.

"What is it for?"

"Let me show you." Mole Desmond was anxious to see where this would lead. "Look through here." Mole Desmond showed Mole Guacha how to view things using the spectacles. One might ask what value spectacles would have for a near-blind mole in the utter darkness of a mole hole. And the answer would be: not much.

"I can't see a goddam thing!" Mole Guacha exclaimed, as he pulled himself out of Mole Desmond's hole. "No more time to waste in *that* mole's hole," Mole Guacha thought.

Seeing his salesmanship mistake, Mole Desmond sought out an acquaintance, Mole Nevus, who lived in a nearby hole. He enticed Mole Nevus to join him up on the surface. Awkwardly lugging the spectacles to the surface, Mole Desmond led Mole Nevus along and the two moles arrived up on the grass of the number five fairway. As a side note, the moles in this community liked the golf course because the ground was always moist—even if the water sometimes had a real bad chemical smell to it—and there seemed to be an unending supply of insects and worms. Mole Desmond was quick to demonstrate the magical quality of the spectacles. Mole Nevus was amazed.

"Where did you find such a thing?" Mole Nevus asked.

"Right here. It was just luck," Mole Desmond replied.

"Would you consider selling it to me?"

"I don't know...It might be very useful in burrowing...being able to see so clearly and all..."

"I'll give you eleven grubs for it," offered Mole Nevus.

"Wow. That's a very tempting offer." After some fake reluctance, Mole Desmond said, "Ok. I guess I can part with them for such a generous amount." So Mole Nevus gave Mole Desmond the location of the eleven hidden grubs and Mole Desmond turned ownership of the spectacles over to Mole Nevus.

It wasn't long before Mole Nevus realized how badly he had been taken. "This thing is useless," he kept saying to himself. "I can't burrow with it. I can't use it in the darkness of the tunnels. Eleven grubs, what a waste."

But Mole Nevus's dismay was short-lived. While struggling to drag the useless spectacles to stow away in his hole, he had a chance encounter with Mole Analemma. When she showed an interest in the spectacles, he seized the moment and unloaded the useless item on her for six earthworms—a loss, but not a total loss. After a demo at the surface, he told her that with the spectacles, down in the tunnels, she would be able to see *through* rocks and things. X-ray vision: not in the vocabulary of moles. So off he went, and off she went schlepping the spectacles with her.

After a while, Analemma realized she was out six earthworms, all for nothing. The spectacles did not function as advertised and were a real pain to lug around in the burrows. So she used her charms to trade the "magical" thing to Mole Poros for a dozen earthworms. She further exaggerated the magical qualities of the thing to entice Mole Poros into the trade.

After several more rounds of trading around the mole community, the street value of the spectacles reached twenty earthworms and eighteen grubs. At that price, only the wealthiest of moles would be able to afford them. Along with the increase in value, the so-called "magical" qualities of the spectacles became quite extensive and wondrous as well:

immortality, invisibility, predator alerts, mate detection, mate attractant, fertility enhancer, grub and earthworm *radar*. All too good to be true.

"*Radar*...sounds good. What is it?" asked Mole Aileron during the trade.

"Hell if I know," replied Mole Dokus. "It was part of the description from the previous owner. I just haven't had an opportunity to use it."

Round and round the spectacles went, one unsuspecting mole at a time. Then, one day Mole Dondon—who was stuck with the useless item for 72 grubs, 90 earthworms, and a pile of locust shells (considered a collector's item in some mole circles)—found a mole, Mole Jardy, who had not heard of the useless spectacles that were being traded around the holes and tunnels.

Mole Jardy was intrigued by all the powers ascribed to the "magical" item. He was considered by many as, perhaps, the most ignorant and stupid of all the moles in the local mole community. Surely Mole Jardy would be the one to gullibly spring for the spectacles, Mole Dondon believed. He also believed that he might recover at least *some* of the price paid for the useless things.

So Mole Dondon began lowering the price. Mole Jardy refused each time, but being so stupid, he did not question why the price kept falling precipitously. Finally, Mole Dondon offered the spectacles for one grub and one earthworm. Bored with all this bartering busyness and flamboyant claims, Mole Jardy flatly refused the final offer and scurried off to do something else. Mole Jardy: either not *always* so stupid or *accidentally* not stupid.

Mole Dondon then realized that there was probably never going to be a mole that would trade for the spectacles and that he was just going to have to eat the loss and abandon the spectacles altogether.

**Moral: When it comes to a chain of fools, beware of being the last link.**

*Postscriptum*: All the false claims and chicanery that went on during the frenetic trading of the spectacles took its toll on the mole community as a whole. Personal relationships went straight into the crapper. Many moles holed-up, avoiding other moles and other mole holes. Many moles stopped speaking to one another and idiopathic "cave-ins" were becoming a little more common than statistics would predict. It was quite a spectacle. And the golfer who originally lost the spectacles was just shit out of luck.

## Monsieur LePont and Sussapuss

ussapuss was a big snake who should have been aware of the imminent arrival of winter. But he was currently enjoying the abundance of prey as many animals of the forest were out and about making last-minute preparations for the cold season to come. Late one autumn evening he found himself chilled to the bone as a cold northern frost came over the woodland area where he made his home. Being cold-blooded, the icy chill slowed Sussapuss down and it became difficult for him to maneuver around and hunt for prey. Days passed and Sussapuss was becoming very hungry. So he continued to brave the cold as he hunted for some animal to kill and eat. But the cold had forced most intelligent animals to hide away in their own homes. Sussapuss could find nothing to eat and was becoming weak. He went back to his nest to wait for a warmer day.

It was still winter, but a warmer spell had arrived. Monsieur Jean-Titier LePont was taking his daily stroll through the peat bog and brambles—a simple, easy path he had forged through repetition and lack of adventure. Although the sun was shining, the air was still very cold and he could see his breath every time he exhaled. Sussapuss was out and about as well. He was cold but he was hungry and was looking for some meat. But all the meat was still in hiding.

Then, Monsieur Jean-Titier LePont happened upon Sussapuss. "What have we here?" he said as he nudged Sussapuss around with his foot. Sussapuss was too weak to even try to respond to Monsieur LePont.

In spite of the frost, Monsieur LePont could see clearly. "Why, it's a snake," he said.

"I need some meat," Sussapuss said with a faint gasp.

Monsieur LePont lifted Sussapuss up off the ground. He decided to play God and save the snake's life. Sussapuss was wriggling around, but seemed harmless enough. So, feeling

God-like, Monsieur LePont returned home carrying the poor starving Sussapuss home with him. During the trip, Sussapuss became unconscious and Monsieur LePont worried that starvation had finally taken its toll on the poor snake.

When Monsieur LePont arrived back at his country cottage, he made a fire in the fireplace and set Sussapuss on the thick rug near the hearth. While Sussapuss was getting warm, Monsieur LePont fixed up a platter of lamb succulents. He was playing God so he wanted Sussapuss's meal to consist of fine high quality meats. He still didn't know if it was already too late for the starving snake. Monsieur LePont set the meat-loaded platter down next to the still unconscious Sussapuss and retired to a large comfortable chair nearby. Gazing at the dancing light of the fire, Monsieur LePont soon became drowsy and after only a few minutes he finally dozed off.

Later, Monsieur LePont awakened to find Sussapuss's tail making tiny movements—he was alive! It wasn't long before Sussapuss was moving around on the carpet by the fireplace. He had already eaten nearly everything on the meat platter, leaving only little specks of muscle fibers and some bits of bloody gel-like fats. Monsieur LePont was very excited. He had played God and brought the starving creature back from certain death.

"Hey you there. How about something to eat?" Sussapuss suddenly and brazenly asked...demanded.

Monsieur LePont was quite put off. Not even a "Thank-you" to the "god" that had rescued him. And now here was this creature demanding something more. Monsieur LePont had emptied his supply of meats and Sussapuss had already downed all of it. Nevertheless, Monsieur LePont complied with the request and handed Sussapuss a small chunk of turnip from his vegetable bin.

"What's this?" Sussapuss asked contemptuously. "I eat meat. Not this crappy stuff..."

Monsieur LePont was fascinated with Sussapuss. The flickering of the fire gave the snake an animated beauty, his body regular, flowing, winding around on itself; his movements graceful and coordinated—fascinating.

Breaking his trance-like state Monsieur LePont replied "I have no more meat. You've already eaten it all." Then, changing the subject, he added, "You are so elegant and regal. You could at least thank me for saving your life…"

"Yeah…thanks," Sussapuss replied grudgingly. "Have you got any mice in this joint?" he asked.

"No. I have a cat…"

"A cat will do…a little big perhaps," Sussapuss said.

Ignoring the implication, Monsieur LePont gazed at Sussapuss with such intensity that Sussapuss was becoming self-conscious. "How about an egg?" Monsieur LePont asked. He was trying very hard to gain the snake's approval and acceptance. The snake sure wasn't treating him very much like a god.

"An egg…from a bird?" Sussapuss responded.

"Yes, from a bird…a chicken." Monsieur LePont reached down to pet Sussapuss. As soon as he touched Sussapuss's scaly skin Sussapuss turned and struck directly at Monsieur LePont's exposed arm. But Monsieur LePont's reflexes were much faster than Sussapuss had anticipated and Sussapuss's head and body went flying right past Monsieur LePont's arm, missing it completely.

"Why you. What did you do that for?" the stunned Monsieur exclaimed. Before he could answer, Sussapuss tried it again, this time going right for the face.

"I saved your life," Monsieur LePont cried out, quickly backing away. "I fed you fine meats and gave you warmth and a piece of turnip—at which, by the way, you turned up your little snake nose. I offered you an egg and you tried to strike me in return. And your piss-poor 'Thank-you', well…"

Sussapuss wound himself up, ready for another strike as soon as the opportunity presented itself. He then retorted, "Don't blame *me*, I'm just doing what comes naturally. After all, I'm a snake…it's my nature.

"Why you ungrateful oversized worm!" Monsieur LePont had reached his limit of disrespect. He stepped over to the other side of the fireplace, grabbed the fire poker, and clubbed Sussapuss to death with it, giving him a few extra, pulverizing blows for good measure. "That'll teach *you*," he said.

***Moral: Going through life basing actions on slogans, aphorisms, and fables will most assuredly lead to disappointment, or death, or both.***

*Postscriptum*: Sussapuss was *double* stupid—Monsieur LePont was not susceptible to Sussapuss's venom anyway. Sussapuss was *double* unlucky—had he survived, Monsieur LePont was planning on putting him in a glass box in solitary confinement and feeding him little bits of dead, junky, dried-up food for the rest of his salvaged life; Monsieur LePont, once again, attempting to play God (as was *his* nature).

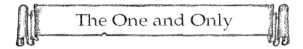

## The One and Only

**nte-Moral: *There are two sides to every story and many of them are unique.***

---

Penelope was an antelope. She was unique. She could run much faster than any other antelope in her herd. She was admired. She had prestige. She was given the position as leader (much to the chagrin of some of the alpha males who felt entitled to the position). Many times Penelope successfully led the group away from danger: predators, savanna fires, hunters, and zoo specialists. Her speed would force the others to push themselves to the limit and to exceed their own expectations.

Penelope was an antelope. She was unique. She could run much faster than any other antelope in her herd. The other antelopes had difficulty keeping up with her. Some would become exhausted and fall prey to predators that Penelope could not see because she was moving so fast. One day while leading the herd, Penelope got way out in front. Isolated and vulnerable she ran right into a mother lion who dispatched Penelope in the blink of an eye. There was enough meat on Penelope's body for the lion and her three young ones.

---

Acker was a duck, a mallard duck. He was unique. Unlike all other ducks, Acker could fly backwards. He developed quite a reputation because of this unique ability. One autumn day, his flock of ducks was flying south, migrating as ducks do when winter approaches. Out of the sky came a falcon. The falcon drew a bead on Acker and calculated an interception angle—the falcon, in its head, drew a dotted line arc from its current position right toward Acker. Acker on the other hand noticed the falcon and before the falcon could pluck Acker out of the sky, Acker started flying backward. This caused the falcon, who was following its calculated line, to completely miss Acker and come up with a talon full of air. Thinking that the other mallards were similarly equipped, the falcon decided to go have a mouse sandwich and a cup of blood.

2. Acker was a duck, a mallard duck. He was unique. Unlike all other ducks, Acker could fly backwards. He avoided predators many times and this day would be no exception. A falcon spotted Acker flying alone among a sparse stand of trees. The trees would offer the falcon cover—cover leading to a sneak attack on Acker. But Acker was much too smart to be caught so unaware. When the falcon zoomed in for the kill, Acker relied on his skill and started flying backward. The falcon missed Acker by a country mile—which is different from a statute mile, which is different from a British nautical mile, which is different from an international nautical mile. The falcon abandoned the hunt since the trees were now obstructing its view and the angles of attack were much too complicated. As the backward-flying Acker watched the falcon fly off he slammed into the trunk of a giant elm tree, knocking him unconscious. He fell to the ground, out cold, but still breathing. An ocelot, who happened to be walking by—and who was having a good day—saw the unconscious duck hit the ground.

"Whoa! What the hell?" the ocelot said looking up into the trees for the possible source of this good fortune. Then, taking advantage of the windfall (the bird-fall)—a helpless bird on the ground—the ocelot ate Acker on the spot. Pretty fortunate for the ocelot, pretty unfortunate for Acker.

———————————

1. Avery was a spider monkey. Avery was unique. Living on a tropical island with many of his friends and family, Avery was the luckiest of all the monkeys. When it came to finding food, when it came to engaging hot monkey females, when it came to narrowly escaping accidental death, Avery was king. But it took many, many attempts before Avery was able to pick just the right numbers and win the spider monkey lottery. And win he did; first prize: an almost unlimited hoard of edible island dates. No other monkey on the island had ever won anything playing the lottery. But Avery did not want to be selfish and so he happily shared his winnings with his friends and family. And

because of his generosity, Avery and his acquaintances were never lacking in edible island dates...ever again.

Avery was a spider monkey. Avery was unique. Avery was the luckiest of all the monkeys. This invited a fair amount of envy and scorn from his fellow islanders. When Avery won the spider monkey lottery he once again demonstrated to the others that he was the luckiest of all the spider monkeys. He collected his prize: an almost unlimited hoard of edible island dates. He ate the dates to his heart's content, sometimes to the point of nausea. But it was not going unnoticed. Soon, other spider monkeys from his extended family came to mooch off of Avery. Not wanting to be an unfeeling louse, he went ahead and shared his good fortune with his friends and family. No one was turned away, and word spread to other spider monkeys on the island—others, strangers, who were neither friends nor family of Avery. But the profligate, unappreciative rapscallions on the island soon caused Avery's hoard to dwindle down to nothing. Of course, all those opportunistic bloodsuckers went back to their own groups on the island without bothering to thank Avery for his generosity. The pillaging of the date supply didn't take very long at all. It was as if Avery had never won the lottery in the first place.

---

Karly was a magical mystical unicorn. She was unique. *Unicorns* were unique, and supposedly she was the very last of them. One day a man named Noah came to her and asked if she wanted to take a ride on his ark. "Where is your mate?" Noah asked. "I need two of you. I have no time to waste." Karly had not seen a male unicorn in a long while. Suddenly, from out of the wild brambles, a handsome male unicorn (name of Glotter) trotted out. "Just what I needed," cried Noah. He directed Karly and Glotter to his ark.

"Not so fast," said Glotter. "I'm not going up into that thing." And Glotter trotted off into the brambles once again.

Unperturbed, Karly went aboard as a single, thanks to Noah's understanding nature. She was asked not to say anything to the others about her single status lest they start asking too many questions. Fortunately for everyone, a flood never occurred. Disembarking from the ark after a long, smelly, crowded stint below decks, Karly decided to search high and low for Glotter. She eventually found him and was impressed with his foresight about avoiding the ark. Karly and Glotter lived a good life together, but sadly, that was the last of the unicorns. Too few unicorns to repopulate the world successfully—no genetic diversity.

 Karly was a magical mystical unicorn. She was unique. *Unicorns* were unique, and supposedly she was the very last of them. As she pranced around one day, she ran into an old bearded man. "My name is Noah and I need to save the beasts of the world. Come and be safe on my ark."

"Don't you need two of us unicorns?" Karly replied.

"Don't worry about that," Noah said reassuringly. "Let's go. I'll find a premium location for you on the ark."

So Karly went aboard the "ark." It was a ramshackle mess of a boat. There were a few scrawny beasts there already...and the whole place was vile and unclean. When Karly attempted to back out of the deal, the old man locked her in. Then the storms came. Karly was frightened since she could not see what was happening as the boat rocked from side to side, tossing Karly all over the deck. When a particularly strong wave hit the boat, Karly fell forward and her horn stuck in the wall. The old man's boat was no match for the storm. He was merely a scam artist impersonating someone named Noah. But he and Karly and all the others went down with the boat and were never heard from again. And so the last of the unicorns was no more.

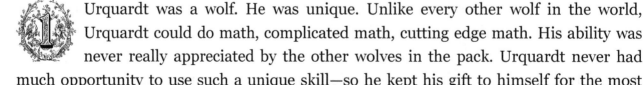

 Urquardt was a wolf. He was unique. Unlike every other wolf in the world, Urquardt could do math, complicated math, cutting edge math. His ability was never really appreciated by the other wolves in the pack. Urquardt never had much opportunity to use such a unique skill—so he kept his gift to himself for the most part. During a particularly harsh winter, the pack was having some serious difficulty in bringing down prey—their hunting skills did not seem to be working. A radical change in leadership did not help. Urquardt merely went along with each new alpha male. New alpha male, same old result: no successful hunts. Many wolves in the pack were beginning to show signs of starvation: glazed eyes, ribs showing, and hair falling out. Urquardt stepped in and offered his services to the current alpha male. He would use his mathematical prowess to calculate the best strategy for the pack to attack an animal, thereby saving them from a terrible fate.

Urquardt went to work and engineered a plan of attack on a buffalo in a passing herd. He instructed every member of the pack in their individual role in the attack plan. He also provided a Plan B if things went awry with Plan A. But Plan B was never needed as Urquardt's original plan was sound, working smoothly and quickly—a buffalo was brought down and the wolf pack was saved from starvation. Urquardt continued formulating plans for different types of prey throughout the winter, and as spring came, Urquardt became a trusted advisor to every alpha male that followed.

 Urquardt was a wolf. He was unique. Unlike every other wolf in the world, Urquardt could do math, complicated math, cutting edge math. When an especially harsh winter made successful hunting difficult, Urquardt offered his services to the alpha male and the rest of the pack. They did not know what Urquardt was talking about. Math? Strategy? He offered to show them, saying that they had nothing to lose except their gnawing hunger. So Urquardt did his calculations and devised a plan to cull out and attack a white-tailed deer—a big healthy one. Highly skeptical, the pack followed Urquardt's instructions, all the while getting lots of advice and critical comments from the alpha male. The attack plan worked in spite of a premature launch due to the alpha male's impatience and desire to maintain his leadership position—he felt threatened by Urquardt's mystical abilities.

Once the pack's bellies were full of venison, their thoughts turned to Urquardt. How did he manage it? Did he really manage it? Or was it just the alpha male's leadership that finally brought them from the brink of starvation? So many questions.

"Urquardt must be bewitched," surmised one member of the pack. That beguiling thought caught the fertile imagination of the entire pack, even if there was absolutely no logic to it at all. Such is the nature of a mob mentality. As an irrational panic began to take hold, the pack became dreadfully fearful of Urquardt, deeming him to be possessed of an evil spirit—the spirit of *Math*! Under the direction of the alpha male, the pack drove Urquardt to the edge of a cliff and despite his pleas, shoved him over the edge and ending his life. This also ended the possibility of Urquardt passing along his advantageous gift to offspring, something that might have advanced the evolution of the wolf species significantly.

---

Gloriana was a Henson's Speckled Goose, a rare type of goose that only existed on one farm in the entire world. Gloriana was unique even in this rarified group. She didn't start out as unique. But she became unique, all on her own. One day, she was about to lay an egg, but by squirming a certain way and fidgeting just right and tightening her muscles in a special sphinctorial manner her egg came out solid gold. Now there have been plenty of stories about such a thing, but none of them have given any credit to the goose herself. And to make matters worse such stories always ended badly for the goose. But in this case Gloriana decided to exploit the gift, all the while being discreet enough to avoid the fate of others that were so blessed. She made sure that only the goose community was aware of her newfound wealth and how she came by it. She had the discipline to limit the laying of golden eggs so that her life would appear normal. All the time she was helping her goose community—the community benefiting immensely from her compassion and generosity.

Gloriana was a Henson's Speckled Goose, a rare type of goose that only existed on one farm in the entire world. Gloriana was unique even in this rarified group. She didn't start out as unique. But she became unique, all on her own. One day, she learned how to lay solid gold eggs. She could do this on demand. Otherwise her eggs were as normal as those from any other goose. Seeing the benefit, she taught other geese how to do it. Soon the barnyard was filled with golden eggs. Knowing what might happen if the farmer got wind of all that gold, the geese hid the eggs in a nearby cave. They loved adding to the valuable stash. They all became so enamored with the laying of golden eggs that they soon forgot how lay real eggs. So, without any offspring, but with a cave full of thousands of useless golden eggs, The Henson's Speckled Goose soon became extinct.

*Moral #1: Uniqueness—how wonderful!*

*Moral #2: Uniqueness—how terrible!*

*Postscriptum #1*: Uniqueness was a cherished gift that helped nurture biological innovations and adaptations as species advanced in the evolutionary development of life on Earth.

*Postscriptum #2*: Throughout history, uniqueness continued to appear, confounding, confusing, threatening, and disturbing various groups; causing them to unite and take up arms...and eventually to beat uniqueness to death...or so they always wanted to believe at the time...every time.

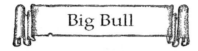

## Big Bull

Big Bull was a dog, a mighty, great dog,
The bravest, as old legends tell.
He fought 'longside soldiers loyal to the realm
And he served them and served them all well.

After the war he was kept in a pen
Till one day they called him again.
They needed his nose to track down a man
And to show them just where he had been.

Big Bull found the killer, sniffed him right out
And justice was soon meted out.
Big Bull got some treats and a pat on the head
And the freedom to roam all about.

One day the young dog heard cries from afar
And alerted the camp's rescue team.
They followed Big Bull and found a young girl,
Neck deep in a cold raging stream.

Before they could stop him Big Bull dove right in
And pulled her up onto the shore.
Big Bull got some treats and a pat on the head
And a warm place to sleep, nothing more.

Being a hero Big Bull was selected—
A journey far south to the pole.
As part of a team he helped the bold men
Fight the wind and the ice and the cold.

But off broke the ice sheet and stranded the group,
Their supplies all got lost in the deep.
Starvation and frostbite soon took their toll
And the journey slowed down to a creep.

Shaking and hungry, desperate men;
The temperature far below zero.
Being so brave Big Bull was selected
For one final act as a hero.

As you suspected Big Bull was eaten
By men who were grateful and full.
A pat on their bellies instead of his head
A tribute to one called Big Bull.

**Moral: To all dogs everywhere: Whatever you may think, to some humans, you're still just a dog.**

*Postscriptum*: The expedition party wound up eating *all* their dogs. Then they began eating each other. With each meal they lived to eat another day. Sooner or later they all froze to death anyway. Meaning? Humans. What are you gonna do?

"Well, enough of that. Basil Hyenoid here again. What did we learn from all of this? Hmmm, I don't know...but this I *do* know: you can't trust the Ordell Ballingo Pest Control Service to get the bats out of your attic. *That* I can tell you. Anyway..."

"Picture this—picture a teenage boy. He's filled with teen angst: competition, uncertainty, dangerous impulses, no concept of consequences, hormonal imbalances, and zit city. You name it. He's got it going. He has a lot going on.

"He decides to run away from home and become a rebel graffiti artist (to attract the chicks). So without any fanfare or hand wringing, off he goes one day with two full cans of black spray paint—the only color that was available from his dad's workbench. Block after block he walks, carrying his knapsack and waiting for inspiration to find him. As his first hour as an independent operator comes to an end, he encounters a large flat field. Anchored in the field are a number of colorful hot air balloons, all of them inflated and ready to head skyward. He sees a large gathering of people milling about, presumably preparing everything for a big group liftoff.

"Noticing an unattended balloon, the young boy boards it and launches himself up and away—much to the displeasure of the owner of said balloon. As the balloon rises higher and higher into the cloudless sky, the young boy watches the people on the ground scurrying around, several of them yelling and shaking their fists at him. As the balloon goes higher, the people below get very small—still anxiously moving around—and the young boy turns his attention (short as it is) to the horizon. Suddenly the smooth ascent is interrupted with a bruising 'thump!' This rattles the teen's brain and startles the crowd below. The young boy looks up and sees the top of the balloon stuck against a deep sky blue ceiling. It's the top of the sky. He cannot rise any higher.

"The young boy feels that he must go up and investigate. He climbs up the rigging, out over the bulging surface (it's very warm), and up onto the top of the balloon (it's very hot). There he can see the balloon butting up against the top of the sky. The balloon is moving sideways with the wind current, causing it to scrape the top of the sky as it slides along.

"The young boy pulls out a can of spray paint and starts printing: S...U...R...E...N...D...He is guiding the balloon along by using his weight—very clever for a mixed-up little teen punk like him. He continues: E...R and moves to a new line: D...O...R...O...Before he can continue, a high-flying eagle comes along and directs a critical comment to the teen monochromist. '*Surrender* is spelled with *two* R's,' the eagle says.

"The eagle's criticism disturbs the inner creative flow of the young boy and his motivation takes a big hit. Unbeknownst to him, the unfinished work has caused quite a stir on the ground—not necessarily from an artistic point of view. Obviously he can't undo what has already been done, so he abandons that first project and allows the wind to move the balloon to a different part of the sky. Following his rebel nature, he re-motivates himself and decides to start a new project. He'll have to create some *finished* artwork (if it can be called that) before the scraping of the balloon against the top of the sky causes a hole to form, releasing the hot air, and...

"The young boy realizes that he has already used up a lot of his paint. Finding a new place to work, far away from his original one, the young boy creates a new, somewhat shorter message, painting in big black letters on the ceiling of the deep blue sky: T...H...E...E...N...D...I...S...N...E...A...R.

"*Postscriptum*, this is Basil Hyenoid saying, 'I have nothing else to say.'"

# Lost

Now in his thirties, Martine DuBallón thought about the times, over the last two decades, that he had come to this meadow with the intention of crossing it and searching the woods beyond. A short distance away, in the town of St. Violet where he lived with his aunt, he would become excited about the idea. But as he reached this spot, he would somehow—always—lose his resolve. He would look across the meadow to the dark, wooded hills on the far side, contemplate it for a moment, and eventually turn back. It was a familiar exercise, but it was one that was making him impatient with himself. This time would be different. There seemed to be a sense of urgency about it. Bringing with him only a sandwich and a small bottle of wine, he planned to remain undaunted and see his quest to its ultimate end, one way or another. He was sure that there were others who lacked the nerve to face a personal challenge like this, but he didn't know any of those people.

So, here he was, on this spring day, at the edge of the meadow, now blanketed with wildflowers, looking across the colorful expanse toward the woods where he became lost as a young boy. Today, in particular, the meadow seemed much smaller than it did then even though the flowers and weeds could still reach up to his elbows. He remembered falling asleep among those trees on the far side. Lying on the ground, late at night, in the darkness of the woods, he was consoled by the familiar aromas of dirt, damp bark, and night air. In and out of sleep he could sometimes hear groups of very official people frantically searching for him; groups led by a mangy set of boisterous, untrained mongrel dogs—dogs that had no idea what they were doing. Having no real leadership, the search groups wandered about for days, randomly and unsuccessfully, while the lost Martine knew that, at any moment, he could easily be carried off and eaten alive by the boogie-boogie. Yet, as Martine recalled, he was unafraid and not particularly interested in crying out for help (or being found). "More likely, complacent and unaware," Martine now thought to himself; "maybe even a little bit intrigued." He had found something special in those magical woods that seemed to help him through it all. Something that was stolen from him shortly before he was finally rescued.

Now, many years later, after several aborted attempts, he was crossing the flowery meadow at Pickering's Glen with a new measure of determination, determination to see this through. In the past, he would talk himself out of continuing, thinking that none of this was worth the effort—a lot of hand wringing, rationalizing, and floundering about. But remembering his bizarre experiences in those wooded hills as a youth—

At one end of the field Martine could still make out the remnants of the private school he had once attended: Summerhall Onizon's Preparatory School for Boys. His wealthy aunt Eileen paid for his tuition since Martine's parents were ill equipped to manage such a thing—both mentally as well as financially. At the time, the St. Violet societal blue-bloods felt that Martine was not fit to attend such an elite, exclusive, and important institution— but that was the way society was, and most likely, always will be, everywhere. The rigors were many. Not only was there academic achievement to be dealt with, but it was the kind of a place where he was routinely evaluated in such things as penmanship, posture, diction, grooming, manliness, and other built-in character traits over which, Martine was convinced, he had no control.

One day, sneaking out of the schoolyard, he wandered into this very meadow, eventually losing his way after entering the nearby woods. His disappearance, of course, caused a furious uproar in the town and made him the center of attention for almost a week. He savored the attention he received when he was finally rescued, but attention was something that he didn't always relish while he was in attendance at the school. Consumed with relief that Martine was found—and unharmed physically—many of the St. Violet adults eventually turned openly hostile toward him for causing such a fuss.

Today, as he began walking through the wildflowers, a cool spring breeze passed over him, making him feel as though nature itself was encouraging him, perhaps even prodding him along. Looking down, he noticed that the cuffs of his white shirt were becoming dusty and discolored with the pollen from so many flowers. This included copious amounts of a weird black powder deposited on him by some tall grass. All of this dust, set loose through the air by his passing, prompted his sinuses to produce a fairly significant amount of fluid, which, when wiped away with his sleeve, left a broad, thick smear of nasty black powder on his face.

As he stood in the center of the meadow, Martine heard a nervous rustling in the undergrowth; some small animal no doubt. "Could it be a wombat?" he asked himself. "What is a wombat anyway?"

[Note to the fastidious observer: The nearest wombat was thousands of miles (kilometers) away.]

The nervous bustling animal, if indeed it was an animal, had heightened Martine's sensitivities so that when a small green grasshopper suddenly popped out of the vegetation and hit him in the face, it caused him to swing wildly with his arms in an attempt to discourage it from any more "attacks."

Moving along, now nearing the far edge of the meadow, Martine could see the dark shadow of a fast-moving cloud briefly drift over the field as the sky was becoming more and more overcast. While he was in school, it *always* seemed to be overcast out here.

In mid-winter, all this vegetation would be reduced to a frozen brown mat on the ground. Martine could feel the crunch and hear it crackle as he walked around on it. On the occasional clear, brisk winter day he would think to himself, "How could it be so cold with the sun shining so brightly? I have no feeling in my right hand!" Just as he was unaware of the black, pasty powder smeared onto his face now, back then he was just as unaware that his nose, with a constant drip hanging from the tip, had turned a bright red on those frosty days.

As a youth, all of Martine's concerns were vague and ephemeral: ghosts, demons, the boogie-boogie. Whereas real, concrete threats were far from his mind and easily brushed off: schoolyard bullies, shards of broken glass, an overgrown pit filled with deadly spikes, snakes with legs, feathered wolves, a headless hermit emerging from his hut. As Martine neared the beckoning woods at the other side of the meadow, today, as an adult, he was thinking, "Is this trip into the woods, with all of its unknowns, really going to be all that perilous?" Sometimes, even the silliest, most mundane event associated with him seemed to get blown all out of proportion by the town's "movers and shakers." On the other hand, many times in his life, he would tell people of a *real* experience, something out of the ordinary, and they refused to believe any of it. Now if he somehow happened to get himself eaten by the boogie-boogie, then that…that would be a *real*, big deal.

Looking to one end of the meadow, Martine could now make out, rising above the school ruins, the remains of the old bell tower standing out like a bony finger pointing at the clouds. It reminded Martine of a similar finger on the hand of the school's headmaster, pointing directly at Martine's nose—pointing out a flaw in Martine's character or admonishing him for some transgression that seemed to be of global importance at the time. The headmaster was a Mr. Peezil, or, as the students more familiarly knew him, "Peezil the Weasel."

Mr. Peezil took his role as headmaster and disciplinarian very seriously. In addition to his administrative duties, every afternoon he was required to teach proper English to a crisply-dressed room full of young boys (including Martine). A scruffy and time-tested Mr. Peezil had interesting ways of maintaining the transitory and fragile attentions of his class. One Tuesday afternoon, filled with overcooked vegetables and questionable meat, Martine fell asleep, involuntarily resting his head on his crossed arms on the surface of his broad desktop. While Martine dreamed of a confluence of masked bandits, lost homework, and a few things more hormonal, Mr. Peezil (continuing to lecture) took a large silver coin from his pocket and casually strolled over to Martine's desk.

"Mr. DuBallón!" Peezil blurted out while evaluating the unconscious Martine and the available desktop space around his head. Martine slowly opened his eyes. But, before Martine could even rise up, Mr. Peezil forcefully bounced the silver coin off the desktop close to Martine's head, producing a loud metallic reverberation that not only rattled the sleeping Martine but the rest of the class as well. There were numerous pockmarked desktops around the classroom, evidencing years of Mr. Peezil's unique educational methodologies. As Mr. Peezil bent over to retrieve the coin off of the floor, Martine, startled and awakened, brought forth all of his luncheon foodstuffs from out his stomach and onto Mr. Peezil's back. Now, according to the unwritten rules of the old school days, heaving at school was probably the most embarrassing thing a young scholar could do. However, the location and prolific quantity of Martine's output provided him, for a while, with a peculiar type of celebrity status among his blue-blooded peers. Parts of the incident, *post-vomitus*, Martine remembers to this day: Mr. Peezil's bony finger aimed at his nose; Mr. Peezil's foul breath close behind; pieces of chipped beef exfoliating off the back of Mr. Peezil's wet shirt; and the sudden disappearance of Mr. Peezil a few weeks later. Perhaps Mr. Peezil was eaten by the boogie-boogie.

Martine approached the shadowy entrance to the woods predictably feeling somewhat agitated at the prospect of actually entering them. Close enough to brush against some of the trees, he crossed into a small bare area, his attention turning to his left where he saw, emerging from the shadows, a large, tightly-packed horde of about a hundred spastically-scurrying wild hares, climbing all over themselves, quickly moving as a group out and away from the woods like some huge amorphous liquid blob or psychotic amoeba. They were eerily silent for such a large chaotic mob. As the hares soon disappeared into the flowery meadow, Martine could track the route of the now unseen wild hares by watching the wave of disturbed wildflowers move through the meadow. He speculated that his mind might be playing tricks on him. But he also reasoned that he was much too clever to fall for that kind of trick.

Puzzled by that wild display, Martine turned his attention back to the woods. Surprisingly, he did not find much at all familiar about them. Venturing into its shadows for only about forty yards (36.576 meters), Martine, looking back, could no longer see any sign of the meadow. But, looking ahead, he could just make out, what seemed to be, the figure of a man, standing alone. A few minutes later, as he approached the figure, Martine saw that it was a one-legged man wearing an orange shirt with vast quantities of matted hair emerging from its openings. The man was standing perfectly still and did not move even as Martine reached out to touch him on the cheek. The man was made of clay. And the "hair" was merely a large colony of spindly-legged black spiders that had taken up residence in the clay man's orange shirt. One might expect an ordinary person to be (fairly) repulsed by all this, but Martine, being such a clever and peculiar sort, instead, removed the man's shirt, shook out most of the spiders, and fashioned a turban-like headdress out of it. Sometimes, Martine was just plain nuts. The orange "turban" smelled pretty rank and although Martine could only imagine what he looked like wearing it, he was quite pleased with himself. Walking away, and as he brushed off the remainder of the spiders from his head, Martine looked back and saw the one-legged clay man run off, disappearing into the darker recesses of the woods, howling as he ran, in a high-pitched voice, "Zhakey-kleesen! Zhakey-kleesen!"

[Note: The more fastidious among us might ask the question, "How could a one-legged man run *anywhere*?" Well, Martine saw it—he was a witness. So it happens to be just one of those things.]

On an overcast day when the sun's light is softened and the air is cool and moist, shadows can lose their sharpness, becoming more diffuse. A place like the woods can turn gloomy and cheerless, the brightest rays of the sun prevented from leaking through the canopy. A certain sense of balance might be observed as a hawk snatches a struggling mouse right off the ground and carries it to its young. Not so much balance as far as the mouse is concerned. What is here? The evidence of new life as pieces of a colorful broken egg shell lie strewn on the ground. New life? Or perhaps just a small dinner for a nocturnal scavenger. Worms can become meals for the very producer of the defunct egg. Ants, building and reproducing, building and reproducing with apparently no point to it at all. Countless life and death dramas, all of them taking place right under Martine's nose.

These types of things meant nothing to Martine, and although quite clever, at times he was almost pathologically unobservant. As a young adult he would travel to foreign countries with his Aunt Eileen. Years ago, Eileen was ditched by her third husband as they visited Grujapur, a small town near Delhi, India. The people in the area assisted Eileen in finding her way back to her home in England so she always felt welcome returning to the place every few years or whenever possible. On one particular trip she took Martine with her.

Out on an excursion by himself, he went sightseeing for several hours, riding on a colorful cross-town bus and not realizing that the man next to him was dead. Martine had stepped over the dead man to get at the window seat and had stepped back over him to get out. He would never have ascertained that the man was dead had it not been for the gasping (hyperventilating) oversized woman who was attempting to replace Martine in that very window seat. She was thwarted when the dead man collapsed forward as she stretched out in front of him, his head burying itself (quite forcefully) into her magnificent crotch. Aunt Eileen humored Martine when he told her of the incident, but of course, like so many other adults, she believed he had made the whole thing up. This led Martine to unconsciously develop a policy of keeping all such experiences to himself, no matter how adventuresome, envy-provoking, or tantalizing. It was a habit that served him well in the future even if he could never fully appreciate it. It gave Martine a kind of stoic stature that was, in actuality, accidental.

Aunt Eileen was aware of some of Martine's shortcomings but was kind enough to keep her observations to herself. She loved him as if he were her own. This provided Martine with a comfort that he did not have with Eileen's twin sister, Martine's actual mother, Bayleen. Although the two sisters were identical in appearance (tall, jet black hair, green eyes, and muscular), their personalities could not have been more different. It was as if a schizoid person was split down the middle, one half (Bayleen) receiving all the darker traits and the other getting the lion's share of the positive qualities (Eileen).

For the most part, Eileen was stable, intelligent, and compassionate. She became very cosmopolitan thanks to the worldliness of her three, now defunct, husbands:

> Husband #1: Benjamin Addleman; Eileen married him for love. Addleman died in a self-inflicted hunting accident. Manly. Left her with nothing.
>
> Husband #2: Richard Ashton-Cropper; Eileen married him for money. He was frozen to death whilst ice-fishing in Scandinavia. Manly. Left her with a fortune.
>
> Husband #3: Garfield Ogden Knox; Married Eileen for her money. Whereabouts unknown (declared legally dead). Cowardly. Left her.

After number three, Eileen preferred a solo and more independent existence, except for her interest in Martine. At this point she had built up a hefty and cumbersome legal name: Eileen Florentine Almondine Addleman Ashton-Cropper Knox. So she just went by Eileen Knox. Taking advantage of her wealth she traveled all over the world. But she would keep up with Martine whenever she could. She even attempted to take custody of Martine at one point but "the Board" denied her request because of her several marriages and heavy travel lifestyle. Martine's real parents could not have cared less, one way or the other.

In stark contrast to Eileen, Bayleen Osentine Almondine led a claustrophobic, stifling life, a situation of her own making. Due to an odd sequence of events, Bayleen had literally stumbled upon Martine's future father, an industrial chemist named Root DuBallón. After a two-week whirlwind courtship, they got married, and, a few months later, little baby Martine appeared on the scene. Bayleen hadn't the brains to find her way out of a phone box, much less manage the everyday challenges of life in the real world—a real world that included tending to her baby boy. She had neither the tools nor the motivation to cope with everyday problems. This led her to lean toward violence as the solution to most everything.

On one occasion Bayleen attacked the neighbor's dog with a twin-edged meat axe for allegedly distributing a trash can full of the DuBallón's private garbage. The dog survived, missing both ears, a fair amount of his tail, and a patch of skin exposing part of his skull. But it was Martine who was implicated and punished. His mother, avoiding blame, had hidden the large bloodied axe under the pillow on Martine's bed figuring that, as a child, Martine would probably take some survivable heat, but she herself might end up in jail. Not surprisingly, the unobservant Martine slept for two nights on that very same pillow without noticing the axe. Martine's father finally discovered the hidden axe when he confiscated Martine's pillow for some kind of "experiment."

[Note: Martine's father spent many hours banging around in the basement of their house, always keeping the basement door locked. What went on in there might have been grounds for a search warrant. But Martine's father really knew how to keep a secret. Although, for the record, his father *had* been taken in for questioning on several occasions. Subsequent residents of the house would discover items that had been left behind by both of Martine's parents, including: a stuffed lion's head with empty eye sockets, seven sticks of dynamite, assorted bottles of acid, a shrunken head, a dozen spent fire extinguishers, twenty-two unused ant farms, a small arsenal of firearms, and a 4-gallon jug of pure mercury.]

In spite of the strange events he had already experienced, Martine redoubled his resolve. His makeshift orange turban was a testament to that—Martine DuBallón was in charge of this excursion, not these mysterious and threatening woods. He turned away from the direction of the screaming fleeing clay man and ventured deeper and deeper into the woods. The overcast sky seemed to get darker as the day progressed, or was it merely the inherent nature of the woods. A few shadows appeared and just as quickly, disappeared, briefly altering the mood of the woods; but the mid-afternoon sun was rarely able to break through the clouds. Martine took a few sips of water from a small spring he encountered. He soon began to consider eating the goose liver and egg sandwich he had brought with him.

Standing by the lightly bubbling spring, he heard a tiny, almost bird-like voice call out, "Hey, you there, in the orange hat, with the dirty face." He couldn't tell where the sound had come from. It seemed to be all around him. "Hey, *you!*" This time the voice seemed more forceful and demanding. As Martine turned in a full circle looking for the source, the tiny voice began to sing:

> *My one true love, a piper snake, crawling 'crost the moss.*
> *Overhead and far away a talking albatross.*
> *How pleasant is the harmless stoat that watches from the stones,*
> *Who soon becomes the furry badger, come to lick your bones.*

Martine did not panic, but this *new* strange occurrence did raise a chill along his spine. If necessary he was prepared to take a powder out of there *posthaste*. But holding him firmly in place was that growing feeling of resolve and a vague sense of familiarity. Cautiously and timidly looking up, he saw, sitting on a low branch of a nearby tree, a comely naked woman staring down at him. She was wearing a short pointed hat with a red and white scarf wrapped round it. The hat looked as if it had captured a small top portion of the wild tangled nest of whitish hair fluffed up all about her head. Her hands rested on the branch on either side of her and she was swinging her legs alternately back and forth, her face sporting a rather insipid little grin and her eyes blinking unnaturally in time with her legs.

"That must be very uncomfortable," he said to her, hiding his uneasiness, "seeing as how you are nude and all."

"No, not really," she replied. "I have quite the callused ass."

"What are you doing here?" he asked her.

"What are *you* doing here, you little bastard?" she replied.

Martine paused, "Hmmm." He looked away, attempting to sort out—whatever. "I am searching for something that I lost in here, in these woods," he answered turning back to her. As an afterthought he followed up with, "As a youth!"

"What does that mean? '*As a youth*'," she asked as she stopped swinging her legs. Her tone had become more confrontational and antagonistic.

"When I was young I became hopelessly lost in these woods for several days."

"If you were *hopelessly* lost, how is it that you are here now?" she asked, taunting him. She began swinging her legs and blinking again.

"What?" replied Martine, unaware that she was just trying to annoy him.

She repeated her question as if rhetorically, "If you were hopelessly *lost*, how is it that you are here now?" She looked away, ignoring Martine, letting him know she was not expecting an answer.

Martine probed his clever mind, looking around as if some snappy answer was going to pop out of the trees. As she stared ahead, obviously ignoring him, he could hear her mumble, "What a stupid little scum-sucking turtle." As he took a breath to make some sort of reply, she blurted out, "What is it that you are looking for anyway?" She stopped moving and looked right at Martine, almost staring him down.

"I'm looking for a small carved stone; it's translucent and blue; it's carved in the shape of a duck; it's a Sapphire Duck." As he replied, he began kicking the leaves and sticks on the ground around his feet, questioning whether or not he should have answered her at all. "I found it while I was wandering about in these woods, as a you…" He stopped, attempting to pre-empt a new round of taunting.

The woman's legs started swinging again, and, looking away from him she asked, "If you found it, why are you looking for it *now*?" quickly adding "Zhakey-kleesen!" as if becoming restless and impatient.

Again, Martine looked about himself as if seeking at least a hint of sympathy from the inanimate surroundings. But before he could answer, the beautiful woman jumped down from the tree branch and came up to him, right up to him, right up to his face, brushing off pieces of bark from her "callused ass."

"The tip of your nose has a drip on it," she said as she flicked at the end of his nose with her thumb and forefinger. "And what does this Sapphire Duck mean to some screwy little beaver like you? What makes you think that something like that is still here after all this time?"

Martine was not aware that there was anything at the tip of his nose as he struggled to restrain his eyes from wandering all over her landscape. Now that she was within breathing distance of his face, she didn't look quite as lovely as she looked when she was sitting in the tree—especially her teeth. They seemed to be sparse, discolored, and splotched with some kind of grey slime. Even at this close range, he could not tell the difference between her real hair and the Spanish Moss hanging from the branches and the

Spanish Moss entangled in her hair. Something small was definitely moving about in there. "Could it be a wombat?" he asked himself.

[Note to the fastidious observer: a wombat is much too large to be living in someone's hair.]

"What was the point of that little pointed hat she was wearing?" he thought to himself. She could have asked Martine a similar question about the big orange spider nest (previously known as "shirt") sitting atop *his* head.

After a pause he tried to explain, "I'm hoping to find the Duck again as it was taken away from me as I lay sleeping, exhausted, after several days without food and with very little water. As for its importance, I believe that it was somehow responsible for getting me rescued."

She stared briefly at him, in silence, then slowly turned away, giving him some welcome space. With her bare back to him she muttered, "That's quite a story. I haven't the slightest notion of what you are talking about. But there *is* a nice little cottage about half a mile (~805 meters) that way." She pointed to an area of the woods that was in the same direction from which Martine had just come. Before he could contradict her, she turned back and faced him, once again singing; singing while looking directly at him, making full eye contact. Gracefully raising her arms, her breasts bobbing about in a final taunt, she lifted herself off the ground and flew up over the canopy, out of the woods. As she disappeared into the clouds in the sky, an almost mystical aura of sunlight seemed to illuminate her—this strange wingless angel: dirty, naked, and antagonistic. Surprised but not intimidated, Martine stood motionless as he watched her disappear. He wasn't buying any of it.

[Note: Those aforementioned same fastidious persons among us might now wonder about this latest preposterous development and they would be right to do so.]

Martine thought about the woman's singing. It was loud and shrill, but not very musical. Nothing in these woods ever seemed to be what it first appeared to be. Unperturbed by these recent events and feeling a bit peckish, Martine sat down on a large fallen tree trunk and began eating his greasy sandwich. No sooner had he taken that first bite, when, out of the corner of his eye he saw something moving. He turned his head and saw the one-legged, shirtless, clay man running furiously toward him. The man was brandishing a twin-edged meat axe, similar to the one Martine remembered from his ba-a-ad experience as a youth. Once again he looked straight ahead, and after a very brief moment of thought, Martine bolted from the tree trunk running deeper into the woods, inadvertently crushing his sandwich in his fist. The clay man, in pursuit, was again yelling, "Zhakey-kleesen! Zhakey-kleesen!"

Running quickly but carefully, Martine leapt very adroitly over all the small logs, branches, and stones in his path. Occasionally, he would glance back to evaluate the situation as the clay man remained relentlessly in pursuit. Coming upon a small creek Martine splashed through it, adding mud, grime, and fragments of vegetation to the menagerie of foreign materials currently adhering to his person. What a mess he was becoming. He could hear the rustle of leaves and branches as the determined, one-legged clay man scrambled his way through the undergrowth. Having only one leg, the clay man was not nearly as agile as Martine, so Martine might have eventually outrun his deranged pursuer.

Again Martine heard the clay man cry out, "Zhakey-kleesen Zhakey-klee...!" The cry was suddenly interrupted. Behind him, Martine heard the sound of the clay man tripping and falling with an awkward crash. He turned to see what had happened. The clay man had tripped over his own one foot. He had fallen against a weathered and partially-disassembled wall of rocks and was shattered into thousands of small fragments of hardened clay—fragments falling into every conceivable nook and cranny among the pile of rocks. The meat axe, real as life itself, lay on the ground, harmless and orphaned.

Bending over, his hands on his thighs, Martine breathed heavily, attempting to catch his breath, all the while keeping a keen eye on the shattered remains of the clay man just in case, by some mysterious magic, all those little pieces of clay re-assembled themselves, and re-animated. Smiling, he thought to himself, "Who ever heard of such a ridiculous thing?" Martine slowly looked over the area where the clay man had fallen. Once he was sure that the clay man was harmless, he grabbed the meat axe, sticking its handle through his belt next to the small bottle of wine that was still with him. The axe was cumbersome and heavy, but Martine felt reassured—he now had something he could use for protection. Considering all the events since he ventured into these woods, he was not going to casually dismiss the idea of actually needing to use it.

Martine was not paying attention to much of anything while he was running, changing his direction this way and that. As a result, he was now, once again, lost. These same bloody woods—lost *again*. Which way was the so-called beautiful cottage? (If there really was one.) Which way was the way out? Currently, with the sky being overcast, the sun could offer no clue. He had heard something (maybe in school) about moss growing on trees, but these trees had no moss (except the strands of Spanish Moss hanging from the branches—and they weren't talking...at least not yet). He wiped the congealed remains of his sandwich on the side of his trousers and wiped off the sweat from his forehead with his black powder-dusted sleeve, adding more black smears to his face. Martine DuBallón was becoming a true testament to filth.

Exhausted from all these events, Martine sat on the ground, drew up his knees, and contemplated his situation. He rested his chin on his kneecaps. Although he could detect a wave of sleep beginning to engulf him, he felt very uneasy about the prospect of falling asleep in this apparently hostile environment. He knew of the boogie-boogie, but the clay man with the meat axe was something new. Perhaps the man was all put out by Martine's absconding with that orange shirt. Although the naked woman seemed harmless, she was really quite bothersome. Martine rolled to one side and fashioned his "orange turban" into a pillow. Resting his head, he fell into a deep and restful sleep.

High above a snow-capped mountain peak Martine's character looked out across the scenery and saw a cool, blue mountain lake. There were no trees at this altitude and every crevasse was filled with packed ice and snow. The character was floating in the icy cold, brittle air, hovering. Then the character dropped down toward the lake, landing on the shore. Overhead some kind of blue dinosaur bird circled. What was that in its mouth? The water was crystal clear, but was so deep that Martine's character could not see the bottom. Then, from the depths of the lake, up rose a number of big silvery fish all wearing neckties and monocles. They all began talking at each other at once, using unfamiliar numerical terms. While they continued to talk, something *really* big began rising up through the water, forcing them all aside. Backing up from the shore, Martine's character could just make out its shape. It *had* no shape. It was a blob. Martine's character believed that this dream-scene situation would eventually devolve into the giant blob's laying chase to a helpless and immobile Martine's character. Or, worse still, the blob would chase him to the edge of a cliff where Martine's character would go over it into a free fall, never actually reaching the ground below (in spite of being able to float and fly previously in this scenario). To avoid all this, Martine's character pulled out of nowhere some kind of ill-defined, projectile-firing weapon and shot the blob several times. But before Martine's character could ascertain the final status of the blob, Martine—the real Martine—awoke with a start.

Martine must have slept for hours since it was now dark. He was beginning to have difficulty distinguishing objects in the foreboding woods. Trees began to look like people. Nocturnal animals were cautiously probing around. He could hear them, but he could not see them. Feeling vulnerable, Martine knew this to be just the kind of situation that the boogie-boogie might take advantage of. Darkness or not, it was becoming challenging for Martine to distinguish between real, surreal, and imagined events as well. He needed to get hold of that Sapphire Duck. What if he were to encounter a...a wombat? How would that compare to an encounter with the boogie-boogie?

[Note: Please excuse Martine's obsession with this Australian animal.]

Feeling glazed over from the cold damp evening air and still drowsy from his nap on the ground, Martine stood up and saw, dimly in the distance, a faint, greenish light. Having no real options and being emboldened by having overcome so much already, he decided to go have a look-see. And so, convinced of his invincibility, the filthy Martine—with only his quest, a small half-empty bottle of wine, and a heavy twin-edged meat axe to keep him company—set out for the source of the light and maybe a respite, a refuge, from all the day's goings-on. The orange, foul smelling shirt—so bloody important earlier in the day— was left behind in a twisted wad.

After walking for a short while, it seemed to Martine that he was getting no closer to that mysterious light; and feeling a little bit frustrated by his situation, he paused for a moment, just to think things through. Looking around in the near dark, he noticed that an owl was watching him from a branch high above him. Martine could just make out its shape against the somewhat illuminated clouds between the tree branches. Yes, it was a big, fat, supercilious, self-important owl. That is what Martine was thinking. The owl wasn't interested in Martine; it was only on the lookout for some food. Martine was much too big for that.

In Martine's weary mind, the owl reminded him of Mr. Glover, the man who took over after Mr. Peezil suddenly disappeared. Mr. Glover was huge (puffy huge) with a coif that might be mistaken for a manicured red topiary. With a hair-trigger temper, he was easily enraged and could turn deep crimson at the slightest provocation—veins popping out and pulsating every which way. He was also a big believer in corporal punishment for any and all crimes against the school order or its academic mission. He was an academia nut. Highly organized, he had a lengthy, detailed list of infractions for which one could receive "licks."

[Note: a "lick" was a whack to the behind with a multi-holed, aerated wooden paddle, the holes' purpose: to reduce air resistance during a swinging delivery.]

Late for school, five licks. Mouthing off, seven licks. Mouthing off to Mr. Glover, 13 licks, and so forth. Mr. Glover would administer the assigned licks to student posteriors during weekly assembly, on stage, in order to maximize the offender's humiliation. The queued- up offenders would parade across the stage, one by one, each receiving his dose of licks. The ordeal could sometimes be lengthy.

[Note: It was excruciatingly lengthy for the observers in attendance as well as the weekly set of offenders. The worst offenders were always saved until last so that they would have plenty of time to "sweat it out" as their turn slowly approached.]

Martine always wondered, "If the punishment was so wretched, why were there still so many violations during the course of a single week?"

[Note: It was a valid question from a clever person like Martine, and being so clever...during Mr. Glover's entire tenure as headmaster, Martine never received a single lick.]

One day, during a routine assembly, at the end of an atypical, very short queue, one of Martine's fellow students named Reznick—a particularly incorrigible offender—was to have a number of licks administered to his behind, up on the stage, for all students and faculty to witness. Martine barely knew the student, but *everyone* was required to attend the weekly assembly. Mr. Glover, proudly displaying his paddle and surveying this eleven-year old threat to society, prepared himself for the big, important event, taking a deep breath. But before he could administer the paddle, Master Reznick pulled down his own trousers, bent over—displaying his bare butt and one-eyed Jack prominently to Mr. Glover—and yelled out, "O.K. start lickin'!"

Feeling the harsh sting of disrespect, Mr. Glover turned red with rage as the boys in the assembly assaulted the auditorium walls with laughter, pounding on the seats, and delivering a torrent of inappropriate noises and cat calls. Reznick, still bent over, looked out across the riotous assembly with an incredibly satisfied smile that most likely remained on his face for the rest of his life. Mr. Glover realized that any level of inappropriate retribution or violence directed at Master Reznick would be witnessed by several hundred young boys and numerous attending faculty.

Frustrated to distraction, Mr. Glover suddenly keeled over, collapsing onto the stage with a loud thud. Later, after all the young boys had been ushered out in an administrative panic, a medical team came into the auditorium and worked feverishly on Mr. Glover.

Eventually they hauled him off. That was the last time anybody could ever remember seeing him.

The somewhat regular, abrupt, and poorly-explained disappearances of several school headmasters may have raised the eyebrows of the cadre of young boys, but a much more serious and somber issue was the disappearance of a number of the young students who attended the school. As community leaders demanded answers, these disappearances eventually led to the closing of the school and its abandonment, leaving its shell to the elements and groups of shameless vandals and scavengers looking to extract from it anything of value. The rigid system in place at the school did not include keeping the young boys well informed—they were never informed about much of anything. It was as if the school's administration was saying to the boys, "You may have seen it with your own eyes, but it never really happened; so forget about it." One day, a student, Pietir Glossom was there, the next day he wasn't. Borden Smythe, present one day, then gone. Overton Schancker, disappeared. Seventeen in all. Willfully unexplained.

Standing in the dark with the distant light beckoning at one side, Martine watched the outline of the owl moving its head around. He thought, "Why seventeen? What made seventeen the significant threshold? Why not close the school at thirteen, or eight, or four?" Even the clever Martine could not dredge up some explanation for the stagnant behavior of the St. Violet community leaders over those disappearances. Was the continued operation of the school that much more important than the lives of those classmates? Could his fellow students have been snatched by the boogie-boogie? Aunt Eileen's abrupt extraction of Martine from the school one day ensured that Martine was not going to become number eighteen. Throughout all of this, Martine's own inattentive parents were oblivious to any of the events happening at the school and the surrounding area.

[Note: Martine's father, Root, eventually (and some say inevitably) blew himself up one summer afternoon and Martine's mother, Bayleen, was placed in a sanitarium for the criminally insane where she became a constant pain in the institution. His Aunt Eileen was very reluctant to ever explain to him why his mother (her own sister) was quarantined there. But that's another story. It was only after both of Martine's parents were out of the picture that his Aunt Eileen was able to obtain legal custody of him.]

After a while, the owl seemed to be very bored with staring down at Martine. That was what Martine was thinking. In actuality, the owl was quite annoyed because Martine's presence was scaring off all the small animals in the area. So the owl very quietly spread its wings and flew off. Martine then decided it was time to move on and so he headed toward the light source once more.

Walking across the debris on the ground was rather tricky in the dark. Diffused light from the distant town of St. Violet illuminated the clouds in the overcast sky just enough for Martine to see his way. After a while he could tell that he was finally making progress toward the greenish light. Then, as he worked his way through a dense thicket, he came upon an open area where a dangerous-looking, run-down, one-room house stood. It wasn't a cottage and it wasn't a shack, but it was fairly large and definitely in a disastrous state of disrepair, seemingly about to collapse at any moment. It had a fire-hazard of a roof that even *looked* leaky—something cooking or burning inside was sending smoke or steam through multiple openings as if the roof were a sieve straining out the smoke from unknown solids below. This could *not* be the "nice little" cottage that the naked woman spoke of. Unless, of course, she was a big fat liar; and she was...a liar.

Creeping up to one of the windows, Martine could see, indistinctly, a very tall but emaciated old woman inside. She was close to seven feet tall (2.13 meters). The window glass, as it was, was so fogged-over with age that he could not make out much of anything else. He found his way round to the house's gnarly wooden door and knocked several times. The door opened outwardly toward him, pushing him back. Appearing in the half-open doorway was the old woman.

Dressed in a dark grey, tattered, loosely-hanging outfit, the old woman had a number of long distorted hairs populating her cheeks and chin; some particularly rebellious hairs were as long as three inches (7.62 cm). She was so tall that Martine had to crane his head back to see up to that face. He could see up her nose. Nasty—nasty in there. She wasn't particularly warty, but her skin looked as rough and bark-like as the roof she lived under. Before being too critical of her awfulness, Martine made a quick assessment of his own state, as he was aware that, with all the foreign substances on his person, he must look pretty awful himself.

Martine was rather surprised when the old woman greeted him with an almost eerie sense of recognition and enthusiasm, and invited him in. She pulled the door closed behind them. Inside he saw three giant metal pots hanging over a large open fireplace and a similar pot, across the room, still producing steam, sitting atop a large, rectangular wooden block. In the center of the room was a heavy wooden table with a set of legs that seemed inadequate for maintaining support of the tabletop. There were a few other heavy iron pots hanging from hooks in various places around the one-room house. The fireplace occupied one entire wall of the house, extending into the room with no defined edge. Apparently the chimney was not functioning so steam and smoke just rose up and filtered through the holes in the ceiling. The smell of it all was so heinous that Martine had to consciously suppress the urge to "spray the Peezil," an expression, invented by classmates, that still lingered in his memory through the years. It had been so long since he had eaten anything substantial that it wasn't all that difficult to hold back.

It was a great relief when the old hag offered him some bread and a carrot (and not "whatever it was" bubbling in those big pots). As he devoured the modest dinner—it was now getting very late—she made him some tea, his bottle of wine all but forgotten. While he rested in a hard wooden chair, she officiously fussed over the three boiling pots, glancing his way every now and then. As he started feeling drowsy she began chuckling and he imagined hearing her leak out some overt laughter as he dozed off entirely.

Even though the potion she had given him had made him unconscious, he had a brief dream where the old hag was dressed in a man's suit, her hair pulled back into a frizzy ponytail. She was doing some kind of weird squatting exercise with her arms outstretched. On her chest was a nametag that read "Boogie-Boogie!" This woke him up with a shock. And as he regained consciousness, he found himself tied to the chair with a length of stout rope. On one of her frequent glances toward him, she noticed that he was now awake.

While the fog in his head was clearing she began looking him over and sizing him up. Once, without uttering a word, she came over to him and slapped him lightly on his cheek a few times with the tips of her fingers. Martine recoiled from her touch.

As he looked around the room from this new angle he saw two things that grabbed his full attention. One was a high shelf in the corner of the room. On the shelf were a number of tiny human skulls. He could not see them all but it looked like there were approximately seventeen! Near that shelf he saw another, lower shelf. This one had only one item on it. It was the treasured item he had been searching for: the Sapphire Duck! Filled with delight about spotting the Duck he was able to briefly dismiss from his mind the distinct and horrifying possibility that those skulls belonged to his former classmates.

Now that he was fully conscious, the tall old hag creaked her way over to him and said, in a weak and gravelly voice, "You don't recognize me, do you? Well, you shouldn't. But I recognize you! Number one, you were whisked away from the school before I could get my bony little mitts on you. Number two, you were whisked away from me when that rescue party found you, probably because the dogs were attracted to that accursed Sapphire Duck. And now you have come here, of your *own* accord. Glorious! Fate is *glorious*! I wonder if you'll taste as sweet now that you are big and tough. If not, then you are truly worthless. You are, however, aged meat. So that's one on the plus side. Oh, glorious fate!"

Martine had some serious objections to this plan as he began to struggle against his bondage. When she turned her attention back to her boiling pots, Martine became aware that, although his hands were tied, he was only bound to the chair around his chest, leaving his legs free. The chair was much too heavy for him to make any kind of mad dash for the door so he contemplated standing up and attacking her bodily. In sorting all this out, Martine was grateful for his gift of cleverness. But while he was congratulating himself, she began sharpening the twin-edged meat axe she had taken from his belt while he was unconscious. It made an ominous metallic singing sound as she ran the stone sharpener across each blade.

Martine was prompted into desperate action by these new developments. Planning to leap across the room and ram her into the wall, Martine quickly stood up. When he did, he hit his head sharply on one of the overhanging metal pots—he hadn't noticed the pot before. The ringing of the metal pot was nothing compared to the ringing in Martine's head as he staggered around from the blow. The pot had become somewhat dislodged from its hook, teetering, and was still swinging to and fro after the blow it took from Martine's head. Alerted to Martine's failed attempt by the vibrating sound of the pot, the old woman rushed to re-secure Martine while he was still reeling. As she forced him back into a sitting position, she brushed against the swinging pot, dislodging it completely. The heavy pot came crashing down on her, flattening her on the floor.

Amazingly, she was able to get back to her feet, but, while she was staggering around, Martine became clearheaded enough to lower his head like a bull, and, charging forward, chair and all, he gave her a massive head butt to the body. The blow rolled her over her preparation area (the big wooden block), spilling out the warm, viscous contents of that large pot, and mixing the old hag in with some yellow-brown meal, caustic syrup, and several oily liquids that were now spilled out all over the place. As Martine attempted to ram her a second time, she slipped out of the way causing him to hit the big unsteady table, upending it. This flipped over a large, beat-up metal bowl containing a gooey mixture of a very different color. That mixture landed on Martine, covering a sizable area of his body. It was oh so sticky and oh so bitter. Backing away from him in quick tiny steps and planning her next assault, the old hag inadvertently backed all the way into the fireplace, setting her raggedy clothing on fire; her smock and skin began smoldering and burning. The room already smelled horrendous even without these new additions. One can only imagine.

With her clothing on fire, her rib cage crushed, and her dinner running rampant around her one-room cottage, she let out a blood-curdling scream in an absolute frenzy, "Zhakey-kleesen!" The flames were cooking her backside as she went over and grabbed Martine, who was still attached to the chair. They wrestled as a threesome on the floor: Martine, chair, hag. In one instance, the mayhem rattled the wooden shelf supports, detaching the upper shelf, and distributing the set of small skulls all over that end of the room. The rolling around of the wrestling trio soon extinguished the hag's fire leaving the back half of her leathery, charred body exposed. As the two adversaries stood up together, they began a unified surge that ended with the whole group slamming against the stone wall of the cottage, totally disintegrating the chair and loosening the restraints on Martine's hands. Martine, now separated from the chair and lying on the floor out of view of the old hag, discovered the twin-edged meat axe that had fallen from the table in the melee. He surreptitiously got hold of the axe and as she came at him with a heavy metal spoon, coming in for the kill, he wielded the axe right smack into the top of her forehead.

[Note: It was very well centered!]

Although it had penetrated firmly and squarely into her skull, she didn't seem to be particularly harmed by the injury, and, strangely enough, seemed to be completely ignoring the axe altogether. Thinking fast, Martine was able to position the heavy tilted table between himself and the old woman. She was having a little trouble moving about because of the axe that was hanging out of her forehead. For a few moments they played cat and mouse on opposite sides of the table, but as Martine's movements brought him near to the door of the cottage he was able to push it open and jump outside. The old hag, seeing that he was outside and wanting to keep him from getting away, vigorously moved the table out of the way and made an awkward leap for the door, axe and all. At that moment, Martine vigorously slammed the door into her face. Hearing a *whump* on the other side, Martine waited and listened for any other sound that might be emanating from the house. Alternately starting and stopping with tiny motions he carefully pulled the heavy, creaking door open. The old hag had hit the door, face first, driving the twin-edged meat axe truly into her brain and turning her head into a Y-shaped kind of structure. The meat axe had one edge stuck in her head and the other edge stuck deeply into the door causing her half-exposed body to hang in a weird kind of arch. When Martine saw her in this absurd state he exclaimed at her in a consciously provocative and contemptuous way, "Zhakey-kleesen to you too, you old hag!" There she was, gurgling, suspended in the doorway, as Martine began gathering his wits and assessing his situation.

He was now fully aware that the old hag had been the one who had stolen the Sapphire Duck from him all those years ago. She had probably taken it as compensation for having to hastily abandon him as the rescue party was, at that point, very close to finally finding him. He had miraculously avoided the fate of the other seventeen. Carrying the Duck, she disappeared into the woods as the rescuers, discovering the young Martine, began shouting and making all sorts of noise. Their chaotic, random search had finally hit paydirt. Of course the rescue party took way more credit than they deserved, dogs included.

Now the old hag was dead, dead! She must be—she must have been—the dreaded boogie-boogie! Returning to the interior of the house and carefully avoiding her body he made his way over to the lower shelf and took down the wondrous Sapphire Duck. Martine's heart was pounding as he examined it. It was truly a work of art—translucent, blue, exquisite, and elegant in its detail. Clutching the Duck tightly in his fist, he now felt a pressing need to get out of the woods quickly and find his way home.

[Extensive Note: The Sapphire Duck was commissioned long ago by some forgotten but wealthy king of some kingdom somewhere, sometime way back, and was sculpted by a deformed and infirm alchemist whose last act on earth was putting the final touches on the little Duck. One day, while traipsing through the undergrowth, the alchemist found a chunk of glowing, translucent stone that had fallen from the sky. When he showed it to the king, the king tasked the alchemist to carve the stone into an animal. The finished sculpture was originally supposed to be a melon-sized charging bull (in honor of the king). But the alchemist was not particularly experienced at sculpting. So after several carving mistakes, the stone had to become a fierce fox, then a proud eagle. The mistakes accumulated and the stone became smaller and smaller. It eventually had to be sculpted into a small duck. In the end, it turned out very well in spite of the errors. In a symbolic sense, one might make the observation, "Just like Martine." As the alchemist took his last few breaths on Earth and in order to secure his own legacy, he attempted to instill a set of magical powers in the Duck. Sadly, since the alchemist was in such poor condition, the powers and abilities were of somewhat questionable value: the power to talk backwards, the ability to see through food, the ability to eat tree bark, an aura that attracts dogs—an aura that attracts *dogs*. In addition, the Duck could detect lies and would vibrate when in the vicinity of someone who was lying. Perhaps the most valuable and long-lasting power of the Duck was to imbue its owner with a special quality causing a listener to believe anything the owner said.]

Leaving the ramshackle house, again avoiding the dripping arch made of dead hag, Martine sensed the arrival of dawn. Not really all that surprised, he saw, from the corner of his eye, that silly naked woman standing near the wall of the house. She had been watching him, as best she could, through the window.

"I see you found your Sapphire Duck you stupid little roach," she uttered in her now familiar tone. Martine quickly shoved the Duck into his pocket—out of sight.

Not really wanting to engage her again, but asking anyway, "What sort of a place is this, this area of the woods? That rampaging horde of hares. A violent one-legged clay man. The old hag. You! You lying, fake angel!"

She replied, in a very dismissive way, "It's all just your imagination, including me!" The second she began her reply the Duck in Martine's pocket began vibrating. Martine didn't notice the vibrating Duck and consciously avoided eye contact with the naked woman. But he began wondering aloud, "What is Aunt Eileen going to think when she sees what a mess I have become?"

Hearing Martine's words spoken to himself, the eavesdropping naked woman, unsolicited, responded sarcastically, "Don't worry. You look fine. She'll never notice." Again, the Duck started vibrating.

Still trying to avoid looking directly at the naked woman, Martine *cleverly* asked, "Do you know the way back to the meadow?"

"Yes!" she replied. "It's that way." She pointed confidently toward the thicket near the old hag's house. Again the wondrous Sapphire Duck started vibrating.

Martine's question was clever because he surmised that whatever direction the naked woman indicated, the meadow was probably in the opposite direction. And that was the direction he took. The Sapphire Duck had no bearing on Martine's decision.

"You're going the wrong way!" she protested.

Without looking back and without saying a thing, Martine raised his hand in a half-hearted wave and continued walking away, still not particularly mindful of the power of his Sapphire Duck.

Turning her attention away from the departing Martine, the naked woman became filled with curiosity about the old hag's house. She went to the front door of the house and slowly peeked into the room through the partially open doorway. Being a strange forest creature herself, she was not particularly alarmed (or surprised) at seeing the old hag's split head attached to the wooden door with the twin-edged meat axe—one edge in the head and one edge embedded in the door.

Carefully stepping around the dead hag, the naked woman worked her way through the doorway and into the house. Once inside, she studied the room and found the whole thing a real curiosity. The old hag that was attached to the door was covered with syrup and yellow meal. Her body was half-burnt and half-dressed. The naked woman looked over the rest of the room, fascinated: boiling pots of mysterious liquids; spilt fluids everywhere; tables and chairs in disarray; a collection of small skulls scattered about the floor; flour, meal, and other materials strewn about all over the room. It reminded the naked woman of many peculiar and unexplainable situations from her own "youth." Whatever the naked woman was, she was quite a package.

Night had turned to day and Martine walked along briskly in the cool morning air of the woods. As noon approached, the sun began peeking out of the clouds. Martine had come to the edge of the woods and into the meadow. At this location he was much closer to the remains of the old school than when he entered the woods the day before. Were all of his experiences just an imaginary mind trip as the naked woman had suggested? He began crossing the meadow where he could see the flattened path that remained after the horde of wild hares had beaten down the wildflowers. At least that part was real. The Sapphire Duck in his pocket was real. The casing of filth and foreign matter on his body was real. The residual image of that mass of wild scrambling hares reminded him of the end of a weekly assembly at school when his fellow students all made for the exits in a mad rush.

By mid-afternoon Martine arrived at the house where he and his Aunt Eileen lived. She had begun to seriously worry about him but up to that point she was reluctant to ask for help, knowing that it would instigate a big, undesirable, hubbub. She had faith that Martine could take care of himself. Despite his appearance, she warmly welcomed him home without criticism because she had always unconditionally loved him as if he were her own.

Martine could not bring himself to believe that all of his experiences were just his imagination; there was just too much concrete evidence to the contrary. Martine no longer wanted to adhere to his policy of keeping these odd experiences to himself. Over the following weeks the stories of his encounters, believed by everyone, raised his stature in the community. Being unobservant, Martine had no idea that the Duck was giving him a limitless amount of credibility. This was fortunate since, had he known, he might have allowed his life to become corrupted—he might have become a politician, a door-to-door salesman, a con-man, or some other kind of charlatan. All Martine knew was that the Duck was a good thing. He kept it with him at all times, cherishing it, for the rest of his life.

It might be worth mentioning that, in their many travels together, Martine and his Aunt Eileen had an opportunity to make their way to a zoo where Martine finally got to see a real-life wombat. It was not what Martine was expecting. How young people can get fixated on one thing or another is always a curiosity to an observing adult.

Martine, with his newly acquired abilities, was able to care for his Aunt Eileen for the rest of her life, just as she had cared for him those many years before. The woods were combed for any trace of the old hag's house. No trace was ever found. But there were always rumors about many other weird things going on in those woods.

[Note to the curious: The naked woman continued to fly around the woods, annoying anyone she met, posing as some kind of shameless angel, and lying her callused and sometimes bark-impregnated ass off. This she did until a monstrous land development ate into her neck of the woods and drove her out...out on that very same ass.]

After all was said and done, Martine believed that it was well worth the effort and risk to search for the wondrous Sapphire Duck. So many times he had come close to death and miraculously stumbled his way out of it, Sapphire Duck notwithstanding. Perhaps it was the power of the Duck, perhaps not. But maybe, just maybe the Sapphire Duck wouldn't have made any difference since Martine was a very clever (if unobservant) person.

So there.

[Note to the fastidious, curious, and patient observers: Thank you for your attention.]

# Late Knight

This story old, I now relate.
No killer, thief, nor reprobate,
But valiant knight with sword held high
To lance the boil, to drain the stye,
And chase all evil from the land.

Young and brave on mighty steed,
He searched the land for one in need
And once upon a new day dawning,
While he stretched his arms out, yawning,
Came a blue bird with some news,

"'Cross hill and dale, across the sea,
A maiden fair as fair can be
Imprisoned in the Black Knight's tower
And destined now to lose her flower.
I come to show the way."

The valiant knight upon his steed
The little blue bird he did heed.
So fast the knight, so fast was he
He did not sink into the sea
And safely rode ashore.

"What ho!" the knight yelled 'neath the wall.
"I've come to fight you, one and all.
To pluck the maiden from your hand
And take her from this awful land.
O Black Knight hear my call."

But to the valiant knight's chagrin
Only silence from within.
When then appeared atop the wall
A sentry who had heard the call
And to the knight he spoke,

"I deign to tell you if I can
You cannot carry out your plan.
The lot of them have gone away
Yet it be just yesterday.
So, be off! O tardy one."

No barking dog, no pompous cock,
Just the wind to foil the shock.
"I cannot now defend her honor.
'Twas my reward to be upon her.
Alas, alas too late."

The knight he gazed into the skies
And thereupon, to his surprise
The blue bird he had met before
And led him to this evil shore,
Approached him once again.

"Far away a band of gnomes
Is stealing babies from their homes.
The gnomes will eat them once they're cooked;
No tiny tissue overlooked.
Make haste O valiant knight."

"Lead on!" the knight said, sword in hand.
"Lead me to that horrid land.
Grateful mothers, babes in arms
Will want to sample all my charms.
And I shall treat them well."

And to the foreign land he flew.
Nothing of that land he knew.
A campfire seen in woods so deep;
Across the ground the knight did creep,
Toward the band of gnomes.

The knight burst in, and mayhem started.
Gnomes stood up, and burped, and farted.
One by one the gnomes were beaten;
But woe! Long since, the babies eaten.
Sad knight, too late, again.

"Here, one by one, these gnomes I've killed
And yet my manhood, unfulfilled.
What sour notes that blue bird sings.
What perfidy its message brings.
And here it comes again..."

"The fault lies not in what I say.
The burden's yours if you delay.
Yet another maiden fair
Lies trembling in a dragon's lair;
And I shall lead the way."

The blue bird flew, the brave knight followed
Sword in hand, and pride thus swallowed.
O'er frozen bridge and desert sand
Snow-capped peak and barren land
The knight rode on and on.

As sunlight waned and north wind blew
The dragon's lair came into view.
Without delay the knight rode in
As if he led a thousand men—
And there addressed the dragon,

"What ho! O Dragon, eyes so red,
I have come to strike you dead...
And save yon maiden hidden there...
And take her from your haunted lair...
And grateful she will be."

The dragon breathed a fiery blast
And to the knight said, "Not so fast!
You may look here all you want.
There is no maiden in my haunt.
Not since yesterday."

No maiden for the knight that day,
A merchant carried her away.
Paid the dragon two pounds gold—
One fair maiden bought and sold.
The brave knight was dismayed.

"What cruelty, the hand of fate
Has me arrive a day too late.
I sought not gold nor hoards of treasure
Just a grateful maiden's pleasure
To satisfy my loins of youth.

"What addled fool or silly dunce
Cannot arrive in time, just once?
And if that bird should here return
I'll light it up and watch it burn;
And feast upon the charred remains."

Seven days went quickly by.
The knight rode where the earth meets sky;
And as the knight had stopped to rest
The blue bird landed on his chest
And appealed to him again,

"I bring sad tidings from a town
Where from the earth all orange and brown
Molten rock with hell's own wrath
Destroys all things along its path—
A town where doom is nigh.

"O valiant knight, O please make haste
Before the town is laid to waste.
Follow me and don't delay
The town is just a mile away."
The knight stood firm and fast.

"The town is full of maidens fair
And you must save their derriere."
The knight did not believe a word
And with his sword he chased the bird,
Unknowingly toward the town.

High upon a wooded hill
Knight and sword, intent to kill.
His missed the bird and cleaved a tree.
The blue bird watched quite silently.
The tree came tumbling down.

"Why do you taunt me, bird from hell?
'Tis you or fate I cannot tell.
And now up here above the town,
I've cut this massive poplar down.
And to what end, what end?"

As he spoke the tree rolled down,
Down the hill and toward the town
Uprooting trees along the way,
An avalanche as some would say.
It all came crashing down.

As molten rock met avalanche
And seared each trunk and every branch
The fiery mass of rock cooled down
And stopped a hundred feet from town
And never rose again.

The valiant knight of twenty years
Rode in to town 'midst shouts and cheers.
From maidens fair with hearts on fire
He finally got his loins' desire.
And savored it with grace.

# The Layout
*A Novelette*

---

## Chapter 1 – Rot and Roll

It was a time of war when Rolf was packed off to the States, away from Europe, away from the conflict; packed off by his aunt and his uncle, Mërt and Gustav von Wartenstahl. They had graciously taken him in after his natural parents were hauled away in the dead of night, escorted by men; men in uniforms; men filled with purpose. Taking Rolf in was mostly an act of duty. Duty and war: both part of the same package in those days.

Living with his aunt and uncle for those many months, Rolf was just beginning to learn about life. Although Rolf's exact age was unknown at the time, his foster parents figured he must be about thirteen based on the number of permanent teeth he had going. His aunt Mërt was an unabashed nudist, while his uncle, Gustav, was involved in a number of illicit activities, the most important (lucrative) being the smuggling of various desirable and popular items in and out of nearby Hungary. They all lived together peaceably enough in a comfortable house in the small rural town of Rotfleisch, Austria—the nearest sizeable town was Wiener Neustadt about 25 miles south of Vienna. Every evening at dinnertime, Rolf would sit quietly, slowly eating his meal, while a grumbling Gustav pored over the "books" right there at the dinner table. Rolf's eyes would discreetly and cautiously move from Gustav's wire-rimmed reading glasses—perched at the end of his (Gustav's) nose—across the table to Mërt's large and wonderfully-shaped, exposed breasts. The vision would completely dominate Rolf's thoughts as his thirteen-year-old body responded with an uncontrollable vigor that Rolf was just beginning to understand and appreciate.

As the war (The Big War) came rolling on in, Gustav and Mërt felt that Rolf would be better off alone in the States than he would ever be in Rotfleisch if, sooner or later, the conflict landed directly on their doorstep. So off went Rolf to America—a traveling adventure filled with unknowns; an adventure that was unenthusiastically undertaken by the young, Rolf Hauswasser.

Rolf's first contact in America was with an immigration officer named Yulis Packer who kept referring to Rolf as Roll Mauswasser. It was an error traceable to the semi-illegible handwritten name on Rolf's immigration documents (not uncommon). Rolf had no way of knowing about the administrative error since he spoke no English; but he did wonder why everyone was calling him Mr. Mauswasser or Rolly or Rollo.

Soon, Rolf (a.k.a. Roll Mauswasser) found himself assigned to an American sponsor family, Abigail and Juliet Pease, two kindhearted sisters who lived together and had, years ago, taken in and raised three other immigrant children. Living with the sisters, Rolf muddled through his teenage years, learning English and learning free enterprise. But, sadly, there were no breasts to be had at dinnertime. In fact, Mom Abigail and Mom Juliet seemed to be particularly skillful at keeping their breasts hidden from him at all times. Strange new culture, this—this America.

From the start, the two sisters referred to him as Little Rolly, a name that he seriously did not like, but he was not in a position to object. They made sure he got proper schooling; difficult at first, but he picked up English fairly quickly. They also tried to instill in him a sense of religion, but religion was a cultural phenomenon that Rolf responded to with complete indifference. He was more interested in some of the grey areas of life in the States—things that were not especially legal. He became street smart and developed a strong instinct for survival, so he was able to avoid any legal repercussions from his engagement in questionable "activities." Just as the sisters kept their breasts hidden from Rolf, Rolf kept his illicit enterprises hidden from the sisters.

By the time Rolf's teenage years came to an end, he had accumulated enough money to strike out and be on his own. He was grateful to the two sisters but, eventually, the time came for him to leave home and make his way on his own. He had developed a healthy network of "contacts" and that allowed him to become quite a self-sufficient operator; so he was able to set up his own place, a modest high-rise apartment in the Big City.

Making a fresh start in the awesome Big City, he felt compelled to do something about his name; he wanted to fit in, to blend in, to become a true American. He decided to drop the names "Rolf" and "Rolly" and so he replaced them with a truly great American first name, "Dominic." In deference and gratitude to his two sister Moms he took their last name as his middle one, "Pease." Wanting to retain at least a tiny amount of his heritage, Rolf took as his surname the English form of his documented last name (Mauswasser). Thus Little Rolly Mauswasser became, legally, Dominic Pease Mousewater. And that is where this story begins.

## Chapter 2 – Family, Business

It wasn't long before Dominic began moving up in the hierarchy of racketeers, purveyors of illicit substances, and other underworld sub-culture groups; but the associated violence was becoming too much of an unacceptable, occupational hazard. So he decided to settle on something he learned about from his Uncle Gustav's activities, something more familiar and less risky: smuggling. He started up a smuggling niche far removed from established organized crime syndicates and built a successful (and cleverly disguised) business that far surpassed that of his Uncle Gustav. Through back channels and his elaborate smuggling network, Dominic was able to traffic in unstamped Turkish cigarettes, pickled eggs, exotic birds, possum-meat sausages posing as chicken, grey-market farm equipment, collector motorcycle knock-offs, counterfeit Cuban cigars, dummy guns, non-regulation (high explosive) fireworks, and many other items that were completely of the Black Market variety. Through all this Dominic became a wealthy man.

Along with his wealth came a deluge of hangers-on, parasites, and characters with nefarious designs on all his money. But there were plenty of women too. One woman in particular caught his fancy, a Mary Lou Galatea. Her breasts reminded him of Rotfleish and dinnertime. Unlike the hundreds of "associates" that were involved in Dominic's businesses, she had no particular agenda and no designs on his money. That appealed greatly to Dominic.

Dominic and Mary Lou were married soon after their first meeting and the couple began putting together a mixed bag of life. Mary Lou never questioned Dominic about his business and remained faithful to him the entire time they were together. Even though they were married and appreciated each other's company (in this way or that), they both had a strong sense of independence—all of it surrounded by Dominic's shadowy world of big money and big opportunity.

They had been married a scant nine months when Mary Lou bore Dominic a wiry, strong, boisterous son. They named him Brisbane, Brisbane Pease Mousewater. It was important to Dominic that his son have an American name. He mistakenly believed that *Brisbane* was a city "down under" in southern California. Mary Lou had never heard of the city of Brisbane. And Dominic did not recognize the irony in naming his son after a former penal colony in Australia.

Almost immediately, Brisbane was left in the care of others. Dominic had little time for rearing the young Brisbane. Dominic was spending all of his time building his businesses and rearing Mary Lou. Brisbane was not Mary Lou's primary concern either as she became increasingly obsessed with staying young and living the good life: plastic surgery, maintenance of a youthful appearance, massages, spa weekends, expensive quack anti-aging treatments, country club activities, social engagements, and extravagant shopping.

One day, as a carefree and sheltered Brisbane approached his fourteenth birthday, Mary Lou mysteriously disappeared and was never heard from again. The overly spoiled and undisciplined Brisbane being minimally affected by the disappearance, demanded, upon risk of an all-out tantrum, demanded that everyone proceed with his damn birthday party. Dominic was out of the country at the time and, hearing about Mary Lou's disappearance, hurried back about three weeks later. With such a large group of associates involved in Dominic's every move, rumors and speculations about Mary Lou were plentiful: she ran off with someone; she just ran off; she was roasted in a tanning bed; she was poisoned by some mysterious quack anti-aging drug; she became disfigured during her twentieth (or so) plastic surgery procedure; she disappeared as part of a plot; she became an integral part of the new Purdle Building's foundation; she was kidnapped (or worse) by a disgruntled business associate of Dominic's.

None of the many imaginative speculations were logical or feasible or true. And perhaps the least likely scenario of them all was one that included Dominic as somehow being involved in her disappearance. He had no motive and getting rid of her served no purpose. She was not unfaithful to him. Even so, long ago, Dominic had pushed aside romantic fervor in favor of the arousal brought on by lucrative merchandise arriving down at the dock—merchandise like a large palette of crates filled with untraceable tins of counterfeit Russian caviar. That was where Dominic's head was. That was where his heart was.

Brisbane's childhood as an overindulged free agent was, for the most part, uneventful—one might even say "ordinary" given the vast supplies of money and the constant presence of crime and no punishment. But there was one particularly memorable event in the young life of Brisbane that would have a lasting effect on him throughout his life.

Living in a multi-story mansion, Brisbane was used to climbing up and down stairways: the sprawling elaborate front staircase; the so-called "secret" back stairway; the tiny, narrow stairs to the attic; and several others. On that memorable day, many years before she disappeared, Mary Lou and an eight-year-old Brisbane were engaged in an extensive Christmas shopping spree at the Newbridge Mall. Most of the items they were buying were for themselves, but everything they bought was to be delivered to the estate, so they were not burdened with carrying all that merchandise around with them. Brisbane was very familiar and comfortable with stairways, but not moving stairways—i.e. escalators. Stepping onto the moving staircase was an unsettling action-adventure for him. Mary Lou had finished an exhaustive cleaning out of all the small, exclusive little designer boutiques—sub-shops on the second floor of a well-known, high-end department store. It was a department store whose business it was to cater to the needs, desires, and tastes of the *crème de la crème*.

As the highly-satisfied consumer, Mary Lou, and the tentative Brisbane stepped aboard the very tall "down" escalator to the first floor, Brisbane lost his footing and fell numerous steps, down, down, down the moving stairs, eventually being driven to the bottom. There, as the surface of the steps combed through them, the escalator's metal teeth cut several striations on Brisbane's forearms. Considering his age and spoiled nature, it was remarkable that he did not cry but emerged from the incident as a pissed-off youngster who had now acquired the first stages of a pathological fear of heights. Mary Lou helped him up, brushed off his shirt and pants, and the two of them left the area as if nothing ever happened. But memory of the event remained with Brisbane—even to the point where using the stairways in his father's mansion was no longer routine nor was it casual or taken for granted.

## Chapter 3 – The Good Life

As Brisbane "matured" into his twenties, his sense of entitlement kept him from achieving anything significant. He was but one of many living on Dominic's huge estate and spent all his days enjoying the fruits of his father's burgeoning success. Brisbane's ambient pursuits included the country club way of life: golf, tennis, swimming, lying about in the sun, indolence, giving critics the fish-eye. He had no athletic aptitude whatsoever so his engagement in any of the requisite and expected sporting activities was comical at best and embarrassing at worst. He did learn how to swim, but only at a level that would prevent him from drowning in an accident. On many occasions he preferred to go down to the marina and lounge about on his family's gigantic yacht. He had no maritime skills so he would just hang around the various decks and cabins doing nothing, listening to music, and sipping all the different alcoholic concoctions he could create with the blender in the galley. During this time Brisbane decided to shorten his name to something a little simpler: just "Bris," rhyming with "bliss." It had a certain "country club" feel to it.

Through all this splendor, Bris was able to develop and maintain a thin, fragile relationship with his father. And, in *spite* of all this splendor, Bris soon became a restless and bored young man. It took a nearly fatal "accident" to finally awaken a sense of reality in him.

It seems that his father, Dominic, got involved with some bullets that were flying around the loading docks one dark felonious night. While some of the "stray" bullets penetrated multiple wooden crates of counterfeit cigars, others found their way into Dominic's body. Heaven forbid that the bullets were actually meant for *him*. The incident left Dominic wheelchair bound and ornery as hell. There was talk that Dominic had "handled" the perpetrators of the violent incident in his usual silent and deadly way, but nothing ever came to light about any of it.

During his convalescence Dominic acquired a large dog, half Airedale and half Irish Setter. He named it Flemmy—Sneezy would have been an equally appropriate name albeit less graphic. When curled up on the floor the dog looked like a big rusted pile of steel wool. Dominic grew to love its companionship and the dog took ownership of Dominic as well. Flemmy's presence seemed to temper some of Dominic's orneriness, but not always.

Bris always had to brace himself against all that orneriness when dealing with Dominic. But, Bris realized that without his father's generation of cash flow there might be some difficulties and possibly actual work for himself in the future. Alas, it was a disturbing and unwelcome dose of reality. To his credit, Brisbane stepped up, maneuvered his way in, and helped Dominic manage the "business"—even though Brisbane's contributions were, for the most part, small and ordinary. Beyond the importation of products, Dominic's empire now included a number of parcels of undeveloped real estate, a few warehouses, and several retail store shells acquired at rock bottom prices. Bris was intrigued and impressed by the extent of his father's empire. With or without Bris's help, the strong-willed, street-hardened, and undeterred Dominic was determined to keep things going at a steady pace. He remained firmly in charge and unfortunately for Bris, Dominic still *owned* everything even though there was always plenty of money available for covering Bris's every indulgence.

Bris noticed that his newly-acquired, yet somewhat tenuous enlightened attitude was beginning to have a positive effect on his life. This mindset was to get further reinforced by a chance event; one where he fortuitously encountered a young woman named Rhonda Proody. It was a typical day down at the marina except for the fact that Bris, instead of drinking and idling about, was actually at work securing several loose storage bins and doing a few maintenance tasks on the family's yacht. While fumbling around on the open deck, he happened to notice Rhonda, sunbathing, face down, on the "boat next door." He had never seen her before. Unfortunately, his swirling fantasies were rudely stifled when a burly goofball emerged from the other yacht's cabin and began stroking Rhonda's bare back. In response to the goofball's touch, she abruptly lifted herself up with a start. Bris was attracted to her immediately. Across the gap between the two yachts she saw the smiling, bug-eyed Bris holding a big storage bin in his arms. As he looked over at her, looking her over, she coyly smiled back at him, showing him an unexpected amount of interest. Then, stepping down into the cabin below, she covered herself with her towel while the burly goofball stood by as if a schoolyard bully had just taken away his favorite ball.

A short time later the burly goofball took off with three of his crude friends for an afternoon of beer and loud, forced laughter. An ironic side note is worth mentioning. On the wooden deck of the outdoor marina café, far away from Bris and Rhonda, the quartet sat around, adrift in a beer fog, each one of the group puffing on a big, thick, dark brown Cuban Chiba-Chiba cigar. They were pontificating on the quality flavor of such fine, rare, and expensive cigars even though the nearby café customers were extremely repulsed by the horrific smell of the so-called "fine" cigars; a smell that was likened to a combination of burning tires, burning hair, and smoldering sweat socks. Unbeknownst to the goofball's group, these "fine" cigars just happened to be some of Dominic Mousewater's imported counterfeits and were probably *made* from tire rubber, hair, and sweat socks (with a few toxic Turkish tobacco leaves thrown in as binder material).

While this unsavory group was getting a generous dose of rubbery chemical smoke and tar, Bris and Rhonda were getting to know each other at the opposite end of the marina—getting to know each other well—their two boats rhythmically floating up and down, up and down, side by side; port and starboard sides touching and bumping together; eventually the two reaching a point of "anchors aweigh."

Rhonda turned out to be Bris's true soul mate. Just like Bris, she would someday come into some money of her own. For the present, though, she had been content to hang around with other characters of the local "jet set" purely out of convenience and laziness. Rhonda and Bris had similar outlooks on life, similar philosophies, and similar priorities. But each of them also had difficulty with uncontrollable obsessive tendencies. These tendencies could raise such a powerful level of fixated tunnel vision that logic, context, consequences, and proportionality would be utterly cast, like so many powdery snowflakes, into the wind. Together, as willing co-enablers, their uncontrolled fixations would sooner or later begin to resonate harmoniously and, in one case, eventually spiral out of control.

With Rhonda and Bris, there was no courtship; none was required. There were no games, no cat and mouse. Rhonda and Bris knew they were made for each other. They knew how to get the most out of big money and how to indulge every whim—now with the added delight of sharing it all, together. They knew what they wanted: more of the same and plenty of it; now, together, the two of them, as a team. In spite of all this pleasantry and compatibility, they both knew there was an unavoidable storm cloud ever-present on the horizon, a monumental challenge that they, sooner or later, would have to face and overcome: Dominic Pease Mousewater.

## Chapter 4 – Cutting to the Chase

As life, business, and romance continued on, another chance encounter introduced Bris to a young freelance writer named Anthony Hill. Anthony and Bris were about the same age. Most of Anthony Hill's work was in interviewing celebrities (on spec) and selling the stories to whoever would publish them. He also had a semi-regular column/feature with his own by line (*The Ant Hill* by Anthony Hill) that could be found in the local second-tier "newspaper," *The Expossiere*. In his column Anthony provided short, bullet-point blurbs containing many of the juiciest tidbits that he happened to run across during his interviews and research. As he was attempting to get an interview with Dominic Pease Mousewater, head of Mousewater Enterprises, he met Bris. Upon learning that Bris was Dominic's son, Anthony reasoned that Bris might be a conduit in getting an interview with the big boss, the mysterious entrepreneur about whom little was known. Instead, he and Bris hit it off and became good friends—the idea of an interview with Dominic was passed over and forgotten. Brisbane Pease Mousewater and Anthony Hill: it was a friendship that would last a lifetime. It was a strange set of events that bonded together two such unlikely characters—a naïve overindulged rich idler and a semi-moralistic and highly literate professional writer. Perhaps Anthony saw a glimmer of hope for Bris since, outwardly, Bris had begun to display a few traces of responsible fortitude.

Over the weeks that followed, Rhonda and Brisbane got to know each other (inside and out) and their plans to get married became more of a reality. All the while, the dark Dominic cloud hovered over them, building, threatening. The happy couple had no way to predict how ornery old Dominic was going to react so they hid their relationship from him as best they could. During this time, Bris's relationship with Anthony also grew stronger, so Anthony was becoming a familiar face around the Mousewater estate as well. Dominic had seen Anthony numerous times and was getting curious about who he was and what he was doing with Brisbane. Dominic was conjuring up all kinds of thoughts, mostly phobic and prejudicial.

On one particular visit, Anthony took Bris aside and the two of them sat on the couch in the living room, behind closed doors. Anthony started, "I know we've known each other for only a few months, but I feel like we've become good friends..."

Bris was becoming uncomfortable and Anthony, uncharacteristically, was grasping for the right words. "You know me...pretty well. Before me, have you ever had a Jewish friend, Bris?" Anthony asked.

"I don't believe so; I don't know," replied Bris with a nervous sense of anticipation in his voice.

"Well, I need to tell you something..." Anthony continued.

Several minutes later, conversation over, the two men emerged from the living room. Rhonda, who had been waiting patiently, was also getting a little bit nervous. Brisbane, with a curious but determined look on his face, announced the he had made a decision—that he would now like to be called "Rip" instead of "Bris."

And that was the nickname he would use the rest of his life. Rip (formerly Bris) came up with it and Anthony gave it his tepid approval—way better than "Bris." Such was the nature of their strengthening friendship; Anthony seemed to be a source of reason and reality in Rip's world of shady enterprises, insulated cultural ignorance, and waterfalls of money. Getting Rhonda to make the change wasn't difficult at all. And Rip's father, Dominic, always called him "Brisbane," so the transition wasn't too awkward or messy. More importantly, the experience alerted Rip to his own lack of knowledge about many things in the outside world. It taught him to move more cautiously and carefully. And except for one monumental exception, the lesson served him well in managing his life and in helping to run his father's business. Oh, but that exception…

## Chapter 5 – The Pre-Nup

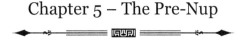

One dismal Tuesday afternoon, in a pit of nervous tension, Rip and Rhonda were preparing to approach Dominic with their plans for marriage. They were standing in the entryway area next to the elaborate stairway to the second floor. Hearing the doorbell, both Rip and Rhonda jumped. It was Anthony. Anthony had arrived at the mansion just in time. He had come to lend moral support.

"Have you seen him yet?" inquired Anthony, his presence helping to calm the nervous couple.

"We were just about to go up there," Rip replied.

"Well, go get 'em," Anthony said as he sat down casually in an uncomfortable, decorative, and fragile chair there in the entryway, opening a magazine he had brought with him. "And good luck!"

"Thanks," the couple said as they proceeded (slowly) up the staircase toward Dominic's room and whatever doom was about to be unleashed. A lot of love and a lot of money were riding on this encounter. Anthony waited patiently in the entryway as the two disappeared into the upstairs hallway.

"You wait here," Rip told Rhonda as they stood in the dimly lit hallway outside Dominic's room. Rip slowly opened the door and went in. Dominic, in his wheelchair, was sitting by his personal fireplace, staring into the flames like a spell-casting wizard making the flames go up and down. Next to him, sitting on the floor was his faithful dog Flemmy chewing on a thick, soggy log of rawhide.

"Brisbane. Who was that at the door?" Dominic said in a very paternal tone.

"It was just Anthony," Rip replied innocently.

"Well, what do you want?" Dominic asked, now with a measure of unwarranted impatience in his voice.

Rip stood silent for a moment. "Well, sir, I want to get married."

Dominic was in complete control of the awkward silence that followed. Something was heavy on his mind.

"No shit...what a shocker," Dominic finally said, breaking the silence as he motored his way over toward Rip at the door. For a moment, Rip thought Dominic was planning to run him down. Rhonda quickly backed further into the hallway in order to remain out of sight. Flemmy, interested, looked toward the door but didn't get up.

"Yes, we're..." Rip turned to grab Rhonda, but she had moved out of reach, forcing him to go into the hall to retrieve her. In the meantime, Dominic was backing up and mumbling epithets. Rip dragged a terrified Rhonda to the door and the tussle between the two of them caused them both to stumble into the room in front of Dominic and his wheel chair.

As Rip and Rhonda stood up, Dominic responded with, "Who the hell is this?"

"This is Rhonda," Rip replied. "We want to get married."

"Holy meatloaf Jesus on a stick!" Dominic uttered. Rip and Rhonda were paralyzed, but determined. Then, to their puzzlement, Dominic asked, "Where is that Anthony person?"

"He's downstairs in the entryway," answered Rip looking around with a bewildered expression on his face.

As for Dominic, perhaps it was the fact that Rhonda resembled his aunt Mërt or perhaps—

To make a long story short, the wedding and the celebration took place only three weeks later, all with Dominic's blessing and financing. It was big, but not ostentatious. Anthony's steady influence may have been a factor in keeping the whole affair under control. It wouldn't be the last time that Anthony's voice of reason would have to prevail. But there would also be times...

Before Rip and Rhonda took off for their superfluous honeymoon at a luxurious hotel suite in the Big City, Dominic had the happy couple join him in his study. Dominic wanted to present the newlyweds with a wedding gift.

"Come in you two, and close the door behind you," he ordered. He motored his way over to his desk where he took out a large envelope containing a number of papers. Handing the topmost set of papers to Rip, Dominic started, "This is the deed to a piece of property; rectangular, thirty-two acres of fairly flat, wooded land near the Big City. It's surrounded on three sides by some prime real estate with lots of hills. The other side is near the Highway 111 turnpike that runs in to the Big City. The two of you can build yourselves a house there on that property."

Dominic then handed Rhonda a second piece of paper: a check. "This is enough for you to begin construction on your house."

Rhonda took the check. "Thank you," she said as Dominic pulled out another sheet of paper from the envelope.

"This last piece of paper is a list of contractors that you should use to build the place. That architect listed there at the top will help you all along the way. He knows everyone on that list. They all *owe* me in one way or another, so they will give you a good price for the work. You can count on that."

Rip and Rhonda didn't know what to say. They graciously thanked him and as Rip opened the door to the study, Dominic made a not-so-subtle reference to progeny, following them out with his wheelchair motor a-hummin'.

## Chapter 6 – Genesis

There was plenty to do in the months following the wedding. Rhonda had been maintaining a penthouse suite in the Big City. She and her four siblings (who lived in Another Big City) were sharing equally in a trust set up by their late parents. Nobody in the group of five was to inherit anything from the bulk of the estate unless each one of the other four siblings became defunct. But Rhonda's share of the trust money provided plenty as far as Rhonda was concerned. Now that she was going to be living with Rip in their new house, she no longer needed the condo. But, before selling it, Rip and Rhonda would live there while their new house was being built. Rip had also been living on a trust fund so they were quite comfortable during the transition period.

First, they set up a meeting with the architect identified at the top of Dominic's contractor list: Peaberry Shortly of *Shortly, Naver, Moore, and Tardy*. Shortly was a highly skilled architect who knew all the ins and outs of getting his creations built. Equally important, he was indebted to Dominic in several ways; debt items that shall remain...undisclosed. It was Dominic's thumb pressure that Shortly was under, not Rip or Rhonda's. But Shortly did not have enough throw-weight to contradict, re-direct, or massage any of Rip or Rhonda's wishes—what they wanted, they got (for a while). So the three of them met and started to work on the layout.

At the wedding reception, at the time, the check from Dominic seemed huge. But now, slowly accumulating, there were many not-so-hidden expenses in making the dream home a reality: permit fees, site excavation costs, road-building (driveway) costs, architect fees, utility installations, and many others. There were also a few "hidden" costs that Shortly was taking care of behind the scenes with several city planners, inspectors, and bureaus. It was the way things got done in the Mousewater world.

"What's going to be built on all this land here?" Rhonda asked Shortly, pointing to the site map. She was referring to the area surrounding their property on three of the four sides.

"I don't know if *anything* is going to be built there any time soon. Those hills are owned by a consortium of developers and investors who have done nothing with it in the seven or eight years since they took over that property," Shortly replied.

"So nothing there will affect our layout?" Rip asked.

"No. Not at all," Shortly replied. "Now, let's look these numbers over. You have the driveway from the highway's frontage road, all the utilities, land clearing costs, fees, permits..." Shortly was mumbling as he focused his attention on the spreadsheet printout. Then, pointing to the bottom line on the sheet, Shortly said, "So, this is how much we'll have left for the house itself." Shortly handed Rip the piece of paper with the final figure shown at the bottom of the page. It was still a substantial amount, but far less than Rhonda or Rip had envisioned for the big mansion they had in mind.

Over the next two weeks, Rip and Rhonda met with Shortly almost on a daily basis, adding a room here, moving around rooms here and there, and modifying each and every small detail in the slowly ripening fruit of their labor—their layout. Occasionally Anthony would accompany them to a meeting, but for the most part he kept his opinions to himself. Version after version of the blueprints were scrutinized and marked up. A stack of paper, eighteen or more inches high, representing discarded blueprints, notes, and ideas was the only real evidence of progress on the project.

Finally, on a bright and windy September day, Rip and Rhonda Mousewater, under the guidance of architect Peaberry Shortly, finalized a plan that everyone was happy with. Although there was a lot of paperwork involved before construction could begin, the process was simplified by the fact that the entire project would be paid for with cash. Once all the papers were signed, construction began almost immediately. Shortly would handle the general contractor and the day-to-day operations so Rip and Rhonda could go on about their business while everything was being built.

The house had a standard set of rooms (large rooms) and only a few extras that the budget grudgingly allowed. There were bedrooms and bathrooms, a kitchen, a modest dining room, a modest living room, a big comfortable den and fireplace, a conservatory, a breakfast nook, and so on. Nothing was particularly fancy, just enough to do justice to Dominic's generous gift and to satisfy Rip and Rhonda's desire for the good life—10,240 ft² and counting.

## Chapter 7 – Up It Goes

"Why are all these rooms so big?" Anthony asked Rip after looking over the plan with the happy couple. "This bedroom is the size of my entire condo."

"Well, we didn't see a need for *more* rooms, so we just made everything bigger. It's all within the budget," Rip replied.

"We could play field hockey in this den," Anthony said, adding "What about furniture? You're gonna need a lot of furniture to fill all this space."

Rip looked at Rhonda. Rhonda looked back at Rip. Anthony looked at both of them as if he had just told the head chef at *Palladyne's* that the Salmon à la Palladyne needed more salt. And ketchup.

"We'll deal with that when the time comes," Rip finally stated.

Month after month went by and construction progressed at an industry-standard pace, while, in his usual small way, Rip continued to help his father manage the family business. All that money. All that money—with money like that, he and Rhonda could *really* do things up right on their new house, furniture too. He and Rhonda visited the construction site only every once in a while, but while there, neither of them could appreciate all of the things, all of the details that were being hammered out and managed in building their special place. Besides, it was more fun to show up and see *big* increments of progress at each visit as the house took shape rather than watch the progress on a daily basis.

One day, while wandering around inside the newly erected wooden framework, Rhonda remarked to Rip, "Why are there so many people working on this? It looks like there are four or five plumbers working on that one sink, and at least three of them are just standing there, watching. And over there, what is that guy doing?" She motioned toward a husky man who was leaning against a stud that was part of one of the framed walls. He was smoking a cigarette and wearing sunglasses and had on a very nice black suit. He seemed out of place.

"I don't know. Maybe it's a union thing," Rip said. "There does seem to be a lot of personnel on the job every time we visit. And that guy in the suit looks like some kind of supervisor."

During all of this construction time, the happy couple wound up spending a lot more time than usual on the Mousewater family's yacht lounging about and anticipating the big day when they could finally move into their new house—their new home. On rare occasions they saw the burly goofball on his yacht, the "boat next door," but the goofball always avoided looking at the two of them and he was soon forgotten.

As the construction neared completion, Rip and Rhonda began to visit Dominic less and less—and, over time, not at all—being fully absorbed in watching the final touches being put on their dream house. It was a sad state of affairs that Rip's recent lack of involvement in his father's business empire went completely unnoticed and had caused no ill effect.

## Chapter 8 – A Day to Remember

There are usually 365 days in a year. Many days go by like a cool breeze on a summer day. Some days, not so pleasant, where little pesky things add up, make those particular days best forgotten. And then there are days that find permanent residence in one's memory. Amidst all the nondescript and uneventful days of the year a handful of days stand out, always.

Such was the case for Rip and Rhonda on one very memorable August day. Construction on their new home had been going on for almost a year and was now complete. At eleven o'clock that morning they were to meet Peaberry Shortly at their new house for their first walk-through. After signing some final papers, their new house would then be ready for immediate occupancy. But earlier that day while Rip and Rhonda were at her penthouse...

"It's positive!" Rhonda shouted from the master bathroom. She rushed out to hug Rip who had heard her scream something but did not understand what she had said. "It's positive!" she said again. "I'm positive. I'm pregnant!" Rip grabbed her and they spun around like two eight-year olds trying to make themselves dizzy. For the most part, the happy couple was excited about the *idea* of having a baby and not necessarily the reality of having a child and raising it.

"Of all days, today, a day when we are going to go and take over our new house," Rip said joyously.

"Yes. Yes," Rhonda replied.

The couple was surrounded by an aura of joy as they arrived at the front door of their new home. Bursting with pride, they could not wait to tell everyone the news. Outside, Anthony was standing there, waiting to greet them; supposedly to act as a witness during the signing of several closing documents. Emerging from the inside, they were greeted by Peaberry Shortly and Simon Q. Latherine, the Mousewater family's attorney. Dominic insisted that Latherine be there to assist and supervise the signing of the final paperwork.

Upon learning about the pregnancy, Anthony, filled with a sincere joy of his own, gave Rip and Rhonda each a big hug. Peaberry Shortly and Simon Latherine both offered their congratulations. Shortly, desiring to "get on with it," gave a set of keys to Rhonda and said, "Shall we go in?"

It almost seemed anticlimactic to go through the finished rooms of the new house. But the tour added even more excitement to Rip and Rhonda's day. At one point, Latherine excused himself, "I'll wait up front. We can talk after you finish your tour." With that, he left the other three to continue on. In their excitement, Rip and Rhonda happened to overlook a lot of small, seemingly unobtrusive defects patently obscured by all the overwhelming gilded grandeur (and size) of the place. Things like crooked electrical outlets, loose faucet handles, missing roof shingles, doors that didn't close properly, leaking pipes and fixtures, a missing door knob, nonfunctional light switches, wall areas with uneven paint, broken floor tiles, sliding glass doors that didn't slide, crooked kitchen counters, unmatched cabinet doors, and many other "little" things.

In the huge master bedroom near the master bath, behaving mysteriously, Shortly took the happy couple aside. "I think you ought to know about something. You were asking about the property that surrounds your lot. I found out yesterday that it's going to be developed... soon."

"How bad would that be?" asked Rip.

"Not too bad. The whole area is slated for a fashionable high-end custom home community. Celebrities and extremely wealthy people will be your neighbors. Even though they will not be right up next to your house, many of them will be able to look down from their yards, down onto your estate below. And then there's the drainage issue..."

"But we'll be Ok?" Rhonda asked.

"Should be," Shortly said with tentative reassurance. "Let's go up front and sign those final closing papers."

Since there was no furniture in the entire place, all the assembled people reconvened in the kitchen where there was counter space available for signing the documents. One at a time, Shortly handed each set of papers to Latherine for his legal approval after which Latherine handed each set to Rip and Rhonda for signing. It seemed like an unnecessarily arduous exercise to both Rip and Rhonda; multiple signatures, multiple copies, notarization, witnessing, on and on. When all the signatures were completed Shortly gathered up his set and left. Anthony was content to wait in the entrance hall while all this legal activity was taking place—unless he was needed to witness any signatures. But Latherine was handling all of that.

Latherine then congratulated the couple, "I hope you are very happy in your new home. Rip. Rhonda." He acknowledged them both. The day had been quite a stunner as far as Rip and Rhonda were concerned. But their lawyer's tone indicated that something else was...up.

Latherine went on, "Rip, it's been a while since you visited your father. Is that right?"

"Not too long, but yes," Rip answered. Anthony, seeing Shortly leave through the front door, joined the group in the kitchen.

Latherine then continued, "I don't think you're aware that your father has become smitten with a newly-hired housekeeper. I mean *smitten*. And...she is all too eager to encourage it. And her youth is adding to the encouragement."

"What?" Rip and Rhonda said together. "How do you know all this?" Rip asked.

"I'm there—regularly. I've seen it. I've stumbled upon the two of them—she's been giving him sponge baths and who knows what else." Latherine was barely containing his turbulent gut feelings.

"What's her name?" Rhonda inquired.

"Jeanette Ovums," Latherine replied, shaking his head as if just hearing himself say the name was causing him to break out in the hives. "I just thought you should know about it. I don't like where all this seems to be headed. My opinion." With that, Latherine gathered up his copies of the papers and put them in his briefcase. As he headed out the door, he added, "You two go over there and see for yourselves. Check out Ms. Ovums. She's a real piece of work. Mr. Hill, watch out for these two, will you?"

The three of them, now alone in the huge but empty house, looked at each other, Rip and Rhonda wondering what to do next. Then Rip broke the silence, "What a day." He then looked over at Anthony who was trying to remain noncommittal.

"I haven't heard of anything so cheesy except, maybe, in the movies," Anthony finally uttered. "I think you should probably go over and check it all out. I'll go with you if you'd like."

Rip went around the house locking the doors to the outside. Rhonda and Anthony closed a few of the open windows. "Why did you prefer to keep it a one-story house?" Anthony asked Rhonda.

"It's Rip's fear of heights, that's all," she replied, closing the last of the open windows.

As Rip was locking the front door Rhonda muttered aloud, "With the baby coming, I think we're going to need more space."

Anthony was expecting some kind of immediate reaction from Rip, but instead, Rip was silent. Then, as Anthony was getting into his car, he heard Rip say to Rhonda, "I think you're right. Yes. I think you're right." Then, as an afterthought, he added, "We should probably get moving on it so that it can all be finished before the baby arrives. As for my father, we'll go visit him tomorrow. I've had about enough for one day."

For those named Mousewater, it was surely a day to remember.

## Chapter 9 – A Piece of...Something

The next day was rainy and cool. Rip and Rhonda arrived at Dominic's mansion in the early afternoon. As they entered the front door Dominic was slowly descending from high above on his wheel chair elevator. Before he reached bottom, out sprung a wiry, scantily clad young woman with a pretty face and hair that looked like a dirty old mop. Red-haired Flemmy came galloping into the room, huffing and puffing, and began randomly jumping around all excited even though he had no idea what for. The young woman grabbed Flemmy in a headlock and proceeded to calm him down; the panting, slobbering dog still showed signs of great excitement even under restraint.

Simon Q. Latherine was correct: Ms. Ovums was quite a piece of work. Rip and Rhonda were introducing themselves to Ms. Ovums as an agitated Dominic came over and interrupted them. "Ain't she somethin'?" Dominic said. A smiling Ms. Ovums quickly scurried over to Dominic, leaned over, and rubbed her hand all over the top of his head as if she were polishing up a bowling ball. Now, his sparse hair was all mussed up. It looked very comical. The whole scene...comical. Except to Rip, who was thinking to himself, "Wipe that shit-eating grin off your face...Dad."

An energetic Ms. Ovums was acting as if she owned the whole place and Dominic along with it. "Well, well, well. If it isn't the happy homeowners. Come to visit dear old Dad I suspect? Well here he is, all cleaned up and cleaned out and drained out. You can see he's smiling. I put that smile on his face."

"I'll bet you did," Rip commented. He turned to Rhonda and said (loud enough for Ms. Ovums to hear), "I'll bet that's not all she put on his face."

Rhonda walked over and gently flattened Dominic's hair back into place. Ms. Ovums was right; Dominic smelled as fresh as a middle-aged man who had just been given a *complete* once-over at the hands of an ambitious—

Rip then said, "Father, we'd like to talk to you. Alone." Rip looked up and glared as Ms. Ovums turned away in a huff, forcing Flemmy to go with her. Rhonda then led Dominic to the study with Rip following. As soon as the door was closed behind them, Rip quickly blurted out, "Rhonda's pregnant. You're going to be a grandfather."

Dominic was obviously pleased with the news but then changed the subject, "Did you see those breasts on Jeanette?" he said to Rip.

"Father, let's focus here for a minute. Rhonda and I are going to have a baby. It'll be your grandchild," Rip said.

"What do you want from me? Money?" Dominic said as he maneuvered over to his desk. Rip looked at Rhonda. Rhonda looked back at Rip. Then the both of them looked at Dominic. He was busy writing out a check. Tearing it off, he handed it to Rip, saying, "That should be enough for a while. Now open the damn door and get Jeanette back. It's about time for some mid-afternoon naked hot tub action."

Not the least bit able to refuse such a generous gift or protest the presence of the questionable Ms. Ovums, Rip pocketed the check and Rhonda opened the study door. Dominic rolled on out, calling for Jeanette. Rip and Rhonda decided to leave the two of them to their own devices. Literally.

"We can do wonders to our layout with *this* money," an excited Rhonda told Rip.

"Yes, indeed," he replied. "Yes, indeed!"

## Chapter 10 – And Now...

When Rip and Rhonda arrived at their own (furniture free) house they immediately began planning new additions.

"We'll need a nursery and a changing room and several more bedrooms for when we have more children," Rhonda was quick to say. "And a bathroom for each bedroom."

"How about a children's playground just outside the bedrooms," Rip added.

"Great." Rhonda wrote down each addition as quickly as they thought them up. "And we'll need some rooms for a live-in nanny while the children are young."

"As long as we are going to have all this construction going on, we might as well add something for ourselves. What do you think?" Rip was hyperventilating.

"How about a home theater. I've seen those in magazines. We could do it up right with all kinds of theater stuff." Rhonda was now hyperventilating as well.

When all was said and done their wish list wound up looking like this:

      Nursery, wet room, bathroom, story cove, and music center (1050 ft²)
      Children's playground with playground equipment and sand pit
      Six new bedrooms each with its own bath and outdoor porch (3660 ft²)
      Nanny's bedroom and bathroom (680 ft²)
      Nanny's sitting room with fireplace and shelves (480 ft²)
      Nanny's kitchenette (345 ft²)
      Garage and driveway for nanny's car
      Rip and Rhonda's Home Theater with seating for sixty people (1240 ft²)
      Theater control room (190 ft²)
      Theater snack kitchen with popcorn machine (240 ft²)
      Video library with shelves (260 ft²)
      Home theater anteroom (220 ft²)

The new additions: 8,365 ft²
New grand total: 18,605 ft²

Peaberry Shortly was glad to make their wishes a reality, but seeing the list, he was a taken aback at the magnitude of the additions. But duty called, so he went right to work on the plans.

## Chapter 11 – Home Theater

Anthony had just finished interviewing Lola Corolla, the movie star. She had been in films such as *Mine of Horror*, *Girls School Blood Slaughter VI*, the tough-guy action thriller *Death Is the New Death*, and the mystery trilogy *The Missing Oyster*, *The World Is My Oyster*, and *Oyster 3D*. She had also narrated a religious *faux* documentary, *Science: Who Needs It?* Anthony was in the mood for celebrating. He had been out of touch for several days—making a living—but now felt free to visit with Rip and Rhonda and was ready to share his own good news. Rip and Rhonda were still staying at Rhonda's penthouse since their dream house was again under construction and they had no furniture there anyway.

"What the-e-e-e fuck!" Anthony gasped when he saw the new plans for Rip and Rhonda's layout. "You haven't even moved in yet. You have no furniture or belongings in your new house. And now you're adding all this space?"

"Guilty," Rip replied, wearing a proud grin and raising his open palm like a witness being sworn in. "My father gave us the money so we're putting it to good use. We even had money left over. We wanted to get it all done before the baby arrives—which is only a few months away."

Anthony was no longer noncommittal, "A home theater, a playground? Why not a bowling alley and... Sixty people? You don't even *know* sixty people...or thirty. How many square feet is this place now going to be? Ten thousand, twelve?"

"Eighteen," Rip said proudly.

Then Anthony remarked, "Well, believe it or not, I just finished interviewing one of your future neighbors, Lola Corolla."

"Who?" Rhonda asked.

"Yes, who is that?" Rip also asked.

Anthony replied, "She's a big movie star. Not the greatest movies, but everyone has heard of her—except you two, apparently."

"We never go to the movies or watch them on TV," Rip added.

"And you're building a home theater?" Anthony could only shake his head.

"We wanted something for ourselves since we were doing so much for our children," Rhonda chimed in.

"So they're going to finish all this by the time you deliver?" Anthony said waving his hand over the plans.

"Sure. Shortly the architect said that there are ways of getting it done in time, so we left it at that." Rhonda rubbed her belly as she spoke. "I think it's turning out to be a really great layout for Rip and me. And for our children."

## Chapter 12 – Out and In

Peaberry Shortly came through for the happy couple and the additions were completed about two weeks before the baby arrived—a girl. They named her Trina Darlene—Trina Darlene Mousewater. She was just an ordinary baby in every way but was a staggering curiosity to Rip and Rhonda. The happy couple never expected so much work, so many sleepless nights, so many fluids; so many fluids that were supposed to be solid. Without furniture in their new house, the family was still living in Rhonda's penthouse. They decided to move all of Rhonda's furniture to their new house and hire a nanny. With brilliant foresight, they had provided rooms in their dream house for a live-in nanny; for just such a need. But now they would have to cough up more money in order to furnish the nanny's rooms (and the nursery). And supplies for the baby.

So Rip and Rhonda moved into their new house, sprung for the nanny's furniture, and hired a nanny, a Ms. Joy Spitz. All of this was costing money, Rip and Rhonda's (normally) discretionary money. Ms. Spitz was a no-nonsense type, a nanny of few words. She could easily blend into the scenery—very unobtrusive. Adequate to the business of being a nanny she was nothing special—no fairy tale governess. Her clothes were too tight and smelled like baked starch, but otherwise she was very clean and polite. Her ways made her a perfect choice for the Mousewater household.

The nursery and the nanny's area were situated on the opposite side of the house from Rip and Rhonda's bedroom so, at last, Rip and Rhonda were able to sleep at night. Rhonda's furniture looked small and insignificant in the large rooms, but it did allow the happy couple to move in and to at least attempt to enjoy their new house.

## Chapter 13 – A New Phase

Introducing Trina to her grandfather was next on the agenda. As Rip and Rhonda arrived at Dominic's estate, baby in arms, they were greeted by Ms. Ovums, again. This time there was no sign of hyper-dog.

Without so much as a "Hello," Ms. Ovums offered, "He's in the study. We've just finished." Ms. Ovums smiled and made an obvious, overstated sweeping wipe of her mouth with the palm of her hand.

"Where's Flemmy?" Rhonda asked, as the threesome barged on in past Ms. Ovums.

"Dead," said Ovums. "Choked on something. But dead. Your father made me put him in the deep freeze before he got too ripe. Good old Dad's none too happy about it."

Rhonda gasped and Rip was actually a bit saddened. They went into the study and closed the door behind them leaving Ms. Ovums on the outside looking in, again.

"Daddy Dominic, here is your new granddaughter, Trina," Rhonda said in a kind of baby talk manner, looking at the baby instead of addressing Dominic directly.

Even though being called "Daddy Dominic" made him want to blow chunks, he made a curly little smile and showed a surprising level of warmth. "I think it's grand," he finally said. "If you two need anything…" He then whispered something softly to Rhonda—the words "Daddy Dominic" were never heard spoken again.

"Money," Rip and Rhonda said together. Rip continued, "There are a lot of expenses with the new house, the nanny, you know…expenses."

The ritual then repeated itself. Dominic wrote out another check and the happy couple was more than pleased with the amount. As Rhonda opened the door to the study, Ms. Ovums was right there, apparently eavesdropping. Ovums begrudgingly let the little family pass as she was ready and primed to continue her handling of Dominic.

"Shall we use this money to furnish our house?" Rip asked Rhonda.

"It's such a large amount, maybe we should put it into the house itself, like an investment. Furniture will come and go, but the house will remain." Rhonda was being logical as far as she was concerned.

"Good thinking," Rip replied without blinking an eye.

Once again the happy couple started creating a wish list. Soon they would deliver the list to Shortly. It was filled with all sorts of additions and amenities and Shortly continued to follow through with new plans and construction cost estimates.

The new list wound up looking like this:

Three new bedrooms each with its own bath and outdoor porch (2160 ft²)
A "Tall Room" (660 ft²)
A "Grey Room" (750 ft²)
A Great Room (1500 ft²)
A Great Hall with Cupola and Balcony (1900 ft²)
Gallery (390 ft²)
Architect's Office (600 ft²)
Architect's Studio (550 ft²)
Layout Room with Model Table (520 ft²)
Basement (810 ft²)
Wine Cellar (Three-Temperature, Climate-Controlled) (320 ft²)
Master Hot Tub (220 ft²)
Double Lane Bowling Alley (1050 ft²)
Walk-in Deep Freeze and Butcher Locker (160 ft²)
Cheese Locker (180 ft²)
Kennels and Dog Runs
Dog's Outdoor Swimming Pool
Kennel Master's Lodge (1650 ft²)
Domestic Animal Veterinary Clinic (800 ft²)
Animal Crematorium (140 ft²)
Construction Center (1750 ft²)
Construction Staging Area
Construction Entrance
Construction Road
Construction Guardhouse (with Bathroom) and Gate (188 ft²)

New additions: 16,298 ft²
New grand total: 34,903 ft².

The basement was to be reached using a series of slowly descending, walled-in ramps instead of a stairway or ladder. This took up a lot of space, but for an acrophobic like Rip it was the only way he would ever agree to have a basement. And, once in the basement, there would be no views down to the ground.

## Chapter 14 – A Phase of a Phase

When Anthony saw the new plans he reacted definitively…

 "What the fu-u-u-ck?! More rooms, more features. You barely have any furniture. What do you need all this for?"

"Isn't it great?" Rip replied, oblivious to Anthony's obvious concern. "It's like an investment. There's a good reason for each item on that list. The bowling alley was your idea by the way. The pin-setting equipment for those two lanes was a little bit pricey so we left out all that mechanical equipment."

"More money from Dominic I suppose," a restrained Anthony said. "What is this gallery and balcony area in this huge "great room" and hall. You don't even have a stairway or some way to get up there."

"Ha…don't plan on ever going up there anyway," Rip retorted.

"What's with all this kennel and dog stuff?"

"We were saddened when we heard about father's dog choking to death so we thought, why not?" Rhonda added.

"You have a kennel, but no dog. You have a wine cellar and no wine. And since when were you planning on eating all the cheese…so you need a cheese locker?" Anthony said. "Just what *is* a cheese locker?"

"It's to store all kinds of cheeses...at an exact, optimum temperature," Rip replied.

"What is a 'Tall Room'? What is a 'Grey Room'?" were Anthony's next questions.

"The 'Tall Room' is forty feet tall. And the 'Grey Room'...well everything, including the walls, is going to be grey. See? Very logical," was Rip's response.

"Tapestries. The tall room is for displaying tapestries," Rhonda added.

Finally, Anthony asked, "Do all these construction management items mean you're planning on adding even more rooms and features after this?"

Rip replied, "Only if necessary. Only if necessary."

Once again, under the disciplined direction of Peaberry Shortly, construction went, for the most part, smoothly and quickly. And surprisingly to everyone, there was plenty of money left over. So as long as the construction crews were still working on the layout and were already going to be on site... Why not take advantage? So, Rip and Rhonda added:

Aviary (1340 ft²)
Luxury Attic (1720 ft²)
Tea Room (840 ft²)
Music Parlor and Music Library (580 ft²)
Walk-In Humidor (290 ft²)
East Side Office (540 ft²)
West Side Office (540 ft²)
Sun Room (610 ft²)
Guest House (2480 ft²)
Butcherary [refrigerated meat locker, butcher block, etc.] (380 ft²)
Fish Locker (410 ft²)
Indoor Grilling Deck (260 ft²) plus an Outdoor Grilling Deck
Breakfast Nook (290 ft²)

Breakfast Dining Hall (880 ft²)

Bakery, Bread Factory, and Donut Machine Room (1250 ft²)

New additions: 12,410 ft²

New grand total: 47,313 ft².

Before starting on the additions to the additions, Shortly requested a meeting with the happy couple in order to iron out a few details.

"We're going to have a problem with your layout," Shortly started.

"What kind of problem?" Rhonda asked.

"Logically, there is no way to physically connect all these areas together unless we add in a large number of hallways and connecting spaces," Shortly said.

"Well then, by all means, let's have hallways and connecting spaces," was Rip's reply without hesitating.

Hallways, passageways, corridors, and connecting areas: 2,640 ft²

New grand total: 49,953 ft².

## Chapter 15 – More of Everything

Anthony was no longer shocked when he visited Rip and the new plans were unveiled. Given the recent history of the layout, the additions seemed perfectly normal.

"This place is not the Palace of Versailles...but it's just as nutty," he remarked to Rip and Rhonda upon seeing the latest additions. He was careful not to say something that might give the happy couple any *new* ideas for future additions. "Do you two realize that you already have over twenty-five bathrooms? That's twenty-five toilets, and sinks, and showers, and tubs. So much plumbing, so much that can malfunction."

One might assume that with all the construction going on that there would be no time left for happy couple intimacy. Well, that assumption would be wrong. A new pregnancy popped up inside Rhonda. And this one was a big one: two for one, twins. By this time Trina was approaching her second birthday, but her parents seemed like strangers to her. Ms. Spitz, the nanny, had become Trina's virtual mother. Adequate to the task—but only just adequate.

One afternoon, Ms. Spitz was sauntering through some of the new rooms on a self-guided tour and ran into Rip and Rhonda.

"Who is that?" Rip asked.

"I think it's our nanny," Rhonda replied.

Enough said.

When the joyous birthing day arrived, Rhonda delivered two big, healthy boys: Orville Pease Mousewater and Amador Travis Mousewater. Orville came first and eleven minutes later Amador appeared from the canal. Eleven minutes: a small timing thing that would later become a brother *thing*. This singular branch of the Mousewater line was becoming a real family, at least in size.

When visiting Dominic to introduce the twins, Rip and Rhonda were again confronted by Jeanette Ovums; she had not changed her curt demeanor and sarcastic tone. Rip felt it was time to broach the subject of Ms. Ovums with his father. Again Rip, Rhonda, and Dominic isolated themselves in the study, but this time with Rhonda guarding against any surreptitious eavesdropping by the tart and curious Ovums. The twins' presence got Dominic into as good a mood as was possible so Rip felt confident in speaking his mind.

"Father, do you realize what Ms. Ovums is up to here?"

"I certainly do."

"You do?"

"Do you think I built up this business by being stupid? I can read people. I'm getting something *I* want. I've never had so much sex in my life. I feel like my prostate is going to explode."

"That may be true, but she's up to no good. She's the most rude, crude...she wants something beyond what you're paying her right now."

"I know that." Dominic was obviously unconcerned about any Ovums treachery implied by Rip. "I stuck her into my will." That comment got a rise out of both Rip and Rhonda. Dominic continued, "She kept pestering me about it, so I stuck her in there, mostly to shut her up. She's not a very subtle person. She knows I might change it again, cut her out of it, at—any—time." Then, looking away scornfully, Dominic muttered, "Always on her best behavior when she's around me. Fraudulent, two-faced little..."

Turning his wheelchair around and raising his arm with his forefinger extended forward, Dominic then declared with some vigor, "But when I wake up from a nap with her head in my crotch, I cannot bear the idea of tossing her out of here; not just yet." Then Dominic turned again and faced Rip straight on, "She doesn't really give a damn about me, so I'm just taking advantage of the situation while I'm still alive and kicking." Dominic turned his wheelchair around again and facing away from both members of the happy couple, he added, "When the time comes, your family is going to be just fine."

All of Dominic's rotating and moving about was making Rip dizzy. Rip didn't say anything more. Dominic did not seem to be his ornery old self—all that sex must have mellowed him out. Rip was beginning to think that his father was smarter than he had given him credit for. As far as the will was concerned, without knowing what Dominic had in mind for the unsavory Ovums, Rip still had serious misgivings; but he had come to the realization that his father was a really devious person. When Rip looked over at Rhonda who was standing guard by the slightly ajar door, she gave him the OK signal and continued monitoring for any sign of Ms. Ovums.

Once again, an energetic Dominic went diving into his checkbook. He didn't seem to care what Rip and Rhonda were doing with all that cash. A spry and formerly ornery Dominic was so pleased with having not one, but two, male heirs that, this time, his gift to Rip and Rhonda bordered on the obscene. As Rip and Rhonda and the twins were departing at the front door, Ms. Ovums came up to them from behind.

"Why don't you two quit stumbling in here and interfering? I've got him, like a fish on a hook, you know," the shameless Ovums said quietly and firmly to their backs.

Rip turned around quickly and pointed his index finger right into her face about one inch from the tip of her nose. Before he could say anything Rhonda grabbed him and turned him away, pushing him to the front door, Rip still trying to look at Ms. Ovums and slowly withdrawing his finger. And out they went, leaving the foaming Ms. Ovums to brood and stew in a cauldron of self-generated internal heat.

## Chapter 16 – Too Much Is Too Much

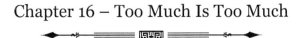

Of course the happy couple was ready to put all that big money to good use. With the newly added hallways and passageways, there were now numerous locations for a major expansion. The couple also celebrated the fact that all the previous indoor additions pushed their dream home's indoor square footage past the one acre milestone. On to acre number two...

> Three luxury bedroom suites each with its own bathroom (3660 ft²)
> Entryway Expansion with guest bathroom (540 ft²)
> Billiard Room and Adjacent Pool Hall (960 ft²)
> Gymnasium (1240 ft²)
> Gym Locker Room, Shower Stalls, and Bathroom (1400 ft²)
> Indoor Pool (1420 ft²)
> Outdoor Pool
> Pool Changing Room (540 ft²)
> Cabana with Sun Terrace, Jungle Shower, and Wet Bar (2150 ft²)

Round Sunken Luxury Den with Central Fireplace (2450 ft²)

Study with Connecting Hall to Library (1680 ft²)

One Story Library with Shelves (1720 ft²)

Parlor (1200 ft²)

Drawing Room (1150 ft²)

Sitting Room (1040 ft²)

Trophy Room with Connecting Hallway to Study (1120 ft²)

Intimate Dining Room (680 ft²)

Formal Dining Hall with 25 ft ceiling (1280 ft²)

Main Steam Room with Connecting Dry Heat Sauna (720 ft²)

Waxing Parlor (430 ft²)

Massage Parlor (410 ft²)

Tanning Salon (380 ft²)

Auxiliary Luxury Attic (620 ft²)

Hidden (Secret) Attic (440 ft²)

Air-Conditioned Doll House (260 ft²)

Rumpus Room (330 ft²)

Four New Hot Tubs (672 ft²)

Model Train Room with Electronics Control Bay (575 ft²)

Model Plane Hanger and Assembly Room (640 ft²)

Hobby Room (430 ft²)

Party Deck

Entertainment Patio

New additions: 30,137 ft²
New grand total: 80,090 ft².

In spite of the huge number of hallway and passageway add-ons, the new, larger list of features was making it increasingly difficult to add rooms that connected *logically* to the existing layout. Several miles of plumbing were already running through and around the house since tacked-on bathrooms could not be peppered around the floor plan in any efficient way. The house was becoming maze-like and convoluted. The sprawling layout's not having a second story was making design and development even more difficult and even less efficient.

Shortly was having to use every erg of his creative energy in massaging each new room or feature into the layout—even if positioning each new addition turned out to be desperately illogical. The mansion was beginning to resemble a patchwork quilt, especially on paper. Shortly was making extremely good money with his fees, but indulging every wild whim of the happy couple was becoming repetitive, tedious, and tiresome. Still, he continued to acquiesce and agreed to forge ahead with every new construction idea. And then...

"What is this sheet, this drawing?" he asked when Rip handed him yet another piece of paper containing some handwritten boxes and lines.

"That's another thing on our list for this set of additions," replied Rip.

"What is it?" Shortly asked...again...afraid of what was to come next. He was rotating the paper around, trying to discern what the diagram represented.

"It's the plan for a simulated underground cave system with a larger cave room at one end equipped with its own wet bar. You see, each of these little boxes is a little cave room with decorative cement formations, waterfalls, fountains, and colorful lighting. And these lines are the connecting pathways. It's really a cavern system, you know, with multiple caves connected together." Rip was showing unrestrained excitement and pride as he described the whole thing.

"And what is this dark line here," Shortly asked, pointing at the map.

"That's a tunnel from our existing basement to the cave entrance," Rip answered. "I didn't think it would be practical, building the underground cave system directly under the house, so I designed it to be further out, away from the house, with only that tunnel actually running underneath. Always thinking, that's me."

"What do you think of this, Rhonda?" Shortly said, noting her display of disinterest in this new "feature."

Quickly responding, Rhonda reached into her pocket and pulled out a piece of paper of her own. "The cave thing was a compromise," she said. "He added the cave...so I got to add the water park." She handed her paper to Shortly who was now expecting almost anything.

There it was: a drawing for a complex water park to be placed adjacent to the new outdoor swimming pool. The water park was to have its own dressing room, shower, and control center. Rhonda surmised that it would be more efficient to have a central water management equipment barn where all the pumps and filters and water feature controls could be housed together in a single climate-controlled environment. The equipment would control both indoor and outdoor pools as well as the new water park and its features: waterfalls, slides, fountains, outdoor hot tubs, grottos, chutes and tubes, splash pools, wave machine(s), sandy beach area, and a multi-speaker outdoor sound system (for adding ocean wave ambience and music to the whole area).

Simulated Underground Cavern System (5660 ft²)
Cave Bar (320 ft²)
Tunnel from Basement to Cave Entrance (950 ft²)
Water Park Facilities (1155 ft²)
Climate-Controlled Equipment Barn (1355 ft²)

Specialty Additions: 9,440 ft²
New grand total: 89,530 ft².

Shortly quit. He'd had enough. More than enough. He left Rip and Rhonda in the lurch. Not even remotely able to hide his disgust, he packed up a few items of paperwork and left the Mousewater property forever, not even bothering to collect a final fee.

## Chapter 17 – The End of an Era

There wasn't much Rip or Rhonda could do. Perhaps Dominic knew of someone else capable enough to finish all the new additions and features. Feeling as though it was an emergency, they went straight to Dominic's place. When they arrived at the estate, Rip and Rhonda were dismayed to see two police cars and an ambulance in the driveway. They both felt two emotions: a sense of panic and a lot of suspicion.

They were delighted to be greeted at the front door by Simon Q. Latherine, Dominic's lawyer, rather than by Ms. Ovums (who was nowhere to be found). But they were shocked to see a large pile of crumpled metal beams and chunks of wood and plaster by the elaborate front stairway; dust covered everything and powdery debris was everywhere.

"There's been an accident. Poor Dominic is no longer with us," Latherine said with an unfamiliar level of compassion in his voice. "It happened over there," he said, pointing at the debris. "Dominic's wheelchair elevator came loose from its anchorage and collapsed onto him. The ambulance attendants have already removed his body from the debris pile. It's out there in the ambulance. I'm sorry. I truly am. Where have you two been? We've been..."

"We were with Shortly. He quit on us. Where is that Ovums woman?" Rhonda asked. She cringed when she saw Dominic's crumpled wheelchair sticking out from the debris.

"She's not here," Latherine said. "One of the housekeepers heard the noise, came in, saw the rubble, and called the police. We don't have to worry with this now, but we'll have to hire someone to come in and clear out all this rubble. But more importantly, there is a section of the staircase that is missing; torn out by the collapse. That will have to be repaired as soon as possible. It's a safety issue. What happened with Shortly?"

Rip replied, "He just quit. Walked right out in the middle of a meeting." Shortly's departure was not much of a priority for Rip, Rhonda, or Latherine—considering the circumstances.

Both Rip and Rhonda were saddened by these events and because of their lack of experience in handling such matters, they left the funeral and all the other necessary arrangements to Latherine.

## Chapter 18 – An Ill-Fitting Send-Off

It was supposed to be a quiet, dignified funeral service. It was not. It looked like a mobster convention with gaudy flower arrangements, lots of black suits and white boutonnieres, and numerous people neither Rip nor Rhonda had ever seen before. Rip began to wonder, "How many of these people are here out of love, how many are here out of respect, and how many are here to make sure he is really dead? And where is that woman, Ms. Ovums?"

Latherine, noticing the arrival of Rip and Rhonda, came over to Rip. "I'm sad to say that...well, according to the preliminary police report, there doesn't seem to be any evidence of foul play...you know by someone...someone in particular...I'm sorry."

"I understand," said Rip. "That's too bad, I guess."

Then Latherine added, "I believe Ovums will show up for the reading of the will, so we'll just have to wait for that—if there is anything that needs to be said, or done."

Then Rhonda remarked to Latherine, "What's going on there—the casket is partially open. I thought Dominic wanted it closed and sealed. He didn't want people gawking at his dead remains—no matter how much they might be able to fix him up. It looks like it's open...not open enough to really see inside, but..."

"That's right," added Rip. "Why is the lid propped open like that...an inch or two?"

Latherine rubbed his brow, then his eyes, and looking down, having already anticipated a question about it, he said, "Well, that's another thing: Flemmy's in there with Dominic. Dominic wanted to be buried with his dog. But let me tell you this, even after the damn dog thawed out, the body was still stiff, like thick tree branches—it had to be jammed into the casket. No matter how hard they tried they could not get the casket lid completely closed with the both of them in there together. The only other alternative was to cut up the dog into pieces, but, believe it or not, the funeral director's professional ethics kept them from taking that drastic step. Not to worry, I've already got a custom-built box on its way for the final burial."

Rip and Rhonda sat down in their reserved seats, right up front near the casket. After a short while, a familiar voice whispered "Hello" to them from behind. It was Anthony. Rip noticed that Anthony was accompanied by a studious-looking female companion. Anthony quietly introduced her to Rip and Rhonda, "This is Whitney Eli, a friend of mine." Neither Anthony nor Whitney was dressed for a funereal occasion, but as far as the mourning couple was concerned, the contrast with all those black suits was very refreshing.

The assistant funeral director took to the podium. "My friends, we are gathered here to pay our final respects to Dr. Salvatore Nicaragua. He was a good man, a healer, a..." The introduction was interrupted by the funeral director himself, "I apologize, ladies and gentlemen..."

The service dragged on for over three hours as many in the assembled throng felt compelled to take to the podium and insert their own comments on the life of Dominic Mousewater. No detail was spared. No tiny reminiscence was overlooked. Anecdotes, anecdotes. Rip did not know any of the people who got up to speak and none of the people he and Rhonda knew bothered to speak at all. There were a chosen few that broke out in song. Some of the singing left the solemn attendees gasping for air.

After the first hour...

"We're taking off. My ass is getting numb, Whitney's getting restless, and the smell of flowers mixed with that dead dog is starting to make me sick," Anthony whispered to Rip. "Did they even bother to embalm that dog?"

"I don't know anything about the dog, but Rhonda and I are anxious to get back and continue working on our layout," Rip whispered back.

At the conclusion of the 3½-hour service, numerous black-clad attendees were milling about just outside the chapel, passing around condolences, reminiscing, providing additional anecdotes, and making comments about others in attendance. Stepping into the adjacent garden area in order to avoid the amorphous crowd, Rip and Rhonda located Latherine and approached him once again. "We're going to need a new architect and a general contractor since old Shortly quit on us," Rip told him.

"I'll see what I can do," Latherine replied. He seemed distracted and preoccupied. "But don't forget about the reading: day after tomorrow, ten a.m. And be prepared for anything, especially if Ms. Ovums decides to show up."

Far away from the large, mumbling funeral crowd, Rip and Rhonda sought refuge in their big empty house. On this day the house seemed especially empty and quiet. It was a rare sad moment for the (usually) happy couple, but they were comforted by the fact that their children were being managed by others. News of the children's dead grandfather should trickle down to them eventually. Rip and Rhonda were both glad to see that Anthony had found a companion, but they did not have any real opportunity to converse with either of them—when Anthony and Whitney stealthily left the service early, disapproving eyeballs in the crowd burned holes in their inappropriate funeral attire.

## Chapter 19 – The Hills

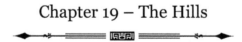

In the unfamiliar land of reality, Rip and Rhonda had no idea what to expect from the reading of Dominic's will. Or what kind of fuss Ms. Ovums was going to make if she happened to show up. So many things to contemplate. While the two of them sat quietly in a pair of cheap folding lawn chairs on an empty concrete slab area in the back of their house, Rhonda sat up, erect. "Look up there," she said, pointing at the hills surrounding their property.

Rip looked to where she was pointing, "I see..."

In their blind zeal to keep construction going on their own property, they had failed to notice the many, many luxury palaces that were in the process of being built in the hills around them. All sorts of designs, all sorts of colors. Walls of glass, brick, stone, pointed roofs, turrets, crenellations, landscaping (something that been developed at a bare minimum on Rip and Rhonda's property). Who *were* all these people? No matter, the happy couple's place was buffered enough around the perimeter so that noisy kids, barking dogs, false burglar alarms, arguing couples—all of that bother would be out of sight, out of earshot, and out of mind. Still, it was more than a little bit unnerving to Rip and Rhonda that all these people would be able to look down at their layout.

The development in the hills was never given an official name. Some people just called it "The Hills." It seemed like the houses just appeared out of nowhere. But the land was prime real estate and so expensive that only the wealthiest of the wealthy could afford to build custom homes there. For Rip and Rhonda, there was something a little disquieting about the way the hills all sloped down toward their property. And then there was going to be all those eyes...

## Chapter 20 – The Paper Dragon

Simon Latherine had set up the reading of the will in his building's conference room so that a building security guard could stand on duty just outside. At first, the only people in the room were Latherine, Rip, Rhonda, and Latherine's secretary (to take notes, if necessary). Since only Rip and Rhonda were officially in attendance, Latherine dismissed his secretary and proceeded to open a large envelope containing Dominic's will. But before Latherine could utter a single word, in barged Jeanette Ovums, carrying a huge carpetbag and wearing a feathery yellow hat that brushed against everything that was nearby. She flung her bag noisily onto the big mahogany table (metal rivets scratching the polished surface), carefully lifted and removed her hat, and plopped it on top of the oversized bag.

While Ms. Ovums got herself all adjusted in her chair, Rip turned to Rhonda and whispered, "I'll bet she brought that bag with her thinking she would need it to carry off big stacks of cash." Rhonda quietly chuckled to herself as she watched a fidgety Ovums finally get settled in.

Latherine started again, "All right. Now that we're all here... Let me say this, to save time. This will was written by Dominic Mousewater himself, in his own handwriting. The signing was witnessed by myself and two others from our law group. It is official and legal.

"First, there are token amounts of money to be distributed among the staff that currently work at Dominic's...Mr. Mousewater's home." In order to preempt any protests from the slowly rising Ms. Ovums, he hastened to add, "That's not you, Ovums. You're separate." Ms. Ovums sat back in her chair, full up to the brim with smugness and a sense of resolved delight. She was quick to give Rip and Rhonda "a look."

Latherine continued, "There are various charities mentioned here, all of them provided with token amounts of money. Those need not concern us. There is a sizable amount to be given to a Mr. Moises DePilleron who is an import supervisor down at the dock. I do not know the man, nor do I know how he is related to Dominic's business, but I will see to it that he gets his designated share. Also there is a generous amount of money bequeathed to a Captain James T. Quirg. I am familiar with this gentleman and I will see that he gets his share."

Then he addressed Rip and Rhonda directly, "A trust fund has been set up for each of your children: Trina Darlene Mousewater, Orville Pease Mousewater, and Amador Travis Mousewater. I would say that each of these funds is generous but not extravagant. Mr. Brisbane Pease Mousewater is designated as custodian for these funds. I have to make it clear that, if there are any *future* children, then—how shall I put it—they are going to have to go it alone."

Then he turned his attention to Ms. Ovums, "Now then, Ms. Ovums, let me read this next section: 'I bequeath to my co-resident, Ms. Jeanette Strappon Ovums, my entire house and all of its contents, except for any books my son Brisbane desires from my personal library and including any books that may be found in other locations around my property. Access to the books shall be granted without question, complication, interference, or obstruction in any way. Removal or sale of books by anyone other than Brisbane is prohibited.'"

Ovums sat up at attention upon hearing her full name announced officially. She was pleased at getting the house, but was curious about the lack of money references and the language about the books. "Is that it, for me?" interjected Ms. Ovums, displaying a crude, visible level of impatient hostility. "Can he do that? The books..."

"That's it for you, Ms. Ovums," said Latherine. "Let me continue. The rest of my estate in its entirety—my securities, my cash, my accounts, my real estate properties, and all my other holdings I pass on to my sole heir and son Brisbane and by extension, his wife Rhonda. This includes the land on which my current house is situated."

"What? What does that mean?" Ms. Ovums blurted out.

"It means that you own the house and all of its contents, except the books," Latherine replied.

"I know, but what does it *mean*?" a pale Ms. Ovums asked again, pulling out a black-looking cigarette and lighting it with a shaking hand.

"It means that you own the house and all of its contents, except the books," Latherine replied again, more firmly this time. "And there is no smoking in here, Ms. Ovums."

With the partially-lit black cigarette flopping up and down at the corner of her mouth, Ovums gathered up her carpet bag and hat and made several exaggerated blustering motions in doing so. Latherine, with a quite evident smile on his face, spoke loudly to her as she left, "We'll be in touch." The security guard at the door made way for her like a matador taunting a bull in the ring—a matador with a deadly sword hidden in a fold of his cape.

Latherine then addressed the happy couple, "Rip, Rhonda, you are now in charge of it all. I will be happy to continue on as your attorney, if that is your wish. That would include, of course, managing the three trust funds Dominic set up for your children."

"Yes. Yes," Rhonda said. Rip nodded in agreement.

"Well then, I thank you," Latherine replied. He then produced a business card from his briefcase and pushed it across the table. "That's the card of an architect that can help you with anything you need for your house. His name is Louis 'Four-Fingers' Licoracci. Also, he can manage the construction aspect of your projects just like Shortly did—anything you two dream up. He is very fast, inexpensive, and is probably better connected, politically, than even Peaberry Shortly. So, good luck."

Rip and Rhonda thanked Latherine for his efforts as they left the conference room. They headed for home and began to contemplate all the complex ramifications of recent events—ready or not. They now had more money than they would ever need to finish their dream home, decorate it, landscape it, and fill it with furniture and art and happiness. When their children were ready for school, only the best private schools would do. Whenever Rip and Rhonda's hillside neighbors looked down on their layout they would have to be impressed...and envious, oh so envious. It was going to be so spectacular.

## Chapter 21 – Louis Licoracci

As a twenty-two year old, Louis "Four-Fingers" Licoracci and several of his buddies were horsing around while partying, drinking, and water skiing—usually a deadly combination. While bobbing about in the water next to the ladder at the stern of their motorboat, Licoracci carelessly got his left hand too close to the propeller and had all of his fingers chopped off. Rich red blood began clouding up the greenish lake water. Although dealing with excruciating pain, Licoracci still had the wherewithal to grab hold of and retrieve three of the fingers using his undamaged right hand, cautiously avoiding the propeller; but his left thumb and left middle finger were forever lost to the deep—probably winding up in the stomach of a ghastly, oversized catfish.

Quick action by Licoracci's laughing and still-partying "friends" was sadly lacking, so Licoracci, with his left hand wrapped in a blood-soaked towel, piloted the boat back to the ramp and hauled himself ashore. His so-called "friends" were AWOL in getting him to an emergency room. Driving a jeep with a standard transmission and an empty boat trailer banging about, and with one hand wrapped in a ball, was not easy, but Licoracci somehow managed to get to a hospital without too much delay, his severed fingers cooling in the ice chest originally meant for beer—it was just in time for an urgent care surgical team to reattach the salvaged fingers. Days later, a secondary procedure was performed: a specialist team was able to replace Licoracci's missing thumb with the big toe from his left foot. In the end, it was one funky-looking left hand—a giant thumb and a missing middle finger.

It took many years, but with physical therapy and determination, Louis "Four-Fingers" Licoracci was able to regain enough function in his hand to become an architect—unofficially. Of course, gesturing disapproval at someone with his left hand was no longer an option. Licoracci's struggles toughened his character and intensified an already superstitious nature, but somewhere along the line he found himself sliding down the all-too-common slippery slope of sleaze.

## Chapter 22 – Way Out

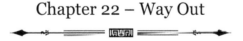

Before construction on the elaborate new additions actually commenced, on a dark and moonless night...

"Wake up! Hey you, wake up," barked the masked man, shaking a sleeping Rip into consciousness. It was a burglar dressed in the *de rigueur* outfit of black turtleneck, ski mask, and blue vinyl gloves. He had come in through an unlocked window seeking a big killing in fence-able goods.

"Hey you! What's the deal here?" he said. Rhonda was beginning to stir.

A groggy Rip answered, "What do you mean? What do you want?"

"Where is everything? There's no furniture, no nothing!"

"Yeah, you said it," Rip replied as he re-deposited himself back among his pillows.

"Hey, hey you. Wake up," the insistent burglar said, shaking Rip once again.

"What *is* it?" Rip said with his eyes closed.

"I can't find my way out. *That's* what it is. Some of the light switches don't work. I can't tell where I am. What kind of a place is this?" The burglar pulled Rip out of bed. Rhonda was now awake and was startled by the sight of the burglar.

"What's going on?" she asked with one eye closed.

Rip answered, "Go back to sleep. I have to show this guy the way out of here." Rhonda fell back down into her pillow.

"You got any cash?" the intruder finally asked as Rip led him circuitously around toward the front door.

Rip replied, "If I say 'yes,' that's bad for me. You'll have to get it out of me. If I say 'no' will you even believe me? If I give you something you'll wonder if that's all there is." Rip learned the art of obfuscation and delay from Dominic and Latherine.

"Just let me out of here," replied the burglar, anxious to just get the hell out. He then stopped and turned, "Oh, one last thing, who are those people over there on the other side of this place? That woman, and those others, kids, looked like."

"Don't know. Squatters, vagrants I guess." Rip knew perfectly well who they were. Without further delay, he opened the front door. As the burglar shook his head and stomped out, Rip said, "Don't come back."

The burglar scurried away and Rip heard him muttering to himself, "Can you believe that shit? Jesus fucking father of time!" The black clad figure disappeared, blending into the darkness—and Rip went back to bed.

## Chapter 23 – Trains and Planes

Construction of the massive set of additions was soon underway. Excavation and tunneling for the cave system proceeded with only a mere handful of disastrous cave-ins. Truck after truck delivered and deposited the gunite used in building the structural foundation for the water park features, the pools, and even sections of the cave system. Large areas of the property were denuded of vegetation, both for the convenient delivery of construction materials as well as for the additions themselves. Room after room and feature after feature, everything in the massive list was designed, contracted, and constructed under the supervision of Louis Four-Fingers Licoracci. His fee would be huge, and he loved it. He never passed judgement on the absurdity or impracticality of any aspect of such a massive project. He was in it for the long haul (and the truckload of money that came with it).

But this set of additions was different from before. Rip and Rhonda had enough money to supply every space (every square foot) with every conceivable amenity; every room, every connecting area, every hallway, every passageway, every feature. No bedroom was overlooked, and there were many. Every bathroom was decorated in a unique style and supplied with appliances and sundries and towels. And there were many bathrooms. The gym was fully equipped; tanning beds; massage tables; no area was left empty. Saunas, steam rooms equipped to the max for major sweat events. The dollhouse had more furniture than Anthony's original apartment. Pool, billiard, and snooker tables were brought in. The bowling alleys were up and running with all kinds of shiny modern automated bowling machinery. Every towel in every location was monogrammed with either RPM or BPM.

The model train room had trains. "Who is that guy?" Rhonda asked Rip, pointing at a man in a train engineer's hat who was working away.

"He's the train man," Rip responded.

The model plane barn was filled with remote-controlled airplanes. "Who is that guy?" Rhonda asked Rip, pointing at a man assembling a model plane at a workbench.

"He's the plane man," Rip responded.

Numerous dead animal heads from all over the world were bought at auction and hung on the wood-paneled walls in the trophy room. Many of the trophy heads also brought in numerous tiny creatures along with them—hitchhikers. The infestation became so extensive that it required the services of professional pest control experts. Before the infestation could spread, the trophy room was isolated and everything fogged and gassed and sprayed. The chemical smell never went away, but no insect, lizard, or any other small creature ever survived after visiting that room. Had any of the trophies (the original animals) been alive in that room during the procedure, the chemical saturation would surely have done them in as well. Neither Rip nor Rhonda thought much about the room and rarely went into it. They did not even recognize half of the dead animals on display. What a waste of dead wildlife.

The new formal dining hall was fully equipped with all kinds of fancy eating equipment: knives, forks, and spoons—all different types. There were silver trays, silver platters, fancy plates, silver pitchers, and an assortment of silver devices, the use of which was a big unknown to the happy couple.

It was an exercise in uncontrolled undisciplined illogical extravagance, unmatched in most of human history; in modern times at least. And, while *new* construction was taking place,

Rip and Rhonda were finally outfitting the "finished" areas of their layout with everything they could think of. What a spree!

## Chapter 24 – A Houseful

Over the next few years, the surrounding hills became more and more populated with celebrities, famous athletes, staggeringly rich business persons, and even a few of Dominic's underworld acquaintances. Most of the new neighbors could look down the hills and view Rip and Rhonda's expanding layout—seemingly always under construction.

The happy couple's children reached their teen years and the lack of true parenting began to show. As a result of their being left to their own devices for so many formative years, and the fact that the siblings were somewhat similar in age, the relationship between them began to devolve into a competitive and rancorous one—blood relations be damned. Ms. Spitz was constantly challenged by the children's spoiled behavior. Their attitudes would be disturbing to most observers if the behaviors weren't so petty and amusing. Private schooling did not mitigate any of the issues. The siblings constantly pecked at each other about gum-chewing, noises made while eating, who broke what, who borrowed what, and who was looking at who...funny. Peck, peck, peck. Buzzards pulling off flesh from a mangled mound of roadkill act with more civility. Ms. Spitz was no longer so much a nanny as an ineffectual professional wrestling referee. A well-paid referee, and adequate nevertheless. All of this turmoil was far beyond the reach of Rip and Rhonda who were always involved with expanding their layout. But, managing all the elements in the layout was slowly, and increasingly taking up more of their time; time that could be better spent coming up with fun new additions and features.

During one particularly cold winter an invasion took place. The luxury attics became home to a large number of raccoons and squirrels, all seeking respite from the freezing temperatures. There were all sorts of animal entry points: holes due to poorly-aligned roof angles and cracks where the roof was missing flashing. Whether or not an entry point was due to poor construction or whether it was the handiwork of industrious, opportunistic nocturnal visitors, the roof was as porous as a pair of twenty-year-old men's briefs. It was cold outside and warm inside so as one fluffy raccoon reasoned, "I must get in." The holes in the roof also allowed a significant number of rats to get into the walls and set up shop for raising families of their own. There was constant banging going on in the ceiling and scratching and digging going on in the walls. Due to Rip's lifelong fear of heights, only one stairway was ever built into the entire layout: the access stairway to the entire luxury attic complex.

That was where all the animals were. So much for using (or visiting) the luxury attics—as if Rip or Rhonda or anyone had ever been up there anyway.

Holes in the roof also led to numerous leaks during rain or snow. Rain was direct—rain coming down, watery leakage following. With snow, the leakage was slow as the snow melted over time. The giant aviary was hit the hardest. All the Plexiglas panels seemed to leak around the edges. It was as if the aviary was no longer an interior part of the house at all.

Construction was always in a manic state—almost unmanageable in scope—so there was never much coordination with existing structures when new rooms and features were added. In the case of the leaky aviary, a tiny slant in the slab allowed all the water leakage to funnel into adjacent rooms of the house.

Rip and Rhonda were always able to carry on, primarily by avoiding the affected areas and ignoring many of the problems. Their children argued over who was to sleep where, shuffling rooms like musical chairs and avoiding the increasing number of "wet" rooms. Each of the siblings eventually found shelter in other bedrooms far away from each other in different locations around the layout. Ms. Spitz was somewhat pleased with that development: she would no longer have to listen to the siblings arguing and picking on one another deep into the night.

When the raccoons broke through one of the ceilings in the house, it was becoming too much. Rip and Rhonda were awakened early one morning with a big, smelly raccoon prancing around on their bed. It had one of Rhonda's silver-backed hairbrushes clenched in its teeth. The raccoon did not recoil in terror when Rhonda screamed at it, but the raccoon slowly and carefully disembarked from the bed and made for the door of the bedroom leaving a little token of its appreciation behind on the bedspread: a half-eaten dead mouse. In the raccoon's eyes, it was obviously a fair trade for taking Rhonda's brush.

It took a dozen or more days for the busy pest control service to finally clear out all the animals. There were so many large, ripped-out animal entry points that fixing all of them was beyond the scope of their pest control business. Louis Licoracci had to be summoned and repairs had to be started.

"I hope all this repair work and cost is not going to have an effect on our layout plans," Rhonda said to Rip.

"Absolutely not," said Rip. "We'll make it work. We always have."

But this kind of thing was becoming a more and more frequent distraction. They always seemed to be fixing toilets: gummed up works, leaks, overflows, flooding, noises. One toilet made a loud banging sound—had the rugby-playing attic raccoons returned? As more and more of the toilets became non-functional Rip, Rhonda, Ms. Spitz, visitors (primarily Anthony and Whitney), and the kids were forced to seek out a functioning toilet (somewhere, anywhere in the layout) when the necessity arose. What a pain. At three a.m. on a cold and wet winter night, going from a warm bedroom, through a maze of rooms, across a patio, by a frozen-over swimming pool, and into the Cabana just to use the toilet— well, something had to be done.

So, onward. The increasingly dissatisfied (but happy) couple had to get Four-Fingers Licoracci to bring in contractors and handyman services to fix the roof and the plumbing and the electrical system and the peeling wallpaper and the mold and the water feature equipment (frozen to death in the subzero cold) and numerous other instances of dysfunction. Not only were contractors required to repair broken items, but there were items that, although supposedly finished, never worked in the first place (e.g. half of the light switches). Rip and Rhonda always seemed to be dealing with whole teams of workers plodding around their house doing this or that, invading their privacy. At night they could smell paint, building materials, wet plaster, glue, cigarette smoke, and whatever remained of the workers' lunches. Lying in bed at night was a small respite from the daily chaos. Even so, both of them had similar recurring visions and/or nightmares about black fingers, dirty fingernails, and butt cracks. And as for daytime hanky panky and other afternoon delights...forget about it.

On one occasion, Rip saw a group of workers huddled around a makeshift barbecue pit, out, away from the house. They were cooking a dead raccoon they had found in the giant dumpster everyone was throwing things into—a stray piece of two-by-four had apparently clobbered the raccoon on the head and sent it to that great luxury attic in raccoon heaven.

"You're not going to eat that, are you?" Rip asked them.

"Nem nem nem," one of them said in some kind of Slavic language. "No English." The worker went back to tending the carcass with a two-foot piece of iron rebar as the animal roasted on the sputtering fire. The raccoon's skinless skull, lying at the edge of the little metal grill, seemed to be giving the assembled group an evil smile. Rip, who had now lost his appetite for any kind of meat, turned and walked away.

## Chapter 25 – Something for the Help

The constant construction, detailed decisions about every little thing, and the high level of maintenance was beginning to overwhelm the happy couple. Management of all the moving parts was especially getting to the incredibly patient Four-Fingers Licoracci. So Rip and Rhonda tasked Licoracci with hiring a full-time foreman to manage the construction, the repairs, and the maintenance. Of course a job like that would require the foreman to live on site so a foreman's residence was built into the layout.

Foreman's Residence: 2,232 ft²
New grand total: 91,762 ft².

An area near the construction entrance was chosen for the building and construction began immediately. Before long, the new, foreman's residence was complete and ready for occupancy. Licoracci hired a stern and capable foreman by the name of Ticker Turlew. This competent (if uncouth) fellow was more than happy to move into the new foreman's residence. Turlew was a former dock-worker operating at the mysterious edge of Dominic's importation sphere. He was familiar with the family even though he had never met Rip. After only a few weeks the foreman's residence was an absolute pigsty. But nobody noticed or cared as long as Turlew kept things humming along.

The first time Turlew and Rip crossed paths was when Licoracci brought Turlew up to the big house with some news for Rip and Rhonda.

"I have some disturbing news for you Mr. and Ms. Mousewater," Turlew said. "There seems to be a lot of pilfering of building materials going on. At first it was only minor, but lately it has become a real problem."

"Will it affect our plans for the layout?" Rhonda asked.

"Most certainly," Turlew replied. "It's slowing things down considerably."

"Heavens," Rhonda gasped. "What can be done?"

Turlew looked at Licoracci, "Well, might I suggest..."

With the appearance of the lost intruder in the dead of night and the apparent ongoing crime spree surrounding their construction site, Rip and Rhonda knew what had to be done.

    Security Office and Bathroom (2300 ft²)
    Adjoining Security Camera and Video monitoring Station (840 ft²)
    Full Coverage Video Surveillance System
    Detention Center (930 ft²)

Jail Cell with Plumbing (120 ft²)

Key Management and Manufacturing Kiosk (340 ft²)

Locksmith Shack (640 ft²)

Guard Towers (8) with One Bathroom Each (3840 ft² total)

Gatehouses (8) with One Bathroom Each (1840 ft² total)

Indoor Pistol Range (2110 ft²)

Armory (1200 ft²)

Vault (790 ft²)

Secret Collectibles Vault (1150 ft²)

Panic Room with Bathroom and Kitchenette (1530 ft²)

Underground Survival Shelter with Full Facilities (4840 ft²)

Main Tunnel to Survival Shelter (1600 ft²)

Network of Secret Security Feature Connecting Passageways (3840 ft²)

Security Additions: 27,910 ft²

New grand total: 119,672 ft²

Total Bathrooms: 74

Construction and maintenance on Rip and Rhonda's layout was being felt in the Big City: resources were being drained away, construction crews were diverted, maintenance and handyman contractors were poached from other jobs. At any given time, hundreds of individuals were at work on Rip and Rhonda's property.

"We have a new problem," Turlew advised Rip and Rhonda. "We have so many workers on site that some of the newer construction efforts are causing damage to completed parts of your layout. And maintenance crews are interfering with construction crews, especially the plumbers. We can probably sort it out using some modern computerized project planning software."

"So what does that mean?" Rhonda asked.

Turlew continued, "It means that we should add a computer center annex to your existing architect's office. In doing so I think Mr. Licoracci and I will be able to coordinate all the activities for maximum efficiency and minimizing damage to existing structures. There's a lot going on here, on your estate, I think you'd agree."

Architect's Computer Center: 880 ft²
New grand total: 120,552 ft²

The new improved system seemed to be working well with both Licoracci and Turlew feverishly completing every whimsical addition to Rip and Rhonda's layout. Excavation for the 200-foot deep survival shelter (including all of its tunnels and passageways) was still taking a lot of time—solid rock layers, ground water issues, routine cave-ins, disgruntled and claustrophobic ex-mine workers. Everything was completed except the survival shelter when...

## Chapter 26 – What the Hell?

Four-Fingers Licoracci was all a-titter when he approached Rip and Rhonda in the main den. He had just come from the one remaining construction area (the survival shelter) in order to have an emergency meeting. "I need to show you something before we proceed," he told them, acting very mysteriously. "If you'll come with me, please." His eyebrows were all raised up and his lips were puckered. Who knows what all this meant.

Licoracci proceeded to open a secret panel, a panel built into the wall of the den and known to everyone—not secret enough. The panel revealed one of the many hidden passages leading to the survival shelter—the last remaining item, still under construction, but nearly completed. The trio crowded their way into the shelter elevator—a sophisticated looking elevator but very noisy. Licoracci was still acting mysteriously as the elevator took the group down to the subterranean construction area 200 feet below ground. Licoracci still wouldn't say what was on his mind. Rip felt very uncomfortable in the small elevator so he just closed his eyes and thought of other things while the elevator rattled and scratched its way down. When they reached the bottom Rip and Rhonda marveled at what had already been finished.

"I had no idea how much of this was already done," Rhonda commented. Even without furniture, decorative accoutrements, or survival stockpiles, the survival shelter looked like a luxury hotel suite: bathrooms, a sitting room, a library, and a kitchen.

"What did you want to show us?" Rip asked impatiently. Two hundred feet down and without a fully functioning climate control system, it was getting very hot.

Without saying another word Four-Fingers motioned for the couple to follow as he cracked open the door to the main bedroom. Before going in, Licoracci turned and asked the couple, "Just a quick question. You have all this space down here, rooms, and this one big bedroom... Well, it occurred to me that you've made no provision for any of your kids. I know it's *your* business, but were you two planning on surviving—whatever catastrophe it might be—and leaving your children behind to fend for themselves?"

After a small pause, Rip said, "What is it you wanted to show us?"

"OK. Check this out," Licoracci said. He opened the door fully and the three of them entered the bedroom with a blast of heat hitting them in their faces. Air seemed to be rushing into the room from behind them. It was all very strange. The large room was empty, but at least half of the floor was gone. Before them was a giant pit radiating heat— enough heat to force them back. With no working air conditioning units or any kind of mechanical ventilation, the heat was stifling.

"Why is it that we aren't already roasted from this heat?" Rhonda asked Licoracci.

"When we started the construction down here, this deep, we had to bore a whole array of air shafts down from the surface in order for the crews to be able to work on this extensive underground complex—you know, to get enough air. Even so, it was hotter than hell for them. Crews had to be shuttled in and out. When this floor caved in, the air shafts were able to let at least some of this powerful heat rise upward and out to the surface on its own. As you can see, most of the heat from this fiery hell-pit just rises straight up through the open shafts and to the outside. Still, the heat is almost unbearable as you can tell. And that sulfur smell. Whew!"

Licoracci pointed out a half dozen openings in the ceiling. "Without some kind of additional mechanical ventilation, those air shafts up there are not nearly enough to handle all the heat coming out of this pit; but without the shafts, we wouldn't be able to stand here—we would be roasted like you said, Ms. Mousewater. Dead already—from the heat, or that sulfur gas, or both."

"So when did they open up this giant hole?" Rip then asked Licoracci.

"Well, day before yesterday, while one of the finish-out crews was working in the sitting room back there, the floor, as you see it here, completely caved in, leaving this gigantic and may I say very deep pit. There was a mad scramble for the elevator, let me tell you."

"Ironic—hmmm—a *survival* shelter..." Rhonda mused.

As Rip tried to look out over the edge, into the pit, his fear of heights got the best of him. He backed away quickly, only catching a glimpse of what was down in the pit. Hundreds of feet down, the bottom was glowing, bubbling orange and black and red and yellow—it looked like lava and was folding over on itself. The glow illuminated the bedroom and the entire confines of the pit, red-orange and hot. The air rising from the pit was so hot that it burned Rip's face if he got too near the edge. Rhonda took a quick look down into the pit and also had to quickly back away. Just as Licoracci said, the hot air was rising straight up and out, almost forming a solid wavy column of heat. The wall on the other side of the room, the other side of the pit, looked distorted by the rising hot air—much like the effect seen over an asphalt highway on searing hot desert day. The rising column of air was causing a funny kind of breeze as air was being pulled from the other parts of the shelter, pulled down from the air shafts in those rooms.

"What do you think it is?" Rhonda asked Licoracci, holding onto Rip's arm.

"Well, I have *my* opinion. You can take it or leave it. But I think we've opened up a cavity exposing the bowels of hell itself." Four-Fingers walked around to one side of the pit and pointed down into it, "If you look closely you can see people down there, burning, tortured. We have stumbled upon hell itself." He squatted down just far enough from the edge to keep his exposed skin from scalding. "That's only my opinion," you understand. He seemed mesmerized by the glow from the pit.

"People? Well, hmm. I think we need a second opinion," Rip said without looking at Licoracci and keeping an eye on the edge of the pit. "Can't we fill it in with cement?"

"Or cover it back up?" Rhonda added.

"There's not enough cement on the planet to fill in a pit this big and this deep. And covering it back up isn't possible either," Licoracci answered. "Even if it were possible to cover it over, would you really want to sleep in this room knowing that below you the fires of hell were burning and boiling and bubbling. And what about all those people down there?"

Neither Rip nor Rhonda knew what people Four-Fingers was talking about—people, what people? Maybe the superstitious Licoracci had been breathing in too much gas from the pit, gas released during construction. But the pit was real enough and the heat was real enough.

Licoracci continued staring down into the pit, his face getting redder by the minute. "I had the project engineer take a look at it. Yesterday, he brought in a geologist. Neither of them could explain it. There's no volcanism in this area; no hot springs or anything like that. It's *hell* I tell you. And those people..."

"Should you be so close to the edge?" Rip asked. "Is it even safe for us to be down here at all?"

"Don't know, but we're here. We're alive—for now," Licoracci responded, still focusing on the pit in a kind of trance. Rip and Rhonda then stepped back a little further with a notion to get on back to the surface.

"What do you suggest we do about it?" Rhonda then asked, gazing at Licoracci at the edge of the pit. She and Rip continued to retreat in small steps, backing away from the pit.

"I've got no friggin' idea," Licoracci responded with a resigned gasp. "I've never dealt with anything like it; don't know what to do about it. What do *you* suggest?" Licoracci kept his attention on the raging pit. Licoracci's squatting so close to the edge was making Rip very uncomfortable and the heat was making Licoracci's face very red and sweaty.

"What about the effect on the rest of our layout? Can't we just cave in the shelter and the elevator shaft? You know, close it off and forget about it without covering over the pit?" Rhonda asked innocently.

Still squatting, Licoracci turned his head and looked up, expressionless, toward Rip and Rhonda. Not having an answer, Licoracci then stood up, ready to leave. He was not overflowing with ideas about how to resolve anything associated with the pit. But the combination of heat, the suffocating lack of oxygen in the air, and standing up much too quickly caused him to lose his balance—he staggered, he tipped over, and he fell, head first, into the pit, waving his limbs as if performing a bizarre (and one-time-only) aerial routine. Without making a sound, his silhouetted spidery form became smaller and smaller until he disappeared into the hellish fiery pit and was completely consumed.

"Wow! Did you see that?" Rip exclaimed. From where they stood, neither of them could actually see Licoracci's final resting place—as if anything was left of him. So it was probably for the best that he just disappeared, silently, winging his way into the fires of hell—*the* hell, or so old superstitious Four-Fingers believed.

"Yeah. That was really something," Rhonda responded. "And all that waving and flailing as he went over the edge."

Rip backed away, further from the pit but still keeping a watchful eye on it. "Yeah, wow! It happened so fast. I mean, one minute he's here, ranting about hell's bowels, bowels with people in them...and then he's gone. Just like that." Rip tried to snap his fingers but they were too slippery with sweat to make any noise. The two of them were so distracted by the demise of Licoracci they had forgotten that they were literally being baked alive by the ambient heat in the room—ambient heat given off by the rising column of scalding hot air over the pit.

"You realize what this means?" Rhonda then asked.

"I guess we'll have to figure out what to do with this survival shelter...and this...this pit," Rip said as he slowly moved forward in order to get another look over the edge.

"Well yes, that too, But. No. I mean we'll have to get another architect if we want to continue expanding our layout." Rhonda began backing away from the pit and toward the door.

"Oh, yes," Rip replied still looking at the pit. He turned and followed Rhonda to the elevator. "And a change of clothes when we get back to the surface..."

The two of them took the elevator back up to the secret passageway. They left the shelter unfinished and never returned to it again—it was not so much a decision as it was a desire not be bothered by it. With all the tunnels and secret passageways it was highly improbable that anyone would ever accidentally stumble upon the shelter elevator, much less be willing to lower themselves two hundred feet down without knowing where they were going to end up. Rip and Rhonda never mentioned anything to anyone about Licoracci. They never reported the incident. Of course official investigations into Licoracci's sudden disappearance turned up nothing—investigations were brief and cursory at best, thanks to the many connections Dominic had made through the years. Even Turlew the foreman was not all that interested in digging too deep into finding out what had happened to Four-Fingers Licoracci. Too many questions...too many bad answers. The crews that were working on the shelter were tasked with other projects. The survival shelter phase of layout expansion was considered complete, but maintenance and repairs, well, that continued on. And on. And on.

Year-round, the heat from the pit continued to rise up to the surface through the six ventilation pipes from the shelter bedroom. Curiously, during winter months, the hot air from below would hit the moist cold air above and produce clouds of water vapor fog that could be seen emanating from the ground almost like six small hot springs. Rip and Rhonda had the area fenced off and explained away the little ground-level "smokestacks" as a kind of natural phenomenon. "Who needs a bunch of fancy fountains when you have something like this?"

And so, the (once again) happy couple went about finding yet another architect (or architect-ish person) to take over. They had even bigger plans for additions to their layout. They may not have considered their three children when designing the survival shelter, but the "needs of the children" provided all the rationalization required for Rip and Rhonda's next big expansion plans. It was going to be awesome.

## Chapter 27 – Uh-Oh

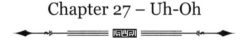

Rolling down her car window, the woman in the driver's seat said, "I'm looking for a Mr. Brisbane Pease Mouse-eater." She was speaking to the guard at the construction entrance to the Mousewater property.

"First of all, it's *Mousewater*, not Mouse-*eater* and second, who's asking?" the guard replied curtly.

"Sorry...I'm City slash County Inspector Maria Agitando and I need to speak to Mr. or Ms. Mouse-*water*." The unfortunate slip of the tongue revealed a certain level of hidden disrespect by the new City/County Inspector. It may be said proverbially that without constant vigilance, what one says many times in private may someday, inadvertently find its way out into the open.

"You'll have to talk to Mr. Turlew if it's about the construction. He's over there in the foreman's house. See that white brick chimney? Pretty sure he's at home...no construction going on today...hasn't been any for a number of days now." The guard pointed to a tall white chimney emerging from the trees only a few hundred feet away.

"Thank you," Ms. Agitando said as she drove on through without getting approval from the guard. She parked her car in front of the modest white brick house of the foreman, gathered up a folder stuffed with papers, and grabbed her insulated coffee mug. While she was preparing all this, Ticker Turlew popped out of the front door of the house, having been alerted by the guard that Ms. Agitando from the Big City was on her way. Turlew had been dreading this day ever since Four-Fingers Licoracci disappeared. Turlew had no experience in dealing with city officials over issues involving the construction because Licoracci had always managed these types of encounters. And in especially prickly situations, Simon Latherine would be called upon.

"Are you Turlew?" she said in a very official way, slamming her car door behind her.

"Yes. What can I help you with?"

"I'm City slash County Inspector Agitando and I prefer to talk to Mr. or Ms. Mouse-water." She was giving the foreman's house the once-over, thinking of her own small apartment. "But you might be able to answer a few questions first."

"Let's go inside and sit down." Turlew motioned for her to follow him.

No sooner than the two of them were seated than Ms. Agitando started right in. "There seems to be a lot of construction going on here on this property and..."

"No. Not right at this moment," Turlew interrupted.

"Well, there has been. Almost every contractor in the Big City has worked out here at one time or another."

"That may be true," Turlew said with a proud chuckle.

"I have not been able to find any record of the construction. Not a single valid permit has been issued for anything on this property. No plans have been filed. As far as the county is concerned, this wooded acreage is vacant. Also, there has never been an assessment of the property for tax purposes. The only way that this oversight could even be uncovered and investigated was because of a deed transferal from a Dominic Pease Mousewater to a Mr. Brisbane Pease Mousewater and ostensibly his spouse, Ms. Rhonda Proody Mousewater. Otherwise, this place doesn't even exist."

Turlew knew that this was trouble and attempted to delay and derail the inspector as much as possible. For a short while he remained non-committal and provided plenty of double talk, but eventually he ran out of impenetrable banter. "I'm only the foreman. If you would excuse me for a moment." He quickly stood up and went into his back bedroom, stealthily shutting the door behind him. Ms. Agitando, armed for bear, was left alone with her exposed papers and her half-empty coffee mug, feeling a bit brushed aside. She waited and waited. And waited.

"Mr. Turlew, Mr. Turlew?" She got no response as she began checking her watch more and more frequently as the minutes ticked by. She could hear someone talking but could not make out what was being said. About twenty minutes later Turlew emerged from the bedroom with a calm, innocent, "aw shucks" look on his face. Ms. Agitando took a deep breath to speak, but before she could say a word the doorbell rang and Turlew rushed to answer it. In walked a well-dressed man, all smiles and congeniality.

"Hello, Ms. Agitando. I'm happy to meet you at last. Seems our paths have crossed many times down at the Big County Courthouse, but we've never met officially. I'm Simon Q. Latherine the Mousewater's family attorney."

After a curious back and forth between Latherine and Agitando, Latherine suggested a more formal meeting at the Mousewater estate on the next day. Although Ms. Agitando was anxious to get down to business, *right now*, she acquiesced to Latherine's request and left Turlew's house gasping for some clean bullshit-free air.

Latherine left Turlew's house and proceeded up to the estate. Having explained the inspector situation to Rip and Rhonda, Latherine provided them with a number of options. They gave him no indication of which option they favored in the matter, preferring instead to leave all the hard decisions to Latherine.

"I have just a few questions for you before I proceed," Latherine stated. To Rip and Rhonda the questions and subsequent discussion had quite an edge to them, but they cooperated fully. They both wanted to get on with the next phase of construction and expansion...without any more impediments. Revealing dark secrets about their layout was further bonding the happy couple with Latherine, much like the bond developed between Latherine and Dominic over the years.

Dante Lorca was a huge ex-football player who had a checkered past filled with street-smart activities and correctional experiences. People in the "business" usually referred to him as "Lorca the Orca" or just "The Orca" even though he did not know the first thing about how to swim. It was quite a while since he was last called upon for services, services required by the Mousewater family. The late Dominic had always trusted him completely in many "impossible" situations throughout the years. Lorca's loyalty to the Mousewater family was probably only equaled by the loyalty of Latherine himself. So now, for the first time, he was going into service for Dominic's son.

The next day, Latherine met Ms. Agitando at Turlew's house once again. Latherine preferred to take his own car from Turlew's driveway over to the Mousewater estate proper. A reluctant Ms. Agitando sat in the front passenger seat. After she had settled in, Dante Lorca appeared in the back seat, seemingly from out of nowhere. The sudden presence of the intimidating and heavy-breathing Lorca startled Ms. Agitando and was making her extremely uncomfortable. She was expecting to be piano-wired at any moment and was very relieved when they all arrived without incident at the front door to the estate proper. Latherine, large briefcase in hand, knocked on the door (since the doorbell was not working, and never had). Rhonda opened the door, welcomed them, and escorted them in and around, this way and that, into the lavishly-furnished parlor. Ms. Agitando could not help but gawk at the elaborate décor and furnishings as the group wound its way around the house. She also noticed all the little things that were broken, crooked, unfinished, peeling, or poorly constructed. As she followed along through the rat's maze of rooms she began to consider how much trouble she would have finding her way back out by herself. Nevertheless, Rhonda's pleasant and cheerful demeanor was having a calming effect. But the armpits of Ms. Agitando's blouse were indicating that, deep inside, she was still really sweating it.

The group came to a halt in a large, tall room with a tapestry hanging on one wall. The tapestry was an inadequate attempt to cover an unsightly defect in the wall. Rhonda then turned toward Ms. Agitando, "Mr. Latherine has explained the situation to Brisbane and myself. I don't see a problem here."

Agitando was baffled by the remark. She was ready to ask where Mr. Mousewater might be but with Ms. Agitando's mouth open, ready to speak, Rhonda broke in, very politely, "If you'll excuse me…" Rhonda stood up and left the room. "What is it with these people?" Ms. Agitando thought to herself.

"Well," Latherine said. "Let's take a look around." He guided Ms. Agitando and Dante Lorca around to many of the standard rooms of the house. She thought about saying something like, "I just remembered a meeting I'm supposed to attend." She knew for sure that they weren't going to buy any of that. So on she went. Occasionally during the "tour" Ms. Agitando would summon up a comment like "very nice" or "this room is very big." Her generic comments were always met with silence from "The Orca" while Latherine provided a few sparse but polite replies. As Ms. Agitando became more and more lost in the Mousewater maze, she lost interest in her official duties and just wanted *out*.

Coming through another passageway, the group entered the luxurious and inviting den, Latherine gathered the group near the secret panel. "This is really something you just have to see," Latherine said as Lorca stood by silently. Feeling extremely intimidated, Ms.

Agitando entered the secret passageway and soon the threesome arrived at the elevator to the survival shelter. Lorca was so huge that the elevator was especially crowded. If Ms. Agitando had not been sweating it before, she was sweating now. And how.

She could feel an increase in temperature as the elevator lowered its way down to the underground shelter. At the bottom, all she wanted to do was get out of the elevator and stretch her arms, having been stuffed in there with the massive Lorca. Entering the main room in the unfinished shelter, she was impressed by its size and how elaborate it was. Since Latherine was so enthusiastic about the *tour*, she began to relax...a little. But the heat and the anxiety were ruining her outfit.

The tour of the shelter was short—there were only a few large rooms. Lastly, as the three members of the group entered the bedroom, she saw the pit—the pit that reached down into the bowels of hell itself, and unbeknownst to anyone but Rip and Rhonda, the last resting place of the now-vaporized Four-Fingers Licoracci.

Lorca seemed to be awfully close behind her. He was nudging her closer and closer to the edge of the pit using his weather balloon abdomen. The heat was unbearable and her coif was now all shot to hell—so to speak. She looked at Latherine trying to evoke sympathy or mercy or salvation but he was busy with his briefcase.

While still looking at his briefcase he said, "Be careful over there, Ms. Agitando. You know, it's so hot in that pit that any living thing that happened to fall in would disappear completely, without a trace, not even DNA would survive in such an inferno." Now acting very officially, he jarringly came to the point, "Here are your options, Ms. Agitando." He opened the briefcase to reveal numerous $10K packs of fairly new one-hundred-dollar bills. He looked at the money and then at Ms. Agitando, raising his eyebrows up and down several times. Then, without turning his head, his eyes looked over at the fiery pit. With a serious expression on his face he nodded toward the pit and then looked back at Ms. Agitando who was being continuously nudged from behind by a big wall of Dante Lorca. Latherine waited impatiently for an answer.

Thinking and thinking and thinking it over, as if she had a choice, a terrified Ms. Agitando finally said, "I believe I prefer the 'green' option over the 'orange' one." With a shaking forefinger, she pointed nervously at the briefcase.

"Excellent choice, Ms. Agitando," Latherine said as he handed the heavy briefcase over to her. "Now, let's get out of here. It's very hot!"

Lorca did not move an inch so Ms. Agitando had to walk around his heavy-breathing hulk in order to get back to the elevator. The trio was drenched with sweat and the elevator ride back to the top was an adventure unto itself—noisy, smelly, sweaty, wet, sticky, crowded. Putting it into perspective, seeing how things might have turned out very differently, the elevator ride (as bad as it was) in actuality didn't seem at all that terrible to the hyperventilating Ms. Agitando. She gripped the handle of the briefcase tightly as the elevator rose up to the surface and the heat slowly faded away.

When all was said and done, Latherine was optimistic that the Agitando situation wasn't just a temporary solution to an ongoing problem. But, for some time afterward, as far as the Big City/County was concerned, the Mousewater property was still just a lot of vacant acreage.

## Chapter 28 – So Far…

Between Rip's lack of interest in the business and Rhonda's increasing obsession with the layout, Simon Q. Latherine was quickly becoming the *de facto* head of Mousewater Enterprises. He was making excellent money for himself and as long as he and his few financial advisors continued to generate unlimited funds for Rip and Rhonda's indulgences, the business moved along smoothly and successfully without participation by the happy couple. All of the shady and ruthless aspects of the business were dealt with by Latherine (and his "associates"). Unlike Dominic, Latherine was fearless when it came to building up the Mousewater empire in full view of more organized groups of underworld characters and families. He was proud of the fact that, although Dominic was no longer in the picture, Mousewater Enterprises had become more profitable than ever before. As profits soared under his guidance, Latherine became fascinated with the ever-expanding array of additions to the Mousewater estate and was more than capable of keeping officials, legalities, and illegalities from getting in Rip and Rhonda's way.

The currently quiescent foreman, Ticker Turlew, knew that he would soon receive new directives from Rip and Rhonda. With help from Simon Latherine in locating a suitable replacement for Licoracci, Turlew hired a new manager to be in charge of the (soon-to-be) next phase of construction. His name was Dick Farmer, a beefy, mustachioed character dug up out of a swamp full of candidates, all of them operatives from Dominic's past—Dominic's presence was still being felt, right out of the grave; a fitting legacy. Farmer was probably the most questionable character yet to be put in charge of such a large and demanding construction project—not necessarily in quality of work or know-how, but questionable in his use of strong-arm tactics in getting jobs completed quickly and cheaply. When Farmer agreed to sign up, Turlew indicated to him that he and Farmer were always to remain on standby until called in by the Mousewaters for a construction summit. They were on standby for a long time.

Rip's friend Anthony might have felt abandoned during all this time had it not been for Anthony's flourishing, lucrative, and time-consuming career as a writer. Many of Rip's neighbors in the hills surrounding the Mousewater estate were willing targets of Anthony's columns and stories. He helped them build and maintain celebrity status and they helped him have an independent career as a writer. Slowly but surely Anthony's subject matter evolved for the better, becoming more and more mainstream, legitimate, and respected. His success made it possible for him and his girlfriend, Whitney, to get married. Soon, they were able to move into a large, high-rise condo of their own—downtown, in the Big City. Rip offered to build Anthony a place somewhere on the Mousewater property, but Anthony (and especially Whitney) respectfully declined. Anthony wanted to be in the "middle of the action" in the Big City and, more importantly, away from some of Rip and Rhonda's neighbors—some of which (and that would include a fair number of hostiles) would potentially be looking straight down on top of Anthony and Whitney's place. Whitney was most concerned about that possibility.

Considering Anthony's career and as tempting as it may have been for Anthony, he was always very fastidious in keeping all of the potential, red-hot, Mousewater "stories" to himself. He was a very loyal friend. It would never occur to him to betray the trust invested in him by Rip. He even went so far as to firmly say "no comment" when a curious celebrity from the "Hills" asked him about the Mousewaters during an interview—he wasn't willing to provide the tiniest tidbit of information, even "off-the-record."

Anthony had long since stopped being surprised by the magnitude or the craziness of Rip and Rhonda's additions, but Whitney was not as casually tolerant when she was exposed to things like the underground simulated cave system or the water park. She kept her critical thinking comments to herself for the most part, but on occasion she de-contained a few choice words when some of the absurdities surpassed her threshold of pain. Although Anthony's eternal loyalty was steadfast and never in doubt for a second, his silent tolerance for the truly outlandish expansions of the Mousewater estate would soon crumble.

Over the months following the passing of Dominic, Rip regularly exercised his right to gather books from Dominic's library. Rip never did much reading but he got immense satisfaction in showing up unexpectedly at the Ovums estate and perturbing the slowly deteriorating Ms. Ovums with his tedious, methodical perusing of the bookshelves. It did not matter that Dominic's directive about Rip and the books was probably in a legal grey area, Ms. Ovums believed it and she had no money to pay for a lawyer to contest it. On the other hand, due to a technicality (rigidly enforced by Ms. Ovums) Rhonda was not allowed to accompany Rip in his intrusive excursions. Only Rip—no one else.

Although Dominic's house now belonged to her, Ms. Ovums had no funds of her own to pay for much of anything. Therefore:

    The elevator and partially demolished stairway were never repaired

    Payments for gas, electric, and water utilities became seriously in arrears

    There was no money for maintenance

    There was no money for food

Every time he visited for a book excursion, Rip felt saddened when he saw how Dominic's mansion was being neglected and allowed to deteriorate.

For a while, the enterprising Ms. Ovums sold furniture and other household odds and ends in order to raise money to keep the utilities from being shut down—and for Ms. Ovums to eat. This solution lasted only until the house was emptied of almost everything. Her first inclination was to sell off the artwork (paintings and sculptures by famous artists). She quickly discovered that not a single one of the items was authentic—they were all forgeries or fake "unknown works." She tried seducing young men and women in hopes that they might be persuaded to share their own wealth with her but this was a monumental failure as well. It seems that they were thinking the same thing about Ms. Ovums and conniving to get at some of *her* "wealth"—who was the exploiter and who was exploitee?

She tried renting the upstairs bedrooms to boarders, but there were few takers; dangerous stairway, lack of furniture, unreliable utilities, the presence of Ms. Ovums. The few that were willing to brave these obstacles all turned out to be penniless glib bums who freeloaded and dragged out their stay for as long as possible, explanations and excuses acting as proxies for cold hard cash...

All except for one tenant, a Mr. Boyd Locust. One night, this particular tenant ripped out all the copper pipes in his and two other bathrooms and made off with them ostensibly to sell for a big profit. He had done this type of thing before in other cities using different false names. His skill at pulling out the plumbing without alerting anyone made him a somewhat pseudo-celebrity known to the authorities as the "Copperhead Bandit." Ms. Ovums was just one of his many victims. As far as anyone knew, he was never apprehended.

As a last resort, she decided to sell the house, but that proved to be impossible. No one was willing to buy just a house when the land under it was owned by someone else—i.e. Brisbane Pease Mousewater.

Ms. Ovums could feel her grip on the house slowly slipping away and she had thoughts of stirring up trouble for Rip and Rhonda. But she was terrified of Simon Q. Latherine and dropped such notions. More than once Simon Latherine had entertained the idea of introducing Ms. Ovums to the ironically-named survival shelter—a contingency plan that he wished would never be necessary. Then one day Ms. Ovums gathered up her few belongings and moved away. Somehow Dominic had masterminded this scenario long before his passing. He may have been ornery, but he was very smart—street smart.

In order to survive, post-Mousewater, Ovums made a plan to seek out another lonely old man or woman—someone who was willing to hire her; a lonely old *rich* man or woman. An aging, sexually-repressed person, living alone, would appreciate her offerings, and would be a perfect match with Ms. Ovums's particular variety of skills. And so she was gone, beyond the Mousewater sphere and far away from the Big City. Simon Latherine was able to regain Mousewater ownership of the entire property and after extensive repair work and refurbishing, the house and land together were sold for a handsome sum. Rip and Rhonda were happy to give Latherine his requested share of the funds. But they were especially happy to add the windfall to their resources for the next layout expansion. When the time was right they would *really* be able to unleash the Kraken.

## Chapter 29 – The Gathering, Part 1

There was an air of unfamiliar tranquility around the Mousewater estate. The children, separated from each other in distant bedrooms and away from Ms. Spitz, were living essentially independent lives. Trust fund money and supplements from Rip and Rhonda kept the children satisfied—extravagant expenditures by the three siblings went unnoticed as did their day-to-day activities. Now in their twenties it seemed that none of the three children had any intention of leaving the estate and living elsewhere. None of them had any type of marketable skill and none of the three had the wherewithal or drive to acquire any. Not surprisingly, the siblings had absolutely no interest in their parents—except for the possibility of someday inheriting a third of all that wealth, and maybe more if fortune waved its hand and took out one or more of the other two siblings in the meantime.

Even as adults, every irksome behavior or personality quirk exhibited by one of the siblings was valid grounds for inter-sibling commentary and criticism: personal appearance and fashion choices; indiscreet and questionable sexual escapades; pranks; social ineptitude; one-upmanship over trivial achievements; and a host of petty personal habits and idiosyncrasies that any normal person would never notice. Much like their parents, there was not an ounce of desire to travel anywhere, or *go* anywhere for that matter. Although the children confined almost all their activities to the estate, money seemed to flow through their hands like shit through a tin horn. Beyond the residency and financial arrangements, the children had nothing in common with each other and their infrequent encounters wound up being just as caustic as ever. Had they not been forced by circumstances to live together on the same plot of land, they would have gone to separate parts of the planet—as far away from each other as humanly possible.

Figuratively speaking, a lot of molten rock had passed under the survival shelter, but ever since their sensibilities were pierced by the stray comment made by Four-Fingers Licoracci in the survival shelter long ago, Rip and Rhonda were determined to do something decent (eventually) for their estranged children. They were discussing the matter quietly—ostensibly in private—when Rhonda made the observation that the children already had two swimming pools, a water park, an extensive model train layout, dozens of model planes, dogs, and many other amenities. What else could they possibly want? Rip shrugged. They had no idea that their conversation was being overheard by Trina who was wandering around the house trying to find the kitchen.

"What are you two talking about?" Trina inquired.

"You, as a matter of fact," Rhonda replied. "We want to expand the layout with things that you and your brothers might want."

"Well, I don't know about them, but I can think of many things that I would like," Trina said.

"Do you know where your brothers are right now?" Rip asked.

"I haven't a clue," Trina replied. "I don't keep up with their comings and goings. They have to be around here somewhere. Nobody ever leaves this place."

Rhonda then said, "Well, go and find them; tell them that we want to have a family meeting this evening; around, say, 7 o'clock—right here in this room. We'd like to find out what they might want as well."

Needless to say, Trina had no intention of locating her brothers or telling them about expansion plans, so it became up to Rip and Rhonda to get everyone together for a meeting. After two days of negotiating the maze and wasting time, Rip located and told each of the siblings to come to a meeting; and to be prepared to discuss their expansion ideas. The meeting was finally held in the formal dining room with all the principals seated around the long expensive dining table (a table that had never been used for a single meal).

"Well...ahem...*family*," Rip started. "I believe we all know why we're here..."

"You want to make up for building a survival shelter that excluded us," Amador said bluntly.

Orville butted in, "I can see why they would want to exclude you, but why me?"

Trina then added, "Why would they want to include either of you. Neither of you is worth the powder it would take to blow your brains to sh..."

"All right. All right!" Rhonda said sternly. "We're here to see what each of you would like to add to our next layout expansion plan. Let's start with Trina."

"Why her?" Amador asked.

"Well, for no other reason than she's the oldest," Rip answered.

A testy Amador then declared, "That always leaves me last. First Trina then Orville. I always have to live in the shadow of that eleven minutes. Eleven minutes and I'm a second class citizen…third class!"

"All right then, you go first," Rhonda said.

"Now wait a minute, that makes me last…or second…*again*. Why can't I be first?" Orville exclaimed.

"No you don't," Trina said jumping back in. The three of them were now standing and leaning over the table, every comment louder than the one before.

Rip and Rhonda watched in amazement as the three siblings went at it this way for several minutes. Finally Rip called a halt to the bickering and said, "I want the three of you to separate; get out of here right now and write down what you want. And stay out of each other's way. Bring your lists to me or your mother and we'll decide what we want to do with your suggestions. I can tell you right now what I would *like* to do with them…or what I'd like *you* to do with them."

Even though that was the end of the "meeting," the three siblings continued arguing and mumbling to each other as they left the room as a group, only becoming silent as each of them retreated into their own adopted area of the house.

It wasn't until the next day that Trina located Rip and handed over her list to him. Trina spoke very sweetly and innocently, "I don't think you ought do anything for Amador or Orville. You saw how they acted last night. How uncivil. How can I stand up against two big old bullying boys, men, like that? My list is very small, modest and practical." Rip took the list and sent Trina away. She got neither a commitment nor even a reaction from him. Her plan to game it by playing the sweet little daughter card on her father was apparently unsuccessful.

A short time later a similar approach was attempted by Amador. He gave *his* list to Rhonda and said, "Trina cannot possibly love you like a son can—a son like me. A son's love for his mother, a son grateful for being born; a mother who carried him in her womb even if it was stuffed tight with that other guy. Orville couldn't wait to separate from you, that's why he birthed out first. So you see, my list should take priority over the others."

Rhonda stroked her chin and took Amador's list. She too offered no reaction to the conspicuously transparent machinations of her son. Thinking about Orville's imminent approach she was expecting the worst, expecting almost anything.

When Orville finally located his mother, Rip, inconveniently, was by her side. "I don't have a list. I don't need anything but my parents love," Orville offered.

"OK. Good," Rip said. "Anything else?"

Surprised by the lack of response, Orville reluctantly turned to leave. As he slow-walked his exit, he looked back, twice, to see if anything had made a mark. His plan had backfired, gloriously. Attempting to manufacture some kind of segue before he reached the door, he turned back and added, "If I had such a list it wouldn't mean that..." He fumbled around, acting all awkward. Then a folded piece of paper "fell" out of his pocket onto the floor. "Since I didn't give you a list, I thought I might be more deserving than those other two." The piece of paper was alive and shone like a beacon there on the carpet.

"What was that? What fell out of your pocket just now?" Rhonda knew exactly what Orville was up to.

"I don't know," Orville said. "I *started* a list, but..."

"Hand it to me," Rip ordered. Orville lifted the paper off the floor and gave it to Rip.

"I think I'll go now," Orville said. He had no skill as an actor and Rip and Rhonda were actually enjoying all of this weak performance art.

"This list looks pretty complete to me," Rip said. "We'll take a look at it."

Orville retreated to his bedroom thinking he had pulled off something worthy of an award.

Rip and Rhonda didn't know whether to laud their children's disingenuous and devious plotting—Dominic's genes in action—or to be put off by the poor execution displayed by all three amateurs.

The three lists were long and detailed. Any normal person would have tossed all three lists into a roaring fire and possibly tossed the three children into the fire with them—or off the property—for good measure. But the intriguing and outrageous content of the lists got Rip and Rhonda's expansion fever raging once again and, rather than rejecting the lists out of hand, the excited couple began building a hefty list of their own. The Kraken was now stirring in its watery domain.

## Chapter 30 – The Gathering, Part 2

Before considering their children's lists, Rip and Rhonda decided to take a short vacation from it all by bingeing on movies and television shows in their home theater, something they had never done before. Thanks to Latherine, soon after the theater was completed, the shelves were stocked with an enviable number of shows and movies—every genre imaginable. Even though many of the selections were old and dated, neither Rip nor Rhonda had ever seen any of them. Entertainment provided by actors and storytellers was a cultural phenomenon they had rarely, if ever, had a desire for—unlike their children who were frequent users of the theater and had added to the library many, many items of their own; Amador's preferences for sleazy and graphic adult films helped to round out the wide range of genres.

Watching old horror movies, dysfunctional families, crime dramas, comedies (which went over the heads of the happy couple for the most part), and any other fare available in their library, Rip and Rhonda became filled with ideas of their own for the next phase of expansion. The names and content of the movies and shows were completely foreign to them so they just made selections at random. Even so, they were getting a good cross-section of fictional stories and a view of the world outside of the Mousewater estate albeit not a completely real one.

And the constantly running popcorn machine and unlimited snacks were beginning to generate a different type of expansion for the happy couple.

There was a time in the 1800's that a number of people believed that everything that *could* be invented had already *been* invented. Was it arrogance or just a forlorn feeling that the world had run out of ideas? For a while Rip and Rhonda began to believe that there were no more worlds to conquer, no more possibilities for features to expand their layout; but with the infusion of new and fresh ideas from their children, and with all the wonderful things they saw in their home theater, they became more inspired than ever before.

They began work on the lists, tossing out duplicate items and items that just weren't feasible. There was so much work to do. At times it became discouraging and the happy couple would retreat to their home theater for another dose of unreality. Of course they would be inspired all over again with new ideas even though that was not supposed to be the intent of the retreat. However, the happy couple soon became the over-saturated couple—watching so many stories was beginning to feel like work and less like recreation or retreat. Several times Rip and Rhonda made an impulsive decision to spend a few days on the family yacht, away from the estate, away from the children, away from everything. A real retreat. But always, in the end, it was time to return to the estate, to get back at it, and to continue on.

After a few final touches, at long last, the full list (in four parts) was complete. It had taken over a year to get it all finalized. It was a year of frequent visits by each of the children, each one inquiring about the status of the project. Never had the children had so much interest in visiting with Rip and Rhonda.

## Chapter 31 – The Gathering, Part 3

So once again Rip and Rhonda met with their three children, all together, in one place—the formal dining hall; but this time with the stipulation that no one was to speak unless spoken to, upon penalty of having one item deleted from his or her list for each violation. Remarkably (but not surprisingly) this threat kept each of the children in near total (if uncomfortable) silence for the duration of the meeting, except when the discussion turned to the relevant sibling and their list. The meeting was expected to be many hours long so food and drink were brought in regularly—it was the first food to be served and eaten in the formal dining hall since it was added to the layout.

"First, let me say this about the survival shelter," Rip began. "Your exclusion was not an oversight. If you three think your mother and I would last an hour in a confined underground bunker with the likes of you three...well, think again." A believable explanation for the oversight, but far from the truth.

"*She's* the troublemaker," Amador blurted out, pointing at Trina.

"OK, that's one item off of Amador's list," Rhonda announced like an administrator as she grabbed her marker and looked through Amador's wish list. "Here's one. Amador's sex grotto is now...OFF THE LIST!" Rhonda put a dark black line through the item; she was not going to put up with any more nonsense.

Rip took over again as the three siblings behaved like caged tigers surrounded by a roomful of meat. "There are a few items that were eliminated from the list and as strange as it may be, some of these appeared on more than one list. The lighthouse is out. The nearest seashore is over twenty miles away—and what would be the purpose? Don't answer that. There is not enough room for an airstrip, so that's out—airstrip, on all three lists, wow. No zip line. No sky ride or monorail. Why would we need a blimp mooring? Don't answer that one either. The giant Ferris wheel and the roller coaster are out as well. Against my better judgement, the heliport and control tower can stay in."

"Yes!" Orville whispered quietly to himself, shaking his fist underneath the tabletop. He was secretly planning to buy his own helicopter and teach himself how to fly it. If his siblings knew about his plan they surely would have encouraged it...vigorously (both siblings assuming, of course, that Orville's first landing would be his last).

Rip continued, "Your mother nixed the rifle range and the skeet range and I nixed the shopping mall. We'll let Turlew and his crew figure out where to put the Captain's Bridge and the cannon deck. Don't know what they're for. Don't care."

Orville wanted to say something but held his tongue.

Heliport
Control Tower with Bathroom (985 ft²)
Captain's Bridge with Bathroom (630 ft²)
Cannon Deck

Additions: 1615 ft²
New grand total: 122,167 ft²
Total Bathrooms: 76

## Chapter 32 – The Gathering, Trina

"Your mother and I have put your three names on slips of paper in this little box. We'll draw a name out and that person's list will be considered first. Then another slip, second. And the remaining one is last. Number one is...Trina. Number two is...Orville. So number three is Amador. Ok that's it."

Amador raised a very suspicious eyebrow about just how that particular order was "randomly" determined.

And so Trina's list became the focus. Rip enumerated the items, "Studios for ceramics, pottery, glass-blowing, woodworking, metalworking, quilting; a discotheque; art and antique galleries; all kinds of sea life tanks and aquariums; a wildlife management center; a bison barn; an equestrian center with riding trails and waystations; indoor and outdoor courts for racquet sports; croquet lawns; an archery range and target course. And, not to get too far ahead of things here, Amador's falconry field will have to overlap part of the archery range and the bison grazing field in order to fit it in.

"And let me add this: if any of Amador's falcons should wind up with an arrow running through it...well, let me assure you three, there's always skid row in the Big City." Rhonda tugged on Rip's arm and softly said, "I didn't know Amador *had* any falcons. Where does he keep them now?" Rip shrugged and said, "Search me..."

Rip continued, "Now, before we go on... Apparently, all three of you wanted some kind of a golf course—different sizes and numbers of holes. We cannot fit eighteen holes, or even nine holes on our property without severely interfering with many other parts of our layout. So as a compromise we will build four holes, a practice range, a putting green, and all the other facilities needed to support the four-hole course. The course itself will have to be all the way around toward the back end of the property; I don't want a stray golf ball landing in my lobster bisque." Rip turned to Rhonda and whispered, "As if any of them is ever going to use the golf facilities anyway.

"But, we're also going to build a place for practicing and playing indoors with modern indoor golf machinery and an indoor putting green. And the indoor miniature golf course will be built near the beach volleyball court."

"Except for the small golf course lake, we cannot build a regular-sized lake on the property. So, Trina, that leaves out the dock, the marina, the fishing pier, the fisherman's shack, the houseboat, the fleet of motorboats, the sailboat, and the floating casino. I believe that covers everything on Trina's list. Do you have anything to add, Trina?"

"Is it OK if I leave now?" asked Trina.

Rhonda immediately rose halfway up from her chair, brandishing an extended forefinger that was firing daggers at Trina, "You stay glued to that chair as if your life depended on it!"

Rip turned to Rhonda and asked, "What is a 'biz-son' anyway?" Rhonda didn't know either.

And so...

Ceramics Studio (2220 ft²)

Potter's Studio (2980 ft²)

Glass Blowing Studio with Furnace (3860 ft²)

Woodworking Shop (1650 ft²)

Metalworking Shop (2150 ft²)

Quilting Studio (1640 ft²)

Discotheque, DJ Stage, and Electronics Control Center (6490 ft²)

Art Gallery (4400 ft²)

Antique Hall (3210 ft²)

Dolphin Tank

Shark Tank

Sea Life Management Center (2120 ft²)

Sea Life Food and Equipment Storage (2230 ft²)

Outdoor Aquarium

Basement Viewing Station (460 ft²)

Indoor Aquarium (1240 ft²)

Bison Barn and Grazing Field

Wildlife Management Office (1230 ft²)

Wildlife Veterinary Clinic (1850 ft²)

Equestrian Center (2255 ft²)

Stables (12 Horses)

Hay Barn

Stable House (4630 ft²)

Riding Trails

Riding Trail Waystations (7) (1140 ft² each)

Four Tennis Courts

Tennis Locker Room (1950 ft²)

Indoor Badminton Court (1770 ft²)

Indoor Volleyball Court (2280 ft²)

Squash Court (900 ft²)

Outdoor Croquet Lawn with Bleachers

Indoor Croquet Lawn with Spectator Stands (4100 ft²)

Archery Range

Archery Course

Four-Hole Golf Course

Putting Green

Practice Tee

19th Hole with Kitchen and Rest Rooms (3460 ft²)

Golf Locker Room (1880 ft²)

Golf Cart Barn

Greenskeeper's Office and Residence (2840 ft²)

Golf Equipment Barn

Indoor Golf Facility (900 ft²)

Indoor Putting Green (460 ft²)

Indoor Miniature Golf Course (3880 ft²)

Beach Volleyball Court

Falconry Field

Trina's List and Other Additions: 77,015 ft²

New grand total: 199,182 ft²

Total Bathrooms: 103

## Chapter 33 – The Gathering, Orville

"Well then, let's take a look at the items we extracted from Orville's list," Rip said as he flipped through the pages in his hands. "I see we have some more athletic items...I don't suppose it has occurred to any of you that not one of you has any athletic aptitude whatsoever."

"Are we allowed to speak?" Trina asked timidly, slightly raising her hand.

"No," Rhonda replied emphatically.

Rip continued. "We have an indoor track and a basketball court, with a locker room. We also have an indoor rock climbing wall with all kinds of climbing accessories. I still don't envision any of you people using this stuff. How tall is this wall thing anyway, Orville?"

"About forty or fifty feet," Orville replied cautiously.

"Hmm. Hiking trails and biking trails all with their own waystations. And why can't you use the equestrian trails for that?" Rip asked.

"Because I don't want to be hiking around in the woods stepping into Trina's horseshit. That's why," Orville said, raising his voice, exploiting the opportunity to say something...anything. Trina raised up about to respond when Rhonda pointed her dagger finger at Trina, lowering Trina back into a seated position.

Rip moved on. "Go Kart track and Kart barn. Motocross course. Do you realize how many truckloads of dirt we'll have to haul in to build a motocross course? You know how that would negatively impact our layout, don't you?"

Orville was quick to respond. "I thought we could use all that dirt we dug out for the cave system and the survival shelter..." Nobody could even mention the shelter without someone in the room cringing. (For different reasons, of course.)

"OK. Good thinking...about that dirt," Rip said sarcastically. Orville took it as a compliment, looking overtly smug at his two siblings. "Now then, Orville, what the hell is a 'blizzard room'?"

"It's a large barn with cliffs and climbing areas covered in artificial snow and ice. It's equipped with a wind machine that blows ice and snow over the whole thing...you know, like for climbing on Mount Everhurst, you know in a blizzard."

"Cooool!," Trina and Amador said in unison. Rip and Rhonda finally exhibited an element of surprise.

"Here is something very interesting: a trolley layout." Rip was intrigued.

Without being called upon, Orville was ready with an explanation. "It's for moving around the complex quickly and easily. Things are so spread out now..."

"I suppose it will require an operator to run the thing," Rip said without expecting an answer. "There's some science stuff in here: drones and robotics, a planetarium, an observatory with telescope. Recording studio, music hall, sound and video control center. A meditation mound with a gong situated at the highest point on the property—you realize that this acreage is flat, flat, flat. And these six jungle huts. We have no jungle, nor do we have anything that resembles a jungle...so we're going to veto those. Otherwise, I guess *this* list is final."

Orville settled back into his chair. He wanted to be excused now that his part was over but he knew better than to ask at that point. Before moving on to Amador's list Rhonda signaled for food and drink to be brought in. Everyone was ready for a break in the action, but Rhonda spoke up as the siblings rose from their chairs, "You three can take a break but you cannot discuss any of this when you leave this room. If we hear anything between you three above a whisper before you return, you can expect consequences."

Of course the whisper loophole was big enough to drive a trolley through—and for the next ten minutes the whispering epithets and accusations sounded like the wind whistling through a haunted house.

Many of Orville's requests added no extra square footage to the climate-controlled spaces of the existing layout. Many of the items did. And the blizzard room was a whopper. Although Orville's list was shorter than Trina's, the square footage was enormous. So much the better as far as Orville was concerned. Rip and Rhonda each had good reasons for removing certain items from the siblings' lists—heights, violence, interference with the existing layout. Their desire to expand the layout—*expand the layout*—adding fresh new features, rooms, and spaces seemed to far outweigh any obstacle, impracticality, or surreal absurdity concocted by their children. Rip and Rhonda's obsessive focus was in full force. It did not matter if anyone ever used any of the new features (or even saw them for that matter). The relentless expansion (at any cost) became an end in itself.

And so...

Indoor Track (8200 ft²)
Indoor Basketball Court (7200 ft²)
Basketball Locker Room (1250 ft²)
Indoor Rock Climbing Wall (1125 ft²)
Hiking Trails (Paved and Unpaved)
Hiking Trail Waystations with Rest Rooms and Snack Bars (12) (420 ft² each)
Biking Trails
Biking Trail Waystations with Rest Rooms and Snack Bars (6) (480 ft² each)
Martial Arts Studio (1600 ft²)
Motocross Course and Cycle Barn
Motocross Observation Booth with Restroom
Blizzard Room (12,640 ft²)
Drone Course and Indoor/Outdoor Launch Bay (550 ft²)
Drone Course Equipment Storage
Drone Management Station, Office, and Control Tower (870 ft²)

Robotics Tech Center and Test Facility (5200 ft²)

Robotics Maintenance Shop (1210 ft²)

Outdoor Robot Pathways

Indoor Robot Pathways (1890 ft²)

Trolley Track, Sidings, and Storage Garage

Trolley Management and Maintenance Barn (4400 ft²)

Trolley Operator's Office (1040 ft²)

Trolley Depots (8) (720 ft² each)

Go Kart Track, Pit, Tunnel, Water Feature, Kart Barn

Kart Observation Deck and Pit Stop Station (2430 ft²)

Recording Studios (3) (540 ft², 620 ft², 1000 ft²)

Sound Stage (5200 ft²)

Audio/Video Production Center (2240 ft²)

Estate-Wide Music/Video Control Center (1260 ft²)

Planetarium (7250 ft²)

Observatory and Telescope with Elevator (9020 ft²)

Outdoor Meditation Mound and Gong

Orville's List and Other Additions: 90,415 ft²

New grand total: 289,597 ft² (6.65 Acres)

Total Bathrooms: 143

## Chapter 34 – The Gathering, Amador

When Rip and Rhonda were compiling the siblings' three original lists, they only threw out items that stood out immediately as undesirable. At that time they did not pause to give a critical look at many of the individual items. So as the group reassembled for a review of Amador's choices, Rip and Rhonda prepared themselves for anything...Amador style.

Everyone was eating when the meeting resumed. Usually the siblings were engaged in back and forth barbs about eating habits, but the rules of the game and the consumption of food material prohibited their usual instinctive hostile banter from getting a foothold. So with a background soundtrack of slurping and loud crunching (much of it deliberate) Rip began again, "And now for Amador's list."

"Surprisingly, there are a number of practical items on Amador's list. Then again— All these items for storing and maintaining our cars...sounds very practical...also the gas fueling station and the 100,000 gallon underground gasoline reserve tank. Expansion of the billiard room to add more pool and snooker tables along with all these gaming areas seems very reasonable. But there is no way to do it since the current billiard room is boxed in by other areas. So we decided to add a gaming wing and move the current billiard room to that location, where all the other gaming areas will be located. Let's have a show of hands: How many here have ever used the existing billiard room?"

An eerie stillness filled the room as the three siblings looked around at each other. The sounds of eating and drinking silenced for a few moments.

"OK. So no surprises there," Rip remarked. We're going to leave the existing billiard room empty as a monument to disuse. And the casino will anchor the whole gaming area with all its amenities. The gaming wing will be built adjacent to the dog track which will be adjacent to the kennels and the dog management area."

"I went through there once! The billiard room..." Orville jumped in, sounding helpful. "I think..."

Rip went on, "We believe these next items are self-explanatory: smoking room, secret smoking room, underground greenhouse, stash cupboard. What is a fungus barn?"

"It's for cultivating mushrooms. It should be underground too," Amador replied.

"Remember, we can't dig any deeper than our basement and cave system," Rip said. "Show of hands: How many here have ever been in the cave system?"

An eerie stillness filled the room as the three siblings looked around at each other. The sounds of eating and drinking silenced for a few moments.

"Next we have a fireworks field, a smokehouse, and a mystery pond. What is a mystery pond?" Rip did not really expect an answer.

"The TV studio and video suite sound OK, but another sound stage? And a secret video screening room?" Rather than belabor these items, Rip wanted to move on to the final set of items. "We have here a bordello room with hot tub, a honeymoon suite with hot tub, a hidden sex room, and a nude beach."

At that point Rhonda interrupted the flow, directing her remarks at the three siblings while tapping her finger on the papers containing the lists, "We appreciate the fact that many of these ideas—many or all—came from movies or television shows that you've seen. But just because they exist in those shows doesn't mean you have to have them or that they exist, or should exist in real life."

"Since when does our estate represent real life?" Trina responded.

Rip wanted to keep things moving, so he questioned Amador, "Amador, what is the purpose of the nude beach? We have the water park, two swimming pools... Show of hands: How many of you have been on that huge water park slide? Let me rephrase that: How many of you have used anything in the water park?"

An eerie stillness filled the room as the three siblings looked around at each other. The sounds of eating and drinking silenced for a few moments.

"Amador, what is the purpose of the nude beach?" Rip asked again.

"We have all those people, up there, on the hills looking down at us all the time. I thought we could have a small pond built with a sandy beach and a number of naked mannequins lying around, all the time, in full view, from the hills. You know, give those gawkers something to look at, you know...for laughs. We could have someone move the mannequins around, take 'em in at night, put 'em out in the morning. Those people in the hills would never be able to figure it out. Are they real or what?"

An eerie stillness filled the room as everyone but Amador looked around at each other. Once again, the sounds of eating and drinking were silenced for a few moments.

"And now we have this final set of items," Rip continued. "Your mother and I decided, early on, that we would not make serious judgements about the items on your lists. We've only vetoed a few. However these last few items on Amador's list were pushing the limit: a dungeon, a wax museum, a Chamber of Horrors, a vintage weapons museum, a laboratory, a *secret* laboratory. And last, but certainly not least, we have a side room connected to the dungeon with a twelve-by-twelve-by-twelve vat of concentrated acid built into the floor requiring almost 13,000 gallons of acid to fill it. Amador?"

"It looked pretty cool in the movie," Amador said defensively.

"One item on the list did not make the cut: in another extension of the dungeon there was to be a large pit filled with alligators. I don't know if fifty or so alligators would survive in the dark, unattended, for any extended period of time and I'm not sure about the huge amount of meat required to feed them and who would be tossing it to them on a regular basis. So that item was considered out of bounds."

The lists were complete and all of the siblings' items discussed or mentioned. Through most of the meeting the three siblings maintained their best behavior. Rip and Rhonda were very impressed by the level of discipline the siblings had displayed even if it was a discipline imposed by the threat of wish-list items being tossed out. Rip and Rhonda felt a quiet sense of satisfaction in finally providing something for their children (things they actually wanted) after years of estrangement. Amador's final list was added to the mix.

8-Car Climate-Controlled Garage (12000 ft²)
Classic Car Climate-Controlled Garage (8000 ft²)

Motorcycle Garage (4000 ft²)

Carriage House (3100 ft²)

Auto Repair Bays

Car Wash

Charging Garage

Mechanic's Quarters (2250 ft²)

Chauffer's Quarters (2860 ft²)

Fueling Station (1430 ft²)

100,000 Gallon Gasoline Tank

Bordello Room (650 ft²)

Bordello Hot Tub (160 ft²)

Honeymoon Suite (840 ft²)

Honeymoon Suite Hot Tub (160 ft²)

Hidden Sex Room (460 ft²)

Nude Beach

Smoking Room (500 ft²)

Secret Smoking Room (600 ft²)

Stash Cupboard (210 ft²)

Fungus Barn (2600 ft²)

Dungeon (9250 ft²)

Wax Museum (2400 ft²)

Chamber of Horrors (1280 ft²)

Vat of Acid Extension (280 ft²)

Vat of Acid

Vintage Weapons Museum (780 ft²)

Laboratory (1240 ft²)

Secret Laboratory (1400 ft²)

Traditional Billiards Room (440 ft²)

Pocket Billiards Room (440 ft²)

Snooker Table Room (680 ft²)

Card Room (920 ft²)

Game Room (800 ft²)

Video Arcade (1550 ft²)

Casino (3640 ft²)

Mechanical Bull Room (320 ft²)

Dog-Racing Track

Track Office and Observation Booth (1230 ft²)

TV Studio (1600 ft²)

Video Suite (360 ft²)

Secret Video Screening Room (640 ft²)

Sound Stage (2200 ft²)

Smokehouse (1250 ft²)

Smokehouse Kitchen (440 ft²)

Smokehouse Deck

Fireworks Field

Fireworks Mgmt Center (340 ft²)

Fireworks Storage (500 ft²)

Mystery Pond

Amador's List and Other Additions: 73,800 ft²

New grand total: 363,397 ft² (8.34 Acres)

Total Bathrooms: 152

Total Doors, Windows, HVAC Units: No one can say

## Chapter 35 – The Un-Gathering

"I believe that covers all of your lists," Rip said to the assembled group still seated around the long dining room table. The table itself had seen its first meal even though the table had been available in the dining hall for many years—and now, possibly it might be the last meal for years.

"We can leave now?" Amador said without hesitating.

"You can go if you wish, but I believe you three will be interested in what's next. If you leave you'll be left out." The siblings sat quietly and attentively.

Rip continued, "There's been a lot of back and forth and moving about...where each of you keep yourselves. So...each of you may build your own place, your own area, somewhere on the property provided it connects to the main house and provided it doesn't interfere with any of the other construction. We're going to do it all...your wish lists...all of it, and more."

"Whoa, daddy!" Orville exclaimed.

"Yes," Rip responded. "And don't call me 'daddy.' "Talk to Turlew...or Farmer. One of them will be able to give you guidance. My advice, take it or leave it...but I suggest you three get together and discuss it—and I mean *discuss* it—so that your new personal areas are as far apart as possible. Any issues you may have...take them to Turlew or Farmer and don't involve me or your mother with any of them."

Rhonda then spoke up, "OK disperse...before we change our minds." The siblings elbowed their way out of the room in the blink of an eye.

With the room now free of the young and entitled, Rip turned to Rhonda and remarked, "I think you were right. It's best that we didn't tell them what else we were planning. What do you think? What'll they come up with...all on their own? Look what they gave us already."

"It'll be interesting, or horrifying, or both. Maybe we should set a limit on them; how much space they're allowed to have," Rhonda replied.

Rip nodded, then said with reassurance, "Turlew knows how to keep a lid on it. I talked with both Turlew and Farmer this morning. We had a long and interesting discussion. Turlew believes all this new construction will, for him, amount to permanent employment. As for *our* list...I can't think of another thing to add."

"Neither can I," Rhonda added.

"Turlew and Farmer have all the lists, and they start tomorrow. We can pass along any revisions. As it stands now, all of the new construction...well, it may take years, but I think we're done. I believe that this is The Big One." Rip's voice was showing a certain underlying level of exhaustion.

Rhonda stood up, gathering the papers together. She stood silently for a moment staring pensively down at the long empty table dotted with uneaten and half-eaten food. Turning to Rip she finally said, "Then what? All we've ever been interested in has been the expansion of our layout. We have ungrateful kids that don't know us. We have repair people here every day. I have no idea how many people we actually have living here. Have you seen our nanny lately? I don't even remember her name. Does she still live here?" Rhonda wasn't really expecting any answers.

"I feel it too," Rip said in agreement. "It seems as if we are dealing with something every minute of every day. No wonder we are unfamiliar with anything but the layout. How many employees have we got working here on a regular basis? Who brought in this food? Who *made* all this food? Half the light switches don't work. Some doors won't lock. Some windows won't open. Some won't close. We measure our layout in acres instead of square feet. We've turned our lives over to Turlew and Latherine and several other lawyers and managers and accountants. I don't even know most of their names. Anthony doesn't come to visit anymore. Anthony. My friend." Rip looked at the papers Rhonda was holding and added, "And still, we just keep going, we must keep going—expanding and adding."

"We must," Rhonda said with a sad resignation.

## Chapter 36 – OCD, Mousewater Style

Late in the evening, long after the meeting with their children, Rip and Rhonda were sitting up in their comfortable bed looking over their own final list. It took a year to develop it and included everything that they could possibly think of. Some of the items were inspired by things they had seen in movies and TV shows. Home theater: blessing or curse? Of course, every list item had some overly compelling reason for its inclusion—it seemed as if every item just *had* to be there. It always seemed so at the time. And—once an item made it into the list, it could never be removed—removing any item would destroy the sanctity of the list.

At one time or another, throughout the day, either Rip or Rhonda, in turn, had the unexplained urge to light a match and set fire to *all* the lists; or rip them up; or eat them whole; or toss them into the survival shelter pit as a symbolic gesture. But along with every such urge there would always be an overriding compulsion to keep the lists; and keep them all intact. It was easy to reject a few of the children's more outrageous offerings—the rejections seemed to add a measure of sanity to the whole business. But there was no such perimeter staked out around Rip and Rhonda's expansion aspirations. Even when taking refuge for a few days aboard the family yacht they continued to think of things to add to the list. They would write their ideas on little pieces of scrounged-up paper and add the items to the main list when back at the estate. So, with a fragile hold on their desire to expand the layout this one last time, Rip and Rhonda looked over their final list with a feeling of excitement and a little trepidation. Rip had the lists in his hand—he was looking at them and yet not really looking at them at all.

Rhonda spoke first, "Do you see anything you want to add, Rip?"

"No."

"Anything you want to delete?"

"No. I think I would just like to give these final lists to Turlew tomorrow and be done with it...on our end. Done with it. Anthony and Whitney will be here tomorrow around noon. Turlew is supposed to be coming up here early, to get an early start." Rip shuffled through the papers while setting forth a big yawn. "I think I'll have Turlew's secretary type all this up before I show the lists to Anthony. I have a strange feeling about Anthony's reaction...or maybe my reaction to his reaction." Rip yawned again causing Rhonda to yawn as well. Allowing the papers to fall flat on his stomach, Rip said, "You know it's going to be at least two or even three years to finish the items on these lists. You realize that, don't you?"

Rhonda sighed, "Yes. But I think...I think it's going to be awesome."

"Awesome. I guess that's the word," Rip said as he and Rhonda both dozed off with the lights on; and the wondrous lists floated around on top of the blanket for the remainder of the night.

The list *was* awesome.

The Gardens:
      Botanical Garden
      Hanging Gardens
      Roman Garden
      Fountain Pools
      Desert Hothouse (625 ft²)
      Landscaping Barn
      Plant and Tree Nursery
      Gardener's Station (1250 ft²)
      Gardener's Residence (2840 ft²)
      Vegetable and Herb Garden
      Maze Garden
      Hedge Maze with Central Gazebo and Fountains
      Greenhouse (Multi-Purpose)
      Orchid Room (1600 ft²)
      Wishing Well
      Fern Grotto (1800 ft²)
      Palm Tree Habitat (3800 ft²)
      Sunken Garden
      Japanese Garden

Zen Garden

Rose Garden

Rock Garden

Orchard (with yet-to-be-determined fruit)

The Business District:

Paris Indoor/Outdoor Café (2840 ft²)

Paris Café Kitchen (660 ft²)

Cafeteria (1900 ft²)

Cafeteria Kitchen (660 ft²)

Pizza Parlor (1600 ft²)

Pizza Parlor Kitchen (660 ft²)

English Pub (1100 ft²)

Main Deluxe Bar (1450 ft²)

Beach Bar (900 ft²)

Coffee Bar (900 ft²)

Indoor Bistro (1680 ft²)

Sushi Bar (1100 ft²)

Japanese Grill (880 ft²)

Shrimp Station (650 ft²)

Delicatessen (900 ft²)

Barber Shop (850 ft²)

Manicure/Pedicure Studio (600 ft²)

Outdoor Amphitheater

New Main House Spaces:

Mosaic Room (600 ft²)

Quiet Room (480 ft²)

Bamboo Room (720 ft²)

Indoor Gazebo (600 ft²)

Vomitorium (550 ft²)

Roman Multi-Stage Bathhouse (2660 ft²)

Concert Hall (4000 ft²)

Lecture Hall (2300 ft²)

Recital Hall (1600 ft²)

Operations:

Physical Plant and Operations (1640 ft²)

Landscaping Vehicles Garage

Mail Room (860 ft²)

Incinerator

Climate-Controlled Storage Center (3400 ft²)

Storage Master's Office (1450 ft²)

Delivery Deck

First Aid Clinic (1230 ft²)

Recovery Room (640 ft²)

Machine Shop (1100 ft²)

Repair Shop (1320 ft²)

Handyman Residence (2300 ft²)

Communications Center (1500 ft²)

Electronics Control Center (1200 ft²)

Electronics Service Center (2140 ft²)

Records Room (900 ft²)

Master Control Center (1230 ft²)

All Seasons Center (2800 ft²)

All Seasons Office (1320 ft²)

Food Services:

Formal Dining Staging Area (770 ft²)

Exotics Pantry (460 ft²)

Garbage Bay (350 ft²)

Chef's Residence (2310 ft²)

Kitchen Break Room (450 ft²)

Pantry Expansion (280 ft²)

Indoor Herb Garden (340 ft²)

Outdoor Herb Garden

Outdoor Barbecue Deck with Self-Grill Campfire Station

The Works:

Guest Castle with Three Turrets (8350 ft²)

Guest Castle Moat with Dungeon Connectivity

Christmas House (4400 ft²)

Snow Generator Station (420 ft²)

Getaway Cabin (2200 ft²)

Log Cabin (2000 ft²)

Boardwalk

Mountain Lodge (3100 ft²)

Ice Pool (500 ft²)

Aegean Villa (5680 ft²)

Sun Deck

Haunted House (2500 ft²)

Museum (3300 ft²)

Secondary Sauna (330 ft²)

Secondary Steam Room (360 ft²)

Sweathouse (930 ft²)

Butler's Residence (3400 ft²)

Resident Servants' Housing (8340 ft²)

Spiritual Add-Ons:

Chapel with Apse (2600 ft²)

Non-Denominational Altar (400 ft²)

Churchyard

Mausoleum (1500 ft²)

Party Deck

Merry-Go-Round

For the Children:

 Trina's Residence (??? ft²)

 Orville's Residence (??? ft²)

 Amador's Residence (??? ft²)


The Ultimate Expansion: 125,055 ft²

New grand total: 488,452 ft² (11.21 Acres of Climate-Controlled Space)

Total Bathrooms: 233

Total Projected Employees: No one can say

## Chapter 37 – The Green Light

It came as no surprise to anyone that Ticker Turlew and Dick Farmer began to question their involvement when faced with Rip and Rhonda's full list and with the three siblings' plans for their individual residences. On the day when the project was arbitrarily scheduled to begin officially there were no drawings, no blueprints, no details—just numerous items listed on multiple sheets of paper. Rip and Rhonda were expecting Turlew and Farmer to map it all out and build it. On the morning of Day One when Rip delivered the lists to Turlew there were a number of contentious moments as Rip, Rhonda, Turlew, and Farmer met in the parlor of the main house to discuss the plan of action. Unfortunately for Turlew and Farmer, there *was* no plan of action. But the happy couple convinced Turlew and Farmer to stay on and build it all. Doubling their fees greased up the convincing operation.

"Do you realize how much all that acid is going to cost?" Turlew asked.

"Doesn't matter," Rip replied.

"We may have trouble finding someone who will fill the vat with all that liquid...all that acid. You realize that, of course," Farmer added.

Rip did not respond to Farmer's comment but instead said, "And by the way we need fifty alligators to stock the guest castle moat. The alligators should be able to enter the dungeon alligator pit using the connection listed on there...on that large list."

Without anything better to say, Turlew just gave a sort of grunt.

Rip was ready to explain. "We weren't originally going with the alligator pit because we didn't think the animals would survive very long in a dark pit, but seeing as they can move in and out from the moat to the dungeon...it'll be a great surprise for Amador, you know, our son."

Turlew spoke up, "I suppose you've thought through all these other items also." Turlew made a hand motion pointing at the stack of papers.

"Of course," Rhonda replied. "How irresponsible do you think we are?"

Not wanting to respond in any way, Turlew changed the subject, "We'll have to build all of this in stages in order to keep a handle on it all." Sensing they were in free fall, Farmer looked to Turlew for any sign that they should immediately pull the ripcord and abandon the Mousewater project before they each wind up doing a header into the ground.

"Stages...of course. I presume that's what all that computer stuff is for," Rip said.

"Yes, but even so..." Turlew replied.

Turlew realized that by turning down the happy couple he would be giving up his residence on the estate grounds and giving up a whopper of a fee. "OK. It'll take a week or two—or twenty—to lay out the plans for all these items...and to organize a staged construction schedule." Turlew paused before continuing and while looking directly at Farmer (but still addressing Rip and Rhonda) said, "I hope you realize that all this construction, use of materials, and number of contractors...all of this is going to attract a lot of attention—especially officials in the Big City."

"Can't Latherine handle all of that?" Rhonda replied.

"I hope so," Turlew said while gathering up all the papers. "We'll let you know when we're ready to start. In the meantime, we'll just continue all the maintenance and repair operations as needed...as usual."

Around noon that same day, Rip and Rhonda were anxiously awaiting the arrival of Anthony and Whitney. Rip was anxious for Anthony to look at the expansion plans and offer an opinion—although Rip had an uncomfortable suspicion that Anthony was going to react logically and negatively. It had been a long time since Anthony visited the Mousewater estate. The last time he was there things seemed to have stabilized—there were mostly repairs, cleaning, and maintenance activities going on; but no new buildings or features under construction. Rhonda had some interest in getting to know Whitney but it could not be said that the reverse was also true.

Without thinking, Anthony pressed the doorbell button and to his surprise the bell actually worked. Anthony and Whitney were welcomed with open arms and although the two couples lived in starkly different worlds everyone felt a sense of warmth as they stood together awkwardly but joyfully in the grand entryway of the sprawling Mousewater main house. Anthony had grown a short beard since his last visit and Whitney's long brown hair seemed quite a bit shorter than before. Everyone looked a little bit heftier—just a little bit. Anthony's casual wear had taken a step up—most likely because his writing career had taken a step up as well.

The foursome wound up in the sunny sitting room, a room situated right next to the closed trophy room. The sitting room had a partial glass ceiling. The permanent chemical smell emanating from the trophy room quickly forced the foursome to move to a different room (a sitting room with a more manageable smell) and, for a while, there they sat, together, enjoying refreshments and catching up on everyone's activities.

At one point Whitney excused herself from the discussion. Following Rhonda's directions she found the bathroom down the nearby hallway and went in...into the cavernous guest bathroom, one of many, many, many. The light switch wasn't working so the only light available was from a small skylight in the ceiling—no windows. The toilet seemed to be almost in the middle of the room and was so far from the side wall that Whitney had to get up and walk over to it in order to retrieve a handful of toilet tissue. The entire time she was in the bathroom the sink faucet was dripping; and the shower plumbing started groaning when she flushed the toilet. There was a large crack in the ceiling over the sink and the industry of some bugs or other creatures had produced several little piles of gypsum powder onto the lengthy (and empty) marble countertop. Multiple wooden cabinet doors were crooked or warped and some only partially stained. The room did not seem to be square, no right angles at the corners, but Whitney could not tell for sure in the dim light. After using the sink, she tried to shut off the faucet but it continued to leak. There was a splash of white plaster or glue on some of the chrome fixtures. And although she waited and waited, the toilet continued to hiss long after she flushed it. It all seemed very sad. In contrast, the towel racks displayed two beautiful, soft, monogrammed towels: BPM and RPM. Whitney dried her hands and returned to the group, perhaps a little enlightened and a little less confrontational.

Any uneasiness Whitney may have had after her bathroom experience quickly dissipated when she rejoined the group and felt the warmth that emanated from Rip and Rhonda. They seemed to be truly unaware that the quality of their massive layout was grossly inferior and basically just a one-story, hellish shell of shit. For Anthony, it was refreshing that the small talk he was used to in the world of celebrity interviews did not exist in the house of Rip and Rhonda. There was an innocence and genuineness that had always appealed to him about the happy couple. Slowly and surely the topic basin was being drained out, but no one in the group wanted to be the first to bring up the subject of new additions. Nevertheless, they all felt the inevitability of it and eventually, the four moved to the formal dining hall where the massive sets of plans were laid out side by side, around the table—plans for every standalone building, every air-conditioned space, every landscape feature, every addition to the main house, every new residence, a site map, the golf course layout. The only items missing were the final plans for the three residences being conjured up by the Mousewater siblings. As the group surrounded the end of the long table Anthony stopped first to peruse a randomly-selected group of plans. Paging through several of them at that location he began shaking his head. He suddenly stopped when viewing a portion of the site map.

"A dog-racing track? A dog-racing track? Are you fucking kidding me? What about some of these other things? A dungeon, a vat of acid, a wax museum, an alligator pit? Rip, what in the world?" Anthony was feeling no restraint, but Whitney, seeing Vesuvius in the pre-eruption stage pulled Anthony aside and ushered him into an adjoining room. Rip and Rhonda stood by, speechless, wondering what that was all about. Anthony and Whitney soon re-emerged, Anthony, visibly, in a much less judgmental state than when they left the dining hall. Most likely, for the first time, Rip and Rhonda began to feel oddly alienated from their layout. Their ambitions suddenly felt like a wedding reception celebrant discovering that the last imbibed stem glass of champagne was maybe *the* one too many.

Very calmly Anthony spoke, "Have you ever heard of a fellow named Charles Foster Jenkins?"

"No," Rip replied.

"He was an important industry mogul who built up a big conglomerate starting with (supposedly) waterproof cardboard boxes and experimental body grooming products. With his wealth, he built a huge compound up in the mountains of Oregon. He named it Mount Oblivious. It was very big and elaborate. I was supposed to have an interview with him at his mountain compound. Never showed. But I did get to see his place. Your place reminds me of his, a little."

"He *was*?" Rhonda asked.

"Ahem. Well, the reason he didn't show up for my interview was because he was eaten by a mountain lion earlier that same day, clothes and all. Tragic. After the lion ate old Jenkins, the lion somehow fell into a ritual meditation pit. One of those where you go in and they pull the ladder up and you have to live down there for a day or two and well...you're supposed to come out of it with all your shit together. While they were extracting the mountain lion from the pit, the beast urped up Jenkins' belt buckle and a couple of Jenkins' toes. That's how they knew what had happened to him."

"And you think his place is, or was, like ours? Is it still there?" Rip inquired.

"When I saw the house it wasn't nearly as extensive or creative as yours...just one big monstrosity on a small mountain top. There was very little flat space for special features because the house was surrounded by steep slopes and sheer cliffs...so the house was pretty much *it*, even if it *was* huge. I don't really know what happened to it after Jenkins was eaten. It was situated so far from civilization that it probably wouldn't have even made a good museum."

The subsequent silence in the room was an indication that neither Rip nor Rhonda understood why Anthony brought up the whole Jenkins subject. Refocusing their attention, Anthony and Whitney politely looked through the table-load of plans for all the additions and at some point began to actually marvel at the combination of enormity, creativity, and surreal nature of it all.

"You have enough money to pay for all this?" Anthony finally asked, very casually.

"Don't know," Rip replied. "We don't even know how long all of this is going to take. We're more worried about calling attention to ourselves. We always have all those nosy neighbors on the hill watching us from their yards, some with binoculars." Then in a contemplative and semi-ominous tone, Rip said "Not every city official is going to let things slide...not the way it's been in the past...one of these days..." Rip became overtly wistful at that point and another awkward silence ensued. Then he broke the silence again, "I think Rhonda and I are going to spend some time on the yacht...let things get set up...get away for a while."

"I think that's a great idea," Anthony said. "If you like, we can come for a visit on one of the nights. We'll bring some wine or beer..."

When Anthony and Whitney finally decided that it was time to go home, there was a feeling of melancholy in the air. The foursome had spent the entire afternoon together, a very pleasant afternoon. Before Anthony and Whitney left, Rip and Rhonda showed them some of the finished areas of the house, now furnished and decorated. The quality of the things *present* in the rooms belied the poor quality of the rooms themselves—the walls, the floors, the doors, all things electrical, everything. The happy couple tried (without much success) to avoid rooms where light switches were non-functional.

And as things became a little too dimly-lit and dreary, Rip broke the mood by stating, very matter-of-factly, "A big advantage to a one-story house, you see...when the electrical circuitry is bad and the lights don't work, we can just add a skylight to the room...as you can see here...problem solved." Rip waved his arm toward the ceiling—the skylight—like a model calling attention to fabulous prizes on a game show. But, in spite of Rip's carefree dismissals, Anthony was detecting an undercurrent of dark reflection, in both Rip and Rhonda.

As the final item on the unwritten agenda the tour seemed to be more obligatory than desirable by any of the four participants. Daylight was turning to dusk. As Anthony was getting into his car he looked back at the pensive couple. They were standing close together on their front porch, each with an arm around the other, standing serenely in the glow of one working porch light (the other one dark). As he waved, he shouted with extreme sincerity, "Good luck!" Rip and Rhonda watched and waved at the car as Anthony and Whitney drove off down the driveway.

## Chapter 38 – The Yacht

The family yacht was where Rip first met Rhonda. He used to spend a lot of time just hanging around on it, making alcoholic concoctions, and doing nothing. At that time it was a refuge from doing nothing at Dominic's estate. Over the years, for Rip and Rhonda, the yacht became a different sort of refuge, a place to get away from all the daily turmoil and intrusive activity at their own estate, their layout.

Dominic acquired the yacht early on as he built up his business empire, but like many things in Dominic's world, it was *there*, ready at a moment's notice, but rarely, if ever, used. In fact, after Dominic's bullet-riddled accident he never ventured to board the yacht again. Rip was about the only person to ever set foot on its decks, but he never took it out for a "spin." In spite of this, Rip made it his personal responsibility to maintain the yacht and keep its engine and other machinery running. The brackish water in the lake prevented the hull from developing a thick layer of freshwater algae below the waterline so Rip's maintenance activities did not require too much exertion on his part.

The yacht itself was huge, well over 100 feet long—it was the largest private vessel in the Big City Lake marina—in fact, it seemed out of place there. Except for the marina area, the man-made lake was almost perfectly round. At one end was the short connection to the Big City Canal. The Canal was made up of two long, straight segments that together made the Canal about twenty miles long. At its end, the Canal widened, leading out to the ocean. The Big City Lake water was not always brackish. Poor management of the City's water resources caused the ocean's salt water contribution to slowly creep up the Canal, eventually making its way into the City Lake and forever altering the makeup of its fish and amphibian life. There was constant dredging going on at the ocean end of the Canal because the shallow Big City River carried and deposited a lot of silt and the poorly-designed City drainage system caused all of the City's storm runoff to flow into the canal, carrying with it dirt, sand, fertilizer, industrial waste, branches, trash, and all sorts of useless debris. In spite of its problems the Canal and the associated docks all along its banks provided the Big City with a substantial amount of commercial trade and imported products—some good, and some, not so good. It was at those very docks that Dominic first put together the pieces of Mousewater Enterprises. And it was at those docks that Dominic had his life-altering accident brought on by a shower of lead projectiles.

The yacht had a sizable, multi-deck cabin with a large galley and a massive amount of storage space. Using the small deck stairways never seemed to bother Rip. In spite of the yacht's size, it could be piloted easily by a single person. It even had its own dinghy which could double as a lifeboat if necessary. When he first obtained ownership of the yacht, Dominic had it fitted with a nameplate fixture so that one of several different yacht names could be installed. There was no practical reason for this since the yacht was never taken from its mooring—not that there were many places to visit in the Big City Lake; and the Canal was always too congested with barges and freighters to take the yacht any further. But in typical Latherine fashion, and presumably for Dominic's benefit, the yacht was registered under a totally legitimate but totally false name—if one could even call it a registration. The yacht didn't even exist—and *if* it did, it was registered under the name of Jack D. Spratt—some recluse from New Zealand who could not possibly be contacted since he didn't even exist.

The next morning after Anthony and Whitney's visit, Rip and Rhonda left the estate and went straight for the yacht. They decided to stay there until all the plans were finalized and construction was about to begin. Rip kept his phone turned off most of the time—he and Rhonda were relying solely on Turlew to get the job done.

At the end of the first week Rip stood on the bow of the yacht looking out over the lake through the masts of a number of small sailboats. The sun was just about to reach the horizon and the sky was starting to be filled with the colors of sunset. Rhonda approached him, but before she could say anything Rip suggested, "What do you say…let's take her out onto the lake."

"Yes. Let's do it."

After a quick recharge of the batteries, the engine was a-hummin' along. However, getting the boat free of its moorings turned out to be a challenge. The ropes had been tied to the docking cleats in a very amateurish way for so long, the knots seemed to be welded into little balls—unsalvageable. Not wanting to waste any time—seeing as how the sun was going down—"Captain" Rip ordered the offending lines to be cut forthwith and the happy couple was on their way.

Rip maneuvered the yacht around the tiny lake several times and then slowed to a halt at the short connection to the Big City Canal. There, he and Rhonda stood on the foredeck and watched the sun finally go down below the edge of the world.

## Chapter 39 – Three Little Pigs

Turlew and his team of architects had only just begun putting together all the plans and organizing various development stages when the first of the three siblings, Trina, approached Turlew with a design wish-list and a hand-drawn floor plan for her new residence. Shortly thereafter it was Amador, then Orville, then Trina (again), then Orville (again). As each sibling discovered the extent of the others' designs, their own design had to be extended in order to maintain superiority. Ratcheting up this way, the three plans were soon dangerously out of control. Turlew realized that, at some point, the sheer magnitude of the three plans would begin to seriously interfere with the existing sprawl—if not physically, then by construction interference and logistics. That loss of control might jeopardize his very existence on the project. There seemed to be no logical end to it all as the designs were in constant flux and extremely dynamic. In addition, the siblings were requesting features that already existed elsewhere on the estate—were any of them paying attention...any at all?

Orville's master plan was to nudge his two siblings' places to the edge of the property by creating an almost tunnel-like linear house several hundred feet long. This would force the other two siblings to put their residences all the way to the edges of the property in order to maintain some kind of separation. In contrast, Amador had come up with a massive multi-story monstrosity that Turlew beheaded upon first encounter—no stairways or second stories allowed. A *single-story* monstrosity *was* considered acceptable however. Trina's creation could only be described as a palace. Although it was the required single story, the ceilings were thirty to forty feet tall with arches and murals. All that seemed to matter in her design was size and *volume*.

Not that Turlew's *normal* quality control was, in any way, stellar, but quality control was now being pushed aside further since Turlew was spending all of his time managing the three siblings and their chaotic design requests. And woe be to Turlew if two of the competing siblings happened to corner him, alone, at his residence, at the same time.

Turlew eventually rounded up the three of them, together—which was quite a feat in itself— along with Farmer and two project architects. Safety in numbers. They all met in Turlew's wildly disarrayed work room at his residence—tools, papers, and books were strewn about the place, and the sibling's plans were laid out on a large table in the center of the room.

Turlew started the meeting and attempted to end it in one breath, "Here it is! This is *it*! I'm going with what I've got now...right now...as of this moment. First you want *this*, then you don't want it. Then you want it again. Move this. Move that. He's got this. She's got that. We cannot go on this way. I cannot *build* things this way—"

Amador attempted to interrupt, "Oh yeah?"

Turlew fired back, picking up a hammer from the table, "Put a lid on it Toreador, or I swear..." He paused for a moment and then continued, "No more changes, no more additions. And I'm going to revise each of these plans so that all three of you have the exact same square footage. End of story! End of meeting!"

"You can't do that," Orville said defiantly. "Do you know who your employer is?"

"Yes I do," Turlew said defiantly right at Orville's face. "Do *you*?"

"Well, we'll see about *that*," Trina said in a huff. And as unlikely at it might seem, the three siblings were finally in agreement on something. They pointed their three petulant, angry pouts at Turlew expecting him to cave in like a deflated ram's bladder, but they were sorely disappointed. Together they left Turlew's house in a combat patrol column and prepared for a group whining session with their parents.

Turlew was unconcerned. He assigned one project architect to each of the three siblings' plans. Together they were tasked with placing the residences as far apart from each other as possible, but still connected to the main house at a reasonable distance. That was the plan; that it was. One of the only mandates that Turlew gave the architects was: "When in doubt, do it arbitrarily."

While Turlew and the architects were continuing their attempts to manage the plans, the temporarily-unified, querulous trio went straight to the higher authorities to complain— i.e. Rip and Rhonda, on the family yacht, on vacation, and not wanting to be disturbed (especially by this particular group). Rip was below deck and Rhonda was on the open area toward the stern as the trio of siblings approached. Surprised at seeing the small stampede heading her way, Rhonda raised her hand, stopping the siblings before they could climb aboard the yacht. The little group stood like a pack of agitated hyenas on the pier next to the port side of the yacht—Amador changing his position constantly among the group; Orville impatiently shifting his weight from leg to leg; and Trina nervously tapping one of her feet on the boardwalk.

Rip suddenly appeared from below and stepped up onto the inboard steps of the deck. He looked very imposing as he cast his stare down on the upset siblings. Before the trio could air their many grievances, Rip waved the three of them back with his arm, after which he pointed his finger directly at them. Then he brusquely and bluntly and ominously stonewalled them all with the warning, "Do not try this again!" Rip turned away for a moment, then quickly looked back over his shoulder, and again pointed his finger at them. If looks could kill... Rip and Rhonda left the deck and disappeared into the cabin of the yacht. They wanted no part of this type of day-to-day turmoil—especially from those three.

The siblings were left hanging, but they didn't dare set foot onto the yacht. The temporary and fragile sibling alliance was dissolved almost as quickly as it formed as the disgruntled group slunk out of the marina, grumbling at each other in the usual way and accusing each other of being the one that had fouled up the conference, causing it to be aborted. Home they went without accomplishing a thing.

The three assigned architects went to work, furiously compiling the wish-lists and the drawings. Each of the architects faced a unique set of challenges; challenges stemming from their assigned sibling's requests—e.g. Orville's sectional diagrams (obviously created at different times) with overlapping areas that could not be reconciled—there should not be a toilet, a bathtub, and a fireplace connected together and opening out toward the middle of the kitchen. The mixture of barely decipherable diagrams from each sibling were difficult if not impossible to coordinate. In some cases the laws of physics imposed the ultimate restrictions. But in all cases, the architects did their best to implement all the features as requested.

When the plans were complete (or so they thought) the architects brought them to Turlew's workroom for a consultation—a design summit meeting. Having worked so closely on the plans for several days, the architects had become inured to the absurdity of it all—all three plans.

"This is nuts!" Turlew remarked as he flipped through the plans. "Ridiculous!" he said as he turned over one oversized page after another. Turlew was overcome with disgust at the sheer audacity of the three siblings and the magnitude of their designs. Then he addressed the three architects directly, "I don't know how you were able to make heads or tails of all those scribblings in putting all this together. For that I congratulate you. But this result is nuts. It's like a surreal mosaic of building construction and floor plans."

The three exhausted architects were feeling intimidated by Turlew's outburst. But those feelings were overshadowed by the sheer relief that they were (supposedly) done with the three designs.

Turlew continued, "What is the square footage of Missy Trina's house..." Turlew looked for and located the summary page. "210,000 square feet?!" He moved to another set of plans, "And this—what is it? What is this? A five hundred and eighty-foot long—long thin house with a rounded central section. It looks like a giant helicopter propeller. Grandmaster Orville's house, yes. And this one..." Turlew was attempting to examine Amador's design. I've seen more organized things coming out of the back end of a rhino at the zoo. These plans look like works of modern art, not something practical or even from this planet. But considering the source and what they represent, these are nothing less than just plain crazy!"

Then Turlew addressed one of the architects directly, "Mr. Mahlmballs would you get me a piece of that clear plastic, over there, please...and a drafting ruler. And Ms. McPuvis, would you please hand me that pair of shears...and that black marker."

Using the drafting ruler, Turlew measured and cut out a correctly-scaled 80' by 80' square of the clear plastic. He then carefully perused the overview plan made for Trina and placed the scaled square over it to include the kitchen and at least one bathroom and one bedroom. Without any further consideration he used the marker to trace a thick black outline around the plastic square and directly on the printout.

"There," he said. "That's Missy Trina's 6400 square foot residence." Turlew then proceeded to do the same to Orville's floor plan and finally to Amador's. The architects didn't know if they should be upset that their hard work was being reduced to a simple square or to be pleased that the three siblings were getting what they deserved.

"Go ahead and make new *final* plans using those squares exactly...and I mean *exactly*. Place those square houses on the site right next to each other with only one long semi-enclosed passageway to the main house. I'll take the heat if and when the time comes. I'll take the heat. And do not, under any circumstances, get involved with those three Mousewater kids."

By getting a firm grip on the situation and acting so decisively, Turlew began feeling a sense of calm as he addressed the group philosophically, "Mr. Mahlmballs, Ms. McPuvis, and Mr. Smith, I want you three to keep this in mind: I think you did a fine job in sorting all this out. I see now that it was an impossible undertaking. But now that it's settled, and I mean *settled*, you can get back to working the other parts of the project after your work on the square residences is finalized. Dick Farmer will take it from there. Any questions you may have, you come to *me*...and *nobody* else."

All squared away:

　　Trina's Residence (6400 ft²)
　　Orville's Residence (6400 ft²)

Amador's Residence (6400 ft²)
Single (Soon to Be a Combat Arena) Passageway to the Main House

Siblings' Residences: 19,200 ft²
New grand total: 507,652 ft² (11.65 Acres of Climate-Controlled Space)
Total Bathrooms: 236
Total Effect on the Layout: Not Much

Without the burden of a single decision concerning the plans for the layout, Rip and Rhonda settled into life aboard the family yacht. Anthony and Whitney visited them several times, making good on their offer to bring along liquid refreshments. As true friends, the four of them could sit on the deck for long periods, in silence, listening to the water lapping against the side of the yacht and the piers. Many times (once with Anthony and Whitney along as well) Rip piloted the yacht out into the lake to watch the sun set over the Big City Canal.

Four weeks quickly went by and the time was rapidly approaching for the happy and tranquil couple to be present, on site, for the construction ahead. But it had been a grand vacation. After confirming with Turlew that all the preparations were completed and that development was about to begin, and with the yacht firmly secured (correctly) in its slip, Rip and Rhonda reluctantly headed back to the estate and whatever might be waiting for them.

## Chapter 40 – The Big One

Daybreak. Plans complete. Contractors in place. A line of heavy machinery waiting for the "opening bell."

This first day would be the last time for many months to come that an early morning crew arriving for work would not encounter one or more night crews, on their way out, ending their shift and leaving for the day.

Turlew and Farmer signaled to the crews and equipment operators to "come on in and get started."

The Kraken was released.

Rip and Rhonda were looking out through the large den windows toward the water park and the hills beyond wondering if they should be watching a different area to get a view of the action—not that they had much interest anymore; not like in younger days. While they watched and waited for the first crew to appear, Rhonda noticed the *Lugardo Plate Glass Associates* decals still adhering to the corner of each large glass pane in the divided light den window; the den was supposedly "finished" a long time ago. Without saying anything, she pointed them out to Rip.

Rip wondered aloud, "I can't decide if things like that bothered me more back in the early days or if they bother me more now."

"Or if we even noticed them at all," Rhonda added.

Turlew and Farmer had decided that the most difficult and questionable additions should be built first—Stage 1. The stages were laid out so that access to and beyond the existing structures, the existing features, and the land itself would not be an issue when delivering materials and performing site excavation. Since the golf course and various recreational fields were located at the rear of the property work began on their excavations first. This would minimize cross-property traffic for later construction. Some of Amador's more atypical items were also first on the agenda—e.g. the dungeon and its features and the dog-racing track. Most of the other standalone buildings (houses, pizza parlor, etc.) were to be built in the final stages. They were self-contained and more or less traditional types of buildings. The guest castle and moat were put in stage one to coordinate the moat with Amador's dungeon. And on and on...

Every day on site, Turlew dreaded the arrival of any one of the siblings, but he knew that he was free of them at least until noon since none of the three was an early riser. What would be their reaction when they got their first gander at the arbitrarily pruned-down squares—stuck together like three flat candy boxes on a shelf? Construction of their residences was not scheduled to begin until the final stage—basically putting off that big headache as long as possible. By then, who knows where things were going to be.

Also on site that first day was Simon Latherine. He was there out of curiosity rather than for any particular legal reason. In spite of his ruthless nature in managing the day-to-day empire oversight responsibilities, he had developed a fondness for Rip and Rhonda. They seemed to be spiritually possessed by their layout obsessions and, to Latherine, they seemed more and more like victims than two overindulgent kids with a grotesque amount of money at their disposal. He had become more than the family lawyer; he was their protector, and friend. He watched the two of them steadily mature through the years and suspected that they had somehow developed a sense of introspection and perspective; something forced upon them by every reality check that had come their way. And, through all his years with the family, and in all his dealings with the happy couple he had never seen them exchange a single cross word in anger—very impressive. They were two people that were truly made for each other.

Over time Latherine himself had changed. He developed a sense of pride in the whole Mousewater estate; not out of admiration of the place itself, but of his own investment in it—his investment in keeping the Mousewater estate completely off the records, without a single building permit, off the tax rolls, and out of the press. That latter accomplishment was no easy task for Latherine given the amount of gawking, daily, from Rip and Rhonda's celebrity neighbors. The neighbors, in spite of their celebrity, in the overall scheme of things were only mere mortals, only human—as in, "What in the hell are they *doing* down there?"

Their interest would have been nonexistent if the Mousewater property was being developed with hundreds of uninteresting, identical, assembly-line houses. But the Mousewater layout was so enormous, unique, and filled with features that, at a minimum, it sparked the neighbors' curiosity—and, for some of the more competitive celebrities it aroused a truly ignorant and misplaced envy.

Anthony and Whitney did not make an appearance on opening day, desiring instead to avoid the initial chaos and then, later, pay a visit to see Rip and Rhonda after things had a chance to "heat up"—and to be able to see some of the construction already "roughed in." A strange feeling of excitement seemed to have taken hold of Anthony; he no longer felt comfortable calling out absurdities and criticizing the layout and some of its more "marginally insane" features. Perhaps Anthony saw some of Rip's inner qualities long before anyone else—that would explain a lot; a lot about an odd-couple friendship that had lasted for decades. Much like Latherine, Anthony watched the happy couple evolve before his eyes. For Anthony, his relationship with Rip—and even Rhonda—was no longer a friendship held together by tolerance, it was unconditional love.

There it was: the biggest construction project that the area had ever seen—that is, if it actually could have been seen, by the average person...on the street. Well, it *could* be seen, seen from the back lawns and fences of plantation-like mansions of numerous celebrities living in the surrounding hills. It *was* seen...and *heard*. Construction on the Mousewater project went on twenty-four hours a day, seven days a week. When the wind was right, the neighbors' mansions were dusted with fine dirt and sand whipped up into the hills, swimming pools were covered with tiny bits of floating sawdust, and the smell of fresh paint and noxious volatile hydrocarbons filled the air night and day. This went on day after day, week after week. It was enough of a nuisance to make the celebrity neighbors want to call the authorities. And they did...call...more than once. Each time, superhero Latherine prevailed. And, as it turned out, it was actually *easier* for Latherine to get the handful of *underworld* households to back off than some of the more temperamental members of the entertainment industry. The noise and the constant clouds of airborne particles and gases continued unabated and the neighbors, resigned to it all, tolerated the situation rather well, even as the continuous and relentless construction dragged on for months, then years. Every neighbor except one.

## Chapter 41 – The Golf Course Issue

The Mousewater golf course, nicknamed the Four By Three by those hostile to its existence, was located at the far end of the Mousewater property. It was one of the Stage

One items built during the big expansion. There were four holes planned, excavated, and started along with the requested number of golfing amenities—quite a list of amenities given the size of the course: locker room, golf cart storage, snack bar, etc. Rip attempted to learn the game as an idle youth but never developed a talent for it nor much of a desire to pursue it. Neither Rip nor Rhonda paid much attention to the construction of the Four By Three or even its presence. The three siblings did show some interest—each of them had added a golf course to their individual wish-list—but their attention could be so easily diverted to other things that its attraction was intermittent and always fairly brief.

On an uninteresting but bright sunny afternoon, Rhonda answered an aggressive knock on the front door at the main house. There were three men standing on the front porch: one dressed in a cheap, ill-fitting suit; the other two were policemen. Before Rhonda could say a thing, the cheap-suit spoke out, "We would like to speak to a Mr. Brisbane Pease Mousewater, please. Are you Ms. Mousewater?"

"Yes. What is it?" Rhonda replied.

At that moment Rip came up from behind, "I'm Brisbane Mousewater. What can I... What is it?" Rip looked out over the men to see a beat up compact car and a police car in the driveway.

The cheap-suit quickly handed Rip a folded piece of paper. "You've been served. Good day." With that, the three individuals made themselves scarce, leaving Rip and Rhonda without further fanfare.

Rip immediately called Latherine before even looking at the folded papers and a very short time later Latherine showed up, ready to go into action. He sat down and looked over the papers for several minutes, paging through them, back and forth. He finally broke the silence, "Those men that came here. One was a process server. He tried to get in here several times, but your gate guards wouldn't let him pass."

"Yeah, well good," Rip said as he turned around, walked over to a small entryway chair and sat down.

"Apparently your neighbor has enough clout to involve the police. Didn't think that was possible. But there you have it..." Latherine sat down and Rhonda continued to stand.

"What neighbor?" Rip broke in.

"A real character named Walter M. Scut. His land abuts yours at the bottom of the hill, way back there in the back." Latherine motioned toward the back where the golf course was located, the Four By Three. "He says that a substantial part of your golf course is on his land..."

"I don't know anything about it," Rip said.

"Well he's pretty agitated what with the downed trees, mounds and mounds of topsoil brought in and built up, re-grading of the whole area. Even the excavation for the small golf course lake crosses into his property."

"How do we know...what if he's just making it all up?" Rip said.

"I doubt if he could have brought the legal action this far if he didn't have some kind of a case. At any rate, we'll have to respond."

Rhonda broke in, "What if we just pay him for that piece of land? Maybe even offer him a premium price. We weren't trying to make... We weren't... I don't know what we were trying to do. Golf..."

"I don't think we're going to get anywhere with that kind of approach," Latherine continued. "Everyone knows this guy. He's famous, infamous, for suing people for everything; every little thing. He's run every business he inherited right into the ground. The only way he stays afloat is by suing his way into and out of all types of situations, whatever he can come up with. Sometimes he sues just for revenge or to legally bankrupt someone merely out of spite. He's really left a lot of mangled bodies behind him...a lot of bodies. His team of lawyers, I *know* some of them. I'm familiar with their methods. They can drag proceedings out for years, decades; drain resources; drive people over the edge. What a bunch of parasitic scumbags. Some high-class neighbor, eh?"

"So what do we do? What *can* we do?" Rip asked.

"Well, at some point we'll have to make a court appearance. I may be able to shield you from some of it, but I plan to negotiate our way out of the suit before anything can even get started. If I can. Traditional methods of getting this guy off your back...well, I'm dubious about success. Even if we prevail, it will be time-consuming and costly—a real pain. Our other options may involve things that you would rather not know about."

"Such as?" Rip asked.

"Why don't you and Rhonda take a few days away from here, down at the marina, on the yacht. I'll come down and let you know how things are going; give you a 'heads up' on what's what." Latherine folded the papers and stood up. "And, we have to make sure this place is empty, no contractors or servants at the house while you're gone. And your kids need to be somewhere else...and not here."

"Well. OK," Rhonda said slowly. She wasn't sure about how they were going to manage the siblings.

"What about all the construction that's scheduled?" Rip asked.

"Let me handle this mess. And try not to worry about it too much. I've handled things that started out far worse than this little piss-ant action." Latherine took the papers and his briefcase and went to his car leaving the happy (but disquieted) couple to begin another "vacation."

Rip and Rhonda gathered up some things and were out of their house so quickly they could almost smell the residual exhaust from Latherine's Mercedes. On the way out, Rip turned to Rhonda and asked, "Are you feeling at all like...all this 'stuff'...all these things going on all the time..."

"Yes," Rhonda said quickly as if she was reading his mind. She glanced at Rip and then back at the driveway. Rip started the engine but the couple sat immersed in silence, the car motionless in front of the house. The only sound inside the car was the humming of the engine which at that moment seemed exceptionally noticeable for some reason. Then Rip broke the silence, "Let's go."

As they rode down the driveway toward the gate, Rhonda continued to focus straight ahead, pensively. The guard waved politely at the mobile couple as they passed slowly through the gate. Rip acknowledged the guard and drove over to the highway. Rip and Rhonda were off to the marina and their mini-vacation while Latherine was off to do his magic.

And magic it was. Before Rip and Rhonda had even been on the yacht for a full two days, Latherine came aboard with the news that the lawsuit had been abruptly dropped.

"So what happened?" Rhonda asked.

"Scut dropped the suit. Wham!" Latherine replied clapping his hands together once. "The golf course can stay exactly where it is and construction can continue—property rights will get sorted out later. No problems there. You know, sometimes I even amaze myself. Hmm...this is really a nice boat you have here," Latherine said as he gave it the once over from where he was standing. "I haven't been down here in a while."

"How did you..." Rip started.

Before Rip could finish his question, Latherine raised his fist and moved his extended forefinger from side to side. End of discussion.

After giving Latherine an abbreviated tour of the yacht, the happy couple thanked him energetically for taking such good care them. He responded by telling them they could return to their house at any time. As soon as Latherine was out of earshot, Rip asked Rhonda, "You want to stay here for a while? A few more days maybe?"

"Yes," Rhonda replied.

Rip then added, wistfully, "All this golf course nonsense. All this lawsuit business over the golf course. It's not even a real golf course. It's not even finished. It's not really anything essential to anything. No member of our so-called family is all that interested in golf. Our kids don't even know whether it's finished or not. They lost interest after only a few days. Can you believe it? And now Latherine is involved. All this for a golf course on a plot of land with a hundred other features just like it...makes you wonder..."

"Yes," Rhonda replied.

Even though the Scut lawsuit situation was quickly and definitively resolved, Rip and Rhonda both felt very uneasy with Latherine's "magic." In the past they never wanted to question any of his methods; he just made life easy for them in spite of the complexity and enormity of the Mousewater world. They never wanted to know more than what he was willing to reveal. So without a game plan, the happy couple just continued to...carry on.

## Chapter 42 – The Golf Course Solution

"What the?" It was two a.m. The black hood went over the head of Walter M. Scut before he knew what was happening. He was partially awake when it happened and was fully awake as he was dragged from his satin-sheeted bed. He had been holding his full bladder in check as he began to awaken, but the abrupt arrival of the masked men and the black hood over his own head caused his bladder to deliver its payload all over the satin sheets and Scut's silk pajamas. Scut's wife, Bubbles Scut, was unaware of the abduction since she had her own, isolated bedroom positioned far away from Walter's. Her sleep was made deeper by a handful of pills that she didn't use sparingly in order to get a good night's sleep.

Walter M. Scut: legal system mosquito and Bubbles Scut's powerful but impotent co-habitant.

After a circuitous journey and some mysterious twists and turns, the black hood was removed and Scut, with his eyebrows melting in the heat and his moist silk pajamas seeming to melt as well, found himself face to face with the boiling, roiling, orange and yellow viscous fluids in the survival shelter pit. He was the first person to experience the room in bare feet. Hot! Damn hot! Everyone was sweating profusely and Scut was getting redder by the second. Then one of the masked men spoke, "Your lawsuit, drop it. Not dropped? You drop…"

"Which lawsuit?" Scut replied. "I don't know which one you mean? I have eight or nine…ahem…right now."

The masked man looked at his partner quizzically and, showing some improvised initiative, especially for a thug, replied, "All of 'em."

"What do you mean, all of them?"

"Drop them all, all the ones you have going right now. If you don't you'll be here again. You won't know when, but next time you…will…be…you will become just so much ashy…uh, *vapor*. Get it?"

"Yes, yes. Let me up! My 'stache is on fire." Thanks to the heat, Scut's pajama pants were now completely dry. All he could think about was the smell of burnt hair coming from the hair on his philtrum.

The masked men quickly and efficiently returned the bloated red businessman to his bed and removed the hood. "If you back out or renege, we'll be back. And remember, if you somehow get yourself dead, your wife is gonna get her hands on all your shit." That alone may have been enough of an incentive for Scut to follow through.

When Latherine learned of the small unexpected twist to the event (that the masked enforcer demanded that Scut drop *all* his current suits) he was more than delighted. It meant that Scut would have no idea who hired the masked men. Such was Latherine's "magic." Such was Latherine's luck.

The unfinished survival shelter was turning out to be worth every cent invested in it; even though no human could possibly survive down there for very long. It was a classic case of finding functionality in something that was designed for an entirely different purpose— like using a hammer to smash a cockroach or using an empty swimming pool to store explosives.

## Chapter 43 – The Fumarole Issue

Turlew and Farmer were contemplating what to do about the fumaroles venting heated air through the ground (the ventilation shaft vents), rising up from far below, from the pit in the survival shelter. It was a strange (actually impossible) phenomenon given the geology of the area. Each of them had been down there only once. Once was enough. As they stood on the bare area of ground watching the hot water vapor rise from the six holes, they had not the slightest inkling about the handful of dramatic events that had transpired right under their feet since the building of the shelter. Then inspiration hit Turlew. They would move the location of the sweathouse from its current planned location near the dog-racing track to the spot right over the vents. The sweathouse would always be ready for use since the natural phenomenon of the fumaroles would keep the place "steamed" continuously. It was an absolutely perfect idea.

Building of the sweathouse was moved up in the schedule and in no time—given the 24/7 construction effort—the shell structure was complete; but the interior work had not yet been started. Fancy vent covers were in place on the foundation in order to give the sweathouse the finished appearance of a luxury spa amenity. But as work on the *interior* commenced, contractors were repeatedly overcome by the gases emanating from the vents—they could not proceed.

Now, the previously, fairly inconspicuous vents had a big conspicuous shell of a building over them. As the days went by, both Turlew and Farmer began to notice the rapid deterioration of the inner walls of the sweathouse shell. The trapped, sulfurous components of the "steam" were basically acid-burning the entire structure. Soon, elements of the unfinished ceiling began crashing to the floor, blocking the release of the gases. The fallen debris itself had also begun to deteriorate, generating a chemical fog of disintegrating building materials and rotten egg gases that prevented any human being from safely or comfortably entering the building. The building would have to come down and the vents left in peace to...*vent*, unobstructed.

But nature, having its own say, brought the building down before a bulldozer could even be summoned. And the sweathouse was once again re-assigned to its original spot near the dog-racing track. Had Turlew and Farmer been paying attention—instead of getting things finished quickly at all costs—they would have realized that with no code compliance hindrances, no expert advice, no scientific knowledge, and no regard for possible consequences, these types of things would wind up being the rule rather than the exception.

## Chapter 44 – The Acid Test

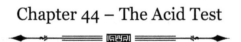

Turlew and Farmer were dealing with a number of issues twenty-four hours a day, seven days a week. Issues. Issues. One of the biggest issues was the recurring number of problems brought on by the building of Amador's vat of acid. Amador had seen it in a movie (or movies) and had to have one. It was, of course, of no concern to Amador that Turlew and Farmer thought the idea was ludicrous and considered themselves crazy to try and make it happen.

First, they had to get a custom-built vat liner that could withstand the presence of the acid. So a twelve-by-twelve-by-twelve tank was built using special acid-proof plastic. Once the tank was in place in the floor of the dungeon, a twelve-by-twelve vat lid was added to cover the vat when not "in use"—"in use," whatever that meant. An electric winch mechanism was added for raising and lowering the lid, and, per Amador's request, could be operated using a hand-held remote control. All of that, extraordinary as it was, was constructed without incident.

What kind of acid was to go into the tank? There were so many choices. Turlew knew nothing about that kind of chemistry. Farmer had limited knowledge. There was hydrochloric acid (HCl), sulfuric acid ($H_2SO_4$), nitric acid ($HNO_3$), hydrofluoric acid (HF), and many others. The easiest to get (with no questions asked) was plain old hydrochloric acid. Concentrated. Deadly vapors. How about a 13,000-gallon vat full?

Turlew happened to be making his usual rounds around the property when he was approached by a big, hairy, tattooed delivery man.

"Are you Farmer?" the hairy man asked.

"No, I'm Turlew, Ticker Turlew, the site manager."

"I was supposed to deliver all this acid to a Dick Farmer, here at this location."

Turlew looked behind the hairy man and saw only a small grey pickup truck. "I don't see any..."

"Got my trucks out there at the gate. Just need a delivery go-ahead and a spot to put the containers. Just say where."

"Trucks?" Turlew asked.

"Yessir. 13,000 gallons, as requested. Can I ask you, sir, what is all this acid for?" Hairy man was chewing vigorously on his toothpick.

"That's none of your concern." Turlew took him to an open area where the containers could be placed.

"You know, this is bad stuff you got here. Acid," the delivery man said.

"Yes, yes. We'll handle it. Just bring it on in and stow it right over there." Turlew turned and went to retrieve Farmer who was dealing with issues in the construction of the castle moat. When he saw Farmer by the rudimentary guest castle, he walked over to him and peered into the primitive moat.

"What do you know about all this acid?" Turlew asked Farmer.

"What about it? 13,000 gallons. You know, pipe it into the dungeon tank. Issue resolved. Check it off the list."

"The delivery guy said something about some containers."

"Don't know. Say, while you're here, we have some issues with this moat." Farmer motioned for Turlew to follow. Looking down at what had already been excavated, Farmer said, "The ground between this point and the dungeon is uneven and there is a slight upward slope to this castle location."

"Which means?" Turlew asked.

"I don't know if we can have the moat water be level with the water in the dungeon pit without some serious site grading and excavation."

"But we've already started on the building itself," Turlew remarked walking around to the back of the castle. Farmer followed. Around and around they went, assessing and evaluating the situation.

"Because the dungeon is lower than the moat—I thought this land was supposed to be flat—dammit," Turlew said. "I guess we'll have to deepen the moat to accommodate the water level. That's probably going to be at least 30 feet down." Turlew sat down on a large block of stone and Farmer sat nearby. They contemplated the situation for at least an hour. Most of the time was spent wishing everything would just go away.

When Turlew returned to the delivery site, waiting for him was a giant wall of reinforced, cream-colored plastic containers. Two husky men and two husky women were adding the final set of containers to the group. Another man was busily operating a weird-looking, three-wheeled, forklift-type vehicle. Turlew was approached by the thick-bearded man in charge.

The thick-bearded man stepped right up to Turlew, "13,000 gallons of hydrochloric acid. Delivered. Sign here and we're good to go." He handed Turlew a pad and Turlew signed off on it.

"How many containers?" Turlew asked.

"260, fifty gallons of acid each. I think there's a couple of extras, can't say for sure, but 260 minimum—13,000 gallons, as ordered, minimum. Good luck. Dangerous stuff. Nasty." With that the thick-bearded man and his crew left the area and Turlew stood silently staring at the imposing wall of containers.

Needless to say, the task of hauling 260+ fifty gallon drums of highly toxic acid down into the dungeon and emptying them into the tank, one by one, was not a task that anyone was voluntarily stepping forward to take on. So Turlew and Farmer, with the help of two other workers (former tin miners) carried the first of the containers down to the edge of the vat. As they carefully poured the liquid into the empty vat, the acid splashed around the bottom with a thin drum-like, resonant sound. But as the gallons of fluid poured out, extremely acrid vapors began to fill the area. In only seconds, it was burning their eyes, noses, and throats. Tiny drops that splashed onto their exposed skin burned like insect bites. Tiny splashes that landed on their clothing made little holes. The four men had to get out, get above ground immediately before they were eaten alive by the acid vapor. Once up top, Turlew again stared at the wall of acid containers and wondered how they were going to get all that acid down into the vat.

It was days before anyone could enter the dungeon, and even then, the air in the place still had a sharp acid smell to it. Turlew and Farmer decided to take a look. Only half of the first drum had been emptied and it was still lying on its side just where they had abandoned it. There were at least three dead rats in the vicinity.

"That might have been us," Turlew remarked.

"Calling me a rat? Farmer said. Turlew puffed out a humpty-grunt as they tried to figure out what to do next.

Back on top, their nightmare continued as Amador made an unwelcome appearance and asked, "What's all this?" He was putting his hands all over the plastic containers.

"That's acid, for your vat," Turlew replied. Just hearing himself say it made Turlew shake his head in disbelief.

"Cool." Amador walked around examining the stacks of containers like an official inspector while Turlew and Farmer watched him without saying a word. Turlew and Farmer were having some very bad thoughts. Then Amador turned away acknowledging neither Turlew nor Farmer. Amador's departure from the area was much appreciated.

In the days that followed, Farmer devised a plan to *siphon* the acid from each container down into the vat. Farmer first attempted to do so by using a garden hose. In no time, the acid ate through the hose leaving a trail of sticky tar-like residue on the ground. No acid ever arrived at its destination. On the second attempt, lengths of PVC pipe were used, but a heroic level of patience was required in order to get the rigid sections of pipe connected at just the right angles and maneuvered into the dungeon pit. Once the pipeline was completed, the process of transferring the acid was tedious. It was messy. Any tiny screw-up got acid on *something*. Anything the acid touched was either corroded or dissolved (including a fair amount of both Turlew's and Farmer's clothes and fleshy parts).

They hadn't been counting the containers; hadn't crossed their minds to do so. Turlew and Farmer just kept the siphoning pump running until all the vats had been emptied. Unfortunately, the thick-bearded delivery man was correct, there were two extra containers in the delivery, and the contents of those two, being 100 gallons more than was necessary to finish filling the vat, had overflowed and covered the floor of the dungeon; the acid eating up any vulnerable thing in its path—including a number of (lucky up to that point) rats. Of course Turlew and Farmer could not monitor the filling of the vat during the siphoning process since the dungeon was uninhabitable—thick fumes continuously filled the room from the first container on. So it wasn't until the air cleared in the dungeon—cleared enough for entry—that they discovered that they had inadvertently (and carelessly) piped that extra 100 gallons of acid into the dungeon; two full containers worth. A thick layer of vaporous acid covered the floor of the dungeon with a haze hovering above the whole surface. The problem was discovered the hard way by the soles of their shoes and the exfoliation of the plantar surface of their feet.

Even if their burning feet had not driven them from the dungeon, the air was so acidic that they would not have been able to stay there for more than 20 or 30 seconds anyway. The only solution was to bring in a haz-mat team to get the acid under control. In the end, the cleanup cost as much as the acid and the vat and the trap door and the winch mechanism combined. And the remote control. But the vat was full and the trap door was finally closed.

## Chapter 45 – The Acid Vat Incident

There were so many things going on at the Mousewater property that the acid vat was promptly relegated to the back burner. It wasn't until Turlew and Farmer had to enter the dungeon to examine the area where the moat water was to reach—for the alligator pit. They were unpleasantly surprised when they found that, even though the vat cover was closed (and ostensibly sealed) every piece of metal in the dungeon had started to corrode—

hinges, knobs, the winch mechanism. Many items of plastic were melting. Exposed wires in unfinished areas were losing their insulation. It had only been a week since the hazard crew finished the cleanup. Braving the acid air, they investigated the situation and found that the vat lid was corroding as well—obviously not immune to the effect of the acid. Since the winch was now non-functioning they had to raise the lid by hand in order to see the extent of the damage.

"Can you hold it there while a get a good look at the underside?" Turlew asked Farmer. Their eyes were watering and their nostrils were starting to burn.

"Sure." Farmer held the lid open at a 45-degree angle while Turlew got a look at the underside of the lid.

"This trap door lid, under here, this lid is eaten all to shit," Turlew remarked, taking stock of how badly it was damaged by probing the lid with a pencil. "This surface is all spongy."

"What do we do now?" Farmer asked, adjusting his position. "This lid is getting heavy. I'm going to go ahead and let it back down."

"Wait. Maybe we should leave it all the way open. It's just going to continue to deteriorate if we close it." Turlew went to the side opposite Farmer and started to push the lid open further. As he did so, Farmer shifted around to get better leverage. His right foot slipped right off the edge and into the vat. His entire body went on in immediately thereafter. Farmer was gone.

"Holy shit on a Sunday!" Turlew said as he stood motionless, still holding his side of the cover. After a few seconds Turlew dropped the lid, his hands burning from acid residue. The lid was now deformed enough to be inadequate in covering the vat completely. As the cover came down, the fog of acid vapor that had gathered over the vat was displaced and billowed up onto Turlew's legs and body and nostrils.

The Mousewater outdoor swimming pool had been in disuse ever since construction began. Its water, green and cloudy and loaded with algae, smelled like a swamp. All kinds of debris dotted its surface; and who knows what was going on in its unseen depths. When Turlew re-emerged from the dungeon—eyes burning, forearms burning, clothes dissolving—he saw the pool, ran over to it, disregarded its stagnant slime, and jumped right in. Workers in the area thought it was humorous and of course could not even imagine what Turlew had experienced.

When Turlew gathered himself together, he called for an urgent meeting with Rip and Rhonda to fill them in. Of course, the first thing *they* did was to call in Simon Latherine.

"Let me get this straight," Latherine said as he and Turlew and the happy couple sat together in the den. "You have a vat of acid in a *dungeon*? Hmmm. The acid is eating up everything, so you..." Latherine pointed at Turlew. "You and Farmer went to investigate. During the investigating process, somehow Farmer lost his balance and fell into the vat...the vat of acid. Is that pretty much it?"

Turlew nodded. Rip and Rhonda just sat silent; another episode, tragic episode; another feeling of resignation reached; reached while pursuing whatever it was they were pursuing.

"Am I to understand that there is nothing left of him?" Latherine added.

"Yes sir," Turlew answered. "I believe so. Maybe some metal. Like a skull plate or metal hip joint or some fillings in his teeth. I don't know."

"And it would be at the bottom of the...uh, vat of acid if there is anything at all?" Latherine turned to Rip and Rhonda, "What do you think of all this? What would you like me to do?"

Rhonda spoke up, "Can you work your magic? Can you make it all go away?"

"Well, it's helpful that there's nothing left of him..." Latherine paused. "Normally we could go to the authorities; maybe say he's gone missing. Something like that. But if it came right down to it, explaining that vat of acid might be a little dicey—especially if the authorities start snooping around this place, searching, with or without a search warrant."

Rip then said, "What would you like us to do?"

"Let me manage this. I'll make it disappear. But...all this stays between the four of us. Understood?" Accepting the reality of the situation, everyone nodded in agreement. The incident was never mentioned again. But the vat of acid was not done with the Mousewater project.

## Chapter 46 – Otilio DiPoto

Otilio DiPoto would never have been a first choice to manage the day-to-day construction, but Turlew was running out of options. He knew DiPoto was discreet and had so many skeletons in his closet that his cooperation (in all things) could be counted on. Not particularly difficult to manage but, in general, DiPoto was one spooky individual: 6'5", very thin and muscular, and always with a menacing look on his face—a face creased with years of working in the sun. His thinness could be attributed to his constant cigarette smoking while working on site. Someone could trace his steps around the property by following the trail of cigarette butts he left behind. He was over sixty and not dead yet. His white hair was dyed black, an unnatural-looking india ink black. Some areas of skin on his head were unintentionally dyed black also. He had a habit of walking around the site without his shirt on, exposing numerous questionable and distasteful tattoos "plastered" all over his sinewy torso. As an indication of his character, it might be said that if DiPoto knew what had happened to his two predecessors, it wouldn't have bothered him in the least.

When Anthony and Whitney next visited Rip and Rhonda they were all introduced to DiPoto. They did not feel comfortable being in the same room with him. Whitney couldn't stand him. Rip and Rhonda had similar queasy feelings about DiPoto. The new site manager was someone to be avoided, when possible.

One of DiPoto's first actions on his very first day fell upon him like a sudden summer downpour. The three Mousewater siblings, together as a unified militant unit tracked down Turlew (Turlew was trying desperately to hide from them). Turlew passed the buck and told them that if they had any questions to take them up with DiPoto, directing them to the guest castle site where DiPoto was watching the deep moat excavation while sitting on one of the large stone blocks, cigarette hanging from his lips. The siblings approached him and brazenly demanded to know why their residences had not been started. They had never seen this guy before, but they got a full dose of him that day. The siblings might have been a trio of puff adders when they first showed up, but when DiPoto got through shaking them down for ten minutes...

Upon DiPoto's recommendation and with Rip and Rhonda's support, the three siblings were shunted off to three separate luxury suites at the Gonoroli Hotel in the Big City. They were banned from the Mousewater estate for the duration. It might have been easier to get an audience with the Pope than for the three siblings to get back onto the site in order to pester the workers, Turlew, and especially DiPoto.

## Chapter 47 – The Summit

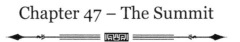

In less than a week, Otilio DiPoto was overwhelmed. Not only was the enormous number of ongoing projects starting to become unmanageable but the very nature of many of the features, rooms, and buildings was confusing and bewildering. In all his years, DiPoto had never had to manage anything like it. There soon came a breaking point and DiPoto had to request a summit meeting with the architectural staff.

Turlew started the meeting, "Otilio, I'd like to introduce Ms. Turquoise McPuvis, Mr. Bando Mahlmballs, and Mr. Bob Smith. Group, this is Mr. Otilio DiPoto." Addressing Dipoto, Turlew added, "These are the top architects on the project." After cursory acknowledgements between the attendees, Turlew continued, "We need to get Otilio up to speed on what we're all doing here."

"What *are* we all doing here?" Ms. McPuvis asked facetiously.

Turlew quickly responded, "OK. OK. Otilio has some legitimate issues regarding many of the projects we are working on. I'm hoping that we can address his concerns and questions. Otilio…"

"What the hell is a vomitorium?" DiPoto did not beat around the bush. "These troughs and shower heads, the large diameter drains, tile floor, huge ventilation system. What's supposed to be going on in there?"

Mahlmballs spoke up, "It's a Roman thing. Romans used to stuff themselves with food and then go into the vomitorium and throw it all up. This is modern version of that type of room…uh, presumably."

"And that's something that people have in their houses these days?" DiPoto asked.

"Well this house has it," Mahlmballs replied.

"All right, what am I to make of this Chamber of Horrors and vintage weapons museum?" DiPoto asked, moving on. "What's going to be put in a "Chamber of Horrors? What *kind* of horrors?"

"Ahem. I'll answer that," Turlew responded. "Those are no longer going to be included. They were slated for the dungeon, but that area is basically uninhabitable."

"Uninhabitable. I see." *Outwardly,* DiPoto seemed to accept the assessment, then, moving on, "So we have an ice pool that is connected to a blizzard room. Either it's ice…or…it's a pool of water."

"Right," Mr. Smith said. "There's ice all around the pool there and the water itself is set at 33 degrees."

"And we're supposed to figure out how to do that I suppose."

"Yes, well...the ice pool is part of the blizzard room complex so that all the associated machinery can be in one place," Mr. Smith added.

"Uh huh. So. Now, according to this set of plans, we're supposed to build an indoor artificial mountain peak out of rocks and dirt inside a big barn, and at the other end of the barn there are two giant wind machines along with a custom-made snow generating machine. They are to be installed for making an indoor blizzard on the mountain peak. This barn is huge...and tall. And there is no provision for maintaining the temperature...the refrigeration or even insulating this building. How is the ice—? Ice pool? All that artificial snow is just going to turn to water before it hits the ground. Have I got all this right?"

"Right," Mr. Smith said.

DiPoto continued, "Don't know how all *that* is going to work. Well. So. Now then, we have a rock climbing wall and a mechanical bull room. Neither of these two items have any safety or protective equipment planned whatsoever. The floor under the bull is merely concrete just like the floor under the climbing wall. There's no padding. The wall has no provision for a safety harness of any kind—that wall is seventy feet tall. Who's going to be climbing that wall at that height with no safety apparatus?"

"Don't know," Mahlmballs replied.

"Uh-*huh*. Here are some other items that caught my eye. We've got what is called a bordello room. It looks like another bedroom and bathroom to me except for the mirrors and this one mirror with the double-ended arrow on it. And what does this mean: secret sex room? Anybody?"

Mahlmballs spoke up, "The arrow there indicates a two-way mirror. We have no idea what the secret sex room is all about. Self-explanatory? They told us that Master Amador will be equipping both rooms himself, but apparently he's not available right now—"

"These little restaurants and other buildings look fairly straightforward, but my question is: Are you aware that all these various standalone places and bars appear to be...identical? The barber shop and salon even have a kitchen. It looks as though one plan was drawn up and then used as a basis for all these other buildings; this wide variety of specialty buildings sprinkled all around the property. That's what it looks like to me."

"You are correct," Mahlmballs replied.

Frustrated with the lack of enlightening information, DiPoto turned to Turlew and said, "I don't think this meeting is getting us anywhere. I'm still not clear on how we're supposed to implement a lot of this 'stuff.' The purpose of all this construction is just as confusing to me as it was before."

Agreeing with DiPoto's assessment Turlew dismissed the architects and began a one-on-one discussion.

DiPoto then said, "And what is a fungus barn? They delivered tons and tons of manure yesterday and just left it out there on the front driveway—a humongous mountain of turkey shit. Must be 25 feet high. It's supposed to be used for the fungus barn, but we haven't even started on that construction yet."

"That was a scheduling screw-up, but the pile will just have to stay there until the barn is complete." Turlew was feeling sympathy for DiPoto and the challenges he was facing.

"Well, it smells pretty bad, it's right out front, and it's going to get completely dried out by the time we move it all to the barn. I'm just sayin'."

"That's the way things go around here," Turlew replied. "I've just learned to accept everything at face value."

"And I have a question about that huge pile of copper...all those copper pipes—different lengths—that we're supposed to use for plumbing. They're not new. They look as though they've been ripped out or salvaged from a demolition site. Some are pretty bent up and twisted."

"Yes, well, we're getting all that copper from an unusual source. Let's just leave it at that," Turlew responded. "I know you have many more issues to discuss, but I think you should follow my example and just go with the flow."

His conversation with Turlew gave DiPoto a fresh (and much needed) viewpoint on what was actually taking place on the Mousewater property. From that point forward he took Turlew's advice and, without questioning anything, proceeded to handle issue after issue as if every one of them was completely reasonable and commonplace—and there would be many challenging moments to come where going with the flow would turn out to be an exercise in swimming upstream.

## Chapter 48 – Going with the Flow

"I see you are police," DiPoto said, puffing out smoke from his cigarette without making anything but furtive eye contact with the officer. "What is it?"

"We have a report that there are nude sunbathers in your yard back there. One of your neighbors called it in. I need to take a look."

DiPoto was no fool. He had years of experience coming up with quick-witted explanations (good or bad) for unexplainable things: "How did that cocaine get in your coat pocket?" "This isn't my coat."

Going with the flow, especially since this was an easy one, DiPoto took the policeman to the beach where ten unclothed mannequins were strewn about in the sand. "We're testing the sunbathing potential of our little beach here, as you can see. You know, suntan lotion, angle of the sun, time of day, you know..." DiPoto was anxious to get the policeman off the property before accidentally running across some of the *real* problem areas.

The policeman walked around the beach area admiring how anatomically correct the mannequins were; but still, they were just mannequins, or dolls, or something—something spooky about it. Amused by it all the officer said, "I didn't think there was anything to it. Doesn't look like much of anything going on here. Neighbors aren't really supposed to be spying on other people anyway. This beach is kinda weird though..." Then, looking around he finally said, "You people sure have a lot of construction going on here..."

"Yes we do. And I've got to get back to it." With that DiPoto escorted the officer on a minimally problematic route through the maze of construction and back to his squad car.

"That's quite a smell coming from that big pile of dirt over there," the policeman said, pointing to the manure as he got into his car. As the police car exited the driveway a large refrigerated delivery truck arrived. It parked next to the giant mound of manure.

"Are you Turlew?" the delivery man asked?

"No, I'm DiPoto. I'm managing the project. "What do you need?"

"I've got 6,200 pounds of raw meats and sausages. Where do I unload all this?"

DiPoto was no longer surprised by these kinds of happenings. He was surprised by the quantity however. Not knowing an alternative, he had the meats stowed in the partially-completed smokehouse—raw cuts of fine meats and sausages, all kinds. Not a good decision. Within 24 hours the meats started to cook up and the smell of deteriorating flesh hovered all around the smokehouse. To make matters worse, the original order was for 620 pounds not 6,200 pounds. And again, the timing was really bad. Eventually all the meats had to be disposed of—something had to be done. So DiPoto was able to sell the entire 6,200 pounds to a fast food restaurant chain—a chain that shall remain unnamed. DiPoto, just going with the flow.

Building the hedge maze was not a particularly difficult task. The maze was designed by Bando Mahlmballs and was very clever and devious. Early on, DiPoto noticed that a person lost in the maze could just plow themselves right through the hedge in order to get out. So the hedges were removed and the maze was built using thin, but impenetrable concrete walls instead of hedges. It was not particularly esthetic, but the maze was diabolical. It was so diabolical that three workers who had tried to explore the maze got hopelessly lost and had to be led out by Turlew and DiPoto. These types of things arose on a daily basis, but DiPoto just went with the flow.

Waystations, waystations, waystations. Turlew was fed up with all the small but feature-filled waystations that were being built seemingly everywhere. There were waystations for the hiking trails, waystations for the biking trails, waystations for the equestrian trails, and waystations for the trolley (more like small depots). Each of these required its own set of utilities. There were places with two or more waystations in the immediate vicinity but were associated with different trails. The trolley depots were larger and had more elaborate interiors. Everything was slapped together quickly and had the characteristic seedy quality of everything else. Seedy, but consistent.

Going with the flow became more difficult when it came to the trolley rail line itself. The two trolley cars were very quaint and attractive in spite of their used condition. They were bought from a defunct amusement park. When the huge underground gasoline tank was built, its intended use was for filling the tanks of all the vehicles at the estate. However, the trolley cars ran on diesel fuel. So an additional tank had to be built just for filling the trolley gas tanks.

Orville, who originally wanted the trolley system, did not realize that it would require someone to operate the trolley cars day and night for them to be of any practical value for moving around the estate. The tracks themselves wound around in an extremely interesting but complicated route in order to visit all the various fields and features—items of interest that were everywhere on the property. In spite of all these issues, the trolley became one of the least objectionable features on the entire estate even though no one was ever hired to run it full time. Rip was especially enamored with piloting it himself, all around the circuit. In doing so he and Rhonda were able to see firsthand the colossal jumble of buildings and features as they rode around the property. It was quite an enlightening but not altogether pleasant perspective. Was their disdain directed toward themselves or the sheer bizarreness of the entire layout? Even though the trolley itself was an unusually enjoyable feature, at least for Rhonda one comprehensive ride around the entire layout was enough.

And then there was the drainage problem. All the features, fields, recreation areas, and especially the golf course were all designed without regard, one to another. As a result, one area would drain into a different area every time it rained and many times the water remained for days or weeks. Soggy ground and heavy machinery would work hand in hand in creating massive areas of glue-like mud with deep ruts in it—ruts that when dried out were like concrete and difficult to even walk over. During the finish-out stages workers tracked mud into every place imaginable. They always seemed to be oblivious to anybody's workspace but their own. When it came to the sorry drainage, go with the flow seemed to be the appropriate philosophy.

When the merry-go-round arrived several months early, DiPoto was truly tested in his go-with-the-flow philosophy. With stacks and stacks of construction materials, unfinished standalone buildings, and features blocking the way, there was apparently no way to get the wide, bulky thing into its place in the back behind the main house. The solution was to turn it on its side and transport it that way.

As Turlew and DiPoto watched the slow-moving process unfold, DiPoto asked Turlew, "Why didn't we just bring it in disassembled and reassemble it here?"

"This was a lot cheaper and faster," Turlew replied. "We got it intact from the same amusement park that we got the trolleys."

At that moment the entire carousel broke free from the hauling flatbed and rolled about forty amazing feet before coming to a halt and landing upside down near the site where the three square sibling residences were scheduled to be built. Its damaged hulk was centered over the area where the single passageway to the main house was planned. Many of the painted horses were crushed under the rubble. It was going to take quite a cleanup effort to remove the unsightly mess.

Rip and Rhonda were constantly provided with unwelcome updates about issues during construction. Normally they would act interested but then pass the buck back to DiPoto or Turlew. In the case of the merry-go-round, Rip came out to the site to examine it personally. "Leave it," Rip said.

"What about the passageway from the three residences? It was supposed to go right through there," DiPoto said as he pointed to the center of the huge defunct ride.

"Make a tunnel through it. Call the upside-down merry-go-round yard art." Rip turned around and went back inside. Indifference and impatience were becoming standard reactions to any problems arising from the projects. Whenever it got to be too much, Rip and Rhonda would take off for a vacation on the yacht. Sometimes, if they spotted Turlew arriving at the marina, Rip would quickly take the yacht out onto the lake. Turlew was left to make all the decisions; sometimes left to twist in the wind. Issue after issue, Turlew and DiPoto managed all the projects and no matter how bizarre the problem, both men were usually able to just go with the flow.

Rip and Rhonda were returning from one of their mini-vacations, when, on the drive home they were hindered by an incredible traffic jam on the highway. A delivery truck had overturned and was blocking traffic on the very lanes that went by the Mousewater estate area. Both the highway and the frontage road were packed with stationary automobiles. The delivery truck was bound for the Mousewater estate when the accident occurred. It was carrying over 570 porcelain fixtures destined to be installed in the various rooms and features in the Mousewater layout (toilets, sinks, and urinals). But the fixtures would never make it to the layout—they were distributed all over Highway 111, the median, and the shoulder. It was newsworthy locally and made good novelty news for national news broadcasts. This was the kind of publicity that the layout (and Turlew and DiPoto) did not need. Watching the news on TV, Simon Q. Latherine readied himself for another round of "magic."

Rip got out of the car to see what was causing the delay when Rhonda yelled and motioned to him to get back in the car. She heard about the accident on the radio and the Mousewater estate was *mentioned by name*. Rip turned onto the median and drove across it to the other side. It was back to the marina, back to the yacht. "Let Turlew and DiPoto handle it," Rip said as the entire mess faded into the distance in the rear view mirror.

## Chapter 49 – Management and Ownership

After three years, most of the construction had been completed (at least outwardly). There was still a monumental amount of incomplete finish-out work to be done on the interior of the buildings. Construction continued relentlessly night and day at a furious pace. Everywhere, at night, massive halogen worklights lit up the entire estate, indoors and out. This attracted millions of bugs so each light had a constant swarm hovering around it. The nighttime light extravaganza also attracted the attention of the very important people in the surrounding hills. Luckily for Turlew and DiPoto, curiosity outweighed the nuisance factor as evidenced by the lack of official complaints from the elite homeowners—all across the hillsides there were binoculars and telescopes trained on the proceedings down at the Mousewater estate.

The quality of the workmanship on the original Mousewater house had always left something to be desired, but the quality of work on all the new additions was not only shabby, in some cases it was outright dangerous—gaps in walls, electrical wire spaghetti, gas leaks, roof leaks, poor paint jobs, nonfunctional lights, disconnected plumbing, no paint jobs, exposed live wires—and of course totally inadequate bathroom fixtures. Mismatched everything. *Working* bathrooms had to be clearly indicated even for Rip and Rhonda. All of this was being built and finished right under the nose of the happy couple who owned it all—owned it all on paper, disowned it all in reality.

Trips to the yacht became more frequent and the mini-vacations turned into weeks of R & R for Rip and Rhonda. Sometimes Turlew would arrive at the yacht and find Rip and Rhonda talking with Latherine or some other stranger in a suit. In those rare instances Turlew could sneak in an audience with the happy couple before they were able to motor out onto the lake. One might consider philosophically: Was the poor construction workmanship evidence of Turlew's passive aggressive spite (the fact that Rip and Rhonda left everything in his hands and were avoiding him whenever possible) or was it just Turlew's desire to get the whole nightmare over with as quickly as possible? In spite of Rip and Rhonda's enlightened and realistic attitude about their dysfunctional children and the absurdity of the layout itself, they still had developed no sense of responsibility. They felt compelled to finish what they started but paradoxically they felt no desire to be a part of it any more.

## Chapter 50 – The Squares

The day had finally arrived: the dreaded return of the Mousewater children; the day they were to take ownership of their individual residences; the day of reckoning for Turlew and DiPoto. Farmer was the lucky one. He was dead. Rip and Rhonda were standing by like security guards...or referees. Standing in the open area between the main house and the squares Turlew, DiPoto, and the happy couple watched as the three siblings jostled their way out into the yard from a side door. They were grumbling to themselves and at each other in typical fashion. If three's a crowd the siblings certainly qualified; they were elbowing each other as if there were twenty of them.

It wasn't surprising that Amador was the first to make a comment. "What the he-e-e-e-ll?" He looked the houses over, up and down, up and down, craning his neck.

Seeing as how the siblings relished branding everything with their individual initials, Turlew had each of the three houses fitted with large brightly-lit letters indicating the owner: TDM for Trina Darlene Mousewater, OPM for Orville Pease Mousewater, and ATM for Amador Travis Mousewater. The signs were gaudy and obtrusive and *bright*, even in the daylight. The signs were such a distraction that the siblings did not even notice the mangled remains of the merry-go-round, not at first.

"What is this?" Orville said as he walked over to the merry-go-round rubble. "Is this a merry-go-round?"

"Not any more," Dipoto chimed in.

"Why are these houses so close together? There's no space in between. They're like three...big...flat...boxes." Trina was the calmest of the three, but was not amused.

"Well go on inside," Rip said. "Use the letters to identify which house is yours," he added with a little bit of mischief in his tone.

Trina's house was in the middle, Orville's to the left and Amador's to the right. They had to enter the side of the main covered passageway, which, at the squares' end, branched into three individual passageways leading to each of the three front doors. It was awkward—the passageways were very narrow. For the siblings, their individual horrors were only beginning. Each of the siblings had given a design to Turlew and each one had been chopped into a square arbitrarily. As the siblings disappeared into their residences, Rhonda leaned toward Turlew and without looking at him said, "I love what you've done with these places. Very creative. Very appropriate."

While the children were inside, the four adults outside could hear muffled exclamations and epithets coming from all three residences. Sooner or later each sibling re-emerged from their respective house, hostile, agitated, ready for confrontation (in other words, the usual).

"My living room is only three feet wide!" Amador shouted.

"My bedroom has no bathroom," shouted Trina.

"And I have no place to eat...except the kitchen...how ordinary," Orville said, following up.

"I know you three have a thousand questions," Turlew said. "But go ahead and move in. You'll learn to love it."

"Where's Latherine? I demand to see Latherine." Trina was ready to storm the Bastille with the family lawyer leading the way.

Unfortunately for Trina, at that moment, as if on cue, Simon Latherine stepped forward from the shadows, briefcase in hand. "What can I do for you, Trina?" Latherine said in a kind of greasy, manipulative way.

"What do you have to say about all this, Latherine?" Trina demanded. Orville and Amador were nodding and saying "Yeah" in solidarity.

"Nice signs...good lettering," Latherine said, indicating that the discussion was over before it began.

Then Rhonda added, "If you don't like your residence, you can always move into a place of your own—but you'll have to pay for that yourself." The three siblings looked at each other with open mouths—consternation with a glaze of pathos.

Turlew was overjoyed that it had gone so well, and some of his irritation with Rip and Rhonda's neglect was definitely tempered by the event. Rhonda's acknowledgment and approval was an unexpected bonus.

"Well then, that's that," Rip said as the entire group of five left the scene; left the siblings to stew in their own juices.

## Chapter 51 – The Wild Life

With such a large project and so few people keeping an eye on things, certain elements of the project were bound to be overlooked. Such was the case with a multi-truck delivery of sea life. Dolphins were delivered, but there was no dolphin tank. Several sharks were delivered, large ones and small ones, but no shark tank. Also arriving at the same time were hundreds of smaller fish, some exotic, some merely for ambient effect. There *was* a place for those smaller fish—they were destined for the huge aquarium. However, the existing aquarium continued to leak and had to be re-supplied with seawater, constantly. The aquarium viewing area was in the basement and the leakage kept the basement floor completely soaked. With the high humidity the entire basement felt moist and sticky. It smelled like a shallow ocean inlet—a fishy fishy pool of saltwater. And, of course, there were no experts on site to manage the correct salt content and alkalinity of the tank water itself so it was anybody's guess if the sea life would soon be sea death—and yet another incident that would have to be managed.

When all the sea life arrived on the same day, there was no permanent place to stow any of it except the aquarium. DiPoto, having no experience with anything concerned with nature, merely had the whole delivery added to the aquarium. There was chaos: dolphins, aquatic life, and sharks all mixed together in one fairly large aquarium tank. The spectacular frenzy could be observed from right there in the basement. The free-for-all was so similar to the behavior of the Mousewater siblings that Turlew and DiPoto were captivated by the similarity. They stood motionless in the basement, looking through the viewing wall, and watching all the Darwinian sea life in action. They watched until an entire group of young, energetic individuals showed up with a pair of policemen.

"We have a court order here to remove these animals to the nearest sea life facility—immediately!" a young woman said as she waved a thick set of papers in Turlew's face. "All of them!"

"By all means," Turlew responded. "Help yourself." Turlew pointed both of his arms toward the clear, leaky aquarium viewing glass.

The group of young people was expecting some kind of confrontation and was momentarily perplexed by Turlew's conciliatory attitude. It was a distraction that was soon shattered when the group got sight of the mayhem and carnage going on behind the wall of aquarium glass. For the next eight hours, with cranes and cradles, all of the dolphins and sharks were extracted from the water. Even some of the smaller sea life was salvaged—those lucky few that had survived the initial melee.

Of course it was up to Latherine to smooth out the whole affair, managing the legalities and illegalities (of course), and somehow keeping all of it out of the media. How he was able to keep such a grotesque incident under wraps is still a big mystery. Needless to say, Trina would never get to swim with her very own dolphins and her shark tank would never materialize; although she would have been right at home in either tank.

Trina *did* get one of her wishes granted with the next delivery.

"I've got forty-one buffaloes out here in these cattle trucks. Where do you want them unloaded?" It was yet another delivery man with yet another questionable cargo.

After looking the trucks over, Turlew guided the drivers into the fields at the very back of the Mousewater property. It was impossible for Turlew to get such a herd of buffaloes (bison) anywhere in North or South America. They were European buffaloes and had to be shipped all the way across the Atlantic—Dominic's legacy of smuggling was alive and well in acquiring the animals.

The bison delivery occurred on the same day that Rip was joyfully demonstrating the trolley system to Anthony. Anthony almost felt guilty that he was enjoying the excursion as much as did. When the trolley rounded the corner near the field where the bison were being unloaded, Rip brought it to a stop so that he and Anthony could see what was happening. Several trucks were parked in the field and numerous wranglers were involved in the operation. Each bison was cheerfully hoofing its way down the unloading ramp at the back end of its assigned truck. It brought to mind an image of animals leaving Noah's ark, single file, after the flood.

"Are those buffaloes?" Anthony asked Rip while the trolley was still in motion.

"Yes I think they are. One of Trina's...things."

"How in the world?"

"Don't ask...but Turlew says they are fairly legal," Rip replied.

"What does that mean...fairly?" Anthony watched as the last of the herd was ushered into the field. "And what is that truck over there?" Anthony pointed at another new arrival.

"I don't know, but it looks like horses," Rip said as he started up the trolley again. He had seen enough for one day.

The horses were delivered to the equestrian center without incident; another item from Trina's list put to bed. Making sure all of these Trina-requested animals were properly cared for took a staff of more or less ten people, all of which had to be on the Mousewater payroll. Between the salaries, the food, the medical attention, and the maintenance of the wildlife management facilities, the animal life was a very expensive add-on to the escalating cost of day-to-day operations at the Mousewater property; a very expensive enterprise given that it was merely a whim of Trina's. Latherine had to be called in several times when Rip and Rhonda's celebrity neighbors complained of the smell from the animals and their deposits—the aromas wafting, as they tended to do, up into the hills.

Amador's whims were no less awkward to manage.

"I'm Gil, Gil the Gator Wrangler. I've got fifty-two adult alligators in my truck over there," the next delivery man informed Turlew. Gil was quite interesting as he was missing his left arm and had heavy, heavy, highly-visible scars on his neck.

"What happened to you?" Turlew said, "if you don't mind me asking."

"Nah. S'okay. Got too close to a gator eight years ago. Snatched me by the arm. Started a death roll. Pulled that damn arm clean off. Scratched me up a sight, too. Don't mind how these *scars* look; not too much. But I do miss that arm. Where do you want these suckers?" The delivery man pointed toward his truck with his thumb. Turlew noticed a woman in the passenger seat of the truck and the gator man noticed Turlew's noticing. "That's my daughter up there, Gayle, in the cab...helps me out with the gator wrangling. Still got all *her* fingers, but only one and a half feet. Good helper though..."

Turlew showed the delivery man the moat and, soon thereafter, fifty-two alligators began puttering around in it, waiting for some kind of meat to be tossed their way. Having been raised and pampered on a farm—a Florida tourist attraction actually—the alligators had certain expectations of their keepers. Turlew wished that the alligators had arrived right after all that meat, that meat that was destined for the smokehouse—what bad timing that turned out to be. Unfortunately, now, *new* meat had to be purchased and delivered and dumped into the moat. The thought of Gil and Gayle's missing body parts was making Turlew uneasy about the whole idea of alligators on the premises; and the prospect of feeding time in particular.

## Chapter 52 – Who's Running This Zoo?

As if all the animal deliveries weren't bad enough and problematic enough, maintaining and controlling such a zoo was becoming a bigger nuisance than anyone could have imagined.

At least the herd of bison was managing itself out in the grazing field. They seemed content to graze and mill about. It was actually a quite beautiful sight with only an occasional confrontation between exuberant males when it came to female pursuits.

The horses were relatively easy to tend, but a lot of veterinary care was always required in order to keep the horses in tiptop shape for riding. Riding and equestrian pursuits—horses at the ready...but nobody in the Mousewater family seemed to be interested in the horses, riding, the trails, or any of it...not even Trina. So the small equestrian staff rode the horses, taking full advantage of the many trails, and cared for the horses as if the horses belonged to them.

Less manageable were Amador's alligators. They needed to be fed—fed regularly if not constantly. Truckloads of meat came in on a regular basis. No matter what dead animal was the source of the meat, it was not cheap—not in the quantity required. And getting the meat into the moat safely and without incident was a hazardous challenge. Turlew took it upon himself to feed the alligators and keep them content, all the while remembering the delivery man's missing arm and all those deep scratches. And just *how* did Gil's daughter wind up losing half of her foot? When dumping big loads of meat into the moat Turlew would watch the alligators go after it, fighting amongst themselves to get the best position for getting at all the tasty goodness. He knew that one bad slip and he would most likely lose more than an arm. One unfortunate slip.

With the accumulation of so many unfortunate incidents, it was becoming clear to Turlew that every little thing was reminding him of some other thing—it was becoming a big blur of memories, mostly bad ones. The fighting alligators reminded him of the sharks and dolphins which reminded him of the siblings. Every time he approached the edge of the moat he thought about Farmer going into the vat of acid. That, and a thousand other incidents and loose ends and legal exposures were permanently logged in his mind. He knew where all the bodies were buried because he buried them—and he did not want to be *one* of them someday.

After things had settled into a routine, Turlew reluctantly invited Amador to come and take a look at the alligators in the moat. Turlew disliked Amador most of all the siblings, but he kept his opinions to himself since Rip and Rhonda always seemed to have Amador's number and that was enough for him.

"Cool," Amador said, predictably. "What's that over there?" Amador pointed to the tower across the open falconry and archery field as if the alligators were no longer of any interest to him.

"That's your dog-racing track. And the kennels are over there, on that end." Turlew was pleased that Amador had taken an interest in something, anything. But Turlew was miffed that Amador dismissed the alligators so casually considering the perilous effort it took to keep those babies happy. "Let's go take a look," Turlew said as he led the way to the dog track.

The dog-racing track was almost complete and all the facilities had only a few finish-out items remaining. But there were no rails around the track and there was no mechanical rabbit mechanism like that found in a real dog-racing track. It was really just an oval track. The handful of dogs in the kennel started barking as Amador and Turlew approached. They were met by Manfred Pippin, the dog handler. He was a real "dog man" and up to that point had never set eyes on anyone from the Mousewater family. He just went about his daily care of the dogs, unfettered, and collected his paycheck like everyone else.

"Are we going to race these dogs, or what?" Amador asked Pippin.

"These aren't the kinds of dogs that do any racing," Pippin replied. He felt put off by Amador's authoritarian attitude since Amador had never laid eyes on anything dog-related during the entire tenure of Pippin's employment.

"Well let's get some dogs and race 'em," Amador ordered. "Don't dog catchers get dogs? Let's get some dogs!"

As Amador marched himself back to the moat, Turlew turned and said to Pippin in a mocking tone, "Well...let's go get some dogs."

Turlew followed Amador back to the moat where Amador was irritated by *something*. "How are these alligators supposed to get into my alligator pit? What is that panel, that grill, there that's blocking the channel? What's going on?" Amador was quizzing Turlew, showing even more disrespect than usual.

"Well, we shouldn't let the alligators go to the pit because of the acid in the dungeon," Turlew replied.

"Well, what good is an alligator pit without alligators? Let freedom ring! Let's get these big boys over into the pit!" With that, Amador lifted the metal grill using the winch handle and proceeded back to his residence without another thought about it.

Turlew was used to this kind of thing so he just mumbled to himself, "Whatever you say little Thermidor. Whatever you say."

## Chapter 53 – Of Alligators and Dogs

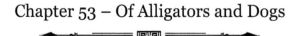

Rather than see a host of pure-bred greyhounds go to waste on such a frivolous enterprise as Amador's dog-racing track, Pippin acquired twenty-four of the most desperate and hopeless dogs he could locate—animal shelters, dog pounds, even some strays he picked up on his own. They were mangy, dirty, and undisciplined, but at least they were no longer headed for a gas chamber or a metal examining table for a euthanasia injection. He carefully managed to keep the new group away from the five dogs he'd been caring for and had become attached to.

It had only been about 24 hours since Amador had lifted the dividing grill from blocking the channel, but the alligators were taking full advantage. The moat was too deep for the alligators to do anything but wander around—crowded uncomfortable captives (predators) between the concrete walls of the moat. No hunting allowed, no hunting for themselves. The channel ran all the way from the moat to the somewhat subterranean wall of the dungeon and connected to the dungeon's alligator pit through a fairly wide opening in the dungeon wall. The walls of the channel were not as deep as those in the moat, not deep at all—especially as the channel approached the alligator pit. And so, the alligators began wandering up the channel, and finding a place to exit from their concrete prison, began to wander all over the Mousewater estate—uncrowded, on dry land. What a welcome change. Eventually, all but three left the confines of the guest castle moat. Some, however meandered all the way down into Amador's alligator pit, preferring to continue along in the channel water rather than moving out onto dry land. It was a deadly choice. Many alligators went through the portal into the dungeon to explore the pit, but enough alligators followed that those already inside could not get out. The exit was clogged with a jumble of alligators. The panicked alligators inside could not get outside because of the giant plug of ancient reptiles. The acid would take a deadly toll on those inside. Alligators may survive a nuclear holocaust, but those unfortunate ones in Amador's pit could not survive a heavy atmospheric vapor of hydrochloric acid—fourteen of them.

Having so many alligators loose on the premises kept the nervous staff busy for days. The remaining contractors (and there were many) were given a much needed hiatus from work on the estate. A few brave souls assisted in the roundup.

"Why round them up? Why not just shoot 'em?" Orville asked Turlew. Orville was sticking his rarely seen nose into a complication where it was not welcome. Orville was unhappy that a bunch of large alligators were wandering all around his residence.

Turlew replied, "Because if we shoot 'em, those nosy neighbors up there are gonna hear the shots and soon there will be police and inspectors and...are you ready for that?" Orville didn't back down, he just let it continue to hang out there.

It was incredibly tedious tracking down and rousting out all the escapee alligators—they knew exactly how to manage themselves out in the wild. Special handlers had to be called to the site to assist in actually capturing them and getting them back into the moat. Turlew closed the blockade grill in the channel and put a sturdy lock on it (ostensibly to keep Amador from starting the mess all over again). Once the handlers had accounted for thirty-two alligators, the round-up became more difficult. The rest of the live alligators had ventured up into the hills and elsewhere off the Mousewater property. But no one cared to look in the acid-soaked dungeon, and the pit, for more of the missing ones. The dead ones began to decay, and if the smell of acid was bad enough, add to that the rotting corpses of fourteen dead alligators. More management nightmares.

Mr. Pippin kept all the dogs safe during the alligator fiasco. The alligators never really got near the kennels or the track. It was quite a surprise when, a week or so later, he saw Amador heading his way, stomping. Turlew was running behind, trying to catch up. Turlew just shrugged his shoulders when Pippin gave him a questioning look, wondering what *this* visit was all about.

"Let's have a dog race," Amador demanded. "I'll help get this thing started. How many have we got here?" Amador was fumbling around acting like he was in charge of something.

"Twenty-four," Pippin replied, keeping his personal five out of this business.

"OK. Let's get 'em down to the track." With that Amador began opening the kennel gates and releasing the dogs. Pippin guarded his five carefully, not letting Amador get anywhere near them. As a kennel gate was opened each dog's own personality kicked in: some stayed put, others hesitated suspiciously, while most of the dogs took off at full speed, heading for the hills, the woods, or any acceptable refuge.

"What the...?" Amador never figured on the unsportsmanlike dogs abandoning their appointed task of racing for his entertainment. He merely went back to his residence and sulked. Pippin never saw Amador again.

Several of the freed dogs got the worst of it, inadvertently stumbling upon one of the remaining loose alligators. Not good. Another small group, led by a self-appointed alpha male, wound up forming a pack whose mission it was to harass the celebrities in the hills, especially one Walter M. Scut; because of the golf course, Scut's property had the easiest and most open access. The dogs were never rounded up and were left to fend for themselves and to enjoy their freedom. Most of them preferred to stay on or near the Mousewater estate, a far less difficult or gruesome fate than they would have had if Pippin had never brought them in.

Tire and Rubber CEO Horace Hiff and his wife Muffy were relaxing in their backyard, stretched out on their redwood lounge chairs, high in the elite hills overlooking the Mousewater property. Horace was sipping lemonade and enjoying a warm afternoon while Muffy was busy with her phone.

"What was that sound; that rustling? Just over there," Muffy said excitedly looking up from her important texting.

"Probably one of those Mousewater mutts again," Horace replied. He was watching the clouds as he continued to sip.

"That's not a dog, Horace. That's an alligator," Muffy exclaimed.

Horace abandoned his cloud watching and slowly stood up next to his lounge chair. "It's a big one too. Much bigger than the last." He extended his executive hand to Muffy and announced, "Time to go inside."

Such was life in the exclusive hills surrounding the Mousewater estate.

## Chapter 54 – The Works

Perhaps it was the final straw. Perhaps not. It most likely was the final straw for *someone*. On paper, Amador's wish-list seemed innocuous enough; bizarre, weird, and impractical, yes. But the consequences of trying to satisfy the whims of such a flippant and aristocratic Mousewater were far too great. Many of Amador's wild and extreme requests had resulted in one catastrophe after another. Equally at fault was the uncoordinated building of feature after feature with only the time frame considered. That was the case concerning one of the last few incidents during the building of the Mousewater layout.

Late, on a dark and moonless night, not too hot and not too cold, the entire family and numerous guests assembled in an area in the middle of the Mousewater property— Amador's fireworks field. Amador had invited them for a late night fireworks display—a display promising to be spectacular and memorable. There were bleachers there, built solely for the purpose of viewing fireworks. Next to the bleachers was a cinder block building, the restrooms—only one of many, many, many such facilities around the layout. Of course the *building* was there, but there was no functioning plumbing. Across the field from the bleachers, about fifty yards away, stood the two associated buildings—the fireworks storage shed and the command center. The entire fireworks complex was a completed feature that Amador was able to enjoy and be proud of, if only briefly. And he was going to enjoy it (to its fullest extent) by showing everyone a grand exhibition of fireworks. He wanted to indicate to them all that his ideas were just as good as those of his siblings—his arch-rivals.

The associated storage shed was filled with all sorts of elaborate and expensive fireworks. Amador spared no expense in getting, what *he* thought, were the biggest and the best. The fireworks command center allowed Amador to control the exhibition while safely ensconced behind its thick concrete walls; and, more importantly, also allowed him to be right in the thick of the action. In setting it all up, Amador knew what he was doing...he *thought* he knew what he was doing.

Rip and Rhonda were in attendance along with Anthony and Whitney. Trina and Orville were there hoping that Amador would get some kind of comeuppance or embarrassment that would allow them to feel better about themselves. Latherine, curious, attended the event as well. Turlew, DiPoto, and many subcontractors also showed up. Some of the contractor attendees showed up just to see what a Mousewater looked like.

Despite the wide range of emotions and opinions among members of the "audience," there was actual excitement in the air as Amador started the proceedings by playing some triumphal music over the loudspeakers. He was going to emcee the show and control the whole exhibition from the command center. He had spent days setting all this up and was acting like a small child with unbridled enthusiasm and pride. And the finale...everyone was going to remember the finale: a hundred and two giant rockets filled with starbursts, sunbursts, supernovae, moon blasts, whizzers, buzzers, wheelers, skimmers, screamers, earth rockers, and numerous other colorful, loud, and explosive elements. It was going to be visible from as far away as the docks.

"Ladies and gentlemen," Amador announced over the loudspeakers, music playing in the background. "This display was designed and presented by yours truly, Amador Travis Mousewater and I want to give thanks to my grandfather, Dominic Pease Mousewater, without whom tonight's extravaganza would not have been possible."

Rip turned to Turlew and asked him, "What did he mean by bringing my father into it?" Rhonda leaned over and listened closely.

Turlew answered, "He got all that stuff from a Mousewater warehouse down at the docks...one of your father's old storage places. Lots of fireworks down there, lots of really good ones. I watched as he was putting all this together. He seemed to know what he was doing. I think he just about emptied out all those old fireworks."

"You know that a lot of those fireworks my father imported are illegal in the States, highly illegal," Rip said quietly. "They are unregulated and years old. Some of those platform fireworks border on dynam..." [ Blam!!!! ]

Everyone's ears were ringing with the first salvo. No one had ever heard anything so loud. It was like a stick of dynamite had exploded—maybe *more* than one stick. About forty feet off the ground a bright ball of light lit up the people in the bleachers as if it were daytime. Numerous lights soon came on in the houses on the hill. And that was just one opening blast—to get everyone's attention, to get the show started. What followed was a brilliant display of beautiful, floral, colorful skyward blossoms of fireworks. They were loud and extraordinary. Amador had outdone himself; and proud he was of it.

The swirling chaos in the sky was magnificent, but the rumbling in the background didn't seem to fit in with the show. Was the fireworks show about to be rained out?

[ Blam!!!! ] Another massive blast and the rumbling became louder. Amador was letting loose with everything he had. He was really going to be lauded for creating such an impressive show—everyone would remember this night and his part in it...forever. And in this instance, Amador was completely right. Even the elite residents in the hills (many now watching the display from their yards) would talk about this night for years to come.

As the rumbling got louder, the survival shelter pit and its volcanic contents came to Rip's mind. Had Amador's explosives set off something in the earth? Turlew was becoming curious about the rumbling. It wasn't from the shelter; sounded more like thunder. The next extended volley of massive air bursts lit up the area and much of the area near and around the field. A few hundred yards away a dust storm seemed to have formed. It was moving in the direction of the fireworks field. Maybe the explosions had triggered an avalanche. But from where? The hills were mostly built up with peoples' mansions.

Another round of fireworks, massive explosions, and the sky and ground were lit up again. That rumbling wasn't thunder, it was a stampede—a stampede of bison! And they were headed toward the light...and the bleachers!

Turlew took charge and ordered everyone into the restroom. The cinder block walls would protect them from the oncoming wave of crazed animals. Being inside the command center, Amador had no idea what was going on, but when he got a brief glimpse of everyone running into the rest room, he decided to launch the rest of the fireworks all at once, including the grand finale. No sooner than he set everything in motion, the bison were upon the fireworks field. The exploding fireworks packages in the midst of the stampede sent the animals into even more of a frenzy, forcing them to chaotically spread out into individual groups.

The wild animals displaced and knocked awry the carefully-placed arrays of fireworks and trampled on them with their hooves—so many of rockets and roman candles and other guided fireworks were launching into the ground or horizontally across the field or not at all. Between the time that Amador initiated the finale sequence and its activation in the field, the bison had already tilted over the large rocket platform (one hundred and two rockets strong)—it was lying on its side at about a 45-degree angle. So much for the grand finale. Now aware of the stampeding herd, Amador, right in the thick of the action, stayed put; he felt safe inside the command center. Some of the fireworks were even pounding on the outside walls of the building.

And then the finale...the hundred and two rockets launched, and although they were not going to be a danger to aircraft in the area, they were still going to produce a display like no other. The group in the restroom could not see anything that was taking place and Amador had only a limited view from the command center. The stampede had passed, but there was still a huge cloud of dust in the air all around the fireworks field buildings. With the thunderous sound abating, the group cautiously emerged from the restroom. They were just in time to see the lower altitude version of the grand finale. The rockets had landed all over the buildings on the layout: the main house, the square residences, the little restaurants, the features, everything. And as each rocket exploded, more fiery debris was splashed about and launched into the air. All the lights in the hills were now on and nearly all of the celebrities were out in their yards watching the spectacle.

The Mousewater buildings were on fire, but the real blazes were masked by the bright and loud explosions from the rockets and their payloads. The neighbors were truly awed by the exhibition, but none of them realized what was really happening to the layout. A day (night) of reckoning had arrived—the result of years of avoiding code compliance and the use of questionable (and highly flammable) building materials. Almost everything was now in flames. Structures like the guest castle (built of large stones) seemed to be unscathed, but the poorly designed internal structure of many buildings caused them to collapse regardless of what the exterior was built of.

The blast from the rockets turned the stampede around and soon the thundering herd was heading back toward the fireworks field. The small assembled group scurried back into the restroom and Amador thought twice about trying to join them—he stayed inside the command center. Once again the huddled humans heard the rumbling beasts all around them. And more dust. It was like trying to weather a hurricane crouched inside a building, wondering if the structure was going to hold up, or if it was about to cave in under the onslaught. It was such a survival scenario that no one even thought about calling for help. The neighbors in the hills could not tell that the buildings were actually burning up—no one called for help. As the noise died down and the bright bursts of fireworks faded out, the people in the hills became bored with it all and went back inside their houses.

And so, Rip and Rhonda's big layout burned and burned. Grassfires were breaking out everywhere.

The assembled group and Amador cautiously maneuvered their way back toward the buildings. The fireworks show turned out to be everything that Amador had promised: memorable. The group watched as ceilings collapsed, beams fell, walls crumbled. Sparks and glowing embers were everywhere. Everyone was stunned, but remarkably, not a single tear was ever shed, not by anyone. As Turlew looked around at the group, faces lit up in the yellow-orange flickering light, he noticed the absence of Rip, Rhonda, and Latherine.

"Where's Mr. and Ms. Mousewater? And Latherine?" Turlew asked around. They seemed to have disappeared. People were wondering if something bad had happened to them. Running true to form, the Mousewater siblings were most concerned about their square residences than they were about their parents. Then it suddenly occurred to Orville and Trina...

"This is all your fault!" Trina said, pointing her finger in Amador's face.

"Yeah. Yeah that's right!" Orville chimed in.

Neither Orville nor Trina knew exactly what they were planning to *do* about it. Beat him up? Murder? Amador just stood still with a "What? Me?" kind of fake innocent look about him.

Soon, what was actually happening became obvious to the people in the surrounding area—this was no show, the blazes had become too enormous to ignore. So three nearby fire departments were finally alerted and dispatched to the Mousewater estate. When firefighters arrived they were shocked to find that there was not a single fire hydrant anywhere on the property or near it. How had this been allowed to happen? Soon the water supplies on the fire trucks were exhausted and the buildings continued to burn.

"We need everyone out of this area!" a panicked Turlew yelled as he tried to get the group away from the huge underground gasoline storage tank. He yelled at the firefighters to vacate the area immediately. No sooner had the area been cleared than the 100,000 gallons of gasoline erupted into a huge fireball of light. The night air that at one time was fresh and clean, the air that earlier smelled like spent gunpowder, the air that was then filled with clouds of bison dust, that air was now filled with smell of burning petroleum fuel.

"Cool!" Amador commented. The group was not amused. The firefighters were *definitely* not amused. And the firefighters were definitely not amused about the careless and haphazard storage of 100,000 gallons of gasoline in an underground tank. What would they think of a vat of acid or a hellish pit in a survival shelter. One can only imagine.

The exploding gasoline tank sent large pieces of metal flying hundreds of yards—metal chunks carrying flames still burning from a layer of residual gasoline. These landed in previously unscathed areas and started small fires as well. Next to go was the smaller tank of trolley diesel fuel. Although its explosion was not as big, new areas of fire were ignited from its flying debris.

Once the last of the explosions had taken place, the bison were content to mill about in their corner of the property—they had "retreated" right back to where they started, right back into their familiar field. Thanks to the many handlers who thought of them as their own, the horses and dogs were all led to safety as soon as the fires broke out. The golf course was a perfect place for a refuge—wide open and far away from the fires and showering debris.

Miraculously, none of the staff was injured or killed in the burning buildings, although no one ever knew what became of the permanent resident nanny, Ms. Spitz. Some people had always assumed that she would burn herself up one day since she had the nasty habit of smoking in bed.

Everyone associated with the former Mousewater estate was ordered off the property for the evening. The fire crews, not knowing what other strange (possibly dangerous) "features" were lurking about on the premises, were not going to be surprised by another incident like the exploding fuel tanks. And they did not want any "innocent" bystanders around if some new destructive force suddenly reared its exploding head.

## Chapter 55 – It's a Wrap

The next day, fires were still smoldering all around the Mousewater property. A smoky haze filled the air. Curious neighbors in the hills watched fire and hazard crews working to keep things under control. Some even ventured down from the hills to get a closer look at what was left of the huge layout that had been such a nuisance from day one. It looked like a serious military conflict had taken place. Hardly a recognizable structure remained. The castle was fairly intact, but the inside was gutted. Most of the smaller infrastructure items were obliterated by the stampeding bison. Stampeded not once, but twice over. One bison had fallen into the half-empty swimming pool and was wading around neck deep in the murky green water, distressed because of its failed attempts to get back out. During the mop-up efforts, a member of the fire crew stood at the edge of the pool looking at the bellowing bison. She wondered aloud, "What in the hell?"

Police were everywhere, picking through debris, looking for dead bodies, looking for evidence. Evidence of what? There was a lot to sort through. A lot of investigating to come. What were the legal implications of a mess like this? And just where were the owners? Even Latherine was missing; he was usually right on top of disasters like this.

One of the few things that did not burn were the hundreds of toilets and urinals and sinks—installed ones, uninstalled ones, and non-functional ones. The white porcelain bowls dotted the landscape like weird giant mushrooms appearing after a storm; giant mushrooms in sea of charred black.

Captain Fred Teacozy of the Big City police was looking out over the burned remains when Fire Chief Damon Straw came over and inquired, "What do you think? What kind of a place *is* this? *Was* this?"

"I don't know," the Captain replied. "It sure looks like some kind of funny business was going on, but I'm not sure what..."

"Has anyone been able to locate the owners?" Straw asked.

"I don't think so, not yet. We're searching the debris for bodies. If someone happened to be inside any of these buildings...I don't think we're going to find anyone alive." The Captain kicked at a few charred pieces of wood and then asked Straw, "You know who the head of this family used to be, don't you?"

"No."

"Dominic Mousewater," said the Captain.

"Dominic...the gangster?"

"I believe so. He's been dead for a while. I think his son owns this property now, or what's left of it. Nobody has seen him, huh?" The Captain continued kicking pieces of charred wood around. "I guess nobody will ever really know *what* went on here, what all this burned up stuff is...is that a water slide over there?"

"Yeah, and one of my crew discovered a live buffalo stuck in the swimming pool over there. And a couple of alligators were crawling around over there by that castle structure; some kind of moat around that one." Straw motioned toward the guest castle.

"Strange place. Really strange," the Captain said. Then he yelled out at a policeman that was looking through some of the debris, "Hey! Lieutenant Moss! Any sign of the owners or bodies? Anything?"

"No, nothing yet, sir," Moss yelled back.

"Well, I guess it's up to the forensic people now. Call me if you discover any bodies." The Captain returned to his patrol car, shaking his head at the crazy wonder of it all. The Fire Chief hung around the rest of the day in case there were any stragglers still left to extinguish—or human remains that needed to be recovered. He was sadly expecting at least one or two bodies.

## Chapter 56 – The Rebirth Canal

It was the middle of the night and one could see the burning Mousewater estate all the way from the marina. Simon Latherine had given Rip and Rhonda a ride down to the yacht. This was not really the original plan, but it was enough of an opportunity that it couldn't be squandered. For many months, all three had been preparing for a golden opportunity like this. As the happy couple prepared to cast off on the yacht, Anthony and Whitney arrived at the pier. They knew what was brewing; Latherine had told them during the chaos. They were not really emotionally prepared for a final goodbye.

Rip had been a really good friend of Anthony's and although he still felt that Rip was highly irresponsible, he saw a decent person underneath it all. Whitney had grown very fond of the happy couple as well. She had never known any couple like them, generally happy no matter what circumstances befell them—a couple happy with each other as well. She respected Anthony's love of Rip and appreciated Rip's loyalty to Anthony. Anthony and Whitney were going to miss the happy couple—miss them very much.

Latherine, too was getting emotional—unexpectedly. He had set himself up with all kinds of resources in a wide variety of places. He could go just about anywhere. Do just about anything. The Mousewater family had given him much.

Anthony called out to Rip, "So I see your renamed your yacht. Staying incognito I presume."

"Yeah something like that," Rip answered.

"What does that mean, Uhura?" Whitney asked.

"Saw it on a TV show. It's supposed to mean "freedom" but I don't know for sure," Rip replied. "We never watched too much television—too busy with everything. Definitely won't miss it. Not where we're going. Latherine got the yacht's name all legitimized. No one will ever know it's us, not by that name. Registered to a Jack D. Spratt, New Zealand. Look him up...if you can." Rip started managing a few last-minute details getting everything ready for the voyage.

"So you're not going to stay here in the Big City?" Rhonda asked Latherine. "You could. You know how to take care of yourself. You know all the tricks. You know, "magic.""

Latherine answered, "I don't think that even *I* could outmaneuver all the different ramifications that are getting ready to uncork up there at the estate. I plan to disappear. I'll be fine wherever I end up. But it won't be prison. You know that's not going to happen. You two should probably be on your way; before someone comes looking for you."

Then Rip asked, "How will you explain our missing yacht? Someone is bound to ask."

"It's already been handled," Latherine replied. "Probably lost at sea at some point. Stop worrying about all this stuff and get out of here."

"What about dock security, out there near the open end of the docks...toward the ocean?" Anthony asked.

Latherine responded quickly, "Captain Quirg. The patrol tonight is led by a captain named Quirg, an old friend of Dominic's; from many years ago. If there is anything that's on our side in all this, it's those docks...and all those folks down there. Lots of friendly faces." Latherine started removing the rope from the rear deck cleat. Once it was neatly coiled up, he handed it to Rip.

"Good luck Rip. Good luck Rhonda," Anthony said as he unwound the forward line from its cleat, handing the rope to Rhonda. Whitney waved goodbye and the happy couple slowly motored out of the slip and toward the lake. Latherine and Anthony and Whitney stood watching as the happy couple waved back. And the yacht, Rip and Rhonda, and storage bins filled with millions in cash and diamonds disappeared into the darkness of the lake and finally into the canal that led to the ocean.

## Chapter 57 – R.I.P.

The layout—what remained of it—was left to rot in the sun. What few structures that were left standing were condemned. One investigation after another looked into how the place came into being, how it met its fiery fate, and how so big an operation could remain undetected and out of the public domain for so long. All the shenanigans, threats, and strong-arm tactics came home to roost—came home to roost but there was no one to roost *on*. The public was fascinated with the exposed and tangled web of lies, incompetence, overindulgence, and scandal brought about by the Mousewater family and its estate. And there was the mysterious disappearance of three of the principals: Rip, Rhonda, and Simon Q. Latherine. For a while, everyone became familiar with the names Brisbane Pease Mousewater and Rhonda Proody Mousewater—three names each, very newsy.

The Mousewater siblings were saddled with most of the many repercussions. Without Latherine they were lost. In the final analysis, and in typical fashion, they seemed to be more interested in assigning blame to each other than in the legal proceedings that threatened their money and their freedom. They each learned, the hard way, that in testimony, "I do not recall" is not a defense. Neither is "Not *me*! It's those two."

As for Turlew and DiPoto, they were in deep, deep koshimuto. DiPoto somehow dug his way back into the criminal underground leaving Turlew holding the bag. The judge in Turlew's case happened to be yet another friend/associate of Dominic's and so Turlew received six months probation—and that was the end of that. Dominic, like so many times in the past, still ruled, even from the grave.

The numerous Mousewater animals were relocated, most given to the handlers who had taken care of them for months and years. There were still some missing alligators. They could be anywhere. The bison were returned to their European grazing grounds, the herd intact and well, despite their ordeal on the Mousewater property and the long trip back. Even the bison that was enjoying the Mousewater swimming pool was returned to its European home.

There seemed to be no end to the wild events at the Mousewater property, even with no one living there and nobody on site in charge of anything. There came a summer storm, a 100-year storm, a storm like no other in recent memory. The unusual drainage in and around the Mousewater property caused the heavy rains to funnel down from The Hills and onto the layout area, flooding the entire property. All the remaining wood, branches and debris from the estate was unceremoniously washed off the property and onto the frontage road next to Highway 111. Hundreds of toilets and other white fixtures were piled up high in a kind of ridiculous-looking porcelain Everest. In a television interview, recalling his part in the previous toilet-highway incident, one Big City patrolman remarked, "What is it with the Mousewater family and all these toilets?"

Of course someone had to take charge of the clean-up. The Big City officials demanded that the Mousewater siblings cough up the necessary capital to clear the area of debris and toilets. As soon as the weather cleared, the task was paid for (by court order) and the debris (basically all that was left of the layout) was gone—dump truck after dump truck of layout remains, possibly landfill for someone else's layout. But nature had yet another laugh at the expense of the Mousewater family. Another deluge, far worse than the first, caused an immense mudslide in the surrounding hills. Mud and slush washed down over the Mousewater property covering it with a new layer of fresh dirt and vegetal matter—including tons and tons of topsoil from the lots of the celebrity houses on the hills. As such, this topsoil was loaded with chemical fertilizers, toxins, pesticides, herbicides, and who knows what else. Not a trace of the Mousewater buildings or features remained visible. Even the six fumaroles had been covered over with many feet of dirt. The Mousewater layout was truly gone.

In addition to the mud, several of the celebrity houses fell victim to the mudslides and ended up at the foothills, on the edge of the former Mousewater property. This included the house of Walter M. Scut—Scut furiously searched for someone to sue over this atrocity but could find no one, not a single *vulnerable* target. And he wasn't about to sue those Mousewater kids. Not if he knew what was good for him.

The mudslide had also unearthed a couple of bodies from the yard of one of the Mousewater's underworld neighbors. The police were quick to react as a member of one of the cleanup crews reported seeing someone desperately attempting to drag a dead body out of the mud and away from the area.

The next year, following the mudslides, up sprang millions of wildflowers all over the former Mousewater property—millions upon millions, toxins and chemicals notwithstanding. News of the phenomenon spread all over the Big City and people came from miles around to get photos of themselves surrounded by the floral beauty—artists and people wanting pictures for family portraits and selfies and book covers and slide shows and clip art and...and of course there was the infamous Mousewater name to add to the attraction. There was so much interest in the Mousewater property that Highway 111 was constantly clogged with cars and trucks; at least during the day. Tourists from far and wide flocked to the place. People from everywhere were coming to trample down the flowers just to get that perfect pic for their stash. Traffic piled up for miles. At that time there were no other trendy scandalous tabloid events available for tourists to gather around so eventually the authorities had to step in and break up the entire circus. It seemed that there was never a true end to anything associated with the Mousewater family.

## Chapter 58 – Brisbane

There was a cool breeze in the air and a bright sun was shining down. Rip had just returned from a trip to the city and was sitting quietly on the rear deck of the Uhura reading the day's newspaper. Water was slapping against the hull of the yacht, anchored several hundred yards offshore from the harbor. Rip's feet were propped up on the bench.

Rhonda sat down beside him and, stroking the side of Rip's head, asked, "Do you want something to drink?"

"Sure. Maybe iced tea?" Rhonda went the galley below as Rip continued to page through the paper in the noonday sun.

Rip and Rhonda had many misgivings about leaving so much behind. They were mostly responsible for the selfish, irascible, and choleric nature of their three children. But, as things began to spiral out of control, the happy couple probably had no other reasonable path than the one they chose. Their pathologic compulsion to keep expanding the layout was responsible for so many catastrophes. But everyone involved was a willing participant—they each walked into hell with their eyes wide open. During the fever, nobody could deter the happy couple from their mission, not even Anthony. As a result, through the years, the entire place had slowly become a house of cards and it seemed strangely appropriate that the whole mess of a thing was brought down by a grandson of the infamous Dominic Pease Mousewater.

Many times Rip would reminisce about the saneness that Anthony brought with him whenever he was around. But there was no denying that the current life he and Rhonda were making for themselves was right for them and no one else.

"Anything in today's paper?" Rhonda asked as she handed Rip his glass. She sat down beside him, sipping from a glass of tea of her own.

"Here's something interesting. They had to evacuate a retirement village that was built on our old property. Rip read an excerpt from the paper, "...it seems that pressure had been building from a series of anomalous hot spot fumaroles hidden beneath the entire area. As a large mound started to well up beneath several of the village buildings, a sulfuric odor engulfed the entire community forcing the evacuation of all the residents. Shortly thereafter, the ground began to separate, releasing gases that had, most likely, been building up for years. The senior citizens were resettled in the beleaguered, but nearby Orville Oaks and the empty retirement community closed down permanently..."

"What newspaper is that?" Rhonda asked.

"It's the Big City Times. Amazing. All the way down here in Brisbane, Australia. Really amazing." Rip folded up the paper and put it down on the bench with his tea glass on top to hold it down. He held out his arms to Rhonda and she slid over and settled herself in them. "What do you say we go down to Sydney for a few weeks?" Rip asked.

"That sounds great," Rhonda replied.

"On my recent trip to Antarctica I was able to swim with the penguins. Water's pretty damn cold; don't know how they manage it. I wanted to ski down one of the black diamond slopes, but they said that all the ski lifts were closed due to bad weather. So I had to settle for some plain old water skiing. That didn't work out either—too much ice floating around. And there weren't any ants down there at the bottom of the world—not that I could tell. Not in that particular area of Antarctica.

At the other end of the world, Arctica, I went over to see the big important Mr. Claus himself. I was more than a little bit peeved when they told me to take a number and sit down. So I left.

"I've been a passenger on board a wooden whaling vessel—first class, of course. I watched as the sailors tossed their nets over the side of the ship. Such skill. They were expecting to haul in dozens of whales, but each time they looked through their catch they found they had only snagged a small assortment of lesser fish. It was a big bust, at least while I was aboard. They accused me of being some kind of jinx and confined me to my cabin.

"We were there when Abraham Lincoln got himself shot. He was in the box right next to us. I think he was only a senator at the time. When we asked for a refund on our tickets...well, sorry, no refunds. Go figure. My ears are still ringing.

"I've surfed on glaciers (too slow) and fresh lava (too slow and too hot). I prefer surfing on water—much easier on my board. Softer landings too.

"But, perhaps my most memorable experience was going to Giza, in Egypt, to watch the building of that giant pyramid. It's situated on the other side of the Nile from Cairo. At least they didn't build it way out in the sticks like they did with the Grand Canyon. When I arrived, they had already finished a lot of the other construction—other pyramids and an animal statue with no nose. I'll bet some construction engineer's head is going to roll for that one. It was fascinating to watch the pyramid-building process. Day after day they hauled those big heavy stones into place. You would think that at least the supervisors would show up for work dressed in a suit. When I tried to walk up the giant construction ramp some security guy stopped me. 'Where do you think *you're* going?' he asked. 'I'm headed up top,' I replied. 'There is no top...not yet,' he said as he ushered me on down the slope. When they told me it was going to be over forty more years before the thing was finished, I decided not to hang around.

"So...those are some of the things on *my* list. Can your bucket list top that? The next item on my agenda will be to head to Indonesia where I plan to have lunch with some fellow called Java Man. With that name I'll bet he makes a damn fine cup of coffee. We'll see."

–G.G.

Be Advised...

# Tales

from the

# Bloody
# Stump

Volume 2

Printed in the USA
CPSIA information can be obtained
at www.ICGtesting.com
LVHW081223240923
758369LV00005B/5